HEIR OF AUTUMN

HEIR OF

Autumn

GILES CARWYN
and
TODD FAHNESTOCK

An Imprint of HarperCollinsPublishers

HEIR OF AUTUMN. Copyright © 2006 by Giles Carwyn and Todd
Fahnestock. All rights reserved. Printed in the United States of
America. No part of this book may be used or reproduced in any man-
ner whatsoever without written permission except in the case of brief
quotations embodied in critical articles and reviews. For information
address HarperCollins Publishers, 10 East 53rd Street, New York, NY
10022.

Eos is a federally registered trademark of HarperCollins Publishers.

Designed by Judith Abbate/Abbate Design
Maps and drawings by Langdon Foss

Printed in the U.S.A.

ISBN: 0-06-082975-3

TODD

For my mother, Lynnette, who gave me the wings to fly.
And for my father, Jim, who gave me the strength to use them.

GILES

for my brother

acknowledgments

THANKS TO OUR lovely wives, Lara and Tanya, for always being first readers (even at three o'clock in the morning). We could not have done this without their unwavering faith, support, and all those extra hours they put in while "the boys" were off fighting in the pits of Nine Squares. Thanks to Ray Bartlett, Aaron Brown, Megan Foss, and Chris Mandeville. Without your insight, guidance, and support, this book would not have become what it is. Kudos to Langdon Foss for the fantastic drawings of Ohndarien, Physen, Nine Squares, and the Cinder and to Eden Dench for her talented hand at lettering. A big thanks to our agent, Donald Maass, for his powerful influence on the book's ending and for being our champion in getting this story in front of a larger audience. And most important, our overwhelming gratitude goes out to Nimue, who gave her life to make this book possible.

book I

A CITY OF STONE AND LIGHT

Ohndarien

Jewel of the Known World

prologue

DEATH BELONGED to her now. She must sit with it for one turning of the moon like her mother had before her. As Copi drew closer to the fire, she heard the music that haunted her dreams. It wasn't real music, not heartbeats, not drums or chanting, not the wind in your ears as you danced. It chirped like a bird, tinkled like silver beads.

In one month Copi would be a woman. Her family would give her a young stallion to call her own. When the colt grew strong she would ride across the Vastness and find a man with many mares to breed with her stallion. And that man would give her many children to ride on the backs of those horses. But first, she must endure one month with the child.

She stepped out of the darkness into the light of the fire. Her sister sat upon a log in front of the flames. Nili's eyes were red and sunken like an old woman dying of the fever, but she offered a weak smile at the sight of her sister.

Nili held the music box in her hands, turning its delicate handle. The strange metal of the box reflected a rainbow of colors in the shifting firelight. As long as Nili kept turning the handle, the box kept singing. As long as the music never stopped, the child would not wake.

Copi looked across the fire at the sleeping girl. Her tiny chest rose and fell as she breathed. She had dark hair and skin so pale blue lines showed through. When Copi's mother told her the child's face was blue, Copi imagined it blue like the sky. But the little girl wasn't the monster from the old women's stories. She was just a tiny child from across the Great Ocean, no more than ten moons old.

The sleeping girl was naked. Her clothes had rotted away generations ago, but no one dared give her new ones. She lay in the snow all winter. She lay in the rain all spring. She did not eat, she did not stir, she did not wake. She dreamed. Her eyes darted back and forth under their lids, lost in a nightmare, but they never opened. No one knew what color those eyes were.

"She's not what you expected, is she?" Nili asked, still winding the music box.

"She's so small, so beautiful."

"She is horrible. She is worse than you can possibly imagine."

Nili stared back at the child and turned the handle, around and around.

"Aren't you tired?" Copi asked her sister. "You've been here a full moon with no sleep."

"No. You will not sleep. You cannot."

Swallowing past the dryness in her throat, Copi asked the question she had been dreading. "Shall I take the box now?"

Nili shook her head. "There is something I must tell you first. It is a story you must remember and pass on to the woman who bears this burden after you. It is the story of how the dreaming child came to us and why she must never, never wake up."

THE FIRST LIGHT of dawn bled into the black sky. Copi sat on the log beside the fire, turning the handle of the ancient box. She couldn't look at the child. She stared at the fire, her feet, the music box, anything but the child. Her first night was almost over. She couldn't imagine twenty-eight more. It was more than any woman could bear.

She wasn't cold, wasn't hungry. Her hand never grew tired. Her back never felt sore. The fire never died down, but it could not hold back the chill of the little girl. It seeped into her bones, and Copi knew she would never be the same. She closed her eyes and turned the handle, on and on and on.

As the sun crested the distant hills, the handle of the box lurched and stopped.

Frantically, she turned the wheel harder, faster. The handle snapped off and came away in her hand. She clutched at the box, let out a cry of dismay. Her fingers fumbled for the tiny nub of the broken handle. She tried to turn it, but it would not go. She pinched it against her knuckle so hard she bled and spun the box instead of the handle. A single note chirped out, then another.

She heard a tiny moan. The child's little hands rose to her face and rubbed her eyes. She arched her back and stretched.

Copi turned the box over and over again, pinching the nub as hard as she could. The music returned, awkward and halting like a horse with a broken leg.

The naked child yawned once, sticking out her little pink tongue.

Copi started to scream.

The child opened her eyes.

They were blue eyes. Pale, pale blue eyes.

I

SHARA'S FATHER called her a whore the day she left home. After ten years, that was what she remembered most about her parents. She could still hear the hate in her father's voice as he passed his final judgment, could see him scowling in that chicken-scratched yard while her mother stood by, head bowed, saying nothing in Shara's defense.

Shara would soon be worth her weight in jewels, but somewhere deep inside she was still a hog butcher's daughter. Despite a decade of training, the smell of pig still drifted into her mind whenever she was scared, whenever she felt lost and out of place.

For the thousandth time, Shara let go of those too-familiar thoughts. They would not serve her, not tonight. She opened her eyes and looked out the window. The sun was setting behind the Windmill Wall on the far side of Ohndarien. The dying light made the Free City's harbor and canals shimmer like liquid gold.

Shara sat on a teak window seat, leaning on silken pillows. She kept her breathing slow as her fingers brushed the tip of her nipple. Her other hand was nestled warm between her thighs. She could feel the energy expanding beyond the edges of her body. Her skin, her white cotton robe, the pillows, the dying light were all becoming one. But that word, "whore," kept her from dissolving completely.

She painted the scene in the air outside her window. Her mind's eye conjured a three-dimensional portrait of her parents. She saw her father's face, swollen fat through the jowls and pinched tight around the eyes. She saw her mother, shoulders habitually curled forward, a strand of her wispy brown hair fluttering in the breeze.

Shara let the accusation build within her. "Whore," she breathed, blowing the word back at her parents, scattering their images like pipe smoke. They swirled away, and she was free of them.

"If I am a whore," she said to herself, "what a magnificent whore I will be."

She shuddered as the last of her resistance fell away. The power hung about her like a haze and she lost herself in it. Reveled in it.

Standing up, she dropped her robe. The woven cotton whispered off her shoulders and down her arms. As it brushed her skin, she gasped and felt her control lurch again. She was on fire. The spell would be powerful, if she could hold the reins.

She walked to the door and ran her sensitive fingers across the dark oak. Beyond her chambers, the school was quiet. The servants were gone for the night. Her fellow students were sleeping in their rooms. Victeris was alone in his tower. She had a brief urge to test her strength against the Zelani Master, but she let that go also. With a smile, she breathed her hubris into the spell along with everything else.

A thrill ran through her, and she nodded.

Now.

Shara opened the door and stepped naked into the hallway. Her bare feet smacked softly on the cool stones. Through the open colonnades, she could see the gardens in the courtyard below. Reaching out with her mind, she brushed the water in the fountain. It felt cool and moist in the hot night, but her thoughts made no ripples on its surface.

At the end of the hall, she turned and headed down the stairs. Her hair slid across her bare shoulders, and she closed her eyes. If this is what the Fourth Gate felt like, she couldn't imagine the Fifth.

Lost in her trance, she almost walked straight into Sybald. The old man cleared his throat to catch her attention. Shara fought to maintain control as her cheeks reddened and her ears burned. The old man looked her up and down disapprovingly. Sybald was Victeris's manservant. The acerbic man was as rigid in his thinking as he was crooked in his body. Like the other students, Shara had feared and hated him while growing up. Now, within a hair's breadth of her full power, she couldn't imagine being terrified by such a tiny little man. He was so old he must have been born ancient.

"What are you doing out of bed?" Sybald asked, holding his candle closer to her face.

"I'm going to the Night Market. Perhaps I'll see a show," she told him. Her voice sounded hurried and nervous, but she stood defiant, chin out, shoulders back, breasts pushed forward. She continued blushing but did not move.

Sybald's wrinkles deepened in his confusion. "Out? At night? What's this nonsense?"

Shara exulted. He didn't see! He didn't know.

Her triumph turned smug. With a wicked smile, she laid a hand on the old man's arm. "But I'm no longer a student, am I?" she said, feeling her power swirl around them.

Sybald nodded as if half-asleep. "No, I guess you're not."

"Would you please open the front gate for me?"

She might be pushing the limits of her influence, but she was on fire. Nothing could stop her.

The old man headed down the stairs. She followed his shuffling steps through the arched doors and across the rose marble walkways to the front gate. As he fumbled for his keys, she looked down at her naked body. Her smooth skin glowed in the darkness. Smiling, she turned back to Sybald as he opened the heavy iron gate.

"Leave that unlocked, would you?"

"Of course," he mumbled, and shuffled back inside.

Shara slipped through the gate, barely able to contain a grin at the power she had, the influence. She couldn't wait for the life she would lead in the next few years. Tonight was her final lesson. After this, she would be ready to pass through the Fifth Gate, into true power and influence. She would escape from under the thumb of any father, husband, or cruel-eyed Zelani-Master and owe fealty to no one. The whole world would open to her. She would walk with kings, whisper in their ears, and change the course of nations.

She continued down the hill toward the city, her glamour wrapped about her like a cape. The Zelani school was set high on South Ridge, overlooking the bay. Moonlight glimmered on the waters that were Ohndarien's lifeblood. She couldn't believe her eyes when Master Victeris had first brought her to the city. Ohndarien, jewel of the known world, was everything her home in Faradan was not.

In the Free City possibilities ran like a hundred roads into her future. In Faradan, there was only one meager, rutted track leading toward a bleak end.

Young women in Ohndarien were afraid their businesses were growing too slowly. Young women in Faradan were afraid to go outside after dark.

Shara imagined her eldest sister, Nelda. The lucky one. The firstborn. She married a kilt-maker's son, and none of Shara's other sisters could aspire to anything better. Now Nelda was punching holes in leather from sunrise to sundown with nothing to show for it at the end of the day except for a thatch roof, a hot meal, and the touch of a drunken and defeated man.

Nelda must already have daughters of her own, daughters who knew all too well the sting of their mother's hand whenever they showed a drop of spirit, whenever their eyes drifted up from the ground. Mothers in Faradan learned to strike their children quickly before their fathers could raise a beefy hand. Feeling a lighter blow was the only kindness a child could expect in the kingdom among the pines.

But Ohndarien was so very different. When Shara first arrived she couldn't believe the way children simply played together in the streets, running around in little chattering packs day or night. Those children grew up without fear. If that wasn't freedom, nothing was.

She breathed in the cool night air, thick with the scent of flowers from the gardens that spilled over the roof of every building.

The Free City was a mythical accomplishment of engineering, built around a series of locks that connected the Great Ocean with the Summer Sea. Endless trade made her the richest city in the world. Her hundred-foot walls kept her that way.

Far below, bright lamps sparkled in the Night Market. Food, drink, song, dance, games, theater—the best in the world could be found at Ohndarien's Night Market, if you had the coin. It was packed with people from a hundred lands from dusk until dawn.

Above the market rose a circular plateau known as the Wheel of the Seasons. The Wheel was the spiritual and political center of the city, and the most beautiful place Shara had ever seen. Most cities boasted a king in a castle, or an emperor in a palace, but the leaders of Ohndarien held council in a garden. Shara had spent countless hours walking with Brophy in those gardens. She'd waded in the fountains, lost herself in the hedge mazes, and slept away warm afternoons under the trees.

At the center of the Wheel stood the Hall of Windows, a stained-glass amphitheater many considered the most remarkable building in the world. But there was sadness mixed with its beauty. A single torch burned in each of the cardinal directions atop the Hall of Windows. The flames held vigil, waiting thirteen years for the return of Ohndarien's Lost Brothers from the Vastness.

Shara continued across Donovan's Bridge into the Night Market. She wandered amidst the shops, naked as the moon above, pretending to look at the wares while studying those around her. They saw what they expected to see. Perhaps she was a haughty strumpet from the Silver Islands. Perhaps she was a cocksure duelist from the Summer Cities, spouting poetic challenges to any who looked his way. They saw anything they wanted, anything but the truth.

With a laugh, she moved on, going wherever she pleased. She walked past the attendants into a private masked ball thrown by an ambassador from Kherif. She strolled through the kitchens of the Midnight Jewel and stole a breast-fruit tart from under the steward's nose. She joined a drunken singing contest between the crews of two trading galleys from Faradan. The bawdy lyrics and guttural accents reminded Shara of sneaking away from her father to watch dueling minstrels on Midsummer's Eve.

That was the night she met her first Zelani.

The haughty stranger had come to the village festival with a squad of the king's soldiers. The man's penetrating gaze scared Shara at first, but he spoke softly despite the hungry glint in his eyes. He called for everyone's attention and showed an enormous coin to the crowd. A hush fell over the village as the poor farmers and craftsmen looked at more gold than they would make in their entire lives. In a quiet voice, the Zelani master said any child who could pick up the coin and return it to him without dropping it could leave with him to study at a new school in the Free City. Then he threw the coin into the bonfire.

The crowd gasped, and a couple of the parents protested, but the presence of the king's men kept that the villagers cowed. Every child was given a chance to approach the fire.

Few children had the courage to face the flames. Those who did yanked their hands back quickly with yelps of pain. None of the children got close to the coin until it was Shara's turn. She strode forward and thrust her hand into the blaze.

The people all around her gasped as she plucked the searing coin from the coals and jumped back with it pinched between thumb and forefinger, a fierce grimace on her face.

Shara's fingers still showed those burn marks, but she never dropped that coin. She never even cried out. Her teeth were gritted in pain, but inside she was soaring as she placed the red-hot coin in Victeris's outstretched palm. It was the first moment in her life that she felt free.

The stranger knelt next to Shara. The firelight flickered across his thin face and smoky goatee.

"Well done, child," he said. "What do you say we give that coin to your parents and teach you how to make a thousand more just like it?"

That was Shara's tenth summer. The last she would spend in Faradan. Her father took the stranger's gold, called Shara a whore, and sent her on her way. She had never looked back.

Reveling in her night of triumph, Shara wandered through the thinning early-morning crowds until a fire-lit doorway caught her attention. She moved toward the noisy café and stood at the threshold. A drunken pipe band tried to overwhelm the laughter and shouting voices in the smoky room. Young women, and older women trying to look young, sat on the laps of drunken men. Some were half-naked, giggling as leering men fondled a thigh.

Others were fully dressed, breasts pushed up into shifting globes, layered skirts riding up their legs.

She stood for a long moment, watching the women work their trade. It had never been so clear to her. She was no whore. These women offered nothing more than a moment's pleasure. Shara would rewrite men's souls.

She turned to go, but a voice stopped her. "Most wait to get upstairs before dropping their skirts."

She suddenly felt cold. He knew. He *saw.*

The thin man sat alone in the closest corner. His eyebrows were black slashes above his dark eyes, giving his gaze a fierce intensity.

The man's gaze traveled the length of Shara's body. His plush fur cloak made him look like a sailor from Kherif, but his features were harder to place. He had a prominent nose and gray flecks in his brown hair. He looked like a man who hadn't smiled in years.

Her heart beat faster, and her concentration wavered. A cool breeze tickled the nape of her neck, and a few of the other men turned to stare at her. Their eyes weren't anywhere near her face.

She gasped and fled out the door. A group of drunken youths stopped and stared as she ran by them.

"Shara!" shouted the sailor from Kherif, sprinting after her.

She doubled her effort, but he reached her in seconds. He was neither tall nor powerfully built, but he caught her as though she were a child and dragged her to a stop. She would have fallen, but he held her up with one hand.

"Let me go!" she demanded.

He did. She stumbled back a few steps.

The young men began to whistle and clap. "Naked women running away from you is a bad sign, my friend," one of them shouted. The stranger shot the boy a deadly look. The youth blanched and said nothing more.

The stranger shrugged off his cloak and offered it to her. His voice was quiet, dark like his eyes. "It will be a long walk home, dressed like you aren't."

Hesitantly, she took the cloak and wrapped it around herself. The cluster of boys continued on their way, laughing and joking among themselves.

"How do you know my name?" she asked, flushed.

"I have found that it is good to know things," the stranger said.

She pulled the fur cloak more tightly about herself. "And who are you?"

"A dog at the feast," he murmured, "A spider in the palace. You may call me Scythe if you have need to call upon me at all."

She elevated her chin slightly. "I doubt I will need to call upon the services of a dog, or a spider."

"More than once, you mean?"

She clenched her jaw, wanting to throw the cloak in his face. But she kept it.

"Would you prefer someone more fair?" he said softly. "A rock lion is certainly prettier than a dog. Black fur. So soft. So powerful. A better companion by far. But then, they eat their young . . ."

"Just because you caught me naked doesn't mean you can treat me like a child," she snapped at him.

Scythe took a step back and bowed gracefully. "My mistake."

"I thank you for the cloak," she said, backing away. "I'll see it is returned to you."

"Keep it," Scythe replied. "Perhaps it will give you some small protection against the lions you bring to your bed."

Clutching the cloak around her, she hurried into the darkness wishing she hadn't heard his words, wishing she didn't know what they meant.

I'M GOING to break your balls with this one!" Trent promised. He wobbled and caught his balance.

Brophy laughed. "Not if you fall first!"

Trent's lips pressed into a line, and he hurled the rock.

Brophy didn't move. The stone whipped past him so close he felt the breeze. It clacked down the scree slope behind him and disappeared over the cliff. Trent was getting better at this. He had his father in him after all.

Each boy perched precariously on a boulder, sixty feet apart. The rocks were particularly jagged south of Ohndarien, thrusting up like half-buried blades. The boys played their game on the knife-edge ridge that separated the two halves of the world. Piss off one edge of the ridge and it ended up in the Summer Seas. Piss off the other side and the yellow stream flowed across the Great Ocean all the way to the Opal Palace.

Throwing rocks at each other was stupid, really. They began doing it out of sheer boredom. Brophy went along with it time after time. Talking Trent out of a stupid idea was always more work than going along with it. Unfortunately, it had become Trent's favorite game. He made certain they played it every time they went hawking.

Brophy bent his knees, cocked back, and threw his stone. It flew high, missing Trent's head by a foot or more. Brophy flailed for a moment, regained his balance.

"Pathetic," Trent shouted across the distance, narrowing his eyes and stilling his body. His wavy black hair fell in his eyes, and he flicked it back with a twitch of his head.

Brophy transferred a rock from his left hand to his right and found his center. He sent his will into the boulder and anchored himself, determined not to move. The last two times they'd played, Brophy had managed to clip Trent on the arm and then the leg, ending the games.

"Get ready," Trent shouted. "And no flinching! You turn coward, I'll pound you."

Trent kissed the rock, aimed, and threw.

Oh hell, thought Brophy.

He winced, but refused to move. He didn't even close his eyes. The rock smacked him square on the mouth and stars burst in his vision. His foot slipped and he went down. The sharp edge of the boulder smashed into his ribs as he tumbled from his perch. Brophy cried out, hit the ground, and slid to a stop on the loose rock. He couldn't breathe.

Trent laughed, triumphant.

Brophy rolled over onto his knees, tears welling in his eyes. He wanted to cry, but he held it in. Not that. Not in front of Trent. He opened his mouth to draw a breath, but his lungs wouldn't cooperate. He gaped like a fish on a riverbank.

Trent's laughter died and Brophy heard scrabbling noises. He thought he might pass out.

"Brophy!" Trent called.

Brophy sucked in a desperate breath. Trent scampered over the jagged rocks and dropped to his knees next to his friend.

"Brophy! Are you all right?"

He continued sucking air. Blessed air!

"Don't mess about!" Trent said.

"I'm all right," Brophy mumbled through a numb mouth. He gasped and put a hand on his ribs. It felt like someone had hit him with a club.

Trent leaned him against the big boulder. Brophy touched his mouth and his fingers came away bloody. He probed the inside of his lips with his tongue. His front tooth felt loose.

"Good throw," he mumbled, shaking his head.

Trent's concern vanished. He laughed and shoved Brophy against the rock. "Damn, you should have seen the look on your face. Why didn't you move?"

Brophy glared at him. "You said no flinching."

"Yeah, but . . ." Trent chuckled. "There's brave and then there's stupid, Broph." He continued laughing as he offered Brophy a hand. Trent had large, powerful hands like his father. He had almost grown to his father's towering height, with shoulders just as broad. When he filled out completely, he would be a mountain of a man. Effortlessly, he yanked Brophy to his feet.

They moved down the rocky ridge slowly to where they'd left their hawks. The hooded hunting birds were perched on the lowest branch of a squat, twisted scrub oak.

"I think you broke my tooth," Brophy said.

Trent chuckled again as he untied his bird. "You should have moved."

"I'm not playing your stupid games anymore."

"Don't be sour," Trent said, giving a deft flip to his hawk's tether. It wrapped around his wrist. "You did good. I was impressed. You're still beating me two to one."

Brophy licked blood from his split lip and tried a smile. Trent was much more magnanimous in victory than defeat. No point in spoiling the moment.

Wincing against the pain, Brophy retrieved his bird. The smell of blood made the hawk nervous, and Brophy stroked her feathers to calm her.

Trent became somber as they walked past thorny bushes along the goat trail back to the city.

"You know . . ." Trent said, his voice low, thoughtful, "we need to come up with a good story."

Indeed. They were supposed to be hunting.

"My father won't think much of our game," he continued.

"No." That's because it's a stupid game, Brophy thought. Trent's father was the Brother of Autumn and the bravest man Brophy knew. He was the first foreigner to take the Test of the Stone in Ohndarien. Krellis wasn't afraid of anything, and he would be the first person to tell Trent it was a dumb game.

"We'll say you stumbled walking up the slope."

"Let's tell him the truth. Let's just—"

Trent's eyes flashed, and Brophy fell silent. Trent's moods came and went like a summer storm.

"No."

"He'll understand, Trent. We're kids."

"You maybe. Not me. No. We'll say we were chased by Physendrian scouts. We were running away, and you fell."

Brophy sighed. He tried to think of a way to stop Trent from telling his father another lie. It must be hard to be the son of a man like Krellis. But Trent would spend less time fighting with his father if he spent more time telling him the truth.

Trent's eyes fell on Brophy's hawk. "What if we break her wing? That will be more believable. We'll have evidence."

Brophy rolled his eyes. "You're not breaking her wing."

"No?" Trent said, his eyes turning flinty once more. "Since when do you tell me what to do?"

Brophy was almost angry enough to get into a fight, but he resisted. He was already too beaten up. And Trent was seventeen years old while Brophy was only fifteen. Brophy was large for his age, but Trent was huge.

"No," Brophy said. "We'll say we were tracking a partridge. I was looking up at the sky and didn't see a sudden drop-off. No need to hurt my hawk." Lying was bad enough, but ruining a good bird to cover up a bad lie was worse. Sometimes Trent didn't think things through very well, but he never liked being reminded of it.

"Well, maybe," Trent said.

They wound their way through the foothills of the Arridan Mountains in silence. Their path led them out of the jagged boulders and down a steep bank into the loose sand of a dry riverbed.

Ohndarien's Water Wall loomed in the distance. The first hundred feet of the siege-scarred wall were solid blue-white marble. The defensive masterpiece had repelled seven Physendrian invasions.

Those massive ramparts were the foundation for five tiers of delicate stone arches that rose three hundred feet farther into the sky. The soaring web of stacked stone supported the world's tallest aqueduct, which carried a constant stream of seawater from the Great Ocean to the enormous locks on the eastern side of the city.

A cavernous tunnel disappeared into the base of the wall, providing the only spot of shadow on the sun-blasted landscape. The impregnable Physendrian Gate stood at the very center of that tunnel. The fifty-foot metal portal was so massive it could only be opened with hydraulic pressure diverted from the aqueduct far overhead.

Once they were within sight of the city, Trent took a deep breath. He was smiling again.

"It was a good day," he murmured, looking sideways at Brophy. "I mean, besides your getting hurt."

"Thanks," said Brophy. His lips were beginning to sting, and every step he took jostled his side, sending a thudding ache through his body. He wondered if he had broken a rib. He'd once seen a dock rat break his ribs when a sudden gust of wind pulled the ship away from the wharf. The boy fell into the gap and was almost crushed when the boat rocked back into place. Supposedly, it happened all the time. Brophy tried to ignore the pain.

"What was your best day ever?" Trent asked.

Brophy gave him a suspicious look. "What do you mean?"

"The best day you can remember. What was it?"

"Not today, that's for sure."

Trent thought a moment, a sly smile came to his lips. "I'll tell you a good day. A while back I went shopping at Master Garm's."

Brophy didn't like where this was going. Garm, Krellis's new master armorer, was the best smith on the Summer Sea, but the man had something that Brophy appreciated more than the heft and balance of a fine blade. He had a daughter.

Femera was a dark-eyed beauty with lustrous black hair that fell all the way to her waist. She moved like a summer breeze and smelled just as nice. She spoke very little, but her eyes sought Brophy's whenever he was around.

When Femera had arrived with her father six months earlier, she instantly became the boys' favorite subject. At least a dozen times they'd invented excuses to go to Stoneside and walk by his workshop. Sometimes they would waste half a day on the off chance that they would see her working in the shop. Trent joked that Master Garm had made many great swords, but he had also made one great sheath. It took Brophy a week to understand that, and he'd blushed to his roots when he did.

"I assume you haven't forgotten his daughter, Femera?" Trent said.

"The rock didn't hit me that hard."

Trent stretched his arms and sighed. "Well, about a month ago . . ." He gave Brophy a playful shove. "That was my best day. Or rather, night." He paused. "Nights count, don't they?"

Brophy felt ill. A sudden ache settled in his stomach.

"What do you mean?"

"Well, my father and I stopped by old Master Garm's to check on the blades we ordered. Femera was there, just putting things in order. I stopped. We talked a little. She isn't much for talking, as you probably know, but . . ."

Trent shrugged and dropped his voice as though there were people around to hear. "She's not so quiet with her skirts hiked up around her waist."

Brophy shook the image of Trent and Femera from his mind. "She is beautiful." He fell silent.

Trent didn't seem to notice his discomfort. "And willing. Oh so willing. You simply have to know how to move a woman."

Brophy nodded. He had no idea how to move a woman. He wondered if he ever would. Trent was good with women, always had something snappy to say. He had already bedded a dozen or more and told Brophy the stories. It wasn't that way for Brophy. He was still a virgin, and it was no wonder. Whenever Femera was around, his jaw clamped shut, and he couldn't say a thing.

"So what was your best day?" Trent asked again as they neared the base of Ohndarien's blue-white wall.

Brophy couldn't compete. To feel Femera's naked thighs on his, to smell her long hair in his face would be a dream come true.

But something had popped into his mind when Trent first asked the question. It didn't seem like the right time, but he said it anyway.

"It was a couple of years ago in the autumn." He cleared his throat. "I'd just turned thirteen and was standing in the Hall of Windows, looking out over the harbor. Aunt Bae was with me and the sun was setting. You know how the light gets when it comes through the stained glass. It lit the entire room in red and gold, just like the leaves outside. I can't remember why we were there, but everything seemed right. I felt . . . Fate. I felt fate all around me."

Brophy smiled at the memory. "I've never felt more Ohndarien. You know? I felt like this was my city. I was a true Child of the Seasons, and I belonged."

Brophy looked over at Trent, but he knew his friend couldn't see it. How could Brophy make him understand?

"I remember Bae's smile from across the room. I could feel her love like the sun on my face. And I loved her in return. I loved everything. The entire world seemed to breathe and I knew I was meant to do something important."

Brophy fell silent, lost in the image. He always lost himself in it. It was the last moment of true peace he had known.

"Important? Like what?" Trent said. There was a strange tone to his voice.

Brophy stared at the ground, not sure what he should say. Trent started to speak, but he was interrupted by the roar of water ahead of them. A flood of seawater rushed from a round hole in the face of the Water Wall as the hydraulic mechanism opened the massive Physendrian Gate and spewed the excess water onto the salt-crusted stones below.

Trent gave his friend a little shove. "Oh Broph! You're such a kid. I tell you about seducing the most beautiful woman in the city, and you tell me about a fall day with your aunt?" He laughed again. "Would you rather sleep with Baelandra or a girl like Femera?"

"It wasn't like that," Brophy snarled. "It was . . ." He shook his head. "You're such an ass, Trent."

Brophy strode ahead, hurrying out of the hot sun into the welcoming shade of the entrance tunnel. He was instantly blinded by the sudden darkness, but marched forward, not waiting for his eyes to adjust. He gave a curt nod to the two guards on the far side of the towering Physendrian Gate.

"Nephew, are you injured?" one of the men asked, using Brophy's formal title. The young man had the round face and easy smile that instantly showed he was from the House of Summer.

"No, I'm fine," Brophy insisted, and hurried on his way.

Trent was just behind him and greeted the two guardsmen by name.

"What happened?" the soldier asked Trent.

Trent laughed and launched into some tall tale that Brophy didn't even bother listening to.

Leaving the darkness of the tunnel, Brophy entered the city of his birth. Standing in the center of the broad, sloping street, he had a clear view of the entire city. The deep blue harbor and vibrant green gardens instantly made him feel calmer, cooler.

Taking a deep breath, he looked across Ohndarien from Morgeon's Seat, the towering lookout pinnacle on top of the eastern ridge, to the churning windmills next to the Sunset Gate. The Hall of Windows glittered in the very center of it all, the jewel that had given Ohndarien one of its many names. The four torches burning atop it added an ever-present hint of sadness to all that beauty.

Brophy sighed and thought back to that day in the Hall of Windows. There was more to the story, but Trent was such an idiot Brophy wasn't about to tell him the rest. He hadn't told anyone that story, not even Shara or Baelandra.

That afternoon was the first time Brophy heard the voice of the Heartstone, the call to take the Test of the Stone, his birthright as a Child of the Seasons.

The singing was quiet at first, a whisper upon a secret wind. But the more Brophy listened, the clearer he heard until there was no doubt whose voice he was hearing.

The moment he heard that beautiful voice, that incomprehensible language, Brophy forgot about his aunt, forgot about everything.

With his eyes still open, he saw a vision of himself running up a narrow set of stairs, urging others to follow him. A man in a dark cloak holding a sword with a pulsing red gemstone in the pommel guarded their backs.

The northern horizon had turned dark and menacing. Black clouds hunched like an enormous beast ready to leap over the wall and devour Ohndarien. Brophy felt an overwhelming desire to stop that beast, halt it, slay it.

The vision faded as quickly as it had arrived and never returned. Brophy had begun to doubt it ever happened, but years later, the mere thought of it made his heart beat faster.

Since that day, the singing of the Heartstone had always been with him. Sometimes she was a whisper in the back of his mind. Sometimes she filled his head like a roaring wind. But he always looked north when he heard her. Whatever shadowy danger was coming for Ohndarien lay in that direction. Far to the north. Into the Vastness, where his father had disappeared so many years ago bearing the Sword of Autumn, an exquisite blade with a pulsing red gemstone in the pommel.

He heard footsteps leaving the tunnel and banished the vision from his mind. Trent grabbed his shoulders from behind and shook him.

"Come on, Broph, don't be such an old woman. I told you my whole story. Tell me yours. What are you supposed to do that's so important?"

Brophy took a deep breath and continued staring out across Ohndarien. "I'm supposed to protect this city," he said. "I'm supposed to take the Test, become a Brother, serve on her council, and stand in her defense when she needs me the most. I'm supposed to find my father and the other Lost Brothers and bring them back to fight by my side."

Brophy clenched his teeth and waited for a snide comment, but Trent said nothing. His friend had turned away and covered his face with his hand.

For a second, Brophy thought he was crying until he moved closer and saw Trent had turned bright red and was biting his lip.

Brophy cursed himself and stalked away as Trent burst out laughing.

"Brophy! Oh, come on!" Trent yelled, running to catch up with him. "You can't go search for the Lost Brothers. I'd miss you too much!"

WILL I EVER KNOW, Baelandra thought, if I saved Ohndarien or betrayed her?

She watched Krellis pull his boots on one at a time, the laces of his breeches dangling undone. He always pulled his boots on first, swiftly and surely, before he tied the laces at his waist. She'd found it odd the first night they spent together, a lifetime ago, and she'd asked him why he donned his boots so quickly.

He'd smiled his crooked smile, and said, "Habit."

Baelandra slid backward along the silk sheets and rested her back against the headboard. She pulled her knees up to her chin and felt the familiar ache in her chest.

The muscles rippled across Krellis's back as he reached for his tunic, hastily cast aside an hour ago on the blue-white marble of her bedroom floor. The sheer size of the man had frightened her at first, but now she loved losing herself in his arms, swallowed by his embrace. Their lovemaking overwhelmed her. Every time.

Almost a decade her senior, Krellis moved like a youth of twenty-five. He still insisted on teaching the sword and spear to every peach-faced young boy with dreams of the Citadel. Everyone knew he was strong, but the towering man still caught the youngsters unawares with his quickness.

Time stands still for him, she thought, but not for me. I will be a dried-up old crone before the years slow him.

Krellis did not look much different than when she had met him fourteen years ago. There was more gray in his beard, a few extra wrinkles around his eyes, but these things did not determine the age of a man. His inner fire never diminished, not by a single flicker. Every generation had its legends, men and women whose fire lit up the world around them. Brophy's father, Brydeon, had been such a man. Krellis was the same, and she'd wagered all of Ohndarien on her ability to outshine him.

Baelandra was barely past twenty when Krellis marched his army to the Physendrian Gate. She was the youngest member of a divided council. The four brothers had been gone for a year, and her sisters wanted peace so badly they were paralyzed in the face of war. It was left to Baelandra to command an army one-tenth the size of Krellis's invading force. So she made a decision. Rather than being devoured by the wolf at her door, she invited him inside and offered him dinner.

Young, ambitious, supposedly wise beyond her years, Baelandra left the protection of the walls and went to face her adversary. The talking lasted three days, two and a half actually. The third night had not held many words. She and Krellis met in his tent as enemies and ended as lovers.

She welcomed the man into her kingdom, into her body, and finally, reluctantly, into her heart. She played the part of the ocean, content to wear him away until he was smooth and shaped to her will.

Baelandra closed her eyes. Oh Ohndarien, have I betrayed you? I will never outlast him. He is stronger than I could have guessed.

She felt him nearing as she would feel the heat from a fire. Her thoughts scattered like seafoam. She softened her expression, smoothed her brow.

His whiskered lips pressed against her cheek, found her mouth. Once again, she opened herself and kissed him. She breathed in his scent, a mix of musk, dust, and oiled steel.

"You are pensive this morning."

"Just thinking about you," she whispered, opening her eyes.

"With such a stern expression?" He smiled. "I don't usually leave women scowling in their beds. I shall have to do better next time."

Baelandra gave him a smile, the Seasons preserve her, a genuine one. But it did not last. She swallowed and swept her tender thoughts away.

She was happy to see his throat tighten, to see that almost-imperceptible widening of his eyes, the smallest flaring of his nostrils. She was not without power here. His love for her was all she had in this battle.

During their third night of parlay, Baelandra had asked him why he wanted to conquer Ohndarien.

"Because she is the most beautiful city in the world."

"Yes. But cutting the heart from a maiden will not make her love you. You will destroy everything you desire if you bring a sword into this city."

Krellis had smiled at her words. "I have found that maidens are not as fragile as they imagine. I may break this city's heart when I bring down her walls, but broken hearts mend. Your maiden of a city will look even lovelier as mother to my sons."

"But why break her heart, when she may give it to you freely?" she had said. "Why bring her a battle when you could bring her a kiss?"

She offered him a chance to spite his brother, to rule in Ohndarien, and to love her. Krellis took them all. He sent his army back to King Phandir and walked arm in arm with Baelandra through the Physendrian Gate. He traded his army for a kiss. She had intended it to cost him his life.

Her plan seemed so secure in the beginning. To join the ruling council, one must take first the Test of the Stone. This dangerous rite of passage was created to test the ruling houses of Ohndarien. Only a few who were not of the blood had attempted it. All had died.

But Krellis succeeded. For the first time in history, a foreigner bore a stone of the council. She told herself she could defeat her enemy without sacrificing a single soldier. But, after meeting that enemy, after loving him, didn't she know he had the strength to take the stone?

At the end of the test, a sliver of diamond fell off the Heartstone into his hand. He thrust the searing gemstone through his own breastbone, into the very center of his heart. Flesh and stone became one as the Heartstone accepted him, and he accepted her. That thought had comforted and infuriated Baelandra over the years. The man had ambition, an overpowering and ugly ambition, but at the same time the mystical stone from Efften had chosen him to be her champion.

When the Morgeons first brought the Heartstone to Ohndarien, they called it their sister. Perhaps, like many women, the stone put her trust in the wrong man.

Baelandra touched the red diamond buried in the thick hair of his chest. She felt where it had burned itself into his flesh. She carried one between her breasts as well. It made them what they were, Brother and Sister of Autumn, what the Physendrians would call a King and Queen.

He reached out a callused hand and touched her stone. A jolt went through both of them, and he smiled.

"I love that," he rumbled.

"You're such a child."

"I prefer to think of myself as a randy youngster."

"That too."

He stood up straight. Muscles rolled across his back as he threw his tunic over his head and pulled it down. "You'd best get dressed," he said, belting on his short sword. "We will be late for dinner with our guests from across the Great Ocean."

She nodded. "Help me braid my hair first?"

He growled.

She gave him an arch look. "It would not need braiding if you did not insist on setting it free in the heat of your passion."

"That's the way it should be," he said.

"And this is the way it should be now," she said simply, turning her back to him and crossing her legs. Krellis sat on the edge of the bed and began braiding. She closed her eyes and let out a long, even breath. Every brush of his fingers made her want him all over again.

"So what are you keeping from me?" Baelandra asked.

She thought she felt him pause for a second, but she couldn't be sure. He continued braiding as smoothly as ever. He was actually quite good at it.

"Keeping from you?" he replied.

"At your age, you can't afford to waste a whole afternoon kissing my belly unless you are about to do something I won't like."

"What could be more important than kissing your belly?" His lips lingered on the back of the neck. "I came here because I love you. Nothing more. Nothing less."

He spoke the words her heart wanted to hear, but he always did. A woman could let that song lull her to sleep. But a Sister of Autumn had to hear beyond the music. Baelandra had ears in the city, she only hoped they were wrong. If dear Scythe spoke the truth, if Krellis still lusted after a throne, this would be the last time she let that man touch her.

THE SISTER OF AUTUMN followed Krellis out of her bedchambers and down the stairs. Her favorite part of her home was the stairway. It arced gracefully around the outside of the house all the way from her rooms on the third floor down to the garden. Open colonnades looked over the harbor, and the smell of the ocean filled the house.

Halfway down the steps, Baelandra noticed a young woman standing awkwardly in the second-story hallway, her hands clutching a blood-spotted bandage. From her plain looks, she was obviously not a Child of the Seasons. It took Baelandra a moment to recognize the girl as the apprentice of her personal physician. Baelandra would have thought nothing of it, but the girl seemed about to run.

"A moment," Baelandra said, approaching the apprentice. "You are Lenendra's assistant, are you not?"

"Yes, Sister." She gave a slight bow. "You have a good memory for faces. My name is Rindira."

"Who is injured?" Baelandra wanted to know.

The healer grimaced. "He asked me not to say, Sister."

"Trent?" Krellis grumbled. The Brother of Autumn took a step closer to the girl, looming over her. "Did my son ask you to hide something from me?"

"No, Brother," the girl admitted, backing away from him. "Actually it was Brophy."

"Show me to him," Baelandra said.

"Sister, he asked—"

She arched an eyebrow.

Rindira sighed. "Yes, Sister. Follow me."

"Baelandra," Krellis said, "We will be late."

"So we will be late."

"If he wants to hide his wound, it is a man's right."

Baelandra ignored him and followed Rindira. After a moment's pause, Krellis went along.

They entered Brophy's room to find him and Trent joking. Brophy's lip was split and oozing blood. He sat on the edge of the bed. His ribs bore ragged, pink scrapes that would soon purple into bruises.

Trent turned pale the moment he saw his father, then shot a vicious look at Rindira, who held out her hands helplessly.

Krellis frowned. "What happened?" he growled.

"Well," Trent began, "it was the damnedest thing—"

"Not you, boy," Krellis cut his son off. He tipped his chin at Brophy. "You. What happened?"

Trent's brow furrowed and he flushed. He looked at Brophy.

Brophy opened his mouth, closed it. Baelandra let out a quiet breath. The boy's curly blond hair and green eyes reminded her of Brydeon at that age. They were so much alike it hurt sometimes. Neither father nor son could ever sell a lie. Her nephew's innocence made her want to smile. Or sigh. Or both.

"We were hunting," Brophy said. He glanced at Trent, who remained stone-faced. "I was staring at the sky, watching my hawk, and didn't see the drop-off. I fell about five feet and landed on a rock."

"A rock?" Krellis repeated.

"Uh, yes. A rock."

"Pig flies, boy. That's the worst lie I've ever heard."

Brophy blushed deep red. He flicked an angry look at Trent.

"We were playing a game," he said.

Trent clenched his jaw.

"What kind of game?" Krellis asked, his voice low.

"It's a stupid game," Brophy said. Baelandra had to give him credit. He never quailed under Krellis's frown like Trent, like so many others. Brophy told them the events of the day. Baelandra hid her mirth, but Krellis was not so successful. The corner of his mouth revealed a bit of his crooked smile.

Krellis shook his head. "What kind of half-wit would stand there and let a rock hit him in the mouth?"

Again, Brophy shot Trent an angry glance.

"Next time, move," Krellis said, smiling as he walked to the door.

Baelandra followed him toward the hallway, but he stopped just outside the door and turned.

"Brophy, would you mind stepping outside for a moment?" he said.

Trent gave Brophy a look of such bitter venom that Baelandra's heart beat faster.

"Aren't we going to be late for the council meeting?" she asked.

Krellis ignored her and stared at his son. The boy could not return the gaze. She wished Krellis wasn't so rigid when it came to Trent. Anyone could see the boy idolized his father. A few compliments would help him more than a hundred harsh words.

Reluctantly, Brophy slid off the bed and walked into the hall. Trent stared at the floor, stiff-lipped and angry. Krellis stepped into the room and closed the door behind him.

"I'm sorry, Bae," Brophy said, with a helpless shrug. "It was a stupid thing to do."

"That's all right, Brophy," she said, lifting his chin to get a better look at his mouth. "No need to apologize to me. Pain is a harsh enough teacher . . . for most people." She arched an eyebrow. He blushed and looked away. The Seasons bless him, he looked just like his father.

The door to Brophy's room suddenly swung open and Trent rushed out. He ran past Baelandra and shoved Brophy with all his might, sending the younger boy crashing into the wall.

Krellis emerged from the room with a weary frown. He flexed his fingers as he looked down at his enormous hand. "Shall we join our guests?"

THE AMBASSADOR'S GALLEY rocked gently in the soft evening breeze. About forty people lingered on the forecastle of the single-masted ship. High-ranking Children of the Seasons chatted with the ambassador's entourage. The Ohohhim ship was exquisite in its simplicity. The gray wood of her decks shone like an oiled blade. The diplomat's ship had none of the bloody-minded carvings of a vessel from Kherif or the gaudy colors of a slave ship from Vizar. The empire on the far side of the Great Ocean kept their ships simple and elegant. Krellis appreciated a well-crafted vessel, but he would happily burn the bitch to the waterline if it would get him off her a second earlier.

He had been trapped here since sundown. The ambassador from Ohohhim had sailed through the Sunset Gate just before dusk. Six hours later, Krellis and the ancient diplomat hadn't done much more than say hello and drown one another in an endless stream of pointless flattery. If Krellis wanted his ass polished, he'd have done it himself.

If there was one thing Krellis hated, it was etiquette. Baelandra seemed to have limitless patience for the formal receptions, the endless dinners, and the polite but meaningless conversations in the gardens. Krellis simply bit his tongue and waited until he could sink his teeth into a ruthless negotiation behind closed doors.

However, it took five years to arrange Father Lewlem's visit, and he wasn't about to jeopardize this meeting. If six hours of pleasantries were required, he would dance to any tune. The Emperor in the Opal Palace had been twenty years old when Krellis first sent emissaries. His men waited for a year to gain their first audience with the "immortal" ruler. Krellis's request for an alliance was politely heard and politely ignored. It was just the same with the second group of emissaries and the third and the fourth, politely heard, politely ignored. They should have sent the men's heads back in a basket. At least that would have been honest.

Krellis took a gulp of the cloying, fermented yogurt the Ohohhim served.

The taste turned his stomach, but he wanted the alcohol. He flexed his fingers as he watched his adversary. The shriveled ambassador hung on Baelandra's every word. The tiny old man's curly hair was dyed jet-black and cascaded to his waist. Like all officials from the bizarre far-western empire, Lewlem covered his face and hands with a white powder that protected him from the sun.

For a people who painted themselves black and white, the Ohohhim certainly lived in shades of gray. It was impossible to get a straight answer from them about anything.

Unwilling to wait any longer, Krellis decided to push the issue. He stood, walking over to the tiny man and his deaf-mute wife. Baelandra saw him out of the corner of her eye and quickly wrapped up the story she was telling about the Midwinter Festival of Lights.

"Father Lewlem," Krellis said to the shrunken ambassador. "I was admiring the ivory handle of your ship's tiller. Is that whalebone?"

The old man clapped his hands together like a small child. "You have a keen eye for beauty. That is my favorite part of this ship, but it is not a whalebone. It is the tooth of a striped walrus that my men killed while in the Vastness."

"Would you care to show it to me? I would love to hear what you know of the land of the horse clans." Krellis raised an eyebrow, hoping the foreigner would pick up on the subtle meaning behind his words.

The ambassador's face lit up. "Nothing would please me more."

The two men walked side by side across the deck to the back of the ship. Hierarchy was extremely important to the Ohohhim. It would have been a mistake for him to walk ahead of the ambassador, which would imply that Krellis outranked him. It would have been just as bad to walk behind, implying that he was subservient.

Krellis reached the tiller and admired the handle. From a distance, he thought it was carved in a spiral pattern, but up close he saw the coils were natural.

"The creature this tooth came from must have been enormous," he said.

Lewlem clapped his hands. "He fed my crew of fifty men for a week."

"I have heard many tales of wonders from the Vastness."

"It is a land of great beauty and unspeakable horrors."

Krellis paused to run his hand along the ivory tiller handle. "I understand your Emperor has a great interest in the treasures of the Vastness."

Lewlem nodded. "His Eternal Wisdom has always been fascinated by items of great power and beauty."

"I was led to believe there is one item in particular that he would like to acquire. Perhaps I could be of assistance."

"Perhaps."

"As we both know, the four former Brothers of the Seasons left this city years ago to investigate a great tragedy that occurred in the far north."

"Reports of this tragedy have traveled across the Great Ocean."

"Ever since that time, those four men have remained in the Vastness, hiding the source of that tragedy."

"This news has also reached the ears of his Eternal Wisdom. You speak of the Legacy of Efften."

"I do."

"The incarnation of God on Earth is dedicated to acquiring any items from the fallen City of Sorcerers."

"I possess information that would be of great assistance to your Emperor's ambition."

Father Lewlem shook his head. "It is not ambition, but sacred duty. The lost secrets must be kept safe from those who would abuse them. Only His Magnificence has the wisdom to wield such power."

"My apologies." Krellis nodded in deference. "I had forgotten your Emperor is not a mortal man with mortal desires."

"You are forgiven. The Emperor is difficult for barbarians to understand."

Krellis's lips tightened at the insult, but he continued on without a ruffle. He could afford a little indulgence in exchange for what he might gain.

"The former Brother of Autumn sent many letters to his sister before his death. I intercepted those letters."

Father Lewlem pursed his powdered lips.

"Do the letters say where the Legacy is hidden?"

"They do."

Lewlem pressed his palms together. "These letters are less than I hoped for, but more than I expected. They might be enough to convince His Eternal Wisdom to extend an offer of friendship."

"I am pleased to hear that. I will make these letters available to you when the Emperor's navy is within sight of Ohndarien's walls."

The ambassador looked Krellis in the face for the first time. "It shall be as you say."

Krellis struggled to keep the smile off his face as he turned and walked back toward the others. He was pleased to see the foreign diplomat fall into step behind him. It was about time the ambassador realized who he was dealing with.

Krellis had just traded a handful of paper for the most powerful navy on the Great Ocean. He had parlayed stories about an infant girl and a music box into a crown that would make him a king of two countries.

Even a barbarian could see that His Eternal Wisdom was a colossal fool.

I 'M READY to sleep with him," Shara said out of nowhere, tossing the words in Brophy's face. She bit her lip, hoping for the perfect reaction, not knowing what it could possibly be.

Brophy stopped in his tracks. People in the crowd had to veer around him as he stood there staring at her. She felt a stab of disappointment, turned quickly, and continued on her way.

The council meeting was starting late. People had grown restless milling and chatting in the Night Market for the last hour. Shara had spotted Brophy amidst the crowd, and they started up a conversation just like always.

The two of them had been friends since they were children. Shara adored him, but she hated the way he followed Trent around like a shadow. Just look at his smashed-up face. She didn't know who was the bigger fishbrain, Trent for coming up with the game or Brophy for playing it.

A lone trumpet atop the Hall of Windows announced the opening of the Wheel, and hundreds of Ohndariens and foreigners joined the procession from the Night Market up to the Council Gardens. A single curving staircase spiraled around the circular plateau known as the Wheel of the Seasons. The stairs were ten feet wide and carved from the living rock. They spiraled around the Wheel one complete revolution before arriving at the top. The beauty of the design was its inefficiency. The trip gave people a chance to change their state of mind, to leave their normal life behind and join a higher one.

Brophy caught up with Shara as she reached the steps. She watched him closely as they started up, walking slowly and stately. She chided herself for being hurt by his reaction. He was still young. He didn't understand much about the real world. But it still stung. He was the only real friend she had, and it mattered what he thought.

"You're going through the ritual then?" he asked. "With Master Victeris?"

"Yes," she said quickly.

He nodded.

"I'll graduate and finally be a full Zelani." She was a year overdue. She'd put it off as long as she dared if she ever wanted to graduate.

"Will you have to leave?"

"I don't know. I will be assigned wherever the council requires."

"Like Syrol and Payter?"

Syrol and Payter were the first students to graduate from the Zelani school in Ohndarien. Shara had been recruited at the same time as the others. She was more talented than either of them, yet she remained a student.

Payter had been sent with an ambassador to Kherif more than ten months ago. Syrol was still in the city, attached to Gorlym, Master of the Citadel. Shara still saw her every now and then. She envied Syrol's elegant gowns and the beautiful silver chain that encircled her waist. The chain was set with the pale blue stone of the Zelani that brought her respect and deference wherever she went.

News of the Zelanis' power was spreading across the two oceans. Master Victeris's mother had revived the secrets lost in the destruction of Efften. After her death, Victeris founded his school here in the Free City. The sorcerers of legend were being reborn in Ohndarien, and Shara would be the latest to join the fabled lineage.

"And when you're chosen, what will you do with them?"

"Don't be stupid, Brophy."

"Will you have to . . . all the time?"

"When they need me, yes."

He frowned, and she gave him an amused glance. "Think of the things I will see, the places I'll go. If I wasn't here, I'd already be some farmer's wife with a screaming baby on each arm and pig shit on my feet. If I was lucky."

Brophy looked back at her, his serious green eyes inevitably drawn to her breasts, barely covered by the gossamer blue gown all Zelani students wore.

"At least I won't be on constant display anymore," she said.

Brophy's eyes snapped back to her face. He grinned sheepishly. Shara laughed and gave him a little shove. He was growing up. Mostly, she found it amusing, but it was also a bit sad.

Men had been sneaking glances at her all night. She had become accustomed to it. People were supposed to look. That's what the split-sided wisp of a dress was for. Still, sometimes a bit of privacy would be nice. Perhaps that was why the glamour was so exciting. Being noticed gave one power, but going unnoticed gave one freedom, which was a different kind of power entirely.

Brophy stayed silent. He always became so serious whenever he visited the Wheel. It was like he aged fifty years every time he passed through an archway into the Hall of Windows. She left Brophy to his silence and looked out over the city as they came around the west side of the Wheel. The dockside piers swarmed with sailing ships, coming and going. The hills beyond were covered with scaffolding, clinging to new construction projects like a net of vines. In recent years, the council had allowed more and more foreigners into the city. The face of Ohndarien was changing as these newcomers built their homes and tried to make their fortune.

The Free City was beautiful all year long, but autumn was especially nice. In a few weeks the trees would erupt into brilliant hues of gold, orange, and crimson. Shara had grown up in the blue-green pines of Faradan. They had their own beauty, but they stayed the same all year. She preferred the turn of the seasons in Ohndarien.

Shara inhaled deeply and slowly exhaled. Breath was the First Gate, the foundation of everything she did.

She turned to her friend, and he smiled. For a moment, the lines between them vanished. She wasn't a Zelani-to-be and he wasn't a Child of the Seasons. They were simply two kids who met swimming in the bay so many years ago.

"I'm scared, Brophy," she murmured.

He looked up, his face full of concern. "Of Victeris?"

Shara felt a flood of affection for the boy. He knew her so well. It was one of the most wonderful things about him.

She nodded. "Yes. There are some things . . ." She paused.

"What things?"

She looked around. There were too many people. She couldn't talk about this here. "Let's just say, when I ran away from the school when I was eleven, I might have had the right idea."

His brow furrowed. "Then run away now."

"No," she said fiercely, then quieter. "No. I've made my choice. I've trained for nine years, and I'm not throwing it away."

He nodded, returning to that serious face he always wore in the Hall of Windows. "I understand. There are some things you just have to do, even when you don't know why."

The two of them reached the end of the stairs. The top of the Wheel was covered with gardens, fountains, and sheltered walkways. It was alive with the color of flowers, the gurgle of flowing water, and the music of birdsong. In the center of it all stood the Hall of Windows, glittering like a huge jewel in the afternoon sun. Four towering archways of blue-white marble supported the domed amphitheater. A delicate spiderweb of copper latticework held up acres of stained glass comprising the walls and ceiling of the dome. Shara felt a lump in her throat as she looked at the beauty and grandeur of Ohndarien's crown jewel.

Why was there so much ugliness in the world when people could create such beauty? Why was there so much fear and doubt when strength and courage were just a thought away? Above all else, Shara hated senseless ugliness. She despised neglect and filth. That was why she would become a Zelani. Shara was born to dirty, little people who hid in their dirty, little hovels, but she would live her life like the Hall of Windows, rising above it all like an icon of beauty, reflecting her light into the world.

Brophy tentatively reached out and touched her shoulder. "Shara, I know you'll get what you want. You always do. You'll do great."

"Thank you, Brophy." She gave his hand a genuine squeeze, then, unable to help herself, she went low to poke him in the stomach.

To her surprise, his hand shot out and caught her wrist. His fingers were warm and firm as steel.

"Be careful, all right?" he said, his serious face making him appear twice his age.

Shara suddenly remembered the man who gave her his cloak a few nights ago. She breathed through the tightness in her stomach and let it go. "I will," she promised.

She stood up on tiptoe to kiss Brophy on the cheek. "Be good. Don't always listen to what Trent says."

Shara felt the boy's eyes linger on her back as she left the procession and joined the other Zelani in front of the Spring Gate. She must stand with the other students while Brophy continued around the circular path to join the Children of the Seasons.

Most of the Zelani students were already there, fifty youngsters ranging from ten to eighteen years old. They would enter last, when the rest of the amphitheater was full. The youngest pupils were still fidgety in their formal clothes, but they would learn decorum quickly. Nervous students did not last long.

Brophy came to the councils because he loved them. Shara, on the other hand, was required to attend. Brother Krellis wanted the Zelani students to be seen. One day, each of them would become attached to the most important friends of the Free City. They were one of the most valuable currencies of Ohndarien politics, and everyone in the world would see what could be theirs . . . if they remained faithful.

Shara took her place next to Caleb, the most senior of the male students. She subtly pulled her foot out of her sandal and ran a toe down the inside of his calf. The boy cracked a small smile, but continued to stare straight ahead, concentrating on his breathing. Of all the older boys, Caleb was the most fun to tease. He was sweet to the bone, but so solemn. She tried to trip him up whenever she could.

Unable to get a rise out of him, she turned to study the crowd making its way toward the Hall. She looked into people's eyes, tried to guess what they were feeling. She tried to imagine what it would be like to be assigned to one of these men. What would they be like, alone in the dark? How could she make their inner fire burn bright as the sun?

Shara's pulse quickened. Without knowing why, she sensed Krellis as he walked up the path. Everyone politely stepped aside as the Brother of Autumn came closer. He was not particularly handsome or finely dressed, but the crowd made way for him like the sea receding from the shore. His black hair was wild, but his face drew everyone's attention wherever he went.

The Brother of Autumn had no Zelani. Some said that Baelandra served that purpose for him, but Shara didn't believe it. He was waiting for the right student to graduate.

After all these years, many Ohndariens still disapproved of the foreign Brother. Despite those who resented Krellis's position on the council, Ohndarien had flourished under his guidance. He'd tripled the size of the army and kept the ports running day and night. Native Ohndariens still mourned the loss of their missing Brothers who went north into the Vastness to honor an ancient, secret alliance. Brophy had never met those men, but he bore their loss like a knife wound.

As Krellis approached, Shara noticed a stooped, ancient man walking next to him. The old man had the powdered, milk-white skin and curly, jet-black hair common to the ruling class of the far western empire. Krellis dwarfed the smaller man, who barely came up to his shoulder. The foreigner hovered next to Krellis, holding onto his shirt like a toddler clings to his mother's skirts. Shara's instructors had told her how the men from

Ohohhom were required to hold on to the sleeve of any man who out-ranked them. The sleeve holder would, in turn, have his sleeve held by an-other man of lesser rank. She'd heard stories of entire processions of Ohohhim walking through their imperial palace in perfect social marching order. Shara imagined them like a line of four-year-olds playing follow the leader.

A tiny woman with the same milk-white face and black hair followed di-rectly behind the ancient Ohohhim. She held on to his shirt just like the man was holding on to Krellis's. The woman could have been fifteen or fifty. It was hard to judge her painted face, especially when she kept her gaze locked on the ground.

Krellis must have felt rather foolish with a line of ghost-faced foreigners hanging off him, but he showed no unease with the strange custom. He car-ried himself with the same grace and fierce dignity as always.

To Shara's surprise, Krellis left the procession and brought the Oho-hhim right up to her. She curtsied as low as she could, as befitted the for-mal occasion.

"Father Lewlem, this is Shara," Krellis said, inclining a hand toward her.

She curtsied again, not quite as low, toward the foreigner.

"She is the Zelani student I spoke of earlier."

"Daughter of my heart, it is a joy to meet you again for the first time," the old man said with a playful twinkle in his eye. She liked him immediately. She had rarely met anyone so old who still smiled like a child.

"Father of my heart," she said, remembering the proper reply from an eti-quette lesson years ago, "I remember you fondly, even though I've never seen your face."

"Would you accept the honor," Krellis asked Shara, "of being Father Lewlem's guide for the rest of the evening? I regret I have other duties I must attend to."

"I would be honored," she replied, without a trace of formality. Krellis had never spoken to her before. He obviously knew she was about to graduate. It thrilled her that he knew so much about her.

Father Lewlem carefully smoothed Krellis's sleeve where he had been holding it and tucked his hands into a fold of his robes.

Krellis quickly leaned forward and whispered in Shara's ear, "Hold on to his wife's sleeve and do not let go until she has given you leave."

Shara looked past Lewlem at the tiny woman standing a few paces behind him. She was so small and meek she looked like a scolded child. As Krellis took his leave, Shara slipped deftly around Lewlem and pinched his wife's sleeve between thumb and forefinger. She stole a moment of eye contact with Caleb, who smiled in approval.

"Shall we rejoin the procession, Father?" she asked, unsure of the protocol.

The old man smiled and clapped his hands together in front of him like a little kid. "Yes, yes, let us see how this 'free' city governs herself."

Shara waited for the Ohohhim to go ahead and followed him along the path. This council marked the first day of autumn, so everyone would enter the hall through the Autumn Gate on the far side of the Wheel.

"In the Center of the World, where I am from," the old man began, "the Emperor speaks and reality follows. He holds the power of Oh on earth and has never been wrong in five thousand years. It is the superior way of life, I say, but I am very curious to see the sleeve you follow here."

Possible replies tumbled through Shara's mind, but she decided to trust the smile in the old man's eyes more than the formality of his words.

"Life would be simpler if we had an Emperor as well. Here in Ohndarien, I am afraid, we are wrong all the time."

Lewlem giggled like a little girl and clapped his hands again.

"Ah, the bluntness of the East, it is a barbarian delight."

Shara smiled back at him, knowing she had read him correctly.

"Please," the old man said, "tell me of your city. I know much that you will say, but I wish to hear the story from the lips of my lovely daughter."

As they continued along with the procession, Shara gave Lewlem the brief history of Ohndarien she had been trained to deliver.

"To explain Ohndarien, I must start at the beginning. Construction of the walls began less than 250 years ago. We are a relatively young city, but unique in the world. The four families that started the construction brought very diverse talents to the table. The Geldars had been living in this bay for hundreds of years, before Ohndarien was even a dream in the mind of Donovan Morgeon. The Geldars made their living fishing, herding, and quarrying marble from the mountain and shipping the blocks both east and west. They were the first to embrace Donovan's vision and provided most of the labor for building the city. They eventually became the House of Summer and the majority of Ohndarien's population."

The glittering sunlight reflecting off the stained-glass dome made it difficult to look at anything else. The intricate beauty of the craftsmanship still amazed her after all this time. Shara pointed out a glittering depiction of the sculpted towers and lush shoreline of Efften, the doomed homeland of Ohndarien's founding fathers.

"The Morgeons fled from Efften when the City of Sorcerers was overrun.

They were one of the few families to escape the slaughter. Though they had been a family of scholars, exile forced them to become merchants. They wandered the Great Ocean for two generations before Donovan Morgeon, at the helm of his first trading vessel, visited the Geldars. He spent the next forty years dreaming of building Ohndarien.

"Morgeon imagined a road over the mountains, carrying goods back and forth in wagons. However, his idea didn't become practical until he met the renowned Master Coelho. The Morgeons became the House of Winter and are the greatest traders and scholars in Ohndarien.

"Coelho was a master architect who had spent his life building the famous Gildheld waterworks. Donovan sought out the master architect when he visited the Summer Seas. Morgeon's idea sparked the tired old man's imagination, and they spent the next year planning the broad strokes of the city. Coelho proposed the ideas for the locks, the windmills, and the Water Wall. The old man was too weak to travel, and he died long before construction ever started, but his genius made Ohndarien possible. His wife and children perfected the plans that Coelho began. His descendants went on to become the House of Spring and now tend the ports and waterworks in Ohndarien."

Shara smiled. "They say Master Coelho still lives in the stone of the walls and the water of the locks."

"I am sure he does," Lewlem said. "The spirits of the dead remain with us forever, just within the shadow of Oh's cave."

Shara made the sign of respect she had been taught and continued with her story.

"Despite a working plan, Donovan's dream could not take shape without the money or military might to start the project. There was no point in building a city if he could not defend it. Donovan went from kingdom to kingdom, back and forth across the two oceans looking for someone to lend him the gold and soldiers to start his project, but his ideas were so radical that no one believed it would work."

"He came to the Opal Palace," Lewlem chimed in. "The Emperor wisely refused his request."

Shara couldn't be sure if the old man was being sarcastic. She hoped he had enough sense of humor to laugh at his own God on Earth, but it was hard to read his face. She nodded respectfully and continued with her story.

"Donovan was finally approached by J'Qulin the Sly, the infamous mercenary commander of the Lightning Swords. J'Qulin had grown wealthy and reviled by constantly switching sides in a series of civil wars between Upper and Lower Kherif. Although J'Qulin had a reputation for being treacherous,

Donovan believed him when he claimed to have grown weary of war. J'Qulin wanted to marry, settle down, and enjoy his riches, but he had a responsibility to his men. They were hated and feared throughout the two oceans. No kingdom would sell them land."

"The Emperor refused this man as well. One could say that your fair city could not have been built without Ohohhim wisdom," Lewlem said.

"I'm sure the world would stop spinning if the Emperor did not hold her center so artfully."

Lewlem clapped again, giggling uncontrollably. "Well spoken, my daughter, well spoken. Please continue with your tale."

The procession had passed through the Autumn Gate's archway of gold and red leaves into the Hall of Windows. The crowd took their seats around a large amphitheater. The soaring dome that enclosed the council chambers was even more beautiful from the inside. The stained glass overhead was angled so that different parts of it caught the light in every season. The feel of the cavernous room changed from month to month. In autumn red and gold glass caught the light most directly. Blue and silver light filled the Hall in winter. Spring brought yellow and pale green. And in summer the stained glass high overhead broke the sunlight into every color of the rainbow.

Shara thought the hall was most beautiful by moonlight, when the entire room was hung in dark blue shadow as if it were deep underwater.

A circle of blue-white marble lay at the center of the auditorium, with eight stone chairs placed upon it. In the very center of the circle was a hole that dropped down to the Heart of Ohndarien, the sacred chamber where the Test of the Stone was given to those who sought a seat on the council.

Shara often caught herself staring at the shadowy opening that led down to the Heart. Brophy would go down that hole someday. He might never come back up. She took a breath and continued her story.

"J'Qulin could have conquered a small city and ruled it by the sword, but he had destroyed so many things in his life, he longed to create something instead. Donovan agreed to trust the man when no one else would, and suddenly he had gold, an army, and a new best friend. J'Qulin married fourteen women, fathered forty children and died at sixty-five with a sword in his hand, defending Ohndarien from the third of many invasions. His children became the House of Autumn and are responsible for collecting taxes and defending the walls of Ohndarien."

"Fourteen wives is very impressive," Lewlem noted. "I myself have only four . . . so far."

The old man looked sideways at her through the corner of his eye. One side of his powdered lips curled upward.

Shara couldn't help smiling. She liked this man, liked him a great deal. She continued with her story.

"The aqueduct, canals, and locks took seventy-five years to build. Donovan Morgeon was carried in his bed on the first ship to sail through the locks from the Great Ocean to the Summer Sea. He was 134 years old. The stories say that he died with a smile on his face the moment his ship sailed out of the city."

Lewlem clapped again. "It is a beautiful story. A very Eastern story, but beautiful nonetheless."

"But our history was not always so beautiful. That is why we have the Brothers and Sisters of the Seasons."

"Eight people to rule one city. Sounds like a wife with eight husbands to me."

Shara glanced at Lewlem's wife. The woman had not said a word nor lifted her eyes from the ground the entire time. She wondered what the two of them were like alone in bed with no one else around.

A hush fell over the crowd as a tall, white-haired woman in a green gown entered the amphitheater through the flower-covered Spring Gate.

"That's Jayden, the Sister of Spring," Shara whispered to her guest. "The torch she carries symbolizes the Brother of Spring who is still missing."

Jayden was nearly eighty and prone to nodding off during council meetings, but Shara had heard that her senility was half an act. The old woman still had teeth, and she wasn't afraid to use them.

A second woman with a torch entered through the evergreen Summer Gate. This woman was in her late forties, blond-haired and plump. She wore a modest gown of yellow and gold. She smiled so broadly that she always looked a little stupid.

"Hazel, Sister of Summer," Shara explained.

Next came Baelandra and Krellis, arm in arm through the Autumn Gate. Every head turned to watch them. The Brother of Autumn was twice the size of the petite green-eyed beauty at his side, but she blazed every bit as bright. Baelandra had always been breathtaking. Her red hair seemed to flicker like a torch in the daylight.

"The woman beside Krellis is Baelandra, Sister of Autumn," Shara explained.

"The sun must be jealous of her beauty," Lewlem noted.

Shara felt a stab of jealousy but breathed it out.

"She is also the youngest woman ever to take the Test of the Stone. Her beauty is the least of her virtues."

As Baelandra and Krellis walked by, the Sister of Autumn noticed Shara and gave her a slight smile. Baelandra was also Brophy's aunt and the kindest woman Shara had ever met. When Shara ran away from the Zelani school so many years ago, Trent and Brophy brought her home, and Baelandra took her in immediately. At the time, Shara thought she had them all fooled. She acted as though she was a lost orphan, not a renegade Zelani student. Baelandra had taken her at her word and said nothing of it. The Sister of Autumn must have known who Shara was all along, but Baelandra bided her time and waited for Shara to make her own decision. When Shara finally confessed who she was, Baelandra had nodded just as she had when Shara claimed to be an orphan.

"And what will you do now?" was the Sister's only question.

Shara had chosen to return and complete her training. She still wondered if Baelandra had known what choice she would make and simply waited for Shara to say it rather than forcing her to return. What would Baelandra have done if Shara chose to abandon the Zelani training?

The two icons of Ohndarien walked past the respectfully silent crowd to take their places behind two of the simple stone chairs.

The last woman to enter wore her dark brown hair cut short like a man. She was painfully thin, with a harsh, angular face, the least attractive Sister by far. She always looked like she was in pain.

"That's Vallia, Sister of Winter," Shara whispered. "Once they have taken their places, the Brother and Sister of Autumn will offer a gift to the others."

Father Lewlem tapped his shoulder, and his wife let go of his sleeve. He turned to Shara and bowed slightly. "Daughter of my heart. Please keep my wife company for a moment; Krellis wished to introduce me to your council."

"Of course."

Father Lewlem shuffled through the milling crowd. Shara was left holding on to his wife's sleeve, not sure if she should let go.

"Excuse me," she asked the downcast woman. "I never heard your name."

The tiny woman suddenly turned around and grabbed the front of Shara's dress, pinching her nipple and twisting as hard as she could.

"Listen, you barbaric slut," she hissed, staring right in Shara's eyes. "I will be that man's last wife."

Shara nearly punched the little woman in the face. A year ago, she might have, but her Zelani training kept her in check. She couldn't make a scene, not here.

"Don't go prowling around him like a cat in heat," Lewlem's wife continued. "I don't fear your Eastern sorcery. I don't fear whatever magic you have tucked under your skirts. If you touch my husband, I will kill you in your sleep."

Shara took two deep, steady breaths. She breathed the pain and anger into her power. When she opened her eyes again, the Ohohhim woman took a quick step backward and let go of Shara's nipple.

"You misunderstand me, lady," Shara said, every word flowing from the fiery maelstrom contained within her body. "If I were attached to Lewlem as a Zelani, you might lose some of his attention, but you would gain something far greater. I would teach him to give you pleasures you have never dreamed of. And he could receive from you ten times what the normal man can contain. You would lose the husband you know, but you would gain an emperor among men. Do not waste your threats on me, Mother. I could be the greatest thing that ever happened to you."

Lewlem's wife stumbled backward. Shara caught her by the arm and gently set her back on her feet. She carefully took the foreign woman's sleeve.

"Look, Mother, the council is about to convene."

AN HOUR LATER, all old business before the council had been decided and they agreed to call a short recess before beginning any new discussions.

Shara directed Lewlem's wife out of the building toward the refreshments. Lewlem's wife stood beside Shara, meek and quiet as before. Flush with power, Shara could feel everyone's eyes on her. She felt their desire, men and women both, like a hundred strings she could pull at will.

She saw Krellis and a young man with coal-black hair and a silver vest chatting under a plum tree. She recognized the tall, thin man, but couldn't recall his name. He was of the Blood, a Child of the Seasons. His name was . . . Celidon.

She remembered him now. He was the third son of the absent Brother of Winter, his older brothers had sailed away to find their father and the other Lost Brothers and never returned.

Shara noticed Father Lewlem on the far side of the clearing and nudged his wife in that direction. Shara had been holding on to the deaf-mute wife's sleeve for the past hour and a half. Her shoulder was starting to ache with the strain. The old man noticed them immediately and weaved his way through the crowd to join them. His wife latched on to his sleeve immediately.

Shara smiled at the ambassador, immediately pleased simply by his presence. "Father, what do you think of our council meetings?"

"Very good. Very good."

Shara wasn't going to let him get off that easily. "No, please, tell me what you really think. Be barbarically blunt."

The old man clapped twice in appreciation. "All this argument over issues is delightful, but isn't it like lifting your skirts and inviting a public debate? Aren't you embarrassed?"

She laughed. "No, not embarrassed at all. We appreciate candor."

"I see that you do. Please, child, continue with your tale."

She nodded. "The end of Ohndarien's tale is one of tragedy and triumph. A few years after Ohndarien's walls were completed, the ruling families began to feud over the power and wealth of their new city. To prevent a civil war, the children of the ruling families locked their parents into a cave below this very hall, refusing to let them out until they resolved their differences. The parents refused to reconcile, and there they stayed." She paused. "You see, we believe that leadership is a duty, not a privilege. Only those who can work with others should be allowed to rule over others."

Lewlem cleared his throat. "What a tragic story."

Shara suddenly felt her control of the situation crumble. Had she offended him? The story must be anathema to a culture as steeped in hierarchy as the Ohohhim, but if he wanted to understand Ohndarien, this tragic tale was at its heart.

Father Lewlem shook his head. "I have heard of this cave and the Heartstone that is kept inside. Is it true that this stone is a legacy of Efften? It is said to possess terrible power."

"Donovan Morgeon's family saved the stone from destruction when they fled the doomed city. They brought it here while Ohndarien was being built. I have never heard it called terrible before, but only a Brother or Sister of the Seasons could answer that for sure."

The childlike smile left the ambassador's face. The old man suddenly looked ancient. "It is hard for one to recognize evil when it surrounds him every day."

The old man's demeanor had changed completely, but Shara could not guess why.

"Have I offended you in some way?" she asked.

"No, child," the old man said. "I thank you for your hospitality."

The old man turned and walked away. His wife followed him, and Shara let the woman's sleeve slip through her fingers.

A trumpet announced that the council was about to reconvene. Shara walked around to the east side of the Hall and joined the other Zelani students. Caleb raised an eyebrow as if to ask her what happened. She ignored him, fearing that she had done something terribly wrong, but not sure what.

Concentrating on her breath, she watched the hole to the Heart, for the first time frightened of what might be down there.

The Brother and Sisters soon returned to their places. Krellis waited for the last of the crowd to filter back inside. When the hall was settled, Krellis called for petitions in his deep, booming voice. Several people stepped forward, but Krellis's eye fell on Celidon, the young man in the silver vest.

Celidon stepped out of the crowd and stood in front of the council.

"Yes, Celidon, what have you today?" the Brother of Autumn asked.

The young man took a deep breath before speaking. "With your permission," he started. His voice was soft and difficult to hear as he spoke the ritual words. "I would give my blood to the blood of Ohndarien. I would make her troubles my troubles, her joys my duties. I would put my life in her service forever."

Hazel closed her eyes and bowed her doughy head. The snowy-haired Jayden rose to her feet, her hand clenched in a fist. Vallia's left eyebrow twitched. Baelandra held her composure, her bearing attentive and concerned as always.

"Brothers and Sisters of the Council," Celidon continued. "I would attempt the Test of the Stone and take up my father's legacy as the Brother of Winter."

Tentatively reaching out with her power, Shara looked deep within the young man's eyes and saw nothing but fear.

6

BAELANDRA CAREFULLY made her way toward the top of the Hall of Windows. The meeting had ended hours ago, and the crowd had drifted from the amphitheater. They would return at sundown to hold vigil while Celidon faced the Test.

Baelandra remained behind, forcing herself to chat with an endless queue of petitioners who sought a moment of her time. She wanted to scream, wanted to call the lightning down on Krellis's head, but she just smiled and nodded, playing the part she knew so well. As soon as she could, she slipped away from the stragglers and went in search of Brophy. There was only one place he could be, on top of the Hall.

It was a dangerous climb up the stairs. They curved up the outside of the vaulted amphitheater to the intersection of the four main arches at the crown of the building. The path was ridiculously steep, and there was no handrail. It was a climb for the young. She'd done it herself many times in another age, before the Test of the Stone, before she became a Sister of Autumn and so many weights had been laid across her shoulders. None of the other Sisters would have tried it, but Baelandra had always been the reckless one. It was in her blood. She was of the House of Autumn after all.

The bay glittered in the dying light. She could see the entire city, from the Windmill Wall to where the locks disappeared into the mountainside. She could see men working the quarries beyond the northern battlements and soldiers training with the trebuchets tucked into the towering arches of the Water Wall.

Taking a few deep breaths, she continued upward. The steps grew less steep as Baelandra neared the top of the arch. It was always strange to see the stained glass up close. It looked normal from up here, just shards of glass held between thin lines of copper. Yet from below, those tiny pieces became a dazzling painting of light.

For a moment, she was that young girl again, wild as a stripeback cub, following her older brother and his friends up the steep steps for the first time. Brydeon had been quiet at that age, a watcher. Mother and Father thought Brydeon would never take the Test of the Stone. Certainly Baelandra would. The fire burned brightly in her from the moment she could cry. But not Brydeon. They thought he was destined to become an academic.

But Baelandra had never believed that. She knew why Brydeon watched. He waited, storing his experiences like a miser hoards his coins. When their father was killed by a rock lion, Brydeon was there. He took up his father's spear and slew the beast, silently and efficiently.

Brydeon wasn't quiet because he was timid. He simply didn't waste anything, not motion, not words, nothing. He took the Test the same way, never spoke of it until the day he stood before the council and announced his intention.

Oh Brydeon, she thought, how has the world become so backward that I remain to lead and you have disappeared?

But you left me Brophy, she thought, my sanity. You left a little piece of yourself to remind me what life had been before I grew up.

Brophy stood exactly where she thought he would be. The boy loved the view from the roof of the Hall. Some days he would spend an hour or more staring to the north, sitting next to his father's torch.

The hall's warden, Charus, was responsible for keeping the four flames alive, but the warden hadn't carried a bundle of branches up the steps in years. Brophy had taken it upon himself to stock fuel for the fires of his missing father and uncles.

Baelandra made no sound as she watched Brydeon's son sitting next to his torch. Brophy's golden curls shifted in the soft breeze. She paused, content to wait until her breathing returned to normal before she spoke to him.

He stood like a statue, his hand over the torch as the flames engulfed his forearm. After a few seconds, he yanked his hand out and shook his fingers to cool them.

The Children of the Seasons were taught to use their minds to increase their resistance to the elements. Brophy had always been particularly good at resisting heat, but he was doing more than practicing his lessons. Baelandra knew how pain of the body could sometimes lessen the pain of the heart.

She scuffed her slipper to let him know she was there.

Turning, he saw her and smiled. Brophy moved to one side of the blue-white marble arch to give her room, and she sat next to him. Brophy offered his hand, and she took it, staring at it for a moment. Her fingers looked so small, a girl's hand in a man's. It seemed only yesterday that his pudgy fist was tiny in her palm.

"Still practicing your lessons?" she ribbed him. Brophy was like his father. His instructors could find nothing bad to say about him. He was quiet, efficient.

"I wasn't studying," he said. "I was just . . ."

"Playing with fire?"

He gave her a half grin.

"How long?" she asked him.

"Almost fifteen heartbeats."

"But you burned yourself."

"No."

She inspected the arm he'd held over the flame. The skin was slightly red and some of his hair had been singed off.

"I'm thinking that only counts as twelve."

He gave her a token smile and took his hand back, hid it behind his side.

"What do you see when you sit up here for hours?" she asked.

"Ohndarien." He said the word like it was the name of a girl he loved.

"What about Ohndarien do you see?"

"Everything. I see all of her. Sometimes I travel the streets in my mind. I start at our house and cross the bridge to the Night Market. I climb the stairs to the Wheel and walk through all the gardens. I splash in the fountains, visit my teachers, ask them questions. Then I go to the Long Market, see what's new, talk to people from all over the world. I visit the blacksmiths on Stoneside. I eat dinner in the Citadel's great hall, listen to the soldiers tell stories."

He glanced at her, smiled a little, then turned away again.

"I can't actually walk around the city and see everything I love in one day, so I do it all from here." He paused, and they watched a galley slip through the vast floating doors of the Sunset Gate. Baelandra squeezed his hand.

"I wish I could see the world through your eyes, Brophy," she murmured. "It is a much more beautiful place."

"If anyone taught me to see this way, it was you."

"I don't think anyone can teach something like that."

Brophy didn't reply. They sat in contented silence, two birds perched on a wall.

"Do you think Celidon will pass the Test?" he asked quietly.

She wondered if he could read her mind. Or had she read his?

"I hope so, I truly hope so. I will help him where I can."

"Celidon is quiet, but he's not dumb," Brophy assured her.

That was exactly what she thought about Brydeon, so long ago. Her brother had held back, waiting for that moment when his words or movements would be flawless. Celidon held back because he was afraid. She prayed she was wrong about him the way her parents were wrong about Brydeon.

"The council could use another Brother," Brophy said, "at least until the others come back."

She nodded cautiously. "Yes."

"I've been thinking about something for a long time."

Her stomach lurched. Don't say it, she thought. Please, Brophy, don't—

"I'm ready to take the Test."

She turned to the north, looking to the horizon with him. She knew she would hear those words someday, but not so soon. He was still a child. She waited several breaths before she spoke. When she did, her voice was steady, neutral.

"That would be very brave. Are you certain you are ready?"

He looked down at her hand in his. His lips pressed together.

"I don't . . ." he began, stopped. "I'm not sure if I'm old enough, but Ohndarien is missing something. I've felt it ever since I can remember. The city isn't whole. And if . . . something happens, I'm afraid Ohndarien will need more than swords to defend her."

"I see."

"I want to bring us back to the way we were before the Brothers left."

Baelandra closed her eyes. "I want that as much as you, but you can never go back, time always moves forward."

"I know, but something is wrong. There is a foreboding." He looked at her. "Don't you feel it?" He turned back to the northern horizon. "If the Brothers wanted to come back they would have done it already. And if they can't come back . . . Isn't that worse?"

Baelandra knew Brophy wasn't just talking about the Brothers. He was talking about his father, the father who never returned for him, the father who never sent word.

"We've been waiting too long," Brophy said. "The torches burn, but nothing changes. It's as if we are stuck in winter, and the spring will never come unless we do something. Ohndarien is missing its shield, its sword, and there is no one to protect us if something should happen."

"Something like what?" She felt a chill on the back of her neck, like a cool breeze, but there was no wind.

He seemed about to say something, but shook his head, then looked at her. "I wouldn't take Krellis's spot. I could become the Heir of Spring or Summer, if they would accept me. We need *more* Brothers, not less."

She knew she had to speak, but Baelandra took great care choosing her next words. This might be the only moment she could influence his decision.

"Your father would be very proud of you, Brophy, but I don't think he would want you to do this."

It was the wrong thing to say. His eyes narrowed and his jaw tightened.

"I'm not a child," he said quickly.

"I know you're not. You're nearly a man, one of the few men of the Blood we have left. I have known for a long time that this might be your decision. But I ask you, as a favor, wait a little longer before you face the Heartstone."

He let go of her hand and stood up.

"I've made up my mind."

She let out a long breath.

"If that is what you've decided, I will not stand in your way, but I would like you to ask yourself one question first. Why are you doing this?"

"What do you mean? I want to help Ohndarien be whole again. I want to face whatever might come, to stand as her protector."

"That is a noble cause, if that is truly your reason."

Brophy's eyes on the horizon faltered. He looked back at her.

"Or are you going into the Heart to satisfy your own curiosity? Are you going as a Child of the Seasons or as a boy angry at the father he never knew?"

Brophy winced as though she had slapped him.

"It is the right thing for me to do," he said. "I know it here." He put a fist against his chest. "Isn't that enough?"

Baelandra took his hands in hers again. He let her, but the softness was gone from him. He was stiff and cold.

"Brophy, you have strength of heart that I've never seen before. But fifteen is too young."

He pulled his hands away. "Don't mother me," he said. "You're not my mother."

His words stung. She swallowed and tried to let them go.

Brophy bowed his head, looked up, and pulled her into a sudden hug. "I'm sorry. I didn't mean that."

She clung to him and wished that Celidon had half of this boy's insight. "It's all right," she murmured into his shoulder. "We all do things we regret sometimes."

Then, fearing she was about to make her own words come true, she said, "Brophy, there's something I never told you about your father."

He pulled back, his body tense again. "What do you mean?"

"I was waiting until you were old enough."

A fierceness lit his eyes, a fire she had never seen before. He waited, quietly burning.

"The Lost Brothers aren't missing. I know where they are, and I know what they are doing there."

"What? Where?"

"They are still in the Vastness. They are trying to keep something hidden that must never be found, something more important than the council, more important than the fate of Ohndarien."

"What do you mean? Why didn't you tell me before?"

"I didn't think you were old enough."

"Then tell me now."

She looked to the west. The sun was close to setting. "I can't. Not today, it's a long story, and Celidon's Test is about to begin."

"Bae, no!" he protested, "You can't say something like that and walk away."

She put a hand on his chest. "Patience, Brophy. The Brothers have been gone for thirteen years. Another day will not matter. We will talk about this and about your taking the Test tomorrow. I promise."

She turned and left him standing by his father's torch.

BAELANDRA HURRIED down the marble path toward the Autumn Palace. The building was mainly used as a school where the Children of the Seasons were trained in the arts of the sword, spear, and unarmed combat. The palace was little more than a covered courtyard with a few attached rooms for foul-weather meetings and weapons storage. Baelandra had a small room on the second floor where she changed before formal functions in the Hall.

She jogged up the stairs and slipped through the unlocked door. Torches were already burning in the sconces even though it was still light outside. Her formal gown had been laid out for her, and there was a small plate of food resting on the table. Grabbing a hunk of cheese, she slipped out of her dress.

A man softly cleared his throat behind her. The Sister of Autumn pulled her dress back over her naked shoulders and turned around.

Scythe stood in the darkest corner. The torch beside him still smoldered.

"What did you find out?" she asked, retying the neck of her dress and turning to the food. It would be a long night, and this would be her last chance to eat.

The man regarded her with his dark eyes for a long moment before he spoke.

"Your suspicions were correct. The Physendrian army is mustering two days south of here."

Baelandra nodded, taking a gulp of cold tea. "How long until they can march?"

"Any day, but they are still training raw troops. It could be several months before they are ready."

"Good, that gives us some time. What about Celidon?"

"He and Krellis went sailing together yesterday morning. The boy announced his intention to take the Test to a friend right after he got back."

Baelandra pulled an olive pit out of her mouth and set it gently on the plate. She took a deep breath and blew out as much of her anger as she could.

"What about the third matter?"

Scythe shrugged. "I could not determine what Krellis and the ambassador discussed."

"What is your best guess? Why is he here?"

"We are on the brink of war. The Opal Empire would make a powerful ally."

"What does Krellis have to offer them?"

"Ohndarien?" Scythe suggested.

"He wouldn't do that."

Scythe raised an eyebrow, but said nothing.

Baelandra shook her head. "My apologies." She picked up a piece of bread, but she no longer had an appetite. "Any chance Krellis and the Physendrian king are working together?"

Scythe shook his head. "No. Krellis hates his brother. The two would never make common cause."

Baelandra nodded. "Once again I thank you for your skill and discretion."

The dark man gave a slight bow. "Shall I leave you now?"

"No." Baelandra paused before speaking. "If I may ask you for one more thing?"

Scythe waited.

"Brophy intends to take the Test."

The former assassin pursed his lips slightly.

"I don't believe he can pass," she said. "He is too young. He has been too . . . sheltered."

"What would you like me to do? Torture the boy?"

Baelandra walked up to her old friend. She lifted a hand as if she were going to touch his face, but paused and let it drop back to her side. "Not exactly. I want you to mentor him."

"Are you sure I am the man you want for this job? You have been critical of my methods before."

Baelandra swallowed past the lump in her throat. "Brophy is strong. He never shied away from hardship."

"Just because you want the boy to be strong does not make it so. We have disagreed about such things in the past."

Baelandra turned away from the bitterness she saw in the man's eyes. She picked up her mug of tea and forced herself to drink. "Then try his mettle, if you doubt me. He has all the skills, Scythe, but he believes the world is good and just. I do not want him to discover that he is wrong at a moment that could cost him his life."

Baelandra did not look up from her plate and she held her breath during the long silence. Finally, Scythe spoke the words she waited for, that she knew he would speak.

"I will do as you ask," he said with a slight bow. "You deserve nothing less."

*S*TEAM ROSE around her. Shara imagined it curling like smoke into her nostrils and mouth. Closing her eyes, she resisted the urge to lick her lips, to trace her hand through the hot water. She hovered on the brink and must hold herself there.

The flickering torchlight shimmered across the skin of the naked young men surrounding her. Theras sat on the edge of the pool beating the deerskin drum in time to her breath, keeping her steady. One of the twins, Baksin, washed her hair, while the other, Bashtin, massaged her feet. She floated free in the bath, each of the male students holding a fraction of her weight as the water held the rest. She floated in a constant caress while Caleb roved over her body, sensing where she was, reminding her to stay at the brink by the liquid motions of his hands, titillating her when she pulled back, halting her if she teetered too close to the edge.

All four boys remained silent. They all had the same purpose, to prepare Shara for the final gate.

There should have been five students guiding her, but Gedge had recently been cast from the Zelani school in disgrace. He and Reela had been with each other behind the backs of their instructors. They broke their vows, shattered their discipline. It wasn't just that they had sex outside their training, outside ritual space. That would be punished, but forgiven, but they allowed themselves to complete the act, and the sound of Reela's climax had betrayed them.

A Zelani used the body and the power of its pleasure as a doorway. Shara had spent the last nine years learning to contain that energy within herself, but she never released it, not once in all that time.

"That energy is your life's blood," Master Victeris would say. "You would not open a vein and spill your blood upon the ground, just as you will not give in to release and cast your power to the winds."

The disgraced students were thrown naked into the streets. Their shame drew quite a crowd. As much as their neighbors revered the Zelani school, they enjoyed it when a student fell from grace. They couldn't resist the jibes, the offers, the rude touching as poor Gedge and Reela fled past them.

Shara closed her eyes and cycled through both sorrow and disappointment. Caleb massaged her shoulders, kneading away her tension. His hand slid slowly across her breast. His fingers brushed along her belly and across her thighs. Her skin sparked along the trail he left and she drew a quick breath as it brought her to the brink again, back to where she should be.

Shara had been so close to losing control so many times. Only the strongest children were recruited, and not one in ten made it this far. The body craved release, the undisciplined mind feared power. Building such sexual energy was a strain, it threatened to overwhelm and destroy. But there was no limit to the power a human could contain within her body if she had the courage to face it and the will to control it.

Shara let go of her thoughts, breathing them out like steam. Each of her attendants felt the ritual as she did. Their erections stood rigid against their bellies despite the heat of the water. They were the most advanced Zelani students, strong and full of will. Together they balanced the energy like dancers on the edge of a cliff. The boys had learned their lessons well. They would make powerful Zelani in a few years.

Unlike Gedge. Unlike Reela.

She heard they were recently married and had found work at the Scarlet Heart, the most respected brothel in the city. It was an honorable and profitable profession, but they would never be Zelani. They gave up their power and for what? One moment's pleasure? For love?

Shara had also pushed the boundaries of the rules, especially with Caleb. At times she had been merciless to the younger boy. She had climbed through his window, woken him with his cock in her mouth. Once, she snuck into the baths when he was meditating. She lay down alongside him as he sat cross-legged on the tiles. She wrapped her body around his and touched herself until she drifted into her spirit, lost in a haze of desire. Caleb never opened his eyes. He never reached for her, never rolled on top of her and pushed her thighs apart to bring a final end to the torture.

That was why Shara chose Caleb. She trusted him. She left that night in the baths exploding with power, and he the same. They were stronger because they dared step so close to the edge. They were stronger because they never stepped over.

Never until tonight. Tonight Shara would take that final step.

She concentrated on diffusing her attention. The edge of ecstasy closed in from all four sides. She steadied her breath and accepted every sensation.

If she focused too much on any part of her body, her desire would explode into orgasm. Doubt, anticipation, her private fears of Victeris, all mingled into a swirling storm of longing. She let her desire flow out the tips of her fingers and toes. She guided it to the very ends of her hair and let it float away into the water.

The boys were there with her. The whole room was one body, her body, and she touched each of its parts delicately, savoring every moment. Each one of these boys had been inside her. She knew them—lips, hands, backs, bellies, cocks, thighs, tongues, and toes—all were familiar to her touch. She felt their heat as if lying naked between four raging bonfires. Yet they held their fires in check, they burned without being consumed.

And what was beyond that control? Shara had an inkling, but those were daydreams, fantasies, not true knowledge. Only the graduates really knew. That secret could only be found beyond the fifth gate, and Victeris had the keys. The Master held the secrets of Efften. He alone could pass the female students.

She had waited long enough. Tonight she would discover what was beyond the fifth gate, or she would fail and follow Reela and Gedge into disgrace.

Shara felt the water, the smoothly shaped stones that lined the steaming tub. She felt the flickering firelight. With her eyes closed, she extended her awareness into the other students. She could feel herself within Caleb's own flesh. She felt the hot water flow around his penis, over his thighs. His desire was hers. His need called to her, thrilled through her, the need to grab her by the hips and thrust deep inside her. It mingled with her own desire until she could not recognize which belonged to whom. To be the entered or enterer, it was all the same, and she was feverish with the wanting.

She drew a swift breath, too swift. Caleb clenched his teeth. His control brought her back, and the energy was held.

She opened her eyes and smiled at him. He smiled back. She breathed herself into him, past the flesh and into the man within the flesh. She felt his generous heart, his playful nature. He had saved her, and he surged with pride at doing so.

Their breathing reversed, and she drew him into her eyes. A chill thrilled through her as they became one for the length of that single breath.

She wanted more of him. She wanted all of them. Baksin, Bashtin, Theras, and Caleb, all of them inside her, in every possible way. But that was child's play, a wicked fantasy. Her preparations were done. She was ready. For nine years she had gathered the energy, it was time for her to take a step beyond mere intimacy, mere self-control, beyond mere love. It was time to step into true power.

The setting sun shot a beam of light through a tiny window high on the rough-hewn western wall. For the last hour, that brilliant square of light slowly crept across the shimmering water of the bath toward where she floated. As the sun dipped below the Windmill Wall, the square of light softened from bright white to orange and finally purple. The last breaths of sunset faded to dark, and it was time to go.

Water cascaded down Shara's body as she stood. Her slick skin glistened in the torchlight. She smiled and silently touched the cheek of each of her attendants, wishing for more, knowing she would never find that pleasure with these men.

Pushing off the algae-covered wall, she swam away from her attendants, crossing the pool with slow, luxurious strokes. When she reached the far wall, she drew in an endless breath as if she would draw the entire world into her lungs.

And she dove.

She stroked smoothly into the tunnel under the wall. Many times she had ducked beneath the water to peer into the blackness. The pool on the far side of the school had a tunnel like this one, heading in the opposite direction. She assumed the tunnels met in the middle somewhere, far beneath the center of the school. No student knew what lay beyond the inky blackness.

The darkness closed around her like a hand on the throat. She released her worries with every stroke, praying she would not run out of breath before she reached the far side. The tunnel kept going down, ever down.

Shara's lungs began to burn. It was too late to turn back. She had swum too far. Her chest spasmed uncontrollably. She let a few bubbles out and regretted the decision at once as she defied her body's urge to draw a breath. The first sparkles crept into her vision. Her stokes became awkward, unproductive.

Wait, it wasn't a sparkle. It was light! The tunnel curved abruptly, leading straight upward.

Flush with hope, she swam for the surface. The circle of light grew larger and larger. She could see the flickering glow reflecting off the surface. With the last of her fading will, she pushed upward and broke the surface of the pool. She opened her mouth and drew a long, slow breath, maintaining control. The first gate, breath, belonged to her. She must remember that and make it so. She would not come to the place of her final test gasping and sputtering like a novice.

When her breathing was slow and easy, she looked around.

The cavern was not unlike the baths she had just left. It was rough-hewn stone, arcing into a dome overhead. No windows opened the walls. There were no doors. A dozen torches lined the walls, illuminating a small, perfectly circular island in the center of the cavern.

Shara pushed the lingering threads of panic from her heart, breathed the fear down her arms and legs, out of her fingers and toes. She left it swirling in her wake as she swam for shore.

Water splashed on the steamy stones as she pulled herself out of the pool. Victeris pushed himself up on the other side of the island at the same moment. She did not question the timing. This was the ceremony. It had a life of its own.

She mirrored him, standing slowly and watching him on the opposite side of the island. He was a tall man, slender and muscled like a warrior. He was nothing like Caleb and the other boys. They had the lithe, smooth bodies of youth, but Victeris was hard, defined. His shoulders and arms stood out like smooth rocks beneath a thin sheen of river water.

His face was rugged and angular, with sharp jawbones and a pointed chin. His long, black hair had two snow-white streaks in it, just above the temples. Thin, dark eyebrows arched over his eyes, giving him an air that was either piercing . . . or cruel.

The natural island was covered with a tile mosaic polished to a mirror shine. Two intertwined spirals—one black, one white—coiled five times around the center.

Drawing a smooth breath, she placed her bare foot upon the dark tile path. Victeris nodded, mirrored her, placing his foot on the white path. He moved to her left as she moved to the right.

They walked slowly, circling the center. On her fifth step, he spoke.

"What is the first gate?" he asked. His voice was deep and resonant, the kind of voice she could close her eyes and dream with.

"My breath," she said, softly and clearly. She matched her breath to her teacher's, watching his chest rise and fall. Moving as slowly and carefully as stalking cats, they circled one another for one complete revolution. Their spiral paths brought them closer together.

"What is the second gate?" Victeris asked. His voice sounded as though it came from everywhere, behind her, above her, in front of her, bubbling up from the water.

"My skin."

She focused her attention on her body, feeling every sensation. The preparation given by Caleb and the others helped her. She felt everything within and without. Each drop of water left a glowing path down her back. The brush of her thighs counted every movement as she sidestepped a second revolution around the circle.

"What is the third gate?"

"My eyes."

She looked into Victeris's eyes, as she had with Caleb before. But this time, she was not the advanced student looking at a younger. This was her master. His energy slammed into her like a physical blow. Caleb gave her love, comfort, companionship. Victeris frightened her. He was raw power. No mercy. No camaraderie. She was the ship, and he was the storm, sweeping her to a place she had never been before.

Her breath quickened, and she tried desperately to tame it.

One foot. Then the next. Round and round. Ever closer to him.

Her fear surged through her, transforming into excitement. She had never desired her teacher before, but it suddenly became overwhelming. She understood at last. Her cravings for Caleb, for Theras, they were nothing compared to this.

She fought to even her breathing, fearing her will would crumble the instant she touched him. She longed to explode.

"What is the fourth gate?"

"My heart." Shara's voice sounded far away, and she knew she was losing control.

The fourth spiral was tight. She could touch him if she reached out her arm. Somehow, she kept her shaking hands at her sides and opened her heart to him.

Her chest shuddered. He rushed past her self-control, filling her with energy. There was no kindness in him, no gentleness, only infinite power.

She thought she cried out, but she couldn't be sure. Everything was hazy. Her discipline cracked. She wanted to flee. Her heart raced. Turn away, she screamed inside. Break the spiral, run back the way you came.

No! She refused. Her foot came down sure and steady. She would never turn away, no matter what. She had come this far. She would be a Zelani.

They spiraled so close their lips hovered inches apart. Each small step was a shuffle. The tips of her breasts brushed against his hairy chest. She sobbed, recovered her breath, somehow maintained her control.

Victeris reached up and cupped a hand behind the back of her neck. His other hand slid along the curve of her ass. His fingertips barely brushed her sex as his hand glided down her thigh, picking her knee up and setting it against his hip. His erection pressed against her. Three quick shudders shot through her body.

"What is the fifth gate?"

"My soul," she whispered.

He thrust inside her, and her control shattered like shale. Her head fell back, then snapped forward. Her body crashed against him. The last sound she heard was his growl as his cock pushed into her, breaking through her, breaking through everything. She lost herself, flying outward, spinning out of control.

She soared above herself, billowing into the room. Below, the Shara-that-was crumpled in Victeris's embrace, wrapped her shaky legs around his waist. He bore her to the floor, crushing her against the tiles, thrusting into her again and again.

Shara filled the entire room, pressed up against the dome, flowed out through the stones. She expanded through the school, into the bodies of the students, out across the city, into the Great Ocean, into the Summer Sea, up into the night sky above.

"I know," she cried to the night. "I finally know!" But the night did not hear. She made no sound. There was no sound.

And so she could not hear her teacher as he spoke to her senseless body below.

"I am Victeris. The source of your power. Your master now and forever. You are mine. When I call, you will come to me. When I speak, you will obey . . ."

NIGHT HAD fallen and a hush hovered in the Hall of Windows. Hundreds of Ohndariens filled the silent amphitheater, holding vigil as Celidon took the Test of the Stone. No one stirred or fidgeted, even the babes in their mothers' arms held the silence. As the moon crept across the sky, the light in the room shifted from pale silver to midnight blue. The stained glass overhead reflected swirling patterns of cobalt light onto the expectant faces of the crowd.

At sundown, Celidon lit one torch for each season and climbed down the ladder into the Heart of Ohndarien. Krellis and the four Sisters followed him into that black hole. They would stand by his side all night aiding the Heir of Winter where they could, but in the end it was Celidon's own heart that would save or betray him.

Just before dawn, Celidon would raise a shard of burning diamond in his hand and thrust it into his heart. If he was strong enough, he would survive the Test and emerge as the Brother of Winter, a full member of the Council. If he failed, the four torches would be extinguished, and Celidon's spirit would remain in the Heart with his ancestors.

Brophy tried to keep focused on the ritual, but his mind kept wandering. Bae's words kept running through his mind. He wished Shara were here. He wanted to tell her everything he'd heard, but there were no Zelani students in attendance. She would face her own test that night.

As a Child of the Seasons, it was Brophy's privilege and his duty to kneel at the very edge of the council platform. For hours he had stared at the gaping hole in the center of the Hall. He kept hoping for a sign, a sound, a flicker of light, but the hole to the Heart was eternally black. Brophy put his hands on the cool stones in front of his knees. Closing his eyes, he willed Celidon to succeed. He imagined the lanky young man standing in the darkness, alone and frightened. It should be me down there, he couldn't help thinking. It should be me, not him.

Only a handful of boys from the four houses had grown to manhood since the Lost Brothers had gone north. It was a startlingly low number. Some male children had died in accidents and fallen victim to childhood diseases, but mostly they had simply failed to be born. Girl after girl after girl found her way into the world.

Of course, Trent was part of the House of Autumn now, but that was different. Trent was an Heir of Autumn in name, but he was not of the Blood.

Trent had chosen to avoid the ceremony. He would certainly make light of the situation. It was difficult for him to be respectful of serious events, but that was no excuse. He should have been here.

Behind the Children stood the guests, foreigners and Ohndariens who were not of the Blood. Some came to add their spirits to Celidon for strength. Some came to witness the spectacle. Some came because it was tradition. But none of them could know what the Children of the Seasons felt. For none of them would ever die down in that black hole or live their lives knowing they didn't have the courage to take the Test.

The night moved slowly. A few of the younger children started crying or fussing. Some fell asleep. Halfway through the night, Brophy felt the beginnings of an uncomfortable urge. He should have relieved himself before taking up the vigil.

An hour later, he couldn't keep a thought on Celidon or the Test. Even Bae's words fled. He kept shifting uncomfortably, transferring his weight from knee to knee in an effort to distract himself. It was hopeless to resist. Brophy stood on stiff legs. Everyone around him noticed as he stepped carefully through the kneeling people. His aunt Hellena frowned at him. He shrugged helplessly and moved toward the top of the amphitheater. Jostling a few of the faithful, Brophy finally managed to make his way to the Autumn Gate and outside the Hall of Windows.

He considered sneaking into the gardens and peeing in the bushes. It was such a long walk down to the Night Market, but on this night of all nights, the idea seemed wrong. Trying to walk quickly, with dignity, he made his way down the long, curving staircase from the Wheel to the Night Market.

A long row of public toilets stood along the edge of the water. A privacy curtain covered the entrance of each green-tiled stall. At night they looked like tiny fortresses, lit by a lamp hanging over each stall on a long, wrought-iron arm.

Brophy cursed his luck as he shuffled up to the six toilets. Each curtain was drawn. He shifted from foot to foot and fought the urge to cross his legs like a little kid.

Blessedly soon, one of the occupants threw his curtain aside. A wealthy trader from Vizar stepped out, wearing the traditional crude clay mask of his people. The facial covering had a long, thin nose and an expressionless mouth that ended just below the bottom lip, exposing the man's chin. A heavy rainbow-colored cloak covered his entire body from neck to toes. Thousands of tiny mirrors had been sewn into the rich fabric, and they twinkled in the lamplight.

Staring was the height of rudeness in Vizar. They wore the masks and mirrors to ward off unwanted glances. Remembering his manners, Brophy averted his eyes and rushed past the merchant into the toilet.

He hastily undid his breeches, aimed for the tile-lined hole, and let out a quiet sigh of relief. The world slowed down and he felt almost drunk with relief by the time he laced his breeches up again.

His thoughts turned back to Celidon as he washed his hands in the waist-high basin and poured a ladle of water down the hole. He had a hand on the curtain when he stepped on something. Kneeling, he picked up a brilliant cloth pouch covered with silver disks. Brophy fumbled with the drawstring and peered inside. The purse was full to bursting with silver.

He threw open the curtain and stepped out, casting about for the Vizai trader. He was nowhere in sight.

Brophy paused, giving one glance back toward the Wheel. He should get back to the ceremony, but the trader couldn't have gone far. He'd probably headed for the line of cafés along the harbor.

Brophy swerved through the milling crowd along the canal's walkway. The Night Market was particularly crowded on this night of the Test. He hurried to a saltwater fountain and hoisted himself up the side of it to get a better view.

There! The mirrors on the man's cloak flashed as he passed under a streetlight. The Vizai walked leisurely, stopping every now and then to look at the wares of the snack vendors in their pushcarts.

Brophy skirted the crowd, running along the edge of the walkway, inches from falling into the harbor. He slowed his pace as he neared the merchant, stopped and respectfully tugged on the short man's cloak.

The trader turned, fixing his gaze somewhere above Brophy's head.

"Yes?" he asked.

Brophy paused, realizing that the man wasn't going to look at him, and somehow that probably made sense. Thousands of years ago, the men of Vizar led solitary lives spread far apart on their barren land. If two men met each other in the wilderness, the weaker man would look away from the stronger. If the two met eyes, it was an invitation to fight to the death. Eventually the confrontations grew out of control. To end the conflict, they all donned masks and stopped looking at each other altogether. The mirrored cloaks were an extension of the same tradition, added after they grew rich trading slaves for silver. But they never gave up the primitive mud masks, as strange and unsettling as they were.

"You dropped this, sir," Brophy said, holding up the pouch.

The trader patted his right side. "Ah," he said. He brought his hands around very slowly and they disappeared into the folds of his cloak. "It appears as though I did." He waited.

Brophy paused, confused by a custom he knew nothing about.

"I thought you might want it back."

"I see," the man said. "That is very courteous of you. And so you are correct. I would very much like that." Still he did not reach to take the pouch, though Brophy held it out at arm's length.

Brophy's brow furrowed. He suddenly felt stupid, as if he were talking to Shara about mathematics.

"Well then, take it," he said. If the Vizai wasn't going to be helpful, Brophy wasn't going to try to guess the right response.

"Ah, yes indeed. What shall be our exchange?"

Brophy narrowed his eyes. He shook his head. "No, I don't want anything. I just wanted to return it."

"Truly? You release it without onus?"

"Um, yes."

"So be it." He reached out and took the pouch. It disappeared behind the mirrors. "I am pleased," the trader said. "I realize that perhaps you are ignorant of our ways. You have done me a great service and released me from any debt. I would return a kindness, also without onus."

Brophy wished he knew what onus meant.

"All right," he said.

"Will you sit and take a cup of spiced cream with me?"

Vizai traders were notoriously tight-lipped and aloof. It was probably a great honor to be invited to drink with one.

Brophy looked back toward the Wheel, then glanced to the west. The moon was dipping close to the Windmill Wall. He had at least another hour, maybe two before dawn. He'd already broken his vigil, it wouldn't matter if he stayed away five minutes or fifty.

"Yes," he said.

"It is good," the trader replied, leading the way to the nearest café. The trader's cloak swished back and forth as he led the way to a table and signaled for a server. Many less-than-pious attendants of the Test sat in the café, sipping warm drinks.

A heavyset woman in her forties hurried over to greet them. She had the round face and corn-colored hair common to the House of Summer. She wasn't of the Blood. Brophy could tell that just by looking at her, but she was definitely Ohndarien. Her family had probably lived here since before the city was built.

The woman recognized Brophy immediately and bent over to kiss him on top of the head. "All our thoughts and prayers are with Celidon tonight, Nephew," she said.

"Thank you," Brophy replied, squeezing the woman's fleshy hand.

"Celidon's a good man, a true child of Ohndarien," she added. "We could use a few more good men around here."

Keeping his gaze on the sky behind Brophy's head, the trader respectfully ignored their exchange.

Brophy ordered for both of them and in a few minutes they had steaming cups of spiced cream.

The merchant brought the thick cup to his lips and sipped. When he set the mug down, he said, "You are from Ohndarien?"

"Yes," Brophy said, blowing on his own cream. It was still too hot to drink. "I grew up in my aunt's house, just on the other side of Donovan's Bridge."

"Ah, you are one of the ruling class."

Brophy shrugged. He wasn't sure what the Vizai counterpart would be to a Child of the Seasons. "I suppose."

Brophy evened his breathing, concentrated, and tried his cream again. The heat did not bother him this time.

"This Test that everyone speaks of tonight, what must one overcome to succeed?"

"I don't know," Brophy admitted. "No one knows until they take it. Those who have taken the Test never speak of it."

"I see."

The trader let the silence fill the space for a long moment.

"I'm Brophy. What is your name?"

"Ah," the trader said. "Names carry a great onus."

"I'm sorry, but I don't know what 'onus' means."

"It is a burden. An obligation. Some might think you yet sought payment for the return of my purse."

"No, that's not what I meant."

"I believe you. I do not think it was your intent to be so rude. Ignorance is almost always forgivable, especially in the young."

Brophy bit back an angry reply and stared at his mug of spiced cream. Perhaps there was a reason people didn't talk to Vizai.

The foreign merchant leaned forward, practically whispering in Brophy's ear. "I must also ask your forgiveness for my own ignorance. I am curious about something which confuses me."

"Yes?"

"Where I come from, one would sell their children into slavery for as much silver as I carry. Even a rich man would pocket the coins and count himself lucky. But you sought me out. You left your vigil to return my pouch to me. Why?"

Brophy shrugged. "It was the right thing to do."

The Vizai laughed abruptly. It looked sinister, the way his living jaw dropped away from the mask, which remained immobile.

"I wonder, then," the Vizai said, "how Ohndarien has lasted this long. True, you have the tallest walls in the world, but within the city there are no walls. There are no guards. The doors have no locks."

"Some doors have locks," Brophy protested.

"But not most."

"No. We don't need them."

"Truly? And what if someone were to steal from you?"

"There aren't many thieves in Ohndarien. Those who steal know what will happen to them," Brophy said.

"And what will happen?"

"They are exiled, stripped naked and left outside the city walls. That's punishment enough for anyone."

"Indeed? Where I come from, thieves are tied to a stake and disemboweled by those from whom they stole. That is punishment. What you do in Ohndarien is merely an inconvenience." He sipped his cream, then added, "I wonder, what you do to murderers?"

Brophy was still imagining the horrible fate of a thief in Vizar. "Well," he said, "it is the same. They are forced outside the walls. But if a murderer is truly hated, people gather on the ramparts and throw rocks at him as he goes. The worst of them never get more than fifty yards."

"Ah, that is good," the Vizai said. "I was beginning to wonder if Ohndariens were made of stone. At least that is some human emotion. A man who cannot hate is not a man at all."

They both sipped their cream.

"Tell me again of this Test. What if this young man succeeds?"

"He will take his place on the council."

"What if there is not an empty seat? Or what if he chooses to claim the seat occupied by this man, Krellis?"

Brophy kept trying to get a glimpse of the trader's eyes, but they were shadowed behind the mask.

"Celidon is from the House Morgeon. He will choose to be Brother of Winter, just as his father and great-uncle were before."

Brophy sipped his cream, trying to find any reaction from the Vizai, but he was as still as the mask he wore and continued to stare at the stars overhead.

"That is why the Test of the Stone works so well," Brophy continued. "Those who want to lead must have the courage, strength, and desire. No one takes the Test lightly. No one takes it out of pride. They take it because they have to, because Ohndarien needs them. Those in power know that if someone is willing to die to replace them, then it is time for them to step down."

"I cannot believe that any person with that much power would give it up so easily. Tell me, when will you take the Test and seize power for yourself?"

Brophy's eyes narrowed. There was no reason why he shouldn't tell this man the truth. He would be announcing his intentions right after talking to Baelandra. Yet, for some reason he held back.

"The Test is a very private matter," he said.

"My apologies," the Vizar said, inclining his head.

"I will take the Test someday," Brophy continued. "When there is great need."

"I'm sure you will."

Brophy looked back at the Wheel. He tried to picture Celidon somewhere inside.

"If it is not a private matter," the merchant continued, "may I ask which house you belong to?"

"I am the Heir of Autumn."

"You are a warrior then?"

Brophy shrugged. "I've been trained in the sword and spear. I've studied every inch of Ohndarien's walls. I know how to defend them."

"So you would take the Physendrian's place if you were to take the Test?"

Brophy shook his head. "Normally, but people have switched houses before if there is need. I could claim any spot I chose. Krellis is the Brother of Autumn, and he is a great man. He stopped the Physendrian invasion twelve years ago. I hope it is years and years before someone has to take his place. And even then, it will probably be Krellis's son, Trent."

"Ah," the Vizai said slowly, "and how do you feel about a foreigner ruling in Ohndarien?"

"I think Krellis is a true Brother. Ohndarien prospers under his guidance."

"Perhaps, yet it is odd to me. You let anyone into Ohndarien as long as they agree to abide by your laws. In this case, you agreed to let one lead. It is a strange choice, and not the safest by far."

"We do not have laws. The council makes recommendations. The people follow them or not as they choose."

"Indeed. But if one refuses to follow the suggestions, one is marked. No one will trade with you or sell you a meal or a room for the night. Such suggestions are very like laws."

"No," Brophy said, frowning. "The difference is that in Ohndarien, you always have a choice. That choice is what makes this the Free City."

The Vizai laughed again. "Ah, truly. Well, thank you. I have enjoyed our conversation greatly. I will enjoy this strange little city for as long as it lasts."

"Ohndarien will last forever," Brophy said, louder than he intended.

"Indeed?"

"Yes. She has lasted for centuries. Why wouldn't she?"

"Ah, but centuries are not so very long. My country has endured for thousands of years. We have seen little cities like Ohndarien come and go many times. The Vizai watched the rise of Efften and her fiery fall."

"You yourself said it. The Ohndariens love their city. And her walls are the strongest in the world. Our soldiers are the best trained."

"Ah yes, perhaps. But there are three times as many foreigners as natives inside these strong walls. Ohndarien's armies are made up almost entirely of those same foreigners. They visit for five years to get the best military training in the world before leaving to sell their services elsewhere. Do you know the wage an Ohndarien-trained soldier claims in Vizar?"

"No."

"The onus is high." The Vizai smiled. "And all that was needed to gain those skills was to promise to serve Ohndarien for five years, then leave and never enter again with a weapon in their hands. Where I come from, there are many men of ill repute who would forget such a promise the moment it is made. What if there were many such men inside this city?"

The Vizai shrugged, drained the last of his cream. "So you see, you are outnumbered by foreigners, you are protected by foreigners, and you are ruled by a foreigner. How long can your 'perfect Ohndarien' last? I think it already fades, and you are too close, and perhaps too young, to see it happening."

Brophy looked down at his cup. He heard the scrape of the man's chair against the tile floor and looked up to find the slight trader standing above him. He still stared over Brophy, never once looking at him.

"Well, young one, I thank you once again for your assistance. I apologize for my rudeness, but I must be on my way. I have another appointment. I hope you enjoyed your drink."

Brophy stood and extended his hand. "Thank you, sir. I did."

The Vizai trader never looked at Brophy's hand, and never offered his own. Leaving a copper coin on the table, he inclined his head and moved back onto the walkway, his cloak swishing about him.

Brophy watched him for a long moment, thinking about a father he never knew and about all the foreigners in Ohndarien.

He glanced at the sky and suddenly remembered why he was here. The dawn was closer than he'd thought.

Spinning about, he raced through the Night Market. He took the stairs up to the Wheel two at a time, headed straight across the gardens to the Autumn Gate and slipped inside.

He worked his way through the tightly packed attendants as quickly as he could. A murmur ran through the crowd. A light flickered deep in the Heart. He'd never reach the front row in time. Standing on tiptoes, Brophy craned his neck and looked down.

The ladder leading up from the blackness shook slightly. Krellis was the first to emerge, followed by Jayden, Hazel, Baelandra, and finally Vallia. Brophy couldn't read a thing on his aunt's face at this distance. He reached into the pouch at his side and pulled out a fistful of flower petals, preparing to throw them, but Celidon did not follow the others. With measured steps, Baelandra crossed to the torch of Autumn and extinguished it.

There would be no Brother of Winter.

9

BAELANDRA CROUCHED in the farthest corner of her balcony, curled up in a ball. She looked out over the bay through the slender pillars of the balcony's stone rail. The tracks of the tears across her cheeks were lost in the soft yellow light of the sunrise.

She remembered the day of Celidon's birth. It had been a difficult labor, and they feared that mother or child would be lost. Baelandra sat vigil with the other women outside Tharra's door. She was only seventeen then, before the Test, before the Brothers left, before everything. She was both amazed and frightened as Tharra's low moans turned to grunts and screams as she fought her third baby into the world. Death hovered about that room, but life pushed through, screaming into the world.

Celidon was born at dawn on Tharra's third day. Baelandra cried when she heard his first squalls from the other room. She remembered Tharra's face, as gaunt and strained as a corpse's, but she was beaming. She didn't see anyone in the room except that tiny new person rooting at her breast.

That night Baelandra longed for her chance to dance that oldest of dances. She wanted the challenge, the intensity, the pure love of that experience. But it was not meant to be, and Baelandra chose another path. That path had led her here, alone and crying once again for the dead men of Ohndarien.

Brophy tapped on the inside of the balcony's archway. Baelandra had already heard him coming, but it was sweet of him to knock. She turned to look at her nephew, the closest thing to a child she would ever have.

"Brophy," she said. "You know me so well."

"Bae."

He sat behind her and put his arms around her shoulders. "I'm so sorry," he said, resting his head on her neck.

"Oh Brophy," she managed to get out. "He was so young, so very young."

"He might have succeeded."

Baelandra held her tongue, sparing her nephew the ugly truth.

"You did. You were younger than he was."

"No," she said softly, almost so soft he couldn't hear it, "No, I am old. I have always been old . . ."

The Sister of Autumn and her brother's son sat in silence. Baelandra enjoyed the warmth of his touch for as long as she could. When the sun behind them lit the garden wall, Brophy stood up.

"Come," the boy said, taking her hands. He pulled her upright. "You need to sleep."

Brophy led her to her bed and pulled back the blankets. She slipped in and he lay down beside her. Baelandra used to hold Brophy as a child when he cried. They slept like two crescent moons, one large and one small. Her nephew found refuge within the curve of her body.

Now he was the larger moon, and she tucked herself into his embrace. He burned so brightly and had more to give than Baelandra ever imagined. It was as if a part of her was inside him, and when she hurt, he felt it. He always knew when to come.

"Never take the Test, Brophy," she murmured. "As long as that man lives, never take the Test. He will be the death of you."

After she said it, Baelandra slowly relaxed in his arms, and her exhaustion overwhelmed her.

BAELANDRA OPENED her eyes just before Krellis pounded on the door. Brophy woke with a start. Still sleepy-eyed and confused, he quickly looked from her to the door and back.

Baelandra sat up slowly and slid her back against the headboard. "Would you give us some privacy, Brophy?" she asked, careful to keep her voice elegant and in control. "Krellis and I have some things to discuss."

Brophy glanced at the door.

"I'll stay," he said.

"No, you will not," said Baelandra, in a tone that brooked no argument. Reluctantly, Brophy stood.

The pounding came at the door a second time.

"Go on, Brophy," Baelandra said again. "Let Krellis in on your way out."

The boy slowly crossed the room. The door burst open a moment before he reached it. Krellis hovered in the doorway, panting like a winded horse. The shattered pieces of the latch skittered across the blue-white marble. His hand clenched the pommel of his short sword and his knuckles were white. Brophy stopped in the face of Krellis's fiery gaze, but he did not back away.

Krellis turned away from the boy and stared at her. A half smile curled the corner of his mouth.

Baelandra regarded Krellis with a stony gaze that veiled her grief. He could surely see the tears dried on her face, but he would not see it in her eyes, not now.

"Go on, Brophy," she said.

Brophy glanced at Krellis's sword.

"It's all right," Baelandra said, as if there were no tension in the room.

Reluctantly, he slipped past the huge man into the hallway. He gave Krellis a parting glare that made her love the boy even more.

Krellis waited a full ten seconds after the door closed before he started chuckling. "I heard there was a man in your bed." He shook his head. "It certainly wasn't the one I was expecting."

Baelandra's rage built inside her, threatening to shatter everything, but she held her feelings in check. She used the furnace inside her to forge her words into daggers.

"If the boy threatens you so much, why don't you just kill him? That seems to be the way you deal with your rivals."

Krellis was still smiling, but the man's jaw muscles stood out in stark relief. "I told you once, never speak of my father."

"I'm not talking about your father," Baelandra spat. "I'm talking about Celidon. I'm talking about Samuel, Garrett, and Broed. I'm talking about every Child of the Seasons you've led to his death."

Krellis took three steps closer to her.

Baelandra rolled out the opposite side of the bed, keeping a barrier between them. "You knew Celidon wasn't ready. You knew he didn't have the confidence, yet you led him into the Heart as surely as if you stuck a dagger in his back."

Krellis picked up the bed and threw it on its side. Baelandra had to jump out of the way to avoid being struck as it fell back to the floor upside down.

"If you are going to accuse me of something, do it to my face. Don't hide behind a tiny piece of furniture."

Baelandra's breathing tripped over itself. For the first time, she was truly frightened of her lover. She felt it deep in her bones.

The two locked stares for a long moment, before Krellis sheathed his sword and cracked his knuckles.

Baelandra's animal fear receded to the background, but she wasn't sure if it would ever leave completely, not after what she saw in his eyes. Baelandra continued, "You can't fool me, I know what happened in the Heart last night."

Krellis shook his head. "A weak man died, that is all."

"No, a young man died because you dangled him over a pit and cut the rope. Celidon would never have taken the Test if you hadn't goaded him into it."

Krellis reached out to touch Baelandra's face. She smacked his hand away.

"Don't you touch me," she said, slow and full of fury. "You will never touch me again. We are not lovers, we are not family. I will do everything in my power to remove you from my city. Twelve years ago, I was afraid of battle. Twelve years ago, I trusted a man I should have destroyed. I will not make that same mistake again."

Krellis sighed.

"Bae, I heard there was a man in your bed. I've told you how I feel about that."

"Do you actually care so much about what I put between my thighs? If you had more spies peering into my heart than my smallclothes, you would know that I hate everything you have become."

"Bae. That's enough." He used the same tone he used to chastise Trent. It was the ultimate slap in the face, to treat her like a child.

"Get out! Get out of my home and never come back."

Krellis shrugged. "Very well."

He reached into his shirt and touched the stone buried in his chest. Baelandra shuddered as a jolt of energy shot through her own gem.

"I will see you at the funeral then, my Sister." He raised an eyebrow at her. "If not before."

Krellis turned on a heel and walked out of her room. When the door clicked shut, the Sister of Autumn bit her lip and clenched her eyes shut to hold back the tears.

10

BROPHY CROUCHED out of sight on the stairway until Krellis's footsteps disappeared down the stairs into the garden. Krellis and his aunt had fought before, but nothing that serious. Brophy didn't want to leave them until he knew everything was all right. He hadn't liked the look in Krellis's eyes when he came crashing through that door, but people dealt with grief in strange ways.

Brophy wanted to press his aunt to continue their conversation from the night before, but he knew it wasn't the time. He had been awake all night. If he was exhausted, Baelandra must be much worse.

With a sigh, he climbed the rest of the stairs up to his room. His bed looked inviting, but he walked past it to his balcony. He needed sleep, but there was something he had to do first. Hopping up on the balcony railing, he jumped for the well-worn tree branch just outside. He grabbed it with both hands and swung his ankles around the limb. Hanging upside down, he crawled to the trunk and swung over to the bough that hung just beyond Trent's balcony. The boys had used the tree to climb over the garden wall between their houses for years.

Trent should have been there last night. His absence had awakened a quiet rage in Brophy. He and Trent would have words, even if the older boy beat him up. Some things had to be said.

Brophy swung his legs back and forth and jumped lightly onto the railing outside Trent's room. His friend lay sprawled on his back, bedcovers and sheets rumpled beneath him. He wore the same clothes from the day before. As Brophy approached, he noticed the bottle in Trent's hand. His limp fingers held it miraculously upright against his chest. Brophy didn't know much about liquor, but he knew an expensive bottle when he saw one. It certainly wasn't the cut-rate dregs Trent usually got from Stoneside.

Brophy peered at the label. "By the winter wind . . ." he murmured. It was Siren's Blood, the doom of the Silver Islands. Brophy had seen it for sale in the Long Market, only in one particular stall, flanked by two huge guards. The wine was said to be tainted with herbs that let men talk to spirits. The one-eyed merchant from Kherif who carried it told stories of how it drove the pirates of the Silver Islands mad. Brophy had always wanted to try it. Who didn't? But he never had the money to buy such an expensive prize. The only person Brophy knew who had drunk Siren's Blood was Krellis, and that was only a rumor.

Brophy knelt by the bed and gently pulled the bottle away from Trent's fingers.

Trent awoke at once, reflexively yanking it back. The sudden move spun him sideways off the bed, and he landed hard on the floor. He jumped straight to his feet as though nothing had happened. Focusing his eyes on Brophy, he gave a magnanimous smile.

"Brophy! There you are. I've been looking all over for you!" he announced with a flourish. Brophy glanced at the floor. Trent had not spilled a single drop. "We have some serious drinking to do."

"This is a bad time, Trent. You should have—"

"I know it's a bad time," Trent interrupted. "A very bad time. That's why we have to drink our way from the bad time to a good one. This bottle and another ought to do it." Trent tossed the bottle to Brophy, who caught the neck while still frowning at his friend.

A slight jingle caught Brophy's attention and a flood of recognition washed over him.

"Where'd you get that?" he demanded, pointing at a multicolored pouch swinging from Trent's belt.

"Where? I bought it in the Long Market, you ninny. This is Siren's Blood." He pointed to a hand that no longer held a bottle. Frowning, he spun around and snatched a second bottle off the table next to his bed. "Siren's Blood," he repeated.

"Not the liquor, you idiot. That money pouch. Where did you get it?"

Trent looked down again. He seemed to get stuck for a second staring at the mirrored pouch, but recovered nicely. "This?" He yanked at the pouch on his belt, pulling the strings tight. It rattled, full of silver. Trent laughed. "You wouldn't believe it if I told you. It was a bad night, Brophy, a bad night. But some good things happen on bad nights, you see?" He furrowed his brow. "Or something like that."

"Where did you get it?"

"Some tiny idiot from Vizar"—he waved his hand at the window—"across the Great Ocean . . . He left it in the shit stall. Might as well have thrown it down the hole."

Brophy studied the pouch. It was the same purse he'd returned to the Vizai merchant. It couldn't be coincidence.

"Did you see who dropped it?" Brophy asked, not sure if he should tell Trent his side of the story. "Did you try to give it back?"

"Give it back? You're such a child."

Brophy didn't laugh.

"Aww, Broph!" Trent frowned. "Ohndarien lives by milking pennies out of slavers and pirates. I just milked this one a bit harder, that's all."

"We don't milk them," Brophy said, in an even voice. "We provide a unique service at a fair price."

Trent sneered. "Don't be an idiot. We've got the world by the balls, and we've grown fat by what we can squeeze out of them."

Brophy almost threw the bottle at the wall behind Trent's head. "If you hate Ohndarien so much," he yelled, "why don't you go back to Physendria where you belong?"

Trent wobbled as if slapped in the face.

"If you were a true Heir of the Seasons," Brophy continued, "you would have been at the ceremony last night. You would have seen Celidon off to the Test. You would have lent your spirit to help him!" Brophy paused, breathing hard. "Why weren't you there?"

"Because I'm going to die in that hole!" Trent shouted back. He flung his bottle of Siren's Blood across the room. It clattered off the wall, spun across the balcony, and disappeared over the edge. His red-rimmed eyes were haunted, and his lip trembled.

"Those bitches will snuff out my torch just like Celidon's. I can just see it. My father will stand there, staring at my dead body, wondering how such a weakling could be his son." He threw his hand again, as though it had something in it. It spun him around and he stumbled into the bed. He didn't try to rise, but lay there half-on, half-off the mattress. His head lolled on the rumpled blankets, staring across the room. He seemed to be looking to some far-off place.

"I'm going to die for that bastard, and it still won't be enough . . ." he murmured.

Brophy stood there, dumbstruck. A long silence stretched between them. Trent stared at the ceiling as though he were seeing the whole thing playing out before him. Brophy walked to the table and gently set down the half bottle of Siren's Blood. He knelt by the bed and put a hand on Trent's shoulder.

"I'm sorry, Trent," he said, "I didn't know that you thought about the Test that much."

Trent shrugged his hand away and leapt to his feet again. "Yeah." He shook his head. "Be a hell of a sight, though, wouldn't it?" He ripped open the front of his shirt, sending buttons bouncing across the stones. "A red diamond, right here. What do you think?" He thumped his chest. "And me walking up to my father in the Hall of Windows, and saying, 'Hop down off that chair, Dad, and kiss my skinny ass.' "

He laughed uproariously, and cast about for the bottle he'd thrown out the window. Not finding it, he looked toward the balcony.

"If we have to die tomorrow, we might as well get drunk today, though, eh?" he announced. "Isn't that a proverb from that one book . . ."

"*The Leaves of Karfel.* No. It's not."

"Well it should be," Trent said, leaping from the floor to the balcony railing. He wobbled there for a second, then leapt for the tree five feet away. He tried to grab a limb, but jumped too high. His forehead hit the branch with a dull thud. Brophy winced and rushed to the railing as Trent plummeted to the garden fifteen feet below.

Trent lay laughing in the bushes at the base of the tree, his head next to the full bottle of Siren's Blood.

"Almost cracked my head on it!" He giggled. "I'm not sure which I'd rather lose."

Brophy let out a breath and shook his head as Trent rose to his feet and tottered toward the garden gate. Brophy jumped to the rail and leapt easily to the branch. He shinnied quickly down the trunk and ran to catch Trent as he slipped through the gate and into the city.

Brophy was only a few feet away when Trent turned around and saw him.

"A race!" he cried, and took off at a sprint. "Last one to the Night Market is a serpent's ass."

Brophy growled inwardly. Trent loved to run when he was drunk. It was one of his more annoying traits. Dreading the effort this might take, Brophy steeled himself and followed.

Trent sprinted all the way along the shore to Donovan's Bridge. The wine lent wings to his feet. He dodged among their neighbors, tossing the bottle of Siren's Blood high into the air and rushing forward to grab it. Brophy didn't catch up with Trent until he was halfway across Donovan's Bridge, balancing atop the railing.

"Where are you going?" Brophy asked, pulling him down.

"To pay my respects," Trent said. "I'm going to the Hall."

"That's a bad idea."

"I'm full of bad ideas," he replied, shoving Brophy back and dancing across the bridge.

Brophy followed his friend as he spun and wheeled through the Night

Market. Trent didn't stop twirling until he was halfway up the curving stair-case to the Wheel.

Krellis's son grew sedate on his walk up the stairs. He was silent and sober as they entered the Hall of Windows and approached Celidon's body. The Heir of Winter was laid out on a bier in the very center of the Hall, next to the Heart. He was dressed in a white robe and covered with winter flowers.

Brophy heard the quiet singing of the Heartstone in his mind. The song stayed with him wherever he went, but it was always stronger in the Hall of Windows. He had never been able to make out any words in her song, but today the tune seemed lost and forlorn.

People hovered in groups, speaking in quiet voices. Trent went directly to the bier and stared at Celidon's corpse.

Brophy steeled himself, preparing for Trent to do something stupid. Bro-phy would drag him away if he had to.

The bottle clinked as Trent rested it against the bier and stared down at Celidon's peaceful face. Slowly, Brophy joined him. Celidon didn't seem harmed in any way, but there was a faint scent of burned flesh. Brophy swal-lowed and tried not to think of what Celidon's chest looked like under the white velvet doublet.

The two friends stood there for a long while. Finally, Trent broke the spell. Pulling the cork from the Siren's Blood with his teeth, he carefully poured a drop onto his index finger and touched it to Celidon's lips.

"Happy dreams, cousin," he said in a husky voice. "Happy dreams . . ."

With that, Trent left Brophy alone at the bier. He lingered for a moment, but found no words for the brave young Heir of Winter. Without a sound, he turned and followed his friend out of the Hall.

Once they were in the garden, Brophy spoke in a low voice. "I'm sorry, Trent," he said. "I'm sorry about what I said before."

"I know," Trent replied. He shrugged. "Me too. I should have been there. It was important."

"You were there," Brophy said, as they walked together toward the wide stone steps. "Just in your own way."

Trent stopped just before the long, winding staircase. He looked at his feet and Brophy waited.

"Broph?"

"Yeah."

"Can you really hear it? The Heartstone singing?"

"Yes. Every waking moment since . . . a long time now." Brophy didn't want to talk about that fateful moment, not after Trent had laughed about it.

"I've never heard it. Not a single peep."

"I know," Brophy said slowly. His heart ached for his friend. He tried to imagine taking the Test without the encouraging call of the Heartstone.

"I've never belonged here, Brophy. It's never been my home."

"Trent, that's not true."

"Don't lie, Brophy. You're really bad at it."

Brophy looked down at his boots for a moment, frowned.

"I'm not an Ohndarien, and I never will be," Trent said, "but my father is determined for me to take that Test. He still dreams of going back to Physendria and reclaiming his father's throne. He wants me to hold his place on the council while he's gone."

"Has he told you this?"

"No." Trent shrugged. "Not directly. But he has a way of saying things without saying them."

"But Physendria is such a horrible place."

Trent's lip curled, and he gave Brophy a sidelong glance. "It wasn't always like it is now. They're just going through a hard time."

"Trent, they've attacked Ohndarien a dozen times. It's a bloody culture. All they know is violence. If we didn't have Coelho's walls—"

"You don't know, you've never been there!"

Brophy paused, let out a breath. Why was Trent defending Physendria? He'd been a small child when Krellis brought him to Ohndarien. He hardly remembered anything about it. "Why does your father want to go back there? What does he care about the Physendrian throne?"

"Every country deserves a good king, and my father knows he's the best man for the job." Trent laughed abruptly. "Even I would make a better king than Phandir."

"But we need Krellis here."

"I know. And that's why he's got it all backward. My father should stay in Ohndarien where Baelandra and everyone else loves him. But with his help, I could go south."

Trent fell silent as an old couple holding hands passed them and headed down the stairs.

"My uncle has more enemies than friends down there," Trent insisted. "With a few good men and plenty of gold, we could reclaim the Physendrian throne. It would be bloody, but we could make it quick and contained." Trent took a deep breath through clenched teeth. "I could hold the throne in my father's name. I could keep the fifteen families together. I could get rid of that vile Nine Squares contest and improve the lives of our people. With an Ohndarien alliance, Physendria could reopen trade routes with the Summer Seas. With reasonable taxes the country would flourish . . . And then," Trent continued, "once your father and the other brothers returned, my father could come south and . . . join me."

Brophy put his hand on Trent's shoulder, squeezed. Trent looked at him with a fierce determination in his eyes that Brophy had never seen before. The two boys stared at each other for a few moments until a flicker of a smile turned the corner of Trent's mouth.

"It's a good idea," Brophy insisted. "You should talk to your father about it."

Trent shook his head.

"Really, you should." Brophy insisted.

Trent took a moment before speaking. "You'd go with me, Brophy, wouldn't you, if I did that? You'd watch my back while I tiptoed through those vipers. I know I could do it if I had you behind me."

Brophy tried to picture himself in Physendria, standing next to the throne, with Trent sitting on top of it. He couldn't hold the image in his head.

"And I'd help you find the Lost Brothers," Trent insisted. "We could do that first. You watch my back, I'll watch yours."

Brophy let go of Trent's shoulder. Trent had always seemed so brave, but at this moment, on the verge of doing something truly heroic, Trent seemed suddenly vulnerable. "You know I'll always be there for you," Brophy said. "No matter where you go."

Trent let out a pent-up breath and dropped his gaze. "Thanks, Brophy," he said to the floor. "That means a lot."

"We should get home. Talk to your father about this."

Trent nodded. "All right, but not right now."

"Trent—"

"No, Broph, not now. Not with Celidon still lying on his bier. These plans can wait. For a little while at least."

Brophy nodded.

Trent paused, then said in a lower voice, "Will you do something for me?"

"Of course."

"Will you get drunk with me? I feel like an ass drinking alone. And I really need to stagger around for a while before I'm ready to face . . . everything." He paused. "I know you don't want to. But will you? For me?"

Brophy didn't say anything for a long time. Trent seemed to be a statue, staring at his boots.

"I don't know," he said. "Do you have anything good in that bottle?"

Trent looked up. He smiled.

Brophy grabbed the Siren's Blood and took a long pull.

THERE'S ANOTHER one!" Brophy shouted.

"Where?" Trent spun around so fast he nearly fell.

"There! There!" Brophy pointed to the dancing point of light in the air above Trent's head. "It's mine!"

Both boys jumped at once, trying to climb one another in midair. Brophy felt a tingle up his arm as his hand just missed the twinkling orb. The delight only lasted a moment before he crashed to the cobblestone streets with Trent right on top of him. The boys fought like two cats in a bag before collapsing into uncontrollable laughter.

Discovering the sparklies was the high point of the day. He and Trent had been chasing the floating white lights through the Long Market for hours.

Brophy didn't believe in the sparklies at first. The way the clouds turned into naked women wasn't real. The little faces that popped out of the harbor weren't real. The potato lady's foot-long nose wasn't real, either. But he and Trent both saw the sparklies, so they had to be real.

Brophy rolled to his knees, trying to breathe. He'd been panting for hours. Hours and hours. He couldn't ever seem to catch his breath, mostly because he couldn't stop laughing. Or was it because they kept running? They had run all over the city since morning and now the sun was about to set.

Trent scrambled to his feet before Brophy. He raised both fists above his head and jumped up and down in mock triumph.

"I caught it!" Trent shouted, twirling around so everyone could see his face. The Long Market was still packed, and a small crowd had gathered to see what was going on.

"I, Lord Trent the Mighty, have captured the elusive sparklie!"

"No!" Brophy scurried on his knees and clambered up his friend's back to get a closer look. "You're a liar. Let me see."

Trent spun away, tucking a fist into his armpit to protect his treasure. He stumbled two steps backward, tripped over a wagon tongue, and flopped into the dusty street.

"No," he announced from the ground. "It's my sparklie. I caught it and I'm going to eat it."

Brophy jumped on him. "You can't eat it," he said, wrestling with his friend, trying to wrench his hand open. "You can't eat a sparklie! You'll get too happy and die. Everybody knows that!"

More than a dozen people paused to stare at them. Trent rolled to his knees, shrugging Brophy away.

"No, no, no," Trent shouted. "I'll eat it and stay this way forever!"

"No, no, no. You'll die," Brophy insisted. "You'll swell up and pop like toasted corn." He reached for Trent's hand again, but his friend twisted away.

"Oh no, I won't!"

"Oh yes, you will!"

Trent jerked around, suddenly putting himself nose to nose with a pair of merchant's daughters who had crept close to the action. They squealed and fled between the legs of a towering man from Faradan. The bearded trader shook his head with an amused scowl.

"Do you think I'll die?" Trent asked the children, completely oblivious of the frowning giant above him.

The smaller and braver of the two girls shook her head.

Trent popped the sparklie into his mouth with a guilty grin.

The wide-eyed girls stared at him.

Trent's brow wrinkled, and a queer look came over his face. Slowly, he grimaced and fell to his hands and knees. His body spasmed. Brophy drew a quick breath.

The smaller girl's bottom lip crept forward into a worried pout. She gripped her father's leg. Trent looked up at her, eyes watering, lips tight. She clenched her father even tighter.

Trent opened his mouth, suffered through two strained pants, and let loose a monstrous burp.

Brophy and the little girls collapsed into fits of laughter.

The rest of the crowd broke up and moved away, many with amused smiles, some in disgust.

Merchants and buyers from a dozen cities had been staring at them all day. Brophy had decided early on that the ones who smiled were the "kid-inside" kind of people. They were little bubbles of joy moving about the city. Sparklies floated around their heads, and Brophy loved them like sisters and brothers. Others glared at them with disapproving frowns. Trent decided they were the "dad-inside" people. Sparklies ran from them, and they were to be avoided at all costs.

The giant from Faradan, definitely a "dad-inside" kind of person, scooped up his daughters and left. The two girls peered around their father's huge shoulders at Trent, who was making funny faces at them as they walked away. Brophy felt his heart swell in his chest. Trent had to be the best friend in the whole world. No one could have fun like Trent. No one could laugh like Trent. No one was so fearless, so funny, so much of a young hero about to emerge.

Before they hid the last bottle of Siren's Blood, a gang of sailors had surrounded them demanding a taste of their wine. Trent had charged right into the lot of them, swinging the bottle like a sword.

"Back, you puddle pirates!" he yelled, cracking a few over the knuckles as they tried to defend themselves. "Begone, you maggots of the sea!" The ferocity of the attack scared them long enough for Brophy to pull Trent away. The five sailors soon got their courage back and gave chase. They hunted the boys halfway across the market, but it wasn't much of a contest. The two boys let them stay close just for the fun of it. It was never hard to outrun a sailor.

Brophy rocked back onto his butt and stared at Trent. His friend's thick black hair caught the fading light, surrounding his face like the mane of a rock lion. Even Shara said Trent was handsome, but as the sun set over Ohndarien, with Trent grinning at the departing girls, he was the most beautiful human being Brophy had ever seen.

Trent turned toward Brophy, and the spell was broken.

"What?" Trent asked.

"You're going to be a great king one day."

Trent's smile faded and the keen sparkle left his eyes.

"Why would you say that?"

Brophy cocked his head. "Because it's true. You're so full of joy, so full of life. That's all you need to rule. To inspire those who aren't inspired. To love the people and let them love you back."

Trent let out half a laugh, but it fell flat. He stared at Brophy for a long time. He seemed about to say something, then didn't. Instead, he turned to look around the market. The hot colors of the sunset were approaching full bloom.

"You know," Trent began, "I don't think my father or your aunt would appreciate two Children of the Seasons lying dead drunk in the middle of the Long Market."

Brophy looked down at himself. His clothes were filthy and wet. Had they gone swimming? He looked over at Trent. His friend's clothes were muddy, too.

Then he remembered. They had been singing a song on the Market Bridge, and a group of "dad-inside" soldiers wouldn't let them cross. The soldiers kept telling them to go back and sleep it off, which was obviously stupid. Brophy had never felt so awake in his life. So they had jumped off the bridge and swum. It seemed extremely daring at the time. Right now, with the sun going down, it seemed a little bit silly.

Trent stood up, steady for the first time in hours. He pointed at the blazing horizon. "We'd best get out of the market before it closes."

Trent gave Brophy a hand up, and they headed back toward the Market Bridge. Everyone had to be off the island by nightfall. The merchants were busy loading the last of their goods into carts to haul them off and store them for the night. The Long Market was an immense, ever-changing city of tents, wagons, and wooden stalls packed with goods from all over the world. There were no permanent structures. Merchants rented space wherever it was available, sold their goods, usually by the boatload, and moved on by day's end. There was always something new and different at the Long Market, and it was easy to get lost.

Neither boy spoke as they wandered east toward the bridge that connected the Long Market with the Night Market. Brophy wondered if the soldiers would recognize them and send word back to Krellis and Bae. Trent must have been thinking the same thing and stayed wrapped in his own thoughts.

As they neared the bridge, Trent suddenly came to life. He tapped Brophy on the shoulder and pointed to a pile of barrels behind an olive merchant's tent. It took Brophy a moment to catch on. The missing bottle of wine!

Trent hurried to the barrels and rummaged through them. In moments, he triumphantly drew out the last half bottle of Siren's Blood.

"Hah!" he exclaimed.

"I can't believe it." Brophy laughed. "We looked all day for that thing!" After the incident with the sailors, they had stashed the bottle and forgot where they left it. They had spent half the day stumbling around the market, looking for that pile of barrels. After searching for so long, finding it this easily was almost a disappointment.

Trent pulled the cork out with his teeth and offered the bottle to Brophy.

"No thanks." Brophy shook his head. "I think I've had enough." It had been a great day, but it was over now. The tide had receded.

With the cork stuck between his teeth, Trent looked a bit comical. He nodded, his face thoughtful. "Yeah. You're right. We touched the sun today, though, didn't we, Broph?"

"At least a couple times." He smirked.

Trent shoved the cork back into the bottle without taking a sip. He opened his mouth to say something and clacked his teeth together again. A mischievous smile flickered on his face. "Then again," he murmured, "perhaps the day's not over after all."

12

ROPHY FOLLOWED Trent's gaze. A dark-haired woman struggled with a broken cart beyond the next row of tents.

Trent breezed past Brophy, clapping his shoulder. "It's Femera," he said.

Brophy blinked and felt a cold pit in his stomach. He didn't mind being around when Trent talked up other girls, but for some reason it bothered him with Femera. He looked wistfully back toward the Market Bridge, but Trent was on a mission. There was no going back.

Trent hurried to the side of a bright green tent from one of the Summer Cities. He peered around the corner at the girl's retreating back. She was struggling to push her awkward load up the bumpy street. One wheel of the heavily laden cart was split along the side. She could barely get it to roll.

"Wait a minute," Trent murmured, as Brophy peered around the tent as well, "This is a perfect opportunity for you. Go talk to her."

"What? Me?"

Trent rolled his eyes.

Brophy looked at Femera. She stopped, rubbed her aching hands, and took several deep breaths.

"What do I say?"

"Ask her about the cart, stupid. It isn't every day you get a chance to save a damsel in distress."

Brophy started forward, but hesitated. Femera looked back and spotted Brophy as he hovered beside the green tent. She smiled immediately.

"Brophy?" She wrinkled her brow. "What happened to you?"

"I, uh, fell in the bay."

"And then rolled in the dirt?" She stood up, her pale blue skirts swirling around her. She wiped her hands on a once-white apron.

"I . . ." he stumbled over the words. He could almost hear Trent's voice in his head. "So, what's wrong with your cart?" Brophy asked.

She stepped back and let him see the wheel. It was a solid piece of wood, cut in a circle with a cotter pin holding the axle through a center hole. It had split along the grain. The entire cart was packed with some kind of reddish brown rock.

She squeezed her aching hands and looked like she wanted to kick the thing. "It cracked going down the steps to the pier on Stoneside. I can barely get it to move."

"Maybe I can fix it. It just needs a new wheel."

She smiled again, and Brophy had to look away.

"You're sweet," she said, "but if I don't get this iron ore to the other side of the market before it closes, the cart won't matter."

Brophy looked toward the Windmill Wall. The sun had already set, and the light was fading. "Maybe we can push it together."

"Definitely," Trent said, emerging from behind the tent. "And I'll help you."

Femera glanced at him for a moment. "Trent," she said in a flat voice.

"Hello, Femera," he said, flashing his most charming smile. "C'mon, Broph, we've got a mission." He grabbed one of the handles and tipped the cart onto its good wheel. Brophy took the other handle. Between the two of them, they pushed the rattletrap cart along at a thumping jog.

"So why are we in such a rush?" Trent asked.

"My father's supplier delivered this low-quality ore this morning. If we don't get our money back before he leaves, we'll have to wait a month until he's back in the harbor."

"We'll make it," Trent said.

Femera glanced west. "I'll hurry ahead," she said, "and try to catch the merchant before he can set sail."

Brophy watched her skirts sway as she ran away from them. Trent gave him a little shove, and he dropped his end of the cart.

"Keep your tongue in your mouth," Trent said. "Unless you're going to use it."

"Shut up and push the cart," Brophy shot back. "I'm doing most of the work."

Trent smiled and started pushing so fast, Brophy had to run to keep up.

Huffing and puffing, they rolled the cart up the market as fast as they could, forcing other people to jump out of the way. It was hard work. Balancing on the good wheel proved impossible. Running on the bad wheel jolted Brophy as if Trent were punching him in the shoulder over and over again. He kept watching the cart, hoping it wouldn't collapse altogether before they got there.

As they approached the south side of the island, the street sloped gently downhill, and their job got easier. A long line of wooden wharves reached out into the bay. Only a few ships lingered at the quay. Most had already sailed dockside for the evening.

"There!" Brophy pointed. Femera stood next to the gangplank of a small trading galley from Kherif. Her prow was carved into a menacing bare-breasted woman with the head of a dog. They turned the cart down a ramp and started pushing it along the wharf. The broken wheel beat the wooden dock like a drum.

Femera argued with a thick-limbed man twirling his pointy beard. He stood in the middle of the gangplank, shaking his head. As soon as he saw the cart, he turned and began walking up the plank.

Brophy and Trent were panting as they rattled to a stop. Femera stood, hands curled into fists, staring daggers at the merchant.

"What did he say?" Brophy gasped.

"The pointy-chinned bastard won't take it back. Said the ore is of fine quality and that the market's already closed."

"He said that, did he?" Trent muttered between pants.

Two deckhands took ahold of the gangplank and began jostling it free. Just as they wrestled the hooks up from their niches, Trent stepped on the bottom, knocking it out of their grip. One of them jumped back, gritting his teeth and shaking a pinched finger. The other one glared at him. Trent ignored them both and walked steadily up the plank.

Femera's eyes widened.

"Dammit," Brophy muttered, but he smirked nonetheless. Trent had his moments. Brophy jogged up the plank as the two glowering deckhands stood in Trent's way.

"I should like to speak with your captain," Trent announced.

"The captain is not to speak with you," the unshaved man grunted in a thick Kherish accent.

Trent raised an eyebrow.

"Considering the unusual state of my attire, I'll forgive you that. You obviously don't know who I am. Go get your captain."

The sailor spat on the deck.

Trent whipped out his dagger and put the tip against the man's throat. He placed a calm, strong hand against the back of the man's neck. The sailor froze.

"I suggest you do as I ask. I am the son of the Brother of Autumn. I assume you know who rules in Ohndarien?" Trent said with a smile.

Brophy put his hand on his dagger but didn't draw it.

The other deckhand, with the crushed finger, glanced at Brophy's dagger. "Best to get the captain," he muttered to his companion.

The man with the dagger at his throat shot a murderous look at his comrade.

"Much better," Trent replied. He released his captive, shoved him back a step, and smoothly sheathed the dagger.

The scraggly sailor felt his throat and gave Trent a look before disappearing through a hatch.

"Your friend has bigger balls than brains," Trent said to the remaining Kherish sailor, still flexing his pinched finger.

"No friend to me. You should've stabbed him."

"I still might," said Trent, with yet another smile.

The captain climbed the ladder from belowdeck. He regarded Trent carefully as he twirled the tip of his beard.

"You are the son of Krellis?" he finally asked.

"Can't you see the resemblance?" Trent replied with a flourish.

"No," he grumbled, but the fire had left his eyes. He pulled a leather pouch out of his pocket and held it out. "This is the money paid for the ore. It is fine good ore. If he does not like to use it, I will find one who does."

The man turned to Femera, giving her a slight sneer over his pointy beard.

"You are to tell your father I never want his business again."

"You won't be getting it," she assured him.

The captain tossed the money toward her.

Trent snatched the pouch out of the air, spun his arm around in a flamboyant arc, and tossed the bag right back to the captain. "Add three more for the cart you just bought."

"Now, wait—"

"The fine for leaving the market late is five coppers. I suggest you pay the three." Trent smiled as if asking a beautiful barmaid for another mug of ale.

Brophy was amazed as the scowling merchant pulled three more coins out of his pocket and slipped them into the bag. Trent held out his hand, and the man slapped the money into his palm.

"Good sir, it has been a delight doing business with you," Trent said. "I am sure tales of your honesty will soon become legendary."

With a silent sneer, the captain headed back belowdeck.

Trent bounced down the gangplank. Brophy followed behind him, shaking his head.

Femera watched Trent saunter up to her and put the coins into her hands. "Justice is served, I believe."

"Thank you," she said, pocketing the coins. "Was the knife really necessary?"

"Some people need to be encouraged."

"Well, thank you. And thank you, too, Brophy."

"I didn't do anything."

"Oh, weren't you pushing half the cart?" she asked. "And weren't you the one who stood ready, giving that second Kher pause when he was about to knock Trent into the bay?"

Trent scowled. "What do you know about it?"

She shrugged. "I know that sailor had a dagger of his own. Probably longer than yours." She arched an eyebrow.

Trent shook his head. "I knew Brophy was there for me."

Femera opened her mouth to reply but thought better of it.

"I can give the money back if you're not happy," Trent said.

Femera shook her head. "I'm sorry, Trent. You scared me, that's all. Thank you. It was a noble thing to do. You almost got yourselves killed, but I still appreciate it."

Trent's brow furrowed. He started to say something, but Brophy jumped in front of him.

"You're welcome," he said for both of them.

Femera began walking back toward Stoneside, her blue skirts swishing like shadows in the darkening evening. "How did you two get so dirty?"

They passed a few soldiers herding straggling merchants out of the market. Trent and Brophy fell in stride on either side of her.

"We were in a fight," Trent said.

"With reality," Brophy added before he could make up another stupid lie. He shot Trent a disapproving frown.

"It looks like you lost," Femera said.

Brophy laughed.

"We got a few licks in," Trent murmured, drawing the half bottle of Siren's Blood out of his shirt. Femera eyed it as she navigated around the departing merchants.

"Thirsty?" Trent asked.

She pursed her lips. "I oughtn't."

"It's a fine vintage, I must say."

"What is it?"

"Taste first, then I will tell you."

Femera looked over her shoulder, then turned back to Trent. She held out her hand. "Give it over."

He handed her the bottle, and she took a taste. Her eyes widened in surprise.

"By the Seasons, that's good!" she said, licking the taste off her lips.

"Best there is," he said, taking the bottle back. He drank deeply and returned it. She took a longer sip this time.

Brophy remembered how quickly the Siren's Blood had begun to affect him. It was no different for Femera, or Trent on his third time around. Not to be left behind, Brophy joined in. The same thrill went through his body every time he swallowed. It was like drinking a smile.

Trent began a long-winded story about one of his hunting trips. He stumbled across a party of Physendrians and led them on a merry chase as they howled for his head like savages from the Vastness. Brophy didn't interfere. He knew the truth of the story. There had been a party of Physendrians close to the wall, but it wasn't Trent who'd outsmarted them and escaped. It was an Ohndarien scout named Thaft. Trent and Brophy heard the tale by the fire in the barracks. Brophy thought about spilling the truth, but he decided against it. He'd already corrected Trent once. To do it twice would spoil the mood. Besides, Femera actually seemed to be enjoying the story.

Brophy thought about Trent kissing Femera on the back of the neck, his hand sliding down the front of her dress. It still made his stomach turn. Why couldn't Trent have left Femera alone? He could have any other girl in Ohndarien. Brophy shook his head. It didn't matter. Trent was who he was. Who wouldn't be attracted to him?

"Waitaminute." Trent stopped and spun around one and a half times. Brophy accidentally bumped into Femera.

"What?" Femera asked, whirling around to look at Brophy, then back at Trent. "What, what?" She giggled. She looked at her hands for a second and back at Trent.

"Why are we going this way?" he asked, as if it were the stupidest thing in the world.

"The Market Bridge?" Femera asked, looking around as if she were suddenly lost.

"Exactly my point. Why don't we go the other way?"

"The Spire Bridge?" Brophy asked.

"Precisely. Why don't we go climb the Spire? It's a perfect night for another adventure. It's clear, not too windy. The view will be incredible. We can watch your friend the iron merchant sail through the Sunset Gate."

The Spire was an eighty-foot natural pinnacle of rock that jutted up from the middle of the harbor. It supported the center of the Spire Bridge, a steep, arched walkway that connected the Long Market to Stoneside. The bridge itself was at least fifty feet high, so ships could sail underneath it. Brophy had climbed the Spire once before, with his aunt, years ago. He remembered feeling like he could see the whole world from up there.

Femera smiled, looking west toward the Spire. "Can you climb up there?"

Trent headed in that direction. "Climb, walk, crawl, fly. However you want to go, we're getting up there."

Femera shook her head and looked back at Brophy. "I'm supposed to go straight home. My father will miss me."

"We won't be gone long," Trent assured her. He turned around and walked backward, facing them. "Just tell him you had to haggle for an hour."

She frowned and turned to Brophy. "I think you and I should leave Trent and go walk the Windmill Wall," she whispered.

"Come on," Trent groaned. "The night is just starting. Worry about your father tomorrow."

Femera glanced at Brophy, and he turned away.

"Come on!" Trent shouted from twenty paces away. He held up the Siren's Blood. "The wine is coming with me."

"Well," Brophy started, "maybe we could climb the Spire first. Then we could walk the wall afterward? The view is really great."

Femera lingered for a moment. She had dimples when she smiled. "I'll go if you go."

She reached out her hand and took Brophy's. Together they ran after Trent. Brophy grinned as he saw sparklies all through her hair. They were even more beautiful in the fading light.

They reached the Spire Bridge just ahead of the last merchants.

"I've never been here," Femera said, marveling at the towering stone. "I've always taken a waterbug across the bay."

The pinnacle was at least twenty feet in diameter where it met the bridge. The walkway encircled it to the east and the west, splitting the bridge in half as though the Spire had grown right up through the center. She trailed her hand along the rock and paced around it.

When she had disappeared on the far side, Trent whispered, "This is your chance. I've already had her, but you haven't. What a perfect opportunity, Broph! Your first time on the top of the Spire. The symbolism is staggering."

"What? No. Are you sure she—"

Femera came around the far side of the Spire. She wiggled her fingers in front of her face as if she had never seen them before.

Trent pulled Brophy around the corner so she couldn't see them. "She's sweet on you, Broph. It's obvious." He thunked Brophy on the forehead. "Any man could see that."

"Maybe," Brophy said. "I'm not sure—"

"That's because you are still a boy." He gave Brophy a playful shove. "Or will be until tonight."

Brophy shoved him back. "Shut up."

"I'll leave you two alone before long," Trent promised. "Don't worry. It's a sure thing."

Brophy blushed just as Femera completed her circuit.

"What are you whispering about?" she asked.

"Brophy's scared to climb up," Trent said.

"I am not!"

"I don't believe you," she said to Trent.

"No?"

"I don't think Brophy's scared of anything."

Trent chuckled darkly. "Oh, he's scared of something."

"Come on, let's go," Brophy said, blushing as he headed for the steep, narrow steps. The Spire had stone stairs that went the first fifteen feet up from the bridge to a man-made landing. Beyond the landing, the spire grew too narrow for steps. Someone had staked a rope to the top to aid the climb up the last twenty feet.

"So what do you think?" Trent asked as he joined the two of them on the little landing. He peered over the edge. "It's a long way down."

"Heights don't bother me," Femera announced. "The Water Wall is five times this high, and I walked over it."

"Well, then, you better hold Brophy's hand. He looks a little scared."

Brophy aimed a kick for Trent's knee, which he easily dodged.

"Maybe I will," she said, taking Brophy's hand in her own. She brought his fingers up to her lips and kissed them lightly. "Brophy's sweet."

Trent nodded and gave Brophy a knowing look. "He sure is."

Trent walked over to the dangling rope and pulled on it a couple of times to test its strength.

"Who built this?" Femera asked Brophy.

"The Spire? It's natural. It's been here forever."

"No silly." She bumped him with her hip. "This platform."

"Brother Morgeon," Brophy said, glad he knew the answer.

"Donovan Morgeon?"

"That's right, the father of Ohndarien himself," Trent interjected. "They say the Spire Bridge was his last brainchild, the last thing he sketched out before he died at the ripe old age of 134."

That wasn't exactly true, but Brophy let the comment slide. "Brother Morgeon got too old to move around in the last days of Ohndarien's construction. He had this platform built so he could supervise the final touches."

"They call it Morgeon's last erection," Trent added. He giggled at this, but he was the only one. Brophy actually thought it was funny, but Femera didn't, so he kept his mouth shut.

Trent shrugged off her silence and handed her the end of the rope. "Ladies first."

Femera shook her head. "You think you're so smooth," she said, tossing the rope back at him, "I'm not climbing up in front of you. You only want me to go first so you can look up my skirt."

"You wound me," Trent said, putting light fingers against his chest.

"No. I know men like you."

Trent shrugged. "As you wish, my love."

He started up the rope, feet braced against the rock as he grabbed each of the thick knots. Brophy started toward the rope, but Femera beat him to it. She winked at him, then started up, as lithe and strong as any boy.

Brophy swallowed again, took ahold of the rope. He caught a flash of Femera's smooth, white calves and looked quickly away. He kept his eyes on the stone in front of his face as she climbed.

"Hey," he heard Trent call from above, "I thought you said you didn't want us climbing up behind you."

"I said I didn't want *you* climbing up behind me," Femera huffed. She paused and looked up at him.

"Why him and not me?"

"Because Brophy is a nice boy, and you're not."

Brophy felt a little guilty, but he couldn't resist sneaking another glance as he waited for Femera to climb over the edge at the top. That time he saw calf, the back of her knee, and even a little bit of thigh. He was blushing again as he hauled himself up the rest of the way. It wasn't like he'd never seen a naked woman before. But this was different. This was Femera.

When Brophy pulled himself over the lip, she was spinning around the top of the Spire staring up at the stars. Trent passed Brophy the bottle with a wink. He drank down a small gulp and handed it back.

"I wish it was taller," Femera murmured. The sparklies hovered around her like a cloud. "I wish we could climb all the way up into the sky."

"That would be fun," Brophy said. He looked up at the stars. They were brighter than he had ever seen them before. "I wonder what a star tastes like."

Trent began singing a bawdy sailor's song, "Three salty dogs, they met a whore. Ya-ho. Ya-ho." He drained the last of the Siren's Blood, ran to the edge of the Spire, and threw the bottle out into the harbor. It disappeared into the night. Brophy never heard it hit the water.

Femera walked over and put a hand on Brophy's arm. "That was strong wine," she murmured. "I'm dizzy. Let's go sit down."

She led him to the southern edge and sat down. Brophy leaned against a lump of rock, and she curled up next to him, laying her head against his chest. Brophy's heart thumped faster than it had all night. He felt hot in the face. If only Trent would leave, like he said he would.

"The way the moonlight catches the ocean is so beautiful," she said. "It looks black, doesn't it, like a huge hole to the bottom side of the world."

"Yeah." He reached his hand around Femera's shoulder and rested it gently on her arm.

Brophy looked across at the Wheel. The torches for the missing Brothers burned bright atop the Hall of Windows. Brophy wondered if his father felt like this the first time he held his mother in his arms.

Trent came to the conclusion of his song, "The salty dogs, they lost their whore. They lost their money. They lost their war. And they were drowned, drowned, drowned. Ya-ho. Ya-ho. Ya-ho."

Femera looked up at the sky again and sighed. "I should go," she said. "I don't want to, but I should."

Brophy's heart lurched.

"Why?"

She laughed. "If my father knew I was up here at night"—she shook her head—"alone, with the two of you, he'd kill us all."

"It's not that bad," Brophy reassured her. "We're not doing anything wrong."

Femera laughed. "You don't know my father. Virginity is very important for a bride in Faradan."

Brophy giggled. "Well it's a little late for that, isn't it?"

She jerked her head up, her brows furrowed, and pulled away from him. "What do you mean?"

"Uh," Brophy blushed. "Well, I mean. What about you and Trent?"

She shot Trent a deadly look. He smiled at her, holding his hands out helplessly. To Brophy's surprise, she started laughing, sharp and venomous. She stood up, her skirts swishing across Brophy's face.

"Is that what he said?" she asked. Her eyes never left Trent. "Me and Trent? Hah!"

Trent's smile curved into a sneer.

Brophy scrambled to his feet. "I'm sorry. I shouldn't have said anything."

Femera turned her anger toward Brophy. "You actually believe I would do that? With him? Take such a peacock to my bed? 'Look at me, I'm so rich, I'm so handsome, I'm such a big man. I can draw a dagger on a man who doesn't dare touch me.' "

Trent said nothing, but Brophy could see his temper rising.

She turned back to Trent. "Inside he is just a scared little boy and always will be."

Trent stalked up to her and cocked back a fist. "You're a lying slut."

Brophy stepped between them.

"Out of the way, Broph," Trent growled. He shoved Brophy to the side and pointed his finger at her face. "You begged me to give it to you, and you cooed when I did."

She glared right back at him. "I might have begged in my life, but never for you, little boy. And I never lie."

Trent slapped her across the face.

Brophy punched him in the jaw.

Trent stumbled, falling to the ground, dangerously close to the edge. He wiped the blood from his mouth.

"Enough, Trent! Don't make it worse," Brophy said. "We're all drunk. Let's just go home."

Trent jumped to his feet and charged. His fist grazed Brophy's temple, but Brophy dodged and brought his knee up into Trent's stomach. His friend grunted and fell to his knees, shuddering as if he would throw up. Brophy blinked, trying to shrug off the glancing blow that could easily have taken his head off.

Femera leaned over and spat on Trent. "Peacock."

Brophy grabbed her by the arm and led her away. "Let's just go home."

Femera couldn't take her eyes from Trent.

"He's a liar," she murmured. "I hope you know that."

"Just climb down the rope."

Trent staggered to his feet and rose to his full height. He was three inches

taller than Brophy and easily outweighed him by twenty pounds. He was obviously still in pain, but he had his breath back. Trent glared at Brophy the
same way he looked at his father. "I can't believe," he started, then took a labored breath. "I can't believe you are taking this little slut's word over mine. I
fucked her. I fucked her and—"

"You never touched me, and you never will!" Femera screamed.

Brophy put himself between them, his heart hammering. "Shut up, Trent!
Just shut up!"

"Why should I?"

"Because you're a liar!" Brophy yelled. He clenched his fists. "You always
have been, and I'm sick of it!"

Trent stared at Brophy for the space of three ragged breaths. His bottom
lip began to quiver. He turned away and stalked to the other side of the spire.

"It's all right," Brophy said to Femera, holding her shaking hands. "He
loses his temper sometimes, but it never lasts. He's good at heart, you just
have to get to know him."

"I don't want to get to know him."

"Come on," Brophy said. "You're shaking. I'll go down first and hold the
rope."

Reluctantly, she nodded, but she kept looking over at Trent. Brophy
started down. He was almost to the bottom when he heard them arguing,
shouting at one another. He jumped down to the ledge and held the rope
steady.

"Femera! Come on!"

He heard a heavy thump, like a body hitting the ground, and Femera
cried out.

"Trent!" Brophy screamed.

He grabbed the rope and hauled himself upward. Suddenly, it went slack.
His fist hit his chest and he fell back to the tiny landing. He almost slid off
the edge, but managed to catch himself at the last second. The rope dropped
into a pile next to him.

"Femera!" he called, but she didn't reply.

Brophy gritted his teeth. Wrapping the rope around his waist, he tied it
tight and started climbing. The Siren's Blood rushed through his veins, and he
couldn't keep his hands from shaking.

"Trent!" he shouted. "Femera!" No one answered.

Searching frantically for small holds, he forced himself upward. He finally grabbed the dangling fringe of the severed rope and pulled himself over
the top.

Trent was just standing up. His hands tugged at the laces of his breeches. Femera crawled away from him, her skirts up around her waist.

"Hey, Loverboy," Trent called out. "Watch this!"

He ran to the other side of the Spire and leapt off.

"Trent!" Brophy yelled. He ran to the edge of the pinnacle and barely heard a muted splash.

"TRENT!" Brophy screamed again. He stared into the blackness.

"Told you I fucked her," Trent shouted from below, his voice muffled by the distance. His laughter faded into the night.

Brophy turned to see Femera standing on the other side of the Spire, looking down. Her pretty blue skirts were dirty, and there was a bleeding scrape on her calf.

Brophy laid down the rope, crossed the Spire, and put a hand on Femera's shoulder. She turned but wouldn't look at him. There were tears on her cheeks, and a drop of blood snaked down from her split lip. She reached up and wiped it off.

"Are you all right?" he asked.

"Of course," she said, her speech strange because of her fat lip. "I'm perfectly fine."

"Did he . . . ?"

She stared at him with a look of utter contempt. "You know what he did to me."

Her lip trembled, but her eyes held a rage equal to Trent's. Another tear slid down her cheek. She left him, walked over to the rope, and began tying it back together. "Don't follow me. If you follow me, I'll tell everyone what you did. Everyone!" she screamed. She started crying again as she grabbed the rope, wincing as she squatted to lower herself over the edge.

"Let me walk you home. I want to make sure you're all right," he murmured.

"You're a little late for that, Brophy," she spat, then dropped over the edge.

He took a gulping breath and staggered to the other side of the Spire. His stomach heaved, and he threw up. By the time he returned to the rope, Femera was gone.

13

BROPHY FELT like a thief, standing in the shadows of the alley across from Garm's workshop. The double doors leading to the blacksmith's forge were shut tight for the night. A few lights still burned in the living quarters upstairs, but Brophy could not see or hear what was happening inside.

The smell of vomit lingered in Brophy's nose. He'd been awake for two days straight and was exhausted. His clothes were still damp and clammy, but he couldn't go home after what had happened. Despite her request to be left alone, Brophy had followed Femera home to make certain she got there safely. He still wanted to make things right somehow.

Garm's daughter had disappeared inside her front door over an hour ago, but Brophy still lurked in the shadows, hoping she would come to a window so he could catch her attention. All he wanted to do was apologize and let her know he would help her any way he could.

Femera finally came to the balcony that overlooked the street. He saw her for an instant as she pulled the shutters closed against the night. Pressing his lips together, he left the shadows and crossed the street. He paused just below her window, wanting to call to her, but he didn't want to make a scene. He picked up a small stone and tossed it at the window. He still didn't know what words could possibly comfort her, but it would be better to say something than leave everything unspoken.

The shutters flew open. It wasn't Femera.

"You!" The girl's brown-haired, black-tempered father shouted. Garm had the stout neck and muscled shoulders of a blacksmith. His burly arms were as thick as most men's thighs. His bristly black beard stuck out from his face like wicked thorns, and his piercing eyes found Brophy instantly in the dim light.

Brophy took a few steps backward. The last thing he wanted was to rouse the father instead of the daughter.

With a growl, Garm threw a leg over the sill and jumped from the second-story window. He landed in a heap on the cobblestoned street, his leg twisted underneath him. Brophy was too shocked to move.

Garm gritted his teeth. He snapped upright and limped toward Brophy, who backed into the alley, stumbling over his own feet. It was a mistake, and he knew it immediately. The alley was a dead end.

Garm snarled and his crooked teeth shone in the moon's half-light. The rest of his face was lost in the bushy black beard and wild hair.

"She was just a little girl!" the blacksmith shouted, his hands bunched into enormous fists.

"I'm sorry," Brophy said, "I just came to say I'm sorry—"

"Shut up!"

Brophy feinted left and sprinted right, hoping to slip out of the alley.

With a roar, Garm lunged and body-blocked him into the wall. Brophy's head bounced off the stone, and he fell to the ground, dazed. Garm grabbed his shirt and yanked him upright as easily as he would a sack of flour.

"She's my daughter!" Garm shouted, limping backward and slamming Brophy into the other wall. The impact drove the breath from his lungs, and he gasped for air.

"My little girl!" Garm slammed him against the wall again. Brophy's ribs flared in pain. "Did you come back for more? Ruining her once wasn't good enough?"

"It wasn't . . . me . . ." Brophy gasped.

Garm launched a thunderous blow to Brophy's face.

Brophy's instincts took over. With no room to dodge, he nodded fiercely and met the fist with his forehead, just as he'd been taught. The blacksmith shouted in pain. Brophy lashed out with his foot, kicking the man in the side of the knee.

Garm stumbled backward. His grip loosened, and Brophy grabbed his thumb with both hands. He wrenched hard, and Garm let go.

Brophy landed on all fours, rolling toward the mouth of the alley. The blacksmith recovered his footing and charged. Brophy spun to the side and swept the man's leg out from under him. Garm crashed to the ground.

"Just tell her I'm so sorry!" Brophy cried.

Even though he was down, Garm was not finished. Gritting his teeth, he levered himself to his knees, pried a cobblestone out of the street, and raised it over his head.

"Papa, no!" Femera shouted from the doorway of the forge.

"Back inside, Mera!"

She ran to her father, trying to block the stone. "Don't," she begged him, "It wasn't him. It was the other boy."

"Watching's as bad as doing," Garm said. His huge biceps bulged, and he hurled the stone at Brophy's head.

Brophy ducked just in time. The wind from the rock's passage whispered through his hair, and the cobblestone shattered on the wall behind him. He backpedaled, trying to get farther from the alley.

Garm pushed his daughter aside and pried up another stone.

"Papa, no! Don't!" She shouted again, interposing herself between the two of them. "They'll kill you. They'll send you out the gate and stone you from the walls." She threw her arms around his neck. "Don't do it."

He let her hug him, but his murderous glare remained fixed on Brophy. He hurled the stone, but his heart wasn't in it. Brophy stepped lightly to the side, and it skittered across the empty street.

"You kings and princes are all the same," he spat, his fury giving way to bitterness.

"I'm not a prince," Brophy protested, wishing he had never come. "I'm nobody."

The enormous man held on to his daughter as if she were a little child. "Call yourself what you like, you rich little bastard. Your type is the same all over the world. You take what you like and throw it away when you're finished. If it were just me, I'd crush your head against that wall and let them stone me. But I got my daughter to think of. You'd best get out of my sight before I forget that."

Brophy opened his mouth, closed it. He almost turned away, but paused, looking back at Femera.

"I just came to say how sorry I am," he whispered to her. "If there is anything I can do . . ."

Brophy's words trailed off. The look on Femera's face made him realize how pathetic they were.

The dark-haired girl helped her father to his feet. With his hulking arm wrapped around her shoulders, she finally looked at Brophy. Her blue eyes flashed.

"You're sorry?" She looked away from him. "Sorry isn't enough, Brophy. Not nearly enough." Femera and her father limped past him through the forge door. Brophy stared after them for a long time. Finally, eyes downcast, he walked home.

KRELLIS STABBED a juicy half sausage and brought it to his lips as he scanned the pages in front of him. Flipping back a few pages, he absently bit into the meat.

A dispatch boy slipped through the half-open door of Krellis's chambers. He padded quietly to the table and dropped off the day's supply of letters and proposals. Never taking his eyes from the page, Krellis reached into his money pouch and flipped a brass coin to the boy.

The boy caught it neatly in one hand. "Like father, like son," he said.

Marking his place with a thick finger, Krellis looked up, brows furrowed. He fixed the boy with a cold stare.

"Drunk as an Islander and rolling around the market like a dying dog," the boy continued with an impudent smirk. "Sounds just like his father at that age."

Krellis slowly drew his dagger with a theatrical scrape. He squinted, as though concentrating on something invisible, and stood up.

The boy seemed to blur. Krellis blinked, forcing his eyes to focus. A tall, lean man in his midforties stood naked before him. The impudent smirk was all that remained of the errand boy.

With one meaty hand, Krellis gripped the edge of the oak table and slid it aside as though it weighed nothing. It scraped loudly against the floor. A few sheets of paper slid away and floated down. Krellis set the tip of his dagger underneath the man's chin. His visitor's eyes narrowed, but he did not move away.

"Your sneaky games might impress your students, but they set my teeth on edge. I'm a dangerous man when I'm on edge," Krellis said, his arm as steady as the wall.

"Just a gentle reminder, little brother," Victeris said. "I can slip a knife into your bedchamber just as easily as you can order a hundred soldiers into mine." He set an elegant finger against the edge of the knife and pushed it away. Krellis shook his head and sheathed the blade.

The Zelani master sucked the stripe of blood from his finger, still smiling.

"We are the shield at each other's backs and the knife at each other's throat," he said, "which, from the outside, must look a great deal like an embrace."

Krellis slid the table back between them, sat in his chair, and picked up his fork.

"Did you come here for a purpose? Or do you simply want to gloat over Trent making a fool of himself in public again?"

"So you know?"

"I know everything that happens in my city."

"I should remind you, dear brother, that at Trent's age you were drinking and whoring yourself to death in the most vile fleshpots in Physendria."

"Was I?" Krellis said. He looked down at his ledger once more.

"In fact, if it hadn't been for the boy's mother, you would be long dead or dying from the slow, suppurating rot of the Cuckold's Revenge."

"Don't bow so low, Victeris. I would have found my mettle with or without her help."

"Perhaps, but Maigery *was* my first student," he pursed his lips reflectively. "The least you can do is give the dead woman a little credit."

The Brother of Autumn gave his sibling a narrow glance, then turned back to his ledger. He ran his finger down the page. "What is your point?"

"Just trying to correct a few errors in your memory. You say you found your mettle. I say you found your mush," Victeris suggested. "No man, woman, or lowly beast can live without love."

Krellis snorted. "Indeed?"

"Absolutely. You may be a master of armies, a fierce commander, but I am master of the human heart." He shrugged. "I don't expect you to understand. Our father didn't exactly fill our lives with much of the precious stuff. But I assure you, it was Maigery's love, not my power, that set you upon the road you walk today."

"I never loved that woman. Even when she held my son to her breast, I never loved her."

"Do you take me for a fool?" Victeris cocked his head to the side. Krellis looked up. "Of course you didn't love her. You saved that for later in life, didn't you?" He gave his brother a crooked smile.

Krellis darkened. He opened his mouth to retort, but his brother cut him off.

"No matter." He waved a hand. "She loved you. That's what's important."

Krellis sneered. "Talking to you is like kissing a snake. Hurry up and pour your poison into my ear, so you can leave, and I can forget you were here."

"I came because of your son."

"My son is my problem."

"If your son prevents you from completing your bargain with me, he is my problem as well."

"Stay out of my family."

Victeris laughed. "Too late, dear brother. I was born into your family four years before you were. Surely you can set aside your plans for conquering the world long enough to hear an older brother's advice?"

"Fine. Speak your advice and go back to buggering little boys."

"Please, your harsh words wound me, and I am so fragile."

Krellis sighed. "Will you ever tire of the sound of your own voice?"

"I humbly doubt it." Victeris's little-boy grin returned. "My advice is this: Move your son to the front of your playing board."

"He is not ready."

"You coddle him and whip him by turns. Neither will make the boy any stronger."

Krellis looked up. His eyes blazed. "Tread carefully, Victeris. My family is my affair. Do not presume you are so well loved that you may overstep your boundaries carelessly."

"Yes, yes, I know, you are strong, you are fierce. You'd as soon spit at me as speak with me. Is that what you would have me think?" Victeris smiled. "I might almost believe it if you had not returned to Physendria to rescue me from our brother's petty tortures."

"I returned for my son. You were an afterthought."

Victeris chuckled. "No one enters the Wet Cells as an afterthought. You risked everything to bring me here to stand by your side, albeit in shadow."

"I owed you," Krellis grunted.

"And now I owe you, and I want to clear my debt. I have plans of my own after our little adventure here. It has been over a decade, you realize. You were not so timid when you gave our father his reward."

"I took the throne from a man who did not deserve it. And lest you forget, I didn't hold that throne long enough to sit in it before Phandir arrived with the royal guard in his pocket. There are very few alive who remember that I was king in Physendria, even if it was only for a few minutes. They now say it was Phandir who cut Father's throat." Krellis frowned and flexed his fingers. "I am sure it is a rumor that he does little to discourage."

Victeris nodded. "Indeed. We both underestimated the cunning of the middle brother. Who would have thought the smiling fool had it in him?"

"Yes. A mistake I won't make again. I took the throne once from a stronger man. I will take it again."

"A moment I await with great anticipation, for it will end my debt of love and my debt of hate, and sever my last tie to everything Physendrian."

"Then be patient, brother. Such things take time."

Victeris arched an eyebrow. "You still must goad Phandir into attacking soon. If that fool drags his feet, all will be lost. Use Trent. Stage a public rift between the two of you. Send him to his uncle filled with offers of an alliance."

"Trent? A spy?" Krellis shook his head. "Do you actually believe the boy is that clever? I thought it was our intention not to underestimate Phandir a second time."

Victeris considered his brother for a long moment. "Surely you see that the boy has a velvet tongue."

"A velvet tongue and a velvet spine."

Victeris found his smile again. "Spines are my specialty. The tongue I cannot duplicate, but I have just the confidence he needs. With a fully trained Zelani at his side, Trent would quickly become a very different man. You did, after all."

"Enough of that." Krellis waved a warning hand. "Do not speak of Maigery again."

"As you wish, but consider what I have said. One of my best pupils has just graduated. I have waited years for her to come to fruition. She may be the most talented Zelani I have ever trained. The girl is spirited and strong, full of fire. Give her to Trent, and she will do for him what Maigery did for you."

Krellis flashed him a lethal glance, but he paused.

"Send him to his uncle," Victeris suggested. "Give the boy a drop of respect and he will turn it into an ocean."

Krellis ground his teeth. "And if he fails? Phandir has used my family against me before."

Victeris shrugged. "You do not expect to rule the world while cringing in fear of a little risk, do you?"

Krellis brought a hand to stroke his beard. "No."

Victeris arched a thin, black eyebrow.

"No," Krellis continued. "Perhaps you are right on one count. It is time for the boy to prove himself, but I don't trust him to match wits with Phandir. Trent needs a mission of a different sort. He is young. He needs a young man's quest. We will send him to find the Four."

"The missing Brothers?" Victeris rolled his eyes. "It's a fool's errand. A myth."

"It is not a myth."

"It may as well be."

"That, I agree with. But I will never rule here as long as I am competing with the memory of four ghosts."

"Still, smarter and braver lads than Trent have tried and failed."

"As far as we know. But none of them had a Zelani at his side."

"Do you really think he will return with the Brothers?"

For the first time, Krellis's mustache curved in a smile. "Why would I want them to return?"

Victeris slowly smiled in return.

Krellis intoned dramatically, "Sadly, the Lost Brothers were found dead at the toil of a monumental task . . ." He resumed a normal tone of voice. "Finally, those damned torches above the Heart will be snuffed, and I shall be a whisper away from truly ruling in Ohndarien."

Victeris nodded. "You are cunning. You have considered all . . . except one thing."

"Indeed?"

"What if he succeeds? What if he finds the Brothers alive?"

Krellis eyed Victeris and his smile faded. "He may find them alive, but he will not leave them alive."

Victeris laughed. "Surely you don't think you can turn that boy into a hired knife?"

"No, of course not. Trent's no assassin, but he will not be traveling alone. This girl of yours, do you have her in hand?"

Victeris paused a moment before continuing. "She is in hand. All I have to do is whisper a name in her ear, and she will do the rest. But . . ." he murmured.

"Yes?" Krellis asked, annoyed.

"You need someone to rule in Ohndarien while you are retaking your throne in Physendria. The Vastness is a dangerous place. What if Trent fails, before he finds the Four? What if your son dies?"

"If he does, then . . ." For the first time, Krellis seemed pensive. He shook his great, woolly head. "No. I know the boy. He will take the easy way home."

"There are things in the Vastness more dangerous than ten Phandirs," Victeris pressed.

"If the boy dies, then he dies!" Krellis snarled. "All men must be tested sometime."

"What will that do to our plans? If Trent does not rule in Ohndarien, then I will be forced to do it. I have no desire to waste my time running a kingdom."

Krellis sneered at his brother's innocent smile. "Then you better hope the magic in your little girl's cunt is enough to keep my son alive."

15

EVEN THE sunlight tortured him. It trickled in through the window, dappling the bedsheet as the leaves outside moved in the morning breeze. Trent shut his eyes against the glare and held his belly. It didn't hurt if he didn't move. It didn't hurt if he didn't breathe. Breathing he could minimize. Unfortunately, he had to move. If he didn't piss soon, he'd explode.

Which would be worse, he wondered. Pissing again or exploding?

"All right . . ." he murmured. "All right!"

He slowly pushed himself upright, keeping one hand on his stomach. He clenched his teeth so hard they squeaked. Carefully, he pulled up his shirt again. He couldn't stop looking at it. The whole side of his chest from hip to collarbone was an ugly yellow bruise. The skin had split along the bottom of his rib cage and his pants were stained to midthigh.

He had landed badly. He knew it from the moment he hit the water. If it weren't for the Siren's Blood, he never would have made it home.

Trent lowered his salt-crusted shirt and looked across the room. On the far side, as far as possible from the bed, the lidded brass bowl stared at him.

I'm an idiot, he thought. *Why didn't I put it next to the bed last time I got up? I could piss from here, spillage be damned. Let the chambermaid clean it up.*

Swallowing, Trent rose to his feet. It wasn't as bad as he had expected. The pain stayed about the same, but he felt wrong inside. His gut was swollen and sore.

He inched across the room to the chamber pot. He'd left his breeches unlaced from the last time. It hurt too much to tie them up. He tried to relax, tried to make it come slowly, but the piss burst from him like a river. His stream shot wide, splashing the wall until he could aim it into the pot.

He didn't want to see, but he stared at it, transfixed.

It was red.

He closed his eyes. His urine splashed on the floor as it slowly petered out, but he was past caring.

He left the laces undone and walked gingerly back to the bed. Only when he sat down did he realize he'd left the chamber pot, again.

Trent couldn't remember the walk home. But he remembered the night before all too well. The images kept running through his mind. The sound of Brophy's voice from far above. The feel of Femera's breast in his hand, her nails upon his wrist. He shook the thoughts from his head.

What if the girl talked? She certainly would. That was just what he needed.

He lay back in bed, prodded the tenderness in his belly. Somehow he kept hoping it would fade.

Perhaps Brophy could talk to the girl, but he would probably just believe her lies all over again.

Trent got the little slut her money back and still she picked a fight with him. Was he just supposed to let her talk like that? He couldn't believe she put up such a fuss. He'd never done anything to her. She was nothing to him. She started it, but Trent finished it.

He still couldn't believe Brophy took her side, after all their years as friends, after those empty promises to watch his back. The bastard probably did her after I left, Trent thought. The way she was wiggling her ass all night, she obviously wanted some.

Trent heard a thump out on the balcony. He winced as he quickly retied the laces on his breeches.

"Who is it?" he asked, relieved to find that his voice was even.

Brophy stepped through the archway, brushing the bark off his hands. Trent sat up and let his hands drift to his sides. Brophy's eyes were red, his hair twisted and matted like gold wool. His clothes were rumpled and stained, his hands dirty. He looked like he was ready to throw another punch.

Finally, Brophy broke the silence. "There's no way out of this, you know," he murmured.

Trent felt his chest tighten.

"You're going to have to tell your father," Brophy continued. "You're going to have to make amends to Femera and Garm. And then . . ." It seemed as though Brophy could barely get the words out of his mouth, "And then you have to leave Ohndarien."

Trent swallowed, feeling like he was going to throw up. "Look, Broph," he started, gritting his teeth. "I don't know what she told you, but nothing happened—"

"Trent!" Brophy shouted. "Everything happened, and you know it!"

Trent felt a lump rise in his throat that he couldn't swallow down. He looked away, but Brophy wouldn't let up.

"They're going to force you out the gate, no matter what you do. If you go to your father first, you can tell him you were drunk and didn't know what you were doing." He almost phrased it as a question. "He might be able to help you, get you out of the city with some money and a pack full of supplies. If you fight this, if you start lying again, the council will send you out the gate naked. You know what they do to rapists who have been thrown out the gate."

Trent forced himself to his feet.

"Listen to me, Broph. Just calm down. We can pay the girl off. It's her word against ours. Two against one. Who'll believe her? She's nobody."

Brophy narrowed his eyes at that. His jaw set. "I believe her. She's telling the truth."

Trent clenched his fist. Brophy glanced at the fist, then back up at Trent. How could he so calmly sentence his best friend to death?

"Don't make me, Broph," Trent murmured. "I can't tell him, not my father."

"You can do it. I'll help you."

"He'll kill me."

"No he won't. He loves you."

Trent barked a short laugh and winced, as pain shot through his side. Brophy didn't seem to notice.

"He might love you," Trent said. "He might love Bae, but he sure doesn't love me."

Spots swam across his vision and sank back onto the bed.

"Don't do this to me, Broph," he said, unable to keep the quaver out of his voice. "Don't make me leave. I can't go out there alone."

"You won't be going alone. I'm coming with you."

Trent jerked his head up. "What?"

Brophy's expression had not changed. "I'll go with you as far as the Summer Cities. I'll help you get established, but then I have to come back. There's something I have to do."

Trent felt something tickle his cheek, and he was surprised to wipe away a tear. "Broph . . ." he began.

"Come on," Brophy said. "Get up, get dressed." He walked out onto the balcony and put his foot on the railing. "I'll meet you here in a few minutes. We'll face your father together. Together we'll tell him."

Brophy stood up, balancing on the railing. He looked over his shoulder, but he didn't turn around.

"Broph, why are you doing this?"

A long silence filled the room.

"Do you really have to ask?"

"I . . . Yes."

Brophy shook his head. "Because you are my brother."

He leapt for the branch, caught it deftly and climbed out of sight.

16

SHARA BLINKED. The knock sounded again. She shook her head. Someone at the door? She sat up, shifted her legs over the edge of the bed. Naked. Where were her nightclothes? Didn't she put them on last night?

"Shara-lani?" The voice spoke her honorific through the door. She didn't recognize the person. A messenger?

"A moment," she said. Something had happened. She stood up, felt between her thighs.

Did she . . . ?

Yes. Victeris came to her last night. They spoke for a long time, of her childhood. Victeris laughed at her stories of the rutting pigs.

She shook her head. She'd never liked watching that, but her father had made her. Said it was a part of the farm, and she should understand it. She'd only told the stories because Victeris seemed so interested. Then she said she was tired, and he left.

But . . . no.

She was sore. They must have . . . She'd said she was tired, but he hadn't left. They'd talked some more and ended up in bed, against the wall, on the floor . . . That wasn't right. A master and a Zelani only coupled during the graduation ritual. Only that once.

Then why . . . ? Shara furrowed her brow. The thought was so difficult to hold on to.

"Shara-lani?" the voice said from the hall.

There was someone at the door. Wait. What had she been thinking? Something about Victeris.

She chased the thought, but it slipped away like a minnow.

The messenger knocked again. She took a deep breath and reached into the man beyond the door. She felt his anticipation, a little bit of fear, curiosity. "Yes, I am here," she said.

Shara let her thoughts go completely. She could think about it later. She followed her breath throughout her body. Her mind calmed, and then cleared. "Enter," she said.

The messenger opened the door and stepped inside. He gave a quick bow. She didn't worry about him seeing her naked. To him, she was garbed in her flowing blue gown, with the Zelani sapphire hanging at her waist.

"Shara-lani, the Brother of Autumn requests your presence in his rooms."

Her heart beat faster. Krellis? In his chambers. Could this be her assignment? Had he chosen her for himself?

"I shall attend him immediately."

The messenger bowed and left.

She smiled. Ten years of waiting and suddenly everything was happening at once. She'd slept for nearly twenty-four hours after the ritual. It was confusing at first to wake up in her chambers, not sure how she got here. But it did not matter; she felt glorious. She remembered the ritual so vividly. All she had to do was close her eyes, and she was back there. Victeris stood naked before her, his hand rough on her thigh. When he entered her it was not like a man sliding into a woman. It was like a wave crashing into the shore. He shattered her. She flew apart like mist. For a moment she was gone. She ceased to exist and was part of everything. It had been glorious. Fleeting, but glorious nonetheless.

The experience changed her. She was different now, worth more than she once was. She didn't know what that meant yet. It was something that might take a lifetime to understand, but she had a lifetime, perhaps more than one if what she suspected was true.

She was a Zelani now. Shara-lani. She was a bonfire walking among candles, and anyone she chose to touch would burn as brightly as she.

Shara took several deep breaths to bring herself back down. She had to be careful. The power was so close. What used to take hours to build was constantly there, ready to flare out of control. The new challenge would be to hold herself back, to stay focused on her audience with Krellis.

She wanted a bath, but she couldn't take the time. She slipped on the gown of her office, fixed the silver chain around her waist, and adjusted it so the sapphire rode the front of her left hip. After a brief glance in the mirror, she left her room.

It wasn't a long walk from the school to Krellis's villa on the shore of Southridge, but she enjoyed the journey. All along the way she played with her new power. She reached out to every person along her path. It was natural to slip into their bodies, feel their emotions, their general state of wellbeing. She even reached into sailors skimming across the bay far below. She could barely see them at that distance, but she could tap into their life force as easily as she could read an expression on someone's face. She must have touched hundreds of people along the way. She gave them a hint of the light she carried with her and left each one a little happier than she found them.

When she passed Baelandra's villa, Shara reached out toward Brophy. She couldn't see him, but she felt him through the blue-white marble of the garden walls. He was upset about something, but she didn't dig deeper to find out what. She wouldn't invade her friend's privacy.

Krellis's villa stood next door. The three-story marble mansion didn't look much different than the buildings on either side of it, but it had a very different feel. It was a man's house. Masculinity had soaked into the stones. It excited her. She couldn't wait to see what lay beyond the marble walls.

Two soldiers stood guard in the archway that led into Krellis's garden. The men uncrossed their spears and let her in without a word. Shara could feel their eyes on her as she walked between them, and she smiled.

Crossing the garden felt like a ritual, much like the swim to her graduation. Shara took the steps quickly on silent feet. The stairs led to a pair of double doors left slightly ajar. Six daggers were carved above the door, exactly where Brophy said they'd be, one for each of the Physendrian assassins who had failed to kill Krellis.

There had been times when she'd feared whom she might serve as a Zelani. What if she wasn't attracted to them? How would it affect her? She suppressed her grin. She wouldn't have to worry about that again. She had no doubts about serving Krellis. Shara pictured the Brother of Autumn in her mind, the way he walked, the way he fenced, the way he'd looked her in the eye. Everything about the man promised that he would be a magnificent lover. She shook her head. Mustn't act like a lovesick maid.

Reaching out a hand, she paused, evened her breathing, and knocked lightly.

"Come," Krellis said, his deep voice rumbling through the door, through her chest.

She pushed the door open and entered. He stood behind a table piled with papers, scrolls, and a few hefty tomes. He looked up, nodded approvingly.

"Good," he said, and looked back at his papers. She stood in silence as he perused the last of them. When he was finished, he walked around the table and stood in front of her. They watched each other in silence for a moment. She held her composure, determined to hide her excitement.

"Victeris tells me that you are possibly his best student yet."

She nodded, but a blush crept into her cheeks.

"He doesn't hand out praise very often," Krellis said. His bushy salt-and-pepper beard, his mane of dark hair, and those glittering brown eyes made him seem like a wild beast, tamed by his own fierce will to walk among civilized men.

"I have done my best, Brother."

He studied her. She remained where she was, looking back at him. Victeris said that a Zelani was meant to be seen. Perhaps this was the last scrutiny of the one with whom she would be joined.

"He also says that you ran away when you were younger."

The steady rhythm of Shara's breathing faltered.

"He did?"

Krellis's mustache twitched. His eyes glittered.

She cleared her throat and forced her breathing back to its natural, even cadence. "I didn't know anyone else was aware of that."

"He says you have a spirited streak."

She suddenly realized this was not an interview. He was playing with her, getting a feel for her. He had already chosen her but was curious. She could have known all of this from the moment she walked into the room, but she hadn't allowed herself to flow into him, to taste his emotions with her powers. From respect, from awe, she wasn't sure exactly why.

She licked her lips. "The spirit is what drives the power of a Zelani."

His mustache twitched again. "Indeed," he rumbled.

She couldn't read anything from his expression. Was that tightening of his eyes disapproval or amusement?

Unwilling to restrain herself any longer, she reached out for the man and let her passions flow into him. Behind that stern exterior, Krellis burned. He was a man of a hundred secret torches. She opened her mouth at the heat of it. Her breath faltered, and the vision vanished. The torches disappeared and she was looking into his eyes once more.

He arched an eyebrow.

This man was not an open book to be read so easily. It made her want him even more.

A knock sounded on the door.

"Come." Krellis looked past her.

To her surprise, Trent entered the room. He looked at her, his brow furrowing. Beads of light perspiration stood out on his forehead. The boy was suffering and lacked his normally cocky stance. She narrowed her eyes. His feelings were jumbled and chaotic.

"Father," he said, inclining his head. He had only taken one step into the room, as though he was ready to turn and flee. "You wanted to see me?"

"You look spectacularly hungover," Krellis said.

Trent shot Shara a quick, curious glance.

"I . . . had a bit to drink last night."

Krellis laughed, suddenly and genuinely. "Indeed? You say that as though the entire city does not know. Siren's Blood. Now that is a drink of men. I know something of it. They say it drove the Silver Islanders mad."

Trent cracked a tentative smile. "Yes, I think I went a little mad myself last night."

"Wine has always been a whore. The more you play the more she makes you pay."

"Then this is one whore I may be in debt to for quite a while."

Krellis walked over to Trent and clapped his son on the shoulder. The boy wobbled.

"If you must suffer, suffer well. A man's mettle isn't only tested on the battlefield, but also by how he handles his drink."

"I shall be fine," Trent said.

"Good man."

Trent grinned.

"You know," Krellis said, "when I was your age, I once got so stinking drunk in Paeler's Port that someone stole the boots right off my feet. You never realize how much shit there is in the world until you have to walk home barefoot." He laughed again, and this time Trent laughed with him.

"Well." Krellis waved a hand. "I won't belabor this meeting. I've brought you here because I have something to say that concerns both of you. Trent, I have a problem, and I need your advice."

Krellis's son jerked back as if stung. His eyes narrowed and he moved forward to stand beside Shara. Trent looked like a dog begging for a bone. Krellis had never asked his son for anything, least of all his advice.

"I have a difficult and dangerous task. I need someone I can trust to take care of it," Krellis said. "I need a good man. Who do you think I should send?"

Trent considered his words carefully. A line of sweat trickled down Trent's temple. It wasn't just the hangover. This boy was in pain.

"Master Gorlym," Trent said, "would be my first choice. He's brave, smart, and the best in the yard with a blade or spear."

Krellis raised his eyebrows and nodded approvingly. "Indeed. A fine choice. But I need the Master of the Citadel to remain where he is."

Trent nodded. "What about . . ." He looked at Shara. "The Zelani master? Victeris?"

Krellis shook his head. "Actually, I was thinking about you."

A smile slowly spread across Trent's face. "Truly?"

Krellis waved a hand. "I had Celidon fit for the job, if he passed the Test. But, well . . ."

Trent's delighted expression faded. "Would I . . ." He cleared his throat. "Shall I take the Test of the Stone, Father?"

"No," Krellis said. "I don't think that will be necessary. But if you succeed in the task, I will recommend you to the council when you return."

Trent relaxed slightly, but Shara could tell he was still tense.

"What is the task?"

"I want you to find the Lost Brothers."

Trent opened his mouth, but nothing came out. Shara looked at Krellis to see if this was a joke. It wasn't. Krellis watched his son with narrowed eyes, as though the rest of the conversation had been a feint, and this the true thrust.

Trent's easygoing grin appeared for the first time that morning, but Shara could see through him. "Are you so anxious to be rid of me, Father?" He laughed.

Krellis laughed with him. "It's not as hopeless a task as people think, and I won't send you alone," he promised. He nodded toward Shara, and her heart slammed against her rib cage. "Your friend Shara has recently graduated. Victeris claims that she's the most talented Zelani he's ever taught. She will accompany you."

Not Trent! Anyone but Trent! Shara kept the expression off her face, but her breath faltered again. The room became ordinary. She couldn't feel either of them anymore.

Trent was vain, spiteful, even cruel at times. She knew him too well from their childhood together. He was often mean on purpose, and whenever he was kind, it almost always seemed to be an accident.

She concentrated on her breathing. If she didn't control herself, they would see right through her. This was what she was here for. This was her purpose. Trent possessed a certain greatness, despite his faults. It was her job to shore up his weaknesses and expand his strengths. That was what being a Zelani was all about, to take ordinary men and make them great. To take great men and make them legends.

Trent's lack of self-confidence drove his cruelty. If there was anything a Zelani could bolster, it was a man's self-confidence. Perhaps Shara was the missing piece that he lacked.

She left her thoughts and realized that Trent was staring at her. He even leaned toward her as though he was still drunk, excited by his prize. Simple desire was flattering. She had long since grown used to that, but Trent's lust was filled with something darker, a rage. Narrowing her eyes, she watched him closely. She had overcome greater hurdles than Trent.

"You will leave by week's end," Krellis said. "That should be plenty of time to prepare. I have some new information that will point you in the right direction. And Milgon has been sorting through maps and stories in the archives. He will make copies of what you need."

"Yes, Father."

"So that's it," Krellis continued. "I leave the details to you."

"Thank you, Father. I won't let you down."

"I know you won't." He put a hand on Trent's shoulder and paused. It seemed to take him a moment to work up the words. "I wanted to say, son . . ." Krellis started. "I wanted to apologize. I know that I sometimes seem cold to you. My father was always very strict with my brothers and me. I should have known better than to follow that man's example, but . . ."

Shara looked at the man and caught the flash of an image that snuck around his defenses. *A young man stood before his own father. He hid a dagger behind his forearm.* Shara forced the image from her mind and concentrated on the task at hand.

Krellis looked to his son and shrugged. "We are what we are trained to be, but I wanted to say that I'm proud of you, Trent. You've made a man of yourself."

Trent seemed to grow two times his normal size. His jaw squared off handsomely, and he looked ten years older.

"Thank you, Father."

Shara caught another glimpse of the image from Krellis's past. *A young*

Krellis and his father were arguing, though she could not hear the words. The young man desperately wanted something. He asked his father for it, begged him for it. But the man spat at his son's feet and turned his back.

The Brother of Autumn closed his eyes and pulled Trent into a sudden, crushing hug.

The young Krellis spun his dagger around and thrust it into his father's back.

Trent cried out in pain.

Krellis pulled back, holding his son at arm's length. His thick, bushy brows pushed together.

"What's wrong?" Krellis's eyes narrowed. "You're hurt."

Trent shook his head. His started to cough and his knees buckled. A drop of blood spattered on his hand.

"Gods!" Krellis cursed.

Shara moved to Trent's side.

"Take him to the chair," Krellis demanded. He strode to the door and shouted down the stairs, sending the nearest guard for a healer. In a moment, Krellis returned.

"What happened?" he demanded.

Shara set Trent on a chair and dug deep into his mind, ignoring any rights to privacy. She saw why his emotions were so jumbled, why he had drunkenly leaned toward her. The boy was delirious. His face was ashen, and his eyelids drooped.

"I, uh, fell," he said, licked his bloody lips.

"Fell? Dammit, boy, where did you fall from?"

"The, uh, the Spire."

"What?"

By the Seasons, Shara thought, it was a wonder he didn't die on impact.

"What were you doing up there? And how did you fall?"

"It was . . . uh . . . Brophy."

"What about Brophy?"

"No, not Brophy. It wasn't really his fault."

"What do you mean it wasn't his fault? What happened?"

Trent labored for each breath.

"We took a girl up to the Spire. Wanted to impress her. Wasn't Brophy's fault. He didn't mean to."

"Mean to what?"

"To push me. We fought, that's all. I mean, not seriously. We . . . do that sometimes. And . . . we were drinking. Siren's Blood. And he . . . the girl. He thought Femera liked him better. She wanted me. Not him. That's all.

She asked him to leave. He wouldn't. I stepped between them and he got mad at me. Shoved me. And I . . . I landed wrong." He closed his eyes languidly and opened them again. "I'll be all right." He offered a weak smile. "Real men can handle their drink, right?" He gave half a laugh, coughed up more blood.

Shara swallowed, looked at Krellis. His face might as well have been stone.

"Brother, the healer," the guard said from the doorway.

"Send her in!" he demanded.

The guard nodded, and the healer appeared. She moved quickly to Trent's side. She was an older woman, painfully bony, with thinning hair. She had the look of the House of Winter.

The woman poked Trent gently in the side and he cried out. She kept a grim, tight-lipped expression, but Shara could feel the matter-of-fact despair that flowed from her. The healer stood up and motioned Krellis to the other side of the room. Shara stayed with Trent, but strained to hear their conversation.

"His entire abdomen is filled with blood," the healer said. She shook her head. "There is nothing—"

"You heal him, or you'll find yourself hanging from a rope," Krellis said in a low voice.

The healer lifted her chin slightly. "Brother, he is too far gone. I could give him dried grayfish to thicken his blood, but it isn't nearly enough. That he is still alive is testament to his strength. It is only a matter of time."

Krellis slapped the woman across the face, knocking her to the floor. She cried out in surprise and pain, gazing up at him with wide eyes.

"Fix him," Krellis growled. He took a step forward.

Shara ran toward them.

"No, Brother," she murmured, breathing a calming cycle. Krellis's emotions burst out of him, into her. She breathed in his anger, cooled it, and sent it back to him as a river of calm. "Come with me," she murmured. "Come back to your son."

Krellis followed her across the room. The healer scrambled to her feet and fled.

"I'm hurt . . ." Trent muttered. "Been hurt all morning."

"It's all right, Trent," Shara said. "You'll be fine. We'll get you some help."

"Thanks, Shara . . . You're so pretty . . ." His eyes flickered shut, then opened again. "Father . . ."

"Yes . . . Trent?" Krellis replied, his voice husky. He took his son's hand. His fierce, dark eyes glistened.

Krellis's father lay dead on the floor. The young man dropped his bloody blade and collapsed to his knees.

"I'm sorry I couldn't help you . . . with your problem."

Krellis shook his head. "Quiet about that. It doesn't matter now."

"Don't . . . blame Brophy. It was just a . . . Not his . . . Not his . . . f . . . ," Trent tried to say, but didn't get the words out. His head lolled back against the chair, bloody mouth open.

He breathed raggedly for a few more minutes before he died.

17

THE AFTERNOON sun filled the balcony with warm light, causing the curtains to glow like spiderwebs. The rest of the room was thrown into shadow. Trent's bier stood on the balcony, a dark silhouette against the glowing light. Krellis bent over his dead son, hands gripping the edge of the marble.

"I gave orders that I was to be left alone," he rumbled.

"I disobeyed them," Baelandra said.

Surprised at her voice, he turned, drawing a long breath and staring at her. His eyes were shadowed, lost in his wild mane of black hair. She could barely see his face through the gloom. She wanted to hate him, but hate slipped through her fingers when she heard of Trent's death.

Krellis grunted and turned back to his son. The man moved like a bear sluggish in winter. She had never seen him like this before.

Light on her feet, each motion a delicate balancing act, Baelandra walked up to the bier. Her breath caught in her throat. Trent was so still, so pale. His lips were ash gray and his eyelids were as white as seafoam. For all his faults, Trent had always filled a room with his energy. That spark of life was gone now, utterly gone.

"Oh Krellis . . ." she murmured, looking up at the anguished giant that she barely recognized. What if it were Brophy on that bier?

She reached across Trent's body and placed a hand on Krellis's cheek. His great tangle of hair parted, and he looked at her for a moment, his red-rimmed eyes glazed with tears. Slowly, he turned his head and kissed her palm.

"Oh Krellis," she said again. She stepped around the bier lightly at first, but then she rushed into his arms. He enveloped her and let out a howl of anguish. His great, shaggy beard rasped against her cheek. He made a strangled sound, as if he would cry but didn't know how.

She grabbed his tortured face and pulled it down to hers, kissed him. She kissed him through her own helplessness. She kissed him with a desperation she didn't understand. He responded fiercely, crushed her to him as if she could save him from drowning.

"He was a good lad," he whispered into her neck. "I should have . . . should have told him."

Baelandra felt his tears come at last, wetting her cheek. She shuddered and whispered into his ear.

"I love you. No matter what, I will always love you."

ROPHY STARED at the chamber pot. The sides glistened red with sloppy usage. A faint pink stain marred the wall behind it. He hadn't paid any attention when he had been there hours ago. He had heavier problems to shoulder, or so he thought.

As promised, Brophy had returned shortly after their conversation, but Trent was already gone. At first, Brophy thought Trent was trying to run away from his punishment like he had as a child. He went immediately to all the places Trent might hide and spent hours searching the city. But now, as Brophy stared at the chamber pot, he wondered if he had misjudged.

Brophy closed his eyes a moment. He took a deep breath and opened them. He should go to Krellis first. Brophy dreaded facing Trent's hot-tempered father, but if Trent was injured, Krellis had to be told. Trent would do almost anything to avoid a confrontation with his father. He had to be found, before he did something stupid, especially if he was hurt.

Brophy left the room, heading down the stairs to Krellis's study.

The house seemed overly quiet in the long afternoon shadows. Brophy walked down the stairs one at a time. He knocked lightly on Krellis's door, but no one answered. He knocked harder, but again no answer. Turning the handle and opening the door a crack, Brophy peered into the dim room.

Krellis's desk had been moved onto the balcony. There was something large laid on top of it, but Brophy couldn't see what it was. He was halfway across the room before he realized it was a body.

"No!" Brophy whispered, running to the edge of the bier. Trent was laid out flat, with hands were crossed over his chest. Brophy hovered there for a moment, hands outstretched. His fingers stayed an inch away from Trent's face, but he couldn't bring himself to touch the body.

It had to be a joke, some sick joke like Trent would play on him. Brophy grabbed Trent's tunic and crumpled against the bier. He buried his face in Trent's chest.

"Why?" he whispered. "Why did you take us up there, you idiot?"

Brophy leaned back and stared at the ceiling, his hands like claws. He wanted to scream, but tears came instead. He cried until he had no rage left for the stupid things his friend always did. He cried until he had no tears left to cry.

Brophy finally left the bier and leaned against the balcony railing. He stared over his beloved Ohndarien. Brophy was empty, washed clean. He didn't even turn around when someone stepped into the room.

Heavy footsteps crossed the marble floor to Trent's bier. Brophy slowly looked at Krellis. The Brother of Autumn was wild and disheveled, like a shepherd warrior from Faradan. His hair stuck out at all angles and his beard was a tangled bramble.

"Tell me, boy," Krellis said. "Was Trent's death an accident?"

"What?" Brophy's brow wrinkled. He shook his head. "It wasn't suicide, if that's what you are asking. Trent jumped, but I'm sure he didn't mean to hurt himself."

Krellis's stern expression betrayed none of his thoughts. "Then why did he jump?"

Brophy shrugged helplessly. "He was drunk," he said, his voice barely steady. He swallowed, tried to get a grip on his sorrow. "And ashamed. Siren's Blood makes you feel like you can't be hurt."

"I know about Siren's Blood." Krellis's face finally softened, and he slowly shook his shaggy head. He closed his eyes and let out a long breath. When he opened his eyes again, he looked at Brophy, but not unkindly.

"What about the girl?"

Brophy looked away. "I tried to stop him, but I got there too late."

"What do you mean, too late?"

Brophy looked back at Krellis. He didn't know what to say.

"What happened with the girl?" Krellis demanded.

Brophy's gaze went to Trent. "He was drunk, sir. He didn't know what he was doing. I don't think it was his intention to go so far with Femera."

Krellis looked down at his son. The huge man flexed his fingers several times and made a fist. "Are you telling me that my son forced himself on the girl?"

Brophy's chest hurt. He nodded.

"Trent said the girl fancied him. He tried to protect her, and you pushed him off the Spire."

Brophy stared at Krellis and shook his head. "No." He turned to look at Trent, and closed his eyes. Of course he lied, Brophy thought. He always lied.

"Are you telling me that my son lied to me with his dying breath, blaming his best friend for crimes that he himself committed?"

"No," Brophy said, trying to find the words. "Trent was always scared to talk to you. He and I, we were going to explain everything together. He didn't want you to think badly of him."

Krellis clenched his fist. "You're a bad liar, Brophy. You always were." Brophy winced to hear the exact words Trent had spoken to him just yesterday.

The wind blew a lock of hair across Trent's face, and Krellis brushed it back into place. "My son fell far short of who we wanted him to be. All the excuses in the world won't change that."

"But he could also be good," Brophy protested, "at heart."

"Good at heart," Krellis murmured. He seemed to look far away, to the future or the past, Brophy couldn't tell. "If only that mattered."

The Brother of Autumn rested a hand on Brophy's shoulder.

"You're a brave lad. Honorable." He paused. "I would have been proud to have you for a son."

Brophy said nothing.

"Sometimes I wish you had been my son." He shook his head. "But fate is not always kind."

Krellis turned and walked away. "But some things are more important than a son. Trent's death made me aware of that. Perhaps I waited this long for him." Krellis waved a hand in the air, let it fall limply to his thigh. "I don't know."

He turned and his eyes leveled on Brophy. His voice became deep and resonant, the voice he used to train Ohndarien's soldiers. "Trent pointed the finger at you. With his dying breath he accused you of murder and rape, and I will let it stand."

Brophy squinted his eyes, turned his head as if that could make him hear better. "What?"

"You will be tried and executed for my son's murder."

Brophy suddenly couldn't breathe. "You said you believed me."

"I do."

"Then how can you . . . ?"

Krellis's gaze bored into him and for the first time, Brophy saw a mindless rage in the man's eyes.

Brophy glanced around for a way out. He considered the balcony, but it was too far to jump. He caught sight of Krellis's sword and scabbard hanging from a peg on the far side of the room.

Krellis followed his gaze. He smiled. "You'll never make it, boy. No point in trying."

Brophy leapt over the bier. He hit the ground running, reaching out to grasp the hilt.

He never even got close.

SHARA WALKED through Baelandra's front door into the garden. She reached out with her mind to touch the young soldier who stood beyond the front gate. He was handsome, small but well built, with dark eyebrows and a long, straight nose. The soldier was probably from Kherif, and he carried himself like a boy trying to look like a man. He wanted her, but he was also afraid of her. Good, she thought. Let him be afraid.

She walked toward him along the marble path. The gate swung inward at her touch. The soldier looked surprised that it hadn't been locked.

"Shara-lani," he said, with a slight bow.

"Yes." She looked him in the eye, but he wouldn't meet her gaze.

"Brother Krellis requests your presence at the Citadel."

Shara set her lips in a thin line. Just yesterday she would have rushed to the Brother of Autumn at the slightest beckoning, but now he was the last person she wanted to see. Krellis was going to try Brophy for his "crimes." Baelandra was enraged. She had spent the whole day at the Citadel trying to speak with Brophy. Shara knew it was useless.

A part of Shara wanted to comfort the Brother in his time of anguish. She might be able to steer him back toward wisdom, but Brophy's life was at stake. She couldn't risk putting herself in Krellis's power until she knew Brophy was safe.

"I am to escort you there immediately," the soldier continued, motioning for her to follow.

Shara finally caught the young man's gaze and held it, timed her breath to match his. She reached out and put her palm on his chest. Each time she breathed in, she pulled a piece of the man's reluctance into herself.

"Go ahead," she spoke softly, sending her desires into the boy's thoughts. "I'm right behind you."

The soldier looked confused, but nodded. He started walking down the street.

A sudden wave of nausea washed over her as she watched him go. A piece of the young soldier stayed with her, stuck inside her, struggling like a butterfly in a web. She took several deep breaths and tried to banish the sensation. It slowly began to fade as the soldier continued up the street alone, but some part of him lingered, an uncomfortable reminder that, for the first time, she had compelled someone against his will. But she couldn't be deterred by a guard. Brophy needed her more than she needed a clear conscience. She swallowed the bitterness and headed across the street in the other direction.

She walked to the small dock in front of Jayden's house and held up a hand. A waterbug, one of the small boats that ferried customers across the bay, veered toward her.

At first Krellis's plan to implicate Brophy seemed foolish. Shara had been in the room when Trent told his story. She was a trained Zelani and she had heard him lie. She would testify, and Brophy would go free. Even if Shara could not speak, anyone who knew Brophy knew he wasn't a rapist or a murderer. And Trent was not renowned for his honesty.

If Krellis was confident that Brophy would be found guilty, then he must have a strong witness. The only person who fit that description was Femera, the victim herself. Someone needed to find out what the girl knew.

The waterbug glided up to the stone quay. Shara was surprised to see a young woman at the tiller.

"Where you going?" the young driver asked.

"Stoneside."

"I can do that."

"How much?"

"Two." The girl's wispy red hair was cut short like a boy's. Her smile was quick and her eyes alert. The waterbug would never be beautiful, but she had charm. Shara didn't trust the girl, but she liked her immediately.

Stepping off the dock, Shara instinctively grabbed the mast as the boat rocked. "What's your name?" she asked.

"Lawdon." The girl shrugged. "It's a boy's name, I know. Blame my father, whoever he was."

Lawdon pushed away from the dock and leapt to the tiny boom, neatly turning it to catch the breeze. The sail filled, and they moved slowly across the harbor. Shara stayed silent. She wanted the girl talking.

"You a Flower?" the kid asked.

"No."

"You came from the Sister of Autumn's house."

Shara looked over her shoulder at Baelandra's three-story marble home. Lawdon continued.

"A man has been watching that place all day. He took off west when you got in my boat."

"You don't miss much, do you?" Shara asked her.

The girl smiled and trailed her hand in the water as she steered. "I have a lot of time on my hands."

Lawdon kept a lazy grip on the rudder as though the boat would sail itself. She grinned. "Me and my 'bug, we're going to go far in this world," she said. "Got big plans. I could use an investor if you're interested."

Shara smiled as they slid under Donovan's Bridge. "What do you think of the Children of the Seasons?"

"The Flowers?"

"Yes. The Sister of Autumn, Baelandra. Brother Krellis. Vallia, Hazel, Jayden."

"Rich. Arrogant."

"Brophy."

"Cute."

Shara laughed.

"Trent?"

Lawdon narrowed her eyes and looked over her shoulder. "What do you mean?"

"What have you heard? About Trent?"

The girl paused, weighing her words carefully. "I heard he was dead."

Shara nodded. "I was there when he died. What else did you hear?"

"All kinds of things. I heard Brophy killed him. Poison."

"Poison?"

"Or a duel." She watched Shara. Glancing away for a moment, Lawdon deftly navigated around a slow-moving galley. "Which was it?"

"I don't know," Shara lied.

"I'm sure it was a duel, then. Trent wasn't of the blood, and Brophy finally gave him what was coming to him. Now Krellis wants Brophy dead. The crazy beggar woman on the Stoneside dock says Trent and his father are the doom of Ohndarien. The blood of the Seasons is failing. The Flowers are dying. They can't make any boys. It's been happening ever since the real Brothers left. Brophy killed Trent to give the Council a good washing. He'll go after Krellis next."

"What do you think of Brother Krellis?"

She shrugged. "The soldiers love him. Sailors hate him. Only makes sense. He taxes the sailors and spends it on the soldiers. He hasn't started taxing waterbugs yet." She winked. "So who cares?"

"Do you think a foreigner should be on the Council?"

"Over a Flower? What do I care? I'm from Gildheld. Everyone I know is from somewhere else. It don't matter. The council won't last much longer, anyway."

Lawdon loosened a line and let the sail luff. They glided gracefully up to a little quay at Stoneside.

The young woman held the boat steady as Shara stepped out.

"You are a credit to your trade," Shara said, putting four coins in Lawdon's hands. She raised her eyebrows just slightly at the amount.

"You need a ride anywhere, anytime, I'm your captain."

Shara smiled. "Keep your eyes and ears open, and we'll talk about it later."

"What about that investment opportunity?" Lawdon called, as Shara walked away.

"We'll talk about it later."

Shara crossed Stoneside, listening to the crowd as she passed. All the talk was on Trent's murder, on Brophy's trial. No one knew what to believe.

She reached Master Garm's shop and let out a slow breath of disappointment. Thick boards had been hastily hammered over the smithy's windows. A lock and chain bound the shop's double doors. A bent pair of tongs lay discarded in the street. A glance inside the window revealed some scattered furniture, old and broken-down. Nothing of value.

Had they run? Or were they removed? Could Krellis force Femera to lie for him? Shara wished Brophy had talked about the girl more. He'd mentioned her a couple of times, and Shara knew he had a crush on her, but he would always clam up shortly after the conversation started. She shouldn't have teased him. She should have listened.

Shara looked around the deserted side street. Someone must have seen something. She crossed the street to the workshop of a brass smith. A small bell tinkled as she opened the door.

The merchant was a tall, narrow-shouldered man with a potbelly. He wore a leather apron over his brown shirt and pants. A mustache drooped from his upper lip, and his nose had been broken at some point in his past. He looked at her with his tiny eyes and smiled.

"Yes, miss? Can I help you find something?"

"Just a question, if you would." Shara smiled and felt him relax. While she concentrated on her words, she matched her breath with his. "Do you know what happened to the smithy across the street?"

She let herself slide past his eyes into his thoughts and memories. She fought back a wave of nausea.

"They just packed up and left," the brass smith said.

She waded through a flood of images in the man's mind. *It was nighttime. Several soldiers helped Garm and his daughter load a small cart. The girl was crying.* Shara felt something else inside him, but it was as elusive as a fish. She lost it.

The brass smith shrugged. "It's a pity. Garm brought a high class of customer to his shop. Many of them stopped here after seeing him. I'm going to lose sales because he ran off like that."

"Was there anything strange about his leaving?" she asked. *The door of the brass shop opened, but nobody stepped through. It slammed shut.*

She hardly heard the man speaking to her as she went over the image, replaying it in her mind. *The door opened and closed. The brass smith stood at the forge, several large vessels by his side. Behind him a wall of tools. The window slightly cracked.*

She pulled out of his thoughts for a moment and realized the brass smith was waiting for an answer.

"I'm sorry," she said. "What were you about to tell me?" Shara delved deep. Something was missing. She felt the answer was hidden there. Somewhere, but she couldn't find it.

"It was the strangest thing," the merchant mumbled. "Must have been a matter o' life and death."

"Must have been," she murmured. *The door opened and closed again. No one entered. The brass smith stood in his nightshirt with a candle in hand. He spoke to nobody. He paused as if someone were speaking to him, but there were no other voices. Nothing.*

A wave of nausea swept over her and she had to grab on to the counter to keep her balance. She swallowed the taste of bile and pressed on.

The merchant turned and glanced at the reflection in one of the pots.

There!

A man's reflection, warped by the shape of the brass. He had black hair, fading to gray at the temples. Black eyes. Black beard.

"Miss, you all right?" the merchant asked.

She snapped out of her trance, looked up at the man.

"Are you all right?"

"I'm fine," she whispered. "Really."

"Seemed like you were going to faint."

"No, I'm all right." Her heart fluttered and she turned to look at the pot she had seen in the man's memory. Her own warped reflection stared back at her, but in the brass smith's memories it hadn't been her. It had been Victeris.

Garm and Femera had not gone willingly.

Shara thanked the merchant and left his shop. The inky feeling in her stomach grew heavier.

This can't be about Brophy. It has to be something else, something larger. Shara needed to talk to the girl, find out the truth and get her to testify before the council.

Shara stood in the alley for a long moment, cycling through the five gates, focusing her mind on the mental image of her master. As a child she had played a game with the other students where they tried to find each other in the baths while blindfolded. Shara had been very good at it. She could easily pick her closest friends out of a crowd just by the feel of their minds.

Shara tried the same thing now with Victeris, extending her attention outward beyond her body. She reached through the city, searching for a hint of recognition. It was dangerous spreading her mind over such a large area, and she grew thin, frayed at the edges. She was losing herself. But she could feel him. She let herself spread even thinner.

And then she had him. She held on to the feeling like a thin thread between pinched fingers. Victeris was somewhere on Stoneside, north and west of her.

Shara headed north through the streets of Ohndarien. She took a wide berth around Bloody Row, the long, crooked street that held Ohndarien's slaughterhouses. A horrendous barnyard stench lingered around the street. It reminded her of her childhood, and she avoided it whenever she could.

The thread took her closer and closer to the Quarry Wall, the blue-white marble barrier that protected the city's northern border. Shara followed it all the way to an old, two-story house near the Quarry Gate, poorly kept, the wood rotting in places. Shara ducked into an alley and took a moment to collect her thoughts.

The safest plan was to return to Baelandra's house. The Sister of Autumn knew hundreds of people who would help her recover Femera and her father, but Shara didn't want to risk losing them again.

She paused, bit her lip. Her mind raced. She would have to face Victeris and take the girl from him. Shara concentrated on her breath, adding her fear to her power. She had been raised on tales of dueling magicians from Efften. For years she had indulged in little fantasies about facing Victeris and defeating him. Now that she had graduated, the idea didn't seem so ridiculous. The element of surprise could go a long way.

Shara wrapped a glamour around herself and left the alley. She crossed the street and peered in the run-down house's front window. The room inside was empty, but Victeris was close. She could feel him. Carefully, she probed the rest of the building, letting her awareness float through the wooden walls. There were two more people inside, an angry man and a young woman.

Keeping her breathing even and steady, Shara stepped through the unlocked front door and crept up the house's narrow staircase.

At the top of the steps, she came to a hallway with three closed doors. Just as she put her foot on the top stair, the left door opened. A burly Farad with a bushy beard walked into the hall and a slender, dark-haired girl followed him. They looked right past her as if she were a painting on the wall.

That must be Femera, Shara thought. The girl was pretty, in a peasant kind of way, but Shara couldn't see why Brophy was so infatuated with her.

The giant man had to be her father, Garm. His fear was palpable, even a normal person could see it. Femera's emotions were harder to penetrate. The girl was empty, as if she had given up on life. Or had all the life drained from her.

They walked past her, and Garm knocked on the right-hand door.

"My lord," he said. "My daughter slept most of the day, but she's awake now. You said we should speak with you when she woke."

Shara's heart beat faster, and she gathered her power. Walking up to the door, she placed a hand lightly on Garm's shoulder. She matched her breath with the big man's and fought the inky feeling inside her chest.

Faint footsteps crossed the room on the far side of the door. The latch rattled, and Shara narrowed her eyes.

Victeris opened it.

"Hit him," Shara whispered. The smith swung his huge fist into the Zelani master's stomach. Victeris slumped to the floor with a grunt.

Femera and Garm both gasped and jumped back. Garm thumped against the wall in the narrow confines of the hallway.

"Run," Shara whispered.

They both stared at her, unmoving. She snapped her fingers and they fled. Garm picked his daughter up and flew down the stairs with her under one arm.

Shara turned to Victeris as he rolled on the floor. She knelt next to the man, put a hand on his cheek, and matched his ragged breathing.

He opened his eyes at her touch. For the briefest instant, Shara felt a rush of fear sweep through the man. Then his black eyes narrowed. She felt his defenses go up, and she attacked, forcing her way past his eyes and into his mind.

Victeris held up his hand as though that might stop the pressure of her will. She gritted her teeth but continued breathing in time with him. When he gasped, she gasped, then drew him back into her cycle. He began panting. She panted with him, slowed his breathing and drew him back in. He crawled backward into the room. She pursued him.

"You don't need the girl," she spoke into his mind. "She has served her purpose, you can forget about her."

"No," he growled. "I won't let you."

Victeris tried to stare her down, tried to counterattack, but she opened her eyes to him and drew his power into herself, overwhelming his flagging will. His body twisted and writhed across the floor. She pressed onward, drawing his breath back to her rhythm.

She could barely keep her mind on the fight. Pulling Victeris's will into her body felt like swallowing a mouthful of tar.

The Zelani master's fingers curled into fists and pounded on the floor. His head flopped against the wood, and he stayed there a long moment. When he rose, the lines of struggle were gone from his face. He stared at her calmly.

"Shara-lani," he intoned.

"Forget about the girl," she said. "Forget about the father. They have served their purpose. Return home, knowing you have completed a job well-done."

"Wha—"

Shara felt a flicker of resistance, breathed through it and let it dissipate.

"Return home," she told him. "You have done well."

"Yes, my lady."

Victeris jerked forward, as if on strings. He walked stiffly across the room and down the stairs. She heard him reach the bottom, open the door, and close it behind him.

Shara staggered to the wall and put a hand on the rough planking. She leaned over and vomited in the corner. By the Seasons, that man's soul was putrid! She had to get that feeling out of her belly, wash the tar from her insides. She vomited again, but it did no good. She had never encountered anything so vile, never imagined it possible.

Her stomach lurched again, but she held it in this time. Breathing steadily, she gained control of her body, wiped her dripping mouth with her sleeve.

Shara wanted to curl up in a ball and sleep, but she forced herself to leave the room and run down the stairs. She hurried into the street and extended her consciousness, searching for Femera and her father. She looked east first, toward their home. They were close, she had almost found them when she felt a cold hand upon her shoulder.

She spun around. Victeris's eyes were aflame and his lips pulled back into a snarl. Shara drew a quick breath.

"I am Victeris," he murmured. Her breath faltered as though he'd punched her in the stomach. A memory echoed through her and her skin tingled. She suddenly felt naked.

No! She focused on him, but he spoke again and her defenses crumbled.

"I am the source of your power. Your master now and forever . . ."

Shara tried to turn, tried to run, but a black cloud filled her mind, and her limbs refused to obey. She held up a hand as if she could stop the magic that invaded her.

"You are mine. When I call, you will come to me. When I speak, you will obey . . ."

Shara fell to her knees and blacked out.

VICTERIS WALKED WITH his arm around Shara's shoulder. He led her down the street toward Bloody Row.

As they neared the slaughterhouses, the stench of animal fear and raw flesh overwhelmed her. The row seemed dark despite the light of the fading afternoon. A few bloody-handed workers looked up from their grisly tasks, but no one said anything.

They passed a feedlot, and the stench of the pigs hit her in waves. Her heart hammered painfully in her chest. Flashes of her father rushed past her, yelling, cursing her. She was running barefoot through the pigpen, slipping and sticking a hand into the filth. She was crying, trying to get up, to get away from the mess, from the pigs, from their horrible squealing and their horrible smell. Her father yelled at her, calling her a worthless little bitch . . .

"Are you all right, my dear?" Victeris asked.

"No, no I'm not," she said, trying not to look at anything. She cringed as she narrowly missed a workman pushing a crude cart filled with severed goat legs. Victeris led her around it. "We'll be through in a moment, my beauty."

She couldn't regain her breath. Something had happened. Something horrible, but her mind was fuzzy. She couldn't remember it, but she could hear a woman screaming in the distance. Using her training, Shara tried to bring her emotions under control. Was she a little girl from a pig farm or was she a Zelani?

"I have to leave," she pleaded. "I don't want to be here."

"Come, my child," he replied, and led her through the door of an inn.

The smoky room was packed with slaughterhouse workers. They gave her and Victeris cursory glances and went back to their meals. The rushes on the floor were pink with the blood from their boots. A dozen girls worked the crowd, serving drinks or sitting on laps. One woman led a drunken man with bloody pants up the stairs.

Shaking her head, Shara frowned. The smoke in the room and the stench of the pigs had left her befuddled. What was she doing?

Shara swallowed and looked up into Victeris's black eyes.

"Follow me, my beauty," he whispered in her ear. "I have something very important to teach you."

Shara let him lead her upstairs, down the hall, and through a door into a small dark room. There was a bed in the corner.

"Why are we here?" she asked. The words felt bloated and awkward in her mouth.

"Because," Victeris purred, walking her slowly across the room, "I own you, body and soul. When I call, you will come to me. And when you come, you will obey."

Shara nodded.

Victeris motioned at the bed. Shara sat down, and he knelt before her.

"Let your hair down," he said. "I like it best when you wear it down."

She reached up and undid the clasp in her hair. Her long, black tresses fell about her shoulders.

"Breathe with me," he said, leading her through the breaths. "Open yourself. Feel the room."

"There are too many memories in this room," she murmured.

"Memories?"

"People leave their thoughts and feelings behind them wherever they go, like a footprint. I can feel them. It's thick here. So many feelings."

Victeris frowned briefly, then his brow smoothed. "What are they like?"

"They glow. The room shines with them."

Victeris glanced around the room before focusing back on her face. "Tell me more."

"This place is a brothel," Shara intoned. "Hundreds of women have had sex with thousands of men in this bed."

His slender hands slid into the front of her gown. With deft fingers, he undid the top knot and loosened the laces. Reaching within, he cupped one of her breasts.

"What does that feel like?" he asked. "What did those men and women leave behind?"

Shara's breath faltered. She swallowed and blinked, looked at the door. "I don't like this place. I want to go."

"Don't fear the intensity, my beauty. Go into it. Feel it. Make it your own."

She smoothed her brow and resumed her breathing.

"What do you feel?" he asked.

"Sadness. Confusion. An unbearable numbness."

He grabbed her waist and pulled her up. With a quick, delicate gesture, he brushed the cloth off her shoulders. Her gown fell to her feet.

Victeris smiled, nodding. "That sounds like the women. What about the men?"

"Desire. Drunken and distant. Frustration. They come here wanting something, yet they leave without it."

"Yes. Go deeper. What is below that?"

"Loneliness. Terrible loneliness."

Victeris pressed her body against his. His breath was rough in her ear. "Deeper."

"There is nothing. Nothing beyond that. Just that desire. Wanting. Hope."

"A hope for what?" he encouraged her.

"For something good. Something pure." She frowned. Again, her breathing faltered. "For something . . . alive."

Victeris looked away from her. His teeth clenched, and he grunted as if he were going to throw up.

"That's what sex is for, creating life," Shara murmured, her brow wrinkling. "The life of a child, yes, but also the spark of life in each of us. That's what a Zelani is. That's what I feel when I use it. Life."

"Life? You feel life?"

Victeris hissed and shoved her back onto the bed. He stared at her, his hands balled into fists.

"What's wrong?" Shara asked.

He took a deep breath, a sneer on his lips. "I want you, my child. You are very special. There is something you have that I want quite badly."

Shara wanted to help her master, wanted to make him feel better. She reached for him, but he pushed her away. "Soon, my beauty, but there is something we must do first."

"Of course," she said.

Leading her by the hand, Victeris took her to the open window. Naked, she followed him outside and across the tiled rooftop to a ladder leaning against the back of the building. Shara looked down and balked. Below, pigs waded through a half foot of mud, shit, and piss.

"Come, my beauty." Victeris tugged her hand.

"No. I don't like this place. I don't want to go down there."

"Why?"

"The smell. I hate the smell."

"How does the smell make you feel?"

"Small. Helpless."

"But there is life down there. All life is beautiful, isn't it? Isn't that what you just said? Life is a beautiful thing."

"No. I'm . . . I'm . . ."

"You are mine, body and soul."

"No, I'm . . ."

"Climb down the ladder, my beauty."

"I don't want to."

Victeris placed one hand between her breasts over her heart. She shuddered, then turned around and put one foot on the first rung of the ladder. After another moment's hesitation, she started down. When she reached the bottom, Shara stepped into the thick ooze. She whimpered and backed up against the side of the inn, trying to get her feet out of the muck, but there was nowhere else to step. The pigs milled about, bumping into her. She squeaked and cringed away from them.

Victeris reached the bottom of the ladder and kicked the pigs out of the way. They grunted and reluctantly cleared a small space.

The sounds of a fight drifted through the thin walls of the inn, but there were no windows on this side of the building. The sun had gone down, and the moon had just risen. There was no one to see Shara and Victeris but the pigs.

"Kneel down, my beauty."

"No," she whimpered, "Please no."

He brushed the side of her cheek.

"Sweet child, I want you to kneel."

Shara knelt, her legs shaking. The pigs crowded in again. A fat sow bumped into her, and she stumbled, dropping one hand into the filth. She kept her clean hand out as if the mud was burning pitch. She began sobbing.

Victeris moved behind her, placing his hands on either side of her hips. She shuddered as he touched her bare skin.

"Put your other hand down, my sweet."

"Why?" she cried.

"Because I wish it. Go to your elbows."

With a thin wail, she pushed her elbows into the muck. Ragged sobs rattled in and out of her shaking body.

Behind her, Victeris slowly unlaced his breeches and knelt in the mud.

"You thought to rival my powers as a Zelani?" he whispered. "You who see memories and talk of the spark of life? You, barely more than a student, thought yourself a master? Zelani is about power, about taking what you want. If you have something that I lack, then I will take it from you. If you have life, child, then I will make it mine."

Shara gasped as he pushed himself inside her. She couldn't move, she couldn't resist. She was a little girl, fallen in the mud, pigs stepping on her, unable to get up.

"This morning you were a Zelani who thought to graduate to master. And now, my sweet," he said, as he slammed into her.

"What are you now?"

"What are you now?"

"What are you now?"

BAELANDRA FUMBLED THROUGH the carved marble box and found what she was looking for. She held up the ornately crafted hair clip shaped like a golden butterfly. When she pushed the creature's abdomen, a tiny knife popped out. The hidden blade had been a gift from Scythe after he returned from Physendria so many years ago. She had never worn it before.

Baelandra tested the edge on her finger. It cut easily and drew a drop of blood.

How had it ever come this far, she asked herself. But she knew. Year after year, she and Krellis had danced their dance. She had tried to soften his heart, remake him into an Ohndarien. Krellis responded with a smile, kissing her and telling her what she wanted to hear. How he must have laughed at her through the years, waiting for this moment to betray her love, to make his political move. She was a fool.

Baelandra dipped the blade into a small jar filled with yellow paste. It was another gift from Scythe that she had never used. She had almost thrown it away several times.

She tapped the tiny blade against the jar, knocking off the excess paste.

If she took the dagger and scratched her own skin, would Ohndarien be better off?

Her mouth set in a firm line, and Baelandra slipped the dagger back into the hair clip. She stood and walked to the mirror. Shaking out her lustrous auburn hair, she pinned it back with the clip. No, it was too late to turn the dagger on herself. She would use it on the one who most deserved it. There was still time to undo what had been done.

Baelandra left her room and swept down her stairs to the garden. She paused in the shadow of a midnight plum tree and looked at the stretch of greenery between her house and Krellis's.

She couldn't believe she had made love to him just two nights ago. She had kissed the tears off his face mere hours before he condemned Brophy to death. What kind of man could do such a thing?

Baelandra slipped from underneath the tree and crossed to the garden wall that butted up against Krellis's house. Her eyes searched the cool, blue-white marble until she found what she sought. The miniature gemstone, mirroring the one embedded in her chest, was chiseled masterfully in bas-relief on the marble. It was so small and perfect that one would never notice it unless one knew to walk thirteen paces from the corner and look to the left. The House of Spring had built doors like this all over the city. No one knew about all of them, but Baelandra knew about this one, and Krellis didn't. It was one of the small secrets she had kept from her lover.

She swallowed. So small, this secret, but perhaps it would make the difference for Brophy. She touched the gemstone carving with her finger. With her other hand, she reached down the neck of her dress and touched the stone on her chest. That telltale jolt shot through her, just as it did when she touched Krellis's stone.

A line appeared in the wall, accompanied by a slight scrape of stone. The door swung wide. Baelandra stepped through and found an identical carving on the opposite side. The door swung shut behind her, closing her in absolute darkness.

Guiding herself from childhood memory, she navigated through a dark storage room into the kitchen. Krellis was still at the Citadel, and the Brother of Autumn did not post guards inside the house, another testament to his confidence.

Quiet as a shadow, she climbed the stairs and paused before the door of his rooms, her gaze lingering on the six daggers carved above the lintel. She shook her head. This was her only course. She opened the door and stepped through, closed it softly behind herself.

The room was empty, but she had expected it would be. She crept to the closet and pulled the door closed behind her, leaving the tiniest crack through which she could see his bed.

A memory of Krellis lying asleep in that same bed flashed through her mind. His body was covered with cuts and bruises. It was the morning after he returned from Physendria with his young son and that Zelani master. He had been away for nearly a month, and they did not make love that night. It was the first night they shared a bed without sex.

Baelandra forced the image from her mind. There were so many pleasant memories, so many times they had laughed and talked together. One by one, she stripped them away, replacing them with his face in the Hall of Windows during Brophy's trial that afternoon. His cold expression hovered before her eyes.

The trial had been a farce. They had locked Brophy in the Citadel, and even Baelandra could not get in to see him. The Sister of Autumn should be mistress of that fortress, but the doors were barred to her. She had allowed Krellis to take over training of the guard because he was better at the job. She trusted him. The Heartstone trusted him, but that trust had led her here.

Brophy's trial went on for hours. Many witnesses were called from the Long Market. They all said the same things, describing how the boys were drunk, fighting and stumbling about the market making fools of themselves. One merchant said he saw them climb the Spire. Brophy was looking up the girl's skirt as she scrambled up the rope.

The healer who watched Trent die had been the first witness who carried any real weight. She repeated Trent's dying words, that Brophy had tried to seduce that poor girl and then pushed Trent off the Spire. It was all Baelandra could do to keep her composure as she watched the faces in the crowd. They believed the healer's story. They believed Trent had told the truth. That boy would slit his own throat to gain his father's approval. Couldn't anyone spot a lie when they heard it?

After the healer, they brought out the girl. Femera stood up and damned Brophy with every word she uttered. Her face was battered and bruised as though she'd been brawling on Stoneside for a week. Her voice quavered and whimpered on cue as she told the story of how Trent had been the soul of courtesy, of how Brophy became enraged when she kissed Trent. How the boys had wrestled. How Brophy shoved Trent over the edge of the Spire just before he forced himself on her. She broke down and cried three times during an hour of testimony. It was a good lie, so full of emotion and shocking detail that it sounded like a play put on by a master actress.

The girl kept looking across the room with haunted eyes, seeking out the Zelani master, Victeris. The vile magician sat three rows back, half-shadowed by a column, nodding as if encouraging the girl to continue.

The crowd went from skeptical to angry to enraged. It was Ohndarien tradition to allow all citizens who attended the trial to stand in judgment of a criminal. Krellis timed his witnesses perfectly. He spent the entire day filling the people with lies. The sun sank behind the Windmill Wall when Femera finished her heart-wrenching tale. The court adjourned for the day, before anyone had a chance to speak on Brophy's behalf. It was no mistake that they would have a full night to circulate gossip about Brophy before he had a chance to defend himself.

Baelandra wished she could talk to her nephew, longed to hear his story. When Femera first entered the Hall of Windows, Brophy looked at her with such sorrow that Baelandra's throat tightened. Femera avoided his gaze as if it burned. But that was the last time Brophy looked at her. He spent the rest of the trial glaring at Krellis as though he would leap over the partition and attack the huge man with his bare hands. If there had not been four guards surrounding him, the sweet boy might have actually tried. Brophy's face bore the bruises of a recent fight, and Baelandra wondered what they were doing to him in the Citadel.

When the trial closed, Baelandra followed Brophy's guards as they hauled him away. She trailed them to the Citadel, demanding to speak with him. Again she was denied by orders of Brother Krellis.

By tomorrow morning, Brother Krellis wouldn't be giving any more orders.

The hours went by, and Baelandra waited patiently. If she was adept at anything by now, it was waiting. Finally, Krellis came to his rooms, giving a parting order to his assistant.

He unbuckled his sword and looped the belt over the post of the headboard. She watched him undress and had a moment of doubt, wondering if she should wait until the second day of the trial.

With Shara's testimony, the opinion might swing the other way. The Zelani was a lifelong friend of both Brophy and Trent. She knew their characters as well as anyone, and she had been there the moment Trent had died. She had heard his lies and knew them for what they were. Shara was twice as charming as Femera. She might be able to pull it off.

But Shara had disappeared. She had gone to speak with Femera and her father and never returned. Without Shara's testimony as a shield against Femera's lies, Brophy would surely be stoned to death outside the Physendrian Gate.

It didn't matter. Even if Brophy miraculously escaped, Krellis had shown his true colors. She had seen the man's ruthlessness and called it effective. She had seen his brutality and called it strength. She had seen all of his qualities and hoped to craft him into a hero, but it was past time for her to do what she must. She should have killed the man before he ever got past Ohndarien's walls.

An hour later, Krellis's breathing became even and slow. She crept from her hiding place and crossed to his bed. She reached behind her head and squeezed her hair clip. The tiny dagger came free without a sound, and she gripped it tightly between two fingers. Krellis's chest rose and fell steadily, his arms limp at his sides. A gentle pulse beat beneath the skin of his throat.

Baelandra steadied herself and leaned forward.

"You are the last person I expected to come to my bedroom tonight," Krellis rumbled.

She quickly palmed the dagger as he opened his eyes.

Baelandra cursed the man's instincts, his unflappable calm. Her sure victory teetered unsteadily. She had no hope of besting him physically, but Scythe said the poison was almost instantaneous. All she need do was prick him.

"I wanted to talk to you," she said, glancing at the covers that sprawled across the edge of the bed.

"Did you?"

"Yes." She sat down as though it was the most natural thing, keeping her dagger hidden.

He brought his massive arms up and put them behind his head. "You didn't come for any other reason?" He raised an eyebrow and smiled.

Her stomach turned. "Now is hardly the time," she said, letting a genuine scowl cross her face.

Krellis shrugged. "Perhaps not."

"I know about the army to the south. I know your brother is about to attack."

"It's awfully difficult to hide an army."

"And I know what you are planning with the Ohohhim," she lied, hoping the bluff would work.

Krellis raised an eyebrow, but didn't say anything.

"I still believe the Heartstone chose you for a reason. When the attack comes, there is no one I would rather have defending our walls."

Krellis smiled at her. "You have no idea what I discussed with Father Lewlem, do you?"

"I know how you feel about your brother. I know you want to retake the throne of Physendria. What I don't understand is why you have to destroy Ohndarien to do that. Why you have to hurt Brophy."

"I'm not destroying Ohndarien, I'm just taking her away from you."

"Why? Why do you want to return to that vile and dusty country that you hate so much?"

Krellis flexed his fingers and made a fist. "Because I choose to."

Baelandra shook her head. "I know it is difficult to set aside the past. But you could have so much more. Here in Ohndarien, with me. Forget Physendria; it's not a prize worth fighting for."

Krellis paused. For a second she dared hope, but then he sneered. "Beauty is in the eye of the beholder."

Baelandra moved closer on the bed. "I know how you feel about your brother, but there is no need to involve Brophy in this."

"I disagree. That boy is this city's last link to the past. If I cut that link, it will be much easier for the people to look toward the future."

"Brophy is innocent," she said. "You know he is."

"My son said he was not."

"But Trent was—"

"And the girl agreed," he interrupted her. "You would think a woman would know which man had been between her thighs. Especially if it was her first time. Women tend to remember that sort of thing."

Baelandra scooted next to him. The blade was inches from his skin. "You are right. I . . . certainly remember."

He sneered at her. "Enough of this game. You are a worse liar than your nephew." Baelandra froze, trying her best to look confused by his words, but he cut through the deception. "Are you going to stab me with that toy or not?"

She lunged at him, thrusting the dagger straight and true for his neck. Quick as thought, he grabbed her wrist, twisted her arm, and pinned her against the wall.

"A weak attempt, Bae. I don't know that I shall even put another carving above the door."

He twisted harder. She gasped and dropped the dagger onto his palm.

He shoved her to the floor and sat back on the bed.

The Sister of Autumn rose to her feet and stuck her chin out. "I didn't come here to kill you," she said. "I only brought the blade as a last resort."

"Ah, yes. Most people hide in my closet for hours when they want to talk to me."

"I wouldn't be so smug if I were you. I'm not the only person in this city who can wield a blade."

"Do you think I care about your little man from Kherif?" Rage contorted Krellis's features and he shook his head. "I'm tired of waiting for this city to quit mourning four Brothers long dead and embrace the one Brother still living. If my son's death is to mean anything, it will herald the change that leads Ohndarien to be the capital of the world."

"Didn't your father try to conquer the world?" she spat. "And his father and his father before him?"

"I wouldn't speak ill of another's family, if I were you. You are related to deserters and rapists."

Baelandra took an involuntary step forward. There were so many nights she could have killed this man in his sleep. Why had she waited?

She flicked a glance at the dagger in Krellis's palm. He caught her gaze and smiled. Lifting the blade to his nose, he sniffed. With a sneer, he threw it back to her. She barely caught it by the handle.

"Go ahead," Krellis said. "After our long history, the least I can do is give you two chances to kill me." He watched her steadily. "Go ahead, my dear. It will be your last act as a Sister of Autumn before I dissolve the council."

"The people will not stand for that."

He smiled at her, an ugly smile. "The people . . .'" He snorted. "The people do not rule here, despite what you like to think. I have the soldiers, my dear. I have the money. I hold the walls and the Citadel. The city is mine. I have been very patient. I have waited a long time, but I am tired of it. There will be no more tests to take the stone. There will be no more torches burning for your missing Brothers. Power belongs to the man with the courage to take it. It has always been that way and will always be. Ohndarien is mine because I have the strength to hold her."

Baelandra smoothed her dress, fighting for control. "No matter how unfeeling and ruthless you think you are, I know better. The Heartstone chose you for a reason." She touched the stone between her breasts. Krellis twitched, and she smiled coldly. "If I cannot make you into a servant of Ohndarien, she will."

Krellis chuckled. "You sound positively religious. I think I liked you better when you were trying to stab me."

Baelandra slid the tiny dagger back into her hair clip and left him lying on his bed, staring after her.

book II

A KINGDOM OF
BLOOD AND GOLD

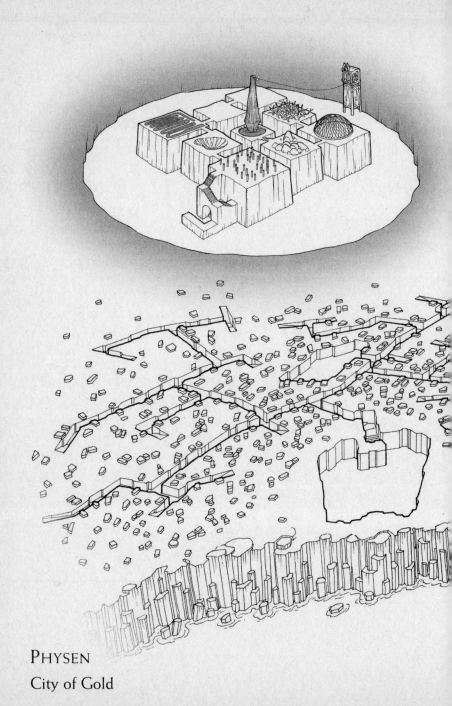

PHYSEN
City of Gold

prologue

A HOWLING WIND RUSHED *from the blue-eyed infant, drowning out Copi's scream.*

The young woman clutched the jagged nub of the broken handle and turned the box. The halting notes grew steady. The child's eyelids fluttered as she rolled onto her side and curled into a ball. The howling wind faded to a malicious whisper as the silver box played on and on.

Copi trembled, crying softly as she fought to keep the music going.

A horse screamed in the distance, its agonized whinny cutting through the night. The box slipped, the broken nub slashing into her knuckle and lodging between the bones. She gasped but kept spinning the music box as the remnants of that howling wind echoed into the distance.

A chorus of misery joined the horse's scream. Tormented dogs howled in the darkness. The people of Copi's tribe shrieked in anguish in their tents far below.

Copi rushed to the child, but she had no free hands, could not pick her up.

The thunder of hoof beats approached, and a young man rode over the crest of Lone Hill. He was not of her tribe, but Copi recognized his broad cheeks and dark eyes from last year's Midsummer gathering. The young hunter leapt from his horse and landed in a crouch next to the fire. His little mare reared onto her hind legs and shied away.

"We have to get out of here!" Copi shouted.

The mingled screams of horror and agony continued in the distance.

"I know," he said, unwrapping the cloth from his waist and scooping the baby up in it. The naked young man quickly twisted the cloth into a sling and tied the baby across Copi's back. She kept turning the box, the broken handle held fast between the bones of her finger.

"What are you doing here?" she asked.

The man whistled, and his mount trotted nervously closer.

"As a woman sits by the fire and watches the babe, a man stands in the darkness and watches them both."

The young hunter turned to his horse and placed a hand on either side of her shaggy nose. He whispered to the creature in the old language and calmed her.

"This is Raindancer," he said, as he grabbed Copi under the arms and threw her onto the horse's back. "Ride her hard. Ride her fast. Far far away from here."

Copi hooked her heels behind the mare's withers. "I will."

The horse jumped at the sound of a hideous snarl.

A hound crept over the crest of the hill. The creature's mangy coat was stretched to bursting over bloated muscles that slithered underneath its skin. Black spines grew all along the creature's back and snout. Fangs thrust out of its mouth like porcupine quills, and its yellow eyes stared straight at Copi. In the shadows behind, several other twisted hounds slunk forward.

The young man swatted Raindancer on her flank. "Haya!" he shouted, and the mare lunged into a gallop.

Copi leaned forward, clinging to the horse's back as they thundered down the hill.

"Run, Raindancer," she whispered. "Run."

I

BROPHY STUMBLED NAKED down the street toward the Physendrian gate. Soldiers urged him forward with the points of their spears. His hands were bound, and he shuffled with a short length of rope between his feet. The dockside hills teemed with people, many who had been at the trial, some who had only come for the spectacle. Brophy saw a few familiar faces in the crowd as the throng pushed and shoved each other to keep up with him.

The jeering mob had followed him all the way from the Hall of Windows. Eight soldiers armed with spears and shields protected him from the rabble, but Brophy's guards could not protect him from the filth and insults the crowd threw at him.

People on second-floor balconies hurled the slop from their chamber pots on him. Brophy kept his eyes and mouth closed as much as he could.

He had heard the words "murderer," "rapist," "traitor," and "coward" so many times they ceased to have meaning. They poured over him like the sewage thrown from above.

Baelandra and the other sisters had not attended the second day of the trial, and neither had Shara. The charade lasted little more than an hour before sentence was passed. They brought Brophy to the stand, and he only had one thing to say. He looked straight at Krellis and held the man's gaze until the entire Hall of Windows fell into silence.

"You know I did not do this thing," he said. "And you know what will happen when I return."

Brophy refused to say anything else. The Sisters were supposed to be there. Shara was supposed to be there. They were supposed to question him, to re-question Femera. It was not Ohndarien justice, and Brophy would not acknowledge it. There were a few voices in the crowd that called for his release, but the vast majority called him guilty and screamed for his exile.

The guard behind Brophy smacked him in the small of the back with his spear. Brophy stumbled forward, his bare feet slipping on the cobblestones.

He went to his knees. The crowd cheered. He had never felt so naked, so utterly exposed.

A gang of young men from Faradan charged through the guards and attacked, hitting, kicking and spitting on him.

"We'll cave yer head in!"

"You're a dead man, little flower."

"—ever touch a Farad lass again!"

With a roar, Brophy leapt to his feet and head-butted one of the young men. He spun, taking a fist to the cheek as he slammed his elbow into the second boy's ribs. The guards rushed forward, hauling the boys to their feet and throwing them back into the crowd.

In the confusion, a small figure darted to Brophy's side. He tried to kick the man, but the rope pulled him up short and he stumbled back to his knees. Looking up into the stranger's cowled face, all he could see was a hook nose and dark, straight eyebrows.

"Don't turn your back on the walls," he whispered quickly. "Watch the stones as they come. The big ones will come first."

"Who—" Brophy started to ask, but the guards pushed the man away and hauled Brophy to his feet once again. He searched the crowd for the stranger, but couldn't find him in the churning mass of angry faces.

The guards pressed onward until they reached the Water Wall. A scowling officer shouted upward as they approached. "Open the gate!"

A man high up on top of the wall flipped a lever, diverting water from the aqueduct. Brophy could hear the seawater rushing down through the pair of pipes. Slowly, the two wheels inside the wall started turning. Metal scraped on stone as the massive Physendrian Gate opened.

Brophy couldn't help looking upward at the Water Wall. Far above, hundreds of people leaned over the battlements to stare at him. Many of them were tossing stones into the air and catching them.

"This man," the officer shouted, cupping his hands around his mouth, "is a traitor, a murderer, and a rapist."

A chorus of boos cascaded down on Brophy from the top of the wall.

"He is no longer welcome in Ohndarien. He is unworthy to share in the bounty of our Free City. Once he walks through these gates, he will never come back."

An unbearable lump swelled in Brophy's throat.

The officer waited for the jeering to die down. "Any man outside this wall is no longer protected by Ohndarien justice. Do with him what you will."

A curly-haired guard knelt and cut the rope between Brophy's feet. Brophy recognized the soldier. He'd played dice with him once at the Citadel. The young man stood and severed the bonds at his wrists.

"I didn't do it," Brophy whispered.

"You should have," the man whispered back. "You're going to pay the price. You should have lifted her skirts when you had the chance."

Another soldier poked Brophy in the back with his spear, herding him toward the open gate. Beyond the dark tunnel, he could see the desolate hills of Physendria.

Brophy had passed through these doors a hundred times to go hunting with Trent. It never occurred to him that they might not let him back in.

Four guards followed him through the tunnel and past the gate. Brophy stopped, protected by the stone archway above. Blinking against the bright, barren landscape, he wanted to throw up. He wanted to smash Krellis's face to pulp on the jagged rocks in front of him.

"Close the gates!" someone shouted from inside the city.

Two gouts of water spewed from the exit tubes on either side of the tunnel, and the gate began to close.

The guards poked him forward with their spears.

A huge rock thumped on the ground in front of Brophy, dropped by an overanxious spectator. Several smaller stones followed before the deluge ceased.

Don't turn your back. The big ones will come first.

He turned around and faced his guards.

"Get going, or we'll run you through," one of them said.

Brophy took three quick steps backward and looked up. Hundreds of stones fell like rain. He waited for them, waited for the last possible second, and then ran back toward the gate.

The four guards blocked his way, but he swatted a spear aside and slipped between two men. A thunderous roar shook the earth as a wave of stones smashed into the ground.

Brophy grabbed a man's spear and spun him into his fellows as they tried to maneuver in the small area. He let go of the spear and ran back into the daylight. He immediately spun around backward, looking for any danger.

"Run! Run! Run!" the crowd kept chanting as they threw the rest of their stones.

Brophy's heart thundered in his chest. Running lightly on his toes, he backed away from the wall.

Rocks fell like hail. There was no way to dodge them all. He kept his eyes open for the big ones, bobbing and weaving as best he could. Two small ones hit him in the side and the arm, knocking him off-balance. He hit the ground and rolled back to his feet without thinking. A stone the size of his head thumped into the parched earth inches from his feet. Another small rock grazed his temple. The flash of pain blinded him, but he did not stop running.

Brophy managed to keep his feet, and he continued backward, gaining speed. More rocks flew, arcing out into the sky, falling inevitably toward him. They shattered on the ground all around him, stinging his legs with broken stone. He gasped as one crashed into his knee, but he kept limping, ever backward.

Ten more steps and he was free. Only the strongest could hurl a rock that far. A few sailed toward him as he slowed to a stop, bloody and breathing hard. He stepped to the side twice, letting the rocks tumble beyond him.

The crowd continued to scream for his blood. One of the guards threw his spear, but it went wide. The last guard ducked through the gate just before it sealed shut with a boom that shook the ground.

The angry voices quickly died down as Brophy backed away. He almost didn't hear the single voice as it rose above the rest.

"Nephew!" someone shouted, from far away. "Don't give up, Brophy, don't give up!"

He turned around and scanned the battlement for the single voice amid the crowd.

A last melon-sized rock came flying out of the sky. It landed just past the others with a wet splat.

The "rock" was actually a cloth sack. He grabbed the bundle and pulled it to safety. Inside were a knife, sandals and some clothes, all soaked in seawater to carry farther. He looked up and saw a lone figure next to the aqueduct at the very top of the wall.

"The Lightning Swords await your return!" the man shouted. Brophy couldn't see his face, but the stranger's reference to the mercenary army of J'Qulin the Sly, the first Brother of Autumn, filled him with an overwhelming joy.

"Tell Krellis to sleep lightly!" Brophy shouted, "I will return! The Heart of Ohndarien protects her own!"

The crowd roared, but any individual responses were lost in the swell of their shouting.

BROPHY HIKED SOUTH through the scrub brush and stunted trees. The clothes in the sack were a little small, but not too bad. His friend on the wall had also included a bowstring and a few iron fishhooks. It would take days to weave fishing line, but he could make a bow. That was as good a beginning place as any.

It was a five-day walk to Physen, the capital of Physendria. He would have to do some hunting along the way. In Physen Brophy could sneak onto a merchant ship headed back to Ohndarien. If he could get past the Sunset Gate, he knew a way to sneak into the Hall of Windows and take the Test of the Stone. He should never have waited. If he had claimed Krellis's spot on the council weeks ago, this never would have happened.

When Brophy emerged from the Heart with a red diamond glowing in his chest, the people would know the truth. The Heartstone would choose who was the true Brother and who was the traitor.

He walked an hour before finding a good tree. It was a gnarled old cypress growing in the shadow of a huge boulder. Its largest limb was long enough to make a good bow.

Brophy went to work on the cypress branch as if it were Krellis's neck. What would have taken an axe five minutes took his knife an hour. But he severed the limb from the tree and began whittling it. He took great care to protect the knife. He couldn't risk breaking it or even chipping it badly. It was his only claw in a land filled with predators.

He tried to keep his anger hot, tried to keep Krellis in his mind, but as he stripped and notched the wood, he felt tired. His fatigue let the anger drift away, and all that remained to him were the tattered scraps of his life.

Tears dripped on Brophy's handiwork. He clenched his teeth and continued carving, but he couldn't stop crying. He hacked viciously at the wood, blinking constantly.

Two men stepped from behind a rock twenty feet away. In his grief, Brophy hadn't heard them coming. The strangers were dressed as Physendrian farmers, but peasants didn't wear polished short swords. Farmers didn't carry steel-tipped spears.

His stomach twisted. Were they Physendrian scouts? Exiled Ohndariens? Brigands awaiting travelers?

Brophy stood, his hunting knife in hand. "I was just exiled," he said. Would they care if he was one of them now?

"We know," the nearest one said. He was a broad-shouldered man with curly gray hair covering his forearms. His partner was much younger and was missing a front tooth. They crept closer, alert as hunters.

Brophy reached to his left hip for a sword that wasn't there.

"I have no money. Nothing to steal," he said, holding out one hand in a pacifying gesture.

The older man grinned. "That's all right, kid. Your head's worth more than a bag of gold."

A rock shifted behind him and Brophy whirled. Two other men came around the edge of the boulder. They were both short and stocky, their arms were covered with the swirling gray tattoos from the Silver Islands. Typical of Silver Islanders, they all had long hair tied back in ponytails.

"I am a Child of the Seasons," Brophy said, fishing for something that might stay their hand.

"*Were* a Child of the Seasons," the older man said.

"We know who you are, kid," one of the Islanders behind him said.

Brophy kept his back to the rock. They'd closed the net quickly. They were well trained.

A calm came over him. This is no different from four-on-one training in the Autumn Palace, he told himself. He would only have to attack one of them to get free.

"Whoever's spear comes closest to the heart gets an extra ten coins," the leader said, chuckling. The four of them stopped, ten paces out, trapping him against the rock. They all hefted their spears, preparing to throw. They weren't going to give him a chance to use his knife.

"And how many coins shall I get for your heart?" another voice said from above.

Brophy craned his neck. A small man perched above him on the edge of the boulder. He wore loose, dun-colored robes and a simple head wrap with a white cloth over his mouth. His prominent nose hooked like an eagle's beak, and his dark brown eyes were inscrutable under the bushy black eyebrows. The deep crags of his brow gave his face a terrible intensity.

It was the man from the crowd! The one who had told him to run backward.

"Save yourself, boy," the man whispered as he leapt over Brophy's head. A curved sword flashed in the dappled daylight.

Three of the brigands hesitated, but the leader with the curly gray forearms let his spear fly. Brophy threw himself to the side. It clacked against the rock behind him and he stumbled to his knees.

He looked up in time to see the leader vomit blood and collapse face forward. A great red line sprouted from his neck to his armpit. The dark-eyed stranger spun around, dodging inside the spear of the gap-toothed brigand. A dagger flashed, and the brigand screamed.

"Look out!" Brophy yelled, as an Islander threw his spear.

The stranger spun as though in a dance. The spear missed his head by inches and plunged into the chest of the gap-toothed screamer. The man's shriek gurgled into silence as he dropped to his knees, bubbles of blood on his lips.

Brophy scrambled to his feet as one of the Islanders attacked the stranger. The Islander swung overhand, but the stranger danced back. His curved sword flashed again, and the two weapons clanged together.

The stranger shifted aside, blocked a thrust. His blade shimmered like a piece of silver string that he waved in beautiful patterns. He made the deadly game look effortless, and the brigand's every strike clanged fruitlessly against his curved sword.

"The other, Brophy," the man said. His accented voice seemed somehow familiar. "Get him."

Brophy spun around in time to see the other Islander running away. He snatched up a spear and sprinted after the man. Scampering to the top of a rock, he cocked back and let fly.

Brophy's spear caught the runner in the hip and spun him around. The man stumbled into a boulder, and his head bounced off the stone with a brutal crack.

Brophy drew his knife and ran up to the moaning Islander. The man rolled on the ground, holding his head, but his eyes were not open.

Brophy hesitated, clutching his knife. He looked at the man's bloody hip where the spear had slashed his skin open to the bone.

"Finish him," said a voice from behind.

Brophy whirled around to see the Kherish stranger only a few feet away. The man's sword still dripped blood.

The boy backed up so he could see both men at once. "He is beaten," Brophy said. "There is no need to kill him."

The stranger walked up to the wounded man and slipped the tip of his curved sword underneath the brigand's chin, bringing his head up.

The man's eyes fluttered open. "No, please," he whispered.

In a blur of bloody steel, the stranger whipped his sword out from underneath the chin, spun around in a complete circle, and chopped through the Islander's neck.

His head rolled across the ground and stopped faceup, staring at the brutal sun.

"But that would not stop him from killing you if he had the chance," the stranger said, turning to face Brophy, who stared at the brutal handiwork with an open mouth. Feeling light-headed, he grabbed a rock to steady himself.

The stranger knelt and cleaned his curved blade on the dead man's clothes with two quick swipes.

"Why did you kill him?" Brophy asked. "We could have tied him up, asked who sent him."

The stranger stood. "I know who sent him. And I killed him so I never have to fight him again. Next time, he may have the advantage."

Brophy stared at the severed head, leaking blood on the ground. He sat on the rock and hung his head between his knees.

"Who are you?"

"You can call me Scythe. I am an old friend of your aunt Baelandra."

Brophy's head was still spinning. "And them?"

"They are old friends of your uncle Krellis."

Brophy looked up.

Scythe walked up to Brophy, dark eyes boring into him. Brophy rose to his feet. He stood half a foot taller, but he couldn't match the smaller man's stare.

"I . . ." Brophy inclined his head. "Thank you."

The little man made a bow. "You deserve nothing less." He sheathed his sword with a flourish. Scythe looked up at the sky, let out a deep breath and relaxed his shoulders. "What are your plans?"

"What do you mean?"

"Your childhood is over, Brophy. It's time for you to grow up. Now." Scythe's eyes narrowed. "Was that an empty threat, that you spoke earlier?"

"What threat?"

"The one you shouted at the entire city. 'Tell Krellis to sleep lightly,' I think you said. You are coming back for him. The Heart of Ohndarien protects her own. Something like that."

Brophy didn't know what to say. He looked at the dead body next to him.

"Are you ready to be the Heart of Ohndarien?" Scythe asked. "Are you ready to protect your own?"

2

KRELLIS STOOD AT the prow of the longboat, torch in hand. Light from the stars danced on the rippling water. Trent's funeral ship was a black shadow in the center of the bay. Twenty men rowed Krellis toward his son's body. All the lights in the city had been extinguished for the ceremony. The boy was wrapped in linen and surrounded by kindling. When the ship was lit, the flames would reach forty feet into the air and take hours to burn.

Burning the boy at sea was Victeris's idea. The Children of the Seasons were entombed somewhere in the catacombs of the Heart. Krellis refused to bury his son like a dog's discarded bone. That tradition, that way of life, was over.

The Physendrians left their dead in the desert for the animals to eat, but Trent was no Physendrian, either. His mother, Maigery, was a Silver Islander and Trent would go to his afterlife as she had.

As the ship grew closer, Krellis could see Trent's body seated upon a throne as befitted royalty. The boy would have been king of both Ohndarien and Physendria one day if things had gone differently. Would he have been a strong king? Would he have been wise and just or petty and cruel like so many Physendrian kings before him?

With perfect clarity, Krellis remembered back to that day in Physen when he had almost become king. How could he forget the bloody dagger in his hand? His father's body at his feet? The empty throne before him?

He took that throne, but he never sat in it. One moment he was a king, the next a slave of his brother as surely as he'd been a slave of his father.

Krellis's eyes unfocused, and he let the memory come.

KRELLIS SET HIS hand upon the golden arm of the throne built for King Phy I. No longer would he watch his father flick commands from this chair. Krellis's words would rule now. Victeris stood beside him, smiling and nodding.

"Sit, my brother. You have earned it. You have done what the rest of us could not."

"I will sit when I am ready." He traced a finger along the delicate carvings on the arm, so subtle, as a ruler must be.

"As you say."

The great doors of the throne room burst open. Fifty swordsmen jogged into the room, forming ranks on either side of the door, creating an aisle for Phandir. These were no ordinary soldiers; each man's right arm was covered with the hairy pelt of a gorilla. These were the incorruptible Apes, the king's elite guard. Krellis's smiling older brother strode in, regal in his breastplate of gold, his feathered cloak the color of flames.

How had that smiling fool won over the royal guard?

"Arrest him," Phandir commanded, pointing to Victeris. "That vile creature murdered the king."

Krellis had not seen Victeris look surprised since they were boys. The eldest brother flicked a look to Krellis that conveyed all.

We have failed, he seemed to say.

And it was over. All of it, in an instant.

Victeris ran for a side door. Three Apes chased him down and threw him to the floor. He did not resist. Even as children, Victeris had always cringed from physical violence. One of the swordsmen kicked him viciously, and Krellis heard a rib snap. Victeris groaned and rolled to his back.

Krellis stood his ground, the bloody dagger still in his hand. He could have gone to help his eldest brother. He could have died trying to save him. He could have waved the bloodstained dagger in Phandir's face and roared that it was he who had killed their father. He could have. But he didn't.

Phandir marched past the Apes as they hauled Victeris to his feet and dragged him from the room. The middle brother stepped gracefully up on the dais, smiling like the fool he seemed, like the fool he was not.

The two brothers faced one another, Krellis standing higher than Phandir for that last, sweet moment. His grip tightened on the dagger. One quick slice would cut the man's throat. One quick slice would bring fifty men down on his head in an unstoppable wave.

"You surprised me, little brother. You had the courage to do what I did not. I hated that man as much as you." He tapped his father's corpse with his toe. "I thank you for silencing him forever, but I am still the older brother. You owe me your allegiance."

Krellis hesitated.

"Will you bend the knee?" Phandir asked, his smile fading for a rare moment.

"What about Victeris?"

Phandir grinned. "Surely you must know what kind of man our brother is. With his death, the madness in our family will be gone forever."

"Victeris may be mad, but he is loyal."

Victeris's unexpected kindness over the past year had been something Krellis had never experienced before. Yet Krellis repaid him with silence as Phandir's guards dragged him away.

"And are you?" Phandir asked. "Loyal?"

Krellis felt the weight of the moment. He could lose everything, even his life, in the next few seconds.

"There is nothing but madness in our family," Krellis said, "Even death will not purge it."

Phandir laughed. He had always laughed too much.

"Victeris's lovely disciple has changed you, my brother. You never used to be so bold."

Krellis took a quick breath at the mention of Maigery. How did Phandir know about her?

"I would not harm her, if I were you," he barely whispered, his voice trembling. He gripped the dagger as if he would crush it.

Phandir waved a hand. "You worry too much, little brother. You always did. Maigery is safe, as is her babe. Yours, I must assume?" He grinned, showing the big, white teeth he was so proud of. "My most trusted men are looking after her. We live in a dangerous world, you know. One cannot be too careful about his family."

Krellis tossed the bloody dagger on the seat of the throne. Red droplets splattered across the gold.

"On that, at least, we agree," he said.

"What shall it be, little brother? The knee or the sword?" The fiendish fool smiled again. "Please let it be the knee, you are the only one in this family I actually like."

The muscles corded in Krellis's neck, and he clenched his teeth as he knelt. "All hail Phandir, King."

KRELLIS GRIPPED THE torch as if it were that dagger from years ago. His men shipped their oars, and his boat drew up alongside Trent's floating pyre. The boy's face was covered with white linen, but Krellis could imagine it under there—sulky, prideful, devious. Trent had looked a bit like Phandir when he smiled.

Krellis threw his torch into the boy's lap. The dry straw of the pyre burst into flame. The fire spread quickly, and he could feel the heat upon his face.

"I knelt for you," he whispered to the fiery corpse. "I bowed to him to save your life."

Krellis flexed his fingers as the flames grew taller. The blaze became so hot he had to fight to keep his eyes open, staring at the burning throne within the pyre.

"All hail Phandir, King," he breathed, tasting the hate on every word.

ROPHY LOOKED BACK. The barren Physendrian hills extended into the distance until they became hazy and indistinct in the heat of the sun. He caught a glimpse of white cloth half a mile back—Scythe, still following him.

With a frown, Brophy licked his lips. The sun blazed overhead. He probably should have rested during the four hours of "high sun," as Physendrians called it, but he couldn't bring himself to do so. Stopping didn't seem to help, anyway. At least walking he got a small breeze on his sweating face. He had used his heat-tolerance training more in the last day and a half than he had in his entire life. He would have been badly sunburned without it.

No, it was better to keep going, even though the horizon swam every now and then. Mirages rippled the edges of the badlands. Brophy had never seen that before, but he'd never been this far south. Trent would have loved it.

His parched lips resisted the bitter smile that tried to come. Trent would have packed a full bottle of Siren's Blood and happily tottered to the other side of the world. Of course he would probably also have molested a local sheep and found some way to blame Brophy for getting her pregnant.

Brophy shook his head. He'd been traveling south and west for a day and a half, dogged by his white shadow.

Their conversation had been short. After everything that had happened, Brophy wanted to be alone. He didn't know who to trust anymore, and he needed some time to plan his next moves. Scythe claimed to be his aunt's friend, but Brophy had never seen him before. It was too convenient the way he showed up the moment Brophy needed help.

So he thanked the ruthless little man for saving his life, and they parted company. Scythe had not tried to stop him. He only said one thing as Brophy walked away.

"If you're not sure who to trust, listen to the man who tells you what you don't want to hear."

That last bit of arrogance still needled Brophy. What was worse, Scythe did not leave him alone, but followed him like a hunter tracking a wounded deer. Brophy kept his original plan and headed for the Physendrian capital. He was determined to lose the little man tonight under the cover of darkness.

He stuck primarily to the rocky ridges, avoiding easy ground where he could. Eventually he would have to turn west and cross the endless barren plain stretching from the hills to the sea, but he wanted to wait as long as possible.

The foothills of the Arridan Mountains slowly faded into the distance behind him. They were named after the mythical serpent Arridus. The entire range was said to be the half-buried spine of the sleeping serpent who was born on the day the world was created. The Physendrian legend claimed that someday the serpent would awaken and swallow the whole world.

Brophy's stomach growled. He was hungry enough to swallow the whole world. Finding water had not been a problem. Tiny springs broke through the bone-dry mountainside, creating weedy little trails down to the badlands, where the water disappeared into the cracks. The spots of green clinging to the moisture were easy to see, but the crude arrows he made didn't fly straight, and he hadn't been able to catch any game. It was three more days to Physen. Food would become a problem before long.

Brophy continued until the sun blazed across the western horizon, spreading rays of orange fire across the sky. He stopped and drank from a tiny spring and stared at the beautiful sunset. Distant clouds caught the dying light as the sun dipped below the jagged plateaus in the distance. Despite his exhaustion, he watched until the sun was almost gone. There had never been any sunsets like that in Ohndarien. By the Seasons, he didn't know the sky could be so beautiful.

Blinking his sticky eyes, he looked for a place to sleep. Casting about, he found a sandy spot between two rocks. It was the best bed he was likely to find. He slumped down. It felt glorious to be out of the sun. The nights were warm, and he wouldn't miss not having a fire.

After giving in to a sweet moment of relaxation, he dug into the sack that his unseen friend had thrown from the Water Wall. There were two plums, one of which he was determined to save for at least another day, and half a loaf of bread. He also had a handful of leaves from the spine flower bushes he found that morning. The plant's fleshy pulp was bitter and made his mouth tingle, but it was edible. There were only a few leaves left, but it looked like a feast after walking all day with nothing to eat. Brophy carefully cut the first leaf in half and scraped the pulp out with his teeth. He chewed the stringy mush, dreaming of the plum that would follow.

Scythe interrupted just as he finished the last leaf.

"I wouldn't sleep there if I were you," the small man said from the top of a jagged boulder some twenty feet away. "Scorpions like that soft sand as much as you do."

Brophy bit viciously into the plum. The succulent juice dribbled down his chin. The previous night, Scythe had come close to Brophy's camp and tried to start a conversation. Brophy had ordered him away. The man left as quietly as he had come, but Brophy had slept uneasily. He'd awoken at every sound and many times at no sound at all, never knowing if he would wake with a knife at his throat.

He realized that he'd chewed the entire mouthful and swallowed without tasting it. It enraged him. His precious plums. The stranger was cheating him out of what small pleasures he still had left. Brophy leapt to his feet and hurled a rock at the man.

"I told you to leave me alone!"

The rock arced unerringly at Scythe's head. At the last second, the little man shifted, and the stone flew past him, inches from his ear.

"You throw rocks better than you dodge them."

"I made it through the stoning, if you remember."

"I would have made it without a scrape."

"Why don't you go back to the wall and prove it?"

Scythe pulled back his hood and unwound the strips of cloth that covered his face.

"I don't know you, stranger," Brophy continued "I didn't ask for your help, and I don't want it."

Scythe remained silent, crouching on the boulder like a vulture. Brophy returned to the sandy spot and lay down, determined to ignore him.

Dusk faded to dark, but Brophy's eyes were still wide-open. He rolled around on the sand, trying to make a comfortable spot.

"You can see their fires," the stranger said.

Pretending he hadn't heard, Brophy rummaged through the discarded spine flower husks, looking for any scrap of pulp he might have missed.

"It's hard to tell, but I'd guess their number is over twenty thousand."

Brophy tossed a husk down. There was nothing left, not a single pulpy string.

"Don't you want to see the army that is preparing to march on Ohndarien?"

"What do you mean?"

"They are right there, maybe twenty miles distant. You can see their cooking fires."

Brophy stood up. The moon hadn't risen yet, and he could barely see by starlight as he scrambled out of his sandy bed and crawled to the top of the steep ridge. He peered over the edge and sighed. Far below him, hundreds of tiny fires lit the dark plain like a cloud of sparks. He closed his eyes and lowered his head to the rock. The gritty stone scraped against his forehead.

"How are you going to stop them?" the stranger asked.

"How are *you* going to stop them!" Brophy shouted. He hated that man. He hated his superior airs, his smug voice, his damned persistence, everything about him.

"Your aunt asked me to prepare you to take the Test. But from what I've seen so far, you haven't got a chance."

"You have no idea who I am."

"I've seen those bruises. I know how you got them. How long did it take Krellis to best you that night by Trent's body? Two seconds? Three?"

Brophy searched for another rock. He found a little one and hurled it into the shadows. It clattered across the ground.

"What will you do the next time you face him? How will you overcome his strength, his speed, his ruthlessness?"

Brophy clenched his jaw and turned away.

"I know you want to take the Test, Brophy, but you are fifteen years old. Your aunt Baelandra was the youngest ever to succeed, she did it at twenty with the full support of all eight Brothers and Sisters. Were you planning on sneaking into the Heart and taking that Test alone? Were you going to slit your wrists first just to make it interesting?"

Brophy gritted his teeth and held his silence.

"Let's suppose you did become Brother of Autumn. What then? Do you expect Krellis to step down and retire peacefully?"

"I'm going to kill him," Brophy said.

"A fine idea. Let's say you succeed. What then? How will you defeat this army? How will you gain the loyalty of the troops trained from boyhood by the man you just killed?"

Brophy's breath hissed through his clenched teeth. "Somehow," he replied.

"Somehow? You haven't thought of anything so far. I don't see why that should change."

Brophy leapt to his feet, grabbed his sack, and started walking away.

"You can't run from life forever, Heir of Autumn," Scythe shouted. "Eventually you'll have to stand still and let it hit you in the face."

Brophy walked for another hour, stumbling over the rocky ground lit only by the stars. When he stumbled across a little patch of sand, he decided to call it a night. He hoped he'd lost the little man in the darkness, but Brophy doubted it.

He rolled around in the sand making a little nest for himself. The top few inches were cool, but the sand underneath still held the day's heat. Brophy tried to relax, fearing the sleepless hours to come. He knew he'd never fully close his eyes with Scythe lurking somewhere out there in the darkness.

Pulling his bag of delicacies protectively to his stomach, he hunkered down for a long night.

FIRE! LIGHTNING! Brophy sat up, clutching at his throat and came away with a hard, wriggling creature. Pain exploded into his hand, and he threw the thing away. His breath seared his lungs, and his neck felt like it would burst.

Scythe leapt out of the darkness, a wicked, curved knife in his hand. He knocked Brophy onto his back and knelt on his chest.

"No!" Brophy yelled, punching the man. Somehow he missed.

Scythe's eyes were tight. His hand lanced out, spearing Brophy just under the ribs. Brophy squeaked. He couldn't breathe. He couldn't move. Scythe slammed him to the ground again.

"Hold still, you fool, or you will die," the man said.

Brophy tried to fight, but his limbs had gone weak. Scythe grabbed Brophy's good wrist and shoved it under his knee.

"Neck's the worst place to get stung, boy. That poison hits your brain, and you're dead. Understand?"

Brophy struggled to breathe. He nodded.

"Then stop fighting me."

He forced himself to go limp.

"Good. Now hold very still. This will hurt a lot."

Brophy's breath whistled. His throat was swelling shut, and he couldn't move his neck.

Scythe jabbed his hand into a leather pouch at his side. "Was it big or small?"

"Wh . . . What?"

Scythe flipped his dagger up and cut a line down Brophy's neck. The stroke was sure and swift. Brophy hardly felt it.

"The scorpion, was it small as your finger or big as your hand?"

"Big . . . Big as my hand."

Scythe withdrew a tiny vial from the pouch. He bit off the stopper and spat it away. "Good. You might be alive in an hour." He dumped the entire thing on Brophy's neck.

Brophy screamed, arching his back. He fought with everything he had, but somehow Scythe kept him pinned. His scream became a wail, then a gurgle. He slumped to the ground again, motionless.

Scythe pressed his fingers against the uncut side of Brophy's neck for a long moment. With a sigh he flopped down to the sand and leaned against Brophy's chest. He glared at the starry horizon and shook his head.

"I hate Physendria."

BAELANDRA STOOD ON her balcony overlooking the garden. Beyond the wall, tall sailing ships and fat galleys rocked at anchor. She had come to watch the sunset, but it had died hours ago. Not even a flicker of purple remained in the night sky. The streetlamps had been lit all over her beloved Ohndarien. They shone like little fireflies, coming alive along Northridge and the distant shore of Stoneside. The evening air had cooled to the perfect temperature for dinner with friends in the Night Market or a walk on the Windmill Wall. It was a night for sex, long and slow under the stars with the scent of lavender drifting into the windows and night sparrows chirping in the trees.

I used to know what it was like to be in love, she thought. I used to know that sweet, aching need for one man. But she could no longer remember it. She could see it, could picture it, but the emotion was gone from her body as if an organ had been ripped out.

Outside Baelandra's garden gate, two soldiers leaned on their spears. Though the guards claimed they were here for her protection, she was a prisoner in her own house. There was unrest in the city, they said. She should stay at home for a few days.

On the first day of her captivity, Baelandra was incensed. She refused to acknowledge their presence and walked right past them. They blocked her way with their crossed spears. After she tried to get around them several times, one of the soldiers slammed the butt of his spear into her stomach. It took everything she had to stay on her feet. Wrapping her dignity around her like armor, she walked back into her house and stayed there.

There were several ways to escape from the building. She knew them well, but there was no point in sneaking off like a thief in the night until she had someplace to go. Her city had been taken from her. She and her Sisters would have to take it back.

Shara was the last person Baelandra had spoken with who wasn't under Krellis's thumb. That was six days ago, when she left to investigate Brophy's story and never returned. Since Shara, Baelandra was not allowed visitors. Hundreds of people had come to the gate only to be turned away. No friendly faces passed those tall spears. Her household staff failed to report to work. They were replaced by strangers, performing the necessary duties in sullen silence.

The lack of news was the worst part. Baelandra had friends in every quarter of the city. Information used to flow to her like streams into a river, and now she was dying of thirst.

One day she pressed a servant girl relentlessly for information. "Just tell me about Brophy," she begged.

"He survived the stones," the girl whispered, but she would say nothing more.

Hearing that Brophy was alive lifted her spirits briefly, but despair slowly settled over her again.

She stared at the darkness atop the Hall of Windows. The absence of those four torches cried out with thunderous silence. It was as if the soul of the city had been snuffed out.

The wind rustled in the trees just off the balcony. Baelandra blinked and tried to focus. She wanted to cry, but she wouldn't let herself. This was her mess. She had created it, and it was hers to clean up. Tears would mean surrender. The last move had not yet been made.

"You should have killed me," she said to him, wherever he might be. "You don't make many mistakes, but that is one you will regret."

"Lady of Autumn, I have news for you."

The voice came soft as a nesting sparrow. Baelandra froze, then forced herself to continue staring ahead at the water. She collected her thoughts. The voice came from the branches to the left of her balcony. Keeping her face locked forward, she watched the tree out of the corner of her eye.

"Who are you, child?" she murmured, carefully throwing her voice that direction.

"I'm not a child. I'm thirteen and nearly grown."

"My mistake, young lady. Who are you and why have you come to me?"

"I have news." There was a slight pause. "News to sell."

This was definitely not someone she knew, but who then? Krellis could have sent the child, but subtle tricks were not his style.

"What is your news and what is your price?"

"I know where the beautiful lady with the blue stone at her waist is being held. I know who is holding her, and I know . . ." Again a pause. "And I know what they've done to her."

Oh Shara, what have I gotten you into?

"And what is your price for this information?"

"A pittance," the young woman said, though Baelandra heard the hesitation in her voice. "One hundred silver stars."

"I see. Who sent you with this information?"

"I sent myself. Five days ago, I picked the beautiful lady up from your dock. I sailed her to Stoneside and waited for her to return. She paid well and she . . . was interested in a business opportunity. When she didn't come back, I decided to find her. I have ways of knowing things in this city."

"I'm sure that you do. I will give you ten silver for your information—"

"Ten! That's an insult. Her life is in danger."

"And then," Baelandra continued as if she had not been interrupted, "I will give you 190 more if you deliver a few messages for me."

The tree rustled. A young girl with short red hair leapt out of the leaves like a squirrel. She caught the edge of the railing, banging her knees into the stone. With a soft grunt, she hopped the rail and rolled into the balcony.

Baelandra watched the guards by the gate. They hadn't seen.

She stepped back into her room, out of sight of the quiet city. The young woman followed her into the shadows. She peered into every dark corner, chewing on her bottom lip.

"Two hundred?" she asked.

"Two hundred."

The girl held out her rough and callused hand.

"You're a waterbug," Baelandra said.

The young woman shrugged. She stuck her hand out an inch farther. "Deal?"

A smile tickled the corner of Baelandra's mouth, and she let it come. It was her first genuine smile in years, it seemed. She took the dirty little hand. "Deal."

BROPHY TRIED to open his eyes, but they were gummed shut. With a grunt, he brought up his right hand and winced. Any movement sent stabs of pain up his arm. He cradled his right hand on his chest and rubbed his eyes with his left.

He was in some kind of cave or a dark room. He tried to sit up, but the whole world lurched, and he thought he would vomit. He lay back down for a moment until the world stopped swinging. His throat was parched, making it difficult to swallow.

More slowly this time, he opened his eyes and looked around. The walls and ceiling were yellow stone. Brophy stared a long time before he made the connection.

Somehow he was in the capital city of Physendria, the City of Gold. The Ohndarien soldiers who told him about Physen talked about the "gold" with a smirk. The only gold to be found in Physen was in the king's coffers or in the yellow stone of the underground palace.

Brophy sat up. He swayed, but this time he realized it was only his bed that moved. He was lying on a circular platform covered with a thin padding. The bed was suspended from the ceiling on four delicate copper chains. A large hole in the ceiling opened up to the sky above. The shaft was flared at the bottom and plated with a shiny metal that reflected the fading light throughout the room.

Brophy held up his aching hand in the pale light. Wrapped in a thin, dun-colored cloth, it was three times its usual size. The skin at the edge of the bandage was a sickly gray color. He looked away.

Gingerly, he touched the left side of his neck. It was swollen almost to his chin. He tried to swallow again and couldn't. Brophy took a deep breath and let it out slowly. At least he was alive.

Swinging his legs over the edge, he tried to stand. The bed rocked on its chains. His neck throbbed, and he gritted his teeth. Enough, he thought. The Children of the Seasons were taught pain control from the time they were seven years old. Brophy imagined the pain as a black cloud within his body. He felt it, turned it over in his mind. He made it larger, then smaller. Soon it became a thing, an idea, not a part of him. He shrank it away to nothing, and it disappeared.

Brophy reopened his eyes. Compensating for the balance of the bed, he hopped to the floor, leaving it rocking behind him. The floor was cool and pleasantly rough on his feet. He stood for a moment, testing the strength of his legs. Except for his bandages, he was naked as a dolphin.

The room was small and circular like the bed, with a writing desk and a wardrobe on opposite sides. Both pieces of furniture were exquisitely crafted. He approached the desk, absently traced a decorative carving of a rat on the front of the drawer. He didn't recognize the wood. It was sage green, burnished to a mirror shine.

There was a single door in the room, with no handle and no visible hinges. Brophy pushed at it. It moved slightly, but wouldn't open. Brophy imagined breaking it down, but laughed at himself. He could barely stand, let alone beat down doors.

The walls were decorated with vivid murals. A giant bird, a crocodile, and a tree full of apes caught his eye. He glanced up at the faint square of light above. The sun was up there, somewhere, but he couldn't see the top of the chimney. If he had been healthy, Brophy could have moved the desk over and tried to climb up the shaft, but not with his ruined right hand.

So, he was a prisoner in Physen. Had Scythe betrayed him? Had that been his true motivation? To sell Brophy to Ohndarien's enemies? Brophy had no idea what a Child of the Seasons would be worth to the King of Physendria.

Brophy tried to remember that fall day with Baelandra in the Hall of Windows. He tried to remember what it felt like to be home, to belong, to be loved. The feeling wouldn't come. Everything he treasured had been taken from him in the last few days. Ohndarien, Bae, Shara, his freedom, his hope. Even his pants were gone.

Brophy shook his head and snatched the quill off the writing desk. He wanted something in his hand if they came for him. The sharp point would be worth one good thrust. He opened all the drawers of the desk. Three were empty and the fourth contained a neat stack of parchment. He crossed the room to the greenwood wardrobe, but it was emptier than the desk.

"I've ordered fresh clothes for you," a dark, beautiful voice said behind him. Brophy whirled around, hiding the quill behind his thigh.

A tall, svelte woman entered the room holding a golden tray. He couldn't tell her age at a glance. She moved like Shara but spoke like Bae. Her raven-black hair glinted blue in the light and was cut just below her ears like a boy-soldier from Gildheld. Her white gown flowed down from a golden necklace around her neck. The dress was belted at the waist by a matching chain. The delicate gold links hung to the floor, drawing a line between her legs. He could almost see through the sheer material. Her bare arms were smooth and sun-browned, strong and graceful.

She held a tray with a golden bowl atop it, tendrils of steam rose from the greenish liquid inside. She had not come through the door, but had appeared through an opening in the wall on the opposite side. With the slightest touch of her hand, the heavy stone door swung shut behind her. Once it was closed, it was indistinguishable from the wall around it.

Brophy looked for a way to cover himself, but there was nothing.

She raised a thin black eyebrow. It was so dark and perfect, it looked as if it had been painted there.

"Are you going to stab me with that?" She inclined her head to the hand he hid behind his thigh. "Or write me a love letter?" She paused, then said, "I suggest you stab me. I despise love letters."

Blushing, he brought the quill into view but didn't let go of it. He looked down and cursed himself the moment he did it. The woman's gaze followed and she studied him with a half smile.

"I wasn't . . . I didn't . . ."

"You wasn't? You didn't? What? We call that device a pen. Should I send for a scribe to teach you how to hold it correctly, or shall I send for a poet to help you speak in complete sentences?"

"I know what it is."

"Well then, that's something." She paused. "As striking as you look, standing there naked and swollen in all the wrong places, I suggest you get back into bed."

Brophy hesitated. He looked at the pen in his hand, at her, at the wall that had once been a door. Brophy set his little weapon on top of the wardrobe and went to the bed. He hopped up and pulled the red feather blanket across his lap. He had to know how that door worked before he could risk an escape. It would also help to know what was on the other side.

"I came to feed you," she said. "But you're awake now. Feed yourself." She placed the bowl on his lap, running a finger down his leg. He took the bowl, and she slowly withdrew her hand.

There was no spoon. He sniffed at it and tentatively stuck his fingers into the green mush, tested it on his tongue.

"We don't poison our guests in Physendria; we drink their blood. It's good for the skin." She smiled sweetly. "Eat. I'll get you some real food tomorrow."

"Am I a guest, or a prisoner?" he asked, forcing himself to swallow a mouthful of mush. It actually tasted quite good, despite the bitter aftertaste of some kind of medicinal. Hungrily, he scooped more into his mouth.

"You've obviously never visited a Physendrian prison."

She shrugged, and the thin fabric rippled over the curve of her breasts. He focused on his bowl of mush. "As I was saying," she continued, "I've ordered fresh clothes for you. They will be ready by the time your strength is up."

His mouth full of food, Brophy stared at her. She regarded him calmly, waiting. He swallowed, paused.

"Don't stare," she said. "Ask a question if you've got one."

"Who are you?"

"My name is Ossamyr."

Brophy stopped eating. He stared at her.

"You're the Queen of Physendria!" he spluttered.

Her lip curled, and she looked down at her hand. "Yes. I suppose where you come from that is a reason to spit," she said. She scooped a fleck of mush from her hand with a golden fingernail and flicked it away.

"I'm sorry," he mumbled.

"As you should be. Yes, I am Queen Ossamyr, only wife of Phandir III, King of Physendria and Lord of the Summer Sea."

None of this made any sense. Was he a hostage? Would they try to use him against Ohndarien? Brophy swallowed hard, then said, "May I ask another question, my lady?"

"See how polite now? Much better. What is your question?"

"How did I get here?"

"A good friend of mine asked me to look after you."

"Scythe?"

"I believe that is what he calls himself now." Her eyes narrowed. "It is rare to survive a scorpion sting to the neck. Scythe must have acted very quickly. But then, he was always quick."

"Quick to sell me to you, you mean."

She leaned toward him, and her dark hair swung forward like strands of black silk. Her eyes narrowed even further. "And here I thought you were recovering your manners. That very small man carried you a very long way. You would have died if he hadn't brought you here."

"You're right, my lady," Brophy mumbled. *Assuming he didn't put that thing on me in the first place,* he thought to himself.

The queen ignored him. "He asked me to extend my hospitality, a great boon that I am starting to regret."

Brophy wondered if he might have wronged the little man. But why would Scythe save his life twice, and then deliver him to the queen of his enemies? It made no sense.

"I just don't understand what is happening."

"Don't whine. Ill-mannered boys outrank snivelers by a long mark."

Brophy took a deep breath before speaking again.

"Why did you take me in?"

"Scythe is an old friend, and queens don't have many friends." She looked down for a moment before looking back at him with a half smile. "Besides, you have a handsome face, a strong body. I'm told you have a keen mind, though I've yet to see proof of that." She pursed her lips. "All of that aside, I took you in because I am your queen. I owe you justice and security. And in return, you owe me your allegiance."

"But I'm not Physendrian."

"The city you were born in lies on the extreme northern tip of the Physendrian peninsula. My kingdom. Three hundred years ago a few brigands built some walls, called it a city, and claimed it for their own. That does not change the fact that you are still a part of Physendria. The crown has not seen fit to knock down that wall and bring justice to the brigands within. Not yet. But we will soon."

Brophy narrowed his eyes. "I . . . thank you for your hospitality."

"Never thank me. I despise thanks."

"I'm sorry, my lady."

"So you can be polite, you're just forgetful when you're scared."

"I'm not scared."

"Of course not."

He scooped out the last of the porridge and swallowed it. She reached for the bowl, and her hand slid across his thigh. He jerked as if she'd stung him. With a faint smile, she put the bowl back on the golden tray.

"Now get some sleep," she said. "I want to see you compete in Nine Squares soon. The local boys have been a weedy lot this year. They could use the competition."

"Nine Squares?" The Physendrian blood sport was brutal and barbaric, a senseless waste of life and limb. "I can't—"

Brophy fell silent as the queen placed a single finger against his lips. She opened her mouth a little, watching him. He could see her tongue for a scant instant. Her dark eyes looked directly into his. "Sleep well."

She left the room, and the thick stone door closed quietly behind her.

6

BROPHY AWOKE in Physendria for the second time. The feather blanket tickled his nose, and he pushed it away, sitting up on the suspended bed. He jumped to the floor, compensating for the rocking movement. His legs felt stronger, his eyes were clearer. At the edge of the bandages, his hand was still sallow and sickly, but the swelling was going down. His neck felt smaller as well.

Carefully, he unwrapped the bandages, wincing as he saw his puffy hand. He flexed, and it responded weakly. Shaking his head, he stripped the bandages from his neck and tried not to look at his hand.

Brophy made a circuit of the room, touching the wall where Ossamyr had entered. He dug his fingernails into the seam, but he couldn't find a way to make it open. Trailing his finger along the wall, he searched for any other hidden doors but found nothing. The normal door was still locked. He leaned on it, pushing as hard as he could. It wouldn't budge.

Brophy tried the wardrobe next. He pulled open the doors, finding neatly folded clothes within. The simple white robe was the same type Scythe had worn to ward off the sun. Beneath the robe was a pair of wildly colorful pants and river-reed sandals.

He took everything out, closed the doors, and laid the clothes on the bed. He wanted a bath before he got dressed, but there was no helping that, so he slipped on the pants, robe, and sandals. The fit was perfect.

After pacing the room a few more times, Brophy fell to thinking about Nine Squares. He didn't know the rules of the game, but he knew enough. It was a kind of military contest based on the nine sacred animals, the nine gods of Physendria. Brophy couldn't summon the details, but his aunt Jayden had once described it as "a senseless game for those who think little of human life." It had something to do with scorpions and beetles and crocodiles. The fifteen great families of Physendria sent champions to die for the crowd's amusement. He couldn't believe anyone would willingly do such a thing.

Martial games were prohibited in Ohndarien. Soldiers from Kherif were even forbidden from practicing their traditional sword juggling. Ohndariens did not consider war a game, and human suffering made poor entertainment.

But that didn't matter. Brophy had no intention of playing Nine Squares. He planned on being long gone by the time the queen or anyone else returned.

Taking a deep breath, he glanced at the square of light overhead.

HOURS LATER, Brophy paced around the tiny room, massaging his aching hand. With a growl of frustration, he kicked the bed. It jerked sideways, swinging back and forth. He'd never been confined before. He couldn't stand it.

Brophy flopped on the rocking bed and stared balefully at the square of daylight above him. After stacking the wardrobe upon the desk, he had been able to reach the tin-lined chimney, but it was impossible to climb. The metal was oiled to protect it from the elements and was as slippery as raw eggs. Brophy fell twice trying to wedge his body into the damn thing and had almost broken his arm. Obviously he wasn't the first person to think of escape through that route.

The door was hopeless. He threw himself against it once. His shoulder still hurt. The hidden door proved just as immovable. He spent an hour look-ing for a secret trigger, but it just wasn't there.

Brophy stared at the ceiling and hatched plot after plot, each more wildly ridiculous than the last. He finally fell to idle fantasies and was deep into his favorite one about cutting off Krellis's head when he heard a scraping noise at the wooden door.

He jumped to his feet. The desk and wardrobe were still stacked in the center of the room. There was nothing he could do before the door swung open. Ossamyr stepped through.

Brophy almost leapt forward and knocked her out of the way, but the hallway beyond the queen was full of armed men. Ossamyr arched an eye-brow at him as he stared through the opening. She calmly closed the door and turned to face him.

Her gown was similar to the one she'd worn before, baring her arms, but this one was slit down the center to her navel, linked by three thin gold chains. The border of the plunging neckline was embroidered with different animals: crocodiles, birds, snakes, apes, and more. Brophy forced himself to look at her face.

The queen stepped into the room and glanced at the stacked furniture. The corners of her lips turned up in a small smile. "Did you get a good night's rest?"

"No, my lady."

"Don't pout, child. It's tedious," she said.

"I'm not pouting. I'm angry."

"Good," she purred, running a finger along the wardrobe's carved doors. "That will serve us well in the arena."

Brophy didn't say anything. He would have to play along until he could discover how to escape.

Ossamyr crossed the room and stood in front of him, close enough that he could feel the heat of her breath on his skin. She smelled of mint leaves. He looked down at her and tried to muster the same fury that had consumed him a moment ago.

"Your anger is wasted on me, Brophy," she murmured, taking his hand, never letting go of his eyes. "Save it. There are others more deserving."

Brophy swallowed. He tried to keep his eyes on her face, but they kept straying to the curves of her breasts.

She turned his palm up and looked at his puffy hand. "You are healing well. Physendria must agree with you."

"I'm a prisoner."

She had large, dark eyes. "None of us can do all that we wish, when we wish it," she said. "I can help you, if you let me. Don't turn from the only friend you have in this country."

Brophy's lips tightened. "Yes, my lady," he murmured.

She released his hand and walked toward the door.

"Come, Brophy. I will show you the city. You can decide whether to trust me along the way."

Pausing only a moment, he followed her through the door.

Four sun-browned young men hunched in harnesses in front of the two-wheeled chariot. Their dark, curly heads were bowed, and they stood remarkably still. The underground hallway was as wide as a street.

Ossamyr's troop of heavily muscled swordsmen stood at a distance, their brass armor glinting dully in the light of the lamps. Each of their right arms was covered with a gray, hairy pelt that ended in a thick-fingered glove. It took Brophy a moment to realize that the glove was actually the severed hand of an ape. He wrinkled his nose as she led him to the cart.

"Is that—?"

"Come along, Brophy," Ossamyr said. She stepped into the chariot and looked back at him. "It doesn't do to keep the queen waiting." She took the reins in hand, her arm flexing as she tightened her fist. He stepped into the chariot, and his gaze moved from the guards to the men in the harnesses. "Is this what they do for a living, my lady?" he asked.

"You might say that." She arched an eyebrow. "They are slaves."

"Oh." He hesitated.

She shook the reins, and the slaves took off down the hallway at a trot. Half of the Apes sprinted ahead, half followed behind.

Brophy hated the idea of slaves. Slave trading was forbidden in Ohndarien, but he could not deny that those traders were allowed through the locks just like anyone else.

The chariot rattled down the hallway, which opened into a deep trench with the sky above. A stone stairway was cut into the walls on either side of the sunken road. Four guards sprinted up one staircase and four sprinted up the other. Flanking the road, they matched pace with the chariot as it sped along below.

"This is the King's Road," Ossamyr explained. "Only the fifteen families may travel it. All others must use the surface."

The depth of the trench shaded them from the morning sun. It was carved from the same gold sandstone as Brophy's room. The sides were lined with cavelike shops. White-robed merchants stared at them as they drove past. Everything was rough and jagged, so unlike the smooth blue-white marble of Ohndarien.

"That underground place we just left was the Catacombs?" Brophy asked.

"Yes."

"That's the king's palace?"

"There is no true palace in Physen. The king owns the entire city and everything in it. The underground Catacombs are simply the most desirable place to live. Someday the entire city will be carved into the ground, but work like that takes time."

There were many other slave-drawn chariots traveling the King's Road, but all of them pulled to the side as the queen approached. Several times Brophy saw the dirty faces of children peer over the edge of the trench, but the Apes ran them away as soon as the chariot drew near.

"My lady, can we see the rest of the city?" Brophy asked her.

She nodded, flicking the reins. The slaves ran faster. The chariot turned off the King's Road up a narrow incline carved into the rock. The ramp was barely wider than the chariot, but the slaves navigated it perfectly, and they emerged onto the surface.

The heat hit him as though he had opened an oven door. He could feel it on his eyes, on his head and back. He broke a sweat before the slaves had pulled them fifty feet, but Ossamyr seemed unaffected.

Half of their escort was suddenly trapped on the other side of the trench. In perfect formation, they used their spears to pole-vault across the fifteen-foot gap. One, two, three, four. Forming up on either side of the chariot, they continued along, forcing everyone out of their way.

The surface of Physen was like nothing Brophy had ever seen. The city was littered with stone-and-wood hovels in a haphazard jumble. Even Stone-side at its worst was never so disorganized. There were no streets, no squares, no fountains. The mismatched buildings slouched against each other like piles of garbage.

There were people everywhere, toiling under the hot sun. Two men slaughtered a squealing pig in the center of the road. They had to jump out of the way as the queen's chariot rolled by. Naked children clustered in tiny bits of shade. An old woman squatted against a building where flies buzzed around a mound of feces.

The smell made Brophy gag. He tried breathing through his mouth, but then he could taste it.

"This is the liveliest time of day," Ossamyr said. "The city will shut down shortly during the four hours of high sun. Even slaves are allowed to rest during that time."

Brophy watched the crowds of naked, malnourished children stare at them with hollow eyes. His grip tightened on the edges of the cart. He jumped when Ossamyr's hand, strangely cool, touched his.

"I know," she murmured, in a voice that did not carry beyond the grinding wheels below them. "I know. Watch, Brophy, and learn. But keep it from your face. For both our sakes."

She continued telling him about the history and glory of Physendria. The chariot wended its way through the ramshackle sprawl toward a looming mountain in the distance. As they neared, Brophy squinted at the ragged peak.

"The Arena," Ossamyr said.

"It's a volcano!"

She favored him with her narrow-eyed stare. "Indeed."

"Isn't it filled with molten lava?"

"Not at the moment." She laughed, shaking the reins. The slaves increased their pace, turned a sharp corner, and descended back into the King's Road. The darkness of the trench was a blessed respite after the heat.

The underground road quickly disappeared into a tunnel at the base of the volcano. Brophy's eyes had barely adjusted to the darkness before the chariot emerged on the far side.

The volcano's interior was hollow. Its huge central core was a cavernous space, rising two hundred feet to the open sky overhead. All around the walls, arched viewing galleries were carved into the lava stone. Brophy gaped. From floor to ceiling, all the way around, those hundreds of galleries could hold thousands of people. His hand gripped the edge of the chariot as he turned around, looking up and up. Ossamyr's cool hand covered his again.

"This is what a king can do," she said.

He was overwhelmed, humbled by the magnificence. It made the Hall of Windows look like a child's toy house.

"But what about the . . . those houses outside. If you can do this . . ."

"All things have a price, Brophy. Come now, wrench your gaze away. You look like a peasant."

The chariot rolled to a stop. The queen's slaves stood straight, their chests heaving, sweat dribbling down their necks and backs. They had stopped on a sloped roadway that spiraled around the volcano. A waist-high wall blocked Brophy's view. He could not see the bottom of the cavern.

The guards formed two lines behind the chariot, creating a walkway between them. Brophy stepped off and offered his hand. The queen took it and landed lightly next to him.

She led him to the wall and looked over. They were about a third of the way up the immense chamber. Far below, the floor of the cavern was a perfect circle a hundred yards across. The area was full of young men and boys drilling with short swords and spears. The clatter of their weapons and the shouts of their instructors filled the amphitheater.

The majority of the arena floor was filled with nine square blocks of stone. The blocks were immense. Narrow bridges connected some of them so one could cross from square to square in a spiral toward the center.

"There they are, our famous nine squares," Ossamyr said, pausing at the edge of the wall. "Those boys you see down there will start the contest as Beetles. They will come running in from the desert at the top of the arena." She pointed to a notch in the rim of the volcano.

"The first nine that finish the run become Jumping Rats. They compete there." She pointed at the first square, which was covered with a series of bone-white wooden posts. Brophy squinted, trying to decide what they were for.

"That is the first of the Nine Squares," she said, "The last man to cross the square will be eliminated, and the eight that survive become Jackals." She pointed to the next square, which was hollowed out to form a large rounded cavity. "The seven that emerge from the pit continue on to be Crocodiles. Then Scorpion, Serpent, Ape, Falcon, Lion and finally the Phoenix."

Each of the squares had a strange apparatus associated with it, from a chaotic web of deadfall trees to a wooden cage filled with hanging ropes. Brophy's gaze lingered on the wicker tower that stood on the Phoenix square.

"What does the last man have to do there, in the center?" he asked.

"He has to walk through fire until he learns how to fly," she said with that half smile of hers. "Not many succeed."

"They burn the tower?"

"They do."

"That's crazy." He shook his head.

She watched him with narrowed eyes, then continued as if he hadn't spoken. "Nine Squares is held every new moon. A hero is most likely to emerge when the world is darkest. There is often less than one winner a year. We are in a particularly dry spell right now. It has been two years since our last champion. As I said before, the local boys have been a weedy lot. We keep waiting for a man with the divine blood."

"Why do they do it, if so few succeed?" he asked.

"Glory, honor, wealth, power." Ossamyr shrugged. "And because they have to. A cowardly boy can ruin his family for three generations."

"A man should not kill for gold or status," Brophy said. "Death isn't an entertainment."

She smiled, laid one of her cool, brown hands on his cheek. "You are a delight. Do you really believe that? That death isn't entertainment?"

"Of course." He frowned, moving away from her hand.

"You've never done anything you didn't want to because your family expected it?"

"No. Never."

"That is very rare in this world."

Brophy turned to the queen. He could sense something behind her words, but he didn't know what it was.

She suddenly seemed closer, warmer. He had an urge to reach out and touch her.

"You would kill to save Ohndarien?" she asked.

"If I had to. That is not entertainment."

"I think you will have to."

Brophy looked at the men fighting below.

"You know my husband is about to invade Ohndarien," she murmured.

"I saw the army on my way south, but you will never break her walls."

She smiled. "Nothing lasts forever."

"Ohndarien will."

"Wishing won't make it so. Physendrian kings have failed in the past, but Phandir has made powerful allies this time. Ohndarien will fall."

The queen's words sent a chill straight through him.

"What allies?"

Ossamyr shrugged. "The Summer Cities are weak. Phandir could conquer every one of them in his lifetime, but we have no forests to build ships on the east side of the peninsula. We need to send our navy through the locks of Ohndarien, but she has stubbornly refused to give us passage."

"Because you have tried to invade us time and again," Brophy said. "We would be foolish to let Physendrian troops into the city."

"It doesn't matter, the whys and wherefores. She has always refused us passage, and now we must take it. If the walls of Ohndarien fall, so will half the world."

Brophy glanced back at the eight swordsmen standing a few feet away.

"Are you now plotting your escape?" she asked.

Brophy said nothing.

"Don't be stupid, boy. You'll throw your life away for nothing. You have a chance to help Ohndarien here. You have a chance to save your family if you keep your wits about you."

"What do you mean?"

"A champion of Nine Squares is not without power. He earns the love of the Physendrian people, which is no small thing. The rich and poor alike love this game. Champions are royalty. They can request any political position from the king. You could take the governorship of Ohndarien after she is defeated. As long as you paid proper tribute to the crown, you could rule the city as you see fit. You could save the Children of the Seasons. You could save Baelandra."

Brophy's eyes narrowed at the mention of his aunt. He imagined her being led through the Physendrian Gate in chains. A painful heat rose in his chest.

"Ohndarien is ruled by the Council, not a governor," he said.

"Not for long. It is your choice, Brophy. One extra sword defending Ohndarien's walls won't tip the scales, but one sword in this arena could make all the difference."

His mind raced. The queen seemed so confident. Could they really take Ohndarien? Baelandra once saved the city by pulling Krellis to her side. Why would she do that if Ohndarien could have repelled the invasion?

"Why don't you just call off the attack? Some kind of agreement could be reached."

"I cannot stop something I didn't start in the first place. Phandir will invade Ohndarien regardless."

"Then what does it matter what I do?" he growled.

A flash of annoyance crossed her face. "Tread softly, Brophy. The words we speak here are not for everyone's ears."

He turned and looked at her guards, well out of earshot.

"Why are you helping me?" he asked.

She smiled her secret smile. "That's my business."

Brophy shook his head. He needed time. He needed to think.

"Come," she said. "There are some people I want you to meet, then I will leave you alone to make your decision."

"You two," she said, pointing at a pair of Apes. "Come with us. The rest, stay."

Two of the men peeled away from the formation to follow dutifully at their heels.

The queen led them down the spiral walkway to the arena floor. More than fifty young men sweated, cursed, and crossed swords. A few trainers watched the small groups.

"Keep your guard up, you idiot," one of them shouted. "Your shield is slower than your wits."

Brophy watched closely as he approached, noting how differently these men were being taught to fight. One of the instructors stood behind his students with a four-foot wooden rod as they practiced their footwork. A smaller boy stumbled, and the instructor smacked his calf with the stick.

"How many times do I have to tell you to stay on the balls of your feet?" he shouted. The boy's legs were covered with bruises.

Brophy let out a soft breath through his teeth. Good teachers found ways to bring out the best in a soldier. They didn't stab him in his weak spots.

Ossamyr led him to a group of men practicing with spears and shields. Many were older then him, but few matched his height or weight. He felt certain that he could beat any of them.

"They are training for the Scorpion square," Ossamyr murmured.

The boys stopped fighting and dropped to a knee as the queen approached. A heavily scarred, bald man stopped in midyell and looked over. He stood almost as tall as Brophy and easily outweighed him by fifty pounds. The big man hurried over to Ossamyr and dropped immediately to one knee, bowing his head.

"My queen."

"Rise, Vakko. I want you to meet someone."

"Yes, Your Majesty." He stood up, his tree trunk legs rippling. His students rose as well. With a nod from the queen, they went straight back to practicing.

Vakko wore a short, dun-colored wrap that looked like a skirt. All of the trainers and students wore the same.

"Vakko, this is Brophy; he might try his hand at Nine Squares."

Vakko squinted at him. "Farad?"

"Ohndarien." Brophy corrected him.

Vakko grunted, and his expression soured. "Ohndariens are soft," he growled. "You sure you want to sponsor him?"

"I have a premonition," she said.

"And you want me to train him?"

"If you think he is worthy."

Vakko grunted.

"Come," the queen said. "Let us discuss it."

Ossamyr led the trainer away, and Brophy was left to watch some of the contestant hopefuls practice. They worked with strangely shaped shields and mock spears. A boy roughly Brophy's age was using the wrong foot stance. Brophy drifted over to the young man.

"You might try pointing your toes toward your opponent," he suggested.

The two combatants stopped, looking at him hesitantly. Both of them glanced at Vakko before turning back to Brophy.

"It feels awkward at first," he told them, "but it will give you more speed and power in the spear thrust."

One of the boys turned his feet forward. He was tall and lanky with long hair tied back behind his head in an unruly tail. The boy's height and long arms gave him a nice reach, but he had no strength behind his strikes. He leaned back and forth in his new stance and grimaced. "With my feet like this, I can't pivot from side to side very well."

"True. But your attacker has a spear. He's coming from the front. You don't need to pivot like you would against a sword, which can come from either side. If you just—"

Vakko's snort of contempt cut Brophy off in midsentence. He stumped over to the three of them. "I think you ought to shut up if you don't know what you're talking about," he growled.

Brophy narrowed his eyes. "I know what I'm talking about."

"That so? Looks like you lost your last fight with a scorpion."

Vakko's students laughed. Other nearby groups stopped their exercises and looked over. They lowered their spears and drew closer.

"I was just making a suggestion," Brophy said.

"All right, boy. Show us."

Vakko snatched the shield and spear from one of the nearby students and tossed them to Brophy. Brophy suppressed a smile as he donned the equipment.

This he understood. He had loved weapons since Bae gave him his first sword. He had actually slept with it for a month. He loved its sleek perfection, its delicate strength. A disciplined swordsman could best a half dozen black-hearted brawlers. Aunt Bae said that weapons in the right hands were the guardians of civilization. Escaping from prisons and battling scorpions was foreign to Brophy, but sparring with spears was not. He would show this arrogant trainer what an Ohndarien could do.

Brophy's hand was still weak, but he could manage a light spear. As he donned the claw-shaped shield, he noticed a lever on the inside and squeezed it. The pincers of the claw snapped together and slowly drew apart again. He smiled. A clever contraption, one could conceivably catch a spear or a shield with the mechanism, but it seemed awkward. Brophy's instructors had always stressed that simplicity was best. Better to be quick, deflect a blow, and get under someone's guard. Still, he would have to stay alert for the tricks that Vakko would certainly know.

The spear was a standard practice weapon. The tip was blunted, but it could still injure if the attacker went for the throat or face. Eyes were sometimes lost on the practice field.

Once Brophy had the shield in place, he squared off against the tall, lanky boy. The two circled each other. Brophy let his opponent attack a couple of times. He was slow and a little bit timid. Brophy could get past his guard easily with a basic feint, but there was no need to embarrass the kid when he was only learning.

Using the feet-forward technique, Brophy smashed his spear against the kid's shield twice in quick succession, knocking him off-balance. The lanky boy stumbled back, hastily readjusting his shield.

Brophy heard a scuffle of feet behind him. He glanced over his shoulder and saw the rest of the boys closing in, shields raised, spears ready. He spun, trying to keep his back away from them, but he opened himself to his original opponent.

The first spear hit him in the small of his back. He gasped and jumped away, catching the next strike on his shield and dodging the third, but there were too many of them. All six students converged, jabbing. Spears punched into his thighs, his back, his shoulders. Brophy went down under the flurry.

"Enough!" Vakko yelled. The ring of boys backed up as he marched forward. Brophy slowly struggled to his feet, breathing hard. He glared at Vakko.

"Had enough, Pointy Toes?"

"You didn't have to do that. I was just trying to teach him something."

"No, I was teaching you something. In Nine Squares, Scorpions fight against five opponents at once. A good defense wins the day, not a good offense." Vakko sneered. "Which is why we all fight with our back foot out to the side."

"I didn't know that," Brophy said.

"Which is why you should shut up and learn."

Brophy stifled an angry retort.

"Vakko," Ossamyr's quiet voice broke the uncomfortable silence. "Do you think he is worthy of my favor?"

Vakko shrugged. "You want him to enter next month?"

"Yes."

"Then no. He's the same age as these sparrows here." He tipped his head at his group of students. "He won't even make Jumping Rat."

Brophy clenched his teeth in silence.

"He's got good height and weight for his age. He's strong. I'll give him that. And Ohndariens are usually fleet of foot with all that senseless wall running. But, in the end, the thickness of a man's blood is what makes him a champion. I've seen some of the fastest boys bleed thin and quit early. No way to know how hard a man's heart pumps until you cut him a few times." Vakko looked Brophy up and down. The scarred veteran put his fists on his hips. "Your boy knows how to hate." He conceded. "Slow and hot. I'll give him that. But one month? No. Give me six, and he'll be ready," he said, then added, "If he can keep his mouth shut. I can't stand braggarts."

"I don't care about this barbaric game!" Brophy exploded. He turned to Ossamyr. "And I wouldn't listen to that man if I did. He has nothing to teach me that I don't already know."

Vakko's huge chest swelled, and he glared at Brophy.

Ossamyr smiled, cold and imperious.

"You think you can defeat Vakko?" she asked.

Brophy looked at the massive veteran. For a moment, he regretted his rash words, but he wasn't about to back down.

"I know I can."

"I'd like to see that," she murmured.

"One-on-one? Or is he going to cheat again?" Brophy asked, flicking a gaze at Vakko. The man chuckled.

"One-on-one," Ossamyr said. She glanced at Vakko.

"Shall I tie one hand behind my back?" he growled.

"I think not. If you are to teach him, he must learn." She took a few steps back, standing in front of her two guards. "To first blood then."

Vakko grinned, showing stained teeth.

Brophy's heart thundered in his chest, but he strove to calm himself. Fear had no place in battle.

Two students brought Vakko and Brophy real spears. Brophy spun his weapon in hand, testing the balance. He shifted it from one hand to the other and inspected the tip. They were broad-headed weapons, like boar spears, except they were only sharp for the first inch. A thick ring was forged behind the tip to prevent the weapon from penetrating farther. They were designed to wound, not kill, but with enough force it wouldn't matter.

The arena fell silent. The other students and trainers slowly gathered around to watch.

The two men squared off and circled. Brophy kept his feet pointed forward and was pleased to note that Vakko did the same. The older man threw a pair of quick strikes, and Brophy lulled him with awkward deflections. After a few passes, he had the man's mettle, but Brophy had been trained to be cautious. He circled and flicked his spear out a few more times to be sure.

Vakko's left leg was weaker than his right, it made him slow to retreat.

The Nine Squares teacher launched another strike and Brophy made his move. He deflected the attack with his shield, feinting a short strike at his opponent's shin. Vakko's shield went low, and Brophy's true strike went high, catching the trainer on the shoulder. His hit was pinpoint accurate. He punctured the skin, but went no deeper. A spurt of blood flecked Brophy's spearhead and he drew back. Vakko would have another scar, but it would heal in a week.

A trickle of blood ran down the trainer's naked chest. Vakko stared at his arm. The crowd of students hooted in approval.

"Your shield is slower than your wits," one of them shouted.

"Should have stayed on the balls of your feet," another called out.

The older man stared at Brophy, his face red. He roared and charged.

Vakko jabbed his spear high and low, making vicious strikes for the shins, for the eyes, for anything he could get.

Brophy blocked the spear again and again, spinning his shield and shifting his feet. The futile clangs echoed through the arena. Vakko began to shout, his face red as he pursued. Brophy backed up, slowly giving ground and wearing the other man down. He saw several opportunities to counterattack, but he had lost his stomach for this fight. He'd already made his point.

With a final roar, Vakko threw his spear and shield away. Brophy lowered his weapons, but didn't let them go. Vakko turned and stalked from the arena, knocking aside an unfortunate boy who got in his way.

"Should have tied an arm behind your back," one of the boys called after him.

The students continued throwing hoots and catcalls at the trainer's back. Ossamyr remained quiet, but her eyes twinkled as though she and Brophy shared an intimate secret.

Brophy felt ill. He stared after Vakko for a long moment, then took off his shield. He went to the wooden rack and carefully put away the weapons.

"I see a champion in you, Brophy, just waiting to get out," the queen said, when he walked back to her.

The rest of the students and trainers slowly drifted back to their workouts.

"I'm done with this. Fighting isn't a game." He looked off the way Vakko had gone.

The queen pursed her lips. "Come," she said. "High Sun is nearly upon us. It's time for you to return to your room."

BROPHY SLEPT lightly that night and awoke when he heard a shuffled step. He opened his eyes, but didn't move at first. Someone was in his room. Moonlight shone through the chimney overhead, reflecting off the metal panes and giving the room a ghostly glow. Slowly, so as not to move the bed, he looked toward the sound. A fully cloaked and hooded figure stood in front of the desk.

Ossamyr pushed back the white cowl. She remained where she was, and they watched each other in the half-light.

"Have you been reconsidering your decision?" she asked softly.

"No," he lied. He jumped lightly from the bed, stopped its swing with his hand. The chains clinked lightly.

Ossamyr's eyes were depthless in the scant moonlight. Her white cloak shone like a pearl.

"I told my husband that Scythe recruited you to be my new Champion. He will only tolerate your presence as long as you make me—and therefore him—look good."

"He will kill me if I don't fight?"

"You are an indulgence he is allowing me for the time being. That is all I can say."

"How does Scythe know the king? Is he a spy?"

"Yes. Although I assume he spies on us as much as for us."

"You don't trust the man?"

"Of course not."

"Neither do I."

"You realize that Scythe asked me to throw you into Nine Squares."

"I guessed as much. Does he expect me to become ruthless like him? Is that why?"

"I didn't ask. I owed him a favor, and I will honor his request."

"Why? What is a Kherish cutthroat to you?"

Ossamyr's eyes narrowed, and Brophy knew he'd crossed the line.

"I'm sorry, my lady," he said.

"No," she said, thoughtful. "I will answer your question. Scythe gave me advice once, when I desperately needed it."

"That's all, advice?"

"And he carried my favor in the arena."

"Scythe fought in Nine Squares?"

"Yes."

"Was he any good?"

"Better than most. His success brought me a certain prominence in Phandir's court. I took that small bit of attention and parlayed it into a marriage proposal."

"Parlayed? You mean fell in love?"

She laughed. "Of course, yes. That is what I mean. I fell in love with the King of Physendria. He swept me away, and we have lived happily ever since. Isn't that the way the story goes?"

Brophy frowned. "I'm sorry, my lady. I didn't mean to presume."

Ossamyr paused, and they watched one another for a long moment. Finally, she reached up to brush a lock of his blond hair out of his face. "Oh, to see the world with innocent eyes."

Brophy turned away. "What advice did Scythe give you?"

The queen walked to the bed and sat down. She scooted to the center of the platform and crossed her legs. Her shimmering white robe cascaded over her knees, pooling onto the bed. When she finally spoke, her voice sounded different, younger and softer than before.

"I was not born into the best of families. My father picked the wrong business partners and lost a great deal of money. He owed the king more than he could pay, and my mother, siblings, and I were in danger of being sold as slaves."

Brophy knelt with his elbows on the edge of the bed, staring up at her.

"When I came of age, my family sold the last of our assets to buy the clothes and jewelry that would make me presentable at court. A successful marriage was the only chance my family had. I failed. I was a shy and bitter child and squandered my chances in sullen silence."

The queen's voice quavered once, but other than that she betrayed no emotion.

"I received a second chance when a small man from Kherif asked to carry my favor in Nine Squares. I had been sponsoring my oldest brother, but he was a timid boy, never anything more than a Beetle. Scythe's success brought me invitations to royal functions, and I put his good advice to use."

"What did he say?" Brophy asked.

"He told me to crawl, he told me to kill, he told me to fuck, to lie, to cheat, to steal. He told me to do whatever I had to do to make my way in this world." Ossamyr clenched her jaw and turned her face away. Her thin hands curled into fists. Brophy put his hand on her knee. She looked down, then covered his hand with her slender fingers.

"It worked," she said. "I did everything he told me. I worked my way into the king's bed. I saved my family. And now I am a queen, ruler of all that I see."

Brophy climbed onto the swinging platform. She took his hand.

"You are the first person I ever told that to," she said in a quiet voice. "I don't usually say such things." She stopped, shook her head. Her black hair fell across her cheeks. "Even a queen can dream." Slowly, her dark eyes found his. She undid the golden phoenix clasp at her throat. The gossamer cloak slipped off one shoulder. She was naked underneath.

Brophy opened his mouth, then shut it.

"Do you understand?" she whispered.

"I . . ." Brophy swallowed.

"Will you make me say it?" she whispered. "Am I not flesh and blood?"

With a shaky hand, he touched her cheek. She pulled him forward. He kissed her, and she wrapped her arms around the back of his neck, slid her legs around his waist.

"Fill me with fire again," she breathed. "I am so cold . . ."

HEN THE LIGHT of morning reflected through the underground room, Ossamyr was gone. Brophy drew a deep breath and rolled to one side. The feather blanket rustled, and the chains of his bed creaked. He closed his eyes again. Of course she was gone. She could not stay. She was the queen.

The queen . . .

He remembered the thrill he felt as her tanned arms slid around him, her skin warm against his chest. He could taste the salt from her sweat. The faint, mesmerizing scent of her lingered. Her breath smelled of mint and something else he could not place.

This was what Shara did. By the Seasons, no wonder Zelani were so highly prized if they could harness that incredible feeling and use it.

Brophy lay back on the bed and relived the moments in his mind. He saw Ossamyr's black hair falling in her face as she hovered above him. Her breasts shifted as she moved with him. He heard her gasp quietly in pleasure.

With a frown, he sat up and jumped from the bed. He had work to do. He still couldn't trust the queen. She was using him. As much as he enjoyed being used, he couldn't let it go on for too long. Ossamyr was playing a game, and he didn't know the rules. Yet.

It looked like, for the moment, he could do more good here in Physen than back in Ohndarien. If the king wanted passage through the locks, perhaps Brophy could arrange a compromise. If he joined their bloody game, he might gain enough influence to save Ohndarien from slavery.

Last night, after their lovemaking, he had promised the queen he would compete. What was done was done. If Baelandra held the walls, Brophy's sacrifice would go unnoticed, but if Ohndarien fell, he might have power to help.

His plans to sneak into the city and take the Test of the Stone would have to wait. Brophy would deal with Nine Squares before Krellis.

He went to the wardrobe and quickly dressed. The door to his room stood ajar. Ossamyr had kept her promise. If he was committed to the games, he was free to roam the city.

Taking a deep breath, he pulled the thick, wooden door open. One of the Ape guards stood on the other side. As tall as Brophy and twice as thick, the huge soldier gave him a glance, then continued to stare straight ahead. The Apes were elite swordsmen, the sixth echelon of the Physendrian military. Only Falcon officers and Lion generals outranked them. And, of course, the king and queen.

He slipped past the man, leaving the door to his room open. The guard paused long enough for Brophy to get two steps ahead, then followed. Brophy stopped. The guard stopped. Brophy backed up. The guard backed up. Shaking his head, Brophy continued.

There weren't many people in the hall. Brophy passed a few Physendrians, richly dressed in feathers and silver, some in gold. A few gave him curious looks, but none paused to talk.

He wandered the halls, trying to remember all the twists and turns. He wanted to be able to find his way out if need be. Along the way, he opened every door he could. Most were locked, but he poked his head into a few rooms. He found a vacant dining hall, a library, a few empty bedrooms, and finally someone's study.

The door was wide-open. He gave the room a cursory glance and was about to move on when he noticed a huge diorama meticulously laid out on a table. Moving closer, he realized the model was Ohndarien. The guard followed silently.

Ohndarien's walls, her locks, her bay, even the Spire was crafted in meticulous detail. Ruffled blue silk represented the Great Ocean to the west and the Summer Sea to the east. Tiny pieces of blue marble represented the houses within. It was beautiful and chilling. It wasn't some craftsman's hobby. This was a war map.

Hundreds of miniature Physendrian soldiers in red massed at the base of the Water Wall. Hundreds of miniature Farad soldiers in brown massed at the base of the Quarry Wall. A vast fleet of blue ships from the west swarmed at the Windmill Wall. The tiny models bore three-pointed stars on their sails, the symbol of the Ohohhim Empire.

Phandir was going to attack Ohndarien, with armies from the north and south and a fleet from the west. It would work. It was the only plan that could. The city could withstand a siege forever unless they were surrounded on all sides.

How had Phandir convinced Faradan? Physendrians hated Farads more than they hated Ohndariens. Why would they join forces?

But Brophy knew the answer. Because they could win. With Ohohhom's help, the two countries could finally overrun Ohndarien and take her for their own. They could do together what they had never been able to do apart.

A man entered the room from a side door, a cape of red-and-gold feathers draped from his shoulders to the floor. The man wore golden armbands emblazoned with a fiery bird. He seemed strangely familiar, his auburn hair curled down to his shoulders, and his dark eyes struck a chord in Brophy. Add a beard, darken the hair, and the man could have been Krellis.

This giant had to be Phandir, King of Physendria.

Brophy froze. An image leapt to his mind of Ossamyr's naked body straddling the king, pushing against him as she pushed against Brophy.

"Well," Phandir boomed, smiling so wide that he showed white teeth. "This is an unexpected surprise. I don't usually get guests so early. It's my planning time, you see."

In one quick motion, the Ape drew his sword and hit Brophy in the back of the legs with the flat of the blade. He crashed to his knees.

"Kneel before your king!" the Ape roared.

Brophy spun about and leapt to his feet. The Ape brought his sword under Brophy's chin, but he jumped back, putting the diorama between them. Gritting his teeth, the Ape followed.

Phandir laughed. "I suggest you listen to him. He'll kill you if you don't."

The Ape stepped between Brophy and the king. Brophy glanced at the open door leading back to the hall, but he wasn't sure he would make it.

"Kneel!" the Ape repeated.

Hesitating a moment, Brophy descended to one knee. As soon as he did, the guard closed the distance between them and whacked him on the back with the flat of the blade. "Kiss the hem of your king's robe."

Brophy did as he was told, astounded by the entire show. Was this how they commanded respect in Physendria? At the end of a sword? It was humiliating. Did they really think loyalty could be bought by such a thing?

"Well done, boy," Phandir said, sounding eerily like Krellis. "Self-preservation is a fine quality." He helped Brophy to his feet.

Brophy longed to have a weapon in his hand. One quick slash, and the whole war could be over. If they had been alone, Brophy might have grabbed the king's sword, but with the hulking guard right behind him, he had no hope.

"Come on, let's take a walk," Phandir said.

Having no choice, Brophy followed. He felt a trickle of blood on the back of his thigh where the Ape's sword had struck. The guard remained two steps behind them, as impassive as before. It made Brophy nervous to have the hulking warrior at his back. It had been a long time since he'd been struck like that. His anger lingered, keeping him on edge.

The king led him across the room to a stairway that spiraled upward through solid rock. As they climbed, Brophy finally found his tongue.

"Thank you for your hospitality, my lord," he said, not sure how to approach this man. There was too much he didn't know about King Phandir.

"Ah, that. Yes. Well it wasn't my idea, I must confess," he said with a jovial laugh. "You're either a spy or a criminal. I ought to have you killed, really." He looked over his flame-feathered shoulder, smiling. "But Ossamyr has taken a liking to you." He sighed melodramatically. "And I'm a fool for love, truth be known. I can deny her nothing. She is determined to have another young man carry her favor to victory in Nine Squares. Nothing to be done about it. The woman is crazy for the contest. No one has won at Nine Squares for twenty months. Quwrence was the last champion, and he bore Helliua's favor, not Ossamyr's."

They reached the top of the stairs and stepped into the open air atop a tower overlooking all of Physen. For the first time, Brophy got some perspective on the city as a whole. The Physendrian capital was built on a dry plateau above a fertile valley next to the river Gesphyn. The sprawling structures, both ramshackle and stout, seemed to continue forever. The city was immense, much larger than Ohndarien. It extended from the ocean to the imposing volcano of the Nine Squares arena in the distance.

"Helliua is the queen's cousin, you see, and Ossamyr's mad with jealousy. Won't rest until she has the next champion. She thinks that's you." Phandir looked Brophy up and down. "I can't say why she believes that. I told her you won't make it past the crocs." He shrugged. "But the woman has a good eye. She's backed a champion four times. That's more than any person in an age, so maybe she knows something I don't."

Phandir clapped Brophy on the back as if they were old friends. "Have a look, young man," he said. "This will be the only chance you get to see Physen from such a height. See there? That's where our soldiers train. That white speck there is The Tooth, the gate to our Wet Cells. And there." He pointed. "And there and there are the three largest markets. Most of the goods in Physen are traded there." He winked. "That doesn't count the black markets, of course. And over there are the winches." He pointed to the southern edge of the plateau. Huge trusses supporting pulley wheels clung to the side of the cliff. The wheels moved immense baskets up and down between the plateau and verdant river valley far below. The lush green riverbank was a stark contrast to the bone-dry city on the cliffs.

"Why don't you live down there?" Brophy asked.

Phandir chuckled. "Spoken like a true Ohndarien, boy. Why waste good farmland by putting someone's house on it? Look on the far side of the river. See that?"

A smaller group of buildings clung to the cliff on the far side, huddled like a band of decrepit gypsies. Brophy squinted. He couldn't be sure, but they looked like ruins.

"That's Sitha. The Old City. King Phy I razed his father's capital and built Physen on this side of the river. Sitha's haunted now. You can hear the dead king singing songs of revenge when the moon is black."

Brophy looked up at Phandir, trying to decide if he was serious. Phandir smiled at him, showing his white teeth again.

"So, boy, tell me. How do you think you're going to fare against our native lads in the dreaded Nine Squares?"

"I'll do my best."

Phandir laughed.

"Best do better than your best. Nine Squares isn't like jogging around a wall." He shook his head, seemingly amused. "Ossamyr favors you, but she changes her friends with the wind. Remember that. No man knows the mind of a woman. The only way to keep her attention is to win." Phandir looked Brophy up and down. "And you have the look of a loser. I despise the queen's losers even more than I despise her pet champions. I don't know why she bothers with you. I should just kill you and be done with it."

The last was spoken with such geniality that Brophy paused, wondering if he had heard it right. "I'm good at contests," he said.

Phandir laughed. "I'm sure. Yes, you seem a very smart young man. Well, tell the other players that. If you convince them that you're *good at contests*, maybe they'll fall over on their backs for you."

Brophy reddened. He had to steer the conversation back to the invasion somehow.

"I wanted to ask about that model I saw in your study," he said.

Phandir waved his hand, still smiling. "It's a toy, nothing more. Go on now, boy. I have work. If I find you snooping in my rooms again, I'll have you whipped. And beaten. And buggered." He laughed.

Before Brophy could respond, the Ape clubbed the back of his knees with his sword again.

"Kneel before your king!" the guard bellowed.

Clenching his teeth, Brophy put his lips to the hem of king's feathered robe.

BAELANDRA STOOD on her balcony looking over the bay. To a casual observer, she was enjoying the morning sunlight, the breeze blowing off the water, but Baelandra's mind was boiling with doubt and fear.

She watched as Lawdon deftly maneuvered her boat through the early-morning water traffic toward the pier. The young waterbug had become indispensable. The four Sisters could not have coordinated their plans without her.

Lawdon dropped sail and pulled up to the dock directly opposite Jayden's house. The Sister of Spring was the oldest of the four, and Baelandra wanted her closest to the boat if there were problems. The four Sisters' homes stood in a row. Baelandra lived on the far left, followed by Hazel, Jayden, and Vallia on the far right.

Baelandra glanced up the street. In addition to placing the guards in front of their houses, Krellis had assigned a squad of men to watch Donovan's Bridge. Anyone moving on or off the island was stopped and searched. She could see people complaining, arguing with the guards, but that was all they were doing. So far.

The Sister of Autumn ran her fingers through her long, windblown hair. So much could go wrong with their escape plan. Timing was critical. If there were any delays, they would be caught. Krellis would not give them a second chance.

Lawdon made a long show of tying up her boat.

Despite the churning in her stomach, Baelandra smiled. Lawdon had a future as an actress, but that young woman had a future as many things if she wished. She was smart, loyal, and full of courage. The waterbug had already earned far more than two hundred silver stars.

Baelandra heard the creak of the cart, right on time. She glanced casually down to her right. Hazel's niece, Quinn, had been flirting with the guards in front of her aunt's house for the past three days. Krellis's men resisted at first, but it was amazing how stupid men became with a pretty girl around.

The men have their spears and swords, Baelandra thought, but some weapons cannot be taken away.

Hazel's guards had come to expect a kind word, a flirtatious glance, and a free pastry every morning. Today there would be more than honey in Quinn's fruit tarts.

The girl's giggle floated up the street. Baelandra took a deep breath of the sea air. Soon.

As if reading her thoughts, Lawdon tied a red scarf around her mast. Baelandra retreated into the bedroom and donned the crude clay mask and mirrored cloak Scythe had left for her. After checking her reflection in the mirror, she frowned. The cloak hung awkwardly off her slender shoulders. The disguise wouldn't hold up under close scrutiny, but she hoped no one would get that close.

She checked the pouch of jewelry, tied securely to her belt, and the thin dagger strapped to her forearm. Wealth came in handy more often than a good blade, but Baelandra was a Sister of Autumn, a descendant of J'Qulin the Sly. Given the choice, she would take the blade every time.

Leaving the room, she headed for the back stairs. There were no guards in the house. Krellis was still courteous enough to keep his dogs outside. She had plenty of time. The sap of the Snoring Tree took a few minutes to take effect. If she emerged too late, it would be inconvenient; If she arrived early, it would be catastrophic.

Quietly, she padded down the stairs and peered around the corner before entering the kitchen. Nothing stirred, no more than a whisper of air.

She hurried through the door of the dry pantry and searched through the thin coating of dust and flour on the wall until she found the tiny gemstone. Resting a finger lightly upon it, Bae touched the heartstone between her breasts.

A jolt of energy shot through her, and the mechanism behind the pantry wall gave a distinctive click. She allowed herself a brief smile. After 350 years, the locks made by Master Coelho still worked perfectly. The heavy door pivoted inward, and Baelandra slid through the opening.

A wall of stone blocked her way.

Her heart started pounding as she pushed on it. The barrier was brand-new. The mortar between the gray stones was still tacky, but the wall was solid. When had Krellis done it? There must have been workmen in the alley for days and she'd never noticed.

For a moment, she considered battering down the wall with a bench or soup cauldron, but she held herself in check. She needed to think through this calmly, time was running out.

She hid the disguise in the pantry and hurried toward the front door. There was only one choice left to her. The drugged guards could be discovered at any moment, and the other Sisters wouldn't move without her. She couldn't be late.

Baelandra hurried across the foyer and opened her front door. She calmed her breathing as she started across the lawn toward her front gate. Krellis's guards watched her with cautious interest as she approached, crossing their spears in front of her.

"We can't let you pass, Sister."

Never breaking stride, she ducked her head and walked right under them. "The cook is sick, I'm just going to the market for a few things."

One of the men grabbed her arm and yanked her back into the garden.

"You're not going anywhere," growled the bear-shaped man with the long beard, obviously from Faradan. His arms were covered with curly black hair, and he sweated profusely in the morning sun.

The other man had a sparse blond mustache and looked like he was from one of the Summer Cities.

"You're making a scene," she whispered, giving a meaningful nod at a few early-morning passersby who noticed the conflict.

The Farad was unfazed. His dark eyes never left her. "I don't care. Get back in that house."

She straightened her dress and continued forward. "I will not be a prisoner in my home. If you want to stop me, you'll have to kill me."

She slipped between them, and the Summerman stabbed her with a spear. She gasped, touched her ribs, and her fingers came away flecked with blood. It was a scratch, but she was still shocked. Her own soldiers, in her own city. She hadn't believed they'd really do it.

"We've orders to kill you if we need to," the Farad rumbled, but it was the little man's spear that had blood on the tip. His fuzzy lip curled into a smile.

"This is boring duty, Sister," the Summerman said. "Believe me, we'll get out of it any way we can."

A thin trickle of sweat ran down the inside of her shawl. There were only a few minutes left. Reaching a bloody hand into her cloak, she pulled out her pouch of jewelry.

"I can pay you," she whispered. Her hands shook as she pulled open the bag, revealing the glittering gems inside.

The men glanced at the pouch, then at each other.

"This is just the beginning," she promised. "I can get you more. Much more."

The Farad shook his head. "If we took that, we wouldn't live to spend it," he said.

"No, no, you could. I have friends. I could get you out of the city. I could take you anywhere."

The big man's eyes narrowed. "I'm not going to tell you again. Get back in the house before I kill you." He lifted his spear and set the razor tip underneath her chin.

"Please . . ." she said, stepping away from the spear. She began crying. "Please. You must . . ." She sobbed, holding the jewels up. "You must." The pouch fell from her shaking hands.

The Farad looked down as silver and jewels clattered to the cobblestoned walkway.

Before he could look up, Bae whipped the blade from her sleeve and buried it in his eye.

The other man didn't have time to even raise his weapon. She took a quick step backward and spun, slicing his throat from ear to ear.

The Summerman dropped his spear and grabbed at his neck. His knees buckled, and he fell on top of his partner. She left the two men flailing in their death throes, smearing blood and jewels across the cobblestones.

Baelandra sprinted for the boat, her dagger gripped tightly in her hand. As she reached Hazel's house, the chubby Sister of Summer ducked through the front gate. Her two guards lay sprawled senseless on the ground.

Thank the Seasons, Baelandra thought. It's working.

The two guards at Jayden's gate cried out and rushed to intercept them. In their haste, they didn't notice the pretty girl with the cart of pastries. Quinn shoved her cart with all her might, and the two guards went down in a tumble of pastries and spears. The Sisters rushed past them.

Baelandra noticed Vallia running along the top of her garden wall. Her front gate faced the side street, shielding her from the guards at the Sister of Winter's gate. The tall woman leapt from the wall, plummeting twenty feet into a hedge just across from the wharf.

"Go on!" Baelandra shouted to Hazel. She ran past the boat to help Vallia. The Sister of Winter was stunned, with a cut on her forehead that painted half of her face red, but she shook off the pain and let Baelandra pull her into a loping jog.

Hazel had already settled herself into Lawdon's boat. Pulling Vallia behind her, Baelandra jumped in, rocking the tiny craft. The waterbug compensated without a thought. She had the sails up and the boat was straining against the line that kept them tied to the dock. Lawdon had a dagger in hand, ready to cut the line. She looked at Baelandra, silently asking for permission.

"Where's Jayden!?" Baelandra asked, craning her neck around to look for the older Sister.

Vallia's guards rounded the corner and shouted at them. One of them stopped to throw his spear.

"Get down!" Baelandra shouted, shoving Hazel out of the way. The spear thudded next to them, pinning Baelandra's shawl to the side of the boat.

The guards tangled in Quinn's cart were back on their feet, racing toward them.

"Should I cut it?" Lawdon asked.

"No!" Baelandra shouted. "Where is she?"

"I'm here," croaked a quiet voice from behind her.

"Jayden?" Baelandra spun around, glanced down. The Sister of Spring clung to the side of the boat with her skinny arms.

"Cut it!" Baelandra shouted, grabbing the old woman by the back of her vest and hauling her aboard.

Lawdon slashed the rope and they shot forward like a leaping horse.

One of the guards leapt from the dock and landed on the small boat. The man quickly caught his balance and drew his sword.

Lawdon jammed the rudder to one side. The tiny craft turned, and the boom swung from left to right, slamming into the guard. He flailed as he went over the edge and disappeared into the water.

They sailed quickly into the harbor. The three remaining guards stared at them from the edge of the dock.

Lawdon stood up, pulled down her pants, and wiggled her ass at them.

Hazel patted the girl on the arm. "Sit, child, no need for that." But she was smiling.

The three soldiers sprinted toward Donovan's Bridge a couple hundred yards away.

"They'll never catch us," Lawdon said, retying her pants. "They won't even get close."

The wind was at their back and Lawdon steered them directly toward the Night Market.

"Jayden, are you all right?" Baelandra asked, helping the Sister of Spring to a seat.

The wrinkled woman pushed her away. "Of course I am, I'm not that old."

Hazel giggled. She seemed composed now that she had regained her breath. Despite the wind pushing her sunny hair all around, she looked as if she were entertaining the other three Sisters in her drawing room. "How did you get in the water?"

"My family built this city," Jayden said, wringing out her shirt. "We certainly know where the sewers go."

Hazel wrinkled her nose and shook her head.

Vallia smirked, but said nothing as always.

Lawdon cut across the bay to the Night Market. Pulling alongside the dock, she jumped out and held the boat steady. The four Sisters helped each other onto the pier.

Lawdon led the way across the dock and up the stairs to the Night Market. The Sisters ran through the empty streets. A group of soldiers shouted at them from the bridge, demanding that they stop. Baelandra grabbed Jayden under the armpit and practically carried the old woman toward the Wheel. They hit the stairs at a dead sprint. Hazel tripped and fell to her face. Vallia helped the heavy woman to her feet, and they kept running.

They took the stairs as fast as they could, losing sight of the guards as they curved around to the north side of the Wheel. Running ever upward, they circled three-quarters of the way around. Hazel was panting uncontrollably. Jayden clung to Baelandra with one hand and held her chest with the other. Lawdon hung back, clutching her seaman's dagger.

"Keep running," Baelandra said. "We're almost there."

"They're gaining!" Lawdon shouted. Baelandra looked back. The guards appeared around the corner.

"Enough!" she said, drawing her dagger and facing the guards. The other three Sisters slowed to a stop, breathing hard. Lawdon hovered at Baelandra's side, her fist clenched around her dagger handle.

Panting and angry, the guards slowly closed the distance between them.

"I already killed two men today," Baelandra said. "I don't mind killing a few more."

A young officer raised a hand, stopping his men. They held back like restless hounds, eyes baleful.

"Sister of Autumn, put down your blade," the officer said.

"No. Not this time."

"You can't win," he said in a calm, rational voice. "Commander Heller has ten men at the top of the stairs guarding the Heart. You are trapped."

"Actually, Heller had eight men," Scythe's voice broke the silence. He appeared around the curve of the stairway, descending on light feet, a bloody sword in each hand. "Now he has none."

Baelandra smiled as Scythe walked past the panting Sisters and placed himself between them and the guards.

"Perfect timing, as usual," Baelandra said.

"You deserve nothing less," the small man replied.

"Scythe?" the leader of the guards said, incredulous.

"Jarll."

"I didn't know you were still here."

"And I thought your five years were over and you'd left Ohndarien." Scythe's dark eyes glinted. "Yet here you are with a sword in your hand. How does a broken oath taste in the back of your throat?"

Jarll darkened, a frown growing beneath his mustache. "Stand aside," he said, "or you will be killed."

Scythe smiled a thin smile. "Somehow, I doubt that."

"Enough chatter!" Jarll's hand cut the air. "We'll take him in a rush. On three."

"I wouldn't do that if I were you." Scythe looked purposefully to the cliff above the guards.

A crowd of Ohndariens lined the edge of the Wheel, looking down at the guards. Merchants, sailors, dock rats, and whores all stood together with makeshift weapons at the ready.

"I brought some friends."

BAELANDRA URGED the other Sisters to continue up the stairs. Krellis's red-faced guards stayed where they were, pinned under the cold gazes of Scythe and the crowd of Ohndariens atop the Wheel.

"You're making a mistake, Sister," Jarll said. "If I have to return with more men, many of these people will die."

A dozen steps up, Baelandra paused and turned to him. "Tell Krellis we will be in the Heart. He is welcome to visit us there anytime, if he has the courage."

"He will tear your Heart to pieces."

Too late, she thought and began climbing again. Scythe followed her silently, but Jarll's voice stopped them both one last time.

"Scythe!" he snarled.

Scythe paused, and Baelandra waited for him.

"You can't stay cooped up in that hole forever. You'll have to leave sometime, and when you do, I'll be waiting."

Scythe smiled. "Be sure to catch me in a dark alley, when the moon is thin. Bring Krellis, if you like." His eyes glittered.

"Enough," Baelandra whispered. "We must leave."

Without a word, he turned and followed her up the stairs. The soldiers did not follow.

At the top of the plateau, the mob of Ohndariens welcomed their Sisters. As she looked at their faces, Baelandra felt a surge of pride she hadn't known in years.

A tall, slight man with salt-and-pepper hair and a fiery gaze stepped to the forefront of the mob. "Lady J'Qulin," the man said, bending a knee. "The Lightning Swords have returned. We are yours to command."

A lump caught in Baelandra's throat at the mention of the House of Autumn's legendary warriors. The slender man knelt before her. She knew him. Faedellin was the steward at her favorite restaurant, the Midnight Jewel.

"Thank you, my friend," she said, grabbing his hands and pulling him back to his feet.

The man had the body of a waiter, but the eyes of a warrior. His profile looked chillingly like a painting of the great J'Qulin, the original leader of the Lightning Swords. The men and women behind him were just the same, fiercely willing and woefully unprepared. They were silversmiths, dock rats, young mothers, carpenters, and stonemasons. They were not warriors.

With a few words, she could turn this mob into a militia. The thought of her beloved Ohndarien in Krellis's hands made her guts twist. But this was not the moment. She would only be leading these brave lambs to the slaughter if she pitted them against trained soldiers. These people had just saved her life; now she must save theirs.

"Hear me, loyal Ohndariens!"

They quieted almost immediately. The morning sun lit their features.

"You have done your city a great service this day. You have rallied to the protection of the whole and fought without spilling a single drop of blood. My Sisters and I are grateful. You have lifted our hearts, and we cannot thank you enough."

Several voices shouted assent, raising their spears, their knives.

"Root the foreigner out of his house!" the host of the Midnight Jewel shouted.

"Toss him off the walls!" said another.

The swell of agreement rose. Baelandra raised her hands, and the crowd quieted again. Krellis would return with more soldiers soon. A confrontation could easily turn into useless bloodshed.

"The Lightning Swords are reborn," she shouted. "Now you must be true to your name. You appeared like a flash from the night sky, and now you must disappear just as quickly."

People shook their heads. Brows furrowed in confusion.

"Now is not the time for this fight," she said, "but I will call on you soon. Go back to your homes. Be ready to strike again. Savor this victory, I promise it will not be the last. Ohndarien will be whole again!"

The cheer was deafening.

Baelandra looked out over the crowd with eyes blazing, nodding to them. The energy of their conviction buzzed through her. She waited a long moment, then held her hands up. The noise died down.

"Go now. Quickly, quietly. Make Krellis's soldiers believe you appeared out of the sky and disappeared just as quickly."

The crowd still hovered, not wanting to leave.

Baelandra leaned forward and whispered to the steward of the Midnight Jewel.

"Faedellin, if I linger, they will linger," she said. "When I am gone, make sure they go, too. Send them safely home, my friend."

The slender man began shouting orders.

Baelandra urged Lawdon forward as the crowd headed off in separate directions. The four Sisters followed the waterbug toward the Hall of Windows. A pair of dead soldiers lay slumped at the base of the Spring Gate. Their right hands had been severed from their bodies. Lawdon skirted around the corpses, hurried into the Hall, and ran down the amphitheater's steps. She paused next to the hole into the Heart, her small knife still in hand.

Hazel, Jayden, and Vallia disappeared down the ladder one at a time. Baelandra paused and turned to Scythe.

"Thank you for returning," she said. "I know the journey is not easy."

He nodded.

"How is Brophy?"

"The boy lives. I left him in Queen Ossamyr's gentle hands."

She looked at him, her mouth open. "That woman will eat him alive."

"Perhaps. Her appetites are legendary."

She frowned.

"I did not plan on delivering him to the queen," Scythe said, "but a scorpion limited my options."

"Was he stung?"

"Yes. But I was quick, and he survived."

Baelandra nodded. At least he was safe, for the moment.

"Were you able to find Shara?" she asked.

His dark brows furrowed, and he nodded. Baelandra bit her lip, expecting the worst.

"She also lives," he said. "The Physendrian sorcerer is still holding her at the inn on Bloody Row." He paused. His anger was palpable. "She has been ill-treated. But I must make more arrangements before I can approach her."

Baelandra nodded. She wanted to know more, but now was not the time. "Do you need help?" she asked.

He shook his head. "I will take the girl, Lawdon, as a lookout. That is all."

"Be careful and return as quickly as you can."

He nodded curtly and turned to go.

"Wait. This entrance will not be safe. Let me tell you—"

"I know another way inside," he assured her.

"How?"

"I have a curious nature." With a quick smile, the small man turned and left. Lawdon rushed to follow him up the amphitheater steps.

Baelandra watched them go, pausing for a moment. What did I do to deserve such loyalty?

When they disappeared through the Spring Gate, she descended the ladder into the Heart. It was a gloomy room, rough-hewn from the dark stone of the Wheel. Any soldiers Krellis sent into the Heart wouldn't get beyond this room.

Baelandra heard the voice of the Heartstone like a distant song on a breeze. The stone's power radiated from deep within the labyrinth, throbbing through the stone in her chest and singing lightly in her mind. She stepped onto the tiny antechamber's floor.

Baelandra hurried to a blank section of wall, found the tiny gem with her finger, and touched the red diamond in her chest. A door slid open, and she slipped inside. The Brother of Autumn could follow her through that door if he wished to face the four Sisters alone. But she doubted he was that foolish. The Heart of Ohndarien protected her own.

Once the door was closed, Baelandra unlaced her dress and exposed her heartstone to light her way. The throbbing red gem lit the rough-hewn passage like a tiny fire.

She descended a narrow spiral staircase into the labyrinth. The sprawling complex of natural caves extended throughout the Wheel and under the city. At the bottom of the stairs, she entered a large chamber filled with stalactites and stalagmites. A side passage branched off in each direction.

The other Sisters were already there. Hazel helped Vallia clean the blood from her face. Jayden finished lighting a torch and fitted it into a wall sconce. The limestone chamber was packed with piles of bedding, barrels of water, and boxes of food. Baelandra had sent a message ahead to Charus, and the Hall of Windows' warden had done exactly as she asked him.

Hazel finished with Vallia's bandage, came forward, and hugged Baelandra.

"That was a fine speech, dear," she said. "You have done us all proud tonight."

Baelandra wanted to cry. She tightened her lips and nodded, hugged the woman tighter. "I wish it had never come to this."

"Of course not. We all hoped Krellis was a true Brother at heart."

"None more than I," she murmured.

"It will be all right," Hazel assured her. "This city is strong. You have seen it today. Ohndarien protects herself."

Jayden and Vallia came closer. The old woman kissed Baelandra on the cheek. Vallia nodded her quiet thanks.

"We're here," Jayden said, looking at each of her Sisters in turn. "Now what?"

Baelandra took a deep breath. "We need to send an emissary to the Summer Cities," she said. "They don't want Krellis in control of the locks any more than we do."

"The Summermen can't agree that water is wet," Jayden said. "They will make fickle allies at best."

"I know, but they must see where Phandir is headed after Ohndarien. We have to try."

The other Sisters nodded in agreement.

Baelandra continued. "We must remain free, here in the Heart, so everyone knows that Krellis's reach extends only as far as the tip of his sword."

"And keep hope alive," Hazel added. "That's the most important thing."

"Exactly," Baelandra agreed.

She looked to each of the other women in turn. Hazel and Jayden nodded in grim resignation, but Vallia shook her head.

"I still say we kill him."

Baelandra sighed. "I know how you feel, but Krellis is not our only problem. He seems to have a plan for defeating the Physendrians. He certainly wasn't worried about the attack. If we kill him, those plans will die with him. I'm not sure I could defeat that army."

Vallia's thin lips set in a harsh line.

"Trust the man's ambition," Baelandra said. "If he defeats the Physendrians, he will want to counterattack to reclaim the throne he lost so long ago. He can't march his troops south if we are still in the Heart, ready to emerge with an army of loyal Ohndariens at our back. He will have to make terms with us. I know this man. He is ruthless when he wants something, and he wants revenge on his brother more than anything else. Ruling Ohndarien is not that important to him. It is a tactical advantage that he would happily trade for a superior one. We may not need to kill him to get what we want."

"We trusted you about him before," Vallia said.

Baelandra lowered her eyes. "I know. I was wrong about him. But right now, we need Krellis. And we need to trust what made Ohndarien beautiful. It is not our job as Sisters to remove him. I learned that the night I tried to kill him. If Krellis is no longer a worthy Brother, it falls to a young man of the blood to step forward, take the Test, and force him to step down. Who are we to second-guess the Heartstone? We must do what we can and wait for Brophy to return."

"Bae's right," Hazel said. "The only thing that makes us any different from Physendria is that we don't kill each other over our disagreements. I don't want to see any man dead, even Krellis. I believe Brophy will come back to depose him. We only have one hope, but that is still hope."

Jayden nodded. "Very well. We wait for Brophy, extend our web of allies, trust Krellis to defend the city, and emerge with claws extended when the time is right. Agreed?"

The three Sisters looked to Vallia.

"I am sick of waiting for men to return and save us," she spat. The grim woman looked at the other three. "But I won't let my anger stand in the way of our traditions. I disagree with your choice, but I will bow to the will of the council."

Baelandra closed her eyes. She felt like they were jumping off a cliff into the dark, but at least they were doing something.

BAELANDRA AND her Sisters spent hours discussing the nuances of their plans. Fatigue told her it must be late at night, but it was impossible to tell so far underground. They eventually ceased planning and curled up in the bedding that the Hall's warden had left for them. Baelandra tried to sleep, but it was impossible. The same overwhelming problems and tenuous solutions turned over and over in her mind, refusing to lock into place, refusing to make sense.

A noise from one of the side passages brought the four Sisters to their feet. Baelandra drew her dagger and hurried forward, peering into the darkness. Lawdon appeared out of the gloom. Scythe followed a few steps behind, carrying a large burden draped over one shoulder.

Baelandra swallowed. It was a body.

Scythe wordlessly stepped into the chamber and laid Shara on the stone floor.

"Oh child . . ." Baelandra's breath caught in her throat. She descended to her knees and touched Shara's cheek. The young woman's thin, pale face was all that could be seen at the top of the blanket that Scythe had wrapped her in.

Jayden and Hazel joined her at Shara's side. "Praise all that you found her," Hazel said.

Baelandra swallowed. "Did you run into any problems?"

"No, but the men Victeris left to watch her have a few problems now."

Lawdon's youthful face was pinched in grief. She knelt next to Hazel, managed to find Shara's hand in the folds of the blanket and gripped it.

Jayden felt for a pulse at Shara's neck.

"She will live," Scythe said. "I had to drug her to get her out of that place. It isn't wise to take chances with a Zelani, no matter what condition she is in."

Vallia brought a torch closer to shine upon Shara's sleeping face. They unwrapped her naked body. She was a bony shadow of the beautiful woman she had once been. Shara's knees were scraped raw, her legs caked with dried blood. The poor girl's entire body was covered with cuts and bruises.

Baelandra clenched her jaw.

The other Sisters looked at each other. Even Hazel's soft face seemed made of marble. Lawdon turned away, but she didn't let go of Shara's hand.

"I couldn't get her until nightfall. There weren't any locks on the door,"

Scythe said, "but the girl wouldn't leave. Victeris must have some kind of hold on her mind."

Lawdon nodded, her eyes brimming with tears. "I watched her through the window. She was crawling naked around the room. I tried to talk to her. I tried to help, but she just kept crawling and crawling around in circles." The young girl squeezed her eyes shut.

"Finding her in that room is something I will remember forever," Scythe said, in a flat tone.

"Her knees were worn to a pulp and she was . . ." Lawdon's voice broke. "She was leaving a bloody streak wherever she went. I wanted to take her away . . . but Scythe told me to wait."

"He was right. You see?" Hazel said. "She is here with us now."

"I'm sorry," Baelandra whispered to Shara, leaning forward and putting her head against the young woman's shoulder. "I'm so sorry."

"How long will the drug last?" Jayden asked.

"Several hours at least," Scythe said.

Vallia nodded, speaking for the first time in hours. "We will have to set up a warding to protect her before she wakes."

"And she will need food and drink," Hazel added.

"Can I help?" Lawdon asked, roughly brushing away her tears. "I'll do anything."

Hazel looked to Baelandra. She nodded.

"Come with me, child," Hazel said.

Hesitantly, Lawdon glanced at Baelandra.

"Go on. It's all right."

Vallia disappeared down one of the dark passageways. Hazel and Lawdon went over to their supplies and began sorting through them.

Baelandra left Shara with Jayden and took Scythe aside.

"Scythe . . ." she said.

His eyes narrowed as if he knew what she was going to say.

"You cannot take revenge upon Victeris."

"You are wrong," he said. "I have made no oath about that man, and I will not."

"Scythe, we are all angry. Don't you think I'd rip that bastard's heart out if I could?"

"It doesn't matter whether you could or not. I can."

"No!"

Scythe raised one of his thick, black eyebrows.

"Listen to me, my friend," Baelandra pleaded. "Shara's wounds go deeper than you can see. Her body will heal, but the force that held her in that room is the most dangerous wound. Zelani magic is subtle and powerful. We cannot kill the man until we undo what he has done."

Scythe's jaw muscles worked. He breathed for a moment before answering. "And then?"

"And then vengeance, if it comes, belongs to Shara, not you."

Scythe hesitated, then nodded. "Very well. What do you need of me now?"

"You must return to Brophy at once."

Scythe shook his head. "My place is at your side. With Krellis gone—"

"Scythe . . ." She let the words between them remain unspoken. It was the wrong time for this conversation. She put a hand on his shoulder. "Please, my old friend. Please. Do as I ask. Brophy is our last heir. He must return to take the Test. Would you have Krellis remain the Brother of Autumn?"

The man's face twisted up. She could see his rage, barely held in check.

She wrinkled her brow. "Scythe, if you go to find Krellis—"

He held up a hand. She saw the old pain in his face. It was there and gone in an instant. "I am no oath breaker. I gave my word to you on the matter, and I will keep it. The Physendrian is safe as long as you wish it."

"I did not mean—" She reached for his hand, but he backed away.

"I will do as you ask. You deserve nothing less," he spoke the ritual words, but they were stiff, lifeless. He turned and disappeared into the dark passage from which he had emerged.

Baelandra let out a long sigh, leaning a hand on a stalagmite as she stared after him. Jayden's raspy voice startled her.

"That man, he loves you, no?"

She swallowed, nodded. "Yes. He has ever since the day we met, many years ago."

"Do you love him back?"

Baelandra looked wistfully at the old woman. "Oh Jayden. I wish I did, for my sake, for his, for Ohndarien. But I don't. Not like he wants." Baelandra turned away. "Sometimes I think my love for Krellis is punishment for what I have done to Scythe."

"Oh, child," Jayden said, giving her Sister's hand a squeeze. "Don't try to make sense out of love. It's a game you'll never win."

10

"T HE LOCKS of Ohndarien were the dream of Donovan Morgeon and the brainchild of Master Coelho," Krellis told Father Lewlem. "Like so many parts of this city, they are unique in the world."

Clinging to Krellis's sleeve, Father Lewlem craned his neck to look at the tunnel in the distance. His wife watched her feet as she followed, attached to his robe with her birdlike fingers.

The three of them walked along the inns and restaurants of Canal Street. The sloping avenue ran alongside the six locks stretching from the bay to the entrance of the tunnel.

"This water comes from the Great Ocean?" Father Lewlem asked.

"That's correct." Krellis nodded, pointing to the far side of the city. A steep ridge rose from the Sunset Gate to the Citadel. A hundred-foot wall, topped with windmills, rode the crest of the ridge all the way from the bay to the highest point in the city.

"Water screws inside the Windmill Wall draw water up from the ocean. The water is pumped up the ridge in a series of pools atop the wall. When the water reaches its highest point there, on top of the Citadel"—he pointed out the towered fortress that formed the southwest corner of the city—"it flows downhill along the aqueduct, runs into a tunnel that cuts through this mountain, and eventually spills into the high point of the locks. We can divert the water both east and west to operate either side."

Father Lewlem let go of Krellis's sleeve long enough to clap his pale hands. "You have mixed the two seas who would never otherwise have kissed." He looked at Krellis with his onyx eyes. "You have tasted the power of an emperor. Did this Master Coelho read of the reign of Oh, the first incarnation of God on Earth, who ordered the creation of the Great Ocean?"

Krellis inclined his head respectfully. "I am certain that he did."

Lewlem clapped. "Certainly he must have, to know the waters so perfectly well."

He took Krellis's sleeve once more, and they continued. Lewlem had shown extraordinary stamina and curiosity for a man of his apparent years. His thirst for knowledge was excruciating. He wanted to see every part of the city. The ambassador had returned from Physen last night, and Krellis had been giving the man a tour of Ohndarien since dawn. Every attempt to discuss his mission to Physendria had been subtly rebuked.

Krellis continued his tour as they reached the end of the street and stepped out of the bright sun into the welcome shade of the tunnel. The passageway was over a hundred feet high to accommodate the tallest of ships. They walked along a narrow passageway, worn smooth from the feet of thousands of sailors.

"The ridge that separates the Great Ocean from the Summer Sea is over a thousand feet tall," Krellis explained. "Constructing locks over the top would have been impossible, so Master Coelho designed them underground, beneath the ridge. The locks and walls were the hardest part of the city to construct. Builders on the two projects competed with each other for generations to see who could finish first. The walls beat the locks by over twenty years."

"It has always been easier to construct barriers between people than bridges between them," Lewlem said.

Was that an invitation to discuss an alliance, Krellis wondered? Perhaps the old man just thought himself clever.

They continued forward. The roar of moving water filled the cavern as seawater from the aqueduct rushed through a tunnel carved into the side of the mountain. The torrent flowed night and day, constantly adding water to the Dark Lake, the canal that ran through the heart of the mountain connecting the eastern and western locks.

Bright lanterns illuminated bas-relief carvings on the walls. Despite the care taken to beautify the tunnels, the locks were still dank and chilly. Condensation constantly dripped from the ceiling.

"Watch your step, Father," Krellis said. "Wet stone has a life of its own."

Lewlem seemed to have no difficulty navigating the path. He looked about curiously. "This is the Dark Lake," Lewlem said, pointing at the canal that ran along the dimly lit tunnel. "And beyond this are the steps down to Cliff Town?"

"You know much about Ohndarien already."

"Only the Emperor knows all. I am merely a small reflection of his omniscience."

The ambassador leaned over the wooden railing and peered into the black water of the canal. "Why do they call those stairs the Foreplay Steps?"

Krellis laughed. "It takes a ship twelve hours to complete the trip through the locks. For a sailor who has been at sea for months, twelve hours is a long time to wait. If a man is inspired, he can leave his ship and walk along this path from Cliff Town to the brothels on Canal Street in less than an hour. The four hundred steps quickly became known as the Foreplay Steps. It is a daunting task to climb them, but a determined man can accomplish amazing things."

The ambassador clapped his hands again. The gesture was starting to get on Krellis's nerves.

"This frankness about family matters in the East is a delight. It is a wonder that humans can brazenly speak of such things with so little shame. It reminds one of animals rutting in the fields."

Krellis let the comment go. After living his life walking in endless lines, the ambassador from the Opal Empire must delight in every opportunity to be rude.

"This is where you keep your trolls, yes?"

"Again, I bow to your knowledge, Father Lewlem."

"I should like to meet one."

Krellis laughed, his deep voice reverberating in the small space, mixing with the sound of the rushing water.

The men and women who worked in the constant darkness of the locks and tunnels were known as trolls. It was joked that to meet an angry troll in the dark was certain death. To meet one in the daylight was certain victory.

"Are they any uglier than normal men, these trolls? It is said they are hideous."

"No. They blink a bit more in the sunlight, but they are just normal men and women."

"A pity, there are so few truly ugly people in the world. Though, I did notice quite a few ugly faces pointed at you as we walked the streets today."

Krellis's smile disappeared. He said nothing, but Father Lewlem continued with his usual childlike enthusiasm. "All rulers must face unpopular decisions. Your recent guidance has made some of your subjects uglier than others."

Krellis shrugged. "Some cannot see what is best for them."

Lewlem clapped deftly, releasing Krellis's sleeve for a moment. "So says the Emperor."

"If the city continues to prosper, the people will remain happy."

"Indeed."

They continued in silence until they came to the far side of the Dark Lake, which ended in a pair of massive water gates leading to the highest bay of the eastern locks. A steady stream of water leaked through the crack between the immense wooden doors that closed off the canal. The ambassador peered over the railing into the vast bay filling with water. There was room for ten ships though only four were presently moored there.

"When the water rises to this level, these inner doors will open," Krellis shouted over the noise of the water. "These ships will be towed west along the Dark Lake and travel down the locks on the far side, passing any eastbound ships going in the other direction. The easterners will enter this lock, which will then be drained, lowering them. Repeat that process six times, and these ships will be in the Summer Sea."

The old man smiled, looking at every detail. "These locks are truly magnificent. The Emperor will be happy to know his ocean is being used so cunningly. Come, I wish to see your Dock Town on the other side."

Krellis flexed his fingers. He had better things to do, but he started down the Foreplay Steps with the Ambassador and his wife right behind him. Krellis had only taken a few steps when the roaring of the water was cut off. The noise faded into an ominous silence as the water trickled to a stop.

Krellis looked over the edge. The bay of the highest lock was not full yet, there was no reason for the water from the Dark Lake to be shut off.

A small group of people jogged across the top of the wooden gates. One after the other, they leapt off the wall onto the narrow path behind Krellis and his guests.

Lewlem clapped. "Trolls, they must be trolls."

"Physendrian scum," one of the lock workers said.

Krellis narrowed his eyes, but he did not slow his pace, nor did he increase it. Lewlem, for once, remained silent.

"You're no Brother of mine," another said to their backs.

Krellis's sword clanked at his hip as he continued down the steps, but he never reached for it. Lewlem followed, constantly looking back. The ambassador's wife trailed last, still staring at the ground.

The taunts became louder, bolder as they progressed. Krellis didn't stop until he spotted a second knot of figures up ahead, blocking the path. The lanternlight flickered off their dingy clothes and dark faces, slick with seawater and grime.

Lewlem let go of Krellis's sleeve and huddled close to his wife. The woman still stared at the steps as if she had no idea what was happening.

"You have something you wish to discuss?" Krellis asked the crowd of trolls in front of him.

The largest of the men, a bony brute missing several fingers, stepped to the front. "We don't want you here," the man growled.

Krellis opened his shirt and bared the lightly glowing stone on his chest. "If any man thinks I haven't earned this stone, let him step forward and take it from me."

The trolls looked back and forth at each other. Krellis turned to show his heartstone to the group behind him. No one stepped forward.

The Brother of Autumn smiled a thin smile. "Come now," he said. "You have me outnumbered, in the dark, on your steps. If I am unworthy to rule this fair city, kill me now and be done with it."

It was impossible to read their expressions in the dark, but no one stepped forward.

"You will never get a better chance," Krellis assured them in a low voice.

They seemed to have lost their tongues and didn't move.

"Perhaps I am not so bad for Ohndarien after all."

He walked straight into the heart of the trolls and motioned for his guests to follow. The lock workers reluctantly let him pass, but as Lewlem neared, one of them lashed out, pushing the old man. "Foreign scum!" he hissed.

In a flurry of silks, Lewlem's wife spun. A dagger appeared from nowhere, glinting in the half-light. Blood striped the front of her robes. The troll screamed. His severed hand tumbled to the stone pathway as he lurched backward, flipped over the railing, and fell into the water.

Slowly rising from her bent-kneed pose, Lewlem's wife stood straight and still as a statue. She kept the bloody blade leveled between herself and the trolls. They scrambled away, stumbling over each other down the pathway, scuttling across the lock gates or down the stairs.

Krellis walked over to the twitching hand on the path. With the toe of his boot, he flicked it into the water far below.

"You see, Father? I told you we would make an excellent team." He paused. "Shall we continue on our way?"

Lewlem grabbed Krellis by the sleeve. His wife cleaned her blade on the hem of her robe with two quick swipes and tucked the dagger into the folds of her clothing. She latched on to Lewlem's sleeve and looked at the ground, meek as ever.

"Perhaps it is time we spoke of your mission," Krellis said.

"Perhaps it is," the ambassador agreed.

11

T HE DESERT was still chilly in the predawn light, but that would change the moment the sun came up. Ossamyr's chariot carried them out onto the blasted badlands, a shifting sea of sand and parched earth. The beautiful queen stood at the front of the chariot, the wind ruffling her short black hair underneath the golden headdress. Brophy could see the curve of her breast through the rippling slit in the side of her gown. He swallowed against his surge of desire. He had barely seen her since they made love two weeks ago.

Sometimes, late at night, he wondered if he had imagined the whole thing, some lingering delirium of the scorpion sting. He remembered her skin against his hands. His hips longed for the weight of her body moving against him. All he wanted was to be back inside her, his arms wrapped around her. But the cold, hard statue of a woman before him had replaced the Ossamyr of his dreams.

Brophy kept his fists locked on the wooden handrail, trying not to look at her. They rode into the desert east of Physen to the beginning of Nine Squares. Ossamyr had wanted him to train for two months, but Brophy insisted he was ready. Ohndarien was about to be invaded. If Nine Squares was the quickest route to aiding his city, he could not afford to delay. He thought the queen would object, but she shrugged and said she would enter his name in that month's list.

Ossamyr's slaves jogged past a huge sundial, seemingly placed in the middle of nowhere.

"Pay attention," the queen said, her voice cold and distant. They neared a towering phoenix carved of stone.

"Those who did well in the previous Nine Squares are allowed the advantage of position in the next contest. Last month's Phoenix receives a half mile head start over the Beetles."

Nine Squares contestants had to stand in the hot sun half the day before racing to the city. The sweeping curve of the phoenix statue's wings would provide great protection from the heat of the day. Standing in the shade would be a huge advantage.

"There is no one there," Brophy noticed.

"The last Phoenix fell from the tower and died," she replied. "He obviously lacked the strength to face the flames."

Fifty yards ahead of the phoenix they came upon a smaller statue of a lion raised on its hind feet, ready to attack. It would offer some shade from the sun as it climbed the horizon. A young man with a shaved head and a bandage on his muscular thigh stood there, talking to a nervous young girl in a shabby chariot. He stopped when he saw them and stared at Brophy with such venom that he blinked in surprise.

"Who was that?"

The corner of Ossamyr's mouth turned up slightly. "Phee."

"Who is Phee?"

"Don't turn your back on him. He will make you pay for it."

"What did I do to him?"

"Not what you did. What I did."

"What did you do?"

"I made the mistake of thinking he was a champion. He is not."

"You were his sponsor."

She shrugged.

Brophy imagined the two of them together, the queen's thigh sliding across Phee's bandaged leg. He gripped the handrail tighter and forced the image from his mind.

Beyond the lion were statues of a falcon, an ape, a serpent, a scorpion, a crocodile, a jackal, and a jumping rat. Each stood fifty yards apart and became progressively smaller. The jumping rat provided no shade at all.

Fifty yards beyond the last statue stood two stone markers covered with carvings of beetles. Roughly forty young men milled between the knee-high spires, talking with each other and their female benefactors.

Ossamyr's slaves jogged up to a cluster of waiting chariots. The chariot rocked to a halt, and the slaves rested against their harnesses, breathing hard. The queen's slaves were by far the most beautiful and well formed. "This is where I leave you," she murmured.

Brophy stepped off the chariot, and Ossamyr leaned over him, wrapping a crimson sash about his waist. Her breast pressed against his shoulder for a fleeting instant. He swallowed, not sure if it was intentional. With a flick of her wrist, she snapped an orange sash out and wrapped it over his shoulder.

"Today you are my champion," she said aloud, and kissed him on the cheek. Then she leaned closer and whispered in his ear. "I long for you. I will visit you tonight. Good luck."

Brophy couldn't catch his breath as she strode away to speak with the other women. He stood there for a moment, watching the sway of her hips until he forced himself to look away.

He wandered over to join the other boys. A thin, well-muscled youth about thirteen years old hovered at the edge of the crowd. As soon as he saw Brophy, the boy broke away and came closer. Brophy recognized him from the arena. Though he had no instructor, he had been there every day, learning what he could from the older boys. He was always tense, though he tried to hide it.

"Hello," Brophy said.

"Hi," the young man replied, his face splitting into a grin. He extended his hand. "I'm Tidric."

"Brophy." He took Tidric's hand and shook it. There was strength in that grip.

"I saw you fight Vakko. You're very good."

"I was well trained."

"I can tell. I'm going to make the top nine this time," Tidric said. One of the boys behind him snickered. Tidric's eyes narrowed. He almost turned around, but stopped himself. "I will," he promised. "I'm faster than these crabs. Besides, three of the top nine from last month were too injured to run this month. At least three new Beetles will make it."

Brophy nodded. "Who is your biggest competition for a spot on the nine?"

Tidric shrugged. "Could be anyone."

Before Brophy could tell him that he ought to know who his toughest competition was, he noticed a group of six young men break away from the pack and stride over to them. Brophy saved his comment and turned to face them.

"You're Brophy," the largest boy said. He had a thin face and crooked nose, a smaller, uglier version of Phee.

"Yes." Brophy looked into Little Phee's eyes. He saw confidence, but confidence came easy with a small army at your back.

"Let me tell you something for free, you piece of Ohndarien shit. Foreigners never reach the final nine. You'd best trip and fall. If you don't, we'll break your legs and make sure you never run again."

Standing on one foot, Brophy raised his right leg slowly and held it at the boy's eye level.

"If you want to break my leg, do it now. Save me the suspense."

Tidric backed up. Little Phee's nostrils flared, he swatted at Brophy's leg and missed. Quick as a snake, Brophy moved his foot in a tight circle, avoiding the hand and sticking his sandal back in Little Phee's face.

"You're dead, Ohndarien," he growled, glancing over his shoulder at the women, then back at Brophy.

Not so confident after all, Brophy thought. "Everyone dies," he said.

Little Phee snarled, pointing a finger at Brophy's face. "My brother's going to wear your manhood on a necklace."

A handsome young man approached Brophy as the others walked away. He was older than most of the boys, perhaps nineteen or twenty.

"You've got iron nerves, New Boy," the man said, smiling. He stood an inch taller than Brophy and was a good deal heavier, all of it muscle. The newcomer reminded Brophy eerily of Trent.

"Iron nerves!" Tidric echoed, slapping Brophy on the back.

He shrugged. "I wanted to know if they meant what they said. They didn't."

"Oh, Sheedar meant it," the newcomer said. "But not in front of the sponsors. They'll try for you somewhere else. Everyone saw what you did to Vakko. They're scared."

"I plan on keeping them that way."

"Good luck." The newcomer chuckled. "They're a tight group, Phee's kinsmen."

"That's right," Tidric added, "Sheedar's his brother. Rejta and Besdin are cousins—"

"A family history isn't necessary," the older boy said, snorting. "He understands the point."

Tidric's eyes narrowed, but he said nothing.

"Phee stands by the Lion?" Brophy asked.

"Yes. The queen's champion." The newcomer's eyes flew wide in melodramatic surprise. "Oh wait, no. Not now. Let me see, that would be you."

"That's you!" Tidric said. "And he hates you."

"He has already—" the newcomer began, but Tidric interrupted him.

"He swore an oath to kill you!"

The handsome boy reached over and grabbed Tidric by the neck and the belt of his wrap.

"Hey! Phanqui!" Tidric flailed as the bigger boy picked him up and tossed him six feet away. Tidric tumbled in the sand and rolled gracefully to his feet.

"You are a gnat with delusions of grandeur," Phanqui said.

"And you're a coward! You run so slow because you're afraid!" Tidric yelled, charging. The older boy laughed as Tidric bore him to the ground. He made no move to defend himself as the flailing blows rained on him.

"Help!" Phanqui called out. "The gnat is kicking me! The gnat is hitting me!"

The other boys laughed, slowly migrating closer. Tidric snapped upright, breathing hard, as Phanqui held up his hands in mock fear. Tidric's young face was mottled with rage. He looked around at everyone laughing at him, spun about, and stalked away.

Brophy held out a hand to Phanqui and helped him up.

"Why tease him?"

Phanqui shrugged, brushing the sand off his bare legs. "He teases himself. Ah, the boy has heart. He's braver than most of this lot, but he lacks patience. A few years from now he'd be a champion, but he won't live to see sixteen. Nine Squares doesn't give second chances."

"And what about you?"

"I've been in the top nine."

"But not the champion?"

Phanqui smiled broadly. "Maybe someday," he said. "You certainly put Vakko in his place. Half his students have moved to other teachers. He beat one of his boys bloody the day after you bested him."

Brophy had heard that rumor. He'd hoped it wasn't true.

"I was angry. I shouldn't have done it that way."

Phanqui shrugged. "Perhaps not, but some of this lot will steer clear of you." He paused. "Or they'll gang up on you. Be careful of Phee's kinsmen. They have been known to keep the best fighters out of the top nine."

Brophy nodded. "You're the king's cousin, aren't you?"

Phanqui raised an eyebrow. "My reputation precedes me, I see," he said, bowing low with a flourish.

"A little. I heard about you. But mostly you look like . . . the king." Brophy caught himself before he could say "Trent."

Everyone began gathering together. The sun had almost risen. The women mounted their chariots and started off, one after the other. Brophy looked to Ossamyr. The queen pushed her dark hair out of her face, but she did not turn to catch his eye.

Brophy joined the other young men as they gathered in a line between the two stone markers. His conversation with Phanqui halted as they took their places. Despite his earlier anger, Tidric came to stand next to Phanqui. The older boy hissed at the younger, and he took a step farther away.

A quiet settled over the group, and the chariots faded into the distance. Predawn light filled the morning sky.

A black-robed official stood next to each of the markers, silently observing. A similar figure stood next to the sundial half a mile distant. He raised a shiny copper disk above his head and clashed the gong just as the first ray of sun peeked across the horizon. Nine Squares had begun. It seemed anticlimactic to simply stand there at the beginning of a race, but this was a race of a different sort. They would spend half their stamina without moving at all.

Brophy closed his eyes and calmed his thoughts. He could hold his hand over a flame for twenty heartbeats, but six hours in the blazing sun would be a different matter. He kept his eyes closed for the next several hours, conserving his strength. The wrong thoughts could sap more energy than heavy labor. He tried to keep his mind blank, but images of his hands on the queen's breasts drifted out of the dark. Eventually he gave up on meditation, opened his eyes, and settled in for a long wait.

As Brophy watched his shadow grow shorter and shorter, he got an idea. "Phanqui," he murmured.

The handsome young man shook his head. "Don't talk. Save your water." Brophy nodded. "I just have a question."

Phanqui smirked. "Ask then."

"Do we have to stand in this line?"

"You can't cross it yet, if that's what you're asking."

"No, just wondering if we have to stand at the edge."

Phanqui laughed. "You're certainly welcome to stand farther away from the finish line." He nodded to the barren desert to the east. "You can start running that way, if you want."

Brophy broke ranks and walked behind Phanqui. Brophy kicked at the sand and dirt with his sandal. He formed a small hill behind Phanqui and stood on top of it. When he finished positioning himself, Phanqui was in Brophy's shadow. Phanqui's permanent smile disappeared.

"What are you doing?"

"No reason we should both stand in the sun. I'll shade you for a while, then you can shade me."

Phanqui's brow furrowed. "I'm not sure if we're supposed to do that." He glanced at one of the black-robed officials.

"Why not?"

"It's just never been done."

"Good," Brophy said, remaining where he was. Phanqui seemed uncomfortable at first, then began smiling. After a moment, Tidric looked over at them hesitantly.

"Would you like to join us?" Brophy asked.

"Sure."

"I don't know," Phanqui said. "Gnats don't cast much of a shadow."

Tidric scowled, then paused. His scowl disappeared, and he stepped back, a poorly veiled look of fear on his face. Another man limped up to them. Brophy met his gaze. The man was easily the oldest in the group, in his midtwenties at least. He was horribly burned. Half of his face was a bubbly mask of scar tissue. His right leg twisted awkwardly underneath him, but his arms and chest were thick and powerful.

"Athyl," Phanqui said, his eyes narrowed, and his lips pinched together in a line.

Athyl flicked a glance at the king's cousin. "Phanqui," he growled, his voice as rough as the sun-blasted ground beneath their feet. He turned his gaze back on Brophy.

"You're the Ohndarien," he rasped.

Brophy nodded. Athyl looked him up and down. Brophy couldn't guess what the ravaged man was thinking. His horribly scarred face prevented any chance of reading his emotions.

"I would take a turn with you." He nodded to the shadow over Phanqui. "If all four of us stood in a row, only one man would have to bear the heat of the sun."

"You're right. Please join us."

Without another word, Athyl kicked a pile of dirt and sand together and stood atop it. He pointed to a space between him and Brophy for Tidric. Brophy's first two companions became unnaturally subdued in the presence of their new friend. They ceased talking and waited out the sun.

After an hour, the other boys began to copy them. The sun hammered down, beating rivulets of sweat from Brophy's scalp, his back, his chest. Standing in the other boy's shadows was a blessed respite.

Brophy's idea became less and less effective as the sun rose directly overhead. The contestants began to drift from their groups and lined up again, crouching and stretching.

At noon, the gong rang again.

With a weary smile, Brophy took off. He'd never stood in the relentless Physendrian sun for half a day, but he'd been racing since he was old enough to run. He'd run the length of Ohndarien's walls a thousand times. Miles evaporated under his feet.

Brophy pulled ahead of the pack with an immediate burst, then set a swift but sustainable jog. Tidric labored to keep up. The boy was fast, but he would never maintain Brophy's pace. They ran together for several minutes. All of the statues whipped past them and they could soon see the contestant from the Jumping Rat statue ahead of them.

"Brophy!" Tidric shouted, faltering.

Brophy spun around to see Phee's kinsmen sprinting recklessly, bent on speed. They could never keep up that pace, but winning the race didn't seem to be their goal. They made straight for Brophy, heavy stones in their hands. Brophy turned just as they threw the first rocks.

He dodged the first two, but a third caught him in the ribs and knocked him down. By the time he got to his feet, they were upon him. Brophy blocked the first punch, ducked low and came up just as the second boy grazed his cheek. Brophy swung his elbow like a hammer, nailing the boy in the eye. That boy went down, but there were six of them, Tidric and Brophy couldn't fight them all.

"You're giving up your chance to win!" Brophy shouted at his assailants, dodging one blow, taking another in the back. He grunted, holding the pain inside.

"This isn't your race, Ohndarien. It's ours," Sheedar said, grabbing Brophy around the waist in a bear hug. Brophy peeled one of the boy's fingers away, ready to break it, when another of Phee's kinsmen punched him in the groin. Brophy doubled over and went to his knees. He expected more blows to land, but they never did. He looked up to see Phanqui clubbing Phee's brother in the head with a rock. Phee's kinsmen leapt upon the king's cousin, as Brophy struggled to rise.

Phanqui was wrestling three boys at once when Athyl arrived. The scarred veteran of Nine Squares grabbed one of their attackers by the arm and twisted.

"Athyl, no!" the boy cried. "This is not your fight!"

The boy's protests turned into a scream as Athyl slammed him to the ground. With a twist of his massive shoulders, he broke the boy's arm.

The rest of Phee's kinsmen gave up and ran. Suddenly Phanqui, Athyl, Tidric, and Brophy were alone with Phee's wounded kinsman whimpering at their feet. Athyl looked at Brophy, his ruin of a face as impassive as the sun-baked earth beneath their feet.

"We'd best run," he said.

"He's right," Phanqui agreed.

Brophy glanced at the boy Athyl had broken.

"He's done," Tidric said. "His sponsor will come pick him up after the contest."

"Will he last that long?" Brophy asked.

"Why should we care?" Athyl rasped. "Come, we run." He turned and began limping at a quick pace. Phanqui and Tidric took off after him. Brophy hesitated a moment longer, then followed.

The race wended through jagged rocks, up and down canyons and across soft dunes. The heat and dehydration were worse than Brophy had imagined, but they were within his capability. He could have outdistanced his three companions, but he held back, running with them. Even at that, the four of them passed many of the others as contestants faltered. Brophy studied Athyl. The scarred man had tremendous willpower. Brophy had never seen the like. His twisted leg was shorter than the other, it looked like it had been broken and set wrong. His knee was turned to the outside, and he could barely bend it. Despite the deformity, he set a staggering pace.

The day wore on, and they kept running. The city was nowhere in sight. Tidric faltered once, fell, and split his lip open on the rocky ground. The boy recovered and hurried to catch up, but he had spent himself. He could not maintain the pace. Brophy dropped back with him for a time, hoping Tidric would find his second wind, but the boy's breathing was labored and wheezy.

"I don't think you are going to make it this time, my friend," Brophy said.

Tidric nodded but kept running.

"Thank you for your help back there," Brophy said. "I would not have made it without you."

Tidric nodded, too tired to speak. He pumped his arms in exaggerated swings, trying to increase his pace.

"Perhaps I will see you next month," Brophy said, pulling away from the skinny boy and pouring on the speed. He caught up with Athyl and Phanqui in the next few minutes. The three of them descended into a valley and ran together through a sprawling boulder field.

As they approached the volcano, the ground began to slope uphill. Spectators lined the path of the race. They grew thicker and more boisterous the closer they came to the city. Phanqui began to fade. He struggled to keep up, fell behind, and struggled to catch them again.

"Go on," he huffed.

"No, you're almost there!" Brophy encouraged him.

Despite the sweat that ran down his face, Phanqui winked. "This mountain's a bitch, my friend. I'll never mount her. Go on. This is where they drop like flies."

"Phanqui . . ."

"Go on." He grinned. "I'll get there next time."

Brophy nodded and left Phanqui behind. He and Athyl continued together. Brophy could not believe the man. His determination was humbling. He was obviously in agony, but he kept on. His injured leg seemed no more than a stick to him. He thumped it in front of himself again and again, launching off his good leg, fighting like a lion for every step.

The path rose steeply as they climbed the flanks of the volcano. Brophy looked ahead. The last hundred yards they would be scrambling upward on hands and feet.

Brophy could have left Athyl behind, but they were in ninth and tenth place, with the eighth runner just in front of them. Athyl had a chance, and he knew it. Brophy could catch the eighth runner, but that wouldn't do Athyl any good.

"I'm spent," Athyl panted, "I will not catch him. I have nothing left." He spoke the words that Brophy was thinking, but continued at the same quick, limping stride, pitting his will against the mountain.

"Catch him, Brophy," Athyl huffed. "Kick his legs out from under him. We will enter the volcano together."

Brophy glanced ahead at the struggling boy. It was one of Phee's gang. The boy would certainly have done it to Brophy if their positions were reversed. And Athyl was right. He wouldn't make it without Brophy's help, just as Brophy wouldn't have made it without Athyl's help earlier.

"What about the crowd? They'll see if I cheat."

Athyl laughed for the first time, a short, sharp huff between his panting breaths. "That's not cheating. That's strategy. They'll love you for it."

Brophy hesitated.

"You don't want to enter that arena without any friends at your back."

Brophy nodded and forged ahead. He kicked the boy's heel, sending him stumbling in the dirt. Athyl caught them in seconds, grabbed Phee's kinsman and punched him in the face. The young man stumbled backward and rolled down the hill.

Athyl took a few more steps and fell to his hands and knees. He panted desperately for a few moments. The man's legs were shaking uncontrollably. Brophy glanced behind him. A group of three runners was only a hundred yards away.

"Come," Brophy said, offering Athyl a hand up. "We're nearly there."

Together, Brophy and Athyl clambered over the rough rocks to the top of the volcano, the eight and ninth runners. As they crossed over the lip, the roar of the crowd became deafening. A band played, and the crowd chanted to urge the runners on.

"Run! Run! Run!" they shouted over and over again.

The arena was packed. Screaming faces were crammed into every gallery. Not an inch of space was empty.

The sudden downhill slope and the roar of the crowd lifted Brophy's spirits. He found his second wind. With a nod to Athyl, he let his feet loose at last and flew down the spiral walkway. Hundreds of people reached out to touch him as he ran by. Brophy passed one of Phee's kinsmen and one other runner before reaching the arena floor.

An announcer hailed each of the runners as they crossed the finish line. The thin-faced man shouted into an immense brass funnel just above the king's box. His deep voice rose above the noise of the crowd.

As Brophy flew past, the announcer called out. "And bearing the royal colors is the rebel prince from Ohndarien, rejecting his lawless ways to return home and bring glory to Queen Ossamyr! Hail Brophy!"

The cheering rose to a crescendo, hundreds of Physendrians waved Ossamyr's orange and red colors in the stands. Brophy jogged to a stop, his throat dry as he fought for air, but it was a glorious feeling. He looked up to the king's box and saw Ossamyr sitting next to Phandir. She gave him a slight smile and a nod. Brophy grinned. By the Seasons, that woman would be naked on top of him tonight.

Fearing what might show on his face, Brophy turned away and watched the final three runners cross the finish line. Athyl was last.

The contestants were allowed a moment to rest, but no one gave them any water. Brophy tried to size up the competition, but his head was swimming as the heat radiated off his body. He walked in small circles until his breath returned to normal.

The musicians finished their song and the crowd quieted. The gaunt announcer began a speech. His words had the sound of ritual, as if he said the exact same thing every time.

"Each man, beast, and insect has his place in the Longest River. Each creature has a part to play in the glory of all. But sometimes, when the world is dark, a flicker of light will appear. A champion will arise and make the great leap upward. A fly becomes a spider, a spider a beetle, a beetle a rat. These nine insects have risen above the rest. They have become Jumping Rats."

The crowd started to chant soft and slow, "Jump! Jump! Jump! Jump!"

"But not all will be worthy to pass beyond this stage to the next. One rat will be left behind as the others fight their way up from insects to gods!"

The crowd roared.

Brophy followed the other contestants up the narrow steps to the first of the nine squares. The immense slab of stone was filled with a haphazard jumble of vertical wooden posts, each rising four feet in the air. The posts were spaced just far enough apart to make them difficult to jump between, but Brophy was not worried. This would be an easy contest compared to running across half of Physendria with no water. All he had to do was be one of the first eight to jump to the far side. As a boy, he and Trent used to leap from crenel to crenel on the Quarry Wall. This was a child's game.

Nine perfectly aligned posts marked the beginning. The Jumping Rats stood in front of their posts. The crowd returned to their chant. "Jump, jump, jump."

The gong crashed.

Each of the contestants attacked his post, climbing furiously. Brophy reached the top of his first, just before Phee, who stood two posts down and glared at him. Sweat still poured off his bald head. Brophy leapt to the next post, then the next. Phee matched him, stride for stride. The queen's former champion suddenly leapt sideways at the exact moment when Brophy hovered in midair. They met at the top of the same post. Phee drove his shoulder into Brophy's back. The crowd cheered.

Even as he fell sideways, Brophy pushed against the post, propelling himself away. It was barely enough to get him to the nearest pillar. He flailed with his arms, grabbing it in a hug. He swung around, narrowly keeping himself from sliding to the ground. Grunting with the effort, he climbed to the top and stood there panting.

Phee glared at him, but wasn't inclined to go backward. He leapt ahead, post to post. Brophy stood and continued on, more cautious now, watching everyone around him.

One of the other boys stumbled and fell on his own. His chin hit the top of a post with a crack that cut through the noise of the crowd. The boy was unconscious before he hit the ground.

The crowd roared at the sight of blood.

The other contestants relaxed as soon as they knew they were safe. They crossed quietly, each of them landing on the far side, breathing hard. Athyl, jumping on one foot, finished last. He gave Brophy a curt nod, but said nothing.

"The mighty Jumping Rats have now become Jackals, fighting and scratching over scraps of food," the announcer called. He leaned over, cupping a hand to his ear. The crowd began chanting.

"Scratch! Scratch! Scratch! Scratch!"

Phee led the contestants across a narrow bridge of stone to the second square. The massive pedestal was hollowed out in the center, forming a rough-hewn bowl. The contestants spread out around the edges of the depression. With a grand show, a black-robed official tossed seven bones into the pit. The bones tumbled down the slope, coming to rest at the very bottom.

"Eight enter the pit," the announcer cried, "to scratch and claw for their food, but only seven will change from scavenger to hunter, climbing to the next level as Crocodiles!"

The crowd howled.

"To the bones, Jackals!"

The gong crashed.

Brophy leapt over the edge and skidded down the slope. Once again, he was first into the pit and found a bone right away. Just as he stooped to pick it up, Sheedar tackled him from behind, knocking Brophy to his knees. A second boy snatched his bone away and struck him across the face with it.

Stars burst in Brophy's vision, and he fell face forward. He tasted blood, but ignored it, forcing himself to his feet. Already the boys were scrambling up the steep sides of the bowl, everyone with a bone except for Brophy. Phee threw his leg over the top, basking in the adoration of the crowd, his bone thrust high in the air.

With a snarl, Brophy launched himself at Phee's brother, but he was too far ahead. Brophy knew he'd never catch him.

Another boy slipped and slid halfway down the slope. Seizing the opportunity, Brophy changed direction and rushed for the boy. He grabbed his ankle and hauled him backward. Both of them tumbled to the bottom of the pit.

The boy leapt up, swinging the long bone at Brophy's head. He ducked, shuffled forward, and punched the boy in the center of his chest just below the rib cage. The kid staggered back. Brophy twisted the bone out of his grip, dodged a feeble grab, and flung the boy to the ground.

Bone in hand, Brophy sprinted for the edge of the pit and climbed out before the stunned boy could catch him. The crowd cheered almost as much as they had cheered for Phee.

The contestants were given a brief moment to rest before they were led across the bridge to the next square.

"Nobody's lucky three times in a row," Phee snarled, as they crossed the bridge together.

"I won't need to be lucky," Brophy said, holding Phee's gaze. "I know how to swim."

Phee sneered.

"The scavengers have become the Lords of the Deep," the announcer bellowed. "Fearsome hunters, but still wallowing in the muck of the lower worlds. Who will have the strength to rise from the swamps and become deadly scorpions?"

The next square was filled with a long, sinuous trench of foul-smelling water. The trough snaked back and forth against itself in nine serpentine curves separated by slime-covered walls.

The crowd began their third chant, shouting, "Deep! Deep! Deep! Deep!"

Athyl drew near Brophy. "Congratulations," he rasped, "You're scraping by, that's all that matters."

Brophy prodded the bruise on his jaw where the bone struck him. "I think I'm learning the hard way."

"Is there any other way?" Athyl give him a little smile. Under his burned skin it looked like a snarl.

Brophy looked at the water. With the black scum floating on top, he couldn't tell how deep it was or what might be living down there.

"You seem a nice kid," Athyl continued. "That'll be the death of you. It almost cost you in the first two squares."

Brophy opened his mouth to speak, but Athyl cut him off.

"Just don't drink the water, no matter how thirsty you are. Understand?"

Brophy nodded, his eyes widening. No one had told him that.

They all lined up across the beginning of the trough. It started wide enough for seven swimmers to jump in at once, but narrowed after the first thirty feet.

"They're going to gang up on you," Athyl said, "They'll try to push you under. If they do, grab their balls, understand? Rip them off if you have to. Remember, it isn't about who finishes first, it's about who doesn't finish last."

The gong crashed.

Everyone leapt in at once. The water was warm and thick. Brophy swam for the bottom, keeping his eyes and mouth clamped shut. He didn't stop kicking until his hands felt the first switchback ahead of him. He swam to the surface and blew the filthy water out of his nose before he took a breath.

The desert dwellers were still halfway down the first row, shouldering their way through the water one hip at a time. Allowing himself a brief smile, Brophy pushed off the wall and stroked forward. Let them catch him now.

He swam quickly down the second lane. Suddenly, hands plunged into the water from above, grabbing his hair and arms. Phee yanked him out, hauling him over the barrier into the first lane where everyone still waded forward. Brophy spluttered, fighting back blindly, but Phee and his kinsmen grabbed his arms and legs and forced him under the water.

Frantically, Brophy searched for the nearest boy's crotch. He caught hold of something, but hesitated and his hand was knocked away. Phee grabbed him around the waist, balled a fist into Brophy's stomach and squeezed. Brophy's air shot out his mouth in a flurry of bubbles. Phee squeezed again and Brophy sucked in a lungful of murky water.

Then Athyl was there, swinging his deadly fists. Phee and his horde fled. Athyl pulled Brophy above water and set him against the side of the trough.

The burned man looked at him steadily, no compassion in his gaze.

"You swallowed the water, didn't you?" he rasped.

Brophy nodded, coughing and drawing a breath. A trickle ran down his chin.

Athyl shook his head. "That's it for you. I told you. Grab their balls."

"I . . . tried."

"Not hard enough."

"What will happen?"

"You'll die, if you're lucky." Athyl's rough laugh didn't make Brophy feel any better. He could already feel a sickly heaviness in his stomach.

"You were a good ally, Brophy," Athyl continued. "Perhaps we'll run together next month, if I don't escape the fire tonight."

He turned and waded casually away, not hurrying. Brophy started after him, but his stomach protested. Clenching his teeth, he fought a powerful urge to vomit and clung to the edge of the trough, his hand slipping on the dark slime.

He barely made it out of the water before doubling over in pain.

12

AYDEN'S GRANDDAUGHTER, Mave, lay naked on the bed when Krellis stepped into the room. He frowned at Victeris, who sat next to the sobbing woman. His brother arched one thin, black eyebrow. His hand rested lightly on a table to his left that held a porcelain pitcher of water, a pot, a cloth and a long, thin knife.

"Is that necessary?" Krellis said, closing the door. He inclined his head toward Mave but did not look at her.

"Necessary?"

"Can't you get your information without dropping your pants?"

Victeris looked as though he'd sucked on a wedge of lemon. "I didn't drop my pants, I dropped hers. Don't tell me you are becoming squeamish since Baelandra left you."

Krellis's cheeks reddened above his beard. "I am beginning to doubt the necessity of your twisted perversions."

Victeris shrugged. "Some dogs just can't be trained to shit outside."

Krellis growled and pounded on the door. He removed a rumpled blanket from the chair and tossed it over the woman. A soldier poked his head inside. "Get her." Krellis pointed. "Give her a hot meal and a bed."

The soldier snapped to action and picked Mave up. Her head hung limply, her eyes open but unfocused.

"If you touch her," Krellis added, "I'll hear of it."

The soldier nodded. He wrapped the blanket around the woman and led her outside. When the door thumped closed behind them, Krellis looked at his brother. "What have you learned?"

"Oh, so my twisted perversions serve you after all?"

"The dog serves me, not his shit."

Victeris paused. The two brothers stared at each other for a long moment. Finally, Victeris smiled. "There are five secret passages leading out of the Heart," he said. "Each is well hidden and . . . dangerous to the uninvited. Would you like me to describe them in detail?"

Krellis waved his hand. "Give the details to Gorlym. He will make sure they are all watched."

"I was hoping you would charge in and take them by storm." A wry smile curved the corner of Victeris's mouth.

"Are you volunteering to lead that charge?" Krellis raised an eyebrow. Victeris said nothing. Krellis waved a hand, and continued, "No. The Heart protects its own. It is far better to know what the Sisters are plotting than to prevent them from plotting at all."

"That sounds like the same overconfidence that got you into this problem in the first place. You are developing a history of underestimating your foes."

"I won't take lectures about overconfidence from you. You are the one who had Shara in hand."

Victeris held his palms up. "This is true, but my guilt does not make you innocent."

"I warned you once," Krellis growled. "I'm not in the mood for your games."

"You looked just like our father when you said that," Victeris returned, but held up a pacifying hand. "Admit it, my brother, we are both to blame. Overconfidence is a family trait. I propose we watch each other's backs. I will use every dirty trick to keep you humble if you do the same for me. Agreed?" His eyes glittered.

"I don't need you to rescue me every time there is a minor setback."

"A setback? To which setback do you refer? When you overestimated your soldiers' competence, when you underestimated the Sisters' resourcefulness, or when you forgot about Baelandra's lapdog from Kherif? What is his name?"

"He has no name. Soon he will have no head."

Victeris wiped a drop of Mave's blood from his wrist and sucked it off his finger. "Perhaps, but he certainly has your spot between Baelandra's legs this evening."

Krellis knocked over the table, grabbed his brother's neck with one mighty fist, and slammed him against the wall. "Don't push me," he said through clenched teeth. "I push back harder than you."

"Overconfidence," Victeris rasped. Krellis looked down to see his brother's slender dagger between them, the point just below his rib cage.

Krellis tossed Victeris across the room. The Zelani master stumbled backward, recovered his balance, smoothed his robes, and sighed.

"What of your visit with the ambassador?" he asked pleasantly.

Krellis grunted. "All is well. He has returned to the Opal Empire to gather his forces. Phandir believes the Emperor has an alliance with him. When our brother attacks Ohndarien, the westerners will land behind him and crush Phandir's army against our walls."

"What makes you think the clapping idiot will honor your alliance over Phandir's?"

"That's why I was hoping Shara would have set sail with him. I would feel a lot more secure with a Zelani in the old man's bed."

Victeris shrugged helplessly.

"Your fondness for your students and lack of discretion with them has put us in an awkward position," Krellis said.

"Shara surprised me. She is more powerful than I imagined. But the girl is not the problem. The Sisters are the problem. They have somehow shielded her from my sight. If we could remove their influence, I could win her back."

Krellis gave Victeris a withering look. "It's too late for that. The ambassador requested her by name, and she was not available. He was very disappointed. I tried to offer him Gorlym's girl, but he refused. I think the old fool is in love."

"I want that girl back," Victeris said, his voice low and steady. Krellis saw a fire in his brother's eyes that reminded him of their father.

"Get in line."

"I've never asked you for anything, but I ask you for this. If the Ohohhim have already set sail, then Shara is of no use to us in that regard. But she is of use to me. I want her."

"Fine."

"Since you do not wish to risk a direct assault—"

Krellis shook his head.

"We could light fires. Fill the caves with smoke."

"No good. Air flows out of the Heart, not in."

"It must flow in somewhere."

"Have you ever stood next to the Heartstone?"

"No."

"Air flows out of the Heart, not in."

"Interesting." Victeris pursed his lips. He thought for a moment, then looked back at Krellis. "We might take hostages."

"Threatening and killing my own citizens is a poor way to begin my rule. My position is still tenuous. Playing the tyrant will not make it any easier."

"Then what do you propose?" Victeris asked.

"Once Phandir is defeated, we will have more options. Those women are not the types to sit around and do nothing. They have already shown that. When they stick their heads out of that hole, I will cut them off."

Victeris smirked. "Is that overconfidence I hear?"

Krellis shook his shaggy head. "Not this time."

Their father's look had slowly faded from Victeris's eyes. He was back to his old impudent smirk. "Then I will wait, for now. I am a patient man. But I want that girl alive. When the time comes, she is mine."

"Very well."

Victeris smoothed his robes and headed for the door. He paused with his hand on the latch. "One more thing. I am curious what you offered Father Lewlem that will buy his assistance against Phandir."

"I offered nothing to the messenger. I made my offer to the Emperor."

Victeris's eyebrows raised and his smirk faded. "And what did you offer the Unseen Monarch?"

"I know what became of the Lost Brothers," Krellis said, waving a hand as if it did not matter. "They seem very interested in this knowledge."

"They are alive? I assumed they all died of some unpleasant intestinal disease in the Vastness."

"No. Some of them still live, or they did a year ago. The fools believe they are protecting the legacy of Efften."

Victeris's eyes narrowed. His impudent smirk faded. Krellis turned, looked at him strangely.

"The Emperor believes the legends are true," Victeris said in a flat tone. It wasn't a question. He studied his brother like a cat watching a ripple of water.

"Yes. And if he is willing to believe in a fairy tale, I'm happy to sell it to him."

When Victeris spoke again, his voice was low, deadly. "Do you have any idea what you're giving away? You should have told me about the Lost Brothers and what they protect. You should have told me immediately."

Krellis laughed. "Trent was right. I ought to send you to the Cinder."

"The Cinder? I thought they were in the Vastness."

"That's where their last letter came from. They moved the child there to keep her safe."

"Our mother and I spent two generations perfecting our powers," Victeris hissed. "Yet Zelani is only one of ten paths the sorcerers of Efften traveled on a daily basis."

"For all the good it did them. They were slaughtered by drunken pirates. Let the Opal Emperor play with his toy. It makes no matter to me."

Victeris watched Krellis with the cold eyes of a snake.

"It should, my brother. It should."

13

VOMIT DRIPPED from Brophy's chin. He breathed through his mouth, his nose filled with bile. His stomach pitched and heaved as if the entire Great Ocean raged inside him. The dim room echoed with his suffering, the low ceiling seeming to creep closer and closer. How could he feel this bad and not die?

He sat on a short wicker stool over the latrine hole. Every time he closed his eyes the room spun, and he vomited out of his mouth, out of his nose, out of his Seasons-be-damned eyes. Even when he had completely emptied his stomach, the retching didn't stop. If he didn't gulp down the soup, dry heaves ripped him apart, twisting his body up like a puppet on mismatched strings. He didn't think he could hate anything more than the vile puke, but somehow puking nothing was worse.

He'd finished praying to the Seasons hours ago. It didn't do any good. Nothing did any good.

Another surge bubbled up his throat, and he leaned over. He spewed most of the green, goopy soup into the bucket in front of him. Ossamyr had sent three pots to him with instructions to eat as much soup as he could, and then eat more.

So far he hadn't managed it. Everything that went down came back up. Athyl was right. Brophy didn't care if he died. He had been in the amphitheater latrine for hours. Four of the Nine Squares attendants carried him here as he trailed vomit across the arena floor. And here he had remained.

During the resting moments between heaves, when he sat thinking, dripping, he imagined choking the life from Phee and his kinsmen. With vomit on his feet, his legs, his hands, his lips, Brophy imagined breaking Phee's arm. He longed for the chance. He was sick of playing the fool, tired of being defeated.

"If you live through the night, you'll have the stomach of a Crocodile," a soft, slightly accented voice said. "I drank some of that water fifteen years ago. I can still scoop a bloated rat out of a sewer drain and slurp it down without so much as a stomach rumble."

Brophy looked up. Scythe stood in the doorway, legs apart and arms crossed, his white robes dusty as if he'd just walked the length of Physendria. The white cloth veil dangled against his cheek, hanging from his head wrap. His features were even more harsh and angular in the flickering torchlight. Brophy gave him a look he hoped was mean, then leaned over and puked again.

"What are you doing here?" Brophy mumbled through wet lips. "I thought you'd be long gone after collecting your reward."

Scythe's eyes narrowed. He paused a moment, then said, "You aren't delivered yet. You're in the middle of the journey, and you still have a long way to go."

With a shaky hand, Brophy grabbed the ladle from the last pot of green soup and brought it to his lips. He got most of it into his mouth and forced it down. He couldn't tell the difference between the taste of the vomit and the taste of the soup.

"Not in the mood for your riddles," Brophy mumbled. "Tell me what you want, then leave."

"I just returned from Ohndarien," Scythe said.

Brophy jerked his head up. His stomach lurched, and he threw up what he'd just eaten. He missed the bucket by half a foot, splashing green goop on the floor again.

Scythe continued. "Krellis has declared himself lord of the city. He put out the torches of the Lost Brothers and placed the Sisters under house arrest."

Brophy gritted his teeth. His visions of strangling Phee changed to visions of strangling Krellis.

"You will be happy to know that the Sisters were more resourceful than Krellis thought. They escaped their captors and found sanctuary in the Heart. Your friend Shara is with them."

"Why are you telling me this?"

"To motivate you."

Brophy's gut rumbled again, but in a different place, lower. He leaned back and another explosion of diarrhea let loose. They had become so un-predictable that he just stayed on the privy seat. Scythe seemed to have a knack for catching Brophy at his most vulnerable moments.

"Your aunt asked me to come here."

"Why?"

"To train you."

"It's difficult to believe my aunt would trust a man like you," Brophy growled. He wished he could just die. Then Scythe would go away. Krellis would go away. Brophy would go away.

"And what kind of man am I?"

"Callous. Brutal. Cold-blooded. Or did you forget what you did to that man outside Ohndarien's walls?"

Scythe shrugged. "It's true. I am all of those things. But if you were more ruthless, you wouldn't be bleeding out your backside right now."

It was too dark in the latrine to know if there was blood in Brophy's feces, but he didn't doubt it.

"Does everyone hate you," Brophy asked, "or just me?"

Scythe smiled mirthlessly. "I'm not here to make you happy, I'm here to make you strong."

"You're doing a lousy job so far. Nothing good has happened to me since I met you."

"Only a fool blames the storm crow for the storm."

"What two-penny singer did you hear that from?" Brophy mumbled.

"Your aunt."

Brophy held his belly and waited for a wave of pain to pass. "Why did you bring me here? If Bae trusted you to help me, why would you bring me here, of all places? I hate it here."

"If you had listened to me, you would never have been stung. The queen was the only person I knew who would help you. Would you rather I left you?"

Brophy didn't answer. Scythe was dodging the truth. One did not just walk into Physendria and command the queen to care for one of her sworn enemies. The queen had told him one version of the story. Brophy wanted to know if Scythe would tell the same. "Why did Ossamyr help you?"

Scythe gave Brophy a sour smile. "She is an old friend of mine."

"Are you her lover?" he asked, stepping on the end of Scythe's words.

Scythe paused, regarded Brophy carefully before he answered. Brophy didn't think he could feel any worse, but he did now. This ruthless little man had lain with Ossamyr.

Scythe let out a quiet breath. "No. I have never shared the queen's bed."

"Liar."

Scythe shook his head. Was that sadness on his face? Suddenly Brophy doubted himself. "No. I carried her favor in Nine Squares. We have remained close ever since."

"You played Nine Squares?" Brophy asked.

"Yes, I did."

"Did you win?"

"Yes, I won."

Brophy rocked back on his butt, watching Scythe's face. The man was telling the truth.

"You got past the fire?"

Scythe nodded. "And all the rest."

"Are you going to tell me it's easy, once you know how?"

"No. It's the hardest thing you'll ever do, if you know how. If you don't, it's impossible."

They watched each other as the silence stretched between them. Scythe licked his lips, and Brophy suddenly realized where he had seen the man before.

"You were that merchant from Vizar who dropped the coins in the privy!"

Scythe nodded. "Yes I was."

"Why? Why did you deceive me like that?"

"I wanted to know what kind of man you were before I agreed to help you."

Brophy remembered the mirrored pouch at Trent's waist. He must have faced the same test and failed. "You say that my aunt knows I'm here? She wants me to fight in Nine Squares?"

"Your aunt asked me to get you ready to take the Test. How I do it is up to me. She needs the Heir of Autumn to return and take Krellis's place, by force if need be."

"What do you know about the Test?"

"I know that sniveling little boys who feel sorry for themselves don't pass it."

Brophy rose to his feet. He took a step forward, and a wave of nausea hit him. He stumbled. Scythe caught him by the arm and set him back on the privy.

Brophy breathed through the wretched feeling, waiting for it to pass. When he could, he looked up into Scythe's shadowed eyes.

Brophy desperately wanted his aunt. He wanted her to put a cool cloth on his forehead and sing him to sleep. He wanted Shara here instead of

Scythe, making fun of him, calling him a little kid, ruffling his hair. He wanted his father, doing whatever a father was supposed to do.

But he didn't have any of them. He had Scythe.

"If I accept, what would you teach me?" Brophy asked.

"What to eat and drink to prepare your body for the heat of the sun. How to drown a man before he drowns you. How to counterattack effectively while hanging from a tree. How to parry with fighting claws. How to climb the burning tower when you can't see or breathe because of the smoke."

Brophy nodded.

"You need strategy," Scythe said. "Your conditioning as a Child of the Seasons is a great advantage. You have physical reserves that others do not, but Nine Squares is a social game as much as it is physical."

"I understand the strategy of the game," Brophy said.

Scythe raised an eyebrow. "Truly? The smell you've created says otherwise."

"I understand their strategy," he grunted. "But I have a different one."

Uncrossing his arms, Scythe crouched down, still watching Brophy's face. "Tell me."

"Nine Squares was created to break the spirit. Every one of these young men is shattered by this contest. It teaches them that they aren't good enough. It teaches them that everyone is their enemy and that they need to lie, cheat, and backstab to get one step farther than the next player. I think Phanqui understands this, which is why he doesn't really try."

"But he still plays," Scythe said.

"They all play. They have no choice, their families are depending on them. The few who get anywhere gather gangs, and then betray them later." Brophy fixed Scythe with a steady gaze. "Is that what you did?"

"Yes."

Brophy shook his head.

Scythe ignored the look. "So you understand it. Who are you going to befriend, then betray in order to win?"

"No one."

Scythe frowned. "Then you will not win."

"Yes, I will, but not by their rules. Nine Squares breeds treachery, isolation, brutality. I won't play by those rules. Physendria is about to invade my home. I'm going to show them that one Ohndarien can succeed with loyalty and honor where a hundred Physendrians failed with ruthless aggression."

"You are trying to beat the game, not the players."

"Yes."

"The game is bigger than you."

"Like Physendria is bigger than Ohndarien?"

Scythe narrowed his eyes. "You have your aunt in you," he said softly, "and your father."

"You knew my father?" Brophy asked, shocked.

"I met him once in Kherif, when I was . . . someone else."

"What was he like? What did he say?"

"He never spoke to me directly. I watched him from the shadows as I watched everyone. He was a good man, and very quiet. He was someone great men notice immediately and fools never see. The Khaba had a strong respect for him."

"I never knew him," Brophy said.

"I know."

"I wish . . ." Brophy started. He shook his head. "I have a basic strategy, but there is still so much I do not know. Will you help me?"

"Help you beat the game?"

"Yes."

"I do not think it can be done the way you say."

"But will you help me try?"

Scythe sighed. He shook his head and broke eye contact with Brophy for the first time. "I am a fool," he said to himself. "But I have been a fool for your family for most of my life. For the part that matters."

Brophy was about to ask him what he meant when he continued suddenly, "I can teach you the tricks I know. But I am no easy teacher, I warn you."

"I am a quick study. If Bae trusts you, then so will I," he said, feeling a sparkle of hope for the first time in ten hours. It was followed by a wave of nausea. He leaned over and heaved into the bucket. Nothing came out. He groaned.

"I believe you are coming out of it," Scythe said, standing up again.

"How can you tell?" Brophy looked up at him miserably.

"It has been a while since your last heave. You will survive."

"Just what I need, more bad news," Brophy said.

For the first time since Brophy had met him, Scythe laughed. A rich, deep belly laugh, it was not what Brophy would expect from the dried-up little man. Like a clap of thunder, it left as swiftly as it had come.

"Tomorrow, we get to work," Scythe said.

14

*S*HARA AWOKE alone in the dark.

She blinked against swollen cheeks, tender to the touch. Her hands ached to the bones, as she curled her stiff fingers. The center of her stomach felt dried up, as if she hadn't eaten for a week. She tried to curl up into a ball and winced. She couldn't bend her knees, the slightest movement sent shocks of pain up her legs.

I must crawl. Master will be angry if he finds me sitting still.

Shara struggled to sit up and saw firelight reflecting off glittering cave walls. Muffled voices whispered in the distance. Was that Victeris?

She rolled over to her knees and cried out in pain.

The voices stopped. Whimpering, Shara crawled a few steps forward. The blanket slid off, the air was cool on her naked body. A thin chain dangled from her neck, and she grabbed it, finding a small pendant. The stone was warm on her clammy hands, and she tightened her grip. Her breathing eased, and she felt better.

A figure stepped out of the shadows. "Are you awake, dear?" asked a soft voice. "Don't get up. Just stay where you are for now."

Shara felt a soft hand on her shoulder. Slowly, she settled back down. "Who are you?"

"It's Baelandra," the woman said. "You're safe. You are in the Heart."

"Where is Victeris?" Shara pushed the woman away. Her heart beat faster, her breaths came in little gulps, and her arms began shaking. She should be crawling.

Shara realized she had stopped holding the stone and grabbed it quickly. The shaking subsided, and she lay back down.

"Victeris is not here," Baelandra murmured. "It's all right. He cannot hurt you in the Heart."

A tall, slender silhouette suddenly appeared out of the shadows. Shara flinched, trying to crawl away.

"That's Vallia." Baelandra put a comforting hand on Shara's shoulder, but it felt like a prickly spider. She tried to shrug it off. "Don't . . ."

"She is awake?" Vallia asked tonelessly, crouching down next to Shara.

"Awake and scared. We need to undo what was done to her."

Shara tried to crawl away from the two women, but she was so weak that Baelandra easily held her upright.

"It's all right," Baelandra said. "We are here to help you."

Baelandra and Vallia lifted Shara to her feet; she winced every time her legs moved. Their fingers crawled on her skin, but she suffered their touch. She couldn't stand without them.

"Do you remember what happened?" Baelandra asked, leading her toward the torchlight.

Shara licked dry lips. "I remember everything."

She crawled through the room, endlessly crawling, waiting for his return.

She lay on that filthy bed as he slapped her, punched her, fucked her.

Her hand sank deeper into the muck. Victeris knelt behind her, his hands on her back.

Shara clenched her eyes, shutting the memories away. She sank to the floor, and fire lanced up her legs. Bae and Vallia pulled her upright.

"It's all right," Bae whispered. "It's over. It's all over."

Shara struggled for breath. "Where is he? Where is he now?"

"Far away. He can't hurt you."

"I can hear him calling. He wants me back."

"Hold on to that," Vallia said, nodding at the pendant. "It will help."

"Yes," Shara said, gripping the stone desperately. Her racing heart calmed when she touched it. Her master's voice became a ghost in the back of her mind.

"We can help you break free of him," Baelandra said. The Sisters carried her a few steps forward. "Victeris has put something deep inside your mind, like a hook in the belly of a fish. That is what you hear, but we can take it out. We can get him out of your head."

"How?"

"Don't worry about that. You've just awoken. Wait until you get your strength back, and we will try."

"No. Now. I cannot stand it."

"Shara, you—"

"Now! Do it now!" she shouted. Her voice echoed through the tunnel.

Baelandra and Vallia exchanged a glance, then led Shara around a corner into a cavern lit by many torches, their light glittering off the bizarre rock formations. The heavyset Sister, Hazel, and the wizened Jayden were waiting for her, sitting next to a lambskin pad spread across the stone floor. Baelandra and Vallia helped Shara sit down.

"You know the Sisters of Spring and Summer?"

Shara nodded at each of the women in turn.

Crawl. She had to crawl.

Vallia began extinguishing the torches by thrusting them into a bucket of sand.

"What is this?" Shara asked, holding up her fist with the pendant locked inside.

"That is a piece of the Heartstone," Jayden said. "The same thing we carry in our chests." The old woman touched the front of her dress.

"The stone was created as a shield against men like Victeris," Vallia said, thrusting another torch into the bucket. The Sister of Winter left a single torch burning. The firelight cast deep shadows on the woman's angular face. "If you were a true Sister, he could never touch you, but the pendant offers some protection to those not of the blood. That is why you still hear his call but are not compelled by it."

Vallia sat down next to the others. Shara looked from face to face. Her head hurt. It was hard to understand what they were saying. "Do I have to take the Test?" Shara asked.

Hazel shook her head. The woman's pudgy cheeks bunched up as she smiled. "No, dear. All we need to do is cut the thread he has woven into your mind."

"What thread?" She blinked, closed her eyes and opened them. It was so hard to concentrate. "He wove something into my mind? How?"

"We don't exactly know," Hazel said, "but it would have to have been when you were very vulnerable. Perhaps during an intimate moment, when you were alone with him."

"My graduation," Shara murmured. Her heart beat faster. "That was the first time . . ."

"Good, good, we'll start there," Hazel said. "Is it all right if we touch you? It will make this easier."

Shara hesitated and slowly nodded. She tried to control her breath, but she couldn't focus. There was nothing to hold on to.

"Lie down here," Baelandra said, patting the lambskin.

Shara leaned back, and Baelandra helped her down. The four women moved into a circle around her. They unlaced the front of their dresses and pulled them open over their shoulders, exposing the softly glowing stones embedded in their chests. The red, white, green, and yellow diamonds pulsed together like a single heartbeat.

Hazel and Baelandra rested their palms lightly on Shara's shoulders. Jayden and Vallia did the same on her thighs. Shara cringed at their touch. Her legs and arms trembled. She didn't want anyone to touch her ever again.

"I want to guide you through that memory, that intimate moment," Hazel said. "Do you understand?"

"No."

"I want you to tell me about your graduation. What was happening the moment before you first saw Victeris?"

Shara's breath came in small gasps. "No . . . I . . . no."

"It's all right. You are safe now. You don't have to go back there," Hazel said. "If you don't want to."

The Sister's hands were hot on her skin. She could hear music somewhere, voices singing in the distance, but she couldn't make out the words. She wanted to tell them that she couldn't possibly go back there, couldn't possibly face Victeris, but she kept getting distracted by the music.

"What's that? Who's singing?"

Hazel and Baelandra exchanged a look, then Hazel spoke. "That is the Heartstone."

"It's beautiful," Shara murmured.

"Then listen to the song. Listen to her voice as you listen to mine."

Shara nodded, letting the faint sounds swirl around her. Her eyes wanted to close. She forced them open, but they were heavy, and started closing again.

"I want you to tell me a story," Hazel continued after a long time. "About a woman named Shara. You are safe in a corner watching this woman named Shara while she takes her Zelani graduation. Can you tell me that story?"

"I think so," Shara said, her eyelids drooping. The orange light on the cave's ceiling shifted and flickered.

"Are you safe in a corner?"

"Yes."

"Good, tell me what you see. What is Shara doing?"

"She's swimming in the underground cave."

"Good. What does Shara do next?"

"She just broke the surface of the water. The island is right in front of her."

"Good. Is there a man there?"

"He's there." The beautiful song faded. Shara couldn't keep ahold of it. She jerked.

"It's all right. You are safe in the corner. Who is he?"

"Victeris. He's climbing out of the water. He's staring at me."

"At a woman named Shara?"

"Yes, at Shara. He wants her."

"Good, what do they do next?"

"They circle each other, drawing closer. I . . . I can't."

"Close your eyes, dear," Hazel said. Her soft voice was comforting. "Don't look at him. I want you to close your eyes."

"All right."

"Good, dear. Now, I want you to leave the corner and climb into the water."

Shara nodded.

"Are you in the water?" Hazel asked.

"Yes."

"Good, go under the water. It's all right, you can breathe. Keep your eyes closed."

"All right."

"Are you under? Can you breathe?"

"Yes."

"Good. Now open your eyes and tell me what you see through the water. I want you to watch a woman named Shara circle a man named Victeris from underwater. Can you do that?"

"Yes."

"What does Shara look like?"

"Her back is to me. She has long, black hair. It's wet, like a wide stripe down her back. She is naked."

"That's good. Tell me what happens next."

"He's touching her. Her breasts . . ."

"Keep watching, dear. What is happening?"

"He is on top of her, fucking her," Shara said in a toneless voice.

"Yes, dear. What else?"

"She's having an orgasm. She's gone, left the room. She's part of everything, the whole world."

"Stay in the water, dear. Look at him through the water. What is he doing while she is away?"

Shara clutched the pendant, her fingernails digging into her palm. She had a terrible headache, she could barely speak.

"He's saying something, whispering into her ear," Shara said.

"What does he say, dear?"

"I don't know. I don't want to know."

"It's all right, you are safe under the water. Close your eyes. Listen to his words. Listen through the water."

Shara twitched, sucked in a breath of air.

" 'I am Victeris,' he says, 'I'm Victeris, the source of your power,' that's what he says."

Shara twitched again. Her hands curled up to protect her face. The pendant's chain pulled tight.

"Is there more?" Hazel asked.

"Yes," she whimpered, then continued. " 'When I call, you will come to me,' he says. 'When I speak, you will obey.' "

Shara ripped the pendant from her neck. She pounded the floor with her fists, twisting and turning trying to get away. Gentle hands held her arms, her legs.

"That's enough," Hazel said calmly. "Come back to me. Come back to my voice."

Shara thrashed, but the Sisters held her in place.

"Come back to me," Hazel said. "Come back to the Heart. You are here with your Sisters, you are safe."

Shara opened her eyes. The four women were still sitting around her. Their heartstones shone in the dim light. Shara blinked, struggled to sit up. Baelandra helped her.

"Don't bend your knees," the Sister of Autumn said. "Keep them straight. They are still healing."

Shara winced, nodding. "What happened?" she asked. "Did I fall asleep?"

Hazel shook her head. She smiled and looked at Shara's hand. She opened her fist to reveal the stone. An inky darkness swirled within the crystal.

"No, my dear," Hazel said. "You just saved your own life."

15

BROPHY STEPPED out of the tunnel into the arena. He paused at the walkway's stone wall to watch the boys training below.

The last two days in bed had been excruciating. Nothing was as horrible as the first night in the latrine, but Brophy was thoroughly sick of the underground prison that had become his home. He was still tired and weak, but it felt good to get up.

He had walked for more than an hour on the King's Road to reach the arena. His Ape guard trailed him in silence. Brophy had nicknamed him Tiny.

Tiny fell in stride behind Brophy as he walked down the spiral ramp to the arena floor. He found Scythe on the far side of the arena, watching the contestants train.

"Wait here," Brophy told his hulking shadow. "I need to talk to my trainer."

Tiny scowled for a moment, but did what he was told, standing with his arms crossed at the edge of the arena.

Brophy walked over to Scythe. The Kher concentrated on the fighter he was watching. His eyes flicked left, up, right as he followed the contestant's sword.

"Are you fully recovered?" Scythe asked.

"No, I'm still weak, but I can do some things."

Scythe shook his head, his eyes narrowing over his hawk nose. "Come back when you are fully recovered. If you are not prepared to be the winner, don't set foot on the field."

Brophy frowned. He almost told Scythe that there were mental aspects to the game that he could learn, but he held his tongue. Bae once said, "If you always understand what your teacher is doing and why he is doing it, you have grown beyond that teacher."

Brophy left Scythe to his studying and walked slowly around the arena until he noticed Tidric. Brophy paused, then walked toward him.

The skinny boy stood by himself, watching the others as he practiced with a short sword. There were a few like Tidric in the arena, young boys with no money who couldn't get trainers to take them on. As soon as the boy saw Brophy, he rushed over. Tidric pumped Brophy's hand heartily, speaking all the while.

"I couldn't believe you caught that pillar after Phee pushed you. It was amazing!"

"Thanks," Brophy said.

"And then in the Jackal pit. You got lucky on that one. By the Nine, you were finished! And then that snail Bellu slipped, and you had him. Zam! Quick as a crocodile. You took him down with one punch!"

"I knocked him out?" Brophy asked.

"No, but he was still woozy when they hauled you away from the crocodile pit." Tidric sobered. "You had them there, too. You were faster than everyone."

"But not smarter."

"Well, anyway, you did really well in the first two contests. Are we going to run together again? Next month I will make it for sure."

"Why do you think next month will be any different?"

Tidric's smile vanished, and his gaze fell to the ground. He gouged a hole in the sandy arena with his toe. "Because I have to win."

"Why?"

"My family is depending on me."

"Ah," Brophy said. "Is that why you don't have a trainer?"

He shrugged again, still studying his twisting toe. "I guess. Sponsors pay the trainers. They don't teach for free. My sister is my sponsor, and we don't have the money for a trainer." Tidric shook his head and looked back up at Brophy. "Doesn't matter. I'll make it without a trainer."

"No, you won't," Brophy said. Tidric had desire, willpower, and a strong body. What he lacked was discipline.

The boy's nostrils flared, and he flushed.

"I'll make a deal with you," Brophy said, cutting Tidric off just as he opened his mouth to retort. Brophy pointed to Scythe. "See that man over there? Go talk to him, see if he will take you on as a student. He won't ask for money. He is . . . a friend of my family. If he agrees to teach you, I will run with you next month and both of us will make the top nine."

Tidric looked over at Scythe. "That man?"

Brophy nodded.

"But he's so small."

Brophy laughed. "You're welcome to challenge him to a duel if he doesn't look impressive enough."

Tidric's brow furrowed. "No."

He left Brophy and walked slowly toward Scythe. Brophy moved on, passing Phee and his kinsmen. One of Phee's cousins, Rejta, made a retching noise and doubled over. Phee coughed and retched as well. Soon, the whole group was grabbing their stomachs, bending over.

Brophy felt a flash of temper, but he set it aside and shook his head at their childish prank. He left the laughing boys behind and continued on his way. One corner of the arena held six massage tables and Brophy spotted Phanqui atop one of them. Brophy made a beeline for the king's cousin. Phanqui looked up, smiling under the ministrations of the old man who kneaded his leg.

"Well, if it isn't the drowned prince of Ohndarien. I heard you shat your entire body out of your ass and died."

"Almost. At the last instant, I jammed my thumb in and saved my life."

Phanqui chuckled. "Good to hear it. I'm glad you're not dead, but you'll forgive me if I don't shake your hand."

Brophy smiled. "I'll forgive you. But I'm curious. Phee and his group are out there, getting better. What are you doing here?"

"Ah, my legs. You set a devilish pace, and my legs are still cramped up. I'll start training in a couple of days."

Brophy frowned. Athyl's leg was all but useless, but Brophy could see him practicing across the arena. Brophy cut right to the point.

"Are you going to make the final nine next month?"

Phanqui grinned. "I'll do my best."

"Good luck to you then." Brophy frowned, turned on his heel, and walked away.

"Brophy, wait!" Phanqui jumped off the table, pulling a rough towel around himself. Brophy turned back around, giving Phanqui a flat stare.

"I'll help you again next month, if you have problems with Phee and his lot."

"Thanks," Brophy said. "But I need help in the arena, not in the desert. You didn't want to get to the arena last month, and it doesn't sound like next month will be any different."

Phanqui looked as if Brophy had slapped him.

"If you want to be in the top nine, go talk to that man over there." Brophy pointed at Scythe, who was shaking his head at Tidric. "He'll get you in the arena."

"Him? He's teaching the gnat," Phanqui said, making a sour face.

"Yes."

"He can't be expensive, then. I have—"

"He's free."

"What?"

"A friend of my family."

Phanqui gave Brophy a tolerant smile. "Look, Brophy, I know you're new here and all, but my teacher is—"

"He won at Nine Squares."

"He—What?" Phanqui's brow furrowed. "When?"

"Twelve years ago."

"But he's so small." Phanqui narrowed his eyes, trying to study Scythe across the distance.

"Go talk to him," Brophy said. "Tell him you think your teacher is better than him. See what he says."

Brophy left Phanqui standing with the towel wrapped around his waist, staring at Scythe. He went to Athyl next. The scarred man stretched his bad leg, grimacing. Brophy knelt next to him. "How's the leg?"

"It can't be worse than your belly."

"My belly isn't so bad anymore, but the smell in my nose won't go away." Athyl leaned forward, touching his toes through a silent snarl.

"Will you be ready to race next month?" Brophy asked.

"I will be there. I got as far as the Serpent square when Sheedar clipped me from behind."

Brophy noticed the bandage underneath Athyl's tunic through the sleeve hole. He shrugged.

For the first time, Athyl showed a hint of a smile. "Phee's little brother. You stuck your foot in his face at the beginning of the race."

"Ah."

"He is decent with a sword. Quieter than I would have thought, too."

Brophy nodded. "I want your help in the next race."

Athyl stopped stretching and looked past Brophy to Scythe, who was talking to Phanqui while Tidric practiced.

"I see you are gathering your own kinsmen."

"It's good to have friends."

"It is, but are they really your friends?"

"What have they got to lose?" Brophy asked.

"We can't all be champion."

"Not true. There can be four champions in four different months."

Athyl smiled. His burned face twisted up wickedly.

"If four of us make the top nine," Brophy said. "We target Phee and his kinsmen in the first few rounds. Then it will be four against a few solos. I like those odds."

"And when we are the only four left?" Athyl asked.

"I'm the best runner. I'll leave first, then Phanqui, then Tidric. You get one more chance to climb the tower. Except this time you'll have more energy and fewer wounds than ever before."

"You would get to the final four and then step aside?"

"I would. You this month. Me next month, followed by Phanqui, Tidric, and whoever else joins us and learns how to beat this ugly game."

Athyl shook his head, his smile fading. "You paint a pretty picture, Ohndarien, but human nature doesn't work that way."

"No, Physendrian nature doesn't work that way. I don't want to win this game, I want to destroy it. If the young men of this country would stop fighting each other, there would only be one man left to fight."

Athyl turned narrow eyes on Brophy. "The king?"

Brophy shrugged.

"There is a price on the heads of traitors, you know. You just made yourself worth a bag of gold the size of my fist."

"I'm betting there is something you want out of life more than a bag of gold." Brophy held Athyl's gaze.

The scarred man calmly glanced to the other practicing contestants before looking back at Brophy. "You have a lot of faith in your judgment of others."

Brophy nodded. "We'll start training in two days. I hope I'll see you then." He stood up and walked away. He didn't look back, and Athyl didn't call out.

Tiny fell into step behind Brophy as he climbed out of the arena.

OSSAMYR CAME to him that night. The door opened as silently as always, but Brophy was waiting.

"I was hoping—"

She shook her head, put a finger to her lips. Her white-feathered cloak slipped from her shoulders, falling into a pile on the floor. She climbed naked onto his bed.

"Ossamyr—"

Again, she shook her head, smiling. Her fingers slid across his belly, and she roused him with her hands in seconds. Brophy took a quick breath, forgetting everything he wanted to say. Wordlessly, she straddled him. They both gasped as he pushed inside her, and she began to ride him.

Ossamyr clenched her eyes closed and threw herself against Brophy with a terrifying intensity. He would have cried out if the queen hadn't kept her hand clamped over his mouth so he could barely breathe. They both reached climax before they even kissed. Brophy screamed into her hand as she shuddered against him over and over again.

Finally, the wave of desire receded, and Ossamyr collapsed into his arms. Brophy couldn't catch his breath, he was left utterly dazed and disoriented. Yet the moment she touched her lips to his mouth, his passion came surging back, and he could not get enough of her. They kissed for hours. He touched every part of her a hundred times. She never let him speak. Without words it was like a dream.

Their hunger built over hours, and finally Brophy couldn't wait anymore. He pulled her brutally to him. Her nails raked his back, her teeth bit his shoulder. All in silence, deliciously agonizing silence.

She drew blood from his neck with her teeth as she stifled her scream. Brophy shuddered with her, and they collapsed onto the bed, rocking slowly back and forth on its chains. The queen was covered in sweat, and the room smelled of musk and desire.

Ossamyr rolled onto her back, closing her eyes as her breathing returned to normal. Brophy reached out to touch the glistening skin between her breasts, running his finger along her breastbone. There should be a stone there, he thought. A red diamond.

He looked up to find the queen watching him. She put a hand over his eyes.

"Don't look at me, not now," she said.

He thought he saw a moonlit tear on her face, but he couldn't be sure.

"Ossamyr—"

Her hand moved from his eyes to his mouth.

"Don't speak. Just . . . be still, with me. Just be still."

He lay back, pulling her closer, and she laid her head on his chest. Her breasts were warm against his ribs, her feverish thigh draped over his legs. Brophy trailed his fingertips along the side of her body, then rested his hand across her ribs and suddenly squeezed.

She jumped.

He tickled her again, and she squirmed away. The queen rolled over and slapped him across the face. "Don't," she demanded, her dark eyes furious.

Brophy grinned and pounced. He pinned her to the bed, tickling her ribs, knees, butt, anything he could reach.

She fought fiercely, smacking her elbow into his nose. He jerked back, put a finger to his face, and came away with a spot of blood. The bed rocked slowly.

"I said don't." Her perfect, dark eyebrows furrowed. She sat up straight, holding her chin high.

"Yeah," he murmured, a slow smile coming to his lips again.

"Brophy—"

He leapt on top of her, pushing her down and tickling her again. She tried to fight back, but he pinned her arms and legs.

"No! Dammit, I'm serious!" She giggled, wrapping up into a ball as he attacked. He didn't give up until she was laughing in his arms.

"Hush," Brophy whispered. "They'll hear you." And tickled her some more. She laughed like a little girl.

Eventually, they collapsed to the bed. Brophy smiled at the queen, and she shoved his face away.

"I'll have you thrown in the Wet Cells for this," she said.

"How long has it been since you laughed?" Brophy asked.

The joy left her face. "Too long, Brophy, too long." She kissed him on the chest and sat up. He reached for her again, but she shook her head, her short silken hair in disarray. Quietly, she slipped to the floor, barely rocking the platform.

He watched her naked back as she crossed the room to her robe. He wanted to jump from the bed and kneel at her feet, tell her how he felt, but he kept his silence.

She lifted her robe from the floor. With a flick of her wrist, the light, feathered garment flared about her shoulders and settled into place, covering her glorious body.

The queen touched a spot on the wall and a crack appeared. She turned back, and her smile made him feel like he was drinking Siren's Blood, but it disappeared the moment she looked down. "I will come back again," she whispered. "As soon as I can."

And she was gone. The wall closed without a sound. Brophy lay back, staring at the moonlit sky through the open square above him. He wondered how he could feel so wonderful and so horrible at the same time.

16

*S*HARA LIMPED down the sinuous tunnel. The cavernous labyrinth had become a prison cell. She'd been lost for hours, and her torch was nearly burned out.

She could barely walk. Every step was a little agony, a petty torture. Her memories haunted her, awake or asleep. She tried to use her Zelani training to control them, but the power was gone. Her sexual feelings had fled beyond recall.

She had been in the Heart for ten days now. Over and over she had done the exercises the Sisters had taught her. Over and over she tried to cut the thread Victeris had woven into her mind. She relived her graduation so many times. She remembered it backward. She remembered it at a frenetic speed and as slow as if she and Victeris had been underwater. She pulled the color out of the room. She relived it upside down. She repeated his words over and over in her head until they bored her. His hook had been removed, his power shattered and broken. She was free.

Free to limp down a dark hallway, lost and alone. That was what Victeris had left her. He had used her up, stolen everything she wanted in the world. She couldn't call the magic. Her willpower was fickle and weak. She was nobody.

Only one thing gave her hope, like an apple dangled before a broken-down horse. Shara had discovered something crucial during her time in the Heart, a possible key to Victeris. That night in the pools, Victeris never once reached his climax. That time and all the other times as well. He never had an orgasm, not once.

This one thing stood out to her like a glowing moon. Why would he do that? Why would he refrain? Victeris, though perverted and dark, was a model of self-control. His every action had significance, so what did this mean?

Shara had been his prisoner for more than a month. He visited her every night, but she was not pregnant. Zelani were taught methods to avoid conception, but Shara hadn't used those techniques during her imprisonment. She should be carrying his child right now, but she wasn't.

Her revelation came quickly when she thought about it. The man must have gone decades without release. That was why he was so powerful. If Shara could shatter his control, she could do to him what he'd done to her.

The idea stayed alight in her mind like a torch in the dark, but it was a fool's hope. She would need her full powers to fight him, and those powers were gone, her will destroyed. She couldn't even find her way out of this damned hole in the ground.

Shara heard a noise behind her. She turned to see a light flickering behind a patch of stalagmites. A figure emerged, and Shara quickly limped away.

"Shara, wait!" Baelandra's voice echoed through the chamber.

With a sigh that verged on a sob, Shara stopped. She couldn't outrun the Sister. She couldn't outrun a snail.

Baelandra drew alongside her, breathing lightly. She glanced at Shara's dying torch, at the shawl covering her shoulders. Shara couldn't tell what the woman was thinking. A month ago, people's deepest desires would have been laid out on a plate. But no more.

"I'm so glad I found you," Baelandra said. The torchlight played on her lustrous red hair, flickered across her features. "We were worried. We thought that—"

"That the madness had returned? That Victeris had called me, and I had to go to him?" Shara said.

Baelandra's expression softened. After a long moment, she asked, "Did he?"

Shara closed her eyes, managed to open them again without tears. "No."

A flicker of confusion crossed Baelandra's face. "Shara, you don't have to run away like a thief. You are not a prisoner here."

"I know." She hung her head, feeling like a little girl. A little girl with skinned knees and pig shit on her feet. Crawling naked through the muck.

A tear did come this time, and she looked away. She rubbed her skinned arms. She couldn't even master her own thoughts. Everywhere she turned, she came back to Victeris.

"I'm sorry," she said. "I just didn't want to have this conversation."

"The conversation where I convince you not to go?" Baelandra asked.

"Yes, that one."

"How does it go?"

"You tell me that I'm still too injured, and you are right. You tell me it's too dangerous, and you are right. And you tell me to wait for the right moment before I face Victeris, and you are right."

"And you say?" Baelandra asked gently, standing small and beautiful in the light from her torch.

More tears came and Shara didn't try to stop them. It was useless. "I say there are fifty students in that Zelani school," she sobbed. "Eight of them are on the verge of graduating. Maeli or Gwynen could be going through that damned ritual with him right now. They may have already gone through it. I can't let that happen, can't let him do that to anyone else."

The muscles of Baelandra's delicate jaw clenched, and her eyes glinted. "Tell me."

Shara wiped her eyes. "Tell you what?"

"What your plan is and how I can help you."

With a sob, Shara threw her arms around Baelandra, and the little woman hugged her back tightly. "I need something before I face him. Something you can't give me."

"Come then," Baelandra said. "I'll take you where you can get what you need."

Baelandra and Shara wended their way through the underground maze. Twice, the Sister of Autumn stopped and opened a hidden doorway by touching the stone on her chest. Shara could never have escaped from this place on her own.

Baelandra came to a ladder that led to a trapdoor in the ceiling. They both climbed into a room filled with endless rows of costumes.

"Is this a theater?" Shara asked, running a finger down the racks of clothes. Masks lined a shelf over the costumes. Demons leered down at her. Feathered faces. A jocular fool. A lion's head. Soldier's helmets.

"Yes, the Blue Lily, in the Night Market."

Shara and Baelandra picked through the costumes, finally deciding on a poor man's ragged cloak and rough-spun tunic. Baelandra helped her change into it. When they had finished, the Sister stood back and gave her a critical eye.

"You look old and decrepit."

"That is how I feel."

Baelandra leaned in and gave her a quick hug. "May the power of the Seasons and the luck of the sailing stars go with you," she murmured.

"Thank you, Bae. Thank you for everything."

Baelandra hesitated, then said, "Can I ask you a question before you leave?"

"I know what you are going to ask, and the answer is no. I'm not going to kill him. Not yet."

Shara looked to Baelandra. The petite redheaded woman nodded, her eyes aflame. Shara squeezed the Sister's hand.

Baelandra returned to the trapdoor and descended into the darkness. Shara slid the rug over the top and left the Blue Lily.

She limped through the Night Market as an old man, a cowl pulled low over her face. A month ago, she would have walked naked, free as a dolphin slipping through the water. She would have appeared as everyone and anyone. A Zelani needed no disguise.

She worked her way through the empty streets. It was two hours before noon and the Night Market was nearly deserted. She paused in a doorway and checked to see if she was being followed. Baelandra warned that some of the exits from the Heart might be watched. There was no way Shara could be sure.

Finally, she reached the Scarlet Heart and walked cautiously through the open doorway into the common room. The remains of a roasted pig hung on a spit over a huge fire pit. A few coals burned in what must have been a raging blaze last night. Shara stared at the pig. Once again she saw herself crawling through the filth. Closing her eyes, she turned away.

An old cleaning woman bearing a soapy bucket and a scrub brush walked through a swinging kitchen door. The matron set down the bucket and put her hands on her hips.

"Sorry, old man." She shook her head. "We're not giving out scraps anymore. Can't feed ourselves or our customers with all the food rationing." She frowned. "It'll only get worse, too, when the Physendrians attack. Mark my words." The woman shook her head again, picking up the bucket. "You think those idiots would learn. Ain't an army in the world can bring down Ohndarien's walls."

Shara pulled back her hood. "I'm not here for food. I'm here to see a couple of old friends."

The woman's lips pulled together like a wrinkled prune. Her eyes narrowed in suspicion. "Who would your friends be?"

"Gedge and Reela. They were former Zelani students. I understand they have come to work here."

The old woman's face softened. "Why the tears, child?"

"I just . . ." Shara drew a shaky breath. "I need to see my friends, that's all."

The cleaning woman pointed with one crooked finger. "Up the stairs, third door on the left. They'll still be sleeping."

"Thank you."

"Seasons preserve you, child. The Wheel keeps turning. All sorrow will pass."

"I hope you are right."

The old woman winked. "I didn't reach this age by being wrong about such things." She turned back to her work.

Shara climbed the steps of the elegant brothel. The lacquered oak banister and paintings on the wall were a stark contrast to the seedy whorehouse where she'd been kept so recently.

Her fist trembled as she raised it to the door and knocked. Three quick raps. There was no answer. An unreasoning panic gripped her, and she turned to go just as a sleepy voice answered.

"Yes?"

That was Reela's voice. Shara stopped, put a hand on the old wood of the door.

"Is someone there?" Gedge asked. His familiar voice sparked the courage within her. She opened the door and slipped inside the immense bedroom. It opened to a balcony that overlooked the bay. The two failed Zelani students lay arm in arm on the bed, draped in a white cloth.

Reela sat up suddenly. "Shara? By the Seasons! Is that you?" She jumped up, not bothering to cover herself, and ran to her friend, throwing her arms around Shara. Reela hugged her tight for a long moment. Shara could not return the hug and Reela slowly backed away, searching Shara's eyes.

"Reela," Shara began, but found it difficult to speak past the lump in her throat. "I . . ."

"Come," Reela said quietly, taking her by the hands. "Come sit down on the bed." Gedge jumped out of bed to help. He was bigger than she remembered, with thicker shoulders, stronger arms. His voice had deepened, and there was more hair on his chest. She had known his body so well, once upon a time.

"Shara," he asked. "What are you wearing? You look as if you've been starved and beaten."

"We heard you left the city," Reela said, "with the ambassador to Ohohhom."

They sat her down on the bed. She tried to speak, to tell them what had really happened, but she couldn't. She hid her face in her hands and sobbed.

Gedge put his big arms around her. "Everything will be all right."

Reela joined them, sitting on Shara's other side and hugging her tightly. Her head barely came up to Shara's shoulder.

"It's Victeris, isn't it? He's done this to you," Gedge asked.

Shara nodded. "He took . . . He took everything from me."

Gedge stroked her hair like he had so long ago. Reela kissed a tear off her cheek.

"Then we will give it back to you," Reela said.

"We'll give it all back and then some."

SHARA AWOKE that night to the sounds of music and laughter. She smiled and pulled the pillow tighter to her chest. The horrors of her torture were distant now, covered over by the exquisite love Reela and Gedge had poured into her. The scabs on her knees didn't hurt as badly as they had that morning. The scabs on her heart were healing, too.

They were artists, Gedge and Reela. With tenderness and patience, they had invited joy back into her body. Shara thought she had become a barren land, unable to grow that kind of joy. But she wasn't barren, just parched beyond recognition. Gedge and Reela rained affection on her until she was full and fertile again.

They had gone slow at first, held her for hours and let her cry. A thousand tiny kisses turned to a light massage. Their tender fingers found every knot of pain and worked it free. The massage faded into longer kisses, lingering caresses as she lay tucked between them. Their hands, mouths, and bodies rekindled the fire within her. Together they brought her to an achingly slow climax that seemed to go on forever.

Shara could feel again. Wisps of her power floated all around her. Desire hummed through her. But their gentle caresses were not the greatest gift they gave. Once they helped Shara, Gedge and Reela turned their attention on each other. As the sun set, they made love to one another as Shara watched, entranced as the golden light moved across their bodies. She had never seen lovemaking like that. She had never watched such purity, such beauty, such love.

Shara had seen sex a thousand times. As a child, she watched animals rutting. At eleven, she had seen a drunken couple fumbling in an alley on Midsummer's Eve. She had joined a dozen Zelani students practicing their craft, had seen their affection and desire, but Shara had never witnessed two people use their bodies this way. It was so achingly beautiful that she cried anew.

Through them, she saw hope. A hope for something new, something greater than she had known before. It was not enough to regain her Zelani powers if they would eventually transform her into Victeris. What Gedge and Reela created with one another was the true power of the Zelani. Victeris twisted the magic to his own uses. He taught his students to shackle their desire, to lock it away in a dungeon. Perhaps he didn't even realize that love was the ultimate result of Zelani power. Love was the only garden from which true magic could grow.

A sudden noise snapped Shara out of her reverie. Gedge and Reela rushed into the room, their beautiful faces pulled tight.

"Soldiers have surrounded the building," Gedge said, quickly closing the door.

Shara sat up slowly. The smile did not leave her face. She was no longer the tiny person Victeris had made her. Her powers had returned, stronger than before and his hook in her mind was severed. It was time for a reckoning.

"They're downstairs, on the roofs, everywhere," Reela said, looking at Shara with such concern that Shara wanted to touch her cheek, smooth the worry away.

Shara stood, thin and naked in the lamplight. The heartstone pendant hung around her neck. "Concentrate on your breath," she said.

Gedge looked at Reela. "Shara, you have to—"

"Yes. I know. This first, then we face them. We must start with the breath."

Her calm infected them, and their Zelani training came to their aid. They breathed through the cycle. Shara took one of Reela's short silk robes and wrapped it around herself.

"You need to leave here for the moment. Cast the glamour, just as we were taught. Escape over the rooftops. The guards will never see you."

"But we never graduated. We never got that far."

Shara smiled, laid a hand on Reela's cheek. "My friends, if anyone in the world is a full Zelani, it is the two of you. You graduated each other, more surely than Victeris could ever have done."

"We don't have time," Gedge said.

"Start with your breath," Shara said. She breathed with them, took their fears inside herself and let them go. The energy roared through her and she gasped at how powerful it was. She looked into Gedge's eyes and saw shock and joy.

"Shara!" he exclaimed.

"Yes," she said. "Breathe. The power is there, waiting for you. Take it. Work your way through the gates, as we were taught. There is more power in your love than any sex I have ever seen. Use it. Build it. You will be invisible to them."

Gedge nodded. Reela simply stared at her. Shara went to the door, paused before she opened it. She turned, resting her hands flat against the wood, feeling it, feeling everything in the room. The salty scent of Gedge. The flowery scent of Reela. The lovely bed, the beautiful view from the balcony.

"Thank you, my friends. Thank you for what you have done. I can never repay you."

"Where are you going?" Gedge asked.

"Come with us," Reela said.

Shara smiled. She sent love and assurance to them. "No. Not tonight. Tonight, I have a date with our former master."

"Shara—" Gedge began, but she held a finger to her lips.

"Go now," she whispered. "I will find you later."

She slipped out the door and hurried down the hall. Four soldiers stomped up the steps as she descended. She felt their determination to find her, to capture her.

Shara's breathing was even and smooth. She opened the floodgate inside her and let it wash over them. "You will let me pass," she said.

They parted for her so quickly that one of them almost tumbled over the handrail. She walked between them. A sickening feeling welled in her belly, but she ignored it. She strode into the main hall where a dozen soldiers had backed the customers and staff into a corner. Two more stood at the doorway.

Shara hissed as she turned her inner river upon the two men at the door. They moved aside, their weapons clattering to the floorboards.

The nasty feeling grew, spread through her like ink spilled on a page. She ignored it and walked outside.

A glamour was child's play. She threw one over herself and walked into the crowd of the Night Market, heading for the Heart. Only one person noticed her as she strode down the middle of the street.

A single, cloaked figure emerged from an alley to her left. The milling crowd parted around Victeris as if he were a stone in a river. He pulled back his hood and smiled at her, a sly, charming smile.

"Hello, Shara," he said. "I did not expect to meet you on this street . . . unchaperoned."

"If you mean your soldiers, they are still fumbling with their manhoods in the Scarlet Heart."

Victeris chuckled. "Impressive," he said. "You have surpassed my greatest expectations."

She felt the warmth of his praise and rejected it. His magic swirled around her, an unwanted touch.

"I've moved beyond you," Shara said. "You can't match me anymore."

"Is that so?" he said. "To my eyes, we seem more alike than ever. You swatted my men aside like insects. And you liked it, didn't you? You've developed a taste for power, and you're really going to enjoy what you've become."

"You have no idea what I've become, but I will enjoy killing you."

"Killing me?" He pursed his thin lips and smiled. "But I am Victeris. The source of your power."

Shara stood defiant. "No, you're not."

"Your master now and forever," he intoned, taking a step toward her.

Your master now and forever.

She backed away from him. "No."

"You are mine."

You are mine.

Shara swallowed, her breath coming faster. "No," she barely whispered.

"When I call, you will come to me. When I speak, you will obey."

Her breath faltered. A couple people in the Night Market turned to look at her. Her knees buckled and she fell to the ground. One of her scabs split open, smearing fresh blood on the cobblestones. She pressed her palms against the cool stone and her whole body shuddered.

"I missed you, my child," Victeris said. "Come closer, let me have a look at you."

Shara crawled slowly to him.

He leaned over, pushing a lock of black hair away from her face. "You are lovely as ever."

His finger slid down her cheek and hooked the chain around her neck. Pulling the heartstone pendant out of her shirt he let it dangle in front of her.

"I don't think this becomes you, my dear. It's so crude—" He yanked on the chain and it snapped. "And you are so graceful."

Victeris tossed the stone into the street. "Come, we have a lot of catching up to do." He extended his hand and pulled her to her feet.

She followed numbly after him. "Yes," she whispered. "A lot of catching up to do."

OSSAMYR DROVE him into the desert again, holding the chariot reins with one slender hand. Brophy hardly noticed the swirling colors of the predawn sky. They rode without speaking, the only sounds were the slaves' breathing and the slap of their sandals on the cracked earth.

When they arrived at the Beetle starting line, he stepped from the chariot, and she began tying her colors about his waist and shoulders. She watched him as a sailor might appraise a new boat. "Good luck," she said.

"Ossamyr—" he began.

Brophy longed for the right words, but he couldn't find them while staring at the impassive face of this queen who was so different from the woman who visited him two nights ago.

She turned from him as though he hadn't said a thing and walked toward the other sponsors. Brophy waited for a moment, looking after her. Feeling like an idiot, he went to stand beside Phanqui.

The king's cousin flicked a glance at the queen. "Do you hate her because she is richer than you or more beautiful than you?" Phanqui asked, giving Brophy a little shove.

"I don't hate her."

"Obviously. To me and to anyone else if you don't tame that gaze of yours."

Brophy glared at him, but he could feel his face turning red.

Phanqui smiled. "It's all right, you can hit me, everybody else does."

Brophy shook his head. "I'd best get in place at the Crocodile statue."

Phanqui nodded.

"I'll be back when the gong sounds."

"This I must see, a Nine Squares contestant running backward."

"Someone has to make sure you finish the race."

"Do you think Athyl will run back, too?"

Brophy shook his head. "He said he wouldn't. He needs the head start."

"It's amazing how fast that man can run on one leg. Imagine if he had two."

"He wouldn't need us, that's certain."

Brophy made his way to his statue and waited for the first gong. True to his word, he walked back to join Phanqui, Tidric, and Phanqui's cousins, Merdol and Roph. This would be the twins' first race. Brophy barely knew the long-limbed and awkward young boys, just starting to get their true height. Phanqui had convinced his aunt he could protect his cousins, and they could use the experience. Brophy was reluctant to include the nervous and undisciplined boys, but they worked hard practicing with Scythe and won him over. Tidric had taken to ordering them around even though the twins were a year older than him.

The five of them took turns shading each other as before. Between the shade and the bitter tea Scythe had been force-feeding them for weeks, the heat was tolerable.

When the second gong sounded, Brophy's gang took off like a wolf pack, setting a brutal pace. Their strategy was simple, catch up with Athyl and fight anyone who got in their way. They barely reached the Serpent statue when Brophy saw a battle up ahead. He turned his run into a sprint and outdistanced his friends in moments.

Phee and his kinsmen, Rejta, Besdin, and Sheedar, had surrounded the scarred man. They took him in a rush, all four grabbing Athyl at once.

Brophy rammed into Besdin, knocking him away. Phee, Rejta, and Sheedar wrestled Athyl to the ground. Phee cursed and backed up as the burned man jammed a thumb in his eye.

Brophy twisted out of Besdin's grip, narrowly avoiding a chokehold. Rolling to the side, he kicked his opponent in the hip, throwing the other boy off-balance. Brophy rolled to his feet just as Phanqui and the others arrived.

Phee held both hands to his injured eye. "Let's go!" he snarled and rushed away, half-blind.

Sheedar and Besdin sprinted after their cousin, but Athyl wouldn't let the fourth boy go. He closed his hands around Rejta's neck.

"I owe you, boy," Athyl rasped.

The kid dropped low and punched Athyl in the stomach. His scarred face twisted into a grisly smile, and he smashed his head into the boy's nose. Rejta fell like a log and didn't move again.

"Is he dead?" Brophy asked.

Athyl's burned face was still twisted into that hideous smile. "No. Want to finish him?"

"No time," Brophy lied. "If we don't hurry, the other Beetles will catch up.

Only Phee, Besdin, Sheedar, and three others are ahead of us. If we catch one of them, all four of us will be in."

Athyl grunted, giving one last look to the unconscious Rejta, and they all ran on. Merdol and Roph stayed with them for a long while, but they faltered in the last few miles. They were happy, though. They knew they were running with the winning group. Brophy thanked them for their help and told them to be ready for next month.

Brophy, Athyl, Phanqui, and Tidric struggled up the mountain and entered the arena as the last four contestants. An ambitious runner tried to get past them at the last moment. Athyl grabbed him by the back of the neck and smashed his face into the wall. The rest of the runners held back as they jogged down the spiral to the arena floor.

Brophy looked to the royal box as his friends leaned over, hands on their knees, taking the only rest they would receive. The royal box was made of a deep, rose-colored wood, polished to a mirror finish. It stood on stilts at the edge of the arena, offering the best possible view of the Nine Squares. Cloth of gold hung from the three sides, a huge phoenix embroidered on each in crimson thread.

The queen looked down on him, nodded, and smiled. But it wasn't her real smile.

Brophy turned away, clenching a fist. Ossamyr would notice if he continued to stare. He turned to Phanqui, who panted through a grin.

"Aren't you the least bit winded?"

Brophy frowned. "No. Just angry."

Phanqui flicked a barely perceptible glance at the royal box. "Did you ever hear about the monkey who stared at a phoenix so long he caught on fire?"

"No."

"That's because monkeys are smarter than that."

Brophy shoved Phanqui to the side. "I wish you could fight as well as you can talk."

"So do I, my friend. So do I."

Phanqui smiled and moved toward the Jumping Rat square with the rest of the contestants. Brophy longed to look back at the royal box, but he didn't. He joined Phanqui at the back of the line.

With the four of them working together, even Brophy was shocked how easy it was to advance. In the Jumping Rat square, Sheedar went for Athyl's bad leg. Athyl dropped him to the stone. In the Jackal pit, the scarred man didn't wait. He grabbed the nearest contestant and threw him off the platform just after the gong, then limped into the pit, picked up a bone and climbed slowly up the other side.

"Not about winning," Athyl rasped as he reached the top. "S'about not losing."

The Crocodile challenge brought Besdin, Phee's last remaining kinsman, within Brophy's reach. Taking a deep breath, Brophy plunged under the water and wrapped up the young man like a snake. Phanqui, Tidric, and Athyl blocked Phee from coming to the boy's rescue. Besdin fought, but Brophy was bigger and stronger. In the end the only thing the boy did was use up his air. Eventually he took that fateful gulp. Brophy rose to the surface, taking a smooth breath as the boy coughed and sputtered, spitting up the vile water.

"Good luck," Brophy said to the boy who had mocked him in the arena, pretending to retch, hack, and cough. Soon enough he would know the truth of it. Brophy stroked slowly through the murky waters to the finish. The rest of the contestants waded slowly behind him.

The long-faced announcer bellowed into his immense brass funnel. "The bottom dwellers have climbed from the muck and become the silent, deadly hunters of the desert, whose sting is certain death. Which five will evolve from the deadly sting to the lethal bite? To change from Scorpion to Serpent!"

The contestants lined up at the edge of the Scorpion square. Phee talked in whispered tones to the sixth contestant, a dark-skinned young man with a serious mien. His name was Goripht, and Brophy had seen him train. He was not a part of Phee's group, but a blind man could see that Phee and Goripht had no chance unless they worked together.

They all donned shields shaped like scorpion claws and took up short spears made to look like a scorpion's stinger, the same weapon set Brophy had used to defeat Vakko.

Brophy flexed the pincer on the shield and tightened the strap. Scythe had shown him many ways to use it. In Brophy's mind, it could never be an elegant weapon, but even a crude weapon could be effective if you knew its limitations.

"Sting! Sting! Sting! Sting!" the crowd chanted, as the six of them took their places.

The gong crashed. Phanqui, Tidric, and Brophy fanned out, attempting to separate Phee and Goripht. Athyl hovered at a distance waiting for someone to turn his back. Each contestant had to draw blood from another. The last to spill blood was eliminated. The Scorpion square had a tendency of starting slowly and ending in a furious melee. Once one contestant had been marked, the rest went for blood like sharks.

Brophy warned everyone to play it safe. With their superior numbers, they could afford to go slowly.

Goripht left Phee's side and feinted at Athyl's bad leg. As the big man backed up, Goripht spun his spear around and tagged Phanqui. Blood flecked his shoulder. Enraged, Phanqui counterattacked, going for the man's face.

In the confusion, Phee struck out, but Brophy slipped inside the strike. He flicked his spear forward and gashed Phee's ribs.

But the move was a trap. As predictable as the sunrise, Tidric yelled and charged forward. Phee twisted, avoiding the young boy's stinger, and snapped his pincers down on the boy's wrist. Bones cracked. Tidric screamed, jerked back, but Phee held tight. The crowd went crazy, shouting and cheering.

Brophy roared and stabbed Phee in the forearm, knocking his shield out of his hand. Tidric fell to his knees, whimpering as Phee danced backward. The gong sounded and the fight was over.

Brophy knelt next to his friend, who cradled his wrist.

"Dammit!" Tidric cursed, trying to control the quiver in his arm. "I . . ." He looked up. Goripht had two red cuts, one on his arm and one on his chest. Both Athyl and Phanqui had scored on him. Phee, Athyl, and Goripht left the square, but Phanqui walked over, crouched down next to Tidric.

"I had him!" the boy said, gritting his teeth.

"You did," Brophy lied. "You were close."

"We have to go," Phanqui said.

"Next month," Brophy said to Tidric, and stood up.

The boy hung his head, cradling his wrist. "Yeah. Next month," he mumbled.

Phee followed Brophy with his gaze and a smug smile as his ribs bled steadily from the wound Brophy had given him.

The announcer's voice boomed through the arena.

"The scuttling stingers have become the deadly descendants of the great serpent Arridus, who will wake one day and swallow the world! But can they rise from their slithering bellies to become the great and powerful Apes, the Lords of the Trees?"

Brophy joined the other four contestants at the edge of the Serpent square. It was a barren area, much like the Scorpion square. The weapons had changed, but the rules were the same. The first four to draw blood on another continued on. One of the attendants handed Brophy a sword. The blade was barely sharp, it would take a stout blow or heavy slash to break the skin.

"Bite! Bite! Bite! Bite!" was the crowd's chant this time.

The hooded attendants drew lots to determine order and tied the boys together with one long rope about ten feet apart. As luck would have it, Phee had the far left end, then Athyl, with Phanqui and Goripht in the middle. Brophy was Phee's opposite, tied at the far right end of the rope.

"You're Goripht?" Brophy murmured to the dark-skinned man next to him. Goripht was a quiet favorite. He had made the top four for the last three months. He'd almost bested Phee in the Falcon square thirty days ago.

The man narrowed his dark eyes. "You are the Ohndarien dog?" he said.

Brophy smiled thinly. "I hope you know how to use that sword."

"Yes, I take it and stick it up your ass."

The gong crashed.

Athyl and Phanqui went after Phee. Goripht yanked hard on the rope, trying to pull Brophy off-balance. Brophy didn't resist. He jumped forward, parrying Goripht's outstretched sword. Now the rope didn't matter, it was all about the best swordsman.

Steel clashed and clashed again. Goripht's sword was a blur, but his technique was shoddy. Brophy parried, studied him. He let his anger work itself through his sword arm. He had been longing for this kind of fight for months.

When Brophy saw Goripht's nostrils flare in frustration, Brophy marked him. A dark red line on his arm. Goripht showed his teeth. Brophy parried a desperate lunge and marked him again. And again. And again. The noise of the crowd swelled. Cheers and whistles rained down on them.

The crowd chanted Brophy's name.

When the gong crashed again. Brophy shook his head and stepped back. Blood streaked down Goripht's arms and chest from a half dozen places.

"Enough!" roared an attendant. "To the next square." The cowled men came forward, untying the contestants. Brophy looked over at his companions. They had both scored on Phee, who now bled from four places, but Phee had managed to tag Phanqui on the leg.

"He's quick," Athyl rasped, as they lined up before the tall, haphazard tangle of dead trees that dominated the Ape square. "And patient. He waits for the opportunity and doesn't miss it."

"I won't either," Brophy assured him.

Athyl gave one of his twisted smiles. "Yes. I see that."

"This is working out," Phanqui said, grinning.

Phee, on the far side of Phanqui, heard the comment but said nothing. He stared grimly at the network of brambles and tree trunks inside the next square.

The announcer stepped up and continued the story. His deep voice overwhelmed the chant of Brophy's name. "The Serpents have risen from the ground. They are now mighty Apes, Lords of the Trees, but what a paltry kingdom to rule when there is the everlasting sky above! Only three will soar on the wings of the Falcon!"

"Remember what Scythe said," Brophy told Phanqui and Athyl. "Your hands are more important than your sword. If they slice you, you don't lose. Only if you fall out of the trees."

"Yes, your highness." Phanqui winked. "This should be easy, we already have one burning monkey on our side."

Brophy smiled as the crowd began to chant, "Swing! Swing! Swing! Swing!"

The contestants kept the same swords they used in the previous square. They moved to separate sides of the platform. The gong crashed, and everyone scrambled into the trees.

Brophy climbed as quickly as he could with a sword in one hand. Some of the branches were barbed. In other places they had been weakened with saws or axes. Every step and handhold had to be tested before it could be trusted. Steadily and surely, Brophy scrambled up through the chaotic limbs. He and Athyl converged in the middle. Phee skirted them, staying close to the fringes, keeping his back to open air. Phanqui watched from below, closing carefully.

"It's only a matter of time," Brophy said to Athyl as he drew abreast of the scarred man. Athyl had his good foot on a solid branch and held a narrower branch with one hand, his blade naked in the other. "We'll have him one way or another."

Athyl nodded, said nothing. Brophy moved in front of him, climbing higher.

Brophy heard something behind him and whirled around. Athyl's sword caught him in the side, raking across his ribs. Brophy grunted and fell backward, losing his grip. Stars burst in his vision and Brophy grappled for a branch, any branch. He caught one. Athyl closed on him, slamming the flat of his blade down on Brophy's hand. Brophy's grip faltered and he fell, smacking and crashing through the branches. He managed to grasp the last branch before the long fall. It snapped. He shouted, half in pain and half in rage, as he slammed into the sand below.

The crowd started shouting Athyl's name.

Brophy struggled to roll over, to regain his breath. His ribs burned. When he looked up, Athyl stood next to him, looking down. Phee hopped from a branch, smiling and shaking his head.

"Why!" Brophy cried to Athyl.

The scarred man's eyes were empty. There was nothing there, no triumph, no remorse.

"I can beat both of them. I'm not so sure about you."

"What? But I would have stepped aside the second we eliminated Phee!"

Athyl's eyes narrowed. He shook his head. "That is a chance I could not take."

He turned and walked out of the square just as Phanqui dropped to the sand and came running over.

DARK CLOUDS bunched and twisted on the western horizon, rolling quickly toward them. The wind of the storm's approach ruffled through Brophy's long blond curls, but no rain had fallen yet.

It was said that Nine Sands, the desert north of Physen, was filled with the spirits of fallen Nine Squares contestants who roamed the parched badlands as ghostly animals. Each took the form of the square that had killed him and preyed on unwary travelers at night. All except those who died in the burning wicker tower of the Phoenix. Their spirits raged as thunderstorms, sweeping across the dunes as they lamented their failed brush with godhood.

Brophy and Scythe watched in silence as a stooped crone in a feathered cape, a young woman with a bitter face, and an angry young boy stood over Athyl's shrouded body. They were his only family members, the only three who had come to this meager funeral. They only stayed for a short time, the crone murmuring ominously about the coming storm. As the family left, scurrying across the shifting sands, Brophy looked at the approaching clouds, wishing Athyl was in there somewhere so Brophy could curse him as he spat lightning and rain.

The betrayal had been stupid, senseless. Athyl might as well have turned the traitor's sword on himself.

"I agree with Physendrians about funerals," Scythe said. "The shorter the better."

Brophy said nothing. Phanqui had fallen in the Falcon square and Phee in the Lion. Brophy could still picture Athyl climbing the burning tower, halting and slow. He'd taken a nasty knife wound from Phee in the Falcon square and could barely use his right arm. Still, the burned man climbed, but when he reached the top, the flames had already ignited the rope. Athyl quickly shrugged on the ceremonial Phoenix wings and flew.

Flew and fell and died. Weakened by flames, the rope snapped before he had gone forty feet. He plunged headfirst to the arena's stone floor. The crowd went wild at the sound of his neck snapping.

Brophy closed his eyes as he tried to banish the memory. His stomach turned, and he held down the urge to vomit. Why did it have to be that way? It was senseless. If Athyl had stuck to the plan, he would have entered the Phoenix challenge with a healthy arm. He would have climbed faster. He would have made it to the rope before it burned. He would still be alive, the Nine Squares champion.

Brophy opened his eyes again and stared down at the abandoned body, wrapped in a frayed black cloth. How could people live this way? How can they bear it?

"Enough," Scythe said, an edge to his voice. The wind howled. "Back to your training."

Without a word, Brophy turned and began running through the desert. A few raindrops pelted his face. Wind whipped across him, picking up sand and dust as it went. Scythe caught up with him and matched his pace.

"Where will the others be joining us?" Brophy asked.

"Forget about the others," Scythe replied.

Brophy looked at him. "What?" More rain fell. In moments it would be a deluge.

"Phanqui came to see me this morning. He and his cousins won't be running with you anymore."

Brophy slowed to a stop. The air swirled, tossing his blond curls sideways. He blinked against the rain. "Why?"

Scythe stopped with him, his hawk's eyes boring into Brophy. "You scared someone, someone powerful. The king can't have an Ohndarien winning at Nine Squares on the eve of an invasion. Threats have been made. Rewards offered for your defeat."

Brophy sneered. He turned and began running again. Scythe followed him.

"I'll talk to Phanqui," Brophy said. "He will run with me."

Scythe kicked out Brophy's foot, and Brophy crashed face-first into the sand. The little man leapt on Brophy's back, twisted his arm, and shoved his face into the ground. Brophy growled, fighting back, but he couldn't break the hold.

"When will you wake up?" Scythe shouted over the wind. "This is not Ohndarien! This is not a run on the wall! This is Physendria, and everything is under the king's thumb. Here you dream only as far as he allows."

"Get off me!"

"I would not be on you if you were watching your own back."

Brophy spat sand from his mouth, wincing at the pain from the wound Athyl had given him. "I know what I'm doing!"

"No you don't," Scythe said in a low voice, leaning close. "You see the world the way you want it to be, not the way it is. You see people the way you want them to be, not the way they are. Open your eyes, Brophy. The world is an ugly, brutal place, and you are alone in it."

With that, Scythe released him and leapt to his feet.

"They saw you disgrace Goripht. You made him look like a drunken ape. They saw you create an army from a gang of Beetles. You wanted to scare them, and you did. And now they will kill you for it."

Brophy stood up, wiped his wet hair back from his face, and blew the sand off his lips. Scythe stood in the rain, the cloth of his hood plastered against his face.

"I won't do it your way," Brophy said.

Scythe shook his head, his brows furrowed. "Then give up. Leave with me, today. I will get you out of here."

Brophy shook his head vehemently. "No. I won't go, not without . . ." he cut himself off. The rain fell hard, blurring the air, turning the badlands into mud. Thunder boomed overhead.

Scythe showed his teeth. "Without what? Without winning? Or without Ossamyr?"

"You don't know anything."

"I know you aren't the first boy she's bedded, and you won't be the last."

"Enough," Brophy growled.

"Beauty is difficult to resist. I may be the only one of her champions to ever refuse her. It drives her mad. She's been trying to bed me ever since."

"Liar!" Brophy whirled on Scythe, swinging at his head. Scythe blocked it and slid to the side. Brophy twisted, but not fast enough. Suddenly, he found himself lurching forward, off-balance. He stumbled on the wet sand. Scythe dropped low, giving Brophy a tiny shove. Yet again, he went down.

Scythe glared down at him, his black eyebrows crouched together. "You mean nothing to her. She is using you like she uses everybody else. When you cease to amuse her, she will shed you like a cloak."

Brophy leapt to his feet. "Get out of my sight!" he snarled. "I don't need you!" He hurled a handful of wet sand at the man.

Scythe blinked, letting the grains bounce off. He shrugged.

"Get away from me!" Brophy yelled.

With a stiff bow, Scythe said, "You deserve nothing less." He turned and disappeared into the driving rain.

19

RELLIS SEETHED as he arrived at the Zelani school. The Master of the Citadel met him at the wrought-iron front gate. Two guards stood at stiff attention on either side, helmets gleaming in the sun.

"Dammit, Gorlym, I ordered you to bring Victeris to my chambers," Krellis said, shouldering his way past the man. "I don't have time for this. The Sisters scheme in the Heart, the city teeters on the edge of civil revolt, and Physendria's army is almost at the walls."

The rose-colored buildings were enclosed by the ornate marble wall. The Zelani school was once the home of J'Qulin the Sly. His pet project had been constructed with a great deal of skill and money. Citizens shook their heads and even laughed outright at the three extravagant buildings connected as a sprawling complex. The school stood out as a gaudy splash of pink on the otherwise cool blue Ohndarien, but the unique promise of the Zelani had slowly changed the prevailing opinion. The rose-colored buildings had come to suggest mystery and magic, luscious young women and beautiful boys instead of bad taste.

Gorlym jogged to catch up with Krellis, then fell in stride with the Brother's long steps. "I know, sir, but he wouldn't come." He paused, then said,

"And I thought you needed to see this with your own eyes. I don't think . . ." He paused again.

Krellis growled. "By the Seasons, Gorlym. I made you Master of the Citadel because you had courage. You're stumbling over your words like a green spear boy."

"I didn't think you'd want anyone else to see this," Gorlym said, flushing.

That caught Krellis's attention. "What happened?"

"I'm not exactly sure, sir."

Krellis glanced sidelong at his second-in-command. Gorlym had never been a timid man, but something had spooked him. "You said all the students are gone?"

"Yes, sir, all of them."

"Where?"

"I don't know, sir. The school was guarded, as you commanded. No one was allowed in or out unless they had permission from you or me."

"Then how did they get out?"

"Well, sir, the guards said that those who passed them had the right permission."

"They bore my seal?"

"I pressed them about that, sir, and it is my impression that they did bear your seal, though not one of the guards could specifically remember it. It is a bit confusing. The guards swear on their swords that no Zelani passed the gate."

"But they could not remember my actual seal?"

"No, sir."

"Damned Zelani," Krellis muttered, striding past the second pair of useless soldiers standing at the doors to the main building. "What use are guards if they can be bewitched by ten-year-old girls?"

"Shall I send them back to the Citadel, sir?"

"Not yet. What about the staff? Did they walk right past your men, also?"

Gorlym flushed. "There were none, sir. Except him," he said, as they rounded the first corner. In the center of the hall lay an ancient, bent-backed man. He was as dead as a three-day fish. His wrinkled arms and legs were tucked into his stomach as if he had been stabbed.

"How did they kill him?" Krellis asked, pausing in front of the old man. He toed the corpse's arms aside. There wasn't any blood, but his mouth was stretched open in a twisted grimace, his bushy brows pushed upward.

"I don't know," Gorlym said. "There isn't a mark on him."

"Who is he?"

"Sybald. Victeris's manservant."

"Perhaps he died of old age," Krellis said in a flat tone, continuing down the hallway.

They climbed the spiral staircase, around and around for several stories, passing a strange array of tapestries. Krellis had not visited Victeris's tower for years. The tapestries were new, and most of them were of men and women coupling in different ways. Some of the depictions were woven with the bright colors of love and romance, some with darker hues and more gruesome subject matter. Krellis frowned and turned away, ignoring the perverse images until they reached the top step. The last tapestry stopped him, and he paused to look at it. It showed a magnificent city with silver minarets that reached for the skies. The city was in flames. In the foreground, a fleet of black-sailed ships brought darkness and death.

The Fall of Efften. He paused for a moment, thinking back on Victeris's strange reaction when Krellis told him about the mythical music box and child. Shaking the thought from his head, he continued on.

As Gorlym said, two guards waited outside of Victeris's rooms, muttering to each other. As they saw Krellis, they stopped talking, and snapped to attention. Krellis strode between them.

He opened the door, ready to beat his brother bloody for the waves he was making during this delicate time. The smell of shit hit him like a physical blow, and he covered his nose with his arm.

"What the—" Krellis growled. Piles of human feces littered the floor. Puddles of urine stood in the hollows of the flagstone. Brown smears painted the walls. Victeris's immaculate desk had been turned on its side. Papers were mixed with human waste. His bed linens had been stripped and lay crumpled on the floor. The mattress sat askew on its frame, streaked with two erratic stripes of blood. It smelled like it had been this way for weeks.

Victeris crawled out from behind the bed and started across the floor on bloody knees, heedless of the filth. He thumped into the desk, circumvented it, and continued on his way. He was naked, and he murmured constantly to himself, oblivious of his brother's arrival.

Krellis stared in shock, then turned and slammed the door behind him.

"By the Nine, what is wrong with you?" he shouted.

Victeris jumped, paused. He rose up on his knees like a gopher. "Krellis," he said, beaming. "My brother, blood of my blood, flesh of my flesh. I'm so pleased you are here." He put his hands back on the shit-covered floor and began crawling again. "I need to tell someone. I need to tell someone who knows."

Krellis ground his teeth. "What happened to Shara?"

"My lady," Victeris intoned. "Shara-lani. She did it. She set me free."

"Set you free? You set her free, you idiot. Her and the rest of the Zelani!"

"No no no. She set me free. I am free, brother."

Krellis flexed his fingers. "Where is she? You had her in hand for more than a month. I wanted to give her to Father Lewlem when the fleet arrived."

"She set me free," Victeris said. "She listened to me. I told her everything, things I have never told anyone else, and now I'm free of it."

Krellis wanted to throttle his brother, but he spoke evenly. "Freed you of what?"

"Our mother's curse. She bound me, bound me to silence." Victeris crawled headlong into a wall. His head cracked off the stone, but he only paused a moment, then continued crawling in a different direction. A trickle of blood ran down his forehead, dripping onto his hands.

"Stop it, or I'll have you tied," Krellis commanded. What had that witch done to him?

Victeris crawled onto the bloody mattress. "You always thought it was Father who made us who we are," Victeris said, clinging to the edge of the bed. "Father was nothing. Father crawled. She made him. He crawled."

With stiff precision, Krellis turned away and opened the door. He stepped out and closed it behind him.

"Bring some rope, strong wine, and sleeping powders," he said.

"Yes, sir." Gorlym gave a small bow.

"And prepare a bath."

The Master of the Citadel motioned to one of the guards, who turned to go.

"And Gorlym," Krellis said, looking meaningfully at the man who was about to leave. "If any of your soldiers breathe a word of this, they die the next day. Understand?"

Krellis's second-in-command paused, then inclined his head. "Yes, sir." The guard hurried off.

Krellis went back into the room. Victeris didn't seem to have noticed his absence. He had crawled off the bed and resumed his circuit of the room, still talking. "Father knew I saw him. That's why he never touched me. That's why he took it out on you and Phandir. You always wondered, didn't you, why he never struck me? I know you did. He was ashamed around me, ashamed. He knew what Mother would do to him if he touched me."

Krellis flexed his fist as his brother stirred up long buried memories. "I know what kind of man my father was," Krellis said. "He had no shame."

"No. He was weak. He crawled."

"What are you talking about?"

"I saw them, when I was very young. A few years after you were born. I fell asleep behind the changing curtain, and I saw them naked. Fucking. Mother told him to wait. Mother told him to hold back, but he couldn't. He lost control of his manhood, and she punished him. She made him crawl. She said he disgusted her and sent him from the room. I started crying, and Father saw me. He saw me and hated me ever since. I promised Mother I would never be weak, I would never lose control of my manhood. I never have. I have never been disgusting. I have never crawled. They crawl. I don't crawl."

Krellis tried to imagine his father that way. He couldn't. There was no way that monster from his childhood could have been the weak puppet of a mother he could barely remember.

Victeris rose to his feet, stiff and awkward. "I have told you now. Shara-lani wanted me to tell you, but there is something else." He blinked, found Krellis, and staggered over. Krellis caught him, his brows furrowing as he held his brother stiffly at arm's length.

Quick as a snake, Victeris snatched the dagger from Krellis's belt and thrust it into his brother's belly. Krellis twisted at the last second. The dagger went deep into his side, through skin and muscle.

Krellis roared and clubbed Victeris on the side of the head. The slender man crashed to the floor, his cheek torn and bleeding, but he laughed and jumped to his feet again, pointing the dagger at Krellis. Putting one thick hand on the leaking wound, Krellis stared at his brother.

"That was for Brophy." Victeris giggled. "She said to say that was for Bro-phy." He lunged again, dagger first. Krellis batted the weapon aside, grabbed Victeris by the throat, and flung him backward. His head cracked against the wall next to the window, and he crumpled in a heap below the casement, mumbling.

"She is my master now and forever. When she calls, I will come to her. When she speaks, I will obey."

Keeping an eye on his brother, Krellis examined his wound. There was a lot of blood, but his guts were not punctured. He got lucky. The seventh and final assassin could have been his own brother, caught in the grips of a witch's enchantment.

Senseless and sprawled on the floor, Victeris continued mumbling. "There's only one more thing I have to do," he slurred. "One more thing to do . . ."

Shaking his head, Krellis stepped into the hallway, slamming the door behind him.

"Sir, you're wounded!" Gorlym said, looking at the blood dripping down Krellis's cupped fingers.

"No one goes in there," Krellis commanded. "No one. Not until I return."

Gorlym turned to the remaining guard. "Run and get a healer, and send three men up here."

The guard sprinted down the stairs and disappeared.

"Lock that door," Krellis said to Gorlym, then started down the steps. He wanted to get away from here, away from the shit-covered, babbling fiend in that room, away from this pink palace with its perfumed halls. He paused in front of the tapestry of the Fall of Efften. Victeris was a strong Zelani, the strongest user of magic that Krellis had ever met. What had that bitch done to him?

Gorlym locked the room and ran to catch up with Krellis. The Brother of Autumn frowned at his second-in-command.

"How many men have seen him like that?" Krellis asked, as they started down the stairs.

"Just a few," Gorlym said.

"I want their names."

"Yes, sir."

"And no one else is to see him. Only me."

"Yes, sir. What about your wound?"

"It's nothing. Hot water, a needle, and some horsehair and I'll live." They reached the bottom of the stairs, strode past Sybald's dead body and into the fresh air. Krellis took a deep breath.

"Sir, what—"

"Shut up, I'm thinking—"

A sickening crunch interrupted Krellis's thoughts, and the two guards at the gate shouted. One of them ran toward the noise and disappeared from sight around the side of the building. Krellis sprinted after them, despite the pain that fired into his side.

Victeris lay at the base of the tower in a splash of his own blood. His broken limbs pointed in awkward directions. His eyes were still wide-open, staring at nothing.

Krellis's run slowed to a jog, then a walk. He stopped and looked down at his brother's smashed face, put his hand against his side, and drew a breath. Three guards and Gorlym stood around the Zelani master's body, and no one said a word.

Krellis thought of the tapestry, the minarets, the flames devouring the city. He glanced up at the tower far above, and his breath caught in his throat.

A young woman in a blue gown stood at the tower window. Her long dark hair flew to the side in the steady breeze. She smiled at the scene below, instantly reminding Krellis of his dead brother's sly grin.

Shara looked away from the body and met Krellis's gaze. His heartstone throbbed under his shirt, and he put his hand to his chest. She raised the bloody knife that Victeris had dropped and pointed it right at him.

Gorlym turned to follow his gaze upward. "What do you think made him jump?" the man said, seeing nothing in the window above.

Krellis clenched his jaw and tore his gaze from the gloating witch. He tapped Victeris's body with the toe of his boot.

"Somebody cover that up," he said in a flat tone. "And pull our men out of here."

Giving one last look to the now-empty window, he turned and walked away.

20

ROPHY SAT beside the wardrobe, staring into the darkness. He was not surprised when he heard a tiny scrape from the wall to his left. Ossamyr stepped through in her white-feathered cloak, the cowl drawn close over her face. She crossed to his bed on silent feet, the light of her lamp glowing before her. His heart beat faster as he watched the way the feathers separated slightly along the curve of her hip. The moon had risen, filtering light into the room, and her black hair shimmered as she pushed back the hood.

"Brophy?" she said softly, turning. She spotted him. "What are you doing over there?"

"Watching you."

He knew she would come, just as she had every night for the past two weeks. Ossamyr said she would give him a rest tonight. Tomorrow he would run in Nine Squares for the third time, and he needed his strength, but he knew she would be here.

After Scythe left, Brophy had continued his training alone. The other contestants treated him like a poxy beggar. Tidric was the only other person who would talk to him. Even Phanqui kept his distance. His sad eyes said that he regretted it, but he never lingered when Brophy was near.

Ossamyr took his hand and led him to the bed. With a quick tug on the cord at her neck, she loosened her cloak. The feathers whispered off her shoulders and piled on the ground. She climbed naked into the swinging platform and winced.

Brophy grabbed her hand. "What's wrong?"

"Nothing. I'm just not feeling my best."

"Why?"

She shook her head, her dark hair swinging. "A warm bath and I will be fine." She looked up at him and smiled.

Brophy untied his pants and climbed in next to her. She did not slide on top of him and make love to him, as she always did. She just lay on her side staring at him. Brophy started to kiss her, but a look in the queen's eye made him stop.

She scooted closer and laid her head upon his arm. Her slender fingers traced a spiral across his chest. Brophy relaxed onto his back and stared at the ceiling. The sting of her rejection faded quickly. He wanted her close to him, that was enough.

"Are you still determined to compete?" she asked.

Determined? No. Required. After Athyl's death, after Scythe's speech, after the last three months of dancing to Phandir's strings, Brophy could not walk away. He couldn't.

He looked at Ossamyr, her smooth skin glowed in the moonlight. The queen's black eyes were old and unfathomable. He had never hated a man more than he hated King Phandir.

"Isn't this what you wanted?"

"So much has changed since then, Brophy." She paused, as if she would say what his heart longed to hear, but instead she murmured, "You have lost your friends and your teacher. You are alone in this contest."

He wanted to ask her about Scythe, wanted her to tell him that she had never laid a hand on the man, that she had not bedded any other man but the king, but he couldn't seem to ask.

"Tidric will run with me," he said. "He cannot compete with his broken hand, but he will help me make the final nine. And Phanqui is still running. He may yet change his mind."

Ossamyr watched him, as though deciding something. "It is not simply the boys. The king will not let you win."

Brophy drew an even breath. "He'll cheat."

"Oh Brophy," she murmured. "It is his contest. Do you think he would let it serve anyone else?"

It was the first time he had ever heard fear in her voice. His resolve strengthened.

"It doesn't matter. I have to win. Now more than ever."

Brophy touched her cheek. Her hair glowed silver with moonlight on one side, gold with torchlight on the other.

She smiled, the edges of her eyes crinkling, but it was not a happy smile.

"Brophy, I—" she started, winced, and sucked in a quick breath. She put a hand to her stomach and sat up.

"Ossamyr!" Brophy flipped to his knees. The bed rocked on its chains and he held her arm, leaning over her.

"Something's wrong," she murmured. "I don't know . . ."

She hissed through her teeth and fell forward onto one hand. She moaned and shifted backward. "Gods, Brophy!" She scooted to the edge of the bed and almost fell. He leapt after her, landing lightly on his feet, keeping her steady.

The queen pushed his hand away and rose. She took a few steps and doubled over. "I can't, it's—"

"Come. Sit down." Brophy led her to the wall. She squatted, putting her back against it. "What's happening?" Brophy asked.

"My monthly cramping, I thought." She let out a thin cry. "But it's worse. Ah!" She clutched her belly and bowed her head.

Something tickled Brophy's bare foot. A thin rivulet of blood snaked across the floor and pooled around his toe. "Ossamyr!"

She followed his gaze. Her thighs were covered in red. "No. It can't be." She put a hand between her legs and stared at the blood on her fingers. "I'm always late. I skip for months at a time."

"What do you mean? You're pregnant?"

"Oh Brophy . . ." She started crying. "Oh no." The blood kept pouring out of her.

Brophy clenched her shoulders. "You said you couldn't have children."

"I never have. But this is . . . It has to be."

Brophy pulled her to him. Her back spasmed under his arms and she struggled to breathe. She clung to him and sobbed, the queen's tears were wet against his cheek. Brophy began to cry with her.

"I told myself I was glad," she murmured. "I didn't want children—" Ossamyr cried out, her hands went to her belly.

"What should I do?" he asked. "Should I get help?"

She shook her head violently. The contraction passed, and the queen tried to stand up. "I have to go, it's not safe."

Brophy wouldn't let her stand. "It's all right," he murmured. "It will be all right."

"I'm sorry," she sobbed. "All those men I've been with and nothing. Nothing. I didn't think it could happen."

He didn't say anything, and Ossamyr did not speak again. They clung to one another for hours. She stared ahead, looking at nothing, and Brophy held her, his knees in the blood of their child. Her thin ribs shuddered against his chest as she cried, and he didn't ever want to let her go.

Eventually, her sobbing subsided, her eyes focused on his face, and she pushed him back. "I have to go. I can't be found here, especially now." She struggled to rise.

"Wait." Placing a hand on her shoulder, he rose and fetched the washbasin. He dipped the cloth in the water and gently began to clean her. Again, her eyes took on that distant look. Brophy couldn't stop himself from crying as he wiped her down. What would it have been? A boy? A little girl? Would he have been a young soldier, an academic, studying long hours in the library? Would his daughter have had her mother's dazzling dark eyes?

When he finished washing her, the water in the basin was dark red. He gave Ossamyr his own robe and mopped the blood off the floor with her feathered cape. Finally, he tied the bloody clothes together in a bundle with one of his old bandages.

Ossamyr had ceased crying. She took the bundle from him and crossed to the hidden door. He stared, unable to move, unable to banish the thought that the tightly wound lump might have been his son, his daughter.

Ossamyr laid a hand on the wall, looked back at him for a moment. He could see the beautiful slope of her nose, the rise of her shoulder where it covered her mouth.

"Thank you for your kindness."

"It was my child, too," he murmured.

"I know." She opened the hidden door, but paused again. "I wish I had met you twenty years ago." She paused, drew a shuddering breath. "Before Phandir. I wish we had met in your Ohndarien."

Brophy reached for her, but she was too quick. The queen stepped through and shut the door.

21

FOR THE third time, Ossamyr's chariot drove Brophy into the desert, but the queen was not with him. She sent a message that she would be at the arena when he arrived. Brophy watched the horizon, watched the slaves' muscles bunch and release as they pulled the chariot across the badlands. He gazed at the gray predawn sand, but no matter what he looked at, the only image he could see was the bloody bundle in Ossamyr's hands as she left his room last night.

Brophy closed his eyes and felt the wind on his face. He listened to the muted sounds of the desert, felt the impending heat of the sun. What was he doing here? The queen lay suffering in her room, and he was to compete in Nine Squares. It wasn't right. He didn't belong here. He belonged at her side.

The chariot jostled and slowed. Brophy saw a cluster of people and other chariots ahead. He narrowed his eyes, trying to see what they were staring at. Something on the ground.

A bloody body lay among the rocks. Brophy clenched his fist, denying the thick knot in his stomach. The slaves slowed to a stop and Brophy stepped down, walked with fated steps until he stood over the body.

Tidric's head was split open, his blood and brains splattered on the ground. The boy's mouth hung open, and his glassy eyes stared at nothing.

Brophy's muscles quivered as he slowly knelt next to his friend. He saw Celidon on his bier, white as the cloak that covered him. He saw Trent on

Krellis's balcony, beautiful even in death. He saw Athyl's body under the sandy burlap. He saw the small bundle in Ossamyr's hands.

Brophy grabbed the slender boy's arm, gripped it tight. He held his tears in, burning them away. Phanqui's first words about Tidric came back to him.

He's braver than most of this lot, but he lacks patience. A few years from now he'd be a champion, but he won't live to see sixteen.

Not because of impatience, he thought. Because of me.

Brophy swiveled on his haunches. Phee stood with Sheedar, Besdin, and Phaggo, his remaining uninjured kinsmen. They all watched Brophy and chuckled to themselves. Brophy walked over to them, measuring his steps.

Phee smiled as Brophy stopped before them. "I would have said the runt didn't have any brains, but what do you know? There they are, lying on the sand."

"Did you do this?" Brophy asked quietly.

"He did it to himself."

Brophy flicked a glance downward, then looked back into Phee's eyes. "There is a spot of blood on your knee."

Amused, Phee glanced down. He touched the red with his finger, brought it to his lips, and dabbed it on his tongue. "So there is. Tastes like gold to me."

Strangely, Brophy thought of Scythe, of the day he calmly beheaded Krellis's assassin. He had been appalled at the time. But staring at Phee tasting Tidric's blood, Brophy understood that deadly calm.

"I'm not going to kill you today," Brophy said. His voice was rough, thick with an emotion that he could not feel inside. His chest felt empty.

Phee and his kinsmen laughed.

"And I was so worried," Phee said.

"I won't kill you, but you'll wish I had." Brophy stared at him. "I promise you, your blood will run."

Phee's kinsmen laughed again, but Phee only managed an empty chuckle. He clapped Phaggo on the shoulder. "Come, my brothers. I smell a championship in the air."

Brophy continued to stare at the four boys as they climbed aboard their chariots and rode away. He returned to Tidric, and said a quick prayer. "Seasons take this courageous friend to the land where the sky is beautiful and bright, where winter does not freeze and summer does not burn."

Brophy climbed back into Ossamyr's chariot and drove to the Ape statue, past a smug Phee at the Lion's statue, and Phanqui, who would not look at him. Except for the slaves, Brophy was alone. Phanqui left the stone falcon and walked toward him. He stopped a few paces away.

"I just wanted you to know that if things were different . . ." Phanqui sighed. "You changed Nine Squares for me. I won't forget that."

"And yet you already have."

Phanqui frowned. "If you were me, what would you do?"

"I am doing it."

"I have family to think of."

Brophy nodded. "We all have family to think of."

Phanqui shook his head. "I just wanted you to know that my cousins and I won't touch you until you get into the arena. After that . . ." He shrugged. Phanqui had difficulty meeting Brophy's gaze. "Just thought you should know," he finished.

Brophy nodded, his gaze cold.

The other boy opened his mouth, closed it, then shook his head and walked away.

"Phanqui," Brophy said. The king's cousin turned around.

Brophy's eyes glinted. "Stay out of my way. I'm not holding back. Not for you. Not for anyone."

Phanqui took an involuntary step back, frowned again, and left Brophy where he was.

They both stood in the shadow of their statues as the gong sounded, and the first rays of the morning sun crested the distant hills. Brophy breathed in steady cycles. He barely noticed the heat of the next six hours. It couldn't compare to the fire inside him.

When the second gong crashed, Brophy took off at a sprint. His feet pounded the cracked earth. He passed Phanqui in a few minutes, heading straight for Phee.

Phee saw Brophy coming, slowing to prepare for an attack. Brophy put on a burst of speed. Before the other boy realized what was happening, it was too late. Phee lunged with a hand outstretched, but he wasn't even close. Brophy showed his true speed for the first time. Phee could not keep up.

The Beetle contest was all but over for him now. He could keep the lead. He had seen these contestants run, and he knew their limits. Brophy could finally run at his own pace. He meted out bits of his inner fire, and his legs ate up the miles. His lead stretched longer and longer. This is just the beginning, he thought. Physendria was finally going to see what one Ohndarien could do.

After an hour, Brophy was more than halfway there and feeling fine. He couldn't see anyone behind him, but he didn't slow down. He wanted to run. For the first time in months he felt he was doing something for Ohndarien. He would push himself all the way. He would—

A burning pain burst in his thigh. Brophy tumbled across the rocky ground, scraping his arm and back on the sharp rocks. Quick as a cat, he hopped to his feet. He looked for the snake, not even daring to rub his throbbing leg before he found it. He saw no snake. Was it a scorpion? Did he kick it up onto his leg?

Brophy saw the arrow on the rocks behind him. His gaze snapped up and he scanned the horizon. Craggy hills, littered with a hundred boulders half the height of a man. There could be a dozen archers concealed up there. He limped back to the arrow and picked it up. It had a blunted tip.

It took him a moment to make sense of it. Phandir didn't want to kill him, the king wanted to slow him down, humiliate the Ohndarien in the arena on the eve of invasion.

Looking down at his leg, he massaged the angry red welt. He waited for the next volley, but it never came. Reluctantly, he started running again, but the first arrow had left him with a limp. Three or four more, and he wouldn't be able to walk, let alone run. His pace slowed even more as he nervously cast about for the hidden archer.

As he descended into the boulder-strewn valley just before the arena, another arrow hit him in the back. Brophy gasped and stumbled, scraping his knees on the rough ground. He could barely breathe. Another arrow skipped off the rocks to his right, just missing him.

Forcing himself to his feet, Brophy sprinted in the direction of the shots. He rounded boulder after boulder. Nothing. He cursed quietly. He couldn't search the whole valley and still make the top nine, but he couldn't turn his back either. He stopped, trying to think.

Rocks crunched behind him, and Brophy whirled, racing toward the sound. He leapt around an outcropping and saw an unarmed man scrambling up the western side of the valley.

"You are wasting precious time."

Brophy spun about to see Scythe. The little man held a bow in one hand and a thin knife in the other. With a deft motion, he severed the string and threw the bow at Brophy's feet. Brophy looked at him, stunned.

"My apologies," Scythe said. "I followed six of them into the desert last night. I was only able to find five this morning." He nodded at the fleeing man, who crested the lip of the valley, silhouetted against the blue sky for an instant, then disappeared. "Until you flushed the last one out." He sheathed his dagger.

"I thought you left Physen."

"So did everyone else, I think."

Brophy nodded. "Why didn't you kill them?" he asked, nodding at the broken bow.

Scythe narrowed his eyes. "I'm not certain. I decided to cut their strings and send them home with the flat of my blade instead." He looked to the south. "Time is wasting. You're not that far ahead of the others."

Brophy paused. Scythe looked into his eyes for a silent moment. A light breeze ruffled his black hair.

"Will I see you at the arena?"

"No one will see me at the arena," Scythe said, his dark eyes shaded under his brow. "But I will be there. Go."

Brophy ran again, leaving Scythe standing in the boulder-strewn valley. He avoided the regular path. If there were other ambushes along the way, he wanted to see them before they saw him. His leg throbbed, but it would stay loose until he stopped. His back was another matter. It ached fiercely deep inside, but he ignored it. Two blunted arrows would not be enough to stop him.

As Brophy struggled up the volcano's slope, he looked back over the desert and saw the crowd that followed. Phee and his little group were in the lead. Brophy wondered how many contestants lay behind them with broken bones or bloodied faces. He shook his head and focused on the incline in front of him. One leg in front of the other. Up the mountain.

He entered the arena amidst the noise of the crowd. Boos and cheers greeted him in thunderous waves.

He spiraled past the spectators all the way to the royal box. The king was there, looking past Brophy as if he didn't exist. Heedless of the danger, Brophy's gaze lingered on the queen. She sat as always, straight and regal, but he saw beyond that, even at this distance. She looked at him, a sponsor acknowledging her contestant, but this time, for the first time, it was more than that. Her eyes glistened, and she gave the slightest sad smile and nodded. Brophy swallowed the lump in his throat.

He ran beyond the royal box and the queen passed from his sight. He finished the race, walked to the edge of the Jumping Rat square and laid a hand on his back. He didn't rub it, just held it there. He didn't want anyone to know that he had been injured, least of all King Phandir. Let the bastard think his ambush had utterly failed.

As his breathing returned to normal, Brophy watched the other eight contestants arrive. Phee and his kinsmen came in second, third, fourth, and fifth.

The crowd went wild, shouting louder than when Brophy had arrived, but there were many boos as well. Brophy wasn't the only one who hated Phee and his thugs.

The sixth place belonged to Spaen, a foreigner from Gildheld. Phanqui followed after, just in front of two contestants Brophy did not know, who completed the nine.

The announcer introduced each of the runners. The man's booming voice filled the arena with a brief history of Phee and his kinsmen, the renegade Ohndarien prince, the capricious poet duelist from Gildheld, and the mighty king's cousin.

"These nine brave warriors have pulled themselves up from scuttling bugs to tenacious Jumping Rats, but who will have the strength to evolve from vicious vermin into fierce Jackals?"

When the first gong rang, Brophy scrambled to the top of a post. No one attempted to stop him and he danced across the pylons with ease, tying with Phee for first place on the other side. The two unknown contestants harried Phanqui. They forced him to the edge of the square. Trapped, he leapt desperately for one of the posts just beyond his assailants. One of them followed, tackling Phanqui in midair. They both plunged to the sand below, but Phanqui managed to twist his body and land on top of his attacker. Phanqui continued to the Jackal square while the other man was eliminated.

The eight boys spread out along the edge of the pit. When the gong crashed, Brophy lingered behind. He did not try to race anyone for the bones. The rest of the contestants made the usual mad scramble, but Brophy waited until all the bones had been grabbed, then launched himself after the last straggler, the second unknown contestant. Brophy had never seen the hairy-chested man practicing in the arena and assumed he had been planted by the king. Brophy grabbed the shaggy brute as he tried to scramble up the far side of the pit. The man fought back, but Brophy threw him to the ground. Brophy leapt on top of him and punched him with all of his strength. His fist cracked against the man's jaw, knocking him cold with one blow.

Brophy let the unconscious man slump to the ground. He turned with the bone gripped tight in his fist and stared up at the rest of the contestants, who all stood on the lip of the pit, watching him. Brophy waited, but none came to challenge him. Slowly, he climbed up the side of the pit. As he neared the top, Phaggo stepped forward, stomping at Brophy's fingers with his boot.

At the last instant, Brophy let go of his handhold and cracked the Jackal bone across Phaggo's shin. Phee's cousin cried out and stumbled backward. The crowd cheered. Brophy took his place in the line, and Phee sneered at him as Phaggo limped away, cursing.

The Crocodile challenge went even more smoothly than the Jumping Rats. Brophy dove as deep as possible and did not come up for air until he was two lengths ahead of the pack. It was an easy swim to the end. Afterward, he sat on the edge of the pool and watched the others chase Phanqui. Scythe's swimming lessons saved the boy as he dove underwater, twisting and squirming out of their grasp. The others continued to wade forward, refusing to submerge. Phanqui finished second and emerged next to Brophy.

Phee and his three kinsmen ganged up on Spaen, the foreigner from Gildheld. They forced him under and held him there for a long time. When Spaen floated to the surface facedown, they continued on, laughing and joking. Two attendants stepped into the pool and fished the body out.

The crowd cheered as the boys lined up and donned their shields and spears for the Scorpion square. Brophy calmed his breathing. He would have to be quick. Even if Phanqui didn't go for Brophy, it was four to one. Phee would never get better odds. He would try his best to eliminate Brophy here.

Sheedar and Besdin were good with spears, but Phee was deadly. Brophy would love to have squared off against Phee, but while they sparred, the other three would strike him so many times he wouldn't be able to draw blood on anyone.

Phee would have to wait. Phaggo was the biggest of them all, but he was the slowest, that made him Brophy's best target. Once Brophy drew first blood, he could concentrate on defending himself long enough to make it to the next round.

The gong crashed.

Brophy ran forward as three spears poked at him. They all missed, but they obviously weren't going to let him separate Phaggo from the crowd. Phee pressed Phanqui while the other three fanned out and corralled Brophy in the opposite direction.

Quickly, thought Brophy. I must be quick.

Lunging to his right, Brophy raised his shield and yelled. Two spears shot toward him. He managed to dodge them both and sidestep quickly to the left. His spear flicked out like a snake's tongue, pricking a dot of blood on Phaggo's thigh.

Brophy danced back, triumphant, but neither black-robed attendant called the hit. Phaggo, Sheedar, and Besdin closed in again, spears pushing Brophy toward the edge of the square. A few people in the crowd booed.

Snarling, Brophy ducked down, seeming to fall backward as he sent his spear forward. Besdin fell for it, lunging to the attack. Brophy slashed his knee. Again the hit was not called. Boos swelled from the crowd.

Phanqui cried out suddenly as Phee cut his shoulder. Phee could have left the arena, but he joined his kinsmen, making it four to one against Brophy. Spinning and dodging, Brophy fought for his life. The spears snaked in every-where. Phee poked him once in his bad thigh.

Then Phanqui appeared, stabbing Besdin solidly in the leg. The young man screamed and Brophy seized the chance. Sidestepping, he took a glanc-ing strike from Phaggo as he smashed his shield into Besdin's face. Blood ex-ploded from his crushed nose. The attendant could not ignore it. He called the strike.

Phee's pincher snapped on Brophy's arm as Sheedar finally scored his own strike, clipping Brophy in the side. With a vicious tug, Phee ripped a chunk of flesh from Brophy's arm. But the contest was over. Phee spat on Brophy and walked away.

Brophy held the pain inside, limping outside the circle. He pulled Os-samyr's sash from his shoulder, ripped a strip from it, and tied it around his arm. He used another strip to staunch the wound in his thigh.

Lacking a hit, Besdin was led from the arena, holding his gushing nose. The announcer called for the contestants to line up again, and Brophy strag-gled to his place.

The five of them moved on to the Serpent square. The attendants went down the line, handing out the short swords, and Brophy glanced at Phee, who smiled. He ran a finger down his sword and showed Brophy the light line of blood on his thumb. Brophy tested his own, but it was as dull as a river stone, nothing more than a shiny club.

One of the black-robed attendants walked down the line a second time and each contestant chose lots. Of course Brophy was last and of course he drew the longest straw. He glanced up at Phandir, but the king was too far away to see his expression.

Brophy got the center spot of the rope. He had no escape. They would tug him left and right.

"I'm sorry, Brophy," Phanqui whispered, as the attendant tied them to-gether. "I have to go after you this time, for the sake of my family."

Brophy didn't even look at him. He had an idea of how to escape the challenge, but he would only get one chance for it to work.

The crowd chanted as the five of them, tied together by one long rope, shuffled into the square. Phaggo and Sheedar flanked Brophy, with Phee on the far right end and Phanqui on the far left. As soon as the gong crashed, Phaggo and Sheedar yanked the rope tight.

Brophy gasped as the air was crushed from his body. The rope was tied in a slipknot. Held fast by the other boys, Brophy could barely move.

Phee and Phanqui charged in. Brophy waited till the last second before redirecting Phee's blade and barely dodged Phanqui. Both sharpened swords sliced right through the rope. Phaggo and Sheedar lurched backwards and fell on their backsides. A ripple of cheers ran through the crowd at the maneuver, and they began to chant Brophy's name.

Brophy dove between Phee and Phanqui. Phee's follow-up strike whistled over his head. Rolling to his feet, Brophy spun around in time to block Phanqui's next attack and deliver a devastating punch to his stomach. The air gushed from Phanqui's lungs, and he fell to his knees. Brophy had no time to follow through. Phee lunged, sword point first. Brophy deflected it and spun again. He lurched between Phaggo and Sheedar, who had just risen.

Phaggo charged, trying to overwhelm Brophy with sheer strength. Sheedar stood ready for Brophy to back away, but he didn't. He met Phaggo's strength with his own. Sparks flew as their swords clashed. The two combatants collided and Brophy head-butted Phaggo, sending the big man reeling.

Brophy spun again, barely blocked Sheedar's swing. Phee fought Phanqui, and for a brief moment Brophy had only one opponent. It was enough to bring a smile to his face. Sheedar realized it in the same instant and stepped back. Brophy feinted, drew a hesitant attack from Sheedar, batted the sword aside and brought his own blunted blade down like a hammer, crushing Sheedar's forearm.

The young man screamed, stumbled backward, and fell off the platform. Brophy turned, breathing hard. Phee hacked relentlessly at Phanqui and the young man buckled under the assault.

Brophy rushed forward to help his friend, but Phanqui's guard failed. Phee slipped through, stabbing completely through his thigh. Phanqui's scream filled the air and he crumpled to the ground, dropping his sword and clutching his leg. Phaggo rushed over to Phanqui and kicked him in the face, knocking the screaming boy back and shattering his nose. The crowd went wild. They stopped chanting Brophy's name and started shouting Phee's.

The gong crashed, and the Serpent square ended. Phee stared smugly at Brophy. Phanqui had passed out. His face was ashen, and his leg drooled a constant stream of blood. Through the haze of his own pain, Brophy wondered if Phanqui would die.

He blinked and realized that Phee and Phaggo had already begun walking to the next challenge. Brophy staggered after them.

"Once in an era," the announcer boomed, "two contestants fall in the same square. You have seen such a day. These three Serpents were so mighty that they slithered straight past the Ape's trees and leapt into the sky, spreading their wings as Falcons. But only two of them shall surrender their wings for the mighty muscles of the king of beasts!"

The crowd's roar was deafening. The attendants led Brophy, Phee, and Phaggo past the Ape square to the Falcon square.

Brophy hadn't faced the Falcon challenge before, but he knew all about it. Each of the three contestants was given a rope anchored at the top of a huge wicker cage. Like tiny birds they swung from the overhead bars, each trying to cut the ropes of the others. The first to fall was eliminated.

Controlling his breathing, Brophy did his best to relax and dispel the pain in his arms and legs as the attendant fastened a cord to his wrist. The cord was attached to the pommel of a dagger.

"Fly! Fly! Fly! Fly!" the crowd chanted, as Brophy crawled up the outside of the wicker cage, opposite Phee and Phaggo. Halfway up, they all stopped, climbed through the bars, and grabbed ahold of the knotted ropes awaiting them. There were dozens of ropes tied around the roof of the dome. Narrow wicker spars crisscrossed ten feet above the ground. If a contestant lost his rope and was lucky enough to land on one of the spars, he could run back to the edge of the dome and get another rope.

Brophy checked his knife. Dull, of course. No doubt Phaggo's and Phee's would be as sharp as their Serpent swords. Brophy closed his eyes for a moment, wondering if he had the strength to continue. He was injured in a dozen places. He blinked his eyes open, had trouble focusing for a moment. He saw Phee smiling at him from across the cage.

The gong crashed.

The three Falcons flew at each other. Phee and Phaggo swiped at Brophy as he passed. Phaggo missed. Phee barely sliced Brophy's shoulder. Brophy's blunt, useless dagger bounced off Phaggo's rope. They all reached the edge of the cage and clung to the wicker.

Brophy couldn't think straight. He couldn't come up with a way to win the challenge if he couldn't cut the lines.

Phee and Phaggo came for him again, springing toward Brophy's perch. Brophy jumped away. They both missed him. He barely caught the far side of the cage while Phaggo and Phee perched right next to one another. They launched again.

With a growl, Brophy sprang to meet them, determined to hurt one of them if he couldn't cut them loose. As the three of them neared the center, Brophy brought his legs up and kicked Phaggo in the face. The big man's head snapped back but he caught Brophy's leg in his meaty fist. Brophy kicked him again.

Phee stabbed Brophy's exposed calf and he cried out, stomping on Phee's hand. The young man cursed and dropped his dagger, which dangled from his wrist on its cord.

Brophy tried to stab Phee, but he twisted and grabbed Brophy's wrist. They struggled for a moment, until Phaggo yanked hard on Brophy's leg, pulling him away. With a quick slash, Phaggo severed Brophy's rope and let him drop.

Brophy flailed desperately and caught Phaggo's foot, clinging like a scorpion. He stabbed his blunt dagger into Phaggo's knee with all his might, and the big man howled. Dropping the dagger, Brophy scrambled up the giant Physendrian like a ladder. Phaggo stabbed at him, but Brophy caught his fist and held the blade at bay.

Separated from the battle and unable to swing back, Phee lowered himself to the spars below.

Brophy smashed his forehead into Phaggo's mouth, into his nose, into his chin. Phaggo reeled, trying to squeeze his opponent with his spare hand but unable to muster the strength. Brophy kneed him in the crotch, and Phaggo dropped his dagger. Snatching the dangling cord, Brophy scooped up the blade. With one mighty lunge, he grabbed the taut rope a few inches above Phaggo's hand and slashed the strap between their two fists.

"No!" Phaggo yelled as he plummeted, smashing through the wicker spars and hitting the ground with a sickening thud.

The gong crashed, ending the game.

The crowd went berserk, screaming Brophy's name.

Brophy breathed hard, straining to hold on to the rope. It slipped slowly in his sweaty grip. He grabbed the rope with both hands, pulling himself up until he grasped one of the knots. Painfully, methodically, he climbed the rope to the top of the cage and clung there for a long moment. He had lost blood, and he was as thirsty as he'd ever been in his life. He couldn't see the people in the stands, they faded into a fuzzy blur.

Closing his eyes, Brophy breathed in and out evenly. His tripping heart settled and his dizziness faded. He opened his eyes and climbed down the cage, favoring his bad leg.

"The mighty Falcons have become kings! But kings of beasts only. Lions have strength and courage, but it will take more than that to face the fire of godhood. Only one will become a king of men! Only one will burn on the eternal journey into the heart of the Phoenix!"

The crowd roared, chanting Brophy's name, chanting Phee's name. All was lost in the tumultuous screaming.

The final square before the test of the Phoenix was simple and straightforward. The Lion square was filled with jagged rocks. Phee and Brophy stood facing one another as the attendants tied the fighting claws to their wrists, putting the grip in the palm of their hands.

"Claw! Claw! Claw! Claw!" the crowd chanted.

Brophy stared at Phee. His opponent sneered.

The attendant pointed them to opposite edges of the square. Brophy tested the blades of the fighting claws. They were deadly sharp. He smiled wearily. Whoever rigged the game didn't think he would get this far.

Once again, he controlled his breathing. He cycled in strength, drawing on his rage yet again. His body was weak, but his will burned with purpose. He would not forget what Phee did to Tidric, what King Phandir was about to do to Ohndarien.

The gong crashed.

Brophy jumped to the top of a rock. Phee crouched and began circling, but Brophy headed straight toward him, hopping from stone to stone. He remembered everything Scythe taught him about using the fighting claws. Don't bother parrying. Attack and dodge, attack and dodge. Take your wounds but give out more.

Brophy lunged, but Phee backed up, keeping a jagged rock between them.

"Look at yourself," he said with a smirk. "You're a mess. You leave a trail of blood wherever you go."

"Then you'll know where to find me," Brophy said, circling the boulder.

Phee kept the stone between them. He tipped his chin at the Phoenix tower. "That's mine," Phee continued. "Tonight, I will be crowned Nine Squares champion."

Brophy glanced that direction, and paused, seeing something that Phee could not. One of the black-robed attendants was inside the tower, climbing through the wicker, soaking the straw with a small barrel of oil.

The crowd, their gazes locked on Brophy and Phee, would never see what they were doing. Brophy set his jaw. The king wasn't taking any chances.

It didn't matter. He looked away from the tower, back into Phee's eyes. "Remember," he said slowly, "I'm not going to kill you."

Phee charged, his claws a blur, but Brophy was quicker.

When it was over, Phee lay bleeding at Brophy's feet. He couldn't raise his right arm, and his left was pinned under Brophy's boot.

"No . . ." Phee mumbled through bloody lips, half-conscious.

Brophy sliced through Phee's twitching thigh. The boy screamed.

"That was for Phanqui," Brophy murmured. "And this is for Tidric." He set the claw at the crown of Phee's head and cut down across his brow, through his eyeball, across his cheek, and off his chin.

The arena shook with the screaming of the crowd.

Brophy cut the claws from his hands, left them on top of Phee's chest, and turned to look up at King Phandir. The attendants rushed to him, bearing a bucket of water and a rag.

"Witness the rise of the renegade prince," the announcer shouted. "Witness his return to the land of his true king, his battle to glorify the name of Queen Ossamyr. No more is he a mere king of beasts. He dares the gods to embrace him as a leader of men, as a lord among us. Can he endure the heat of the Ninth God, the burning Phoenix? Is Brophy of Ohndarien a mere mortal, or will he rise to divinity and become the right arm of our beloved King Phandir, voice of the gods!"

The black-robed attendants washed the grime from Brophy's body, and hastily bandaged his wounds. He must be presentable before they took him to the king.

No contestant attempted the tower of kings until he was blessed by Phandir. As they washed him, Brophy watched the king's box. The king murmured something to Ossamyr, and she gave him a weak smile. Brophy's heart twisted inside him.

He was lost in a haze of fear, pain, and fatigue. The gouge that Phee had torn from his arm had soaked the entire bandage. His other wounds seeped anew. The thin strips of white cloth would not hold back the blood for long.

The attendants led him up the stairs to where the king stood in a cape of fiery feathers and golden armbands that gleamed in the bright light. His red hair looked like the ruff of some great bird of prey, and his eyes regarded Brophy coldly, though his lips carried that amused smirk. King Phandir always looked like he was smiling, but the king's smile was just like the king's gold, a gleaming bit of show.

Brophy spared a quick glance to Ossamyr. Her red feather cape was draped over the back of her intricately woven wicker throne. Her tanned skin shone, more beautiful and perfect than the gold around her neck. She nodded politely, but her eyes lingered. She smiled at that moment, and Brophy saw into her heart. He wrenched his gaze away.

Four Apes stood at the edges of the box, ever attentive. Brophy recognized the guard he called Tiny among them. Before one of the Apes could smack him with a sword, Brophy knelt and kissed the hem of King Phandir's robe.

The crowd continued to chant Brophy's name.

"So," King Phandir said in his jovial voice, leaning to look at Ossamyr, "your Beetle has become a Lion."

The queen nodded gracefully, that perfectly crafted smile on her face. Brophy kept his eyes on Phandir. Once again he wanted to snatch the man's sword and turn it on him.

Brophy's name reverberated throughout the arena as the crowd continued chanting.

"You always had a great eye for little boys, my queen," Phandir said. "But I think this one will burn as well as he bleeds."

Brophy stared hard at Phandir. "Do you hear that?" he murmured, just loud enough for Phandir and Ossamyr to hear. "That is the sound of what one Ohndarien can do."

Phandir grinned even wider. He leaned forward. "They are going to cheer just as loudly when you die."

"I wonder how loud they will cheer when you die," Brophy whispered to Phandir. The king's face reddened. He opened his mouth to say something and paused. His smile returned, but not as relaxed as it once was.

The king looked away, waved a hand at Brophy. The Apes moved forward, practically shoving him down the stairs. Brophy stumbled as pain lanced through his bad leg. He barely caught himself, slowing his descent until he stood with the attendants.

The announcer called out again. "And so our would-be hero will face his final challenge. He must pass through the flames, letting them burn away his mortality. If his heart is pure, he will fly to the king's side, but if his heart is full of doubt, the fire will claim him, and he will burn as the gods demand. The Ohndarien prince will have his chance to emerge from the shadows and join the gods, a ruler in service of the Nine! To become a Phoenix!"

"Let the tower burn!" Phandir's voice boomed above the crowd. Normally, the contestant was allowed to line up at the edge of the square before the tower was lit, but not this time. The oil-soaked straw caught immediately, and the flames leapt up the tower.

With a shout, Brophy hobbled across the length of the arena toward the rising flames. Brophy pushed his bad leg, ran past the Jumping Rat square, past the Jackal square. He skirted Crocodile, Scorpion, and Serpent, cursing his legs as he tried to run faster. He kept glancing at the blazing tower. The flames were already higher than most contestants would face when they were a quarter of the way up the tower. He rushed past the Ape, Falcon, and Lion squares, spiraling toward the center.

The tower rose out of a moat of the same brackish water that filled the Crocodile square. Brophy pushed his damaged leg into a sprint and dove into the muck. He swam deep and fast, ignoring the pain. His body was his to command, it would follow his will.

Rising within feet of the raging flame, Brophy took a deep, smooth breath. The air was a furnace already. He calmed himself, took three more deep breaths, and focused, using the techniques of heat resistance he had learned as a child. Splashing moat water onto the burning wicker, he created a small aisle on the tower. It smoked and sputtered.

He dipped his head and swallowed as much of the vile water as his stomach would hold. Fighting the urge to gag, Brophy grabbed the smoking wicker and began climbing. He did not move to the inside of the tower like most contestants. He clambered up the outside, closing his eyes, climbing blind as Scythe had taught him.

"Your eyes can only hurt you," Scythe had said. "You can't see anything in the smoke. Feel your way. Feel the strength or weakness in the wicker. You must become a part of the tower to beat it."

My hands are iron, he told himself. *This heat is a breeze upon my skin.*

Brophy clambered up the crackling wicker, breathing sparingly through his nose. He chose poorly once, cracking through and almost falling onto the raging bonfire below. His stomach lurched. His concentration strayed and his fingers blistered.

Iron. My hands are iron. He sucked in a quick breath of smoke.

Climb. Just climb. Higher. Faster.

He found his next hold and continued upward. Before long, his hand swatted at air. He blinked. Smoke swirled around him, stinging his eyes. He had made it to the top.

Feeling with his hands, he located the rope. His stomach lurched, and he let it come this time, vomiting onto the burning cord. The flames hissed and sputtered. He vomited again, cupping his hands underneath and splashing it over every bit of the rope. He hoped it would be enough.

Brophy dared to open his eyes for a moment and found the feather-covered Phoenix harness, just starting to burn. Moving blind, he shrugged it on just as Scythe had taught him. He didn't bother with the buckles, just held onto the straps and prayed his grip was still strong enough.

He climbed back to the rope and fitted the pulley wheel in place. With his eyes closed, he couldn't tell if the rope had burned too much already. It didn't matter now, it was out of his hands.

Brophy leapt from the Phoenix tower.

The sudden jolt ripped one of the straps out of his hand. But he held on to the other one, dangling by one shoulder. The rope held. He soared over the arena, crossing the Lion square and rolling steadily toward the king. The screams of the crowd were deafening.

Brophy slid to the bottom of the rope and slammed into the handrail of the royal box. He clung there, blinking his gummy eyes, barely able to see. He could hear nothing over the screaming of the crowd, but he thought he saw Ossamyr stand. Phandir put a hand on her arm, and she stopped.

The rope went slack, falling behind him in a burning trail. Brophy pulled himself painfully over the rail and fell to the wooden floorboards. Someone touched his face, and it felt like sandstone against an open wound. He opened his eyes and saw Ossamyr.

"And so," she said. "The Lion becomes the Phoenix."

22

ROPHY AWOKE with a start. He ached all over, and for a moment could not remember where he was. There was no breeze, but he felt the air acutely on his skin. He shifted and the blanket scraped him. There was someone else in the room.

"Bae?" he asked. No one answered. He sat up and the bed rocked. Chains creaked and his memories came rushing back. He was in Physendria. He was the Nine Squares champion.

He blinked, touched his gummy eyes tenderly.

"Ossamyr?" he asked.

"No," said a dark voice with a Kherish accent.

"Scythe."

"Yes, and keep your voice down. I am not an invited guest."

"A moment," Brophy said. "I'll light a lamp." He shifted to the edge of the bed. Scythe put a hand on his arm, and Brophy winced again. His skin was as tender as a baby's.

"No. You're still sleeping, and I'm not here."

Brophy nodded. The pain was making everything distant and fuzzy. He fought to clear his head. "Scythe?"

"Yes."

"I forgot to thank you. For the archers. The training."

"You are welcome." Scythe's shadowy figure made a small bow. "It was what I was sent to do."

"I never would have made it up that tower yesterday without you."

"It was three days ago."

"Oh . . ."

"Yes. Many think you are immortal. They are still guessing how you survived the flames."

"My training as a Child of the Seasons."

"I know that. They do not. Some whisper that you actually have the blood of the Phoenix. Braver souls whisper that you've come to reclaim the throne."

"I wish it was that easy."

Scythe was silent for a moment. "You did well, Brophy. I thought you dead when you disappeared into that smoke. Phandir won't underestimate you again."

"It would be hard to underestimate me right now."

Scythe chuckled. "You are practically untouched."

"Tell that to my leg, my arm." But Brophy smiled. Scythe was right. Brophy's wounds didn't hurt nearly as much knowing that he had succeeded.

"So that leaves me with one question," Scythe said.

"Yes?"

"What do you plan to do at the ceremony when they find out you have awoken? Your victory celebration will be combined with a call to war."

The celebration to honor a new champion was held in the Nine Squares arena with all of Physendria looking on. There the king would present nine solid gold statues of the Physendrian animal gods to Brophy. Afterward, he would be allowed to make a request of the king.

"I considered smuggling a blade into the ceremony," Brophy said, "and killing the king where he stands."

Scythe's dark eyes glittered as he shifted. "You might succeed, right before you die. Phandir was never much of a swordsman, but his Ape guards are deadly."

"But I realized you would already have assassinated him if it could save Ohndarien. That's what you used to do, isn't it?"

Scythe stayed silent for a moment, then said, "According to Physendrian law, Krellis would become king after Phandir's death. Ohndarien would fall without a fight."

"Exactly, which is why I hadn't planned on attending the celebration," Brophy said. "I've had enough of screaming crowds, but I'm going to miss those nine statues. Did you keep yours?"

Scythe snorted. "Gold statues do little more than attract thieves. I thought you planned on becoming governor of Ohndarien."

It was Brophy's turn to snort. "I've learned a little something of Physendria by now."

"I'm glad you see that. I was starting to wonder. Are you ready to take your Test?"

Brophy watched Scythe in the pale light for a moment. "Yes. I've accomplished all I can here. It's time to return to Ohndarien and face Krellis."

"I couldn't agree more. Take the Test, sever his connection to the Heartstone, and I will do the rest," Scythe said.

"You'll have to get in line. You aren't the only man who wants his head."

Brophy could barely see Scythe's smile. "We'll fight that battle when we come to it," the little man said quietly.

"My escape plan's a bit thin at this point," Brophy admitted.

"You can leave with me. Tonight." Scythe said, "I have a ship waiting on the river. You could be in Ohndarien in three days."

Brophy saw the passion in the man's eyes. He set his lips in a firm line. "I was hoping you would say something like that, but I can't leave yet. Not without . . ."

A long silence stretched between them. When Scythe spoke, his voice was thick with disdain. "Do you actually think the Queen of Physendria would run away with you?"

"Yes. You think you know her," Brophy said, "but you don't."

Scythe growled. "You thanked me for saving your life. I am calling in the debt. Leave with me tonight. That is all I ask."

Brophy was glad Scythe could not see his face. "I can't," he whispered.

"Everything will have been for naught. Your sacrifices. Your victories. Don't throw your life away for a woman who doesn't love you." His voice trailed off.

Brophy took a deep breath before speaking. "I don't know if she will go with me. I don't even know how she truly feels about me." He swallowed past the tightness in his throat. "But I have to ask her. I have to know."

"The gods are cruel, Brophy," Scythe murmured. He seemed to be talking to himself. "Go then. Ask her and see what she says. If she refuses you, you will never be able to escape. Even I could not save you from the Wet Cells."

"I know, but I must try."

"I know," Scythe echoed. "I would do the same."

"You would?"

"If I were in love," he clarified, clearing his throat. His voice was short and clipped again. "You may be the finest warrior in Physendria, but there is no defense against a woman who owns your heart."

Brophy looked up at the faint light coming through the chimney. "Can you take me to her?"

Scythe sighed. "I suppose I must."

Brophy lit a candle, and Scythe quickly found the mechanism that had confounded Brophy for months. The hidden door swung open.

"How did you do that?" Brophy asked.

"I have been in this room before, years ago. The queen used this same door to visit me."

"Did you . . ." Brophy forced himself to ask the rest of the question. "Sleep with her?"

"Sleep with her, yes. Fuck her, no. I told you before, I refused her."

For the first time, Brophy believed him. "Why?"

"Because I chose to."

Brophy knew better than to press the matter any further.

He nodded and motioned the candle toward the door. The two slipped through the opening and crept into the darkness. The tiny flame barely lit the passageway. The tunnel soon came to an end. Scythe paused. His nose seemed twice as long in the harsh shadows.

"We could still leave," he murmured. "Will you risk all of Ohndarien for this woman?"

"Yes."

Scythe let out a long breath. After a moment, he held out his hand. Surprised, Brophy took it. Scythe clasped him on the forearm, his grip like steel. "I will be here when you are ready. I pray to the Seasons that she will be with you. If she betrays you, yell 'For Ohndarien' and charge back to this space in the wall. I will have it open, and we will get a fair head start, at least."

"Thank you . . . my friend."

"You are welcome."

"Scythe . . ."

"Yes?"

"I'm not wrong."

"So you say."

"Here. The candle." Brophy held it out to him, but the assassin shook his head. "No. I am the dark. Let the fool who stumbles across me hold the candle."

Scythe touched something in the shadows and the passage opened to reveal Ossamyr's bedroom. Her bed was round and three times the size of his, suspended from the middle of the room. Luxurious silks and oversized pillows were draped across the platform. Mirrors reflected the moonlight to glorious effect. It seemed like a ghostly daylight. Three tall wardrobes stood next to each other. Across the room was a dressing table with an oval mirror almost as large as the bed. Colorful tapestries covered the walls.

At first, Brophy thought his luck had failed him, that Ossamyr was not in her room, but just as the stone door slid silently into place, she appeared from a side passage.

Her face was drawn and her deep tan seemed pale in the ghostly moonlight. She wore a simple white shift, but even in such common clothing she was radiant. She noticed him and started.

"Brophy . . ." Her brow furrowed. "You shouldn't be here," she breathed.

"I had to come."

Her brow smoothed as she understood. "You're leaving."

"Yes."

"But—"

"I want you to come with me."

The queen froze. For an instant, she seemed younger, Brophy's age. She closed her eyes and swallowed with difficulty. Her hand trembled at her hip. "You shouldn't have come here . . . Just for me," she whispered, almost to herself.

Tears welled from her closed eyes, one slowly slipped down her cheek. "They will kill you if they catch you here."

He crossed the room and knelt in front of her. "I love you," he murmured, taking her hands.

"Oh Brophy . . ." she paused. Her beautiful face tightened as though she was in pain, then something released inside her. She let out a little whimper, and her features smoothed out. Her dark hair swished against her cheek as she hung her head. He could barely hear her when she spoke. "The Nine help me, but I love you, too."

"Then come with me."

Her dark eyes caught his. "Now?"

"It is the only time we might succeed."

She drew a deep breath, looked at the hidden door. "Scythe?"

Brophy nodded. "He is ready. He has a ship waiting."

She closed her eyes, and Brophy's heart sank. Scythe's warnings leapt to mind.

"And so Ohndarien will fall?" she asked.

Brophy clenched his teeth. "We can go to Ohndarien. We can defend her walls."

"And what if we did? Could we stop the entire army?" She squeezed his hands. "Oh Brophy. Watching you, your determination, the light of your soul . . . It has made me dare to believe. But if we leave together and Phandir takes his prize, what will become of us? What will you become if Ohndarien falls and your loved ones are slain?"

She stroked his cheek, brushed the hair from his face. "The attack is poised. One extra sword will not save the city."

"You said it yourself, a Nine Squares Champion wins the love of the Physendrian people. I've already done that. Scythe says that many of them think I am immortal. Surely facing a divine champion on the opposing battlements will make a difference. Phandir has painted Ohndarien as a city full of brigands. I have made her a city full of heroes."

Her dark eyes glistened. "It will not be enough."

Brophy shook his head. "If the city falls, she falls. But I will be there, sword in hand defending her. I would like you to be by my side."

The queen blinked, opened her mouth to speak and closed it again. Finally, she said, "We have two choices that I can see. We can leave, take our chances or . . ." She paused

"Or?"

"Or we can kill him."

Brophy opened his mouth, but nothing came out. She stared somberly into his eyes. He had never seen her like this, ravaged by sorrow, so earnestly determined. He could read every emotion on her face.

"But only a man can rule in Physendria. Krellis would take the throne."

Her lips curved in disdain. "Let him try. A quarter of the royal guard answers to me. I could snare another quarter easily if Phandir were dead. The other half would be leaderless. Let Krellis come south and claim his birthright. He would find himself in the Wet Cells before he entered the city. No, Brophy. I could seize the kingdom if we were quick. And I could hold it. Phandir is certainly not loved in this city. Many would flock to me."

Brophy's heart beat faster.

"Would it work?" he whispered.

"I could manage it," she said. "With your help. You must swing the sword, but I could take the kingdom."

For a glorious moment, Ohndarien was freed from the specter of war. It dangled before Brophy's eyes like a gift.

"I have thought on it since . . ." She swallowed. "Since my last night in your room. I have thought on it day and night up to this very moment. But I never believed . . . I never thought you would come back for me. I thought you and Scythe would be long gone."

Ossamyr struggled to draw a breath, and Brophy squeezed her hands. "It is risky," she continued. "A hundred things could go wrong, but it might work." Her voice trembled when she spoke. "The man deserves to die. I would take this throne and make Physendria a kingdom to rival all others. We could both have everything we wanted with one quick thrust of the sword."

"What about Scythe?"

"Do you think he would help us?" the queen asked.

Brophy hesitated a moment, then said, "If it will save Ohndarien, he would."

A ghost of a smile flitted across the queen's face. She pulled on Brophy's hands and drew him to his feet. "Listen closely," she whispered. "We will only get one chance."

23

THE WALL closed seamlessly behind Brophy, and Ossamyr crossed to her bed. She put her palms on the silken covers and spread her fingers, barely able to catch her breath. Could the Nine be so generous? She knew she was being reckless. They could so easily die for this. All her childish daydreams of spending the rest of her nights in Brophy's arms were suddenly real. Real enough to bleed, real enough to die in her arms.

She felt the soft slickness of the sheet under her fingers, felt the old scars on her heart. She had thought such wild, tender feelings were lost to her forever.

For the first time since she understood power in Physendria, for the first time since she offered her lips to a man she despised—for the first time since she spread her legs to take a step up, Ossamyr didn't care about consequences. Her heart thundered in her chest, and she couldn't find that calm control she'd maintained for so many years. It fled from her, left her spinning and giddy and happier than she had felt since she was a little girl.

Taking a long breath, she let it out slowly. A weary but satisfied smile came to her lips. She closed her eyes and enjoyed the moment. He came back for her. He risked everything he holds dear . . . for her.

The queen's door swung wide, smacking heartily into the wall. Ossamyr started, then held herself perfectly still. She didn't turn. Her fingers curled into claws on the bed. She relaxed them, smoothed the covers. Phandir stepped into the room, grinning.

"My beautiful queen." He chuckled.

Oh, the Nine were cruel. They were bitter and vengeful, and always had been.

She swallowed down a tight throat and swiveled around, her face suddenly a cold mask. He crossed the room and took her chin in his huge hand, tipped it up. He looked into her eyes.

"You rival the gods. What a performance! Who would have thought you would become this amazing when I plucked you from your mother's house a decade and a half ago? You are exquisite. I have always been amused by your dalliances over the years. I thought your idea of turning a Child of the Seasons into a puppet ruler in Ohndarien was clever, if a long shot, but avoiding my recent embarrassment by goading this boy into assassination is brilliant. I couldn't have thought up a better plan myself. Truly, we were made for one another." He let go of her chin, tossing her head to the side. She remained that way for a moment, staring at the edge of the bed, her short hair flung across her cheek, then raised her head again to look at him.

The king paced across the room. "Tell me, my love, when were you going to spill this glorious plan to me?" His smile froze in all its overflowing charisma. "Tonight?" he asked, measured and even. "Tomorrow, just before the ceremony?"

Ossamyr stared at him for a brief moment, a sardonic smile curved the side of her mouth.

"Tonight, my love. Of course."

"Of course. I love surprises. Do you think Brophy will enjoy the surprise we will plan for him?"

Ossamyr licked her tight lips. She said nothing.

"Or should I prepare a surprise for you?" Phandir asked, grinning like a skull.

"I live to serve, as you know."

"Yes," he said, drawing the word out. "I know it all too well." He strode casually to the door, put his toe at the edge and kicked it shut. It slammed against the doorjamb. His fingers traced the wood for a moment before he shot the bolt.

"Now, my love," He walked slowly toward her. "Let us consummate our blessed union and justify the love of the gods that has brought me such a brilliant wife."

Ossamyr slowly held out her arms. "Come. I've grown tired of boys."

He picked her up under the arms and tossed her on the bed. She bounced once, and the platform rocked. He grabbed her ankles and slowly pulled her toward him. Twisting his hands into the sides of her shift, he ripped the dress from her body. She drew a quick breath, forcing her mouth into a smile as he pushed her legs apart. Her hips twisted away, resisting as if they had a mind of their own. But he turned her back, pressing hard on each side of her hips.

"Tell me more." The king smiled. "Some of the details were difficult to hear. Tell me the entire plan from beginning to end."

Ossamyr laid her head back as he climbed on top of her.

"Yes . . . my love," she said to the ceiling. "Yes, my king."

24

WHEN BROPHY returned to his rooms that night, he thought the morning would never come. He lay on his bed, staring up at the starry glow from the opening overhead. The cut in his thigh and the gouge in his arm throbbed, and his tender burned skin kept him from moving, but the pain, the doubt, everything he had suffered in Physendria seemed worth it.

He slipped into a daydream and saw Ossamyr in the Hall of Windows, wearing wedding white in the Ohndarien fashion. No red-feathered capes or gold jewelry. No Physendrian colors of blood and money.

Brophy waited for her under the dome, with his father standing next to him. All of Ohndarien had packed into the Hall of Windows. Aunt Bae and Shara sat in the first row, smiling. Even Trent was there, a little bit drunk and winking at a fetching maiden in the row behind him. Ossamyr walked toward him, followed by a train of attendants that extended all the way outside.

The dream shifted. Ossamyr sat on the edge of his bed as a babe suckled at her breast. Brophy peered over his wife's shoulder, and the little blond girl smiled at him. He imagined that same girl five years older. Brophy led her up the stairs to the top of the Hall of Windows.

He imagined running along Ohndarien's walls, barely able to keep up with his long-legged son, who had his mother's dark eyes.

He fell asleep, disappearing into his dreams.

THE KNOCK shook his door, and he started. Tiny stepped inside the room. "The queen will be here in moments," the gruff man said, his lip curled into a sneer.

Brophy shook the sleep from his head, slid off the bed, and went to the wardrobe, pulling out the blue-feathered cape, white shirt, and brightly colored pants he was supposed to wear. Though he had conquered the Phoenix tower, none but the king and queen were allowed to wear the red feathers of that fiery bird.

Brophy stood outside his room next to the Ape when Ossamyr arrived in her chariot. Climbing up next to the queen, he wanted to tell her of his night's dreams, but he looked at her stony façade and decided against it.

"We are watched," she said quietly, her chin elevated, every inch the queen. He nodded. He felt like he was going into battle naked, but Brophy's dreams bolstered his courage.

The queen had planned everything to the last detail. Brophy knew he could beat Phandir, but the rest was in the queen's hands. All I have to do is swing the knife, he reminded himself. Wait for Ossamyr to clear her throat, one swift stab, and it's all over. Brophy had never killed anyone, not even Phee. The closer he got, the harder it became.

They rode in silence along the sunken King's Highway to the arena. No sun-browned urchins ran along the top of the trench. No other carts scurried to get out of their way. All had gone to the arena to see the Nine Squares champion crowned, to see the beginning of the Ohndarien war.

As they neared the arena, Brophy could hear the music, the crowd chanting. It swelled louder and louder the closer they came. He kept his breathing steady as they plunged into the darkness under the volcano. The queen slipped the dagger into his hand. With a smooth motion that would have impressed Scythe, Brophy concealed it in a slit he had crafted in his ceremonial cloak. The Apes never saw.

They emerged into the arena and the crowd went wild. Their chants were deafening, drowning out the music, drowning out every other thing.

The queen had coached him on every motion, every social nuance that was expected of him, but Brophy had never looked upon so many faces at once. The arena had not been this full when he actually won at Nine Squares. Every gallery was packed, and the crowd overflowed onto the arena's dirt floor.

"Wave," Ossamyr said through the side of her mouth. "Smile."

Brophy stuck his hand into the air. The crowd exulted, shaking the ground with their shouts.

"Is Scythe here?" she asked.

"Somewhere. He promised to watch my back. He didn't say how."

She paused, nodded.

After one victory lap around the arena, the announcer fought to be heard.

"All hail! The renegade prince from Ohndarien returns to his rightful homeland! He comes in our time of need, a hero rising from the darkness to burn in the brightest light! Under the banner of King Phandir, Brophy will show the city of northern bandits what happens when they turn their backs on their true lord and master! I give you the Ohndarien blade master. I give you the king's newest knife. I give you the Nine Squares champion! I give you Brophy!"

The crowd exploded once more into raucous shouting. Brophy barely heard the announcer's lies as Phandir loomed in his mind.

"Are you ready?" Ossamyr asked in a dead tone as the chariot rolled to a stop.

Excitement and fear rushed through him. He was not an assassin, he reminded himself. He was saving lives. "I'm ready."

Brophy and the queen ascended to the royal box. Phandir stood facing the crowd, smiling as he always did. He held out his hand to Ossamyr, who took it and stood beside him. Four Apes hovered within a sword's swing of the king. Brophy surreptitiously spotted Ossamyr's man among them, to the left and behind. He flicked a gaze over the crowd around the box, but Scythe was nowhere to be seen.

Obeying his instructions to the letter, Brophy knelt and kissed the king's cloak. He was presented with the nine golden statues, and he asked for governorship of Ohndarien as his reward. Ossamyr had told him to say "the Physendrian city of Ohndarien" but Brophy left that part out. It was a small victory. Phandir smiled smugly down at him. Brophy's conflict fled as he looked at the tyrant. It would be better for everyone when this man was dead.

Phandir looked across the teeming throng of Physendrians. Brophy stood behind the king's left shoulder as Phandir held up his hands for quiet. The tumult died away to an eerie silence.

"Tomorrow, we march to reclaim Brophy's home."

The crowd cheered madly. Phandir waited, and they quieted again.

"Tomorrow, we march to reopen the doorway to the east."

They cheered again, louder this time. One drunken reveler screamed at the top of his lungs just as the audience began to quiet. Phandir smiled, pointed in that direction.

"Tomorrow, we march our first step toward reclaiming control of the Summer Sea."

The cheers rose again. Phandir had to shout over them.

"Tomorrow, we march to a glory that will never end!"

The crowd went wild. Phandir nodded, waiting, waiting . . . Finally, he held up his hands, and they quieted once more. Phandir turned to Brophy.

"Will you lead our armies to victory?" he asked, speaking to Brophy's face but loudly enough that everyone could hear. "Will you return your home city to its rightful king?"

The noise of the crowd slowly began to swell, chanting Brophy's name.

"What do you say, Brophy?" Phandir asked again.

Ossamyr coughed lightly.

The dagger fell into Brophy's hand. "For Ohndarien!" he screamed, and plunged it into Phandir's heart, slamming his palm against the pommel to drive it sure and true.

The blade bounced off a hidden metal breastplate. Brophy's eyes flew wide as the king fell to the floor. A sudden pain jabbed the back of Brophy's neck. He brushed it away, watched a tiny dart spin across the wooden planks.

He leapt upon Phandir. A dagger could find a throat as easily as a heart.

Two Apes grabbed Brophy's arms. He twisted, cutting one across the wrist. The man cursed and his grip went slack. Brophy slugged the other Ape in the face and yanked himself free. He kicked the man in the groin and slapped stiff hands on either side of his short sword. With a quick wrench, Brophy twisted the blade free, caught the handle, and spun about.

Ossamyr was kneeling next to her husband, squeezing blood from a tiny bladder across his shirt. She looked up at Brophy, tears in her eyes, and opened her mouth to say something, but she didn't. She looked away.

Brophy stumbled backward. He felt cold, as if someone had thrown icy water into his face. She lied to him. She chose Phandir.

Ten Serpent swordsmen, wearing their distinctive fanged headdresses, streamed up the steps to the box.

Brophy's vision swam, and he blinked. His arm felt heavy, his sword wobbled.

The first two soldiers raised their weapons.

"No!" Phandir roared.

The soldiers surrounding Brophy hesitated, but they did not back away. His knees wobbled. He clenched his teeth and held them steady. He was having trouble breathing.

Phandir's other two Apes helped him sit up. "This one is mine!" the king shouted, his voice carrying to the crowd. He stood, covered in false blood, and grabbed a sword from one of his men. "This treachery will end. Here! Now!"

Brophy tried to look at Ossamyr, but he couldn't see straight. Everything blurred, and he stumbled to the side. He realized his sword arm had fallen and tried to raise it again.

Phandir attacked, cutting down at Brophy's neck. Somehow, Brophy got his guard up and blocked the first blow. The second cut his arm. He dropped his sword. With a grim smile that wobbled in Brophy's vision, Phandir clubbed Brophy with the flat of his blade. He took ten hits before he collapsed to his knees, falling face forward onto the hard wood.

"To Ohndarien!" Phandir shouted.

"To Ohndarien!" the crowd chanted.

"To war!" Phandir shouted again.

"To war!"

"To victory!" Phandir cried for the third time.

"To victory!" They screamed, and Brophy felt the boards vibrate against his cheek.

Ossamyr's voice spoke, close to his ear.

"I'm sorry, Brophy," she said, cold and distant. "Forgive me. I had no choice."

THE SOLDIERS bound and gagged Brophy, paraded him around the arena on their shoulders. The king had been right. The crowd yelled just as loudly for his death as they did for his victory.

The king's men threw him in a chariot and rode out of the arena. As the noise faded away, Brophy's vision slowly returned. Three Apes rode with him along the King's Highway, five Serpent swordsmen ran in front, two behind.

"You're awake," one of the Apes said to him.

Brophy stared back. Ossamyr's face flashed through his mind, helping Phandir, gazing up at Brophy with that look.

I wish I had met you twenty years ago. Before Phandir. I wish we had met in your Ohndarien.

"I think you'll really enjoy the Wet Cells," the driver said, smirking. The other two Apes laughed.

And I love you. The Nine help me, but I do.

Lies. All lies. And now Ohndarien would fall for his stupidity.

A huge crash jolted Brophy upright, and a wave of heat swept over him. Three wagons full of burning straw plunged from the rim of the King's Highway, landing on the soldiers in front of the cart. The chariot lurched to a stop as it slammed into the burning barrier.

The driver whipped the slaves to turn around, but they screamed as they burned. An arrowhead sprouted from the driver's throat. His eyes opened wide, and he toppled over the edge of the cart.

"Ambush!" one of the remaining Serpents shouted, and took an arrow in the chest. He screamed and stumbled backward, slamming into the wall and scratching at the arrow sticking out of him.

Another Ape leapt from the cart and was shot by a cowled archer at the edge of the trench. The guard gurgled and went to his knees. The last Ape grabbed Brophy and jumped to the ground, using him as a shield. The Ape backed slowly toward the two Serpents behind them.

A feathered shaft suddenly quivered in his eye. Brophy crashed to the ground as his captor went limp. The remaining soldiers looked at Brophy, hesitated a moment, and fled.

Scythe threw back his hood and climbed down the rough-hewn walls of the sunken highway. He was only halfway to the ground when he leapt backward, landing in a crouch right next to Brophy. Two quick slashes of his dagger and Brophy's bonds came away. He cut the gag next.

"Can you run?" Scythe asked, pulling Brophy to a sitting position. Brophy shook his head and stared at the flames.

Scythe grabbed Brophy's arm and lifted him across his shoulders. With a grunt, he rose to his feet and charged through the flames. The heat flashed past them. Brophy smelled singed hair.

Scythe ran to a nearby sloping exit and pounded up the incline. In the distance, a warning horn blew. As Scythe reached the top, he set Brophy down on his feet.

"Come on!" he shouted. "I can't outrun them if I'm carrying you."

"No, you were right . . ." he mumbled, sitting down. "I meant nothing to her. She used me like she uses everybody else, then shed me like a cloak."

"That doesn't matter. I can get us out of here, but you have to go now!"

Brophy stared back at the trench from where they'd come. "You were right. The world is an ugly, brutal place, and I'm alone in it."

Scythe slapped Brophy across the face. "I have a ship waiting, but she won't wait forever. Get up, man!" Scythe's head snapped up. Slowly, Brophy followed his gaze. A crowd of Serpents charged up the incline from the King's Highway, their swords drawn.

"Run for Bae, run for Ohndarien if you won't run for yourself!" Scythe shouted, shaking Brophy's tunic in two fists.

"Leave me alone," Brophy murmured. "Just go."

Scythe let go of his shirt, and Brophy slumped to the ground.

"As you wish," he said in a tight voice. "You deserve nothing less."

He ran between two buildings and was gone.

book III

A LEGACY OF PAIN
AND GREED

THE CINDER
The Cursed Isle

prologue

OPI CLUNG TO *Raindancer's back as the little mare pounded down the slope. The young hunter she'd left behind screamed. His dying wail chased her down the hill, but she kept the music box playing, turned it around and around. Hisses and growls filled the moonlit night. She looked toward her tribe's encampment. Dark figures leapt between the tents, biting and slashing one another around the campfires.*

Raindancer neighed and pulled up short, tossing her head and galloping to the right. Copi squeezed the little mare with her legs, urging her forward. They crested a rise and plunged into the valley where her tribe's horses grazed.

She gasped. The herd was charging straight at her. The sleek, beautiful horses had become feral predators, biting at each other with catlike fangs, rearing and lashing out with wicked hooves.

"Away, Raindancer!" she screamed. The mare whinnied and threw her head to the left, cutting across the rim of the valley, but the monstrous herd stampeded after them.

Raindancer's head bobbed as she galloped faster than Copi had ever ridden. The twisted herd thundered after them, their growling whinnies came closer and closer.

Continuing to turn the music box, Copi used her legs to guide her mount toward the river. The mare charged down the bank and splashed into the water. The impact almost swept Copi from the horse's back. Water flew on either side of them, and Raindancer struggled toward the other side.

The screaming herd charged into the river right behind them. They shrieked and flailed. Their spiny necks and red eyes disappeared below the frothing water.

Raindancer carried Copi and the child across the current and climbed out on the far bank.

"It's all right," Copi whispered, patting Raindancer's dripping neck. The terrified mare danced sideways, looking back where their pursuers had submerged. Copi began to sob between breaths. "It's all right—"

A black, thorny head poked out of the near side of the river. Blowing water from its nostrils, the cursed horse snarled and showed its long, sharp teeth. Another head splashed up, snorted and howled. Raindancer wheeled about and clambered up the bank. The entire twisted herd emerged from the river and gave chase.

The little mare galloped across the moonlit plains. Hours passed as the lone horse pounded across the Vastness with the howling pack of monsters in pursuit. The cursed horses closed the gap by inches. The little horse gave her all, but she could not pull away. Pursued and pursuers ran tirelessly, the frenzied horses driven by an inner fire, Raindancer driven by the magic of the music box.

Her lathered steed ran unerringly toward the Great Ocean. As the sun crept over the flat horizon, they rushed across the beach and plunged into the surf. The mare leapt over the rolling waves, fighting through the breakers until they were in deeper water.

The blackened horde crashed into the water. Their muscles squirmed under their sleek coats as they fought the waves rolling over their flanks, their backs. They continued mindlessly forward until the surging surf finally closed over their heads.

Copi whimpered, turning the box, keeping the music playing. She stared at the roiling water.

"Keep going, Raindancer," she whispered. "Just a little more."

The mare's head bobbed forward as she struggled out to sea.

RELLIS AND Gorlym stood on the Quarry Wall and looked north, watching the Faradan army gather at the top of the meticulously carved mountainside. For three hundred years Ohndariens had mined the famous blue-white marble from that stair-stepped quarry. In two days it had been overrun without a fight.

Farad soldiers swarmed across the highest step, setting up their camp and preparing defenses as if Krellis was stupid enough to leave the safety of his walls to attack an army perched on a cliff. But they would get it back. Before long, those bearded invaders would scurry back over that rise into the wasteland they called a kingdom, their tails tucked between their legs.

"How would you estimate their number?" Krellis asked, his narrow eyes already counting.

"No more than twelve thousand troops. Several thousand more in support. Our scouts say they have ladders, battering rams, and siege towers."

"They came prepared. This smacks of Phandir, not the boy king of the north." Krellis kept his hand steady on the rampart.

"They can't get the towers down the cliffs," Gorlym said. "They'll have to dismantle them and reassemble below."

Krellis grunted. "What is the latest count of Physendrian troops outside the Water Wall?"

"Twice the number of Faradan."

"We are outnumbered three to one."

"Yes, sir."

"What about their navies?"

"Our last report says forty war galleys sailed north from Physen."

"And the Summer Sea?"

"Faradan has seventeen ships within sight of Dock Town."

Krellis took a deep breath. "The arrival of Faradan is unfortunate, but only a distraction. The Ohohhim should land behind Phandir's force in three days, a week at the most. Once Physendria falls, young King Celtigar will beg us for peace. I assume you can hold this wall for three days?"

"I can hold it for three months," Gorlym said, frowning. "I am not worried about Faradan, sir. What is outside will stay outside. It is the internal threat that worries me. Our forces have been divided ever since the Sisters emerged from the Heart and took the Night Market. I've heard that a third of the city would rise against us if those women attacked."

"I will worry about the Sisters. You worry about Ohndarien's walls."

"Yes, sir."

Footfalls pounded up the walkway, and both Krellis and Gorlym turned. The runner stopped just in front of them, gulping air.

"A message, sir," he huffed, "from the Citadel."

"Speak," Krellis said.

"Your offices, sir. Robbed. Three men killed. One injured."

Krellis's eyebrows crouched together. "My office?"

"Yes, sir."

"What was taken?"

"Papers, sir. From your desk. Nothing else. No valuables."

Krellis's face turned red.

"Who did this?" he growled. The boy blanched and took a hesitant step backward.

"The injured man said . . ." The boy hesitated. "But he must be mistaken, he is almost dead."

"Tell me," Krellis raised his voice.

The boy winced. "He said it was a woman, sir."

"The Sisters!" Gorlym hissed.

The boy shook his head vigorously. "No, sir. A foreigner. Small, with curly dark hair and a powdered face."

Krellis looked past the boy, staring at nothing. He ground his teeth.

"What is it, sir?" Gorlym asked. "What was taken?"

Krellis spun around, slammed his hands on the battlement. "The Emperor's fleet won't be landing as expected," he said, his voice suddenly hoarse.

"Sir?"

"We are alone."

Gorlym looked at the boy, who had turned pale. The Master of the Citadel looked back to Krellis, his face grim. "What do we do, sir?"

Krellis stood upright and stalked away. "It looks as though you may have to hold these walls for three years."

2

B AELANDRA'S BLUE skirts rippled behind her as she stood on the edge of the Wheel and gazed out over the Night Market. Was this what Efften was like in her final days? Despite Ohndarien's beginnings, she would never have thought to compare the two cities until this night. A seemingly unstoppable army stood at their walls, and treacherous magic flowed like a river inside the city.

As she walked down the curving staircase, Baelandra reread the letter she had just received. It was from Prince Reignholtz, one of the most powerful rulers of the Summer Cities. The Sisters had sent Lawdon to him over a month ago with an offer of an alliance. As always, Reignholtz's reply was brief:

> Lady Baelandra J'Qulin, Sister of Autumn, my friend,
> I have presented your offer to the Summer Princes, we are carefully considering the matter.
> As you requested, I will keep the young woman who delivered this message safe aboard my flagship until these dangerous and unpleasant times have passed.
> The silk merchant you mentioned in your letter was happy to pay me half the sum he owes you in exchange for absolution of his other debts. I will see that the young woman receives the entire sum when she comes of age. It should be enough to buy her the finest ship on the Summer Seas.
> I must admit that she is a spirited young woman, and not at all pleased by your decision that she be kept out of harm's way. The ankle she broke climbing out a porthole is healing nicely, and I have transferred her to more secure quarters.
> Again I hope for a prosperous future between our people.
> May the sun shine upon all that you see.
> —R.

Baelandra had read the letter five times, each time more infuriated at the shortsighted fool. *We are carefully considering the matter.* Didn't those sun-addled princes know where Phandir was headed if Ohndarien fell? She knew an alliance with the Summer Cities was a long shot, but it still rankled to hear their oh-so-polite refusal.

Baelandra reached the bottom of the steps. The streets were packed with Ohndariens practicing with weapons, fletching arrows, building makeshift barricades.

Shara and her young Zelani owned the Night Market. Since Victeris's death, Shara had taken the Zelani and made them her own.

Had Baelandra been given the choice, she would have stopped Shara from creating her conclave of magicians, but Shara had graduated the males the night of Victeris's death without asking anyone. After that, it was out of Baelandra's hands. The male students initiated the rest of the females almost immediately. Baelandra couldn't have stopped them if she'd stood in front of them with a sword. The young Zelani left their school and marched straight to the Heart. Those first few nights had sounded like a brothel.

Against the advice of the Sisters, the young Zelani marched out of the Heart and took the Night Market the day Phandir's army arrived at the Physendrian Gate. Krellis's soldiers tried to retake the Night Market three times. Each time they charged across the bridges with sword and spears in hand. Each time a line of unarmed Zelani stood calmly in their way. One by one the trained soldiers tripped and faltered, dropped their weapons, and ran back the way they'd come, knocking their fellows down along the way.

Before long, the Lighting Swords took it upon themselves to guard Donovan's Bridge, and a group from the House of Summer manned fortifications facing the Market Bridge. After that, Krellis posted hundreds of soldiers on both bridges. Their little war turned into a tense stalemate.

Krellis didn't want potential enemies scattered all over the city. He was allowing safe passage across the bridges to anyone who wanted to join the tiny kingdom of the Night Market. Thousands of loyal Ohndariens had crossed the lines, but Krellis did not allow them to take any food or weapons. With every loyal Ohndarien that joined them, Baelandra's love of her people increased, and their food reserves dwindled.

She reached the Blue Lily, the theater the Zelani students had taken over after reclaiming the Night Market. She ducked into an alley and headed for the theater's back door. A young student, perhaps thirteen years old, stood sentry.

"Sister," the young girl said. "Shara-lani is expecting you. She should be on the main stage."

"Thank you, child," Baelandra replied, avoiding the young Zelani's gaze. The feral look in the prepubescent girl's eyes turned Baelandra's stomach. It was a look that had become all too familiar lately.

Every day the new mistress of the Zelani came to the Sisters with her plans. Shara suggested poisoning the enemy's water supply. She suggested assassinating the Master of the Citadel. She offered to capture other officers and subject them to a Zelani interrogation. She even suggested causing a mass hysteria among Krellis's loyal citizens. It was obvious that she loved Ohndarien. It was also obvious that she had changed.

The Sister of Autumn passed through the door and hurried past the scenery and costumes piled in the theater's backstage area. She could hear moans of pleasure from several different voices in the distance. The recently graduated Zelani practiced their art with a fanatical passion.

Shara had certainly regained her power, but she never truly recovered from her revenge against Victeris. She was falling prey to the same power-hungry disease that destroyed the mages of Efften. Baelandra no longer recognized the sweet, spirited girl she had liked so much.

"Shara-lani!" Baelandra called out, not wanting to interrupt their rituals. She had no desire to see what they were doing on the theater's stage.

Moments later, the curtain brushed aside, and Shara stepped through it, tying a robe around her waist. She was no longer the skinny, abused girl whom Scythe had rescued. Weeks of eating and practicing her art had made her radiant again. Shara's dark hair was tousled, but her eyes glowed in the dim light. Baelandra's heartstone throbbed as Shara approached.

The sounds of passion continued on the other side of the curtain.

"Baelandra," Shara said. "I've just received confirmation. What we suspected is true."

The Sister felt a pressure on the outside of her skull, like a headache trying to get in. "The ambassador's wife was in the city?"

"Yes. I snuck into the Citadel and questioned Krellis's wounded guard myself. I saw her face in my mind. There is no way the man could be lying. The Ohohhim stole the information they wanted, the letters Krellis was planning on trading for an alliance."

"You first heard of these letters from Victeris?"

"Yes, we spent a great deal of time together before he died."

"Is there any way he could have lied?"

Shara laughed. "No. That man was nothing when I was through with him. I destroyed him body, mind, and soul."

Baelandra turned away from the twisted smile on Shara's face. A wave of nausea swept over her, and she wanted to throw up.

"I see. So the Ohohhim know that the Lost Brothers are hiding the Legacy on the Cinder."

"Yes. I believe they will wash their hands of this little war and head for their true goal. Why do they want this Legacy? What is it?"

Baelandra swallowed, she noticed the heartstone pendant she'd given Shara was no longer around Shara's neck. "The Legacy is a weapon of terrible power. A curse. The absolute worst that the sorcerers of Efften ever created."

Baelandra paused, searching the uncaring expression on Shara's face. "I can only hope the Ohohhim want it for the same reason the Brothers want it, to keep it away from everyone else."

Shara raised an eyebrow as if she highly doubted that possibility. "How could we turn this information to our advantage?" she asked. "Could we bring the Legacy here and trade it for the Ohohhim's assistance?"

"No!" Baelandra said. "It must not be brought here."

Shara eyed the Sister, her lips pursed.

"Trust me, Shara. I would rather see Ohndarien fall."

"Very well." She pointed to the roll of parchment in the Sister's hand. "Is that a message for me?"

Baelandra handed her the letter. "No, but I wanted you to read it. If nothing else, at least Lawdon is safe."

BAELANDRA RETURNED to the Autumn Palace. She needed some time alone in her chambers to decide what should be done about Shara. She desperately wanted to help the girl, but she couldn't afford to blunt her best weapon.

As she stepped through the door, a man cleared his throat.

"Scythe!" she exclaimed, almost rushing to him, but she held herself back.

He stood in the corner, dusty and dirty. The knee of his loose pants was torn all the way down to his boot. A thin cut above his thick black eyebrow had crusted shut, but he stood there as strong as ever.

The Sister of Autumn crossed to him in a stately walk and took his hands in hers. Despite their years together, there was always a line that she could not cross.

"It is good to see you again, my friend," she said. "You are a hard man to worry about, but still I manage. Where is Brophy?"

Scythe's lips pressed together, and Baelandra's heart skipped a beat. "No," she whispered. Her knees quivered and Scythe was there, holding her up, keeping her steady.

"No," Scythe said. "Phandir threw him into the Wet Cells."

"But he lives?" she said, glancing into Scythe's dark eyes.

"He was alive when I left him. Who knows how long he will last down there. A month at most. Perhaps only days."

"Brophy is strong," she said, but her insides ached at the news.

"He was a broken man when I left him."

"Oh Scythe . . ." She began to shake. "How? How did it happen?"

"You would have been proud of him, my lady," Scythe said. The assassin's voice became husky. "He won the Nine Squares championship. He was a lion among jackals. They tried to kill him, they rigged the game, they cheated him at every turn, and he bested them all. All save one."

"Who?"

"Ossamyr. He fell in love with the queen. I knew she would try for him, I did not know he would fall so readily to her charms."

"He's just a boy, Scythe," she whispered.

"I know. I warned him. But it is beyond me to undo the workings of the heart," he said in a flat tone.

Baelandra looked down, her auburn hair falling across her face. She nodded. In a quiet voice, she asked, "How did she betray him?"

"In every way. She dashed his hopes in front of everyone." He paused.

"What, Scythe? Tell me."

He cleared his throat. "I do not know if he will ever come back. I tried to rescue him. We would easily have made our escape, but he lay down to die right there in the middle of the street."

Baelandra put a slender hand over her mouth and turned away. After a moment, she took a deep breath and set her jaw. She would not give up her brother's son so easily.

"We have to try. We have to find a way to get him out."

"We would have to carry him—"

"Then we carry him," she said.

He nodded and fell silent. Finally, he said, "Phandir would trade him for the city's surrender."

Baelandra didn't know which was worse, that Scythe would suggest such a thing or that she actually paused to consider it. "You know I can't do that," she finally said.

"Then our only option is an escape. As far as I know, only one man has ever broken anyone out of the Wet Cells."

They stared at one another in silence for a long moment. Baelandra bowed her head.

"Krellis," Baelandra finally said, closing her eyes.

"Krellis," he echoed.

BAELANDRA, SHARA, and Scythe waited for Krellis on Donovan's Bridge. Faedellin and the Lightning Swords had gathered behind them. Gorlym stood at the apex of the bridge's arc, fifteen feet away from the trio. As though intentionally creating a mirror image, Gorlym's soldiers gathered behind him on the shores of Southridge.

Baelandra wore her council robes, red and orange for the falling leaves. Her auburn hair flickered like a fire in the breeze. Shara stood to her left, her long blue dress smooth and perfect. Her black hair shone in the sunlight, fanning behind her like a curtain. The silver Zelani chain with its beautiful sapphire sparkled at her hip, trapping her gown at the waist and drawing attention to the curve of her legs.

Baelandra's heartstone pulsed, and she shifted uncomfortably. She reached two fingers through the buttons on the front of her dress and touched the diamond shard embedded in her flesh. Krellis was close.

"Remember," she murmured to Shara and Scythe, "we don't want violence."

"Speak for yourself," Shara replied, her narrowed eyes burning a hole through Gorlym. Syrol, Gorlym's Zelani, had abandoned him when Shara killed Victeris. Shara seemed to take it personally that a Zelani had once served Krellis's second-in-command.

"I still say we kill the man," Scythe said in his quiet voice. "His soldiers are trapped in this city just as we are. If Krellis dies, they will fight for you just as they fought for him."

"Or they would revolt, throw open one of the gates, and take their chances in Physendria or Faradan," Baelandra said curtly. "No. This internal conflict can only weaken us. Morale is already low. You cannot predict what another fracture in leadership would cause."

"And if he doesn't agree to your demands?" Scythe asked.

Baelandra stayed silent for three heartbeats. "Then we kill him and take our chances," she said. Scythe gave a thin smile and turned his gaze forward again.

Krellis stepped through his army of soldiers and crossed the bridge to stand beside Gorlym.

Scythe moved his hand to the pommel of his sword. Baelandra could ask almost anything of him, but she couldn't make him be civil toward Krellis. Only his oath kept him from leaping upon the huge Physendrian.

Sometimes, during her worst daydreams, she saw the inevitable battle between them, but never to the end. She could not guess who would win if their swords ever crossed.

Krellis said something to Gorlym, then walked alone to the center of the bridge. He stopped just short of the trio.

"Baelandra, Shara." Krellis inclined his head to both of them, but his lip curled as he turned his gaze to Scythe. The Brother of Autumn snorted and looked back at Baelandra.

"Krellis." She inclined her head gravely.

"You sent for me." The big man tapped his chest.

She nodded. "I want to offer an alliance for the defense of Ohndarien against her common enemies."

He frowned. "What are your terms?"

"We offer you complete command of the armies and the treasury. We offer the services of fifteen full-fledged Zelani to aid your senior officers. We offer a unified front to face our enemies."

"And what do you ask in return?"

"The council will be reinstated. The four Sisters will handle the distribution of food and other domestic matters."

"And after the battle is over?" Krellis asked.

"We offer Ohndarien's aid in your quest to regain the Physendrian throne, free passage for Physendrian ships through our locks, and a long-term alliance between our people."

"Meaning I am no longer an Ohndarien in your eyes?" He gave a mirthless smile.

"Were you ever?" she asked.

"I see. You are starving, and you offer me the privilege of feeding you. You are surrounded and outnumbered and you offer me the promise of future conquest. I am not impressed."

"We offer you friendship in a time when you desperately need friends," she said.

He laughed, a short, sharp bark. "I need troops and supplies, not aged councilors, hungry peasants, and arrogant whores."

"How long do you think it would take for my Zelani to cut the throats of your officers?" Shara breathed.

Krellis turned his gaze upon her. "You're only going to cut their throats? I thought Zelani were unnaturally compelled to play with their food."

Shara sneered. "Be careful, little Brother, or you'll find yourself crawling home."

Baelandra's stomach churned, and she had to swallow down an unpleasant taste in the back of her throat, but Krellis simply raised an eyebrow. "If you are so powerful, girl, tell me what I'm thinking right now."

Shara's eyes narrowed and she concentrated on his face. Krellis's heartstone pulsed faintly red through the linen of his shirt. Shara's lip curled and she looked away.

"Stop it," Baelandra said. "This bickering is pointless."

"What else do you have to offer me?" Krellis asked, crossing his arms over his chest.

"What else do you want?"

"You could return to my bed." He smiled a thin smile.

Without looking at Scythe, Baelandra put her hand on his, stopping the sword that was halfway out of its sheath.

Scythe glared at Krellis, who regarded him calmly. "I could kill you before your men could nock an arrow," Scythe said in a low voice.

"Only if Baelandra lets you take your sword out." He smirked.

"She is the only thing that keeps you alive."

"I will take that bet, Kher, anytime." Krellis touched the pommel of his own sword.

"Enough!" Baelandra raised her voice. "We need each other. Can't anyone else see that? We are surrounded by enemies, yet you squabble like chickens. If you were children, I would paddle you raw and send you to bed without supper."

Krellis flexed his fingers, and Scythe slammed his blade back into its sheath.

"Would you send us to bed separately, or in pairs?" Krellis asked with a half grin.

Baelandra sighed. "Krellis, I would happily spread my legs for you if it would save this city. But you would not find what you are looking for. The time we shared is gone forever."

Krellis grunted.

"What do you want to seal this alliance?" she pressed. "What will it take to unite us?"

"Two hostages."

Baelandra paused, stunned. Could he be serious? Could it be that easy? She raised her chin, knowing who one of those hostages must be. "Who?"

"You." He nodded at Baelandra. "And him." He inclined his head toward Scythe.

Baelandra's throat constricted. She turned to Scythe. His face betrayed nothing. "For myself, I agree," she said softly. "But I cannot speak for another."

Scythe didn't look at her. He focused his gaze on Krellis for a long time. "This is what you want?" Scythe asked, though he did not turn toward her. "There are other roads we might travel."

Baelandra swallowed hard. "It is the best way," she whispered.

Scythe slowly closed his eyes, his jaw muscles tensed and released. He opened his eyes again. "I will do this thing if you ask it of me."

He owed her nothing, but she owed him her life, twice. She owed him the life of her beloved nephew. Owed him for Shara's life. Owed him more than she could ever repay, and yet she must ask him for another favor. "I do," she said, her voice so quiet she could barely hear herself.

He nodded once. "Then I will do as you ask," he murmured, but he would not look at her. "You deserve nothing less."

Then he turned to Krellis. "You would be a fool to keep me imprisoned when the fighting starts."

"I will make that decision when the time comes," Krellis said.

"Then we have an understanding." Baelandra cut them off.

Krellis nodded. Scythe said nothing.

"Good," she said. "Now. There is one more thing before we can complete our bargain."

Krellis frowned, shaking his head. "I think I have given quite enough."

"Nevertheless," Baelandra said, "we require one thing more. It is simple and will cost you nothing."

"Indeed? And what would this insignificant request be?"

"We need to know how you got into the Wet Cells."

Krellis blinked. His brow furrowed, and he narrowed his eyes, flicked a glance at Scythe, then back at Baelandra. Slowly, his gaze settled on Shara. She stared back at him, raised an eyebrow.

"I see," he murmured, an indecipherable expression on his bearded face. "What did you want to know?"

IT WAS strange to be back in her house after such a long exile. Nothing had been touched, but Baelandra felt as though someone had rearranged all of the furniture, put it in wrong places. It was as though strangers had been living here for months, laying a careful layer of dust over everything. If any of them survived the days to come, would this place ever feel like home again?

Baelandra knelt and put the jade comb Brophy had given her into the trunk. She stopped and frowned; with a shake of her head, she took out the comb and set it on the dresser.

Seeing Krellis again brought back old hopes. He could have been such a great man if he had just let go of his past. She wondered if anything she loved about the man still survived, buried deep inside him.

"Almost ready?" Scythe asked from behind her. She jerked her head up. He always moved in and out of rooms like a ghost. Krellis could never sneak up on her, but Scythe did it naturally. She never knew when he was with her until he spoke.

"Almost," she said, frowning at the half-filled trunk. "I have never moved into a cell before. I have no idea what to pack."

She smiled at him, and he smiled back, one of his rare moments. Baelandra swallowed, took another dress off the bed, and put it in the trunk.

"This is the first time we've been alone in months." He spoke her thoughts.

She swallowed again, feeling a tightness in her belly. She should have foreseen this. Perhaps she had. Of course she had.

"Yes," she murmured, letting out a quiet breath. Like a little girl, she wanted to continue packing and ignore the tone of his voice, the meaning in his words. But she was not a little girl. She looked him in the eye, waiting. For all that he had done for her, she could at least give him herself, as honestly as she could.

"I would like to ask you something," he said quietly, staying where he was. He watched her so simply, so certainly. Her heart wrenched within her chest.

"I'll tell you anything, you know that," she said.

"Do you still love him?"

She opened her mouth to speak and found her voice gone. She bit her lip, praying to the Seasons that she was not blushing. "No," she said.

He said nothing, merely watched her face. Was she lying to him? Did she even know the truth herself?

"Scythe," she said, her voice low and husky, "I could never love him after what he did to Brophy." She remembered Krellis's ruthless accusations, his single-minded drive, the way he set the boy up, twisted the testimony. She remembered, and her resolve strengthened. A part of her loved the man still, despite it all. She could not deny it. Perhaps that part would always be there, but her soul knew the difference. Krellis was their best chance to save Ohndarien, but he would never be her lover again. She did not know much, but she knew that.

Whatever shone in Baelandra's eyes in that moment must have been the sign Scythe was waiting for. He crossed the room. It had always been odd to look into Scythe's eyes. The first time she saw him, he slew three men while at death's door. He seemed huge at the time, but they stood at the same height. It always surprised her when she noticed how small he was.

He brushed a hand across her cheek, moving back her wavy auburn hair.

She licked her lips, waiting for him to kiss her, wondering what she would do when he did.

Instead, he said, "When you are as short as I am, you never kiss a woman for the first time until she is lying down."

Scythe scooped her up behind her knees and shoulders and tossed her on the bed. She bounced twice and laughed in surprise. He leapt after her, landing lightly on his toes. He knelt slowly, lowering himself onto her hips as he looked into her eyes.

"This is the last chance we may get," Scythe murmured, his fierce black brows turned upward slightly. She had never seen that expression on his face before, uncertain, vulnerable.

"I know," she whispered.

He paused. "Is this what you want?" His brows came together and his body tensed.

She nodded, putting her hands behind his wiry shoulders. "Yes."

He smiled like a little boy, then leaned down and kissed her, his body pressing against hers. She wrapped her arms around his back, brought her thighs up on either side of his narrow hips. His body trembled as though he were cold. She swallowed, turned her face away. He kissed her neck as one slender hand deftly unfastened the buttons on the front of her dress.

She closed her eyes, willing herself to love this man, willing herself to give him this one small thing in return for everything he had given her.

Scythe stopped kissing her. His hand left the buttons of her dress. She opened her eyes. His face was tight, resolute. It was the face he wore before she asked him a favor, the face he wore before he killed a man, and after. It was a face she knew too well.

"You are thinking of him."

She shook her head quickly. "No. I'm not."

He watched her for a long moment. Carefully, methodically, he began re-buttoning her dress.

She grabbed his hands. "No, please. I want this."

His hands were gentle, but unstoppable. "You want this like an honorable merchant wants to pay his debts."

"No, Scythe, that's not—"

His open, frank look stopped her.

"Scythe, please," she said, sitting up, interrupting him. Her dress lay open at the top, the last three buttons still undone. Her heartstone glimmered red. "Give me time, please . . ."

He slid off the bed and offered her a wisp of a smile, his dark fingers touching the edge of the covers. "Time has run out for us." He shook his head. "I should not have come here, but I needed to know."

He strode quickly across the room. Baelandra leapt from the bed and ran after him, caught him just as he entered the hallway. She grabbed his arm and turned him around.

"I want to give you this, my friend, my . . ." She tried to say 'love' but could not. "Be my lover. Please, I am asking you."

"No. In this, I deserve nothing less," he said in a husky voice. He shook her hand loose and continued walking.

"Scythe . . ." She hurried after him for a few steps, but knew she could not catch him. She would never be able to catch him again. "I wish I could. Please know that I want to."

He stopped and her heart beat faster. She opened her mouth in anticipation. Oh please, she thought, turn around.

But he merely turned his head, his profile dark against the light behind him. "We all wish for things, Baelandra."

He turned and went down the blue-white marble stairs.

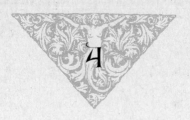

*S*UTOM'S PALMS began to sweat. The carvings were recent. Flecks of stone scattered the barren ground around the little statuettes. He picked a figure up and held it close to his face so he could see the details in the darkness. It was an elegant woman with long, sweeping hair and an imperious look to her face. The other carvings were just as beautiful, like little idols from a barbarian shrine. He had almost overlooked them in the foul mist that haunted this place, but the vapors cleared for just one moment and revealed the secret of the Cinder.

He set the carving down gently and crept farther into the alcove between two boulders where the carvings were hidden. Every surface of the rock was covered with a vast panorama of carvings. Squinting in the darkness, he could barely make out an intricate carving of the Blue City. It depicted the vile fortress in painstaking detail, from the Water Wall to the windmills and the bay.

The Empire was saved. The wizards of the Blue City were on this island, just as the letters said. Father Lewlem would be pleased, and Sutom would progress countless sleeves closer to Oh.

A light tinkling sound caught the scout's attention. He crept out of the alcove and opened his ears to the sound, opened his eyes to find the enemy.

Sutom had been trained since childhood in the arts of silence. Few of the Children of Oh could bear the loneliness of his work. But he had been blessed with a serene heart, a keen mind, and deft feet. He was proud to serve His Eternal Wisdom in these lonely, barbaric places of the world.

Quiet as the wind, he crept closer to the sound. It had to be the baby's music box. Father Lewlem would be most pleased, indeed. The horsewomen of the Vastness had spoken of the mystical box that always accompanied the Legacy.

When he was certain no one had seen him, Sutom padded across the dry, porous rock toward the sound. He stayed close to the largest formations, using every scrap of cover in this bald, fuming land.

The childish tune emanated from a cave lit by the soft, red glow of a fire from deep within. Sutom crept closer and paused before the entrance. A chill ran through him. The infection of the wizards was inside. His skin crawled as if dipped in oil, and his throat felt thick.

Certainly this would be enough evidence, but Sutom had had to make certain with his own eyes . . . Crouching low, he peered around the edge of the cave like a serpent.

A noise behind him! A foot on rock! And then another and another, rushing toward him!

Launching himself forward, Sutom sprinted up the hill into a thick bank of noxious mist. He whipped his head around. The fog swirled away, and he saw the glint of moonlight on a naked blade.

The scout's feet gripped the volcanic rock, and he ran faster than he ever had in his life. All would be lost if the wizards of the Blue City caught him. Sweat beaded on his forehead. His legs ached, but as he raced from the sound of rocks crunching under his pursuer's feet, he could hear the wizard's even breathing. The devil was gaining.

With a grunt, Sutom crested the jagged ridge and plunged down the other side. The slope would give him an advantage. The wizard behind him might have the large body and long legs of an easterner, but he could never be as agile as an Ohohhim scout. He could not—

Sutom smacked headlong into a furry, fetid belly. He spun sideways and fell to the rocks, covered with an overwhelming stench. An enormous black creature lunged at him. Its guttural roar pierced his ears. Sutom rolled farther down the slope, and the creature bounded after him, stomping on his leg and slashing him with its claws. Sutom threw himself down the mountain, desperate to escape. He tumbled down the slope and slammed into a rock. Sutom shook the stars from his vision, tried to rise, and screamed. He fell back and gasped. His thighbone jutted out of his leg just above the knee.

The perversely misshapen bear lumbered down the steep slope, causing a small avalanche in its wake. Its limbs barely seemed attached to its body, stretching and distorting its mangy coat as it ran.

The scout fumbled for his blade, but it was gone from his belt. He jerked his head up to stare at the thing coming down the hill.

The malignant bear roared, rising on its hind legs, twice as tall as Sutom. Oozing flesh spotted with tufts of brown hair covered its body. Jagged, yellow teeth flashed beneath glowing eyes. Black saliva flew from its mouth as it roared again, its huge, hairy arms spread wide. Claws as long as Sutom's hand jutted from the paws at contorted angles.

A figure flew out of the darkness. A sword flashed.

Hot blood splattered across Sutom's face, and the creature's roar became a wet burble. Its hairy head tumbled past the scout. The great, mottled body continued forward, and it swung blind, the claw crashing onto the rocks inches from Sutom's arm. The headless creature rose to its feet, lurched past him, and rolled down the hill out of sight.

Sutom stared into the fog, jerking his head back and forth, trying to see both the bear and the man who killed it. The headless creature never reappeared, but a faint light illuminated the vapors, and an emaciated man emerged from the swirling mist.

The glow came from the stone embedded in the center of his chest. He wore nothing more than a pair of tattered pants that hung loose on his gaunt frame. With an economical swipe, he cleaned his blackened blade on a rag hanging from his belt, set the tip of the sword at his hip, and sheathed it.

"You are from the Blue City," Sutom said between pants.

"Yes." The sorcerer crouched next to Sutom, his weather-beaten face spotted with the creature's blood.

"Please don't kill me," Sutom said, clutching his shattered leg.

"I'm sorry, my friend, but you are already dead." With a surprisingly delicate touch, the thin, starkly muscled man lifted Sutom's hand away from his thigh. The wound reeked like the creature that caused it, and vomit surged into the back of his throat. Inky tendrils were already spreading outward from the gash. The dark fingers of the infection spiderwebbed across his skin, creeping across his belly and onto his chest.

Sutom whimpered, his eyes huge as he stared at his doom. He could feel the vile wound growing, reaching for his heart. Sutom had been in the Vastness when they discovered the Ohndariens' handiwork. He saw what became of the Children of Oh when touched by that corruption.

"No!" Sutom gripped the man's forearm. It was like grabbing a steel bar. "Please! Don't let it take me."

The barbarian wizard's mouth tightened a little. He let out a slow breath and looked away for a moment. "I cannot save you. Your wound is too great. I'm going to have to kill you."

"Yes," Sutom begged through clenched teeth. "Yes, yes. Do it quick, you devil. Finish your handiwork."

Sutom thought he saw a tear in the Ohndarien wizard's eye as he drew his sword and thrust it into the scout's heart.

The pain vanished, and suddenly Sutom felt much, much better.

5

$\mathcal{S}$HARA BOBBED naked in the water, clinging to the wooden plank. She took a dozen hasty breaths, then a dozen slower breaths, then a dozen very long breaths as she rested from her swim. The journey across the open ocean in the dead of night had been longer than she had expected. Her magic sustained her, her body glowing with the power, but this was only the beginning of the nightmare journey. She had already taken too long. If she didn't hurry, Brophy would have to wait another twelve hours.

The cliffs south of Physen blotted out half of the starry sky, and she kicked backward, keeping her distance from them. The waves were deceptively gentle at this distance, but they would crush her if she let them carry her into the jagged rocks.

Krellis said there would be archers watching the cliffs, but they would have a hard time spotting her. She had dyed her entire body with juice of the midnight plum, and her black hair was bound tight against her scalp.

The Kherish sailors had been afraid to talk to her on the journey south, and Shara nurtured that fear. The men had stared in hungry amazement as she stripped naked on the deck, black as a starless sky, and leapt from their ship, tied to a sackful of iron. The sack rested on a wooden plank, following her as she paddled several miles from the ship to the shore.

Shara clung to the wood as the waves urged her toward the cliffs. Without the plank, the iron would have dragged her to the bottom of the ocean long ago. The saltwater constantly stung where the rope had chafed her waist, but she funneled the pain inward, adding it to her power.

Her eyes glittered as she scanned the base of the cliff and remembered the conversation that had led her here.

"It is a fool's errand," Krellis said. "Leave the boy."

Shara sneered at the man's arrogance. "Baelandra said you broke into the Wet Cells. Does that make you a fool, then? Or a liar?" she replied.

"You are not me."

"Try me," she said softly. She put her hands flat on the table between them. The strap of her gown fell off one shoulder, and she glanced at it. She sent the tendrils of her power to caress him, tried to pull him into her.

He arched an eyebrow. "You can take the entire dress off if you like, Zelani. You won't get your claws into me."

Her smile turned sour. "Is this how you honor your bargains?" she asked. She slipped the strap back onto her shoulder.

He grunted. "We have much to discuss," he said. "If you are truly serious."

"Do I seem frivolous?"

"Then you had best hope that Brophy is in some condition to fight. It took all of my brother's powers and my strength to get us out of there. Victeris lasted six months in that hellhole. That is how strong he was."

"I know all about your brother's strengths."

Krellis's eyes flashed.

"Is six months a long time?" she asked, pleased to see the man squirm.

He smiled thinly. "Longer than anyone in ten generations."

"And how many have escaped?"

"Just the two of us."

"How?"

"What do you know of the Wet Cells?" Krellis asked.

"I've heard of them, just as everyone else."

"Then listen, because you cannot know them by the rumors. The first King of Physendria knew that any lock could be picked and any guard could be bribed. So he made stone his jailors. He turned the ocean into his executioner."

"The prisoners are locked in cells that fill with water," Shara said. "Everyone from Gildheld to the Opal Palace knows this."

"No." Krellis shook his head. "Not locked. Trapped. The Wet Cells are carved deep underneath the volcanic cliffs of Physen, deep enough to connect with the old lava tubes that roar with the tides of the Great Ocean. The cells are hacked out of this jagged rock. There are no locks. The prisoners are thrown into the cell and caged by an iron grate with no hinges, no winches, no mechanism to raise it. The grates were forged directly into slots carved in the rock, and the only way to open one is to lift it straight up, a feat that requires at least ten men."

"How many guards are in the cells?"

"Two." Krellis leaned back in his chair, and it creaked under his weight. She stared back at him, cold and impassive.

"What about the inside of the cells?" she asked.

"A torture device. There are no public executions in Physendria. Any mention of the Wet Cells causes more fear than a dozen headsmen. The Wet Cells are a death sentence. They are a cold, damp, and lonely place. Pitch-black. For the last few weeks, young Brophy has been sleeping on jagged volcanic rock. They'll feed him twice a day, of course, but he'll shit where he sleeps. His lullaby will be the ravenous roaring of the ocean in the empty lava tubes."

Shara tried to pry into his mind again and failed.

His bushy mustache twitched. "And that is the best time of day. That's low tide. As the tide rises, the sea will seep into his cell through the endless warren of tiny pockets and gaps in the volcanic rock. At first, the waves will simply lap against his feet, cooling his fever perhaps, washing away his filth. But as the tide grows higher, the waves will rush in and out of his cell, battering him into a mind-numbing exhaustion until the cell is completely filled with water. If Brophy wants to live, he'll have to climb to the top of the bars and reach the tiny pocket of air that remains between waves, gulping breaths whenever he can."

"But he can survive?"

"There is enough air. King Phy wanted to wear his prisoners down, break them completely. At some point, the mind or the body will give out, battered by the tides or despair. But until then, there will always be just enough food. Just enough air."

Shara clenched her teeth, wishing Krellis were floating in that prison.

"He was brilliant, our Phy I," Krellis said.

"A fiend."

"Yes. Unlike a woman who twists a man's desire until he is a slave to her will."

Shara smiled and leaned forward onto the table, giving him a better look at what he was already staring at. "What else?" she asked.

Krellis flexed his fingers, popping the knuckles in his fist. "The only entrance to the Wet Cells is in the center of Physen's main barracks."

"Why not go in that way?" she asked.

"Why not lift the Water Wall and walk underneath?" Krellis narrowed his eyes. "Even a Zelani could not do it. The door to the prison is called the Giant's Tooth, a massive thing made of nine tree trunks, each over three feet wide and a hundred feet tall, lashed together with iron bands. It weighs tons. Not even fifty men could budge it, but the ocean can. When the tide is high, the door floats. It is forced against the top of the doorway like a portcullis in reverse by the unstoppable pressure of the ocean. When the tide is at its very lowest, the door sinks, opening briefly between the waves. A quick man can roll through the gap before the Tooth crushes him. Every few years a careless guard gets eaten by the Tooth."

"What a shame."

"Isn't it?" Krellis leaned back in his chair again. "Every twelve hours, the Tooth starts chomping. For about two minutes. The entrance is set into one wall of a sunken courtyard where Physendrian troops gather for inspection. There are always hundreds of soldiers standing at the entrance when the Tooth opens. Two guards roll out of the darkness and two more roll in. It's always two, unless they send in a crew with a new prisoner or to bring out a body." He paused. "Still want to enter that way? Can you enchant hundreds of soldiers at the same time?"

Shara said nothing.

"So, you can either burrow through solid stone, chop through a three-foot-thick wooden door, or overcome hundreds of men and roll through the door when it is open."

"Or?"

"Or you can do it my way."

"Then tell me."

"Then listen," he had said. "Listen to every detail, because one blunder means death . . ."

Shara let the memory fade and bobbed in the water, scanning the dark base of the cliff for the landmark. Her suspicions trickled back. If Krellis wanted Brophy dead, why would he tell her the truth? Wouldn't it be better to lie to her? He could rid himself of two enemies and avenge Victeris in one swift stroke. All it would take was one bit of misleading information.

The last thing she asked Krellis before leaving Ohndarien was why he agreed to help her rescue Brophy.

The Brother of Autumn shrugged. "Because Baelandra asked me to."

"She also asked you not to exile him in the first place."

"I've had a change of heart. I'm sure that's something a woman like you can understand."

Shara hadn't believed him at the time, and she still wasn't sure she believed him, but she had no other options. It she wanted to take Brophy back, this was the only way to get him.

The underground cave was her first challenge. Holding her breath and fighting the surf, she must swim through a submerged tunnel blinded by the dark and dragged down by the weight of the iron she carried. The end of the porous lava tube held a pocket of air during low tide, and that was only halfway to the Wet Cells.

Shara spotted Krellis's landmark, dark against the shadowy cliffs.

"If you come in from the southwest," he had said, "swim toward the tallest freestanding outcropping. There is a natural indentation over the place where you'll have to dive. It looks roughly like a pyramid."

And there it was, just as he'd described, covered with barnacles. Her heart beat faster. He'd told the truth about that, at least. Of course that wasn't a lie that would kill her.

She began her breathing and cycled through the five gates, gathering her power. As she did, she remembered the five rites of initiation she had performed on that first night after besting Victeris. The pools below the Zelani school sang with magic as her former master crawled through his own shit in the tower above. Caleb had been inside her, then Teras, Baksin, Bashtin, and Zale. She imagined their hands on her body, their breath matched with hers, their eyes open and trusting as she filled them with more power than they could possibly imagine.

She had hoped for a glorious union with Caleb, but something had changed between them. In the end, it had just been business. A sweet, powerful business, but with none of the romantic allure she once imagined. It was no matter. Her life was different now. Romance paled next to the magic. She was no longer the foolish girl who had let Victeris dominate her.

Her thoughts stoked the fire within her body. Over the past weeks, Shara could slip into desire as easily as a dress. She felt her own mind, swirling with the knowledge of her task, filled with thoughts of Brophy and the rituals with her fellow Zelani. She felt the depth of the ocean, indifferent and hungry. It pulled at her. She added her determination to the spell. She added her distrust of Krellis, her hatred of Victeris, her desire for Brophy. She added it all.

Shara drew the knife attached to her roped bundle and cut the plank free. The bag of iron sagged slowly in the water, reached the end of its tether and pulled insistently against her waist.

Shara took several deep breaths and stroked to where the waves crashed against the bottom of the pyramid. With one last deep breath, she dove. The rope tugged at her. The salt water stung her chafed waist, but she swam deeper and deeper, following the load until she reached the bottom.

The mouth of the cave was right where Krellis said it would be, and she stroked closer. The bag of iron dragged behind her. A surge of water carried her into the tunnel, propelling her forward. She bounced off jagged rocks as she went, taking the wounds and swimming onward. A few cuts meant nothing if she couldn't find the pocket of air at the end of the tube and get her next breath.

The water changed direction and Shara clung to a jagged outcropping to keep from being sucked backward. In moments the next wave came, and she was hurled forward once again.

Zelani had incredible control over their breath, but as she continued into the blackness, fears gnawed at her. Memories of her own initiation came to her, the underwater swim, the betrayal at the far side.

What if Krellis lied, sending her into a dead end? What if there was a branch in the tunnel that he never explored? What if she had already taken it and was swimming deeper and deeper to her eventual death?

Feeling light-headed, Shara swam onward. The rope pulled taut, stopping her. She yanked frantically. It wouldn't budge. Her chest spasmed, trying to draw breath, but she fought it and swam down, hand over hand on the rope. She found the bag wedged into a nook and wrestled it free. Her lungs burned, but she slung the weight over her shoulder and held the rope with her teeth.

She swam farther and went up, hit her head. Nothing. No escape. She swam forward another few feet and tried again. Her arms were lead, but she pushed against the water, against the weight of her anchor, swimming forward, ever forward.

Another surge of the tide threw her onto the jagged floor of the lava tube. The water receded and she could suddenly breathe. Clinging to the rocks, she sucked in a desperate breath around the rope in her mouth. She spat it out and drew another breath, deeper and longer. The next wave came in and threw her forward again, rolling her across the rough ground.

Shara clung to the side of the tunnel as the wave receded, refusing to be pulled backward again. She hauled the bag out of the surf and set it on a shelf.

Bracing herself in absolute darkness with water up to her thighs, she fought the tide as she gasped for air. The water grew shallow as the floor inclined upward. Soon she was able to lie down for a moment beyond the hungry pull of the sea. Krellis had led her true.

So far.

When she felt ready, Shara sat up and pulled the bag to her, hand over hand in the darkness. The ropes were rough and frayed in places where they had scraped against the sides of the tunnel.

She cut the lines away with the knife, and opened the bag. Withdrawing two round stones, she smacked them together. A spark lit the darkness for an instant, and she squinted. The sharp smell of sulfur from the rocks seemed out of place so close to the ocean. She clacked the fire stones again. Another spark gave her a brief vision of what the cave looked like. With repeated clacks, she created enough light to see the opening to the next leg of her journey.

She was in a jagged tunnel about five or six feet across. Dozens of smaller tunnels, only a foot or two wide, branched off in every direction. Most of them went nowhere. Krellis said he'd had to come back to this cave seven times before he found a path to the Wet Cells. He could only search for a few hours before the rising tide forced him back outside.

He had spent six days returning to this cave, crawling over jagged stone, constantly stung and battered by seawater, never completely certain he would get through. He used a hammer and chisel to break through a few tight spots.

She couldn't imagine it, especially for a man like Victeris. What would possess Krellis to go through such a nightmare to rescue that demon?

If Krellis had spoken true about the markers to the Wet Cells, she should be able to get through in time. But this cave would completely fill with water by high tide. This brief gap of air only lasted two hours of each cycle. She had timed her midnight swim as carefully as possible, but she could only count on a little more than an hour before the tide surged in behind her, trapping her in a watery death.

After clacking the rocks several times in front of Krellis's old scratch marks, she opened the bag and withdrew the leather gloves and a pair of leather pads for her knees. She had cursed this bag for its bulk many times in the ocean and the tunnel, but now she wished she had a leather helm, shirt, and pants as well.

She crawled into the tunnel, pushing the bag in front of her, and clacking the stones together for brief flashes of light. Sometimes the passage was tall enough that she could crouch and waddle forward. Sometimes it became so narrow that she pulled herself painfully through, scraping her belly, breasts, and legs. How could someone as large as Krellis have made it?

She found out how moments later when she ran into a dead end. Krellis had not come this way.

With infuriating slowness, she backed down the tunnel, taking more time to clack the fire stones together and look carefully at what she had thought were Krellis's scratches. She found her mistake and continued down the next passage.

She couldn't be sure how long she spent in that timeless darkness, the volcanic rock biting at her skin, pulling at her hair, but the ocean roared constantly, reminding her that it was coming for her.

When she felt the cool rush of water on her legs, Shara despaired, doubled her efforts to scramble forward. She was already past the point of no return. Her pocket of air was gone. If she didn't continue, she would drown.

Shara came to another open area and clacked the rocks. Three forks in the tunnel. She looked closely at all of them. Two had scratch marks next to them and led straight up. She heard the water behind her surge forward and disappear. Which scratch marks should she choose? Why hadn't the bastard told her about this? Was this his betrayal? Was this—?

A man's voice echoed down the tunnel to her right.

Grinning, Shara leaned her head into the opening and strained her ears to make sure she hadn't imagined it. Yes, it was there. The slow, deep tones of a man's voice. Shara reached out with her magic, following the voice to its source. Yes. A man. Two men. Someone she didn't recognize and . . .

Brophy! He was alive. Blessedly alive.

She pushed the bag up the tunnel, crawling only a short distance before it opened up slightly . . .

Into a rusted iron grate.

Shara clenched her teeth. Behind her, the ocean rushed and receded. She worked her fingers through the grate and pulled on it. It creaked but did not give. Someone must have discovered how Krellis had broken in and made certain no one followed after him. She sat back, heedless of the sharp stone biting into her skin. She rummaged in her bag. She could use the iron to—

No. Not that way.

Turning her attention forward, she closed her eyes and breathed. She only hoped the two guards holding Brophy were strong. She would need that strength.

The magic thrummed through her, and she reveled in it. Power surged through her like a black wave, and Shara began to sing.

6

DATHYL WOULDN'T shut up.

"Did you know they're calling you the Ohndarien Lion? Y'ought to be proud of that. Stand tall. Keep your head above water." Dathyl chuckled. "Swim tall. That's all I'm saying. If you give up, then what are you? The Ohndarien Fish? You don't want that . . ."

Brophy sat cross-legged on the floor of his cell, waiting for the next tide as Dathyl blathered on. The water was coming soon. Already the lowest corner of his cell glimmered in the torchlight. Little waves splashed and drew back. He wanted sleep, wanted warmth, more food. All the things he was supposed to want. He kept his breathing even, pushing back the cold, tempering the rumbling in his stomach, bolstering his energy.

Twenty guards had rotated duty with Brophy over the last three weeks, and they had all bet on how long the Nine Squares champion would last. Dathyl's time wasn't for another month, and he insisted on giving Brophy inspirational speeches every time he had guard duty. The earliest guesses had already lost, though there had not been many of them. Most had high expectations of the Ohndarien Lion.

Brophy tried to sleep, but Dathyl kept talking to him. The ignorant ogre never shut up and didn't seem to realize that Brophy would drown much sooner without sleep.

When Brophy came to the Wet Cells, he wanted to die, but as that first tide came surging in, he found giving up was a lot harder than he thought.

Scythe could have kept him from this. That thought had almost driven Brophy to despair in the first week. But there was always hope. Nobody could take that away from him. The ocean would have to fight him to the last.

". . . think about the honor of Ohndarien." Dathyl continued. "If you crack off and give up this early, what'll they think of you? They'll say, 'now there goes a 'darien who's not worth his salt,' they'll say. You want them sayin' that about you? You want them . . ."

It had been thirty-nine tides since Brophy's first night in the Wet Cells.

He waited, half-asleep, for the fortieth to begin. Brophy faded out, leaning his head against the cell wall.

He dreamed of swimming with Shara in the glittering bay outside the Summer Gate. Trent stomped and shook his fist at them from the shore. "Ohndarien Lion!" Trent growled in Dathyl's voice. "Wouldn't want to be a fish!"

Brophy and Shara laughed, ignoring him. Brophy swam after her, but she always stayed ahead of him, swimming as smoothly as a dolphin. No matter how hard he swam, he couldn't catch her. She looked back and smiled, her long black hair fanning out in the water.

His dream changed suddenly. A haunting song descended from the sky. Clouds rolled in, obscuring the sun, and it grew cold. Shara paused, and so did Brophy, looking up. They bobbed in the bay, treading water and listening to the beautiful voice that made his blood run cold.

"Did you hear that?" Shara asked with Dathyl's voice.

Brophy blinked. Shara vanished, and he looked up at his idiot guard. His dreams pulled at him, that beautiful voice urging him to fall asleep again.

"It's Llyella, the maiden of the depths," Brophy murmured, smiling. "She's come for me at last."

"Who?"

"Llyella," he said, closing his eyes. "She sings sailors to sleep, calling them to her watery embrace."

"Well that bitch can't have you for another month," Dathyl said. He stood up, grabbed the torch, and disappeared down the tunnel. Brophy drifted back to sleep. The water would be back soon. He needed to sleep.

A man's grunt and the sharp pang of breaking iron jolted him awake. He sat up, blinking. He suddenly felt sick to his stomach. It wasn't just hunger. It was something worse.

He looked around. Dathyl was gone. A wave splashed against Brophy's leg, and he stood up. Again, there was a groan of metal followed by a pang and a splash. Brophy put his hand to his heart; it suddenly felt very empty and wrong.

He stumbled to the grate and pressed his cheeks against the cold bars. Out of the darkness, he heard the last sound he ever expected to hear, a man's cry of pleasure. It set his teeth on edge. He peered into the gloom, straining against the thick bars. It felt like the air was heavy with oily smoke, but nothing obscured his vision.

Dathyl had taken the torch, but he hadn't gone far. Within the ring of light, Brophy saw both guards. Mashed between them was another figure, dark as night but definitely a woman. Both guards had stripped down to their boots, shuffling awkwardly as their own movements threw them off-balance. The black woman writhed against them and both men humped her like beasts, one in front and one behind, thrusting urgently.

Brophy tried to turn away, but he couldn't make himself. It was awful, arousing him and disgusting him at the same time.

The woman whispered to the guards, encouraged them. Her hands ran through Dathyl's hair while her thighs wrapped around Locklen's waist.

"Yes." She rocked against them. "Feel the fires growing inside you. Feel the flames make you strong."

Their panting grew faster, moving toward orgasm. As they neared, the shadow woman put her feet on the ground. She twisted her hips out from between the two men and stepped away. They reached for her, but she held up a hand. They stopped as if on strings. Descending before Locklen, she took him into her mouth as she pulled his breeches up. Releasing him, she retied the laces.

"No," Locklen growled in a deep voice. "I want—"

"Shhhhh . . ." She put her fingers on his belly, and he froze. Still on her knees, she turned and did the same to Dathyl, fastening his pants.

"Now, my giants." She rose to her feet, took their wrists like children and led them to the bars of Brophy's cell. "When our work is done, I will reward you."

Dathyl's eyes glimmered red as if they held a fire. He breathed in quick, short gasps, and the veins stood out on his neck. He looked thicker, his shoulders heavier than before. Locklen was the same. His lips pulled back from clenched teeth, and he stared at Brophy like a zealot. Brophy stepped back from the bars. They both looked like Athyl or Krellis, dangerous men, beasts that would rip him apart in seconds.

The shadow woman led them over to Brophy's cell, and he backed into the corner. "Now lift," she purred.

"By the Seasons!" Brophy exclaimed, seeing her blackened face for the first time. "Shara!"

"Hush, Brophy," she murmured. "Not now." She stroked Locklen's back with a finger, touched Dathyl's heaving shoulders. "Lift, my warriors," she said in her throaty voice. "Lift."

Suddenly speechless, Brophy watched as Dathyl and Locklen bent and grabbed the bars of the huge grate. The two of them pulled, grunting, but the grate did not move.

"Lift, my warriors!" Shara said, louder. "Nothing can stop you."

They screamed, their necks bulging, veins standing out starkly on their burly forearms. Brophy rushed to help them. He grabbed the bars and pulled, feeling like he was trying to lift a mountain. A wave surged from the back of the cell, cascading across the guards' boots and Shara's black shins. The grate creaked and rose a few inches. Shara slid a small block of iron underneath.

"Rest, my giants, rest," she murmured. They let the grate slam down onto the hunk of iron.

Brophy panted from his exertion. He had a hard time believing the blackened woman before him was really Shara. He couldn't look at her. Despite his terrible fatigue, he wanted her. His body ached with the anticipation of sliding his hands along her smooth skin, of touching the dark V between her legs. He shuddered, tried to shake the horrible feeling away. "What are you doing!" he cried. She shot him a fierce glance and shook her head.

"Now, my giants, again." They grabbed the bars and heaved. Brophy strained with them. Again, the grate creaked up another notch. Shara withdrew a longer piece of iron and wedged it next to the other one. The grate came down again, almost open enough for a man to slide underneath. The water washed across their legs, ever rising.

She let them rest.

"One last time, my giants, and then you may rest forever." Calf deep in water, they pulled one more time on the grate. Brophy heard a wet snap somewhere in Locklen's arm, and the grate sagged, stopped. He looked up, panting. Shara had the third length of iron wedged in place.

Locklen's left arm hung limply at his side, but he didn't seem to notice.

Shara looked at Brophy. "Come, my friend. You're free."

He hesitated, not wanting to get near her.

"Now, Brophy," she hissed.

He took a breath and plunged underwater, scrambling beneath the grate. He surfaced and backed a step away. "What have you done to yourself?" he whispered.

Her eyes narrowed, and her lip twitched, then the flash of anger was gone as though it had never been.

Her dark flesh glistened in the torchlight. He ached to throw her up against the bars and thrust up into her. Clenching his teeth, he turned away.

"Sweet Brophy . . ." She reached out and touched his shoulder. "Be calm. I am almost done here."

His skin shivered at her touch. Her voice was the rasp of a crone, her gesture wicked and ugly. Acid splashed up his throat as the breath of power touched him. He stumbled to his knees and vomited.

"Shara! Stop it!"

Her eyes flickered coldly. "Never mind him, my giants," she said to the others. "Under the bars. Both of you."

They pushed themselves under the water and squeezed through the narrow space beneath the grate. They stood leering, arms hanging at their sides like puppets.

"Remove the iron," she murmured to Dathyl. He knelt, took the medium piece and hammered at the longer one. It sprang free, and the grate crashed down, trapping the two men inside.

"You are nothing," she hissed at them.

"Shara—!" Brophy began.

She held up a fierce hand to him, continued to speak to the men behind the grate. "You are weak. You are fools. You are nothing, you deserve to die in this cell."

The guards seemed to shrink. Locklen screamed, holding his arm and collapsing to his knees.

Brophy's stomach turned again, and he splashed up the hall, away from her. The corridor sloped up, and in moments he was on dry ground. Weak and wobbly, he staggered up the tunnel to the guards' room at the bottom of the spiral stairs that led to the Giant's Tooth. Locklen's screams quickly dwindled to pathetic whimpers.

Two torches burned in the small room. There were three tables set at haphazard angles and a scattering of wooden chairs. A pair of cots had been provided for the guards. There was nowhere to go. The Giant's Tooth wouldn't open until low tide, hours from now.

He turned around. Stained black and naked as the night, Shara walked calmly up from the cells, her hips swaying.

"Stay away from me," he whispered.

"And why would I do that, Brophy? We have nine hours to wait until we can escape. I will make you a god in that time."

She walked closer, and he forced himself to stay where he was. Her eyes were strangely warm as she spoke. "I will make it sweet, Brophy, not like it was with them. With you it will be beautiful. I will be gentle."

His heart thundered painfully in his chest. He wanted her so badly, he couldn't get away from it. She walked closer, and he held out his hands. She leaned forward and kissed his fingers. His skin shivered.

"Don't do that," he whispered.

"Do what?" she said, smiling playfully. "I think you want me to do that."

"No."

She brought her other hand up to his arm. "I've come for you. Scythe said you wanted to die, but I knew you wouldn't give up. You fought the ocean. You dreamed of escape, and now I am here. Let me help you." Her hands slid down his chest and past his naked stomach.

He grabbed her wrists. "Don't." His penis responded to her touch, growing painfully hard, but his stomach lurched. "No. Not this way."

"Shushhh," she whispered, stepping closer, taking one of his fingers into her mouth. "It will be beautiful."

Brophy grabbed her wrists and squeezed as hard as he could. "I'd rather be back in that cell."

"You used to want me, Brophy," she said, backing him against the wall, pressing her body against his. "You wanted me, but you wouldn't say so, couldn't say so. But we can do it now. We can do it for hours . . ." She lifted her leg, brushing her thigh against him.

He reached for her waist.

"Yes," she purred. "Like that."

His hands clamped solidly on her hips, and he pushed her away, gasping at the effort it cost him. He swallowed back salty bile as her power curled around them.

Her eyes flashed. "We have to do this," she hissed. "In nine hours there will be a hundred men down here looking for you. You are weak, starving, and broken. You'll never make it out of here without my help."

Brophy shook his head. "Not like this. Never like this."

"You think you could stop me?" she said, gliding a light hand across her breast. "I could make you crawl if I wanted, dear Brophy. I could make you love me for it."

He fought the tendrils of magic slithering into his mind. His thoughts became fuzzy, his manhood throbbed against his pants. With a growl he lashed out and slapped her across the face.

Wet hair flipped across her cheek with the force of the blow. She stumbled backward a few steps and steadied herself against the table. Slowly, she looked back at him. A snarl curled her lip, and she laughed. "You're such a child, Brophy. You always were. You never could face the truth. If you don't make your enemies crawl, they'll do it to you."

She looked up at him, her dark eyes piercing. He stared back at her. "I don't believe that, Shara, and neither do you."

She pushed the wet hair out of her eyes. The oily tendrils of her magic receded.

"What's happened to you?" Brophy asked, "Your eyes are filled with so much pain, so much . . . malice."

"Pain?" she scoffed. "I'm not the weak girl you once knew. Not anymore. Do you have any idea how powerful I can make you?"

"I liked that girl. She was my best friend."

Shara's smooth, even breathing faltered. Her brow wrinkled as she grimaced and swallowed painfully.

He stepped forward and put his hands on her shoulders. "I'm so glad you're here, Shara. I've longed to see you for days. I've dreamed about you. But I can't see you like this. What you're trying to do to me is terribly terribly wrong. Can't you feel it? That oily twisting in your gut? Please, don't do this . . ."

He tried to draw her into a hug, but she pushed him away. "Do you have any idea what I went through to get here?" she hissed, baring her teeth.

His heart thundered painfully. He was so tired. He couldn't think straight. He reached for her again, trying to hold her. "Just stop. Please stop." He couldn't think of anything else to say.

"Dammit, Brophy!" she yelled, shoving him back so hard he stumbled into the wall. "Don't you understand! Krellis has seized Ohndarien! With his damned heartstone, I can't stop him! Everything is out of control!" Her breath was ragged, her eyes wide with terror. She grabbed him by the arms, shaking him violently.

"Ohndarien needs you! Baelandra needs you! It's getting worse and worse and worse!" she screamed. "And I can't stop it! I can't stop it! I need you! I need you, Brophy, before it's too late!"

She fell to her knees at his feet and started crying. He slumped down next to her, cradled her head against his chest.

"It was . . . He was . . ." She couldn't speak through the sobs.

"It's all right. It's all right. Just breathe," Brophy muttered. "Just breathe. It's going to be all right."

"I'm so sorry," she sobbed. "So sorry. You have no idea what I've done. He's still in me, in my blood, in my heart, in my bones. I can't get him out. I can't get him out."

Brophy clung to her.

"I can barely remember who I was before Victeris," she whispered. Her breaths came in little pants. "The magic rages inside me like a hunger. I want more, Brophy. I want to hurt them all, hurt them as badly as I can."

"Yes . . ." Brophy said, "I know."

"How could you? How could you know? You loved Trent when another man would have cut his head off. You loved me, and I was just a . . ." she trailed off.

"A pig butcher's daughter?"

"Yes."

She tried to pull away, but he wouldn't let her. She finally wilted into his arms, letting him bear her full weight. "I'm so lost. I'm afraid I'll never find my way back again."

"Yes, you can. I know you. I know you can."

"Oh Brophy," she sobbed. "How can you still believe in me? How can you still care?"

"Come here," he said. He led her to one of the cots and they lay down together like two crescent moons. He wrapped his arms around her, and she held his hands. Her skin was covered with scrapes and scratches that he hadn't seen because of the dye on her skin.

Brophy pressed his cheek against her bare back. Her skin was cold, and he held her tight to keep her warm.

After a long moment, she slowly wiggled around in his embrace. "I have something for you," she whispered.

Shara reached back and untied a silver chain from her hair. She pulled the necklace free and held it up to Brophy. A diamond pendant filled with swirling rainbow colors hung from the chain.

"A heartstone?" He reached out and took it in his hand. "Where did you get it?"

"It was a gift," she said. "I lost it once, but Baelandra found it. I . . . I didn't want it back at the time, but she made me promise to give it to you when I found you." She smiled weakly. "And I found you."

Brophy took the chain and slid it over her head. "Why don't you hang on to it for a little while longer?"

Shara pressed the stone against her chest. The ever-changing colors shone through her fingers.

Brophy buried his face in her neck. "I've always loved you, Shara," he said. "Before I even liked you, I think I loved you."

"I know," she whispered. "I always knew." She moved back, looking deeply into his eyes. Her gaze did not hold the tortured pain of before, but rather an exquisite sadness. Slowly, softly, she kissed him.

The taste of her lips was so sweet, so tender. Something inside him let go and for the first time in months, Brophy heard the heartrending voice of the Heartstone singing in the back of his mind.

"I always loved you," he murmured, and fell asleep in her arms.

7

BROPHY . . ."

He awoke to Shara's soft voice, to her hand touching him gently on the chest.

"The tide is dropping, Brophy. We have to go now."

For a moment, he thought he was back in Ohndarien lying side by side with Shara in the shade of a plum tree. He opened his eyes, and she wobbled slowly into focus. He saw her dark skin, the deepest purple. Only the whites of her eyes caught the flickering torchlight. The smell of plum came from her skin, not a tree overhead.

It all returned to him through the fog of sleep. The aching muscles, the bone-deep exhaustion from swimming day after day, trying to stay afloat, trying to stay alive.

He smiled weakly, reached up a hand, and touched her soft cheek. "Shara."

She climbed off the cot and pulled him to a seated position. "The Giant's Tooth will open soon," she said, "and then the guards will come. It will all be for nothing if we don't go now."

Nodding, he grunted and stood up. His body protested as though he'd just run Nine Squares again. He gritted his teeth against the cramps in his legs and wobbled as Shara reached out a hand to steady him. He'd finally reached the limit of his reserves. All he wanted was to lie back down and sleep for a week.

"Hey, sleepyhead," she said, "let's not die in the Wet Cells. Not after all of this."

He forced his eyes open and looked down at Shara. She was long and slender in the flickering torchlight, dark with the juice of the midnight plum and as naked as a drawn dagger. A warrior woman. A powerful Zelani. His best friend from childhood. And now what? They'd only kissed once, but they already felt like lovers.

He pictured Ossamyr vividly in his mind, and his heart twisted. The queen was so beautiful, so unreachable, so unknowable. She was the fiery touch that burned up his youth. Ossamyr had slain his childhood as surely as Nine Squares.

But that long-lost child he used to be had loved Shara all along. Ossamyr had damned him to this place, but Shara had risked her life to pull him out.

Shara smiled at him. "Come on, Brophy. You can do this. We can do it together."

His eyes flicked to the ground. When he'd first met Ossamyr, he'd run headlong toward her, always grasping, always wanting more, like he was chasing a bird he would never catch. And she led him along just far enough to drop him into a chasm.

"Brophy . . ." Shara said. She cupped his chin, tried to move his head up to face her, but he couldn't meet her gaze. If he looked into those eyes, he would fall all over again. He'd never be himself again. It would change him forever.

"What's wrong?" she asked.

Steeling himself, he finally turned to face her. "I'm . . . sorry," he said. "I wish this had happened for the first time years ago."

"I know." She closed her eyes and nodded. "How sweet would that have been?"

Brophy pulled her to his chest, leaning his cheek against the top of her head. The touch of skin against skin sent a tiny thrill through the fog of his exhaustion.

"There were so many times I wanted to kiss you, but I never had the courage. I always felt like a child next to you."

"I was the same," she said, returning his embrace. "I just didn't see it. At least you had the wisdom to know you were still a child."

He kissed her on top of the head. "I can't even remember what that was like," he whispered.

"We both grew up far too fast these last few months . . ."

Brophy held her close to him, breathed in the scent of plum and seawater. He nearly fell asleep on his feet when she shook him gently.

"We have to go," she insisted. "The guards."

"I know," he said, breaking the embrace. "But I'm not myself. I think it's all catching up with me."

"Just a little bit farther," she said. "Once we're out, we'll be safe."

He nodded. They each grabbed a torch from the wall sconces, and she lead him out of the guardroom, down the sloping tunnel to the Wet Cells. They passed Dathyl and Locklen, trapped in Brophy's cell. Locklen lay unconscious against the wall, his ruined arm hung limp at his side. At first Brophy thought he was dead, but then the man twitched in his sleep.

Dathyl also sat against the wall, next to the bars, but his eyes opened sluggishly when they approached. Brophy knew how that felt. With Locklen's arm ruined, no doubt Dathyl had swum for two. He glared balefully at them.

"You'll never make it out of here alive, Ohndarien," Dathyl sneered. "You're dead on your feet."

"At least I'm still *on* my feet."

Dathyl sneered, grabbed the bars, and hauled himself upright.

Brophy was glad to see they were both still alive, but he couldn't resist returning a bit of the hospitality they had shown him. "At least you'll only have one more tide to get through before they send enough men to get you out."

The former jailor made a rude gesture through the bars. Brophy managed a weak grin. "Don't crack off and give up this early, what'll they think of you? They'll say, 'now there goes a 'sendrian who's not worth his salt.' Swim tall, my friend, swim tall."

"You'll never get out!" Dathyl screamed at them as they walked away. "No one escapes the Wet Cells!"

"Come on," Shara said, pulling him forward. "We've done enough to those two already."

Brophy followed her to the end of the tunnel. She knelt before the twisted metal gate that had once barred the exit. Brophy could hear the distant rumble of the tide far down the tunnel.

"This is the way I came in," she said. She reached into a canvas sack hidden just inside the dark tunnel and pulled out a pair of leather gloves and thick pads for his knees. "Put these on, you need them more than me. It is a long rough crawl. It was narrow for me and will be worse for you."

Brophy donned the pads and gloves with sluggish, fumbling fingers and followed her through the jagged tunnels. She chose the way confidently as though she had all of the intersections mapped in her mind.

After half an hour, Brophy's back and sides were cut and bloody, his cloth pants shredded on the sharp rocks. Shara waited patiently for him as he slithered through a narrow opening, losing skin every inch of the way. The roar of surging water was only a few feet away.

Brophy was finally able to stand up. They had emerged into a long, sloping tube about twice the height of a man. The surf rushed in and out, frothing over the rough surface like a beach full of daggers. The torchlight played off the jagged walls.

Shara walked into the surf up to her knees. "We can rest here for a moment," she said, looking back the way they had come. Her dark eyes glittered. "The tide is nearly out. It is a long swim, I want to make it as short as possible."

Brophy sat down just beyond the reach of the surf and tried to slow his erratic breathing. "It's a long swim?" he asked. He couldn't seem to catch his breath, and the worst was yet to come.

She nodded. "Yes. It's a very long swim."

Brophy pulled off his gloves and tossed them aside. Every movement was an effort. "I'm sorry, Shara. I don't know if I can. Whatever strength I had, it's spent. I thought I could, but . . ."

Water splashed as she strode back up the incline and knelt next to him. She pushed his hair out of his face, and he looked up at her. Her dark eyes searched his as her hand traced behind his ear, along his jaw.

"I can give you the strength," she said, "if you'll let me."

His chest tightened. "With your magic."

"It's what Zelani were meant to do."

"What would that be like? Would you make me a puppet like Locklen and Dathyl?"

"No. I will never do that again." She wedged the torch into a fissure in the rock and took his face with both hands. "With you it would be different."

"Why?"

"Because you could let me in. Because I would give you what you want, what you need, not what I want."

Brophy's free hand shook, and he pressed it against the floor to stop it. He'd trusted Krellis, too. He could still feel the powerful man's fist striking the back of his skull. He'd trusted Trent, and his friend's last words had condemned him to exile. He'd trusted Femera, and she had lied. He'd trusted Ossamyr, and that had nearly been the end of him.

Brophy stared at the dark water. He didn't think he could make an easy swim right now. This one would be the hardest of his life.

"What will you do then?" he asked hoarsely.

"Let me show you? I don't blame you . . . After what you've seen me do. I'm not proud of what I've become, but can you give me a chance to make it right? I came here to rescue you, and you saved my life instead. Will you let me finish saving yours?"

He swallowed hard, his hands gripping the rough rock underneath him. "All right," he said in a slight whisper. "I'll trust you. I'll trust . . . This one last time."

She pushed back his hair again, slowly, deliberately. Her lips touched his, and she kissed him, long and wet. He tasted the salt on her tongue and felt a thrill of fire go through him.

"Come," she whispered pulling him to his feet and leading him into the water. "Come with me."

They waded down the tunnel until they floated on the water, rocking with the tide as it surged forward and slowly receded. She touched him on his arms, his legs, his chest. Her fingers trailed sparkles across his skin. Every touch seemed to go straight through him.

"What are you doing?" he asked, finding it hard to catch his breath. He could barely see her in the distant torchlight. Her blackened skin melded with the dark water, and she seemed to be everywhere at once.

"Breathe with me," she said. "That is the first gate. The breath."

Shara took a deep breath, and Brophy joined her. He exhaled and gasped as the pain and weariness flowed out of him.

"Keep breathing," Shara said. "Slow and steady."

With every inhale, energy surged into his body. With every exhale, pain and fear left him.

"Let go," Shara whispered in his ear. "Let me do my work."

Brophy closed his eyes and relaxed. Shara's magic drifted into his body like mist. He had never felt anything so wonderful, so tender.

He laughed when she removed his tattered breeches and tossed them to the side. She let out a low moan, placed her hands on his shoulders and slid up the length of his body. Wrapping her legs around him, she teased him for a moment. He was so hard, already aching for her. They rose and fell with the tide, and she suddenly pushed herself onto him.

He gasped. A fireball of energy coursed through him, rushing through his body and out his fingers and toes. His aching muscles seized, then relaxed, then filled with power. He pulled her to him, water splashing as he grabbed her thighs, her back. He moved with aching slowness, sliding in and out of her, each movement more overpowering than the last.

"Yes!" Shara exclaimed suddenly, arching above him. Her orgasm swept through him like a flash of lightning. His body vibrated with excess energy. He shouted, lifting her into the air above the water as though she weighed nothing.

"Enough!" He laughed. "Any more and you will kill me."

She grinned down at him, dark wet hair plastered against her dyed skin, hanging down around him. "Are you ready then, my love?"

"Yes," he gasped. "Oh yes. Let's go home."

They swam to the end of the tube, where it disappeared underwater.

"Just follow me," she said, "and everything will be all right."

Brophy's whole body was vibrating. He couldn't wait to swim, couldn't wait get to the far side and be inside her once again.

Shara took a deep breath, and he joined her. His lungs seemed to fill with twice as much air. She gave him a quick smile and dove.

Brophy swam after her, swam for all he was worth.

THE SEA BREEZE blew wildly through Brophy's hair, and he breathed deeply, clinging to the mast at the top of the crow's nest. He closed his eyes, sent a prayer of thanks to the Seasons.

The Kherish vessel cut through the waves on an early-morning breeze. He was free. They were headed home. It seemed years since he had run backward through the Physendrian Gate with stones raining down on him, but now he had a chance to return and make things right.

The ship's captain was an old friend of Scythe. He and his crew risked a great deal waiting so close to the Physendrian coast, never knowing if Brophy and Shara would emerge from the Wet Cells.

Brophy's perch rocked far to port, then leaned back to starboard as the sleek ship rocked the waves. They had just rounded the northernmost corner of Physendria. The Narrows extended to the east and beyond them, Ohndarien. He could not see the Free City's walls from this distance, but he could see the dip in the mountain chain that her locks cut through. Brophy could picture his home in his mind. He could feel the windmills turning with the wind that blew past him. The Heartstone sang in the back of his mind, sounding louder every moment.

"I have put you off for too long," he whispered to the wind. "I won't fail you again."

A golden feather swept past him, so close it brushed his cheek. Brophy turned with it. The crazy wind eddied around the crow's nest, whipping the feather around in a circle. Hooking his foot around the mast, Brophy lunged out into the air, his hip resting against the rail as he snatched the feather out of the sky.

He paid for the sudden movement with a wince of pain, but he didn't mind the price. There were scabs all over his stomach from crawling through the tunnels. He had left a lot of skin behind on his way out of the Wet Cells, but he'd also left his anger. He'd left behind his despair.

He had never seen a feather this color before, vibrant gold, with tiny veins of dark brown. It was small and curved. He searched the skies for a bird that could have shed it, but there was nothing.

The crow's next shifted again, leaning to the other side. Brophy steadied himself and noticed Shara coming up the rope ladder. She also had a feather, held between her teeth. She winked at him as she climbed. The purple on her skin made her look like something out of a storybook. An ethereal faerie from the Southwylds.

He helped her over the edge onto the platform and plucked the long, black feather from her mouth.

"What's this?" he asked.

"I might ask the same." she said, taking the golden feather from his hand.

"I just caught it." He spun his hand in a circle. "It was swirling around the mast."

"That one blew against my chest as I was climbing." She pointed at the sleek black feather in his hand. "I was going to give it to you, but you stole it from me first."

Brophy grinned as the sheer joy of being free coursed through him. He felt like himself again. He was free to catch a feather from the wind. Free to give it to the woman he loved.

She leaned over, awkwardly tried to kiss him as the crow's nest tipped back and forth. Brophy laughed as he clung to the mast with one hand and her with the other.

"You keep mine. I'll keep yours," he proposed.

She nodded. "All right. This one's the same color as your hair," she said, tracing its curve. "And the same shape. I think I'll make a comb out of it and wear it in my hair."

Brophy stared at her, memorizing every bit of her. For a moment, she wasn't a powerful Zelani. She was just a young woman, a child delighted by a child's treasure.

"And I'll wear yours," Brophy said, looking at the black feather, the same raven color as Shara's long hair. "On my heartstone necklace . . ." He nudged her. "If you ever give it to me."

Her hand went instinctively to the pendant over her heart. She shoved him back. "You're so impatient," she said with a sly grin. "You're like a little child."

Brophy scoffed, "Only to an old lady like you."

Shara huffed and went low to poke him in the stomach.

His hand shot out and caught her wrist, just as he had so long ago on the Wheel. The wind swirled around their perch. A sailor in the rigging shouted to his companions below. Brophy held her arm, held her gaze with his own. She didn't look away.

He leaned over and kissed her, softly at first, then desperately. He wanted to hold on to the moment forever, but even as their lips parted, the feeling faded. It had always been fading.

"I love you," she whispered, saying the words for the first time.

Brophy's chest filled with a bittersweet glow. "Why couldn't this have happened a year ago? Why did it have to be now, when there's so little time?"

She shook her head. "I don't know. You were just a kid. And I . . . was trying so hard not to be."

He nodded. "Even now, I feel like I've barely seen you in the past two days. I hate to waste any time sleeping, but we've both been so tired."

"How do you feel?" she asked. She wore a Kherish dress, and its long sleeves ruffled in the renewed breeze. The skirts rippled across her legs and fluttered out behind her. It looked strange on her, covering her dark arms and legs, not like the provocative clothing Shara would normally wear.

"I'm sore," he said, "and weak. But I'm finally awake. By the Seasons, I'm more awake than I've ever been."

"And now?"

The tone of her voice was strange, and he looked at her carefully. "To Ohndarien, of course. Isn't that where we are headed?"

"We are currently sailing north. The captain will turn the ship east unless we tell him otherwise."

"I have to take the Test. Krellis has ruled for too long."

She nodded slowly, but her eyes betrayed her.

"You don't want to go back to Ohndarien?" he asked.

"I will go with you wherever you want."

"But you don't think we should. Why?"

Shara took a deep breath and looked to the east. "Krellis isn't our only problem."

Brophy nodded. "I know, but first things first. I'll take the Test and send Krellis out the Physendrian Gate, right into the teeth of Phandir's army. Then we'll deal with the rest. If we're going to solve these problems, we've got to take them one at a time. Nine Squares taught me that."

"Ohndarien is facing a lot more than nine opponents."

"So Faradan joined with Physendria?"

She nodded. "Krellis planned for it, but his allies betrayed him."

"Then they're smarter than I am."

She gave him a smile. "Ohndarien will suffer the most for this betrayal, not Krellis."

"Who were his allies?"

"The Ohohhim."

Brophy raised his eyebrows. "The Opal Empire makes no alliances."

"Krellis had something they wanted."

"What?"

"The location of the Legacy of Efften."

"The what?"

"The Legacy, it's some sort of weapon that the Brothers went to the Vastness to protect."

"The Brothers? How do you know this?"

"Baelandra told me. Didn't she tell you?"

Brophy shook his head. "I think she was going to, but we ran out of time. Are you sure the Brothers are in the Vastness? They haven't sent word in years."

"Krellis intercepted their letters."

Brophy clenched his teeth. His fist gripped the rail. His father had written him letters, and Krellis stole them.

She laid a hand on his arm. "Exiling Krellis will not help our city now. Ohndarien will still be overrun. Krellis will be dead, but Phandir will rule. Is that what you want?"

"No." He closed his eyes, and it seemed as though the music of the Heartstone faded away, lingering as a whisper in the back of his mind. He opened his eyes again. "What do you think we should do?"

She let out a long breath. "Go back to Krellis's original plan. Bring the Ohohhim fleet."

"But we don't know where they are, the Vastness is huge."

"I know where they are."

Brophy stared at her. "You read the letters?"

She shook her head. "It was difficult to probe Krellis. The man has a towering will and the Heartstone protects her own, but one thing burned brightly in his mind—the Ohohhim betrayal and the Lost Brothers' letters. I caught that much. The Ohohhim fleet has gone to the Cinder."

"The island in the north? Near the Vastness?"

She nodded.

"Why would the Brothers go there?"

"I don't know that, but if the Ohohhim want the Legacy, they will hunt for it on the Cinder."

Brophy looked down at his bandaged hands.

"So the question is, my love," Shara said, her light fingers taking his hands in hers, "where do we go from here?"

Brophy remembered his vision, climbing up the Hall of Windows with his father behind him, fighting with the Sword of Autumn. As much as he hated turning away from the Test once more, the pieces were falling into place too perfectly for him to ignore.

For years he'd longed for that vision to be true, but all that time he feared it was just the wishful thinking of a lonely boy who wanted a father. Now it looked like the Heartstone was right all along.

Brophy looked back across the sea, and Shara moved behind him, pressing her body against his back, wrapping her arms around his waist. His heart ached, and the music of the Heartstone receded to the back of his mind.

"To the Cinder, then," he said in a hoarse voice. "We go to the Cinder."

9

BROPHY REACHED for the latch on their door as quietly as he could. The boat leaned, and he grabbed the doorjamb to steady himself. Timbers creaked as the sleek Kherish sailing ship tacked across the wind, carrying them swiftly north.

Brophy opened the door an inch and peered inside. Shara was perched on a window seat looking through the glass. The soft light of the setting sun made her skin glow. She wore a white, long-sleeved tunic that was too big for her. The laces were loose at her throat, revealing one shoulder and the heart-stone pendant at her throat. The shirt draped down her body like a short dress, giving a delicious glimpse of her long legs. She had tucked one foot underneath herself and the other was braced against the window well to keep her stable as the boat rocked.

"I had a dream about you last night," Brophy whispered through the crack in the door.

Shara smiled but didn't turn around. "Was it a good dream?"

Brophy opened the door, hanging on the jamb as the ship climbed another swell.

Shara turned to him. Her black eyes sparkled as she smiled. "You look good," she said. "You shaved."

"I borrowed the captain's razor."

"You look good."

He smiled. "You said that."

"Did I?" She looked down. Her long black hair slid across her cheek. She tucked it behind her ear with a finger and held up an arm, pulled back the sleeve. "It's almost gone." Her skin was still a light lavender color from the midnight plum juice.

"It's about time. Seven days since Physen."

Brophy descended two steps into their tiny cabin and sat on the floor next to the window. Shara reached down and cupped his cheek with her palm.

He paused, feeling her touch, then murmured. "Sometimes when it's dark and I hear the sound of the ocean, I think I'm back there. I don't know how much longer I would have lasted if you hadn't rescued me."

"No, you rescued me," she murmured. "I was lost in the dark, and you led me out."

He reached up and pressed his hand against her face. The boat shifted, listing to the other side. Shara held him in place.

"I want to stay on this ship forever, with you," he said. "Keep making love to you."

She climbed out of the window seat and led him to the bed. The ship listed back, and they tumbled into the cot together. "We could." She glanced into his eyes, a hint of a smile on her lips. "Keep sailing to the Vastness. Tame some horses and ride them into the mountains. Sleep in caves for the rest of our lives."

He kissed her, nuzzled his cheek against hers. "Oh Shara . . . I wish we could."

She nodded, pushed her fingers into his curly blond hair. "Perhaps after. We'll build a cottage on the Petal Islands, raise goats like the Geldars before Master Morgeon ever dreamed of Ohndarien."

Brophy picked a splinter off the wall next to him. One sailor called to another on the deck above. "I'd like that very much."

He paused, savoring the vision, then his brow furrowed. "Are you sure this Father Lewlem will listen to you?"

"Yes. I don't know if he will agree to our plan, but he'll listen at least."

"And the Brothers will listen to me."

"But will they give up the artifact?" Shara asked. "What if we can't get them to trade this Legacy of Efften for an alliance against Phandir?"

"They must. It's Ohndarien's only hope."

"I know, but that doesn't mean they will do it."

Brophy fell silent, picked another splinter out of the wall.

Shara shrugged, propped herself up on an elbow. The loose neck of the shirt slipped off her shoulder. Brophy eyed her skin. She pushed his hair out of his face, stared into his eyes.

"So," he said. "Can you read my mind?"

"I don't need magic to read your mind. It's written on your face." She rolled on top of him. "We have three more days," she breathed, "before the world finds us again."

With aching slowness, they made love, exploring each other's bodies as if it was the first time, as if they had not made love every night of their seven days at sea.

An hour later, Shara lay with her head on Brophy's chest, as the ship rolled side to side. Brophy gazed up at the low, wooden ceiling, his eyelids heavy.

"Tell me about your dream," she said.

"I flew," Brophy mumbled, holding her snug against his chest. "You stood in the moonlight on the top of the Hall of Windows, watching me. Your hair blew behind you like a cape. I flew over the Water Wall, over the eastern locks and Dock Town, over Stoneside and across the bay. Ohndarien glittered like a jewel. The lights of the Night Market joined the lanterns on the ships reflecting off the dark water. I flew and flew, around and over the city, finding something new and wonderful with every turn. I felt like a hawk protecting its nest. My chest ached with pride."

Shara began to breathe rhythmically. Brophy's head swam, and he grinned as her magic gathered. His skin tingled, and his eyelids fluttered closed.

"Sleep, Brophy," she whispered.

"What are you doing?" he murmured.

"Sleep, my love . . ."

He drifted into sleep as if floating on a soft pillow. Colors flew past him, a blend of white and blue sky. They cleared, and he found himself atop the Hall of Windows. The torches of the Four Brothers burned around him and he looked out over the city of Ohndarien.

"She is worth fighting for," Shara said. Brophy turned and saw her next to him. She wore the long, loose shirt from the ship. It fluttered in the breeze, rippling against her thighs. "Worth dying for."

He looked down at his arms, his hands. He was naked. "What is this?"

"A dream, my love. Your dream." She turned and stepped backwards onto the air. She didn't fall.

He laughed, and she tugged his hands, pulling him beyond the sloping edge of the Hall. "Shara!"

"Come. Let's fly."

He followed her as they floated farther out. The Wheel passed below them. "How are you doing this?"

"Magic." She winked.

"Wait," he said. "Why are you wearing clothes and I'm not?"

She smiled. "It's your dream."

He touched her shirt and it dissolved in a shimmer of sparkles. She spun away, diving toward the bay. He chased her, reaching to grab a toe, but never quite getting there. They pulled up and streaked along, brushing the tips of the waves. He caught her and pulled her to him. Their bodies entwined, and they flew upward again, kissing. The Spire whipped past them.

"I never want to wake up," he murmured, tasting her neck, her ear. He buried his hands in her floating hair.

"Then sleep, Brophy. Sleep and love me. We will take what eternity we can find in your dreams."

10

B ROPHY HAD never seen fog so thick. It rolled in waves, as if it were an ocean itself, lying on top of the water. A seagull's call came down from the crow's nest. The Kherish scout ship leaned hard to starboard. Brophy thought he heard another ship behind them, cutting through the water. The Ohohhim were everywhere in these waters, patrolling every approach to the Cinder.

It was their third attempt to reach the island. The previous two they were almost discovered, but Captain Ahbren's seamanship saved them both times. In his hands, the little Kherish scout ship flew over the waves faster than any of the Ohohhim war galleys. Two nights in a row they fled back out to sea, disappearing into the mists with their black sails.

An Ohohhim commander on the ship behind them shouted something to his crew, but the voices faded as the ship missed them in the fog and sailed farther away. But sound did strange things across the water. It was impossible to tell if they were a mile away or just out of sight.

"They say this place is cursed," Shara whispered when the last noises of the Ohohhim ship faded.

They stood at the prow of the Kherish ship. Brophy's hand rested on the wooden snout of a dog-headed, bare-breasted woman. The grotesque carving stared fiercely forward over the waves. Under the captain's orders, there was no light on board. They had been flying black sails since twilight. The dark sea slid slowly past as they crept into the fog.

"We're close," she whispered, taking hold of Brophy's free hand.

He peered into the swirling fog, but he couldn't see anything. "How can you tell?" he asked.

"I can smell the sulfur. And the sailors are nervous."

"They'll be glad to be rid of us," Brophy said.

Captain Ahbren, a taciturn fellow with a bushy mustache and bad breath, had not told his crew where they were sailing until the ninth day. Brophy had been getting ugly stares from the crew ever since they learned where the ship was bound. Sailors had always shunned the Cinder, and most captains would sail an extra day or two to stay out of sight of the volcanic island. Everyone knew someone who knew someone else who sailed too close to the forsaken island and never returned.

"The captain must owe Scythe an extraordinary debt to have brought us this far," Shara said.

Brophy nodded.

"There it is." She pointed. Brophy followed her gaze and caught sight of a rocky outcropping through the haze and darkness. He wrinkled his nose at the fumes. The Cinder was a volcanic island that had exploded eons ago, leaving little more than the ragged edges of a vast crater poking above the ocean. The sea rushed in to fill the crater, forming an island the shape of a crescent moon with a bubbling bay in its center. The volcano still spewed noxious fumes underwater. A constant torrent of steam billowed up from the center of the crescent, boiling the ocean and sending noxious gases into the air. The stench of sulfur and brimstone hovered for miles in every direction.

As he looked upon the dark, mist-wrapped island, Brophy thought of a dream he'd been having for the last few nights. It started as the dream where he and Shara flew above Ohndarien, making love in the sky. But then it changed. Black clouds surrounded the city like the sulfur mist surrounded the Cinder, trying to blot out the tiny light that struggled to shine at its center.

Brophy touched the heartstone pendant at his neck, side by side with the black feather. The heartstone pulsed insistently. He hoped, as a Child of the Seasons, that he could use the shard to sense the lost Brothers, just as Baelandra and Krellis could sense each other through their stones.

At a whispered command, the sailors in the rigging dropped the mainsail. The Kherish trader coasted slowly toward shore. Brophy turned as the mustached captain hurried down from the upper deck and walked over to them.

"We go no closer," he said, in his clipped accent. He nodded toward the swirling mist. It parted for a moment, and Brophy saw an entire fleet of ships.

"By the Seasons . . ." he whispered.

"The Ohohhim," Shara said, her lips pressing together.

"Yes," the captain replied. His mustache twitched. "No farther."

"There must be two hundred ships there," Brophy said.

"We will row you from here," the Kherish captain said. "I owe Scythe this debt, but not the lives of my crew."

"Of course," Shara said. Brophy noticed the way she used the tone of her voice to reassure him.

The sailors lowered a rowboat into the water. Shara grabbed two packs full of food and water as Brophy buckled on the sword she'd brought for him from Ohndarien. They followed four sailors over the ship's railing and climbed down to the rowboat.

The men were silent as they rowed Brophy and Shara through the sulfurous fog to a small, desolate shore. The prow scraped onto a gravelly beach, and the sailors hastily hopped overboard. They held the boat steady as Brophy and Shara climbed out. One of the sailors, a man with shoulder-length salt-and-pepper hair, made a strange gesture in the air.

"Azeel keep the monsters from you," he said as his comrades pushed the boat back into the water. They leapt to their oars and pulled hard. Mist swirled around them, and they disappeared.

"They think we are doomed," Shara said, staring after them. "I overheard them talking yesterday while you slept. They say that monsters are attracted to the island. They climb out of the ocean and crawl over the desolate ridges looking for the passage back to the netherworlds. One sailor said they look like anything—men, women, horses, wolves, even mice or insects."

"Do you believe him?"

Shara's hand closed over his, and he felt his doubts drift away. "That we are doomed? No. That there are monsters . . ." She paused. "Does it matter?" she asked, looking into his eyes. "Would you stray from your course?"

"No."

"Then do not listen to their legends."

"The captain said he would send a boat back for us in three days, if possible."

She raised an eyebrow.

Brophy nodded. "He won't be coming back."

"It doesn't matter. We can't leave until the Ohohhim agree to save Ohndarien. We'll sail back with them, or not at all."

He cupped her cheeks with both hands and stared into her eyes for a moment. "Thank you for coming with me," he said.

She smiled. "This place isn't so bad. It smells better than my father's farm."

"Come on," he said, touching a finger to the pendant. It thrummed through him. He could feel something to the north, on the opposite side of the ridge. "We have a long walk ahead of us."

SHARA AND BROPHY worked their way along the eastern edge of the island, climbing ever upward. There was a thin moon out, but the swirling mists often made it impossible to see. The ground was steep and jagged. It reminded Brophy of the run up the outside of the arena in Physendria.

After an hour of hiking, Shara stopped and held up her hand. Laying a finger against her lips, she crept to the edge of a barren ridge. Brophy followed. There were no plants of any kind on the island. It was all rock and gravel, blasted and forsaken. The swirling mists gave some cover, but they were fickle allies, shifting with the breeze.

Scooting the last few feet on their bellies, they looked over the edge of a rise at the sheltered beach below. Soldiers from Ohohhim were methodically setting up their camp fifty yards away. A line of men ferried poles and canvas up the beach from the rowboats; their fair skin was easy to spot in the moonlight. Like pale ants they walked single file, packing up and loading. The mists parted once, and the enormous Ohohhim fleet could be seen offshore.

Shara shuddered.

"What is it?" he asked.

She winced. "I don't know. There's something out there, in the water. I can feel it."

She looked up suddenly, and grabbed his hand. "Hush! Breathe with me." Brophy matched his breath to hers, closing his eyes as she worked her magic. The chip of heartstone around his neck vibrated.

An Ohohhim scout party appeared around a twisted outcropping of rock, their eyes flicking left and right. The four of them moved quickly through the dark. Two of them looked straight at Shara and Brophy but did not see them. When their footfalls faded, Shara let go of Brophy's hand.

"Thank you," he murmured, looking back at the encampment. They watched in silence for a time. "There are so many of them." Again, she shuddered. He squeezed her hand as she trained her eyes on the lapping waters below.

"Something's coming," she whispered.

A soldier screamed far below. The surf frothed, and five gruesome beasts lumbered out of the water. They were four-footed creatures, stocky like oxen, but their elongated snouts bristled with sharp teeth. Lopsided shoulder muscles bunched under their black skin. Heavy hooves sloshed in the sea as they stampeded up the beach. Tufts of hair bristled all over their stout bodies, and broken horns twisted up from their heads, black and slimy with rotting seaweed. Seawater drained from their mouths, straining through yellow teeth, and their dark eyes shone in the moonlight.

They thundered up the beach and charged the nearest Ohohhim. One man froze while his comrades ran. A beast impaled him on its horns and kept on running. The man screamed as he was carried along.

A warning horn split the night.

The creatures did not stop to feed. They left the dead behind and charged into the tents, ripping apart the canvas and the men inside.

Ohohhim soldiers shouted to each other, drawing swords and grabbing spears. Officers barked orders, and the terrified men formed battle lines. As one, they rushed to brace the monsters. The twisted oxen impaled the Ohohhim on their great horns or tore them apart with their long teeth.

The Ohohhim did not break ranks as the monsters charged through them. The soldiers stabbed desperately and died for it. An Ohohhim stuck a spear clean through one of the beasts, skewering its rib cage. The spearhead burst out the other side, but the beast turned and bit off the soldier's arm. He screamed and fell to his knees, blood spraying the sand. The beast twisted about and chomped through the soldier's head.

Shara covered her mouth, and Brophy watched as more Ohohhim died. A hundred became sixty, and still the beasts came on. Sixty became forty.

More troops began to arrive from the ships in the harbor. Boatload after boatload landed to aid their comrades. This time, they threw their spears from a distance, staying clear of the creatures' deadly horns. When one of the oxen fell, the soldiers moved in with desperate determination. They chopped the legs off the creatures, who continued to growl and snap from the ground, unable to move.

The beach swarmed with soldiers by the time the last beast fell. There was no roar of victory, just a sudden lull in the frenetic activity, accompanied by the moans of the dying.

Brophy's heart hammered painfully in his chest. The beasts didn't die. Black blood seeped from their severed limbs, but they bellowed and growled just as they had when they were whole.

"Bring the torches," one of the officers yelled. "Check for infection. The injured must die."

Brophy couldn't look away as the foreigners turned on their own men, slaying the wounded. One man hobbled toward the sea with a broken leg. Three spearmen ran him down and stabbed him repeatedly as he died in the surf. His cries for mercy were lost in the surging of the waves.

"We should get out of here," Brophy said, breathless.

Shara nodded.

"That way, straight up the mountain," he said.

Again, she nodded.

The two of them took off at a run, scrambling up the slope on hands and knees. They didn't stop until they reached the summit. Panting, they collapsed into a tiny shelter formed by two rocks.

"What were those things?" Brophy asked when he finally got his breath back.

"I don't know," she whispered.

"They made me sick to my stomach, just like . . ."

"Just like I did in the Wet Cells?"

Brophy nodded. "The Kherish sailors were right," he said. "This island is cursed."

"What if we run into one of them? What if we run into a dozen?"

"We stay as far away from the water as we can," he said.

She pulled him to his feet. "Come on."

A S THE SUN ROSE, the mist lightened. Whenever the clouds and fumes parted, the sun beat down ruthlessly on the ruined island. The Cinder made the deserts of Physendria look like the land of plenty. Nothing grew anywhere, not even a trace of scrub grass.

Shara and Brophy left the volcano's ridge and descended toward the boiling bay at the center of the island. A continuous cloud of billowing steam erupted from the water. At night, they had seen a faint red glow somewhere below the surface.

Without any vegetation to hold the soil, the slope had been cut away by rainfall, creating a veined network of ridges and grooves that snaked down to the water. The ground was constantly shifting and unstable.

The two of them hurried down the slope and began walking along the barren shore. Shara tested the water with her finger. It was too hot for comfort, but not boiling this close to shore. The swirling winds blew noxious gases toward them, then the same winds cleared them away.

Sweat streamed down Shara's face. Her Kherish dress clung to her as if she'd gone swimming. They had almost emptied their waterskins. If Brophy didn't find the Brothers soon, they would have to look for a water source. There had to be natural springs somewhere. The Brothers couldn't have survived so long if there weren't, but it was hard to imagine a natural spring bubbling up from the side of a volcano.

They held cloths over their faces as Brophy led Shara around the beach. He kept one hand locked on the stone around his neck, following the impulses that pulled him forward.

Brophy stopped, coughing. He looked back at Shara with watering eyes. "The pull is very strong here," he said. "We are close."

They continued along the rocky shore. The cliffs grew taller and taller to their right, disappearing into the mists. The sloping shore narrowed, forcing them closer to the boiling bay. The fumes lingered against the rocks and Shara began to get light-headed.

"Just a little farther," he said, clenching the heartstone necklace.

"We'll be swimming before long," Shara said, eyeing the water. She pulled her wet skirts to the side and tied a knot high on her thigh to keep them out of the way.

He led her farther into the mist. They had to clamber along the jagged cliff face at the edge of the shore. A false step and they would slide into the bay. Brophy turned right, walking into a narrow fissure that split the cliff wall. The crack was about ten feet wide and extended into the mists. Coughing into her shirt, Shara drew a shaky breath and continued shuffling along.

The fissure grew deeper and narrower as they moved inland. Soon it was about as wide as Brophy and Shara standing shoulder to shoulder. The bottom of the crack turned uphill.

Brophy forged relentlessly upward. Shara leapt after him. Her wet clothes pulled at her, but the heat diminished the farther they climbed from the bay.

The fumes began to clear. Orange light filtered down from above, the sun's rays trickling into the fissure, lighting the higher layers of mist.

Brophy looked above them. "It reminds me of the Hall of Windows in autumn," he said. "The light, I mean."

Shara coughed into her fist and shook her head. "I don't see how you can compare any of this to home. Ohndarien is blue. This place is gray. Brown-gray. Orange-gray. Yellow-gray. All gray."

He stopped, a sheepish grin on his lips. "I just said the light looked like—"

Shara gave him a little peck on the cheek. "I know what you said." She smiled. "You dream even when you're awake, don't you, Brophy?"

"I didn't mean—"

"Brophy?" a man's dusky voice asked from above. Brophy spun toward it, looking up. He stepped between Shara and the noise. Metal rang on metal as Brophy drew his sword. The chip of stone at his throat glowed orange.

"Brophy, is that really you?" the voice said.

Shara grabbed his hand, pointed to a tiny shelf of rock above them. A gaunt man with jet-black hair crouched like a spider overhead. His cheeks were sunken, his skin mottled and peeling from a dozen sunburns. A crude rope tied tattered pants around his waist, and a white diamond gleamed in the center of his bare chest. He carried a long sword in one hand, holding it easily. The blade shimmered in the strange light and a huge diamond glowed on the pommel.

Shara and Brophy drew a breath at the same time.

"Celinor?" Brophy asked, unwilling to believe his eyes.

The man's arms were corded with muscle, and he looked like he hadn't eaten in a month, but his green eyes shone with an inner light. He leapt from his perch, bounding off the wall like a mountain goat, landing neatly on his feet. He stood up straight, not quite as tall as Brophy. The white diamond pulsed in his chest in time with another at the end of his sword. He sheathed his blade with the quick efficiency of a lifelong warrior.

"Yes, I am Celinor. It's really you?" the man asked. "Brydeon's boy?"

Brophy's sword hovered between them for a moment, then he put it away. "Yes. I am Brophy."

The man laughed. It was a strange sound to hear from him, deep and resonant. "Of course you are!" he said, pulling Brophy into a hug. The boy returned the embrace, reluctantly at first, but then in earnest, clapping his uncle on the back.

Celinor broke the hug first and held Brophy at arm's length, moving him around like a child even though Brophy outweighed him by thirty pounds.

"By the Seasons," Celinor continued, "I took you for Brydeon himself at first. Thought I was hallucinating, after all these years. Finally losing my mind." He gave a quick shake to his head. "But that's the last thing to go here. The mind stays sharp long after the body fades. But of course you're Brophy. Who else would you be with those shoulders, that stride? You have your mother's hair."

"And you are the Brother of Winter," Brophy said.

Shara saw it now. Add a month's worth of good meals, and the man would look just like Celidon.

"Yes. I guess you wouldn't remember me. The last I saw you, you were just a babe." He paused. "You certainly have the look of your father about you."

"Where is my father?" Brophy asked, a sudden lump in his throat.

Celinor glanced at Shara. "Well . . . the letters." He looked back at Brophy. "We told you in the letters. Years ago."

Brophy swallowed hard. He closed his eyes. He knew what Celinor was going to say. But how could that be? His dream . . .

Celinor frowned. "I'm sorry, son. I thought you knew." He took a deep breath. "Brydeon died years ago," he said, his voice low. "He saved my life. Saved the child, but . . . I'm sorry, Brophy. I can take you to his grave, that is all."

SHARA STOOD next to Celinor as Brophy approached his father's grave. It was nothing more than a pile of black rocks on a narrow ledge, set between two other monuments just like it. Sulfurous mists gathered and swirled away. A long shard of red diamond rested atop the cairn. Shara felt Brophy's anguish swelling inside him. She wanted to comfort him, but she held herself back.

"Come," Celinor murmured, taking her hand and leading her up out of the canyon and out of sight. "Sometimes a man needs to mourn alone." He sat her down on a rock and settled himself cross-legged on the ground facing her.

"There is too much death on this island," he said. "Tell me of other things. Tell me of you and Brophy. He has a strong heart, like his father. You have done well to choose him. Are you his wife?"

Shara surprised herself by blushing. "No. I am a Zelani."

Celinor narrowed his eyes. "A Zelani? A sorceress of Efften?"

"A sorceress of Ohndarien."

"They have sorceresses in Ohndarien now? Of all ten types?"

"Ten?"

"Zelani is but one of the ten paths a mage can follow to her power. Didn't you know?"

"No. I thought there was only one."

He waved his hand. "It isn't important. The secrets of Efften are best left forgotten." He cocked his head to the side, still gazing into her eyes. For the first time since Victeris, she felt like she was being read, except Celinor's scrutiny was gentle and kind. She felt power behind it like a storm on the horizon, but he did not invade her mind.

"You couldn't have come at a better time," Celinor said. "With the Ohohhim searching the island, my strength is stretched thin. So thin. We will need your help."

"You have been here for fourteen years?"

Celinor nodded.

"What do you eat?"

He shook his head. "We do not eat. We do not sleep. You cannot sleep."

Shara swallowed.

The Brother of Winter waved his hand. "You'll find out about that soon enough. First, tell me about yourself. You are a Zelani, but what does that mean in Ohndarien? You are not married to Brophy?"

"We are lovers, but not married."

"Zelani is the path of sensuality. You can lend your strength to your lover." Celinor nodded. "Is that why Brophy shines like a polished gemstone?"

"Brophy shines wherever he is."

"Yes, yes. A woman does not need the magic of Efften to make a man shine." He shook his head, his long black hair swishing across his shoulders. Strangely, he was clean-shaven. With his tattered appearance, she would have expected him to have a long, straggly beard. His eyes narrowed. "I can smell the magic on you, but you do not turn my stomach." He looked at her chest. "You are not a Sister, but you have communed with the Heartstone?"

"Baelandra gave me a stone to wear for a short time."

"Ah." He nodded. "The same stone that Brophy carries now?"

"Yes."

"I understand. I did not find you so much as you found me."

"I suppose so."

He paused for a moment, but his eyes held hers with a raw intensity. The silence was uncomfortable for her, but he did not seem to notice. "Brydeon's little sister was always headstrong. Did she send you north?"

"No. It was Brophy's decision."

"Ah." Again, he paused as though he were asking silent questions of her soul, receiving answers she could not hear. "You have no corruption within you," he said at last.

"Corruption? Like the beasts that come out of the sea?"

"You've seen them."

"Yes. I felt them coming before they attacked the Ohohhim."

"You are lucky there was someone in their way. Those poor creatures reek of malice and hate. They are the opposite of life. When you saw them, you wanted to vomit?"

"Yes."

He nodded. "That is how it feels. Those who are sensitive react to them more strongly than others. This is what Efften left us. This—" Celinor waved a hand around. "All the evil that you feel in this place, is just a fraction of what Efften wrought when she collapsed."

"Is all of this caused by the Legacy?"

He paused again. She couldn't read his mind or his emotions. He was shielded, just like Baelandra, Krellis, and the other Sisters.

"Yes. The Legacy," he said. "I haven't heard her called that in years. Did Baelandra tell you what we are hiding?"

"She said it was a weapon of terrible power."

"Ah." Celinor nodded, then waved a hand. "Enough of that for the moment. Tell me of Ohndarien. How does she fare? And my family? Tell me of my family."

"Your younger sister, Vallia, still rules on the Council."

"Is she as serious as ever? The Seasons know I tried, but I could never get her to laugh."

"She is. The children she teaches joke about being able to cut glass with the tip of her nose."

He laughed. "Ah yes. She was always the serious one. And no man yet, I wager."

"None that I know of."

"And what of my wife?"

"Hellena is well, though sad. She still waits for your return. Deep in her heart she believes you will come back to Ohndarien, though there are many that have given the Brothers up for dead."

"Yes." He sighed. "Yes, she would." He closed his eyes. "And I wish that I could return to her, but . . ." He blinked. His eyes focused on her again. "Tell me of my son."

"Your older sons sailed north to find you. They—"

"I know about my older boys," he said. "They perished defending the child." He paused. "Tell me of my youngest. Tell me of Celidon."

Shara licked her lips, hesitating a fraction of a second. Celinor saw the truth in her eyes. He let out a long breath. "I should be used to it by now," he murmured. He bowed his head, and tears came to his eyes. Methodically, he blinked them away. "Ah Shara . . . But you have brought hope to me. A small hope, perhaps, a fleeting one. To see two young people, bright and beautiful, it eases my heart in a way you cannot know." He touched her cheek. "Tell me," he whispered. "Tell me how Celidon died."

"He took the Test of the Stone," Shara said, her voice hoarse as she felt the man's pain. "Baelandra thinks he was betrayed by Krellis."

"Ah."

"You know of Krellis?"

"I know about the man," Celinor said.

"Baelandra believes he led Celidon to failure."

"No. It would be easier to believe that, but Celidon's failure is his own. It doesn't matter if you have friends or enemies at your side. In the end, you live or die by the strength of your will." He closed his eyes. "In the end, you take the Test alone."

Shara took his gnarled hand and sent comfort to him through the cycles of her breath.

"Thank you." Celinor looked up, piercing her with his green eyes. "Whatever you are doing, it helps. This is one of the things a Zelani can do?"

"Yes."

"And you are not a Child of the Seasons." He mused.

"I am originally from Faradan, but my heart belongs to Ohndarien now."

"Yes. She captures the heart that way."

Shara almost didn't say what came to mind next, but she had to. "Ohndarien is under siege. We came north to find help."

"Help from who?"

"The Ohohhim."

He raised a black eyebrow. The subtle shift in his mood was unmistakable. "Why would the Opal Empire help Ohndarien?"

"They seek the artifact you protect. They believe it possesses the secrets of Efften."

"Ah. And you came here to convince me to give them this artifact in exchange for their assistance?"

Shara nodded. "Yes. Without them, Ohndarien is lost. She is besieged by Faradan and Physendria and will fall very soon."

"I see . . ." he said wistfully.

"I've met their leader, Father Lewlem. He's a good man. You should speak with him; perhaps we could come to some sort of alliance."

"You hoped we would surrender the Legacy into his keeping, for Ohndarien's sake?"

Shara nodded.

Celinor rocked forward onto his feet and stood up, extending a hand to her. She took it, and he pulled her upright. "Come, then. Why don't you look upon this Legacy? Then tell me if you would give it to the Ohohhim, even to save Ohndarien."

CELINOR LED Shara farther up the slope to the tiny mouth of a cave. He pointed into the center of the dark opening. "There is a fire within."

The opening was hidden behind a jumble of rocks. She would have to crawl on her belly to get in.

"What is in there?" she asked.

"The artifact you seek."

He didn't look Shara in the eye, but turned and walked away. She crouched, peering into the cave. Her stomach heaved. She had to close her eyes and turn her face away. There was something vile in that cave. She could feel it humming in her bones, tight and frantic. The faint tinkling of a music box drifted out of the darkness. Shara recognized the haunting tune from her childhood. Her mother used to hum it as Shara fell asleep.

If the key to saving Ohndarien was in that cave, Shara would have to face it. She swallowed her disgust and crawled through the gap. The passage grew taller and wider as she crawled toward a small fire flickering at the back of the cave. She crept forward through the darkness, slowly rising to her feet as the tunnel expanded.

A young woman dressed in rags sat on a rock next to the flames. She had tanned skin and black hair and was constantly turning the handle of a silver music box that lay in her lap.

As Shara approached, the young woman peered into the darkness. Her red-rimmed eyes finally focused. She reached a thin arm toward Shara, waving her hand through the air as if trying to touch a ghost. Her gaunt face cracked into a smile.

"You have come," the shriveled young woman said. Her voice sounded distant and fragile. "Thank the winds and the sky and the forever plains."

Shara walked into the firelight. She wanted to run back the way she came, but she felt oddly compelled to go closer. She couldn't look away.

On the stone floor next to the young woman lay a baby, no more than a year old, with pale skin and rose lips. She slept, her eyes darting madly underneath their closed lids.

"She's not what you expected, is she?" the girl asked, still winding the music box.

"Is that her? Is that the Legacy? She's just a child, so small."

The stranger shook her head. "She is horrible. She is worse than you can possibly imagine."

Shara looked closely at the sleeping babe. Her tiny chest rose and fell with her breathing. This little one was the source of that sickening feeling Shara had been fighting ever since she landed on the island.

Shara ripped her gaze away and knelt next to the young woman. She had the face of a fourteen-year-old, but her eyes were strained, constantly focusing and unfocusing. Her shoulders curled forward like a crone's. She seemed as if she would blow away in the wind.

The music box she turned glimmered in the flickering firelight. It was made of exquisitely wrought silver, except for the brass handle, which looked crude and heavy.

"What are you called?" the young woman asked.

"Shara," she said, feeling numb.

"I am Copi."

Shara nodded, unable to take her eyes from the child.

"One moon, that was all," the young woman said, steadily cranking the wheel. The delicate notes sounded hollow in the confines of the little cave. "Only one moon. I was to take my turn and become a woman. I would be given a stallion to ride across the Vastness." She drew a sobbing breath. "I don't want to be a woman anymore. I just want to stop. I just want it to be over."

"How long have you been here?" Shara asked.

"Fifteen years." She closed her eyes and bowed forward, curling over the music box. Her hand continued turning as though it were a separate thing, no longer part of her. The girl's index finger was scarred and crooked. It pointed away from her hand at an odd angle as if she could not bend it.

Shara turned back to the sleeping child. Her little lips puckered repetitively as if she were trying to nurse. Was this child the weapon that the Ohohhim sought? What kind of people would want such a thing?

Unable to look at the child for long, Shara turned her back to Copi. "Who is she?"

"Just a child. Nothing more. The horror is inside the child, locked in her dreams."

"You don't look more than twenty," Shara whispered.

Copi let out a little puff of air. "The body does not age, she does not let us. But the spirit stretches thin. Celinor is the same. I do not know what we have become. I don't know how we endure."

Shara wanted to use her power to ease the girl's pain, but she couldn't concentrate. Arousal seemed impossible in this place.

"The women of the Vastness have guarded this child for the past three hundred years," Copi said. "As long as there is a woman to turn the handle, the box will keep singing. As long as the music never stops, the child will not wake."

Shara didn't ask the obvious question. After standing in the child's presence, it wasn't hard to imagine the horrors that would be unleashed if she ever woke up.

"I have waited so long for you," Copi said. "Have you come to take her from me?"

Shara leapt to her feet and backed away. Her head spun, and she felt the walls of the cave closing in. "No. I can't do that."

"You are the first woman I have seen since the baby opened her eyes. Please. You must. I cannot go on forever."

Shara saw herself a hundred years from now, sitting alone in the dark, turning that handle. She felt like her whole life was being ripped from her. Brophy, Ohndarien, her power. The baby was like an endless black pit she could fall into and never hit the bottom.

"No. No. I'm sorry, no." Shara turned and ran toward the light at the end of the tunnel. She fell to her hands and knees, wriggling through the tiny opening. The bright sun blinded her as she crawled out of the cave. She couldn't breathe. The First Gate had been taken from her.

Shara knelt on the jagged rocks until her breath returned to normal. She kept her eyes closed for a long time before she finally opened them.

The landscape before her was twisted and broken, shrouded in the swirling mists. She sat on her haunches and hugged her knees to her chest. She could still hear the faint notes of the music box coming from the cave behind her.

It was over now. Everything she and Brophy had hoped for was over. She couldn't run from this burden, not after what Brophy had taught her. She could still feel the baby back there, hovering like a black wave about to crush her. No matter how far she ran, that wave would catch up with her.

The tinkling of the music box came closer and closer. Shara looked back in the tunnel and saw Copi creeping forward, the music box tucked under one arm while she held the handle with the other. The hollow-eyed young woman crawled out of the narrow gap and set the box down next to Shara.

"I'm done," Copi said. "My time is over." And she let go of the handle. The silver box gave one final tinkling note and stopped.

Shara grabbed the handle and turned it as fast as she could. The song returned, harsh and frantic. "No! What are you doing?" she screamed.

Copi crawled the rest of the way out of the cave and kissed her softly on the cheek.

"I am sorry, my sister," she said quietly. Her eyes lingered on the box for a moment longer, then she stood and staggered down the hill toward the ocean. She let out a sob of laughter, then collapsed to the stony ground and died.

BAELANDRA CONCENTRATED on her breathing, waiting until her body and mind slipped into perfect harmony. When the moment sang to her, she spun into the first stance of the Floani form and leapt from the ground. Her breathing remained easy and controlled. She stretched the breath, flung her legs into the splits in midair and landed precisely, swiveling slowly into the next stance.

One move flowed to the next as she leapt around the room, twisting and spinning. She finished the form and remained standing lightly on one foot. The trance faded. The tingling, invincible feeling seeped out of her as her conscious mind rose slowly back to the surface.

Her foot started wobbling, and she gave up on the dance. Exhaustion replaced euphoria, and she sank to the floor, sweat running down her neck.

She had spent the last two weeks of her imprisonment practicing the meditative arts she had learned as a child. She could feel her mental strength and discipline returning—she had never felt so close to the Heartstone—but the sense of peace and serenity that her teachers had spoken of eluded her.

At least Krellis had the decency to lock her in one of the officers' rooms in the Citadel, rather than a cell. Her quarters were elegantly furnished with a beautifully carved table, an enormous feather bed, and a small fireplace in the sitting area; but she hated this place more than anywhere she had ever been.

Her two young guards refused to speak to her. They only opened the door when they brought food. Even then, the first thing to enter was always a spearhead, forcing Baelandra back. They took no chances.

She had never felt so disconnected from the events of Ohndarien. There was a Physendrian army at the Water Wall and Farad troops outside the Quarry Gate, but she might as well have been on a remote beach in Vizar.

Hearing footsteps outside, she rose to her feet. She was still breathing hard, her forehead dotted with perspiration. Her skirt was hiked up and tucked into her belt at her waist to perform the dance.

The door creaked open, and a spear was thrust through the crack. "Call out so I know where you are," the guard demanded.

"I'm here, in the center of the room," she replied.

A young man opened the door wider and stuck his helmeted head inside. The thin young man had a long face and an even longer nose. His eyes were large and always looked sad, even when he smiled. She overheard his name once, Tyrlen.

"Brother Krellis requests your presence with him on the Water Wall. The Physendrians are attacking."

Baelandra leapt forward. She yanked the hem of her dress out of her belt and let it fall to floor length again. Grabbing her sandals from the corner, she slipped them on. "Lead the way."

"Yes, Sister," he said, but didn't move. "I was instructed to warn you. If you attempt to escape, your friend from Kherif will be killed."

Baelandra sneered. "Fine, let's go."

She pushed the door wide and breezed past him. The young soldier hurried to catch up as she rushed down the dark hallway. The Citadel was the first structure Morgeon had built, and the crude fortress had withstood several attacks before Ohndarien's blue-white walls were completed. From time to time they passed a coat of arms. There were dozens of them throughout the hallways, one for each Master of the Citadel.

Tyrlen led Baelandra up a spiral staircase to the Citadel's battlements. They emerged into bright sunlight a little bit north of the Water Wall, and Baelandra could hear the sounds of battle in the distance. She rushed toward them.

The young guard grabbed her arm. "Sister! You are to remain here. Krellis's orders."

She twisted her wrist, broke his grip. His sword rang against its scabbard, and she turned to face the point of his blade.

"You must stay here, Sister," Tyrlen said.

The clash of steel and sounds of the dying rose from below.

"My city is at war, and I belong on the wall. Run me through if you must," she said.

The youth said nothing, but she could see the doubt in his eyes. She turned her back on him, ran toward the battlements.

The Citadel was built on top of a hill overlooking a wide valley. The famous Water Wall dropped down from the fortress, crossed the valley, and climbed up the mountain on the far side. The towering arches that supported the aqueduct were built atop the hundred-foot barrier.

Men were fighting on the steps of the Water Wall. If there was a skirmish on the ramparts, then the Physendrians had already scaled the walls.

Baelandra sprinted toward the sounds of battle. She ran over a bridge across the aqueduct and onto the steps where the Water Wall met the Citadel.

Ohndarien defenders in blue-and-white uniforms fought a large group of armed men in civilian clothes. The Ohndarien soldiers held the high ground and seemed to be standing fast, but beyond the stairs the entire Water Wall was empty, completely undefended.

Baelandra ran to the outer battlements and peered over. "No," she whispered.

The vast Physendrian army filled the valley like an ocean. Squads of Crocodile pikemen, Scorpion spearmen, and Serpent swordsmen went on and on.

A dozen massive siege towers crept toward the base of the wall. The rolling buildings were almost as tall as the battlements. Teams of oxen pulled the wooden monstrosities closer at a grinding pace as hundreds of men pushed from behind. Physendrian soldiers crowded the tops of the towers with ladders in hand. Archers clung to the sides, arrows at the ready. They would arrive in moments, and the wall was empty of defenders.

A boulder smashed into one of the towers, thrown from an Ohndarien trebuchet. Shards of wood exploded from the rocking platform. Men screamed as they fell, but the tower did not stop.

"Where are the soldiers?" Baelandra snapped a glance at her guard, but he was as shocked as she.

"I . . . I don't know, Sister."

Again, Baelandra looked down the length of the battlements. What was Krellis thinking? Two hundred men could hold that wall against thousands, but none guarded the most vulnerable stretch where the siege towers were bound. There was no way Ohndarien could reinforce the wall in time.

"This is insanity!" She looked over the battlements again. A cold sweat trickled down the back of her neck. The attacking troops were clustered in the very center of the valley against the base of the wall. That could only mean one thing.

The Physendrian Gate stood open.

Baelandra charged to the inner edge of the wall to look down into the city. Physendrian soldiers poured through the narrow gap into the streets. A dense line of defenders braced them, but they could not hold out forever against that many invaders. With the wall and the gate intact, Ohndarien could have held out until starvation claimed them, but they could not hope to brace Physendria soldier for soldier.

They had to get those gates closed.

"You were ordered to stay put," a voice boomed to the side of her.

Baelandra spun around. Krellis walked up the stairs, away from the skirmish some fifty feet below him. He sheathed his sword.

"What have you done?" she shouted, running toward him. "Did you sell Ohndarien to Phandir?"

He laughed.

She slapped him. "You think this is funny?"

Krellis's laughter died away, and he rubbed his face. Flexing his fingers, he forced a smile. "I thought you were never going to touch me again."

She swung at him a second time, but he caught her hand.

"Bae," he said in a softer voice. "You know I would never treat with my brother. If I wanted Ohndarien at the end of Phandir's leash, I would have given her to him years ago."

She shook off his grip. "Then what treachery is this?" She pointed at the fighting on the stairs.

Krellis smiled. "Look a little closer."

She studied the individual men in the battle. Swords clashed, and shield smashed against shield, but she noticed some of the men were smiling. The wounded hid grins while they lay on the steps.

"There is no blood," she said, stunned into confusion. What was this farce?

"That's my girl," Krellis returned, winking. "Your Zelani were the kernel at the center of this plan."

She frowned. "What are you talking about?"

"There were Physendrian agents in Ohndarien. They'd been hiding among us for months. I knew about some of them, naturally, but I didn't know about all of them. It turns out I didn't know about most of them. There were hundreds posing as soldiers and merchants, but your Zelani ferreted them out. I had the spies killed this morning before they could gather. Our soldiers dressed in their clothes and took their places."

"And carried out a mock attack?"

Krellis smiled. "Of course. Those are my men down there, pretending to fight each other, but, alas, my poor brother doesn't know that. He thinks they are his vanguard. In his eyes, they have been brilliant in sweeping the wall clean, opening the gate, and pinning our defenders on the stairs." He pointed where she had just been looking inside the city. "Hundreds rush into that narrow tunnel as we speak, but I have archers and soldiers on the other side of the wall, slaughtering them as they emerge."

"But the siege towers . . ."

Krellis put his hand on her shoulder, and she shrugged it off. He pointed past the mock battle on the stairs to the long, flat part of the wall. "You're going to have to look again," he said. "Look hard. Do you see anything different on the ramparts?"

Baelandra narrowed her eyes. The top of the wall where the soldiers should be wasn't Ohndarien's classic blue-white marble. It was gray, and it glistened as if wet. "There's a foot of water along the walkway, or . . . No, what is that?"

"Watch."

The first siege towers pulled up to the walls. Dozens of Physendrian soldiers threw ladders against the ramparts and climbed up. They poured over the battlements, one after the other. Half of the invaders slipped and fell as soon as they jumped onto the wall, disappearing beneath the surface. They flailed through the goopy liquid that filled the walkway. One soldier slipped and fell from the wall, plummeting to the ground below. Those who maintained their footing found themselves wading in foot-deep gray sludge.

"What is that?"

Krellis chuckled. "Whale oil. Barrels and barrels of it. Shipload after shipload of whale oil."

Warning cries went up from the first arrivals. Some of them tried to go back down the ladders, but too many were coming up.

"Brother," a soldier said from behind them. Baelandra turned to see Krellis's assistant holding a burning torch.

Krellis grunted, took the flame. His face became stern, and he stood still, holding the torch and waiting. Baelandra watched, mesmerized by his cruel efficiency.

"Finish this," Baelandra whispered. "Do it and be done."

A slight flicker of his smile returned. "I want a few more fish in my net before I pull it up."

Baelandra tried not to think about the young men on the ramparts. Most were just a little older than Brophy. Krellis waited until the steady flow up the ladders ceased. Warning cries filled the air, but the attackers were still locked in a hopeless jam.

Krellis cocked back his arm and threw the torch. It arced over the steps. The mock combatants ceased their charade and turned to watch. The torch descended, landing at the base of the staircase. It flickered for a moment.

The first flame rose high, spreading quickly. A river of fire flowed along the wall, engulfing the hapless invaders. Screams rose with the fire, and Baelandra turned her head away.

"You're going to miss the best part," Krellis said. "Watch."

Reluctantly, she turned back. The sight caught her breath. A hundred-foot wall of flame crowned the entire Water Wall, licking the arches that supported the aqueduct above.

"Any moment now," Krellis murmured.

A spout of flame shot out from the wall, arcing over a siege tower. Screaming Physendrians jumped from the top like wingless fireflies.

"How . . . ?" Baelandra couldn't see what had launched the flame.

"I replaced some of the rampart stones with wax."

Another spurt of fire shot out, catching the edge of a second tower and setting it aflame. Another spurt went, then another.

"And now they're melting," Baelandra said.

Spout after spout erupted from the wall. In moments all but one of the siege towers were ablaze. The flames poured down the towers and splashed over the tightly bunched troops below. Burning soldiers fought each other to get away, spreading the flames as they fled.

"And look over here," Krellis said, pointing beyond the inner edge of the wall. A fountain of flame arced backward into the city, right over the opening of the Physendrian Gate.

"Krellis!" she said.

"Don't worry."

The Ohndarien defenders had pulled back, drawing the Physendrian forces farther into the city, trapping them under the deluge of fiery oil.

"You've set our own city on fire!"

"Only a part of it," Krellis replied. "And we will put that out when the dying is done." He pointed upward at the towering aqueducts hundreds of feet above. "Remember, we have all the water we need."

Baelandra ran to the outside of the wall again. The lone siege tower creaked in the heat, abandoned on a field of flames. Phandir's entire army fled across the badlands.

"I told you, the blood of the Phoenix runs in my veins," Krellis said.

Had you foreseen this, she asked the Heartstone. Is this why you chose him, because no Ohndarien could be so cruel, so ruthlessly clever?

Krellis waved his hand over his head.

Shouts of "Close the Gate!" were relayed along the length of the wall.

A pair of soldiers atop the aqueduct pushed a lever that would divert water to operate the gate's mechanism. In a few moments, the Physendrian Gate clanged shut, smashing dozens of burned bodies beneath it.

Krellis waved his hand again.

Shouts of "Make it rain!" were passed from man to man to the top of the wall.

Those same two soldiers turned the lever farther. Water roared out the side of the aqueduct and cascaded down the arches' supports. A deluge poured into the streets raining down on the dying flames. Cheers rose from the soldiers in the city below.

"It is not over," she said to him in a dark voice. "They won't let this stop them."

"I know," Krellis said, with a cocky half smile. He placed a hand on her shoulder. "But we must savor our small victories where we can."

13

WHITE FUMES curled around the ridge as Brophy stared at the thin shard of red diamond in his palm. He sat next to his father's cairn, his scarred boot touching the base of the perfectly wrought pyramid. The rocks of the cairn, rough as they were, had been chosen with care, forming a reverent structure that stood almost five feet tall.

The piece of heartstone around Brophy's neck thrummed, and he wasn't surprised when he heard his uncle's voice right behind him.

"Your father was the best of us," Celinor said. "None of us would have had the courage to do this if it weren't for him."

Brophy continued to stare at the stone.

"Did one of those corrupted creatures kill him?" Brophy asked.

Celinor made a strange sound somewhere between a laugh and a grunt. "Not one. Many. It was a gang of corrupted humans. They are the hardest to kill. Brydeon and I were trying to lead them into a trap. Another second or two and we would have escaped, but I let one get too close. She lunged for my calf, and I went down." Celinor paused. Brophy kept looking at the red diamond in his hand.

"We all made a promise to leave each other for dead if it meant saving the baby," Celinor continued. "I would have left him if our positions had been reversed. But not Brydeon. The J'Qulins have always been headstrong. He came back for me, and we fought the world's last stand. They killed him for it. In fourteen years, it was the worst battle I've seen."

"How long ago?"

"At the very beginning, when we first got here."

"You made this cairn?"

"I did."

"Thank you," Brophy said.

"He was my Brother."

Letting out a long breath, Brophy tucked his father's heartstone safely into his pocket.

"I have something else for you," Celinor said. Brophy finally looked at his uncle.

A long sword in a battered silver scabbard lay across Celinor's open hands. A giant red diamond glittered at the pommel, grasped by silver roots. The handle was made of red and silver wire, elegantly swirled into tiny leaves. The stylized branches of the glimmering steel cross guard swept up on either side of the sheathed blade.

"I assume the Heir of Autumn knows how to use this?" Celinor said.

Brophy rose slowly as Celinor handed the blade to him. As soon as Brophy touched it, he could hear a faint singing. It was the sword from his dream, but without his father to wield it.

"This stone—"

"Is a part of the Heartstone. The Swords of the Seasons were forged when the council was formed almost three hundred years ago."

"I can hear her, she sounds so close."

Celinor nodded.

Brophy drew the blade, and the voice surged in his head. The huge red diamond at the pommel shimmered in the muted light. He looked down its length. The shining steel was flawless, the balance perfect.

"It's the most beautiful sword I've ever seen."

"You will need it before long, I fear. The stone makes it one of the few weapons that is effective against the corrupted."

Brophy's gaze fell on Celinor's own sword, strapped at his waist. The clear diamond sparkled at the pommel.

"The Swords of Spring and Summer were lost in the ocean when Thorn and Kayder drowned. I'm glad I was able to salvage the Sword of Autumn. Your father would have wanted you to have it."

"Thank you."

"Come, Brophy," Celinor said gently. "The time for grieving is short on the Cinder. There is much you must know before the battles come."

Brophy sheathed the weapon. He took off his old sword and fixed the new one to his belt. "Last night I saw some kind of hideous oxen climb out of the ocean and attack the soldiers from Ohohhim. They lost eighty men to kill a half dozen."

"Those creatures are the corrupted. They were once normal animals, but they became twisted into something hideous and powerful by the worst of Efften's magic."

"Will they come up this far on the island?"

"Oh yes. They seek her always, yearning to finish what she started."

"Her?"

"Yes, the Legacy is a child. A little girl less than a year old."

"A child? How can that be? You have guarded her for fourteen years."

"She is the daughter of Darius Morgeon, Efften's greatest archmage. That baby is the best and the worst that the fallen city ever created."

"I don't understand."

"Do you know what black emmeria is?" Celinor asked.

Brophy nodded. Vallia had taught him the legends of Efften as a child. The black emmeria was a disease, a curse that the mages brought upon themselves. Probably the very same illness that had plagued Shara before she rescued him from the Wet Cells. "I think I felt that once. It made me ill."

"I know that feeling well. That baby is a vessel, a container for enough black emmeria to destroy the world."

"How?" Brophy asked. "A baby couldn't be a mage that powerful."

Celidon sighed. "Normally you would hear this tale upon taking the Test. But you need to know, so I will tell you now."

Brophy's uncle pointed to a rocky outcropping at the edge of the cliff. "Let's sit over there," he said, "so I can keep watch while we talk. The Ohohhim are already looking for us."

"Why are they here? If the child is that dangerous, why do the Ohohhim want her?" Brophy asked.

"The Opal Emperor has been searching for the Legacy for years. He has sent his army here through greed and ignorance. If they knew what she was, they would never have tried. Come, I will explain it all."

Brophy followed his uncle into a jumble of boulders. They had to crouch to crawl into a little alcove between the rocks.

Flat stones had been carefully arranged between the boulders to make more comfortable seats. Every rock face within arm's length of the makeshift chairs had been meticulously carved. Brophy instantly recognized the Windmill Wall and the Hall of Windows amid the depictions of leaves, flowers, animals, and people.

Sitting down, they could see the shore of the boiling bay through the mist, but they remained hidden from sight.

"I've spent a lot of time here over the years," Celinor explained.

Brophy touched the carvings. He missed Ohndarien so badly, and he had only been away a few months. He couldn't imagine how Celinor felt.

A number of exquisitely carved stone figurines sat on a rocky shelf at the back of the alcove.

Brophy picked up a half-carved statue of a young boy.

Celinor took the little statue away from him and placed it lovingly back on the shelf with the others. "It's my youngest, Celidon, as he looked when I left Ohndarien so many years ago."

"I'm sorry—" Brophy started.

Celinor shook his head. "We must care for the living before the dead, and there is much you still need to know."

Brophy nodded.

"The story of the child goes back three hundred years," the Brother of Winter started. "She was born on the island of Efften, the greatest city in the world. The sorcerers used their magic to create a land of unimaginable beauty and prosperity. But too much success bred jealousy and greed among the mages. They threw themselves into ever-larger and more elaborate projects trying to outdo each other. They scoured the world, gathering slaves to work on their monuments. Using their magic, they enhanced and manipulated these slaves into building their fantastical city.

"But power always comes with a price. The magic they used created a backlash of hatred and resentment from the people they controlled. This black emmeria began to consume Efften and her slaves. But rather than change their ways or curb their ambitions, the mages found a trick to avoid paying that price. They created stones that would contain the black emmeria, storage bins for the refuse of their magical greed."

Brophy hated to admit that Shara had been tempted by that same dark path. He remembered his revulsion of her in the Wet Cells. If one person could build up that much malignancy in a few months, what could an entire city of mages build up over generations?

The Brother of Winter continued. "The kingdoms of the world grew to resent their voracious neighbors and united against them. Efften responded with fury and sent her navies to crush their enemies.

"The pirates of the Silver Islands always hated and feared the magic of Efften. When the sorcerers' fleets sailed, the pirates seized the opportunity. They swept over the mage's unprotected city, slaughtering and burning all they could find."

Brophy listened in silence. He knew this story well; he had heard it since he was a child.

Celinor continued. "Darius Morgeon, the city's greatest archmage, had warned his colleagues where their pride would lead them. While others rushed to the city's defense, Master Morgeon chose to face Efften's demise with grace and dignity. Refusing to spill more blood in a hopeless cause, he decided to spend the final moments of his life singing his infant daughter to sleep.

"His colleagues had other plans. If Efften was to fall, they decided to wreak a horrible revenge on the people who would destroy them. They broke every vow they had ever taken and released their imprisoned emmeria into the world.

"Morgeon heard of their plans and rushed to stop them. He knew that much black emmeria would feed upon the living until it consumed the world.

"The Archmage arrived too late to stop them completely. They had already shattered many of the containment stones and loosed their evil. Those mages were the first to die for their vengeance.

"Master Morgeon did the only thing he could. Unable to stop the emmeria, he redirected it. He corralled the darkness and trapped it in the only magical vessel he had, his infant daughter's dreams."

"How?" Brophy asked.

Celinor shrugged. "I have heard that only something completely innocent could contain that kind of evil."

Brophy had a brief memory of washing the blood from Ossamyr's thighs. "How could Morgeon have done that to his own child?"

Celinor closed his eyes. "Sometimes a father doesn't have any choice."

Shaking his head, the man went on. "Capturing the emmeria nearly killed Master Morgeon, but he used the last of his strength to enchant his daughter's favorite music box. As long as the handle continued to turn, his daughter would never wake, and the darkness would remain trapped in her dreams."

"How did the child get here?" Brophy asked.

"Master Morgeon's eldest daughter smuggled the baby out of Efften as it burned. The teenage girl brought her younger sister to the shores of the Vastness and left her in the care of the horse tribes. Of all the people in the world, she believed they were the least likely to succumb to the child's influence. For three hundred years, the women of the Vastness took turns turning the handle of the music box. Until one day, the handle broke. The music stopped, and the baby opened her eyes."

"What happened?"

"Copi, the young woman who was watching the child, jammed the nub of the broken handle between her knucklebones and kept turning the box. The music started again, and the child fell back to sleep. She was only awake for a moment, but the damage was done. Any living creature that the child looked upon became infected by the black emmeria.

"The infection spread as the corrupted attacked everything around them. Copi's entire tribe was transformed into blackened and twisted monsters determined to kill her and the baby. Their horses were infected, birds were infected, insects, the grass, and the trees."

Celinor ran his finger along the carving of a tree in front of him. "I have been to that place. It is still a barren wasteland from horizon to horizon. The evil seeped into the soil and has remained there ever since. Any creature that wanders into that cursed place becomes infected."

"How did Copi survive?"

"Courage and luck. The power of the music box saved her and her mount from the corruption. She rode day and night, all the way to the sea. A horde of corrupted horses chased her all the way into the surf. Her horse kept right on swimming with Copi and the child on her back as the corrupted creatures sank to the bottom of the ocean.

"Horse and rider were sustained by the same power that keeps the baby alive. They did not age or tire, they had no need of food, water, air, or sleep. Copi's horse carried her all the way to the Cinder, and this is where she remained."

"Where is the horse?" Brophy asked.

"After it carried her all this way, Copi set it free. The beast walked a hundred feet up the beach, lay down in the sand, and died."

Brophy nodded.

"The Heartstone alerted Ohndarien's council when the disaster occurred. Your father convinced the four Brothers to travel north and investigate. We discovered that barren hill where the child had awakened. That is where we fought the first of many battles against the corrupted. We followed the creatures here and have been protecting the baby ever since.

"It's a good thing we did. Anything tainted with the black emmeria is drawn to the child. Most of them crawl along the bottom of the ocean to reach this island. It can take them years, but they always emerge here eventually.

"That is why we cannot bring the child to Ohndarien. Imagine the swath of destruction across the Vastness and Faradan as the corrupted traveled south."

"But these creatures can be killed?" Brophy asked.

"Yes, with the heartswords. I've killed hundreds of them."

"If you have killed so many, how are there any left?"

Celinor shook his head, his lips tight. "The slightest scratch from an infected creature can spread the infection. The worse the damage, the faster the transformation. Eventually, you become like one of them. My sons came north to help us. I had to kill both of them myself."

Celinor glanced at the statues of two young men on his altar.

"Why does it have to be you?" Brophy asked. "Why does Ohndarien have to fight this evil?"

"Because we are the only ones who can. Our bond with the Heartstone makes the Brothers the perfect protectors of this child. We cannot be corrupted by black emmeria and, to a limited extent, we can heal those who have been touched by it." Celinor fell silent for a moment. "A Brother cannot be taken by the infection, but the fangs and claws of the infected will kill us just like any other man."

"You could not heal your sons?"

"I stabbed each of them through the heart as black hair bristled out of their necks, as fangs grew out from their mouths, as they clawed for my throat. No, I could not heal them once they had gone that far."

"Isn't there any way to destroy the emmeria completely?"

Celinor shook his head. "That is what the Heartstone was supposed to be. Master Morgeon's eldest daughter, mother to Ohndarien's founder, Donovan Morgeon, used the last knowledge of Efften to create the only weapon against this evil. She crafted the Heartstone to repel black emmeria. It protects against the foul sorcery and its residue. But Donovan's mother was not as great a mage as Darius. She tried to transfer the evil from her baby sister into the stone, but the Heartstone was not strong enough. It would have shattered long before it could contain all that was locked in that tiny girl's dreams."

"The music box is the only thing that keeps the child asleep?"

"It is."

"Don't you think this burden would be better shared by more protectors?"

"I would not bring that baby any closer to civilization than I had to. We would just put others in harm's way and provide fertile ground for the spread of the infection."

"But we have other problems," Brophy said. "Ohndarien is at war. She will soon fall to the Physendrians. Do you want that?"

"My current task is barely within my ability," Celinor said. "Ohndarien is beyond me now."

"Even if she will be destroyed?"

"Better Ohndarien than the world."

"But what if we gave the child to the Ohohhim? If we could convince them to protect the baby as you have, then we could save both."

"I know why you came here, what you want me to do, but trusting the Ohohhim is a risk we cannot take. I see the child as an abomination, but there are others who would see her as a weapon. We cannot give these foreigners a power they do not understand and cannot control."

"Shara believes their leader, Father Lewlem, is a good man. Is it not worth the risk to save Ohndarien?"

"Ah, Brophy . . ." Celinor sighed. "Fair Ohndarien seems a dream to me now. Her blue walls and rushing water, the Night Market with all her charms, a winter evening in the Hall of Windows . . ."

"Then help me save her!" Brophy said.

Celinor snapped out of his reverie. "I cannot." He shook his head. "It's just not possible."

"That's absurd! You won't even help me try?"

Celinor paused a moment, then said, "There is something I want to show you. After you see it, I think you will agree with me."

The Brother of Winter crawled out of his lookout and headed up the rocky slope. His thin body moved gracefully over the rocks, leaping from one to the other.

They crested the hill and saw a body crumpled on the ground. Celinor rushed forward, fell to his knees next to the young woman. Her eyes were closed, and she looked smooth and peaceful. Only when Brophy came to stand next to his uncle did he realize that she wasn't breathing.

"She fulfilled her obligation a thousand times over," Celinor said sadly. "She was ready."

"Who was she?"

"The keeper of the child." He bowed his head, touching his fingers to her eyelids. "Sleep well, noble Copi. Sleep well and may the Seasons be beautiful where you have gone."

"If she is the keeper, then who is watching the child now?"

Celinor's bright green eyes looked up into Brophy's, but he said nothing.

Brophy followed Celinor's gaze to the dark mouth of a small cave. He thought he could see a flicker of firelight deep inside.

14

A FAMILIAR nausea came over Brophy as he crawled into the cave. The Sword of Autumn began glowing, casting an eerie red light in the narrow tunnel. As the passage grew wider Brophy stood and ran toward the fire at the back of the chamber. He swallowed back the bile that rose in his throat.

Shara sat on the far side of the flames, calmly turning the music box. She glanced up at him, and he wanted to cry out, rip the box away, and take her into his arms.

"What have you done?" he cried. "How could you take the box?"

"How could I not?"

Brophy swallowed. He drew closer and saw the child lying on the ground. "By the Seasons . . ." He gagged. "What's wrong with her?"

"More than you can possibly imagine," Shara said, her voice distant and toneless.

"She is right, Brophy," Celinor said from behind him. The skinny man stood silhouetted by the faint glow from outside. "Someone must turn the handle."

Brophy let out a breath. "We can't stay here," he whispered to Shara. "We must return to Ohndarien."

Shara closed her eyes and bowed her head. Her hand cranked the music box's handle over and over again.

"There has to be a way," Brophy insisted. "Can't we at least talk to the Ohohhim?"

Celinor placed his hands on Brophy's shoulders. "Ohndarien is beyond our reach now. We must concentrate on the baby."

Brophy spun around, knocking the man's hands away. "We have to try!"

Celinor sighed and continued. "There are too many Ohohhim now. We have to get the child away. There are a few more islands to the north. We will take the baby there."

"How?" Shara asked.

"Tonight we'll swim out to one of the foreigners' boats. With the soldiers ashore, the ships will be lightly guarded. We can take one by force and disappear into the mist."

"At least let me talk to the Ohohhim first," Brophy said. "You know nothing about these people."

"They have been to the corrupted lands!" Celinor snapped. "They have seen what this child can do, and still they seek her!"

Brophy grabbed the pommel of his sword.

Celinor paused and took a moment to compose himself. "Brophy," he said calmly, "I will do anything to protect this baby, even if it means killing you. Do not force me to make that choice."

"What about me?" Shara said, standing up. She held the box awkwardly in one hand and continued to turn the handle. "Will you kill me if I choose Brophy's plan over yours?"

Celinor narrowed his eyes. "Shara, you never would have accepted the child if you planned on giving her up."

"I didn't choose this burden, it was dropped at my feet!"

Celinor lowered his eyes. "I know, I am sorry. I tried to take the baby from Copi many times, but she refused to pass her to a man. She said there was some pain only a woman could bear."

Shara nodded.

"Please," Celinor begged her, "don't give the child to that foreign man, however noble he seems to be."

Brophy looked at Shara, but she wouldn't meet his eyes.

"Wait!" Celinor cocked his head, listening. A hound bayed in the distance. He looked back at them, his heartstone shone in the darkness. "The time for words is done. The next battle is upon us."

He moved swiftly, snatching up a tattered sling from the side of the cave. With practiced ease he wrapped it around Shara's neck, avoiding the silver box. The music continued to play. He scooped up the child. Her limbs moved slowly in any direction they were pushed, as if she were underwater. Celinor set her gently in the sling and turned to them.

"Are you with me?"

Brophy nodded. "For now."

"I will do what I can," Shara said. "But my magic is lost to me. I have no power."

"Just keep turning the handle," Celinor said. "Brophy and I will do the rest."

The Brother of Winter led them out of the cave and down the slope to his lookout. He held a finger to his lips and leaned over the edge of the cliff. Brophy followed, though Shara held back a distance, the music carrying eerily in the fog.

A line of Ohohhim soldiers, each pinching the shirt of the man in front of him, crept along the edge of the boiling water. Several pairs of dogs with low, stocky bodies and powerful legs pulled at their leashes. The hounds snuffled the rocky ground, pulling their handlers forward.

"They're tracking our scent," Brophy said. "We led them right to you."

"Don't blame yourself. With that many men, it was only a matter of time," Celinor said. "We can still avoid them. I know these canyons better than any man alive."

He led them back up the mountain and into the slot canyon. They descended a series of switchbacks that ended in the bottom of the fissure where they first met Celinor.

"This way," he said, clambering around the fallen rocks. "You should know. The volcano still erupts. We are headed into an area full of vents that spew poisonous fumes. Stay close to the baby if we must go through them. The magic that protects her will protect you as well." He jogged ahead. Brophy peered behind them. He thought he could see movement, but it could have been a trick of the mist.

They ran up the canyon. Celinor led, with Shara in the middle and Brophy trailing. She continued to wind the music box endlessly. They stopped when a foul-smelling hole blocked their path. The canyon continued on the far side. An uncomfortable heat and foul smell hit Brophy in the face as he peered into the steaming shaft. It reminded him eerily of the Wet Cells.

Celinor turned an ear toward the volcanic vent. "She sounds quiet for now," he announced. "We can get around over there." He pointed to a jagged ledge to their right.

"Quickly now. Brophy, you first. Climb with one hand, hold Shara up with the other. I will take her other side. Her hands must be free."

Together they inched along the narrow ledge, with Brophy keeping Shara upright as her feet navigated the crumbling stone. Celinor climbed easily, keeping a steady hand on Shara. A dog bayed behind them.

"They're close," Brophy called back.

"It doesn't matter. When we get to the other side, the dogs won't be able to follow."

The path was treacherous and took precious time. Brophy slipped once, almost dragging Shara down with him, but Celinor held her steady, supporting both of them until Brophy got his footing. They made it to the other side.

"All right," Celinor said. "This vent spouts regularly. If luck is with us, she will keep them from crossing."

They continued up the canyon when the stone on Celinor's chest suddenly blazed.

"The corrupted! Watch the sky," he yelled.

The man's sword rang on its sheath as he drew and sliced in one motion. A hideous squawk made Brophy jump. A wing fell to the ground on either side of Celinor amidst a spray of black blood. A few greasy feathers floated down.

The creature was twice the size of a normal hawk and as black as a crow. Its beak was almost as long as Brophy's hand and it hooked in a jagged curve. Its wings flopped on the ground amidst a smear of black entrails.

Brophy drew the Sword of Autumn. It sang in his mind.

"Shara, protect the baby," Celinor shouted. "Cover her with your own body if you must. And keep turning the handle!"

No sooner were the words out of his mouth than the air filled with the screeches of the corrupted birds. They dove into the narrow canyon, falling from the sky like stones. Shara crouched over the baby as they came for her. Celinor struck two out of the sky just before their claws touched her. Brophy slashed a third, slicing its wing off. The bird squawked, hit the ground, then got up and hopped toward Shara. Brophy hacked it in two with his next stroke.

The birds were everywhere, and Brophy swung all about, always staying close to Shara. They covered her, pecking and scratching as she curled herself around the baby. Brophy's arms worked desperately, slicing away one bird after another, knowing that one missed stroke could kill her.

Celinor fought by his side, hacking a bird with every stroke. His diamond burned like daylight. In moments, he had killed the last of them. Brophy had never seen anyone move so fast.

Celinor instantly knelt next to Shara, who crouched over the baby on her knees. Her back was covered with little red marks that darkened slowly to black. Laying his hand on her, he closed his eyes. The stones on his chest and sword shone brighter. The wounds went from black to red. They still oozed blood, but they looked like natural, normal wounds.

"Are there any more?" Celinor asked, turning her to face him, looking at her chest, her arms, her neck.

"I-I think that is all," Shara said.

He nodded. "Good." He turned to Brophy. "Are you cut? We must make sure that—"

Celinor grunted and staggered backwards. An arrowhead protruded from his thigh, wet with blood. Brophy spun around. A squad of Ohohhim archers had reached the far side of the vent. Before anyone could speak, another volley of arrows flew toward them.

Celinor leapt forward, batting two arrows out of the air with the flat of his sword. Brophy stepped in front of Shara. An arrow whistled past them. Another glanced off his scabbard and spun to the ground.

A half dozen Ohohhim started across the ledge as the archers nocked another round of arrows.

"Run," Celinor said to Brophy. "Take the girl and run!"

The hounds barked constantly, pulling at their leashes.

Brophy hesitated.

"Run, boy!" Celinor's gaze bored into him. His heartstone flashed. Brophy grabbed Shara's arm and sped over the loose rocks, their footfalls echoing off the canyon walls. They had gone a hundred yards before Brophy shook his head, clearing it. Celinor's voice had set his feet moving before he'd decided to run.

"He compelled us," Shara said as they slowed to a stop. "He used a magic akin to Zelani."

"It's his heartstone," Brophy growled, heading back the other way. "I have never seen it used that way before." His breath came fast and hard. "Come on."

"Brophy!" Shara cried. He spun around. She knelt, opening the sling farther to see the baby. "Oh no," she said. "Oh no." He rushed to her side.

There was a tiny scrape on top of the baby's downy head. Several tiny black tendrils radiated out from the wound, staining the pink flesh.

"Come on!" Brophy roared, hauling her to her feet. "We have to get back!" They ran together through the twisting gorge.

A distant rumble grew louder and louder until a thunderous crack split the air, and the ground shook. A wall of smoke rushed up the gorge toward them. Brophy scooped Shara and the baby into his arms in one quick motion. He knelt and pushed them against the wall as the smell and heat hit them like a searing wave. Brophy clenched his eyes and mouth shut as Shara kept winding the music box.

They were buffeted by the searing wind; the hissing roar went on and on. Brophy kept his eyes shut tight, but his body rebelled against holding his breath for so long. His lungs felt as if they would burst, but he kept his mouth closed. He thought he would pass out, but the agony dragged on. He desperately wanted air, but he didn't need it. The sensation sent chills through him.

The swirling hot gases finally dissipated. Brophy stood up as the fickle breezes cleared the air. Shara rose to stand beside him. They shared a quick glance, then walked slowly back the way they had come.

Celinor's body lay in a swirling eddy of deadly gas. Three arrows stuck out of the Brother of Winter, and his gaunt face looked skeletal now that the life had left him.

The Brother had made his last stand in a narrow stretch of canyon. Three Ohohhim had been hacked apart by Celinor's deadly blade. Others sprawled where they fell, killed by the gas. On the far side of the gap, several hounds lay unmoving, their tongues hanging out of their mouths.

Brophy dropped his sword and rolled Celinor over. The Brother's heartstone slid from the hole in his chest and Brophy grabbed it before it hit the ground. The long, thin shard of diamond pulsed in his hand.

The only sound to be heard was the deep rumble of the volcano.

"Brophy, we have to go," Shara said. "We can't stay here."

"I know." He placed his hand on the puckered pink scar over Celinor's heart. "Sleep well, my kin. May the Seasons be bright and beautiful where you have gone."

Brophy slipped the heartstone into a pocket and picked up his sword. He froze when he saw a dark scratch on his wrist. Black tendrils had begun to snake away from the wound.

A hound bayed in the distance. Brophy looked back at Shara. The music of the magic box floated around them, mingling with the mist. He bowed his head.

"We better go," he said, unbuckling the Sword of Winter from Celinor's waist. He looped it over his shoulder and rose.

"Brophy," Shara said, pointing farther up the canyon.

A small woman with black curly hair and a powdered face stood in their path with a long knife in each hand. A squad of Ohohhim archers rushed up behind her, arrows at the ready.

Brophy looked the other way. A dozen spearmen rounded the corner, their hounds straining against their leashes.

"Put your sword away," Shara whispered. "It won't help us anymore."

15

BROPHY SHEATHED his sword as the Ohohhim soldiers surrounded them.

He inched closer to Shara and held up his hands. She stood half a head taller than their captors, but that didn't make her feel any safer. Razor-sharp spearheads hovered inches from her chest and back. She felt an urge to throw an enchantment over them, but her powers had fled the first instant she saw the child.

"We came to talk to Father Lewlem!" she said.

"Silence!" one of them shouted. "Don't let the witch speak."

Lewlem's wife stepped forward, her eyes widened as she neared the baby. Her jaw clenched, and she looked up at Shara.

"Mother Lewlem," Shara said. "Please, we must speak with your husband."

The tiny woman tucked her blades into the folds of her cloak. "Is that the child?" she asked, pointing at Shara's sling. Her powdered face tensed, and her breath came in shallow gasps. "Give her to me. Now."

Shara glanced at the soldiers. They hovered, staring at the sling.

"Wait," Brophy said, holding up his hands.

"He's infected!" one of the spearmen shouted, pointing at Brophy's wrist.

Three soldiers lunged at him, spears thrusting for the kill. Brophy threw himself to the ground, rolled away, barely evading the sudden attack. He came to his feet with sword in hand.

"No!" Shara shouted. "Stop it!"

The Ohohhim charged, and Brophy danced back, batting their weapons aside.

Lewlem's wife reached for the sling, Shara spun away, dumping the baby onto the ground with one hand as she kept the music playing with the other. She lifted a foot over the babe's head, which rested on a sharp rock. "I'll kill her!" she shouted. "I'll do it!"

"Halt!" Mother Lewlem barked, her blades suddenly in hand.

The spearmen backed away from Brophy, turning to look at the child. They recoiled. One retched, but managed to keep the vomit down.

"It's the Legacy," one of them murmured.

"Back up!" Shara demanded. "Back up!"

At a gesture from Lewlem's wife, the foreign soldiers all backed away.

"I will give this child to Father Lewlem and no other," she said as Brophy rushed to her side.

"He is infected, he must die," one of the Ohohhim whispered to Lewlem's wife.

"Let me see your wrist," the tiny woman said, her voice barely more than a whisper.

Brophy shifted his blade to his left hand and held his wrist out. Shara winced. Black tendrils extended from a small scratch all the way around his arm. One had snaked down as far as his fingers.

"Why doesn't the infection spread?" Lewlem's wife asked.

"We will explain that all to your husband," Shara insisted.

"Then follow," the Ohohhim woman said, hiding her blades for a second time. "We will take you to him."

Brophy picked the baby up and tucked her back into Shara's sling.

They were escorted through the narrow canyon in tense silence. As they passed through a thick bank of mist, Shara whispered to Brophy. "Are you all right?"

"I can feel it growing," he whispered back. "But I'm fighting back the way I fought your magic in the Wet Cells. The heartstone on the sword seems to help. If I take my hand off, I can feel a blackness surge inside me."

"How long until you are completely infected?"

"I don't know. The wound is small. A week? An hour? I don't know."

The mist cleared and he moved closer to her. "Let me see the baby."

She pushed the music box to the side and drew back the edge of the sling. A black spot the size of a coin blotted the crown of the baby's head, inky tendrils snaked all the way to her face.

Brophy glanced to the soldiers all around them.

"She's worse," he whispered, so low she could barely hear. "It won't matter how long I last if she dies." He fished into his pocket and drew out his father's and Celinor's heartstones. He touched them to the baby's forehead and she twitched. "Keep these on her as much as you can." He gave the stones to Shara. "And this." He removed his necklace and winced. He paused, then slowly put it around the baby's neck.

Lewlem's wife stared at them, but Shara ignored her.

"Are you sure you are all right?" she asked Brophy.

The strain was evident around his eyes. "For now. If Celinor cured your wounds, one of the Sisters should be able to help the baby. But we need to get her to Ohndarien."

Shara nodded, remembering Baelandra's words.

It must not be brought here. I would rather see Ohndarien fall.

Shara kept her thoughts to herself and followed the white-faced foreigners through the narrow canyon. They marched in long lines, each one holding the sleeve of the man in front of him.

LEWLEM'S WIFE led them down the mountain toward their camp on the beach. A warning horn blew as they approached, and dozens of soldiers ran up the hill in little lines to greet them. A crowd of soldiers trailed them as they marched down the slope. All activity in their camp stopped as Shara moved through the tents. The black-haired boys stared at her and the baby in mute astonishment. Lewlem's wife led her to a line of rowboats along the shore.

"You may come." She shook her head as she looked at Brophy. "He must stay."

"No," Brophy said, his hand gripping the pommel of the Sword of Autumn. "If she goes, I follow."

"It's all right," Shara said. "I will go alone. It will be all right."

"What if they—"

"What? Kill me? Kill you? Brophy, it all depends on this meeting."

Brophy's eyes narrowed. "Shara . . ."

She shook her head and climbed into a rowboat. "Wait for me. I'll return."

No one spoke as six soldiers launched the boat and stroked past the breakers into the sea. The oars creaked steadily, and Shara found herself turning the music box to the same rhythm.

The Ohohhim took no chances with her. Four soldiers rowed, and the other two held their naked short swords pointed at her throat. With each rocking of the boat, a sword tip pressed lightly against her collarbone.

The Ohohhim ships loomed as they approached, their shiny black hulls like polished obsidian. The little rowboat wended through them until the soldiers found the one they sought. The ship creaked, swaying over them. Small waves splashed along the side of a hull.

"Daughter of my heart, it is a joy to meet you again for the second time," Father Lewlem said, leaning over the ship's railing. His robes had been exchanged for loose black pants. "Of all the places in the Emperor's world, I did not think to find you here."

"Father of my heart," she replied. "I remember you fondly, though it has been too long since I have seen your face."

A rope with a loop in the end snaked down the side of the ship. Moving carefully across the wet wood, Shara stepped into the loop. She hooked an elbow around the rope, resting the music box gingerly on top of the sling, and continued turning the handle. Men on deck hoisted her up the side of the ship and set her on her feet, then backed away, their eyes fixed on the baby.

A muted howl rose from below the deck. Shara glanced around, no one else seemed to have noticed it.

Lewlem's wife climbed over the ship's railing and stood behind her husband, pinching his sleeve. Lewlem's eyes were wide as he stared at the bundle in Shara's arms. He pressed his palms together.

"Is that the Legacy?" he asked. "Is that The Child Who Lived?"

Shara moved the music box aside and drew back a flap of the sling.

His brow wrinkled, and he stepped away.

"What have you done to her! What have you done to that child?"

Shara looked down at the baby. The infection had spread across half her head.

"You have corrupted her!" Lewlem shouted, unable to catch his breath. "You have poisoned her with your foul magic."

"No," Shara said, backing up against the rail. "We were attacked, she was injured, she needs to be healed."

Horror turned to despair on the old man's face. "But she is the child who lived. She is immune."

His wife whispered something in his ear.

The ambassador hung his head and struggled to compose himself. His bony little hands were clenched into fists. The baleful eyes of the crew seemed to accuse Shara from all directions. "This is unexpected," Lewlem finally said.

Another muted howl arose from below deck. Shara looked around, but everyone else ignored it.

"Come," Lewlem said. "I arranged for refreshments in my cabin." He turned and walked aft. His wife fell in line behind him, pinching his sleeve. The desolate crew parted slowly to make way for her. Shara took a deep breath and followed. The trio descended the steps to Lewlem's cabin.

A round wooden table had been bolted to the deck at the center of the small room, and three chairs encircled it. Chunks of steaming fish had been arranged on a plate in the center. A loaf of bread and a pitcher sat next to it.

"Please sit," Lewlem said, sinking into one of the chairs. Lewlem's wife followed, and Shara did the same. He scooped some fish into a bowl and set it in front of Shara. His old hands were shaking. The ambassador did the same for his wife, then filled his own bowl. His wife then poured wine for each of them.

"Thank you," Shara said.

None of them touched the food.

Lewlem folded his hands in his lap. "I apologize for my earlier outburst. We must illuminate these events," he said.

"The Legacy is not what you expected," Shara said.

"No."

"What were you seeking?"

"A child, such as you carry. A music box, such as you spin. But not this child I see before me."

"What was she supposed to be?"

"A house for all the lost magic of Efften. A great vessel of healing. A tool to undo what the leaders of Ohndarien have wrought upon the world with their foul magic."

Shara stared at him a long moment until she understood what he was saying. "Fourteen years ago—"

"We know what happened in the Vastness. A great evil was unleashed, but an infant child and a young woman escaped the destruction. The women of the Vastness told us what happened. They saw the four sorcerers from Ohndarien emerge from the corrupted lands and follow the child across the sea. The horsewomen know about the child. She is the only thing that can hold the evil back, yet the Ohndarien sorcerers have kept her away all this time. They, who caused the corruption in the first place.

"I accompanied His Eternal Wisdom when he came to the Vastness to investigate. Many of our soldiers were infected. No matter what we tried, we could not heal them. We believed this child possessed the healing power we need."

Shara shook her head. "You are right about many things, but you are a victim of a misunderstanding. The Ohndariens did not unleash the corruption you have seen. This child did."

A flicker of annoyance crossed the ambassador's face, but he nodded for her to continue.

Shara relayed the story of the child to Father Lewlem as she turned the handle of the music box. When she finished, he sat back, his fingers steepled against his chin. His forehead was wrinkled in thought.

"So you see, the Brothers have been protecting the baby, fighting to keep her from letting the black emmeria into the world again," Shara said.

The ambassador paused, closed his eyes. "Then our mission is for naught. I would like to doubt you, but now I have seen the child. The power that destroyed our soldiers flows from her like a foul wind. Despite our short time together, I believe you. Your words ring true."

"I am sorry, Father. But perhaps there was another reason you came to this island. We need your help. Now that the baby is infected, we have to get her to Ohndarien to cure her."

"There is a cure?" Lewlem's eyes lit with a fierce hope. He leaned forward, clutching the edge of the table.

"There is another artifact of Efften called the Heartstone. It resides in the center of Ohndarien and was created to repel the black emmeria that the child carries. Each of the Brothers carried a piece of that stone, burned into his flesh. These heartstones allowed them to withstand the corruption and to heal it in others." Shara revealed the top of the child's head. One of the dark tendrils had reached as far as an eyelid. "If we do not get the child to Ohndarien soon, she will die, and nothing will stop this corruption from spreading."

"Yes." Lewlem nodded. He turned to his wife. She rose and shuffled quickly from the room. "We will bring your friend on board and set sail immediately."

Another howl sounded from below, and Shara shivered. Memories of the black oxen and corrupted birds leapt to mind.

"Father, what is that noise?"

His wife returned to the cabin and came silently to Lewlem's side, pinching his sleeve. Without a word, Lewlem stood. "Come," he said. "Let me show you something." He nodded toward the center of the room, and his wife looked up at him, shook her head slightly.

"Yes, Heart of my Heart, we must. If there is any path from here, surely it lies with Shara-lani."

Lewlem's wife glanced at Shara, seemed to look her up and down, then her eyes focused on the floor again. She let go of Lewlem's sleeve, knelt before the rug at the rear of the room and peeled it back. Underneath was a trapdoor. She pulled it open. A surprised snarl came out of the darkness. Then, silence.

Shara glanced at Lewlem.

"Come," he said. "It is safe enough." He led the way down the steep wooden steps. She followed, descending into a large cargo hold. A foul stench hovered in the gloom.

"Bring her to me!" an enraged voice shouted out of the darkness.

Lewlem's wife slipped past Shara and turned up the wick on a swinging oil lamp. The added light threw shadows behind the ribs of the ship, splashing orange on the thin sheen of water that sloshed across the hull.

At the far end of the hold hung a man, suspended in midair, shackled at the wrists and ankles and around the waist. Velvet padding lined the cuffs, but they were covered with bite marks.

The man screamed and yanked mightily against his bonds as Shara stepped off the ladder. The chains clinked and swayed as he thrashed, then pulled tight. He strained, pulling with all of his strength, but he could not free himself.

"Give me the prize, give her to me!" the hanging man screamed.

To Shara's amazement, Lewlem and his wife bowed in reverence.

Shara sloshed forward, peering into the gloom.

"Be wary, my daughter," Lewlem said. "Step no closer."

The prisoner was not quite a man. His bare skin was black and bumpy. Uneven spines ran down the center of his chest and the outsides of his arms. His black hair hung lank and greasy over the hard ridge of his protruding brow. Long fangs pushed past his scaly lips. His waist was covered with a loincloth, but otherwise he was naked. His engorged muscles bunched and flexed like snakes writhing under his skin, even when he wasn't moving.

Shara flicked a glance at his hands. His fingers had too many joints and did not end in fingertips, but tapered thinner and thinner until they ended in pointed flaps of bloody flesh.

"I want her, give her to me!" the creature rasped. His thick tongue licked the front of his teeth. It was covered in blood, and a trickle ran down one of his fangs, dripped into the water. "Give me the baby. Give me the baby!" He gnashed his teeth.

"By the Seasons," Shara murmured. "Who is he?"

"I'm your master," the man growled, his breath rattling in and out of his lungs. "I have never been wrong in five thousand years."

Shara turned to Lewlem and his wife. Their heads were still bowed in deference.

"Give me the child," the thing said in his guttural voice. His fingers flexed as though he were crushing the baby's head in his hands. He turned his red eyes on Lewlem. "Set me free! I command you!"

"You know I cannot do that, my lord Emperor."

"Treason!" he roared, thrashing against the chains.

"This is the Incarnation of God on Earth," Lewlem said quietly, his voice thick with emotion. "His Eternal Wisdom, the Emperor of Ohohhom."

Shara breathed hard, trying to assimilate what she was seeing and realizing why the Ohohhim were so desperate. Their entire culture revolved around this one man. If his condition were known, the Opal Empire would fall.

"Give me the child!" The creature snarled. Thrashing in his chains, his undulating muscles strained to the breaking point. "I need her!"

Shara looked at the moorings of the chains. They were strong, built into the very structure of the ship. He would have to rip the hull in half to break free, but she wondered if he could. Despite herself, she stepped back.

"Set me free!" the Emperor roared.

"You know I cannot do that, my lord," Lewlem repeated as though he had said it a thousand times.

"Please," he whimpered, going limp in his bonds. "I command you. Let me touch the child. Just let me touch her."

"Come, Shara-lani," Lewlem said. "Let us retire to my cabin."

"No!" the Emperor shouted. "Stay. Don't leave me in the dark, not in the dark!"

They climbed up through the trapdoor as the Emperor shrieked behind them, thrashing against his chains. The white-faced woman closed the trapdoor and slid the thick rug over it, but it could not completely shut out the howls of rage.

"Please, sit," Lewlem offered. "And I will tell you our story." The food had been cleared, and their untouched wine had been replaced with a different vintage.

"That young man was still an unweaned babe when he was recognized as the latest incarnation of His Eternal Wisdom," Lewlem began. "Since he was old enough to read, the Emperor was fascinated by the stories of ancient Efften. He studied every book that could be found, never satiated, spending lavish amounts for information on that old and powerful island kingdom. It is near fourteen years ago, as you said, that strange and disturbing reports came from the Vastness."

Lewlem swirled the wine in his glass. "His Eternal Wisdom asked to be taken across the Great Ocean. It was a highly unusual request. No emperor has left the Opal Palace in five thousand years, but His Eternal Wisdom has never been wrong, so we did as he asked. We sailed to the Vastness to witness the stretch of corrupted land." Lewlem shook his head. "His Eternal Wisdom entered this land with his bravest guards. At the end of his first night, the Emperor and his entire escort became as you see him now."

Lewlem turned back to Shara. "We captured the Incarnation of God on Earth. We hunted and slew his escort at the cost of many men."

"Oh Father . . ." Shara said.

He shook his head. "We know not why His Eternal Wisdom chose this path. It is beyond our mortal comprehension, but we trust that all will be revealed.

"Since then, we have done everything we could to obtain the Legacy of Efften from Ohndarien. It took a long time, but we stole the information bit by bit. After we met Krellis, we knew we must be correct. He offered the child to me for aid in a long line of betrayals. The man's heart is black with deceit and ambition. We thought the Brothers had hidden the Legacy of Efften, preventing her from healing the damage that they had wrought, refusing to undo what they had done, refusing to let the light of the child into the world again."

He paused, closed his eyes. "But now we have seen the child . . ." Tears welled and streaked down Lewlem's powdered cheeks. To her surprise, Shara noticed that his wife was also crying.

"Brophy will take the Test," Shara said. "If there is a way to heal your emperor, he and the Sisters will find it."

"I apologize for our tears," Lewlem said. "Your words bring hope where we have felt none in many years. Such emotions are a parent's weakness." He reached out and took his wife's hand. The woman's dark eyes met Shara's, pure and unflinching.

"Parents?" Shara asked, leaning back in her chair.

"Oh yes. His Eternal Wisdom is our son."

16

KRELLIS WATCHED the Physendrian and Farad armies swarm across the ocean and assault the Sunset Gate. He still couldn't think of a way to stop them from doing it. Ohndarien's western defenses had been designed to resist navies. The Sunset Gate was slightly taller than a ship, half the height of the other walls. It was poorly suited to repel soldiers who walked on water.

Krellis cursed Father Lewlem again. With an Ohohhim fleet on the Great Ocean, they could have broken this attack in a few hours. The Farads had felled hundreds of trees and rolled them down the slopes into the ocean. In the gentle waters of the strait, they lashed those trees together to form huge rafts, then pushed them up to the gate. Krellis tried setting them on fire, but the logs were mostly submerged. No fire would catch. The catapults and trebuchets were useless. They crushed soldiers as the men ran across the shifting rafts, but they couldn't break the logs underneath.

Krellis had a dozen ships packed with Ohndarien archers waiting for the attack just inside the gate. His men fired at will for half the day, but they could only kill so many. They were running out of arrows, and the invaders had plenty of men. Ohndarien defenders still held the walls to either side. They had managed to stand their ground this long, but it would not last. Once the invaders broke through the Sunset Gate, it was finished.

The Farads had launched a major assault against the Quarry Gate while the Physendrians attacked the Water Wall. With all of his best manpower at the locks, the rest of the walls were thinly defended. Soldiers and civilians alike fought for Ohndarien, but they were beset on three sides. A breach was imminent, even if it didn't come at the Sunset Gate.

Master Gorlym stood next to Krellis on J'Qulin's Arm, a mighty stone walkway that extended west from the Citadel, defying the sheer drop to the base of the ridge. The walkway rose almost five hundred feet above sea level and gave a clear view of Ohndarien's western edge, from the Windmill Wall to the Sunset Gate. Krellis turned to Gorlym. "What is your assessment?"

Gorlym had been frowning for three days. His armor was flecked with bloodstains, but his counsel was as calm and accurate as ever. "We can hold for a couple of hours. Maybe a day."

Krellis nodded, looked back at the carnage below. "I agree," he said. "Pull the men back in waves precisely the way we planned it. We'll make our stand in the Night Market."

"What of the soldiers left on the walls?"

Krellis shook his head. "They will die for their city."

Gorlym grunted. "Yes, sir. What shall we do with the Sister of Autumn and the man from Kherif?"

Krellis looked down at his hands. "Yes," he mused. "Bring Baelandra to the Night Market. Drug her if you have to. Do not let her run free like last time, or I'll have someone's head."

"And the man?"

"Use arrows. Kill him in his cell. Don't let any of your soldiers near him."

"Yes, sir."

17

THE AMBASSADOR'S ship slid down a swell under full sail. The Kherish vessel Brophy and Shara had taken north was certainly seaworthy, but the Emperor's flagship was the most graceful vessel on the Great Ocean. Constructed of gray ironwood, its elegant bow curved upward like a Kherish sword. No carvings adorned its hull or even the stern of the ship. It was sleek and effective like the Ohohhim themselves. They had outdistanced the rest of the fleet almost immediately and left them hours behind.

"We are almost there," Brophy said. His hands clenched the pommel of his sword, and he softened his grip. The creeping black corruption covered his right hand and had spread to his shoulder. Dark tendrils reached toward Brophy's chest like roots. He had already cut his lip on his own teeth. They were sharp as a knife and growing longer. Sometimes his body felt numb. Every few minutes, he had the urge to grab the baby from Shara's arms and dash her little head against the deck.

The child was wrapped in a white bandage that kept Brydeon and Celinor's heartstones bound against her wound. The amulet was draped around her throat, and Shara carried the Sword of Winter on her hip. All the heartstones helped slow the corruption, but the child was still getting worse. The infection covered her entire face and chest like a scaly mask. A few tendrils ran all the way down her legs. Brophy had no idea how much time they had. If he was losing control, surely the child was that much closer. The baby had always been as still as stone, but now she squirmed whenever Brophy came near.

The Ohohhim had crafted a new sling for Shara. The leather garment held the baby securely against her chest. A separate pouch held the music box with the handle sticking out so she could turn it with one hand, leaving the other hand free. The new sling was essential for Brophy's plan. Shara must have one hand free to swim while still turning the music box. They had already tested the box by dunking it in a barrel of water. The liquid muted the sounds, but did not affect the baby.

Shara lifted a leather flap and peered at the child. "She's fading."

Brophy put his hand over Shara's shoulder, careful not to crush her in his grip. The baby twitched and let out a tiny grunt.

"I know," he growled. Clenching his teeth, he cleared his throat and spoke normally. "I feel the same. I can fight it, but my mind wanders so easily."

"Oh Brophy." She looked at his neck, then looked away.

"What?" He reached up and felt a few long hairs, stiff as quills, protruding from behind his ear. He suddenly wanted to hit her, smash her nose with his fist. He moved his hand back to the Sword of Autumn and drew a breath. "Just one more night, and it will be over. One way or the other."

Father Lewlem shuffled forward to join them at the prow. His wife trailed behind, eyes on the deck and Lewlem's robe pinched between her fingers. "My worthy friends," he said, "there are enemy ships ahead. We dare not come closer without the rest of the fleet."

"We can't wait," Brophy hissed.

Lewlem's wife stepped between them, but the old man pushed her gently back. "I understand this and I agree," he said. "But it is nearly nightfall. I suggest you wait and continue on in a smaller boat under the cover of darkness." He pointed to the east. Dark clouds bunched on the afternoon horizon, purple and black. "The coming storm should cover your passage as well. It will be here in less than an hour."

Brophy nodded.

"I will get ready," Shara said.

"No," Lewlem replied. "Please do not take offense, but Shara-lani will remain."

Shara shook her head. "The baby cannot wait that long. We must take her to the Sisters immediately."

Lewlem pursed his lips. "You misunderstand me. My wife, Medew, will take the baby and accompany Brophy. Shara-lani will remain."

"No!" Brophy roared, lunging toward Father Lewlem. The man's wife stepped between them again. Brophy towered over the tiny woman with her hands still tucked in her cloak. He barely held himself back, breathing through gritted teeth. A growl rumbled in the back of his throat. He could kill the old man before that bitch got her blades out. He knew he could do it.

Brophy stared at Lewlem's powdered face until his breathing was back under control. "You don't need her as a hostage!" he hissed. "I'm coming back."

Lewlem inclined his head. "Of course. But Shara-lani must remain. As soon as his Eternal Wisdom is cured, we will attack the invaders."

Brophy snarled and tore himself away, stalking across the deck. Didn't that pasty-faced runt understand what he was going through! He needed Shara by his side. He needed all the help he could get!

He drew the Sword of Autumn and swung it as hard as he could, burying the blade in the wretched ship's railing. The sword's gem blazed beneath his hands. He clenched it, until his ragged breath returned to normal.

Shara walked up behind him and put her free hand on Brophy's arm. "It's all right," she whispered. "They have placed great trust in us. We should return the favor."

Brophy nodded, struggling to get his temper back under control. He felt like he was trying to roll a boulder up an endless hill. If he relaxed for one second, he'd lose control.

Finally, he pried the sword out of the ironwood railing and started to sheathe it.

"Maybe you should keep it in your hand from now on," Shara suggested.

With a sneer, he thrust it back into the scabbard and walked back to Lewlem. He wasn't beaten, not yet.

"I'm sorry," Brophy said to the ambassador.

The old man nodded. "There is no shame, all can see the burden you bear.

We will make ready the boat," Lewlem said, bowing and shuffling away. His wife followed him.

Shara cupped Brophy's cheek as her other hand continued to turn the handle of the music box. The tinkling music was driving him mad, and Brophy wanted to smash it to pieces.

"I want to go with you," she said.

"I know," he replied, forcing his jaw to relax. Perhaps it wasn't such a bad idea that she stayed away from him. "Stay safe. I know what a strain the child is, let someone else carry her for a while."

Shara leaned forward and kissed him on the cheek. "Even now, you think of others."

Brophy pulled away. He didn't like her touching him.

"What if the city has fallen by the time you get there?" Shara asked. "What if you can't find the Sisters?"

"Then I will take the Test and do what must be done."

"Alone? While fighting the infection?"

"I don't have any choice," Brophy snarled. He reached out a hand, his fingers curled like claws. He could crush the child's skull in one fist. It would be so easy.

With a grunt, Brophy pulled himself away. He stalked to the ship's railing and punched the gash his sword had made. The wood cracked.

"Get her away from me!" he snarled, breathing through clenched teeth.

She nodded and left him standing by the rail.

BROPHY YANKED on the oars of Lewlem's rowboat, glaring into the driving rain. Sheet after sheet of water pelted them. As long as he was moving, he could keep the rage at bay. It was sitting still that drove him mad.

Mother Lewlem held the rudder in one hand and turned the music box with the other, the baby snug in the cunning sling. The waves tossed them about, but the tiny woman stared down the throat of the storm, giving ground where she had to and holding true when Brophy thought the boat would capsize.

The white powder had long since washed off the tiny woman's face, but her skin was just as pale underneath. Brophy could see the strain in her body language, but the woman showed nothing on her face.

Brophy knew they were in the Narrows near the Sunset Gate, but he couldn't see a thing. With the rain slashing at them, the Physendrian armada could be smashed to twigs or Ohndarien collapsed to rubble, and they would never know.

Lightning lit the sky, and Brophy spotted a thick lump in the storm-tossed waters ahead. He stomped twice on the deck. The boat started to turn, but the warning was too late. The dark lump was a huge log rising on the swells. It rammed the little boat, and Brophy was almost pitched overboard.

"What are you doing!" he shouted at the stupid woman.

Medew shouted something into the wind, but Brophy could barely make out the words.

"What!"

"What did we hit?" she yelled louder.

He tossed the oars aside and lurched to the side of the boat. "A log," Brophy shouted back. "It's a whole damned tree."

He grabbed the gaff pole and leaned over the side. "We are breached! It's punched clean through."

Lightning flashed again. Brophy craned his neck around. Another bolt of lightning lit the Narrows. As far as he could see, the water was full of logs, bucking and rocking on the waves. They filled the strait from shore to shore.

"By the Seasons!" he roared, flinging the gaff pole at the log. There were no trees in Physendria. How did they get here?

He hurled himself over the side and tried to shove the boat free. His feet slipped on the wet wood, and he couldn't get it to budge.

"Who's there?" a man's voice shouted through the rain.

Brophy spun around. Dark figures scrambled across the rafts toward their mired boat. "Who goes there?" the man called again. "These waters belong to King Phandir."

One of the Physendrian soldiers raised a horn to his lips and blew. The deep honk rivaled the noise of the storm. Another man pulled back a bow. The arrow whistled past them in the dark.

Brophy drew the Sword of Autumn. Another arrow whistled past his head. A firm hand grabbed him by the collar and pulled him backward. He slipped on the wet log and a wave swept him into the ocean.

Brophy spluttered and kicked in the raging sea but managed to hold on to the sword. The waves closed over his head, and he quickly lost all sense of direction in the dark and choppy seas. Medew jumped in next to him.

"No fighting," she shouted, paddling awkwardly with one arm, turning the handle with the other. "Swim. Swim under the rafts."

Brophy shook his head to clear it. The sudden shock of cold water had calmed his rage.

"Follow me," she said, and dove.

Brophy sheathed his sword and swam blindly after her. Thunder boomed overhead, sounding eerily quiet under the water. He fumbled through the darkness and hit his head on something. Flailing wildly, he tried to find the surface. Medew's strong hand closed over his wrist, and his need for air subsided.

Brophy looked about, but he couldn't see anything underwater. He groped for her and grabbed the leather sling. Brophy's lungs spasmed, but he refused to draw a breath. Holding on to Mother Lewlem with one hand, he scrabbled along the underside of the raft with the other, pulling them forward foot by foot in the pitch-darkness. They finally emerged on the far edge.

His head broke the surface and he coughed up a torrent of water. Mother Lewlem bobbed next to him.

Lightning flashed, and he looked back the way they had come. Soldiers swarmed over the little boat in the distance.

"These waters belong to Ohndarien," he spat at the distant figures. If they had been any closer, he would have climbed back on that raft and killed them all.

Medew tugged on his shirt. "Where from here?" she asked, blinking against the rain. The music box's childish tune warbled about them, nearly drowned out by the roar of the storm.

Brophy looked across the shifting sea of logs. A lightning flash revealed Ohndarien's walls looming in the distance.

"To the Heart," he said, rage and fear mixing in his belly. "Before it's too late."

18

RAIN POUNDED down on Ohndarien that night, but she was alight with torches and lanterns, alive in a way she had never been before. The city was overrun. Farad soldiers lined Stoneside. Physendrians held Dock Town and the Long Market. Krellis destroyed both bridges as the armies entered the city. The only way to attack the shores of the Night Market was by boat.

Krellis stood at the edge of the seawall, Master Gorlym at his side. The piers glowed with the lights of their sentries. Barricades had been built all along the shore, but Krellis didn't fool himself. They weren't hundred-foot walls. It had taken Physendria and Faradan a little over a month to break through the greatest defenses in the world. It would only take them a few hours to break through the crates of fishnets and barrels of sand that made up the Night Market's barricades.

After those defenses fell there was only the Wheel. The last stand would be made there. The invaders could mount an attack from all sides. Their own lines couldn't hold much longer than a day, a week at most. One way or another, Physendria would decimate them. It was only a matter of time.

Once again, Phandir had arrived with superior forces and taken what Krellis had held for a short time.

A Physendrian galley pulled slowly around the bay. It was difficult to see the ship even thirty feet out. It carried an announcer who shouted into the night, repeating the same message over and over again. He stood at the prow behind a wooden barrier bristling with arrows. A few of Krellis's finest archers had shot the first announcer. They were more careful now.

"The loyal forces of your rightful king, Phandir III, son of the Phoenix, long may he reign, will attack at dawn," the announcer bellowed across the distance. "Any who remain on this island to stand against him, man, woman, or child, will be executed. Any subjects loyal to the king who leave this island tonight will be spared. There are ships in the harbor to assist you if you swim. Any who leave the island will be spared."

The announcer paused, then started again. "The loyal forces of your rightful king, Phandir III, son of the Phoenix, long may he reign, will attack at dawn . . ."

Krellis glanced down the line of rain-soaked defenders. None met his gaze. They all stared at the galley. Krellis wouldn't be surprised if Phandir attacked in the night. Nothing was more demoralizing than having to await your doom in the cold and wet.

Krellis longed to meet his brother's announcement with words of fire and steel, but he held his tongue. The time for speeches was past.

He turned and left the wall. Though the soldiers huddled deep into their cloaks, he left his shirt open at the chest, letting his heartstone remind them who he was.

Gorlym fell in step behind him. "There are three ships circling the island making the same offer," Gorlym said as they walked.

Krellis grunted. "Are the men listening?"

"They are listening. No one has made a move yet, but it is early."

"The lifelong Ohndariens won't budge. You can be sure of that. They'll die for their beloved city. But it isn't them I'm worried about."

"The soldiers."

Krellis nodded. "These men weren't born here. The jewel of the known world doesn't glimmer quite so bright this evening. Why not serve Physendria instead of Ohndarien?" He waved a hand. "If we try to stop them, it will only be worse. If a man wants to run, he'll find a way."

"Yes, sir."

"Of course, if you catch any deserters, make a bloody public example of them."

"Yes, sir."

"And spread a message through the officers. Tell them to remind the men that Phandir may spare their lives, but only long enough to sell them into slavery. Tell them there are twenty slave ships from Vizar waiting outside the Sunset Gate for that very purpose."

Gorlym looked at him. "Is that true?"

"It could be."

Gorlym paused long enough that Krellis shot him a glance. The former Master of the Citadel nodded. "Is there anything else, sir?"

"Yes. I need to know if you will still be here in the morning," Krellis said, not looking at the man.

Gorlym paused. "Will you, sir?"

They walked in the rain for a while. Neither said a thing.

"You have your orders," Krellis finally said.

"Yes, sir." Gorlym left as they reached the brothel that Krellis had made into his temporary headquarters. The Scarlet Heart's courtesans had not been happy about being rousted from their roost, but the brothel was comfortable, roomy, and most important, it had a view of the entire bay.

He thumped up the steps that snaked along the outside of the building to a second-floor landing. When he banged on the door, a short, stocky guard opened it. Relf was as ugly as a hog, but quicker and stronger than he looked. The man was as a damned good soldier, extremely competent and constantly underestimated by his foes. He stood aside immediately as soon as he saw Krellis. "The food you requested is on the table, sir."

"Good."

"The woman is awake, also. I heard her moving."

"Thank you."

The pig-faced man looked up at him, waiting for something. Krellis knew when one of his men needed a word of encouragement, but tonight he could not tell the soldier what he wanted to hear.

Krellis opened the first door on the left. The bed took up nearly a third of the room, but there was plenty more space for a writing desk, dressing table, and three wardrobes. Lavish, brocaded curtains hung over the windows. It was the madam's own room, but the opulence was wasted on him. He'd chosen it for the view.

He strode past the open-air balcony to the bed. Baelandra slept soundly, her slender legs tucked up against her chest. Her wrist manacles were bolted to the stone wall behind the headboard. They'd had to cut a hole in the expensive rosewood. The madam would have a fit if she saw it, but she wasn't likely to see the room ever again.

A small table next to the bed held a bowl of stew and a crystal decanter of wine. Working at the clasp at his neck, Krellis whipped off his cloak and threw it on the edge of the bed.

"I know you're awake. There's no point in pretending."

Baelandra opened her eyes. She pulled the chain tight and slid closer to the headboard, farther away from him. Her green eyes watched him with cold fury.

"How long have I been here? How long have I been drugged?" she asked, her voice slow and rough.

"Three days," Krellis said. He tugged at each finger of his glove, removed it, and started on the other one, then tossed them both on top of his cloak.

Baelandra's nostrils flared. "Why?"

Krellis gave her a crooked smile. "You've been known to appear out of closets with knives in hand."

She tried to keep her venomous gaze fixed on him, but he saw her glance at the steaming stew. He sat on the bed next to her, and she flinched away, scooted as far from him as her short chain would allow. He scooped up a spoonful of stew and tapped it against the side of the crockery bowl. After blowing on it, he raised the food to her mouth. She turned her head away.

"I've had enough of your sleeping powders."

"If I'd wanted you drugged, you'd still be drugged." He moved the spoon to her mouth again. She jerked her head the other way.

Krellis sighed.

"How long have Phandir's troops been inside the city?" she asked.

"They breached the walls two days ago."

"You've sold us all."

He shook his head.

"Any word of Brophy?" she asked. "Has he returned?"

"No. There has been no word since the Kherif ship left for Physendria."

"And Scythe?"

"He escaped."

Her lip trembled and she flushed. "You killed him, didn't you?" she whispered. "You bastard."

"Why ask questions if you aren't going to believe the answer?"

"Is there anything you say that I could possibly believe?"

"I doubt it." He offered her the stew a third time. Baelandra shook her head.

"It's not my manhood. Just barley stew. I know you're hungry. Most Ohndariens will have a lot less to eat tonight."

She waited a long moment. The spoonful had stopped steaming. Like a bird, she leaned forward and snatched a bite, chewing resolutely as she stared at him. He fed her spoonful after spoonful. She took them greedily and didn't stop until the huge bowl was almost empty.

"Did you hear my brother's offer? The one he is shouting across the bay?" he asked.

"I heard it. Is it a bluff?"

"No."

"It doesn't make sense. Why attack? Our supplies are exhausted, and they've only had a few days to prepare."

"Ohohhim ships rounded the point this evening."

"In the storm?"

"They seem determined. I can only guess at their purpose. Perhaps they are coming to fulfill their bargain." He sneered.

"You've heard nothing from them?"

"Not a word."

"How many ships?" she asked.

"Two hundred."

"Two hundred! By the Seasons, how many men do they have?"

"Like the stars in the sky."

"Are they here to help us?"

"I would guess they plan to take Ohndarien for themselves."

"If they are here to help us, how long do we have?" Baelandra asked.

He shrugged, reached for the decanter of wine, poured a glass, and lifted it to her lips. She shook her head, and he drank it himself.

"A day perhaps."

"If they've rounded the point, they'll be here by morning." She pulled at her chains, frowned, brought her feet up underneath her.

He shook his head, filled the wineglass again. "No. While you were in the Citadel, Phandir filled the Narrows with huge log rafts. The Ohohhim can't sail into the city until the logs are cleared. Or their forces will have to come over the logs like Phandir's did. Still, my brother only has two days at the most. The Ohohhim will find a way to assault the gates. Phandir will want to finish us quickly so he can turn his attention to defending his new prize."

"Then we have no chance?"

"Unless the Ohohhim take the city and give it right back to us." He snorted. "No, we will be overrun in the first wave."

"I see." Lightning flashed outside. "And what are you going to do?"

He paused, held her gaze. "Escape through one of the tunnels leading out of the Heart. I've made arrangements with several officers in Faradan. They will smuggle me through the Quarry Gate."

Her nostrils flared, and her lips pulled back in a sneer. He looked away.

Someone knocked at the door.

"What?" Krellis roared.

Relf spoke through the door. "Sir, there is a woman here to see you."

"Tell her to wait," Krellis growled.

Baelandra looked at him as though he was a roach. "Who is she? Your backup plan when I refuse to sleep with you?"

"Bae—"

"You have done many things I despise," she spat, "but I never took you for a coward."

"Baelandra . . ." Krellis said, his voice low. "I could take you with me. Just say the word."

She laughed in his face.

He continued calmly. "I'm asking you to go with me. I . . . want you to go with me."

She stared at him, slowly shaking her head. "How could you possibly think I would go with you?"

Krellis said nothing.

"You betrayed my nephew. You killed Scythe, the most loyal man I've known, who lived only for a kind word from me . . ." She choked, but her eyes were on fire. Clenching her teeth, she continued on. "You gave Ohndarien to Physendria. Tell me, my *love*." She added cruel emphasis to the last word. "What do you have that I could possibly want?"

"I still love this city. I did what I thought was best for her."

"Stripping her of her tradition, her dignity, the very things that make her beautiful and unique? And then fleeing as she is overrun by an army you enticed to fall on her?"

"I . . ." He hesitated. "My plans had a very different outcome."

"Did they?"

"Yes. But I chose the wrong allies."

Her mouth set in a line. "Yes. I am very familiar with that particular mistake."

Lightning flashed, illuminating her hard features, her cold glance.

"Baelandra, don't stay here. It's pointless."

"My heart belongs to Ohndarien," she said, touching the stone in her chest. Krellis flinched. "I live and die with her."

He looked away, fought for his voice, and it came out dark and husky. "At least let me give you your life. Do something with it. Save yourself for revenge if you must."

"Revenge is your obsession, not mine."

"Why live if not for revenge?" he shouted suddenly. "Phandir will pay for this day. He will pay dearly!"

Baelandra closed her eyes. "What's the point in killing a man if he has already destroyed everything that you love?"

Krellis swallowed, waiting for his breathing to return to normal. He stared at the woman chained to the wall. "Do you still love me?" he asked.

"I should ask you the same," she said. "Or more important, did you ever love me?"

"By the gods," he murmured. "Would I have let you leave my chambers alive with that poison dagger in your hair if I didn't love you? Would I have tolerated you and the Sisters in the Heart? Would I have sent Shara to save Brophy—"

"He wouldn't have needed saving if you hadn't betrayed him in the first place."

Krellis clenched his fists. "I regret that," he said. "Trent's death made me . . ." He struggled for the words. "I wanted to stop loving you, but I couldn't."

Bae closed her eyes. Her jaw muscles clenched. "Then stay," she whispered. "Fight with us. Do not let Phandir take this city while there is breath in your body. Your heart is bound to this place. You passed the Test when no one, not even I, thought you could. There was a reason for that."

He shook his head. "I passed the Test because of my brother's magic. Nothing more, nothing less. The influence of a Zelani."

"No. The Heartstone cannot be fooled. You have a purpose here."

He looked out the window at the thousands of torches on the far shore. There was no way to win this fight. He would not let his death become a grand and wasted gesture. He was not meant for that. "Not anymore."

He stood. "You have made your choice then?"

"There is no other choice I can make."

"I see."

He left her on the bed and strode to the door. She rattled her chains as he touched the handle.

"Krellis, I beg you. Don't leave me chained like a dog. For the love you claim you bear me, set me free."

He turned slowly, his brows furrowed. "Sorry, my love. You are a dangerous woman and always will be." He left the room.

"Krellis!" she called as the door shut. "Krellis!" she screamed again, her rage muted by the thick wood.

"The woman is waiting inside," Relf said, pointing to the room at the end of the hall.

Krellis ignored him and stepped into the closest room, slamming the door behind him.

With a roar, he grabbed the full-sized table and threw it against the wall. A vase shattered on the floor. He flipped the bed over, grabbed a chair, and smashed it against a chest of drawers.

"Sir, are you all right?" Relf asked through a crack in the door.

Krellis threw the broken chair against the door. "Leave me be!" he shouted.

The guard snapped the door shut, and Krellis was left alone, clenching his fists so hard his fingernails bit into his palms. He stood like that until his ragged breathing slowly came under control. Picking up a broken table leg, Krellis twisted it in his hands and snapped it in two. He let the pieces clatter to the floor.

Taking a deep breath, he stepped into the corridor again. Relf watched him with wide eyes.

"Who is she?" Krellis asked.

"I . . . I don't know, sir. She had this." He handed a piece of paper to Krellis. It bore Gorlym's seal. Krellis's brow furrowed. Without another word, he walked through the door at the end of the hall and shut it behind him.

The woman stood at the balcony, covered by a full cloak and cowl. As she heard the door shut, she turned, pushed back her hood.

Krellis's eyes widened. He laughed, though he wasn't sure why. "By the gods . . ." he said.

"Isn't the phrase 'By the Seasons' in Ohndarien?" she asked.

"I'm speechless," he said, inclining his head toward her.

"You say that as if it is a rare thing. I remember how very little you talked the last time I saw you." She looked him up and down. "You haven't aged a day."

"Leaving Physendria has been good for me."

"Perhaps I should have done it years ago," she said.

"Perhaps you should."

He watched her closely, wondering what had caused this unbelievable meeting. Her breathing was too fast, and her eyes kept darting to the door.

Krellis scanned the room. Had she brought assassins? Was she the assassin? She had obviously convinced Gorlym to trust her. Or perhaps Gorlym wanted him dead now.

"Did my brother send you?"

"No. I came on my own."

"You take your life in your hands. If Phandir found out—"

"I don't have much to lose," she said. Her voice was odd, resigned. He remembered her very differently. Vivacious, daring, spirited, cunning. She was the only one who could effectively banter with Phandir.

"It seems to me that the Queen of Physendria has a great deal to lose."

"You've obviously never been a queen," Ossamyr said.

"No. A king once, but never a queen." His mouth crooked in a smile.

"I came to ask a question. Will you answer me?"

Krellis fought to put the pieces together. What could her game be? He could imagine King Phandir standing in this room much more easily than his wife.

"I would be honored." He played along, thinking quickly of what he might ask in return.

"Is Brophy here? Has he returned?"

"What?"

"He is Baelandra's—"

"I know who he is, Ossamyr. I exiled the boy." He laughed again. "Surely that Kher did not have the truth of it. You're not smitten?"

Her chin lifted. "I owe a debt. Is he here?"

"Last I heard, he was in your Wet Cells."

"He escaped."

Krellis chuckled. "Doesn't everyone?"

She crossed the room, laid a slender hand on his arm. He glanced down at it, then back at her. "If he is here, I need to speak with him, please."

"To what end?"

"I can get him out of the city. I will take you as well, if need be."

He walked past her. "I must tell you, Ossamyr, seeing you here in my rooms has caught me completely unprepared. That you are here for Brophy confounds me. The woman I remember would smile and whisper sweet nothings as she slit her young lover's throat. I do not know how to treat with you. Tell me you aren't in love."

"Does it matter?" she asked.

"I'm sure it would matter to Brophy. He thinks you betrayed him. The Kher, Scythe, said you ripped his heart out and made him eat it."

Her gaze dropped to the floor.

"And this bothers you?" Krellis said. "What is a betrayal among lovers and families? Betrayal is as common as scorpions in Physendria."

"And in Ohndarien?"

He frowned. "And here I was having such a fine time talking with you. Brophy is not here. Even if he was, I would not tell you where."

Her fire diminished. She nodded. "I understand." She flipped her cowl up again. "Thank you."

She turned to go, and he grabbed her arm.

"I never trusted you," he said through his teeth. "And Brophy was a fool to fall into your trap, but I have to say, I never thought you would betray your husband."

Half of her face was covered by the wet cowl. "It runs in the family." She tried to yank her arm from his grip, but he wouldn't let her go.

"But since you are here, and I have so graciously answered your question, perhaps you could answer one of mine."

Her eyes searched his. Her breathing came even faster. "You may ask."

"Could you tell me, perhaps, if Phandir is currently within the city walls?"

She hesitated. His hand tightened on her arm.

"Why?" she asked.

"If I knew where he was, I could eliminate him. He has sent enough assassins after my head over the years. I would like to return the favor, but I would come personally."

She relaxed. Another surprise. If this was one of Phandir's ploys, she was playing her part flawlessly.

"What makes you think I would tell you such a thing?" She raised one of her thin, dark eyebrows, yanked her arm again. This time he let her go. That was the Ossamyr he remembered.

"You are here tonight, serving the cause of true love."

"Mock me and I will leave."

"Try to leave and I will have you whipped."

Her eyes narrowed, and she smiled a thin smile. "You would like that, wouldn't you?"

"I've dreamed of it since I can remember."

"I had whips in my room, and yet you never came to me." She pushed her cowl back again, shook out her short black hair.

"I valued my throat the way it was."

"Such a timid boy."

"Where is Phandir?"

"He is in the city."

"Where?"

"Assassinating the King of Physendria is not as easy as you make it sound."

"And easier than you might guess." Krellis's mind began piecing the plan together even as he spoke. "I think you want him dead."

"You seem to think many things."

"You've shared his bed for twelve years. You must hate him."

"And if I did?"

"I heard that Brophy took a stab at Phandir before they threw him in the Wet Cells. Could it be that you engineered that?" Krellis shook his head. "In front of the whole of Physendria. And then you yanked the rug from underneath his feet."

Ossamyr's smile became stiff.

"But not on purpose," Krellis guessed. "Did Phandir catch you? Did you trade your life for Brophy's?" He paused, seeing it all on her face. "And so you gave your toy to the king, but it stung this time, did it?"

"Krellis . . ." she warned, her smile gone.

He held his hand up. "No matter."

"What makes you think you can succeed where Brophy failed?"

Krellis laughed. "He's a fifteen-year-old boy. I have had years to plot my brother's demise. We can have it tonight, if you tell me where he is."

"How?"

"Imagine if you will, this pleasant scene." Krellis strode across the room, taking his time. "Fifteen Physendrian guards drag me before his royal majesty. They caught me trying to escape the walls. Think of how Phandir's face would

light with joy seeing me on my knees, nose bloodied, face red. Think of that
gloating smile. We all know how he loves to gloat."

"A fine plan," she said. "Shall I truss you and beat you now?"

"And imagine his face when the Physendrian guards throw off their helmets and cloaks and reveal themselves to be my fifteen Zelani."

Her brow wrinkled. "We heard Victeris was dead."

"You heard right. Victeris did not graduate them. His successor did. We
have fifteen. They could strip the minds of the elite guard in seconds. They'd
be fighting each other for an hour before they realized their king was dead.
In that time I could break my dear brother's neck with my bare hands. Or slit
his gizzard. We both know that Phandir was never much of a swordsman."

"I see," she said.

Krellis suppressed a smile. He had her. He could see the sparkle in her
eye. "All I need to know is where he is."

"And then what?"

"We begin the game. How many of his officers would support me if I took
the crown?"

She paused. "More than you might think. Many would flock to you.
Most, if I supported your cause."

"And will you?"

She nodded.

"I would give you Physen," he said. "I will rule the kingdom from Ohndarien, but you could govern Physen."

"I want nothing," she said. "Except to see Phandir's plans in ruins, especially now at the moment of his triumph."

Krellis moved closer. He could smell her breath. Mint leaves, just as he
remembered. "What did he do to you?" he asked quietly.

"It doesn't matter."

"Doesn't it?"

"If it did, I certainly would not tell you."

He shrugged. "No matter. I will save my city. You will have your revenge.
Then the only question left to answer is whether we can trust each other."

"I don't trust you. I trust your ambition," Ossamyr said.

"A wise bet. That still leaves your ambition. Why would you hand the
crown to me instead of taking it for yourself?"

"I don't want it."

"I don't believe you."

She smiled, though her eyes remained cold. "You should. I'm not doing
this for you. I'm not doing it for myself. I'm doing it for Brophy."

19

BROPHY AND MEDEW bobbed in the ocean at the base of the Windmill Wall. The rain pelted the water all around. Lewlem's wife remained utterly calm. It was almost unsettling. She floated in the raging seas, stoically turning the handle.

"One mistake and we are dead!" Brophy shouted over the roar of the storm. "We must to do this together. If I lose my grip on you, I'll drown."

Brophy glared at the marble wall above him. It rose so high its top disappeared into the falling rain. The water lift was in there, the huge screw constantly turned, catching pockets of seawater and spiraling them upward at a diagonal slant until they spilled into a holding tank at the top of the wall. Brophy and Trent almost rode the lifts once. They had even come this far before, bobbing in this same spot. In the end, they decided against it, swam back to the gate, and drank themselves silly.

The trick was actually getting into the screw without drowning. Brophy had seen drawings in old tomes written by Master Coelho. As the water screw turned, a pocket of air and water would be lifted from one spiral of the wooden corkscrew to the next. Once inside, they would be raised higher and higher until they were spit out on the top of the wall. It was so large that a human being's weight was nothing.

Finding the entrance of the immense screw would be perilous. If the scoop came around and cracked you on the head, it would grind you up like sausage. The lift spun relentlessly, slave to the windmills above. They would have to time it perfectly and hope that nothing interrupted Medew's turning of the handle.

"It'll be moving fast," Brophy warned. "Stay close." She nodded, saying nothing. Her mouth was set in a tight line. The tiny Ohohhim woman balked at nothing. Not the burden of the baby, of breathing water, nor swimming down blind into a huge, turning screw.

They dove. He felt the water churning at the mouth of the lift. The scoop swept past them. The revolution was quick tonight with the wind of the storm. Battered by the turbulence, they moved close to the opening. In the darkness, Brophy couldn't see the edge of the scoop as it came around again. He could only hear it and hope they were in the right place.

Medew's hand clenched tight to his shirt. The water sucked them forward as the scoop came around again. Brophy grabbed her arm and swam as hard as he could.

They slipped through the gap and collided with a thread of the screw. It spun him around in the darkness. Polished wood slid underneath them and they tumbled as it revolved around them. The water sloshed and slowly settled. Brophy struggled to the surface and raked his claws against the screw, growling.

He couldn't see Medew, but he heard her cough and sputter. The warbling tune of the music box surfaced with her, and the endless grinding of the screw echoed in the tight space. They swam constantly in the sloshing pool, trying to stay away from the edges of the screw. Brophy kept a clenched fist on Medew's sling.

"We'll be out of here soon," he shouted, his voice nearly lost amid the scrapes and groans as the screw made its revolutions, ever turning. The lift took them up and up until they spilled along a narrow trough and dropped into the holding tank.

The rain continued to fall, splashing all about them, and they kept low in the water. He drew the Sword of Autumn underneath the surface. If they were walking into a fight, he was ready for it.

Brophy pulled himself out of the water and crouched on the ramparts, squinting against the rain. There wasn't a guard in sight.

"It's clear," he hissed at Medew. "Hurry."

The woman hooked her foot over the edge of the wall and levered herself out of the pool. The water slowly drained from the box and the tinkling music returned.

"Where are the soldiers?" Medew asked.

"I don't know. The Physendrians should have posted guards on the wall." Brophy wiped the water from his face and continued down the walk.

He kicked something and looked down. It was a hand, still gripping a sword. A trail of blood smeared the rain-soaked stones where the wrist had been severed. Brophy crouched next to it. He had a sudden urge to taste the blood, but he suppressed it.

"Come on," Brophy said. "We have to hurry."

They found the nearest access stairway and raced down the steps into the city streets. Brophy led Medew to an old warehouse at the base of the ridge.

They clung to the shadows of the wall as a trio of soldiers ran by. Brophy recognized the Serpent helmets even through the haze of rain. A low growl rumbled in Brophy's throat, and he stepped out of the shadows toward their retreating backs.

Medew's hand touched his arm, and he spun about. His fist clenched tight on the pommel of his sword, but she gazed into his eyes unafraid. With one slender finger, she pointed to the black tendrils on his forearm.

"We must hurry," she whispered.

Brophy shook his head. Clenching his teeth, he mastered himself. "Fine," he whispered hoarsely.

He spun and led the way. They crept along the wall and ducked through an unlocked door. The warehouse was mostly empty, and Brophy headed for a narrow staircase leading down into the cellar. He stopped at the bottom of the stairs and turned to face a blank wall.

Brophy had never been into the depths of the Heart, but Baelandra had told him about three secret entrances. One of them led from this warehouse near the Citadel. Only the life of the Heartstone could activate the secret doors, but Brophy had a piece. With this shortcut, they could bypass the entire Physendrian army. They would be in the Heart in minutes. He grabbed the heartstone from around the baby's neck and pressed it against a little divot in the wall.

Nothing happened.

Brophy scraped his pointed fingernails down the stone. "The bitch lied!" he snarled.

"It's all right," Medew whispered. "Try again."

Brophy growled, turning to the tiny woman. He imagined ripping her rib cage open, exposing the beating heart beneath.

Mother Lewlem returned his fiery gaze, calmly cranking the music box. Brophy glanced at the baby's feet dangling from the sling. The corruption had reached all the way to her toes. He snarled and wrenched his eyes away, gripping the Sword of Autumn with both hands.

Breathing hard, Brophy took a hand off his sword and turned the pendant over, pressing it against the wall once more. He concentrated on the stone, willing it to respond. The call of the Heartstone was weak in the back of his mind, like a whisper in a storm. He concentrated on that faint call until it grew louder and louder. Rock ground against rock and a line appeared in the wall. Brophy roared, clenching his claws. With a guttural laugh, he threw the door open and ran down a dust-covered stairway. Medew followed, and they descended into the darkness below the city.

Running his claws along the wall, Brophy found a sconce and withdrew a torch wrapped in oilskin.

"There's nothing to stop us now," he panted. "I'll light a torch, and we'll be there in a few minutes."

After a moment's fumbling, he found the flint that had been left on a shelf below the sconce. A few strikes against the stone wall, and a spark flew to the pitch-soaked wood, but it did not light.

He tried again. Another spark fell on the wood, but did not catch. Medew crept a few feet past him into the darkness.

"Dammit," he hissed. Brophy scraped the flint against the wall over and over. Faster and faster he bashed flint against stone. A shower of sparks fell on the torch, but would not catch.

Brophy roared and smashed the flint against the wall. It shattered in his hand, slicing it open. He screamed, punched the wall. He threw the torch into the darkness, then grabbed the sconce and yanked on it, cursing and screaming until it ripped out of the wall.

His guttural voice echoed in the narrow hallway. He barely heard the sound of running feet and snapped to his senses.

That bitch was running! That bitch was running away with the baby!

Brophy charged into the darkness, following the sound of the retreating music box, following the faint glow of the stolen Sword of Winter.

"Give me the child," he roared. "She's mine! Mine!"

20

SHARA STOOD in the rain staring into the night. Brophy was out there somewhere, fighting the battle of his life, and she was stuck here for the sake of diplomacy.

Her powers returned steadily after Mother Medew took the child from her. She could easily compel the Ohohhim to let her go. But she had made a promise to Brophy. She would not use her magic against an ally, a friend, no matter the cost.

The Ohohhim had done everything she asked. She had no right to expect anything more, but it still ripped her in half to be so far from Brophy when he needed her most.

Lightning flashed, and Shara saw a small figure shuffling across the deck. She walked aft and met Father Lewlem near the mast.

"You have suffered long enough, daughter of my heart," he said. "My men have prepared a boat for you. The need for separation is over. Go, find the man you love."

"What do you mean?" A thrill ran through her, but it was followed by the cold prickle of suspicion. "I thought you wanted me as insurance for Brophy's return."

The old man shook his head. The rain had washed the powder off his face and his wrinkles stood out in sharp contrast to his pale skin. "Keeping you here was the only honorable way for you give up the child. And your sword."

"My sword?" Suddenly, it all made sense.

"She's going to kill him! Medew's going to kill Brophy as soon as they get inside the city!"

Lewlem held up his hands. "No, no. Only if she has to. Only if absolutely necessary."

"And who is she to judge that," Shara shouted.

Lewlem lowered his eyes and shook his head. His long wet hair hung in his face. "Your friend is very far gone. I saw the way he looked at the child the last few days. If he were to lose his fight with the corruption, the sword my wife carries is the only thing that can stop him."

Shara bit back her anger.

"If you had gone with Brophy," the ambassador insisted, "you would never have swung that sword. You have neither the skill nor the desire to land that blow. Even if it meant losing the child."

Shara willed away the image of Brophy snapping the infant's neck.

"Perhaps you are right," she admitted, her anger replaced by a sinking dread.

"Sometimes wisdom is a terrible burden," Lewlem admitted. "I hope your Brophy can continue to follow the sleeve of Oh through the darkness, but I could not take that chance."

He motioned toward the back of the ship. "Come, the boat is waiting. Lend our cause what help you can."

21

BROPHY LUMBERED through the darkness snarling and wheezing, dragging his sword along the ground behind him.

"I'll find you . . ." he mumbled, "I'll find you, you bitch, and I'll rip you open."

That witch with the painted face was gone. Gone! Disappeared into the black and twisting tunnels. He'd never find her in this maze of endless passages.

"I'll taste your blood . . ." he rasped. The tip of the Sword of Autumn made a ringing scrape along the tunnel floor.

The baby was the key. Kill the baby, and his chains would be broken. Kill the baby and he would be free to rush across the face of the earth, feeding, feeding, feeding forevermore.

He wiped the froth from his chin, scraping his cheek with his claws. The baby was the key. The baby must die.

He slowed as he saw a shimmering light in the distance. His skin crawled as the swirling rainbow colors shifted across the cave wall. A foul breeze wafted down the passage, stinging his eyes.

He grabbed the sword in both hands and crept forward, peering around a corner into a small chamber packed with stalactites and stalagmites.

Raising his blackened arm, he shaded his eyes from the repulsive, multi-colored light. He heard strange music that made him sick to his stomach. It was hideous, vile. It, too, must die.

A misshapen gem the size of his head sat on a pedestal in the center of the room. It was lumpy and scarred as if dozens of pieces had been broken off it.

The singing became louder and louder, roaring through his mind like a storm. He spun in a circle, hands pressed to his ears, trying to keep the noise out. He had to stop that sound.

Raising his sword high overhead, Brophy charged into the room. He brought the blade down like a hammer on the gemstone. There was a blinding flash, and the clang of steel on stone echoed in the tiny room. His sword dropped from numb fingers, clattered to the ground, and he staggered back.

He shook his head, hissed. The gemstone remained unharmed.

With a howl, he leapt forward and seized the fiendish stone with both hands. He cried out, hands gripping the jewel as his body convulsed. It wouldn't move. He couldn't let go. The diamond held him fast.

A howling wind flew out of it, blowing his hair back, squeezing the water from his eyes. He thrashed back and forth, desperate to get away.

"Let me go!" he screamed. A sudden stabbing pain shot through his hand, and he flew backward.

Brophy fell to the floor, and the rushing wind slowly abated. His mind cleared. The two voices warring in his head faded away.

He looked at his hand. A long, thin shard of blazing diamond was embedded in his palm. The inky blackness around the wound receded. His claws shortened, thinning into normal fingernails. The skin around the shard became translucent, radiating light like the Heartstone.

The rest of his skin was still covered with the net of inky tendrils. His teeth were still too sharp inside his lips, but the maddening hunger, the mindless rage slunk back into the shadows of his mind. It remained there, wounded, waiting.

He rose to his feet. The glowing red shard throbbed. The top was multifaceted like the heartstone in Baelandra's chest, and it tapered to a bloody needle point that jutted through the back of his hand.

Brophy remembered touching his aunt's heartstone as a tiny child, the singed flesh as Celidon lay on his bier, Shara's shimmering pendant, taking the diamond from his father's grave, Celinor's gem as it fell from his chest.

But this was his heartstone, the searing diamond he was supposed to thrust into his own heart. His Test had begun.

"No . . ." he murmured. Not yet. He wasn't ready.

The melody that had been his constant companion for years turned ravenous. A rush of wind swept through the chamber.

He couldn't pass the Test, not now. He'd already failed. The black hunger lurked in the back of his mind. The Heartstone would kill him.

Staring into the shifting colors, Brophy reached out for the Heartstone, his bleeding hand hovering inches from the surface. His heart beat so fast, so hard his chest ached. A red drop fell on the stone, and a jolt shot through his body. He placed his palm on the stone.

Brophy's whole body locked up, and he fell to his knees against the pedestal. The fire burned through him, and he cried out. Rainbow colors splashed across the rough-hewn walls of the cavern, dancing and shifting. Her voice roared, building to a chaotic crescendo. It spread through him, filled his arms, legs, and chest, moved up his body and into his head. Images flashed past like mist on a hurricane wind.

"No!" he cried out, yanking back, but his hand remained on the huge gemstone. He couldn't let go, couldn't get away.

His thoughts swirled and disappeared into her. The only images of his mother vanished. His memories of running into Baelandra's outstretched arms were swept away upon the howling tempest. Shara, laughing and touching his hair on the Kherish sailing ship, sucked away. His deepest, most personal memories fled into the gem, leaving him empty. Alone.

Foreign images flew in to replace them. He saw her intentions in vivid detail. His childhood vision flashed across his thoughts, charging up the steep steps, black clouds rushing past the city walls. But this time he knew where that path led, he knew where it ended.

"No . . ." he murmured. "Not that . . ."

The wind swirled around the room, voices and images clashed in his head.

"I can't . . ." He clenched the searing diamond shard in his fist. "I won't . . ."

The visions flew through him again. Over and over. Insistent. Undeniable. He saw them, so many of them. All with the same ending, all save one. Brophy sagged against the stone, pressing his burning face against the cool gemstone. Her voice bored into the center of his chest and his heart slowed, thumping in great, desperate beats. Those images, the many paths into his future began to fade, one by one.

His head fell forward as his strength ebbed. "I can't do it . . . I won't."

The fire swirled tighter and tighter, constricting his heart. It stopped beating.

His limp body draped down the pedestal. Only his hand remained fastened to the Heartstone, reaching above his head.

For an eternal moment, he fought her, knowing he could not win. He let out a long, hissing breath and surrendered, gave his life to her, accepted her visions, accepted his fate.

His hand slipped away, and he slumped to the floor. Her voice turned soft again, lifting him up, filling him with energy like Shara's Zelani magic. Rolling over, he pushed himself to his knees, breathing hard.

With a cry, Brophy grabbed his heartstone and yanked it from his hand. Blood gushed from the wound and splattered on the floor.

Even now, surrounded by the soft song of the Heartstone, he had a choice. He could still flee with Shara, build that hut with the goats grazing outside and a child at her breast.

Clenching his trembling jaw, he pressed the deadly shard against his chest, covered it with one hand, then the other.

He took a shuddering breath and fell forward, thrusting the red diamond through flesh and bone into the very center of his heart.

K RELLIS CLOSED the back door of the Blue Lily and took a long breath. The marble theater was famous for the four pure blue marble columns of its façade. Ohndariens once congregated on her balcony during intermissions, sipping drinks and looking out over the bay. Nothing but water congregated there now.

Krellis shrugged his cloak up on his shoulders and stepped into the rain. The Zelani were useful, but they made his skin crawl. They were like rats that had suddenly multiplied, all of them little pieces of Victeris. The Zelani master had never been able to get his hooks into Krellis, but a crowd of rogue Zelani was certainly a double-edged blade to have in one's sheath. If they ever turned on him, it would be an ugly day.

The young magicians had taken over the theater and made it their home. Their leader, a handsome young man named Caleb, claimed that it appealed to their sense of the dramatic. Krellis hadn't been sure if it was a joke or not, so he didn't laugh.

The beautiful young people began preparing themselves for Krellis's plan before he even left the building, slowly slipping out of their clothes. They invited him to join them, but he had no stomach for the oversexed witches. Baelandra came immediately to mind, and he left them to their rituals. In truth, he didn't care if they flayed the skin from their bodies in preparation, so long as they were there when he needed them.

Krellis strode into the street. The alley between the theater and the restaurant next door was being resurfaced, leaving a smattering of muddy puddles between piles of new cobblestones.

The storm had not let up. Rain pelted him as his boots sloshed through the muck. His cowl sagged with the weight of the water. He stopped for a moment and stood in the middle of the alley, considering a return to Baelandra. He could tell her of his plans.

No. She had made her decision. She would rather die than be with him. She had been very clear on that point.

Krellis wiped the moisture from his beard, crossed the alley, and took refuge under a staircase. Let Baelandra hear from someone else how he had saved the city. When he ruled all of Ohndarien and Physendria, he would exile her. Let her live as a foreign oddity on the floating courts of the Summer Seas, passed from noble to noble until they tired of her, until they cast her aside like so much flotsam.

Krellis took a deep breath, and thoughts of Baelandra drifted away. The battle neared. He longed to cut a swath through his enemy. He longed for the divine joy of it, the fleeting feeling of immortality as other men died around him.

Krellis decided that he would produce no more heirs. Even if his plan went perfectly and he held the crown of Physendria, his line would die with him. He would rule long and well and let his family be remembered for that, not for the failings of his brothers and father. Yes, that was what—

Krellis winced at a sudden pain in the center of his chest. He massaged it, rubbing the hard point of his heartstone. The pain spread throughout his body as if the little diamond was on fire. He hissed, clutching his shirt. His muscles twitched, and he gritted his teeth. By the Nine, what was it?

Slowly the pain faded. Krellis looked up and saw a fully cloaked man standing in the center of the alley with a hand over his heart, mimicking him. Squinting, he watched the figure raise his fist higher, touch his forehead. The hand dropped suddenly to his side, fingers splayed open.

That was not a mocking gesture. It was a Kherish battle salute.

Scythe pushed his cowl back, and a curved sword slipped up between the folds of his cloak until the tip pointed at Krellis's chest.

"Is your conscience bothering you?" the Kherish assassin asked.

The pain had almost gone, but Krellis felt a strange hollowness inside.

"I told Baelandra that you escaped," Krellis said. "She didn't believe me."

"Then she is gaining wisdom at last."

"How did you do it?" Krellis asked, drawing his sword. The last time he'd seen the man, Scythe had been shackled to the back of a barred cell. "I told them to take no chances with you."

"Unlike Baelandra, I know what kind of man you are. I did not wait for an order I knew would come."

"So how did you do it?"

"Also unlike Baelandra, I do not consort with my enemies. I kill them."

Krellis laughed.

Scythe nodded. "That will be your last laugh." His voice was dead and even. "I've broken an oath for the second time in my life by coming here."

"Don't tell me you let a woman hold you back all these years." Krellis sneered, stepping out from under the staircase into the rain. He pushed back his own cowl, his fingers twitching against the cool metal of his sword's grip.

Scythe showed his teeth. "You need not worry about that anymore."

They slowly circled each other. Krellis's heavy boots pushed into the mud with each step while Scythe danced lightly around the puddles.

"You are undone," Scythe broke the silence.

"Not by you."

"No," he said. "I will take your life, but Brophy has already taken your heart."

Krellis's brow furrowed. "Brophy?"

"He returned to Ohndarien tonight, just as he promised he would. He entered the city through the water lift. I made certain the way was smooth for him, all the way to the Heart."

Krellis's free hand wanted to go to his chest, but he wouldn't give Scythe the satisfaction.

"The Heartstone has forsaken you, 'Brother,' " the assassin said. "Now, let's see what kind of man you are."

Krellis growled. "The fool boy is taking the Test alone?"

"Not such a fool," Scythe said. "Not such a boy. Not anymore."

"It doesn't matter. What has been lost can be retaken."

"Not this time."

Lightning flashed. Krellis roared and charged.

They met with a crash of blades.

23

"W̶E LOST the city when we lost the wall," the soldier in the hall-way said. The Silver Islander's thick accent was muffled by the distance and the door. From the number of boots that came up the stairs, Baelandra guessed there were at least four new-comers outside her door, possibly six. "Staying in a lost fight don't make you brave, it makes you dumb. An' after that, it makes you dead."

Baelandra kept her breathing even and steady, drawing on the exercises she had been practicing during her incarceration. If she stilled her body and her mind, she could make out the heated conversation going on right outside her door.

Krellis had left, and his soldiers were talking about deserting. Perhaps the coward had already fled into Faradan. Her breathing faltered, and the muffled voices disappeared. It didn't matter. Krellis was beyond her power now, but Ohndarien was not.

She calmed herself again and listened to the islander.

"Ohndarien's been a sweet whore t'me," the man said. "Don't mistake me. But I'm not chucking my life into th' gutter for a bunch a' Flowers. They're done. We won't last an hour when th' Snakes decide to attack. Now listen, Piggy. We all leave or we all stay. Can't leave a body behind to raise th' alarm. Everyone else is in. You're th' last one."

"We can't," Relf said. "Krellis will be back soon."

"The Brother's gone for good. He slapped his ass into a catapult and flew over th' walls. Or his Ohndarien witch-whores made him invisible, and they scurried away like a pack a' rats."

"Don't believe everything you hear," Relf said. "The Brother will kill us if we leave our posts."

"Why are you afraid a' one man when ten thousand are waiting in line ta kill you?"

"We can't go," Relf said. "Everyone hates a deserter."

"How you get so stupid, Piggy?" the Silver Islander spat. "I'm not going to ask you again."

"I know, but . . . Everyone hates a deserter," Relf said again.

There was a quick scuffle and a man's cry was cut off in a wet gurgle. Baelandra closed her eyes.

"What did you do that for?" another soldier demanded. "You said you were just going to scare him."

"Shut up, Finn. It's not my fault he's too dumb ta scare," the Silver Islander growled. "I won't see ten men gutted for one moron."

"You didn't have to kill him."

"That Piggy was gonna squeal. You want ta die 'fore we get out?"

Finn was quiet for a moment, then asked, "What do we do about the Sister?"

The islander chuckled. "Go kiss her if you like. She's already chained ta the wall."

"She's a Sister," Finn said.

"What are you, afraid a' royalty? Queens lie down as easy as whores, after you push their face into th' pillow. Do what you will, but I'm getting out of this city before dawn."

"I should at least unchain her," Finn said. "It's only right."

"You as dumb as Piggy? She'll sound th' alarm in a second." The Silver Islander snarled. "Now are you coming, or you want ta stay with your friend?"

"I'm coming."

The guards tromped down the steps. Baelandra listened until she was sure they were gone.

Flipping backward, she planted her feet against the headboard. She couldn't let the Physendrian soldiers find her like this, alone and chained to a wall.

Baelandra leaned back and pushed against the headboard with all her might, groaning as the metal dug into her wrists. The chains trembled as she strained against them, trying to rip her hands free. She soon became light-headed with the strain.

With a whimper, she fell back to the bed, breathing hard.

She cast about the room, and her gaze fell on the bowl of soup that Krellis left behind. Scuttling to the edge of her chains, she balanced on the edge of the bed and reached for the soup with her feet. Her toes fumbled against the table, an inch short. Taking a breath, she tried again, stretching her body out completely. The chains creaked tight, and she steadied her legs. Her toes touched the rim of the bowl. Carefully, she coaxed it to the edge of the table and cupped her feet underneath it.

Her stomach muscles trembled as she slowly brought the bowl closer. She set it on the bed and repositioned herself. She picked it up again and slowly leaned backward. Gripped between shaking toes, the bowl hovered over the manacles. She dumped the last of its contents, and the little bit of remaining stew dripped down her hands and forearms.

She dropped the bowl, and it tumbled off the bed. Baelandra worked her wrists back and forth, slicking them down with the greasy soup. Taking several deep breaths, she calmed herself. Then, with another quick flip, she spun around and slammed her feet against the headboard once more, yanking against the chains.

She wriggled her hands, trying to slip through the cuffs. Pain shot up her arms, but she ignored it, working her hands back and forth, back and forth. The chains shook.

Growling in frustration, Baelandra fell panting to the bed again. She thrashed, kicking and cursing Krellis's name. It was no use. The cuffs were barely wider than her wrists. She would have to break her hands to get them through.

Baelandra felt like she wanted to throw up. She wasn't sure if she could do this, but she had to try. Concentrating on her breathing, she slowed her chaotic thoughts. She thought again of her childhood, of the exercises they encouraged her to practice over and over. Meditation. It had been Baelandra's worst subject. She would need to separate herself from her body's needs and concerns. She must shut everything out except her one purpose.

The stone on her chest pulsed softly when she reached that calm state. She pulled all of the energy out of her hands. She made her hands weak and small, insignificant. They were a baby's hands.

She took all of that energy and sent it into her legs. They started trembling. Baelandra took a deep breath and launched herself backward, slamming her feet against the headboard. It cracked, and she screamed as she yanked her hands against the cuffs. Bones snapped, and both hands came free at once. She screamed and tumbled off the bed.

Baelandra gasped, tears welling in her eyes as she rolled to a sitting position. She cradled her ruined hands, biting back the pain. Both thumbs twisted toward the palm at an unnatural angle, and her wrists were smeared with blood.

She sat there for a moment, rocking back and forth. Using her heartstone, she stilled her mind again, sucking the pain into the stone, away from her hands.

When she opened her eyes and stood, her hands became dull, throbbing things. She flexed her fingers gently, but did not dare to move her thumbs. Gingerly opening the door to the room, she crept outside and down the hall.

Relf lay in a pool of his own blood. His glassy eyes stared unflinching at the ceiling.

Kneeling next to him, Baelandra gingerly undid his cloak. She banged her thumb against his brooch and curled over, gritting her teeth. When her head stopped swimming, she rose and draped the cloak over her shoulders.

She slipped out the door onto the landing. She hadn't seen such rain in a decade. The storm had raged all night, but it was finally breaking up, fading to an intermittent drizzle. Her bare feet slapped down the wet steps, and she ran into the flooded street, heading for the Blue Lily. Rallying the loyal Ohn-dariens would begin with the Zelani. Loyalty spread like wildfire whenever the sorcerers were around. She was almost there when she ran into a crowd of people gathered in the mouth of an alley.

Approaching slowly, Baelandra tucked her hands protectively inside the cloak and wormed her way through the crowd. The Zelani stood there, along with soldiers and many civilians.

Baelandra's heart skipped a beat, and a little gasp escaped her. Krellis's body lay in the mud in the center of the alleyway, his great woolly beard stained with blood. He was missing his sword hand. Several cuts striped his arms. The wound that had killed him was in the center of his chest, a deep red hole just beneath his ribs, near his heartstone.

It had been so easy to imagine him dead, imagine him suffering for the things he had done. It was different to see it in the flesh. Krellis had not lied. Against all odds, Scythe had escaped.

She slowly descended to her knees next to him.

"Oh Scythe," she murmured, bowing over Krellis's bloody body. "You have ended it at last."

Shaking her head, she threw back her cowl. A whisper went through the silent crowd as her long, auburn hair fell free, tumbling down her shoulders.

She pushed aside Krellis's shirt with her bloody fingers. His heartstone had gone dark. She would never feel that jolt again. She would never—

Baelandra sat up straight. The stone was empty and lifeless, but she did not feel that loss she had felt when Brydeon died. Her brother had been miles away, and she had known of his death, had felt it like something ripped from her chest. Yet Krellis lay here, and she had felt nothing.

Baelandra touched her own stone and it thrummed with life, if anything with more vigor than before. And that meant—

"Brophy," she murmured, standing up. She looked back at Krellis's body. Was it Brophy who had killed Krellis?

No. She would recognize Scythe's sword work anywhere. He always sliced off the weapon hand first. In Kherif it was a sign of contempt if a swordsman could take your hand before he took your life. But that meant Brophy was in the Heart. Had he taken the Test alone?

Someone grabbed her by the shoulder. "Sister, what should we—"

She shoved him aside, wincing as it jostled her tender hands. Dawn broke through the edge of the clouds, lighting the top of the Hall of Windows.

A signal horn split the silence.

Another horn followed, and another. Baelandra looked toward the sound. "What is it?" someone asked.

"It's the attack!" one of the soldiers shouted. "They're attacking. Run!"

The crowd began to break up. Some soldiers started toward the water, others paused.

"No!" Baelandra shouted. "Stop!" Most of the crowd stopped, looked back at her. A few continued on, disappearing down the alleys or side streets.

"We stand!" Baelandra said. "Ohndarien is our home! Will we let them take her without a fight?"

"We can't win," one of the soldiers said.

She ripped her dress open, exposing the heartstone that blazed between her breasts. Pain lanced through her tortured thumbs, but she steeled herself. "Ohndarien belongs to us!" she shouted. "We built her stone by stone. I will not abandon this city to some bloodthirsty king from the south!"

Many drew closer. The red glow of the stone reflected off their wet faces.

A handsome young man with short brown hair and dark eyes came forward. She recognized Shara's friend Caleb, one of the Zelani.

"Sister, Brother Krellis is dead. His soldiers are fleeing. We have no hope."

"No hope?" she said, walking in front of the motley group, looking into every eye. "The attack has begun, yes, but we are still here to meet it. You say the Brother of Autumn is dead, and I tell you he has risen! No prince from Physendria, but a true Child of the Seasons has claimed the stone."

A murmur ran through the soldiers and citizens alike. Baelandra listened for the one word that would complete her speech. Someone said, "Brophy?" and she jumped on it.

"Yes!" she shouted. "Brophy swore to return and put an end to Krellis, to put things to rights in Ohndarien, and I tell you he is here!"

"Is it true?" Caleb asked. "Has the Heir of Autumn returned?"

"Yes."

"And Shara-lani?"

"Is with him," she said, hoping it was true.

Caleb smiled. "Then we fight," he said. "I will not be the one to tell Shara I fled when she left us to defend the city."

"Nor I," said another Zelani.

The two words were repeated a dozen times as all of the Zelani said them.

"Ohndarien has never fallen, and she never will!" Baelandra shouted. "We will rally at the Wheel. Abandon the Night Market! Fall back to the Wheel!"

"Yes!" A soldier said, thrusting his spear into the air. A cheer went up from the other soldiers and citizens alike. "To the Wheel!"

As they began to move off, Baelandra turned to the Zelani's leader.

"Caleb," she said.

"Yes, Sister."

"Take your Zelani and spread out. Cover the island. Tell everyone. If they are running, let them run. If they are standing firm, get them up the stairs. Ohndariens defended the Wheel long before the walls were built. A few men can hold an army on that stairway if it is done properly. Get everyone there, and we will have a chance. Go now!"

Caleb turned to the other Zelani.

"Selese, you take the western tip of the Night Market. Gedge and Reela, southwestern. Bashtin and Baksin, go north . . ."

The young man glowed. Baelandra had to force herself not to be swept up by his words. One Zelani stayed to shepherd the crowd to the Wheel. The rest left to warn the other defenders.

In moments they were gone, and Baelandra stood alone in the middle of the muddy alley with Krellis sprawled at her feet. Horns sounded again in the distance, but when they ceased it was quiet. She looked down at Krellis, closed her eyes and said her last good-bye.

A footfall splashed behind her. She opened her eyes.

"I didn't think you would go far," she said, turning.

Scythe stood behind her, half of his cloak thrown open, exposing his sword arm. "You should take your own advice and get to the Wheel."

Silence fell between them.

His shoulder hidden under the cloak slumped a little lower than the other.

"Are you wounded?" she asked.

"I can fight," he said.

"Of course," she whispered, then cleared her throat and spoke louder. "You always could."

"And you?" He nodded at her hands.

She brought them up for him to see. Her twisted thumbs were swollen and turning purple. "I will not hold a sword, if that's what you're asking. But I will fight to my last breath."

A flicker of a smile lit his stern features.

She watched his face in the pale red glow of her heartstone.

"I should have let you kill him years ago."

"Yes, you should."

"But I couldn't."

"I know," Scythe said. "I should have broken my oath years ago."

She nodded.

"But I couldn't," he said softly.

"Scythe, you have already given so much without receiving anything in return. I've given you no reason to love me, no reason to give your life for this city, but Ohndarien will need you in the coming fight. Can you forgive a foolish woman?"

He reached out a hand, darkly tanned and striped with blood. The hand of a lifelong warrior. He cradled her ravaged fingers, and his smile returned.

"You deserve nothing less."

24

SHARA RAN toward the Market Bridge in the uniform of a Physendrian Falcon officer. Her feathered cape fluttered behind her, and any who saw her stepped aside. She dodged her way through the Croc pikemen, with their thick green shoulder armor and long pikes, through the Scorpion foot soldiers, with their short spears and pincer shields, through the

Serpent soldiers, lightly plated in green-enameled armor, standing in perfect lines.

The Serpents were the best trained, the most deadly, and they seemed to go on forever. They fought like a moving wall, short swords slashing through the spaces between their line of shields. Shara's glamour made her invisible to all of them. They saw an officer in a hurry and moved aside.

Lewlem's men rowed her through the storm, and they reached the logjam in the Narrows just after dawn. They set her ashore, and she entered the city from the north, climbing an abandoned Farad siege tower. She had stolen the feathered cloak and scepter from a dead officer on Stoneside. Once she had them, it was easy to supplement the disguise with her glamour. She slipped through the Physendrian army all the way across the Long Market.

Phandir's troops had lashed an emergency bridge made of heavy rope and wooden planking to the shattered remains of the Market Bridge. The Night Market lay undefended, completely overrun with Physendrians.

The foreign army bunched at the base of the Wheel, where the Ohndariens fought like badgers backed into a hole. The curving staircase was packed with attackers, trying to reach the top of the plateau, but the long line of soldiers was jammed. They could not move forward.

Squads of Jackals, poorly trained draftees, wearing nothing more than rags, threw ladder after ladder against the edge of the Wheel. The Jumping Rats, bearing bows decorated with dead rats, loosed arrows at the defenders on the lip of the Wheel. As Shara ran up, a defender screamed and fell from the plateau into the seething mass of Physendrians.

Dozens of Serpents and Crocs streamed up the ladders, and dozens died, falling with arrows sticking out of them. One lucky Serpent actually made it to the top. He was quickly cut down in a flash of swords and spears.

"You! Falcon!"

Shara looked to her right. A Lion general beckoned to her. Reluctantly, she went to him. He was flanked by two Ape guards, huge and stoic. Their long swords hung heavy at their hips, and they watched everything with a cold stare, as the battle raged around them.

"Take this lance of Crocs to the northern side," he growled. "We need to draw some of those Ohndarien dogs away from the main assault."

One of the Ape guards eyed her strangely. She returned his gaze and let her magic flow into him. He looked back at the carnage without a word.

"Yes, sir," she said.

Shara left the Lion, ignoring his orders and heading into the thick of the battle. She heard a voice rise above the din. She peered to the top of the wall.

A thin woman with a bow in hand shouted commands to the Ohndarien defenders. Vallia wore a white leather vest cut low between her breasts, and a blinding light blazed forth from her chest.

Shara looked for the best way to get to the top of the Wheel, but that was what every Physendrian soldier wanted to do. The men trapped on the stairway jostled one another as defenders hurled rocks from above. As she watched, a rock the size of her head sailed over the edge of the plateau, crushing a Jackal's skull and sweeping two Crocs over the edge of the stairway.

She could never make it up that way. Spinning around, she looked to the ladders.

A throng of Serpents clung to a ladder near her, trying to make the top. Vallia shouted again and a rain of arrows decimated the Serpents, who plummeted to the base of the Wheel. Two crested the plateau and fought valiantly for a few moments before three Ohndarien spearmen skewered them and sent them over the edge.

A cluster of Jackals carrying a dozen ladders over their heads shoved their way to the front of the battle.

"Let them through!" the general shouted.

The draftees charged the cliff and threw all the ladders up at once. Ohndarien defenders rushed forward with forked sticks, pushing at the ladders. The Lion commander bellowed again, and two ranks of Rat archers shot a volley of arrows at the defenders. A squad of Serpents scrambled for the ladders. Shara charged forward, grabbing one of their arms. The Serpent tried to shrug her off, but she caught his gaze.

"Let me go first," she said.

The frightened young swordsman nodded and let her go ahead of him. Scrambling onto the wooden ladder, she flew up the rungs. The ladder next to her was pushed sideways and fell to the ground amidst shouts and screams. An Ohndarien defender plummeted past her, an arrow in his neck.

An arrow whistled past Shara's ear. She clenched her teeth, kept her breathing steady, and continued climbing. She was almost to the top when a woman with a long, gray braid and a forked stick jammed it against the top rung of the ladder. It wobbled, teetering. Shara clung to the rungs. The defender shifted her grip on the stick and prepared to shove it over.

"Wait!" Shara shouted.

The gray-haired woman froze, gazing at her. Bile rose in Shara's throat, but she forced it down. Her ladder thunked back against the edge of the cliff. Ladders to the left and right of her crashed to the ground. Only Shara's remained upright. The Physendrians clambered up behind her.

"Stop!" she shouted. Her magic flowed into them, and they hesitated.

"Loose!" A Falcon officer boomed from below.

Suddenly the air was filled with Physendrian arrows.

"Duck!" Shara yelled at the gray-haired woman she had manipulated. The defender threw herself to the ground and shafts flew overhead to clatter against the plateau all around her.

Shara scrambled to the top of the ladder and leapt onto the Wheel. She and the woman faced one another on the ground, no more than a foot apart. The gray-haired woman was shaking and had tears in her eyes. She gripped her stick with white knuckles.

Shara breathed deeply, letting her attention flow into the frightened old woman. "You are brave. You are fast. You are stronger than you ever believed possible," she murmured. A joyous tingle replaced the nausea.

The woman's eyes glistened, and she set her jaw. With a scream, she launched herself at the ladder just as a Serpent's head appeared. She smashed the forked stick straight into his face and pushed. The soldier clung to the ladder, sending it crashing to the ground far below. The gray-haired woman charged the next ladder, where three more Physendrians had already gained the plateau. A handful of uniformed soldiers shouted and rushed over, flanked by a crowd of citizens wielding homemade spears and clubs. A potbellied butcher swung a cleaver into one of the Serpents.

Shara rolled to her feet and saw Vallia, still bellowing orders in an inhumanly loud voice, her heartstone shining like a star on her chest. The Sister of Winter picked up a Physendrian arrow, nocked it in her bow, and sent it flying back at the army. A spearman screamed and fell to one knee, clutching his thigh.

Stripping off her feather cloak, Shara rushed over.

"Vallia!"

The Sister of Winter turned. They both crouched underneath another volley of arrows. "Shara," she said. "You have returned." Her normal speaking voice was just the same as always, quiet and contained, though she panted as she spoke.

"Have you seen Brophy?" Shara asked.

Vallia shook her head, grabbed an arrow and nocked it. "At once," she shouted to her archers. "Aim for the Falcon's head!" She let loose. The officer below dove for cover behind his men.

"What about Baelandra?" Shara asked.

Quick as a breath, Vallia nocked and shot again, then crouched. She tipped her chin toward the other side of the Wheel. "She was on the stairs when I last saw her. With Scythe." She stood, and yelled, "Again!" before letting her deadly arrow fly to its mark. This time the Falcon went down.

As Shara ran across the Wheel, her feet sank into the deep mud between the marble paths. She neared the Hall of Windows and saw more dead and wounded laid out at the base of the dome. Harried old women and young children attended to them. One man with a nasty head wound begged for water.

Shara passed a young man who shouted, thrashing on the ground as a woman in a blood-spattered apron tried to calm him down. "Get it off my leg!" he cried. There was nothing on the young soldier's leg. It was missing from the knee down.

Shara reached the far side of the Wheel. Rocks had been piled along the rim by the stairs, and dozens of defenders lined the edge, flinging the stones down on the enemy. She rushed to them and looked over.

"By the Seasons," she murmured. Hundreds of Physendrians were crammed onto the stairs. Scythe held them at bay, his sword hovering in front of them. The attackers held back, reluctant to engage him. Three bodies lay sprawled on the steps in front of the Kherish assassin and none of the Crocs, Scorpions, or Serpents seemed ready to leap over and be the first to face his bloody blade.

Scythe's clothes were stained red, and he frowned in concentration as he waited. Baelandra stood beside him, teetering on the edge of the stairs. The bare-breasted Sister held a six-foot-tall bronze shield, protecting Scythe from the archers below. Her heartstone splashed crimson light over the battle.

"Loose!" a voice shouted from below.

A wave of arrows flew at them. They clacked against the side of the plateau or clanged against her immense shield. Baelandra held her hands strangely, as if they had been cut or broken.

"Forward, you shivering maggots! Stay together! I want his liver on a plate!" a Physendrian officer roared.

Four Scorpion spearmen ringed by tall shields marched to the front of the crammed stairway, pushing all others aside. A Rat fell off the staircase, screaming. Two Crocs and a Serpent fell back, pushing themselves against the side of the plateau as the heavily armored spearmen moved forward. Scythe danced toward them. Spinning, he hacked through the shaft of a spear and caught the lip of one shield, flipping it open.

Before the Scorpion could close the gap, Scythe slipped under two spears and cut the man down. The soldier screamed and collapsed on the stairs.

Scythe danced back just as a flight of arrows whistled past him. Baelandra jumped forward and blocked the missiles.

Panting, Scythe beckoned the rest with a nod of his head, but no one wanted to fight the man.

A Serpent was thrust to the forefront by his fellows. His blade rang against Scythe's once, twice, but not a third time. The Serpent missed his parry and Scythe slashed him through the stomach. Three more swordsmen scrambled over the bodies, trying to take Scythe in a rush. The Kher backed up a step, parrying furiously. One of them made a desperate lunge. Scythe stepped back, kicked the man's knee out. The Serpent screamed and crumpled to the stairs. Sweat and blood dripped from Scythe's face as he parried the other two. He backed up another step, and the throng pressed forward again. He only had twenty steps left to go. Once he reached the top, he would never be able to hold them all back.

Shara moved among the rock-tossing Ohndariens, whispering to them one after the other.

"Your aim is deadly," she said to a teenage boy. The boy squinted and hurled his stone. It cracked off the head of a Croc, who disappeared into the swarming mass.

"You kill with every throw," Shara said to the boy's mother, who fought next to him. The woman raised a huge stone over her head and brained an officer fifteen feet below.

Shara spent another few precious moments bolstering the abilities of the defenders, then ran to the Heart. The Physendrians were endless. Ohndarien's defenders would run out of rocks long before the Physendrians ran out of heads to crush. They needed every advantage they could get. They needed Brophy. She needed Brophy.

And he needed her.

Shara raced down the marble path, sprinting for the Hall of Windows.

25

BROPHY'S EYELIDS FLUTTERED.

He drew a sharp breath and rolled over on his back. The stalactites of the natural cavern glowed with a dim, shifting light, and the Heartstone's song filled his mind. She did not speak in words, did not think in words. Each note was an image, a vision portrayed in bright colors.

The walls of Ohndarien rose brick by brick, built by the labor of hundreds of people in love with a dream. Brophy's mother strained, her face beaded with sweat as she gave birth to a squalling baby boy. A teenage Baelandra screamed, holding a hand in front of herself as she took the Test of the Stone. Brophy's father turned and looked back at the Windmill Wall as he sailed away, the sea shimmering behind him and sunlight catching his red hair. Shara and Brophy slept arm in arm on a tiny cot in a torchlit room. Krellis snarled, in the rain, clutching a fist to his chest.

Brophy blinked again. He sat up, looked down at his arms. The infection was gone, the inky tendrils had vanished. He was free of it, free and whole once again. He craned his neck down to look down at his chest. The red diamond blazed within his flesh, lighting the darkness. He was the Brother of Autumn. For the first time since Trent died, he knew exactly what he must do.

His father's sword lay beside him, the pommel pulsing in time with the gem on his chest. Not his father's sword anymore. His sword. The Sword of Autumn belonged to the Brother. He picked it up, and the red diamond flashed.

He sheathed it and turned to the Heartstone. The lumpy, misshapen crystal contained a storm of chaotic hues rolling and twisting around each other. She still sat atop the stalagmite that had been cut and polished to create a pedestal. Brophy had expected a monolith of diamond as tall as a man, exquisitely proportioned, the precious gem at the center of Ohndarien, the jewel of the known world. But the Heartstone was in her natural state, unshaped and unpolished. Her surface was covered with long chips and scars where she had given up pieces of herself to her family. The Heartstone wasn't a piece of jewelry to reflect light and twinkle with an imagined perfection. She was like a person, rough, scarred, imperfect, and achingly beautiful.

Brophy placed his hand on the stone and felt a rush of love flow through him. The colors swirled brighter near his hand. He traced the gouges and scrapes on the Heartstone's surface, and she glowed in response. She had seen him at his very worst. He remembered every moment of his nightmare journey to her chamber. Thank the Seasons that Medew had been so swift, so nimble in the twisting passages. If he had caught her and the child, he could never have stopped himself. His face burned with shame, but the emotion fled quickly, flowing down his arm and disappearing into the stone.

The Heartstone knew him better than he knew himself. Every petty and spiteful thing he had ever done was laid bare, just as every moment of love, tenderness, and joy had been relived in heartbreaking detail. Her song flowed into his mind, incessant and determined.

"Yes," he murmured. "I know." He could rest no longer. He must go. A lump caught in his throat, and he swallowed it down. Every joy had its price. He just hadn't expected it to be so high.

A sad smile came to his lips. But he could not complain. The path she had shown him was better than he thought possible. Putting both hands on the stone, he held on to her as though he would be swept away. Gently, he lifted the Heartstone from the place she had rested for three hundred years and tucked her under his arm.

Brophy left the chamber and ran down the tunnels, the Heartstone lighting his way with an array of colors. He felt the twists and turns like the veins in his own body. Even without the light, he would know which way to go.

As he neared the exit, he saw a lantern bobbing in the passage ahead.

"Brophy? Is that you?" Shara called.

"Shara!"

They rushed together, embracing, kissing. She clung to him, burying her face in his neck for one sweet instant. He closed his eyes. Surely he could spend one second, just one more blessed moment with her. Her lips felt like velvet against his neck. He took a deep breath of her hair. She smelled of salt spray and sweat, and that little bit of sweet fragrance that was Shara's alone. Far too soon, he let her go.

I'm going to miss you, he thought. You more than anything else.

Shara backed up and touched the Heartstone. "Is that—?"

"Yes."

"What are you doing?"

"What must be done."

Her brow furrowed. She searched his eyes in the strange light. "Brophy, what's wrong—?"

"Not now," he said, shaking his head. "We don't have time."

"Tell me what's wrong." She put a light hand on his arm.

"The Test was . . . hard," he said, his heart twisting with the lie. But he couldn't risk the truth, not until the final moments. They must trust him as he trusted the Heartstone.

"You're the Brother of Autumn?"

He nodded. "Perhaps I will warrant a Zelani now," he said, smirking, trying to steer away from deeper emotions. He had a brief vision of Shara ducking under the low lintel of a simple hut, cradling a squalling baby, their baby. The Heartstone had shown him that, too. There was no deception in her, only possibilities and choices. They could still flee the city, live their lives together in the Vastness, but Brophy had made his choice.

"The corruption. Did you—?"

"It's gone."

"So you can remove it!" The joy in her voice almost made him cry.

"Yes."

"Then we've got to get you to the baby. Come on." She grabbed his arm and pulled him down the tunnel. "Medew is this way."

"What about Baelandra. Did Medew find her?"

Shara shook her head. "The city is falling," she said. "Baelandra is somewhere up there in the middle of it. I believe the Ohohhim will counterattack soon. Lewlem doesn't have time to wait. If the city falls, the Emperor might never be cured. We have to hold the Physendrians back until they arrive."

Or we could run away, Brophy thought again, seeing that fading future for one more moment, that little hut and Shara's smile as she held their black-haired, green-eyed child.

"I know," he said.

"You . . ." she looked at him again, placed her palm on his cheek. "What's wrong? What's different?"

He must be careful. If he let her, she would read everything in his eyes. His heartstone would block her powers, but only if he was careful. He forced a smile and closed his heart to her. "We have to hurry," he said.

"Yes." She grabbed his hand, and they ran down the tunnel. "Hazel let me in. She's wounded."

They ran through a torchlit cavern full of empty crates and discarded bedrolls. Shara headed straight for a cramped staircase, and he followed her up. Moments later he saw natural light up ahead, just beyond the doorway to the antechamber beneath the Hall of Windows.

Hazel lay crumpled at the bottom of the ladder as though she had fallen there. Mother Lewlem knelt beside the Sister, comforting her with her free hand while the other constantly turned the handle of the music box.

Brophy met Medew's eyes, wanting to apologize, but knowing there was no time. She gave him a curt nod and looked back down at Hazel.

The sister's belly had been sliced open. Blood soaked her yellow dress all the way to her knees. Brophy looked back at Medew.

She shook her head. "This woman will not live."

"Brophy . . ." Hazel said weakly, her blue eyes flickering open. "You came back to us." He knelt next to her, took her pudgy hand.

"Sister."

"The Wheel is lost," she croaked. "They have broken through every-where."

"No!" Shara cried.

Brophy nodded. "Where is Bae? Where are the other Sisters? I need their help."

Hazel opened her mouth to speak, but blood came up instead. Weakly, she pointed up to the square of light at the top of the ladder. She slumped back, her breathing ragged.

"May the Seasons take you to the land where the sky is beautiful and bright, where winter does not freeze and summer does not burn," Brophy murmured, touching Hazel's golden hair.

Brophy's gaze locked on the baby. Her eyes moved madly underneath their lids. Her face was completely black and scaly, lost to the corruption. Lit-tle yellow fangs poked out from her lips.

"I'll go find Bae," Shara said quickly.

"No," Brophy said. "We stay together. I need you close."

Shara stopped, her eyes wide at his deep voice. "All right."

"Will you follow us, Mother?" he asked of Medew. "There is something we must do before I can heal the baby." She nodded, laying her free hand on the Sword of Winter at her hip.

Brophy tucked the Heartstone under his arm and clambered up the lad-der. Shara and Medew followed.

They emerged into the Hall of Windows. It was filled with Ohndariens. They huddled in the aisles, between the columns, by the stained-glass walls, each of them clenching a dagger, a sword, a spear or pitchfork. He heard the clang and crash of battle outside. A single scream split the air.

At the Summer Gate, three spearmen held the Physendrians back, using tall shields to protect themselves. At the Autumn Gate, Master Gorlym and another man swung their swords like madmen.

Physendrians swarmed the Spring Gate. They rushed through the gap and were met by a rain of arrows from the dais in the center of the Hall. The invaders toppled over, and Ohndarien defenders leapt to fill the gap.

Baelandra stood beside Scythe, who held the Winter Gate on his own. Unlike the attackers at the other three gates, the Physendrians at the Winter Gate were reluctant to engage the Kherish swordsman. Brophy's plan solidified in his mind. He would need them both.

"Scythe! Bae!" Brophy pushed his way through the crowd.

Baelandra turned to see him, though Scythe remained focused on his grisly task.

"Brophy!" his aunt shouted.

A Scorpion lunged bravely, trying to bowl into Scythe using his body. The Kher spun, his sword a blur. His attacker grunted and crumpled to the ground. Brophy could not see where Scythe had cut him, but the soldier did not get up again. Two Serpents shouted and rushed forward to take Scythe while he was off-balance.

Except Scythe was not off-balance. One of the soldiers screamed as Scythe's sword slashed through his arm and neck. The other fell back, gagging on an Ohndarien arrow that suddenly quivered in his throat.

Baelandra and Scythe fell back. Four Ohndarien soldiers rushed forward and took Scythe's place, pushing back the tide.

Brophy ran to meet them halfway up the stairs. Bae was flecked with blood, and Scythe looked like he had bathed in it. Bae's hands were twisted and swollen and Scythe limped, one arm tucked at his side.

"Brophy!" Bae breathed, falling into him. She held a huge shield on one arm, but she wrapped her other arm around his neck. "It is so good to see you, even at the last—" She stopped, looked down at the Heartstone he carried.

"What have you done?" she asked, bewildered. She saw Mother Lewlem slowly turning the music box, the sling around her neck. Baelandra paled and stepped away from her. The music box sang its child's tune.

"Brophy no!" she shouted. "You didn't bring her here!"

"Yes," he said, looking directly in Baelandra's eyes. He grasped her shoulder with his free hand. The gem on his chest flashed red. "I need you to follow me, Bae. I need you to follow and not ask questions."

"Brophy—" she began, glancing again at the stone on his chest.

He gave her a tight smile. "Ohndarien is not finished yet," he said. "Come on. Stay close."

Brophy turned and ran for the edge of the hall. Shara and Lewlem's wife jumped to follow. Baelandra hesitated, then jogged after as fast as she could. Scythe limped behind without a word. Brophy took the amphitheater steps two at a time as the others struggled to keep up.

He broke into a sprint as he neared the stained-glass wall, put his shoulder down, and slammed into it. Glass shattered all around him. Brophy stumbled outside, ripping away the lattice of copper and colored glass that clung to him like a fishing net.

Physendrian soldiers were everywhere, hacking down stragglers, killing the wounded. A group of Rats ripped the shirt from a screaming Ohndarien woman and forced her to the ground.

Brophy leapt onto the steps carved into the support arch, and Shara stayed right behind him.

"Brophy!" she yelled. "What are you doing?"

He could feel her presence questing at his thoughts, lightly, lovingly. He shut her out. "Trust me, Shara," he murmured, knowing she would hear him over the din of the battle below. "Stay close. I need you close."

Brophy ran up the curving slope of the dome. Shara and Lewlem's wife stayed right behind him. Baelandra and Scythe labored up the steps, falling steadily behind. Brophy neared the top and turned. He let some of his fervor flow to them through his heartstone. He would need them. They must be strong.

He looked out over Ohndarien. She was in flames. Buildings burned throughout the Night Market. Smoke coiled up into the sky, becoming one with the dark clouds. Physendrians crawled through his beloved city like ants. Bodies, Physendrian and Ohndarien, littered the plateau of the Wheel. The wails of the wounded and dying had become a horrific chorus. Brophy tore his gaze away.

"Shara, Medew," he said, setting the Heartstone on the ground between his feet. "Hang on to me. No matter what happens, do not let go." Lewlem's wife pinched his ragged sleeve. Shara touched his shoulder.

"Brophy—"

He gave one terse shake of his head. She fell silent. Baelandra and Scythe caught up with them.

Baelandra panted. "Brophy, you must tell me what you are—"

"Not now!"

She sucked in a breath. Brophy turned his hip toward Scythe. "Take my sword," he said.

Scythe hesitated, glancing at the pulsing red stone on the sword's pommel. Brophy nodded. "You will need it," he continued. "I'll be with you. I'll help you if I can."

The Kherish assassin met Brophy's eyes. He reached out and unsheathed the sword. The red diamond flared, and the fleeting vision from Brophy's childhood flashed through his mind. All the pieces were in place, just not as he had expected them to be. But the moment had come, and Brophy felt the hand of fate all around him.

"Bae," he said, "grab on to Scythe. Don't let go, no matter what happens." Brophy turned away from them. He must trust them now, as they trusted him.

I love you, he thought. His mouth formed the words, but he felt cold. He thought he felt Shara squeeze his shoulder. Had he said it aloud?

Ohndarien stretched out before him, quickly disappearing beneath the billowing smoke. He remembered the city as she should be, as he had fallen in love with her, with her lights gleaming like jewels. With her sultry Night Market and lively Long Market. With the Citadel rising like a dark protector on the horizon, with life and prosperity flowing through her locks. With the Heartstone at the center of it all, beating steadily.

The fight for the plateau was over. Only the Hall of Windows resisted Physendria now. A pack of Ape guards in tight procession appeared around a cluster of burning trees, moving closer. Brophy paused, watching. Phandir emerged behind the Apes, resplendent in his golden breastplate and crimson-feathered crown. Ossamyr walked next to him, radiant in her gown of fiery feathers.

Brophy's sight had never been so clear. Even from this lofty height, he saw every curl of copper in Phandir's beard, saw the lines at the edges of Ossamyr's eyes, those lovable lines he had kissed once upon a time.

Now, he said to himself. It must be now or I will never do this thing.

Brophy yanked the music box away from Lewlem's wife. The sling tipped and the baby tumbled out, but Medew caught her before she hit the ground. The music stopped.

He hurled the box at Phandir.

"Brophy, no!" Shara screamed, lunging forward to grab it, but it sailed beyond her reach. He caught her arm before she slipped. "Brophy!" she yelled.

He pulled her back, crushed her to his chest as the box flew through the air. "Stay close, my love," he murmured into her hair. "I need you close."

The box shattered at Phandir's feet, silver twisting, gears and wheels skittering across the stone.

"Hold tight to me," he said louder, as he set Shara on her feet. He scooped the baby out of Medew's arms.

The child scrunched up her face, her little fists flailing weakly. She rubbed her blackened eyes and yawned. Her tiny fangs shone in the light.

Brophy raised the child over his head, facing Phandir's entourage. The King of Physendria looked up and pointed. Phandir said something to Ossamyr and laughed at his own joke. The queen's eyes went wide. She shouted to Brophy. He could see her perfectly, her ruby lips, her large eyes, her dark skin, but he could not hear what she said.

With a kick of her little legs and a plaintive cry, the baby opened her eyes.

26

SHARA SCREAMED and fell to her knees, clinging desperately to Brophy's leg. She closed her eyes as a howling wind spun past, pushing them this way and that. A thousand separate screams of terror were carried upon that wind. Shara's voice was lost in the ocean of suffering, but she couldn't stop yelling, couldn't take a breath.

Brophy turned in a slow circle. Shara and Medew stumbled with him. If they stopped touching him, they were lost.

Shara put her fist to her head. The screams wanted in, they clawed at her eyelids, her lips, at the tips of her ears. It was like being touched by a hoard of Victerises everywhere at once, but Brophy held the chaos at bay. Through her closed eyes, she could feel his heartstone shining like a red beacon.

Slowly, the screams faded, echoing off the distant walls. Shara realized she had stopped shouting. The absolute silence terrified her more than the screaming. It was as though the soul had been ripped from the world.

Shara opened her eyes and stared at the city. A seething wind whipped around them, threatening to knock them off the stairs. Dark clouds roiled and spun overhead, blotting out the sky.

She looked down to the Wheel below. Physendrian soldiers twitched and flailed their limbs. They scrabbled across the ground like wounded crabs, tearing at their clothes, at their faces.

The infant began crying. Shara looked up at Brophy. He stared unblinking at the city below, mouth open, arms down, barely holding on to the baby.

The child drew a shuddering breath and wailed again. Brophy shook his head, looked down, and brought her to his chest. He cradled her there, slowly turned to look at Shara.

"We have to hurry," he murmured, as though sleepwalking. The baby balled her fists and screamed. Little tears beaded at the corners of her eyes. Medew was on her hands and knees, staring down, panting as if she were going to throw up. Baelandra and Scythe clung to one another on the steps, shaking in the aftermath.

"We are lost . . ." Baelandra mumbled, her head twitching. At the base of the steps, a mottled, long-limbed creature flipped to its feet, scratching claws along the stone. It ripped a Serpent helmet from its head and shook its body like a wet dog. Turning its muzzle skyward, it howled. Other animal cries rose all over the city.

The creature looked up at them with glowing red eyes and began climbing. Bloody saliva dripped from its mouth. Behind it on the courtyard below, a grotesquely enlarged man with bladelike claws leapt upon a misshapen beast that had fallen on all fours. The clawed man tore bloody chunks from the other beast.

Shara turned around, watching all of the corrupted people rise and roar. The battle lines had disappeared. Ohndariens turned on Ohndariens. Jackal fought Ape fought Serpent. Swords clashed and claws ripped.

"Shara." Brophy's steady voice broke her away from the grisly sight. "Bae. I'm going to need you both. Scythe, you must protect us as long as you can. The corrupted will come for us. They feel us, hate us. Mother Lewlem," he said, holding out the baby, "please watch over her. I don't want anything to happen to her. She's been through enough."

Lewlem's wife took the baby in shaky arms, held her tightly. The child continued crying.

The long-limbed howler finally reached them, scrambling up the staircase like a ladder. Scythe leapt in front of it. The Sword of Autumn flared, and he hacked through its arm. It clawed at him with its other arm, never noticing the missing limb. Scythe blocked the strike with his sword and sliced open its belly.

The howler fell upon the Kherish assassin, snapping its jaws at his neck.

He cried out and backpedaled, bringing the Sword of Autumn down on its head. The blade cleaved through the creature's skull, spilling brains onto the landing. Still it came on, biting into Scythe's leg. He growled through clenched teeth.

Medew leapt forward, hacking into the monster's back with the Sword of Winter. With two quick strikes she severed it in half. Its legs slid away, bouncing down the stairs. Scythe yanked himself free. With his other foot, he kicked the beast. It slipped down a half dozen steps, holding on with its one remaining arm. Medew severed its hand, and it tumbled down the steps out of sight.

Brophy reached down and picked up the Heartstone. It swirled with rainbow colors, the only spot of light under a dark sky.

A spiny man crawled like a spider up the steps toward Scythe. Light and quick, the creature feinted left and came right. Scythe barely dodged and slipped on the bloody steps. He spun away as the man-spider lashed out, raking his ribs with long claws.

With a grunt, Scythe raised the Sword of Autumn overhead and hacked into the monster's shoulder, narrowly missing its neck. It hissed, snapped at Scythe's face.

The Kher jerked back, escaping the fangs by inches and rolling to his feet. The thing leapt straight into the air and sailed over Scythe. He shouted, but his sword flashed in the light. The beast crashed to the landing, missing a leg. Scythe stepped forward and hacked its head off. It thrashed as the head bounced off the landing and thumped out of sight.

Scythe kicked the blind body after, then stood breathing hard, his eyes wild.

"Brophy, what have you done?" Baelandra said, her eyes wide and her auburn hair a twisted tangle.

"Bae, please. You've trusted me this far, trust me one step further. We need to do this together as Brother and Sister. We need to take everything I have loosed and put it back into the Heartstone, like sucking the poison from a wound."

Baelandra shook her head, her gaze going out to the snarling city. "Are you sure? There are so many of them, Brophy, how can we help them all?"

"They will help themselves. Those who hate the corruption will fight it."

"They don't seem to hate it, they seem to love it."

"Some will be seduced by the darkness. We just have to hope there are a lot more of us than them when it's done." He sat down cross-legged in the center of the landing, setting the Heartstone between his legs.

"Show me," she said. She sat down opposite him, put her swollen hands on the diamond.

"Brophy, let me help," Shara offered, kneeling next to them. Brophy's distant gaze refocused on her. He looked into her eyes and smiled, beckoned her closer. She leaned in, and he kissed her.

"Thank you, Shara. For everything."

"Brophy, please . . . How can I help?"

"Your part is the most important. Find your breath. Gather your magic. I will tell you when."

"What am I to do?"

His hand lingered on her cheek, then slid off. "I will tell you when."

Another monster charged up the stairway. Its grotesque head grew two faces, and two extra arms sprouted from its ribs. It keened like the wind, charging for Scythe. He twisted to the side, drove his sword through the thing's guts. It screamed and slashed him across the neck. With a gasp, Scythe went to one knee.

Medew darted in, spearing the two-faced monster through the eye with the Sword of Winter. With a gurgling growl, it charged at her. She danced back lightly, keeping her footing, the baby cradled in the sling. The monster charged past her off the edge of the stairs. The glass shattered, and it plummeted into the Hall of Windows.

Brophy and Baelandra leaned forward, their fingers overlapping on top of the Heartstone. Brophy nodded. He started chanting, barely louder than a whisper.

"What are you doing?" Baelandra asked.

"Listen to her song," Brophy said. "Sing with her."

Baelandra nodded, and the two of them began to sing.

"Can you feel it?" Brophy asked.

"By the Seasons! It's everywhere, all around us."

"That's the black emmeria. Pull it into the stone. Draw it in with every note."

"I can't. It's horrible."

"Give it to the Heartstone, let it flow through you."

They continued to sing with their eyes closed. Baelandra calmed as her voice grew louder. Her crippled hands relaxed and pressed against the Heartstone. Brophy's eyebrows furrowed in concentration. His blond curls whipped around him as the furious wind blew straight through him, disappearing into the Heartstone.

Shara cycled through her breaths, taking herself from the first gate to the fifth in moments. Her power hovered about her like the air before a lightning storm. She longed to use it to help Scythe and Medew, but she waited for Brophy's signal.

The wind roared toward them from every direction. The swirling colors in the Heartstone slowed, then dulled. They became lighter and lighter shades of the rainbow, fading to gray.

Another creature slowly approached Scythe on all fours. Thick, stiff hair burst from one side of its neck. Its ears had become thin and pointed at the top, thrusting through a mane of wild brown hair. Its eyes shimmered like gold coins. Letting out a purr, it skittered closer and stopped. Its claws clicked on the stone.

Scythe pointed the Sword of Autumn at its nose. Its head twitched as though it had heard something, and it let out a thin mewl, looking frantically at the sky. Its ears drew closer to its head, shortening and rounding out. A howling gust of wind flew out of the creature's mouth. Its eyes lost their metallic luster. The bristle of fur grew backward, pulling into its neck and disappearing. Claws retracted and became fingers.

The corruption fled and the creature became a woman. Bewildered, she slipped and began to fall down the stairs. Scythe reached out and caught her hand.

"Climb," he said. "You are safe now." Sobbing, she scurried past him and crouched at the far corner of the landing, staring at them all with wide eyes.

The noise of the city changed. The clash of swords continued, but the snarl of corrupted creatures was met with the shouts of people. Those who had expelled the corruption in themselves now fought for their lives against those who had embraced it.

"Too much!" Bae shouted. The Heartstone had darkened, swirling with an inky blackness.

"I know," Brophy intoned. "Keep going."

"We can't—!"

"Keep going."

The Heartstone trembled.

"Brophy!" Baelandra shouted. "You'll destroy it!"

Brophy opened his eyes and took his hands off the Heartstone. "No. I won't."

"We can't put any more in. It will shatter, and everything will escape."

"I know." Brophy paused, looked at Shara, then back at Baelandra. "I'm going to take it into myself. I'll hold it as the baby did before."

"What?" Baelandra shouted.

"No!" Shara's breath caught in her throat. She reached for the Heartstone, trying to take it away from him. She began crying. "Brophy, please. We'll use . . ."

"We'll use what? The baby? No. This is my path. I will follow it to the end."

"You don't know what you are doing!"

"Shhhh . . ." He put a gentle finger on her lips. "Don't fight me. Help me. I can't do it alone."

Tears streamed down Shara's face. Baelandra was crying, too. "No, Brophy," she said. "I will do it. Let me do it."

He shook his head. "The Heartstone chose me. I've known I was meant for this since I was a boy. Just do as I say."

Baelandra set her jaw and fell silent. Tears streaked through the blood on her cheeks. Scythe leaned over, resting a hand on one knee, his sword touching the steps. He stared down the slope of the Hall, waiting for more of the corrupted.

"All right," Shara sobbed. "Tell me." She put her shaky hands over his, began breathing evenly. Brophy lay down and set the Heartstone on his chest, touching it to the red gem embedded there.

"Remember on the Kherish ship?" he murmured. "The dream? How we flew over the city?"

Shara nodded as she sobbed.

"Take me back there. If I have to be somewhere forever, that's where I want to be."

She sniffled, blinked her tears away.

"Can you do that?" he asked, closing his eyes.

"I . . . I can do that," she said.

"We'll lock the black emmeria in my dreams," he murmured. "I will keep it there. But you must never let me wake up. No matter what."

"Brophy—"

"Promise me."

"Oh Brophy!"

"Promise."

She hesitated so long that he opened his eyes again. His gaze burned. She knew every moment she hesitated was a battle for him. "I promise," she sobbed. He closed his eyes again.

"Bae, finish what we started," he said, his voice sounding far away already. "We have most of it. We must get the rest. Send it all through the Heartstone, into me."

Baelandra nodded. "I will do it," she whispered. "I love you, Brophy." Her voice caught in her throat, and she fell silent. She put her hands on the Heartstone. The black swirled within, and she closed her eyes.

"Finish what we started," he murmured, softer. "Keep Ohndarien safe. Don't let her die."

Shara breathed with him, touched his forehead with both hands. She swirled into his thoughts, found him as she always did, bright and beautiful. She slipped into his mind, brought him back to their shared dream.

"Come," she said. "Let us fly."

They floated out from the Hall of Windows. They flew over the Ohndarien they had known as children, untouched by the black emmeria or the war.

"Forever . . ." he murmured.

They flew over the surface of the lapping waves. He caught her and pulled her to him, kissing her fiercely. Their bodies entwined, and they flew upward again.

Brophy's arms slowly relaxed and fell limp at his sides. His eyes darted underneath his eyelids. Shara sang to him, keeping her hands on his forehead as Baelandra leaned over the Heartstone. The swirling black became swirling gray. Faint colors appeared, growing brighter.

The sky slowly returned to normal, gray clouds scudding off into the blue.

"It is working," Shara said.

Mother Lewlem knelt next to them and pointed to the west. "The Ohohhim have entered the city," she said. Shara looked up.

A swarm of soldiers scrambled over the Sunset Gate, running over the ramparts.

Baelandra gasped and sat back. The Heartstone swirled brilliantly. It slid off Brophy's chest and rolled to a stop at Shara's knee. Brophy's own heartstone was dark as congealed blood. His eyes twitched underneath their closed lids, but his body was still.

Scythe slowly limped over to join them. The tip of the Sword of Autumn hovered an inch above the stairs. His bare arm was painted red, and blood dripped steadily from his clenched knuckles, dotting the blue-white marble. His neck was a ragged mess where the two-faced monster had clawed him. He stopped, swaying. Baelandra leapt to her feet and rushed to him.

"Is it done?" Scythe slurred, his voice as unsteady as his feet.

"It is done," Baelandra said.

A faint smile turned the corner of his mouth. He dropped the Sword of Autumn from limp fingers, and it clattered at her feet. The red diamond flickered and went out. He gave one last shuddering breath and collapsed.

Baelandra lunged for him, but his body rolled all the way down the stairs to the ground far below.

epilogue

A HOODED WOMAN walked carefully through the Night Market. It had been three weeks since the Nightmare Battle, as they were calling it. Most of the cafés and brothels were open again. Clusters of drunken Ohohhim soldiers wandered about the shops in little lines, each holding the sleeve of the man in front of him. Giggling Ohndarien children made a game of joining their rows. The pale, black-haired soldiers couldn't go anywhere without dragging half a dozen children along with them.

Despite their serious faces, the soldiers from the Opal Empire took it in good humor. They knew they were well loved in this city. Their skill and courage fighting the corrupted during the Nightmare Battle had made an impression that would last for generations. The Ohndariens had treated them as royalty since the purging of the city. There was little food or drink to share with them, but there certainly weren't any virgins left in the foreign army.

The fleet would return to the Opal Empire tomorrow. The Night Market was full tonight, packed shop to shop with the white-faced soldiers as they enjoyed their last night in the Free City.

The cowled woman lingered a moment in the shadow of a fountain next to a café. She knew she should move on, but she was reluctant. She watched the children for a moment longer, listening to the conversations of café patrons sipping their drinks.

"I heard that King Celtigar is going to sign a treaty . . ."

"The Summermen aren't meeting much resistance in Physendria. They've already taken the eastern shore. They'll go after Physen next, and who's to stop them?"

"It's true then. She gave birth to twins! Two baby boys."

"Yes. Old Jayden's granddaughter, Tara. She delivered twin boys last night. Happy and healthy as you please. They're the first new Nephews in more than a decade. The Flowers will bloom again."

Yes, the cowled woman thought, all save one. She looked up at the Wheel. A single torch burned atop the Hall of Windows.

Breaking away from her shadow, the woman made the long trek up to the Wheel. Recent rains had washed all of the blood from the stairs, but the stone was still scarred and pockmarked from the battle.

Trading ships had begun to trickle back into the city, and makeshift tents and shops were erected along the Dock Town quays. The Long Market had not been reopened. It still bore the memory of the dead. The entire island had been laid with a mile-long pyre to burn the bodies of those who fell in battle. The hundred-foot logs from the invaders' rafts had been dragged ashore, dried, and used for fuel. The flames reached higher than the walls and burned for two days. The ashes had been given back to the sea, but no one had suggested reopening the Long Market yet. The grief was too fresh.

The cowled woman's husband had been somewhere in that pyre, but she had no idea where. The bones of the corrupted had burned with all the others. Friend and foe alike shared the same grave.

The battle had not been between Physendrian and Ohndarien at the end. It was man against beast, the saved against the corrupted. All those who escaped the child's influence fought together for their lives. Ohndarien, Physendrian, Farad, and Ohohhim banded together to destroy the inhuman creatures spawned that day.

The woman reached the top of the steps and passed a short, half-carved pedestal at the top. She had heard that it would soon hold a memorial to Scythe, the Kherish warrior who held back the entire Physendrian army before the Nightmare Battle. He'd fought like a man possessed. Unstoppable.

She crossed the flat plateau to the Hall of Windows. Coppersmiths had set up scaffolding all around the amphitheater, already repairing the damage to the stained glass.

Two weeks ago she had attended the joint funeral of Sister Hazel, Brother Krellis, and Scythe. She had not been back, though council meetings had been held every day since. All were welcome to attend, and there was still much to discuss.

She entered through the Autumn Gate and sat at the back of the amphitheater. The council had just ended, and a cluster of people hovered around the Sisters, waiting for a word with the remaining Ohndarien leaders. A line of three Ohohhim broke from the group and headed up the stairs toward the cowled woman. She recognized the Emperor. Young and fair, he had directed his men with grace and civility during their stay. He became an instant favorite of the people and promised to return every year on the anniversary of the battle, so Ohndarien and the Opal Palace would forever follow the same sleeve.

The young Emperor was quick to flash that bright, charming smile, but his eyes were old. People said he was heartbroken by the horrors he had seen during the Nightmare Battle.

An old man and a woman carrying a baby trailed behind His Eternal Wisdom, clinging to his robes. The cowled woman watched the sleeping baby as the trio passed. Some said she was the three-hundred-year-old baby from Efften, the one who held the corruption inside her dreams. Looking at the sweet little thing, it was hard to believe that she could have caused such destruction.

The trio passed the woman, and she turned her attention forward again, waiting a long hour until the last of the petitioners left the Sisters alone. The Sister of Autumn, Baelandra, started up the aisle toward the Autumn Gate. When she drew close, the cowled woman stood.

"Sister, may I have a word?"

The petite Sister paused, turned a weary smile on the cowled woman. "Of course," Baelandra said. Her lustrous auburn hair shone like copper in the lanternlight. The little woman seemed taller than she actually was. Her fierce dignity towered over them all. Her hands and forearms were still bandaged in stiff clay, but she seemed even more elegant for it. It was said that she had broken both of her hands fighting the corrupted.

"I know you are tired," the woman replied. "But there is a question I must ask."

Baelandra nodded. "Please do."

"I was one of those who saw the eyes of the child. I heard the roar, and I was . . . changed by the magic within her."

Baelandra's gaze softened, and she took the woman's hands. The clay casts were stiff and awkward, but the Sister's fingers were warm.

"I am so sorry for your pain," she said, "but you are not alone. Everyone in Ohndarien was changed in the same way. I, too, would have changed, were it not for the heartstone I carry."

"I remember everything," the woman said. "The memories are stronger than any others I possess. I liked it at first, wanted it. I loved the strength, the power."

"Power can be very seductive, especially to those who have never had it."

The woman hesitated, slowly nodded. "My husband was corrupted beside me. I . . . I killed him. I ripped him apart with my bare hands."

The Sister of Autumn pulled her into a soft embrace. "I'm so sorry."

The cowled woman began crying. Baelandra's hand stroked the back of her head through the hood.

"It was not you," Baelandra murmured. "It was centuries of hate and cruelty working through you."

Slowly, the woman pulled back, and Baelandra let her go.

"No." She swallowed. "No, you are wrong. It was me. I wanted to kill him. He deserved to die."

Baelandra cocked her head, peering into the woman's cowl, but the woman turned her face away.

"I'm sorry, Sister. This is not what I came to ask you." The woman wiped the tears from her face. "I did not mean to cry. I just want to know why. Why did I return to normal when so many remained corrupted?"

With a gentle hand, Baelandra brought the woman's chin up again. "Because you have a good heart. You are a woman who loves more than she hates."

"I don't understand."

"When the black emmeria was released, it sought a home. Hate is drawn to hate, and everyone keeps some locked inside themselves. Everyone was corrupted. But when the Brother of Autumn and I used the Heartstone to draw the power back, everyone who had been infected was given a choice. Those who loved the evil, who reveled in their newfound power, kept it. They remained corrupted. Those who recoiled at what they had become rejected the black emmeria, and they fought for their true selves. They helped us remove the corruption."

"But Sister, I am not one of those people. I have done such—"

Baelandra touched her shoulder, and the woman fell silent. "It does not matter what you've done in your past. When the moment came to choose between love and hate, you chose love."

"But I . . ."

"Remember that," Baelandra said. "Some people think themselves fair, yet they stain the world with their touch. Some think themselves ugly, yet they fill the world with all the beauty of the Seasons. Always remember that you chose love at the moment when it mattered most."

Baelandra kissed the stunned woman on the cheek and continued up the aisle toward the Autumn Gate.

"Sister!" The woman called after. "Please, wait. One more thing."

Baelandra turned. "Yes?"

The cowled woman hesitated. "May I . . ." She faltered.

"Go ahead."

"May I see him? May I look upon him just once, the boy who saved us all?"

The Sister of Autumn smiled sadly. Her eyes glistened, and she blinked. "Follow me," she said, turning and walking through the Autumn Gate.

Baelandra led her up the steep staircase along the curve of the Hall of Windows. They stopped as soon as the top landing came into view. A blue-white marble gazebo had been built at the apex of the dome. A single torch burned on its roof. A handsome young man lay on a stone slab in the middle, his arms crossed upon his chest and a long sword in his grip. The blade glimmered with the red light that came from the giant stone in its pommel. A pretty young woman with long black hair cradled the boy's golden curls in her lap as she sang to him.

Baelandra and the cowled woman paused in the distance, listening to the beautiful words.

"We keep him here because he always loved the view of the city from atop the hall," Baelandra said.

"He holds the corruption in his dreams now, just as the little girl did?"

Baelandra nodded. "Yes."

"And if he should wake, would the corruption escape again?"

"We considered removing him from the city for the safety of all. We discussed this at length in council, but we agreed to take the risk. For his sake. No one wished to expel him after his sacrifice."

"That woman, she is the Zelani, Shara-lani."

"Yes. The Zelani take turns watching over him, but Shara-lani is here more often than not."

The cowled woman hesitated a moment. "May I go to him? I want to see his face."

Baelandra nodded. "Go ahead."

The woman walked up a few steps. Baelandra's voice stopped her.

"Ossamyr."

The woman froze. Slowly, she turned. After a moment's hesitation, she pushed back her cowl. Her dark eyes were lined with red, her short, black hair hung in disarray. She bowed her head and took one reluctant step away from the gazebo.

"Talk to Shara while you are up there," Baelandra said. "I think the two of you have a few things in common."

Ossamyr paused. "I—"

"The Zelani school will reopen soon," Baelandra continued. "Perhaps they could use your help in caring for him."

A single tear started down Ossamyr's face. "Yes," she murmured. "Yes, I will do that."

"Good." Baelandra gave her one last tired look and smiled. She turned and climbed out of sight below the curve of the dome.

The Queen of Physendria turned and walked up the stairs toward the sleeping Brother of Autumn.